The first romance stories Stephanie Laurens read were set against the backdrop of Regency England, and these continue to exert a special attraction for her. As an escape from the dry world of professional science, Stephanie started writing Regency romances, eight of which were published in the UK. Subsequently, she turned her hand to longer historical romances set in the Regency period. The first, *Captain Jack's Woman*, was published in the US by Avon Books in 1997. *Scandal's Bride* and *A Rogue's Proposal*, the titles featured in *Marry Me*, were two of the first books she wrote about the masterful, arrogant Cynster clan. The other Cynster novels are: *Devil's Bride*, *A Rake's Vow*, *A Secret Love*, *All About Love*, *All About Passion*, *The Promise in a Kiss*, *On a Wild Night*, *On a Wicked Dawn*, *The Perfect Lover*, *The Ideal Bride* and *What Price Love?*. She has also written four books about the seven dashing bachelors of the Bastion Club: *The Lady Chosen*, *A Gentleman's Honour*, *A Lady of His Own* and *A Fine Passion*.

Stephanie's last fifteen releases have been *New York Times*, *USA Today* and *Publishers Weekly* bestsellers. Stephanie lives in a leafy suburb of Melbourne with her husband and two daughters, along with two cats, Shakespeare and Marlowe.

Visit Stephanie's website at
www.stephanielaurens.com

STEPHANIE LAURENS

Marry Me

TWO CLASSIC CYNSTER NOVELS

SCANDAL'S BRIDE

&

A ROGUE'S PROPOSAL

AVON BOOKS

An imprint of HarperCollins*Publishers*

AVON BOOKS
An imprint of HarperCollins*Publishers*

Scandal's Bride and *A Rogue's Proposal*
first published in the USA in 1999 by Avon Books,
an imprint of HarperCollins*Publishers*, Inc.
This combined edition first published in Australia in 2006
by HarperCollins*Publishers* Australia Pty Limited
ABN 36 009 913 517
www.harpercollins.com.au

Published by arrangement with HarperCollins*Publishers*, Inc.,
New York, NY, USA. All rights reserved.

Scandal's Bride and *A Rogue's Proposal* copyright © Savdek Management Pty Ltd 1998

The right of Stephanie Laurens to be identified as the author of this
work has been asserted by her under the *Copyright Amendment
(Moral Rights) Act 2000.*

HarperCollins*Publishers*
25 Ryde Road, Pymble, Sydney, NSW 2073, Australia
31 View Road, Glenfield, Auckland 10, New Zealand
77–85 Fulham Palace Road, London, W6 8JB, United Kingdom
2 Bloor Street East, 20th floor, Toronto, Ontario M4W 1A8, Canada
10 East 53rd Street, New York NY 10022, USA

Laurens, Stephanie.
  Marry me: two classic Cynster novels.
  ISBN 978 0 73228 324 7.
  ISBN 0 7322 8324 8.
  1. Cynster family (Fictitious characters) – Fiction.
  I. Laurens, Stephanie. Scandal's bride. II. Laurens, Stephanie.
  Rogue's proposal. III. Title.
A823.3

Author photograph © James Flaagan
Cover photograph by Mary Javorek
Stephanie Laurens lettering on cover by Patricia Barrow
Cover design adapted by Katy Wright, HarperCollins Design Studio
Typeset in 10/12 Times by Kirby Jones
Printed and bound in Australia by Griffin Press on 70gsm Bulky Book Ivory

5 4 3 2 1   06 07 08 09

Marry Me

Scandal's Bride

The Bar Cynster Family Tree

(at the beginning of this story)

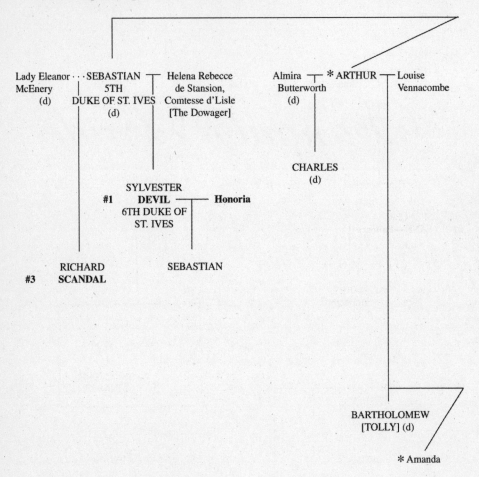

Lady Eleanor ···SEBASTIAN ─┬─ Helena Rebecce
McEnery   5TH   de Stansion,
   (d)   DUKE OF ST. IVES   Comtesse d'Lisle
                    (d)   [The Dowager]

Almira ─┬─ *ARTHUR ─┬─ Louise
Butterworth   Vennacombe
   (d)

                                         CHARLES
                                           (d)

              SYLVESTER
     #1   DEVIL ───── Honoria
             6TH DUKE OF
               ST. IVES

     RICHARD   SEBASTIAN
#3   SCANDAL

                                    BARTHOLOMEW
                                     [TOLLY] (d)

                                         *Amanda

MALE CYNSTERS named in capitals   * denotes twins

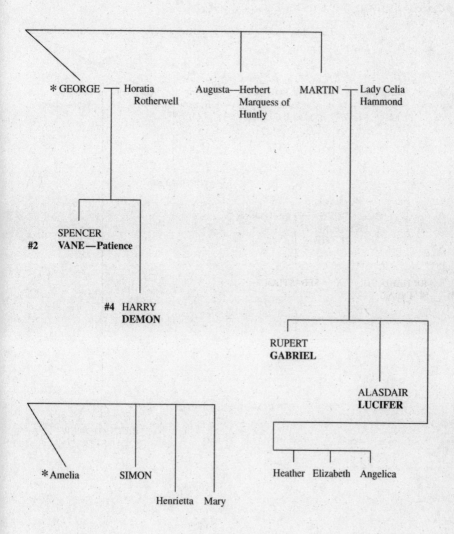

* GEORGE ┬ Horatia
         │ Rotherwell

Augusta—Herbert
         Marquess of
         Huntly

MARTIN ┬ Lady Celia
       │ Hammond

#2 SPENCER
    VANE—Patience

#4 HARRY
    DEMON

RUPERT
GABRIEL

ALASDAIR
LUCIFER

* Amelia   SIMON

Henrietta   Mary

Heather   Elizabeth   Angelica

Prologue

❧❧❧

December 1, 1819
Casphairn Manor, the Vale of Casphairn
Galloway Hills, Scotland

She'd never had a vision like it before. Eyes—blue, blue—blue as the skies over Merrick's high head, blue as the cornflowers dotting the vale's fields. They were the eyes of a thinker, far-sighted yet focused.

Or the eyes of a warrior.

Catriona awoke, almost surprised to find herself alone. From the depths of her big bed, she scanned her familiar surrounds, the thick velvet curtains half shrouding the bed, their mates drawn tight across the windows beyond which the wind murmured, telling tales of the coming winter to any still awake. In the grate, embers gleamed, shedding a glow over polished wood, the soft sheen of the floor, the lighter hues of chair and dresser. It was deep night, the hour between one day and the next. All was reassuringly normal; nothing had changed.

Yet it had.

Her heart slowing, Catriona tugged the covers about her and considered the vision that had visited her—the vision of a man's face. The details remained strongly etched in her mind. Along with the conviction that this man would mean something, impinge on her life in some vital way.

He might even be the one The Lady had chosen for her.

The thought was not unwelcome. She was, after all, twenty-two, long past the age when girls invited lovers to their beds, when she might have expected to play her part in that never-ending rite. Not that she regretted that her life had been otherwise, which was just as well, for her path had been set from the instant of her birth. *She* was "the lady of the vale."

The title, one of local custom, was hers and hers alone; none other could claim it. As the only child of her parents, on their deaths, she'd inherited Casphairn Manor, along with the vale and its attendant responsiblities. Her mother had been the same, inheriting manor, lands, and position from her mother before her. Each of her direct female ancestors had been "the lady of the vale."

Cocooned in warm down, Catriona smiled. Just what her title meant few outsiders understood. Some thought her a witch—she'd even used the fiction to scare away would-be suitors. Both church and state had little love of witches, but the vale's isolation kept her safe; there were few who knew of her existence, and none to question her authority or the doctrine from which it sprang.

All the inhabitants of the vale knew what she was, what her position entailed. With roots buried generations deep in the fertile soil, her tenants, all those who lived and worked in the vale, viewed "their lady" as the local representative of The Lady herself, older than time, spirit of the earth that supported them, guardian of their past and their future. They all, each in his own way, paid homage to The Lady and, with absolute and unquestioning confidence, relied on her earthly representative to watch over them and the vale.

To guard, to protect, to nurture, nourish, and heal—those were The Lady's tenets, the only directives Catriona followed and to which she'd unstintingly devoted her life. As had her mother, grandmother and great-grandmother before her. She lived life simply, in accordance with The Lady's dictates, which was usually an easy task.

Except in one arena.

Her gaze shifted to the parchment left unfolded on her dresser. A Perth solicitor had written to inform her of the death of her guardian, Seamus McEnery, and to bid her attend McEnery House for the reading of the will. McEnery House stood on a bleak hillside in The Trossachs, north and west of Perth; in her mind's eye, Catriona could see it clearly—it was the one place outside the vale in which she'd spent more than a day.

When, six years ago, her parents had died, Seamus, her father's cousin, had, by custom, become her legal guardian. A cold, hard man, he had insisted she take up residence at McEnery House, so he could better find a suitor for her hand—a man to take over her lands. With his rigid fist clamped on her purse strings, she'd been forced to obey; she'd left the vale and gone north to meet Seamus.

To do battle with Seamus—for her inheritance, her independence, her inalienable right to remain the lady of the vale, to reside at Casphairn Manor and care for her people. Three weeks of turmoil and drama later, she'd returned to the vale; Seamus had spoken no more of suitors, nor of her calling. And, Catriona was quite certain, he had never again taken The Lady's name in vain.

Now Seamus, the devil she'd conquered, was gone. His eldest son, Jamie, would succeed him. Catriona knew Jamie; like all Seamus's children, he was mild-mannered and weak-willed. Jamie was no Seamus. In considering how best to respond to the solicitor's request, she'd been much inclined to start as she meant to go on, and reply suggesting that, after the will was read and Jamie formally appointed as her guardian, Jamie should call on her here, at the manor. Although she foresaw no difficulty in handling Jamie, she preferred to deal from a position of strength. The vale was her home; within its arms, she reigned supreme. Yet ...

She focused again on the parchment; after an instant, the outline blurred—once more the vision swam before her mind's eye. For a full minute, she studied it; she saw the face clearly—strong patriarchal nose, determinedly square chin, features chiselled from rock in their angularity and hardness. His brow was concealed by a lock of black hair; those piercing blue eyes were deep-set beneath arched black brows and framed by black lashes. His lips, held in a straight, uncompromising line, told her little—indeed, that was her summation of his face—one meant to conceal his thoughts, his emotions. From chance observers.

She wasn't a chance observer. Presentiment—nay, *certainty*—of future contact compelled her; she focused her mind and slid beneath his guard, behind his reserved facade, and tentatively opened her senses.

Hunger—hot, ravenous—a prowling, animalistic urge, swept over her. It caressed her with fingers of heat; its tug was even more physical. Beyond it, in the deeper shadows, lay ... restlessness. A soul-deep sense of drifting, rudderless, upon life's sea.

Catriona blinked, and drew back, into her familiar chamber. And saw the letter still lying on her desk. She grimaced. She was adept at intepreting The Lady's messages—this one was crystal clear. She should go to McEnery House and, at some point, she would meet the restless, hungry, reserved stranger with the granite face and warrior's eyes.

A lost warrior—a warrior without a cause.

Catriona frowned and wriggled deeper under the covers. When she'd first seen that face, she'd felt, instinctively, deep inside, that, at long last, The Lady was sending her a consort—the one who would stand by her side, who would share the burden of the vale's protection—the man she would take to her bed. At last. Now, however ...

"His face is too strong. *Far* too strong."

As the lady of the vale, it was imperative that she be the dominant partner in her marriage, as her mother had been in hers. It was written in stone that no man could rule her. Not for her an arrogant, domineering husband—*that* would never do. Which was, in this case, a pity. A real disappointment.

She'd immediately recognized the source of his restlessness, the restlessness of those without purpose, but she'd never met anything like the hunger that prowled within him. Alive, a tangible force, it had reached out and touched her, and she'd felt a compulsion to sate it. A reactive urge to soothe him, to bring him surcease. To ...

Her frown deepened; she couldn't find the words, but there'd been a sense of excitment, of daring, of challenge. Not elements she generally met in her daily round of duties. Then again, perhaps it was simply her healer's instincts prodding her? Catriona humphed. "Whatever, he *can't* be the one The Lady means for me—not with a face like *that*."

Was The Lady sending her a wounded male, a lame duck for her to cure? His eyes, those hard-edged features, hadn't looked lame.

Not that it mattered; she had her instructions. She would go to the highlands, to McEnery House, and see what—or rather, who—came her way.

With another humph, Catriona slid deeper beneath the covers. Turning on her side, she closed her eyes—and willed her mind away from, once again, seeking the stranger's face.

CHAPTER
One

❧❧❧

December 5, 1819
Keltyburn, The Trossachs
Scottish Highlands

"Will there be anything else, sir?" An artful arrangement of sleek, nubile, naked female limbs sprang to Richard Cynster's mind. The innkeeper had finished clearing the remnants of his dinner—the feminine limbs would satisfy that appetite still unappeased. But . . .

Richard shook his head. Not that he feared shocking his studiously correct gentleman's gentleman, Worboys, standing poker-straight at his elbow. Having been in his employ for eight years, Worboys was past being shocked. He was, however, no magician, and Richard was of the firm opinion that it would take magical powers to find a satisfying armful in Keltyburn.

They'd arrived in the hamlet as the last light left the leaden sky; night had fallen swiftly, a black shroud. The thick mist that had lowered over the mountains, hanging heavy across their path, obscuring the narrow, winding road leading up Keltyhead to their destination, had made passing the night in the dubious comfort of the Keltyburn Arms an attractive proposition.

Besides, he had a wish to have his first sight of his mother's last home in daylight, and before he left Keltyburn, there was one thing he wished to do.

Richard stirred. "I'll be retiring shortly. Go to bed—I won't need you further tonight." Worboys hesitated; Richard knew he was thinking of who would brush and hang his coat, who would take care of his boots. He sighed. "Go to bed, Worboys."

Worboys stiffened. "Very well, sir—but I do wish we'd pressed on to McEnery House. There, at least, I could have trusted the bootboys."

"Just be thankful we're here," Richard advised, "and not run off the road or stuck in a drift halfway up that damned mountain."

Worboys sniffed eloquently. His clear intimation was that being stuck in a snowdrift in weather cold enough to freeze the proverbial appendages off brass monkeys was preferable to bad blacking. But he obediently took his rotund self off, rolling away into the shadowy depths of the inn.

His lips twitching into a slight smile, Richard stretched his long legs to the fire roaring in the grate. Whatever the state of the inn's blacking, the landlord hadn't stinted in making them comfortable. Richard had seen no other guests, but in such a quiet backwater, that was unsurprising.

The flames flared; Richard fixed his gaze on them—and wondered, not for the first time, whether this expedition to the Highlands, precipitated by boredom and a very specific fear, hadn't been a trifle rash. But London's entertainments had grown stale; the perfumed bodies so readily—too readily— offered him no longer held any allure. While desire and lust were still there, he'd become finicky, choosy, even more so than he'd already been. He wanted more from a woman than her body and a few moments of earthly bliss.

He frowned and resettled his shoulders—and redirected his thoughts. It was a letter that had brought him here, one from the executor of his long-dead mother's husband, Seamus McEnery, who had recently departed this earth. The uninformative legal missive had summoned him to the reading of the will, to be held the day after tomorrow at McEnery House. If he wished to claim a bequest his mother had made to him, and which Seamus had apparently withheld for nearly thirty years, he had to attend in person.

From what little he'd learned of his late mother's husband, that sounded like Seamus McEnery. The man had been a hothead, brash and vigorous, a hard, determined, wily despot. Which was almost certainly why he'd been born. His mother had not enjoyed being married to such a man; his father, Sebastian Cynster, 5th Duke of St. Ives, sent to McEnery House to douse Seamus's political fire, had taken pity on her and given her what joy he could.

Which had resulted in Richard. The story was so old—thirty years old, to be precise—he no longer felt anything over it, bar a distant regret. For the mother he'd never known. She'd died of fever bare months after his birth; Seamus had sent him post-haste to the Cynsters, the most merciful thing he could have done. They'd claimed him and reared him as one of their own, which, in all ways that mattered, he was. Cynsters bred true, especially the males. He was a Cynster through and through.

And that was the other reason he'd left London. The only important social event he was missing was his cousin Vane's belated wedding breakfast, an occasion he'd viewed with misgiving. He wasn't blind—he'd seen the gleam steadily glowing in the eyes of the older Cynster ladies. Like Helena, the Dowager, his much-loved stepmother, not to mention his fleet of aunts. If he'd attended Vane and Patience's celebration, they'd have set their sights on him. He wasn't yet bored enough, restless enough, to offer himself up, fodder for their matrimonial machinations. Not yet.

He knew himself well, perhaps too well. He wasn't an impulsive man. He liked his life well ordered, predictable—he liked to be in control. He'd seen war in his time but he was a man of peace. Of passion. Of home and hearth.

The phrase raised images in his mind—of Vane and his new bride, of his own half-brother, Devil, and his duchess, Honoria, and their son. Richard shifted and settled, conscious, too conscious, of what his brother and cousin now had. What he himself wanted. Yearned for. He was, after all, a Cynster; he was starting to suspect such plaguey thoughts were ingrained, an inherited susceptiblity. They got under a man's skin and made him ... edgy. Dissatisfied.

Restless.

Vulnerable.

A board creaked; Richard lifted his gaze, looking through the archway into the hall beyond. A woman emerged from the shadows. Wrapped in a drab cloak, she met his gaze directly, an older woman, her face heavily lined. She measured him swiftly; her gaze turned frosty. Richard suppressed a grin. Spine stiff, her pace unfaltering, the woman turned and climbed the stairs.

Sinking back in his chair, Richard let his lips curve. He was safe from temptation at the Keltyburn Arms.

He looked back at the flames; gradually, his smile died. He shifted once more, easing his shoulders; a minute later, he fluidly rose and crossed to the fogged window.

Rubbing a clear space, he looked out. A starry, moonlit scene met his eyes, a light covering of snow crisping on the ground. Squinting sideways, he could see the church. The kirk. Richard hesitated, then straightened. Collecting his coat from the stand by the door, he went outside.

Abovestairs, Catriona sat at a small wooden table, its surface bare except for a silver bowl, filled with pure spring water, into which she steadily gazed. Distantly, she heard her companion, Algaria, pace along the corridor and enter the room next door, but she was deep in the water, her senses merging with its surface, locked upon it.

And the image formed—the same strong features, the same arrogant eyes. The same aura of restlessness. She didn't probe further—she didn't dare. The image was sharp—he was near.

Dragging in a swift breath, Catriona blinked and pulled back. A knock fell on the door; it opened—Algaria stepped inside. And instantly saw what she'd been up to. She swiftly shut the door. "What did you see?"

Catriona shook her head. "It's confusing." The face was even harder than she'd thought it; the essence of the man's strength was there, clearly delineated for anyone to read. He was a man with no reason to hide his character—he bore the signs openly, arrogantly, like a chieftain.

Like a warrior.

Catriona frowned. She kept stumbling across that word, but she didn't need a warrior—she needed a tame, complaisant, preferably readily besotted gentleman she could marry and so beget an heiress. This man fitted her prescription in only one respect—he was indisputably male. The Lady, She Who Knew All, couldn't possibly mean this man for her.

"But if not that, then what?" Pushing aside the silver bowl, she leaned on the table and cupped her chin in one hand. "I must be getting my messages crossed." But she hadn't done that since she was fourteen. "Perhaps there are two of them?"

"Two of whom?" Algaria hovered near. "What was the vision?"

Catriona shook her head. The matter was too personal—too sensitive—to divulge to anyone else, even Algaria, her mentor since her mother's death. Not until she'd got to the truth of the matter herself and understood it fully.

Whatever it was she was supposed to understand.

"It's no use." Determinedly, she stood. "I must consult The Lady directly."

"What? *Now*?" Algaria stared. "It's freezing outside."

"I'm only going to the circle at the end of the graveyard. I won't be out long." She hated uncertainty, not being sure of her road. And this time, uncertainty had brought an unusual tenseness, a sense of expectation, an unsettling presentiment of excitement. Not the sort of excitement she was accustomed to, either, but something more scintillating, more enticing. Swinging her cloak about her, she looped the ribbons at her throat.

"There's a gentleman downstairs." Algaria's black eyes flashed. "He's one you should avoid."

"Oh?" Catriona hesitated. Could her man be here, under the same roof? The tension that gripped her hardened her resolve; she tied off her ribbons. "I'll make sure he doesn't see me. And everyone in the village knows me by sight—at least, this sight." She released her knotted hair, letting it swish about her shoulders. "There's no danger here."

Algaria sighed. "Very well—but don't dally. I suppose you'll tell me what this is all about when you can."

From the door, Catriona flashed her a smile. "I promise. Just as soon as I'm sure."

Halfway down the stairs, she saw the gentleman, short, rotund, and fastidiously dressed, checking the discarded news sheets in the inn's main parlor. His face was as circular as his form; he was definitely not her warrior. Catriona slipped silently down the hall. It was the work of a minute to ease open the heavy door, not yet latched for the night.

And then she was outside.

Pausing on the inn's stone step, she breathed in the crisp, chilly air, and felt the cold reach her head. Invigorated, she pulled her cloak close and stepped out, watching her feet, careful not to slip on the icing snow.

In the graveyard, in the lee of one wall, Richard looked down at his mother's grave. The inscription on the headstone was brief: *Lady Eleanor McEnery, wife of Seamus McEnery, Laird of Keltyhead*. That, and nothing more. No affectionate remembrance; no mention of the bastard son she'd left behind.

Richard's expression didn't change; he'd come to terms with his status long ago. When he'd been abandoned on his father's doorstep, Helena, Devil's mother, had stunned everyone by claiming him as her own. In doing so, she'd given him his place in the ton—no one, even now, would risk her displeasure, or that of the entire Cynster clan, by so much as hinting he was not who she claimed he was. His father's legitimate son. Instinctively shrewd, ebulliently generous, Helena had secured for him his position in society's elite, for which, in his heart, he had never ceased to thank her.

The woman whose bones lay beneath this cold stone had, however, given him life—and he could do nothing to thank her.

Except, perhaps, to live life fully.

His only knowledge of his mother had come from his father; when, in all innocence, he'd asked if his father had loved his mother, Sebastian had ruffled his hair and said: "She was very lovely and very lonely—she deserved more than she got from her marriage." He'd paused, then added: "I felt sorry for her." He'd looked at him, and his slow smile had creased his face. "But I love you. I regret her death, but I can't regret your birth."

He could understand how his father had felt—he was, after all, a Cynster to the bone. Family, children, home, and hearth—those were what mattered to Cynsters. Those were their quintessential warrior goals, for them the ultimate victories of life.

For long, silent minutes, he stood before the grave, until the cold finally penetrated his boots. With a sigh, he shifted, then straightened and, after one last, long look, turned and retraced his steps.

What was it his mother had left him? And why, having concealed her bequest all these years, had Seamus summoned him back now, after his own death? Richard rounded the kirk, his stride slow, the sound of his footfalls subsumed by the breeze softly whistling through snow-laden branches. He reached the main path and stepped onto it—and heard crisp, determined footsteps approaching from beyond the kirk. Halting, he turned and beheld . . .

A creature of magic and moonlight.

A woman, her dark cloak billowing about her, her head bare. Over her shoulders and down her back spread the most glorious mane of thick, rippling, silken hair, sheening copper-bright in the moonlight, a beacon against the wintering trees behind her. Her stride was definite, every footfall decisive; her eyes were cast down, but he would have sworn she wasn't watching her steps.

She came on without pause, heading directly for him. He couldn't see her face, or her figure beneath the full cloak, but well-honed instincts rarely lied. His senses stirred, stretched, then focused powerfully—a clear case of lust at first sight. Lips lifting in wolfish anticipation, Richard silently turned and prepared to make the lady's acquaintance.

Catriona strode briskly up the path, lips compressed, a frown knitting her brows. She'd been a disciple of The Lady too long not to know how to couch her requests for clarification; the question she'd asked had been succinct and to the point. She'd asked for the true significance of the man whose face haunted her. The Lady's reply, the words that had formed in her mind, had been brutally concise: *He will father your children.*

There were not, no matter how she twisted them, very many ways in which to interpret those words.

Which left her with a very large problem. Unprecedented though it might be, The Lady *must* have made a mistake. This man, whoever he was, was arrogant, ruthless—dominant. *She* needed a sweet, simple soul, one content to remain quietly supportive while she ruled their roost. She didn't need strength—she needed weakness. There was absolutely no point sending her a warrior without a cause.

Catriona humphed; her breath steamed before her face. Through the clearing wisps, she spied—the very last thing she expected to see—a pair of large, black, highly polished Hessians, directly in her path. She tried to stop; her soles found no grip on the icy path—her momentum sent her skidding on. She tried to flail her arms; they were trapped beneath her cloak. On a gasp, she looked up, just as she collided with the owner of the boots.

The impact knocked the air from her lungs; for one instant, she was sure she'd hit a tree. But her nose buried itself in a soft cravat, mid-chest, just above the V of a silk waistcoat. His chin passed above her head; her scalp prickled as long hairs were gently brushed. And arms like steel slowly closed about her.

Instinct awoke in a flustered rush; raising her hands, she pushed against his chest.

Her feet slipped, then slid.

She gasped again—and clutched wildly instead of pushing. The steely arms tightened, and suddenly only her toes touched the snow. Catriona dragged in a breath—one too shallow to steady her whirling head. Her lungs had seized; her senses skittered wildly, informing her, in breathless detail, that she was pressed, breast to thigh, against a man.

Not just any man—one with a body like warm, flexing steel. She had to lean back to look into his face.

Blue, blue eyes met hers.

Catriona stilled; she stared. Then she blinked. It took half a second to check—arrogant mien, decisive chin—it was he.

Narrowing her eyes, she fixed them on his; if The Lady had made no mistake, then it behooved her to begin as she meant to go on. "Put me down."

She'd learned the knack of commanding obedience at her mother's knee; her simple words held echoes of authority, undertones of compulsion.

He heard them; he angled his head, one black brow rising, then the ends of his long lips lifted. "In a minute."

It was her turn to listen and hear the intent in his deep purr. Her eyes flew wide.

"But first . . ."

If she'd been able to think, she'd have screamed, but the shock of his touch, the intimate warmth of his palm as he framed her face, distracted her. His lips completed the conquest—they swooped, arrogantly confident, and settled over hers.

The first contact stunned her; she ceased to breathe. The very concept of breathing drifted from her mind as his lips moved lazily on hers. They were neither warm nor cool, yet heat lingered in their touch. They pressed close, then eased, sipped, supped, then returned. Firm and demanding, they impinged on her senses, reaching deep, stirring her.

She stirred in his encircling arm; it locked tight about her. Heat surrounded her—even through her thick cloak, it reached for her, enveloped her, then sank into her flesh. And grew, built, a crescendo of warmth seeking release. His hot hunger had infected her. Utterly distracted, she tried to hold it back, tried to deny its existence, tried vainly to dampen it down.

And couldn't. She was facing ignominious defeat—with not a clue of what followed—when the hard hand tilting her face shifted. He altered his grip; one thumb pressed insistently in the center of her chin.

Her jaw eased; her lips parted.

He entered.

The shock of the first touch of tongue against tongue literally curled her toes. She would have gasped, but that was impossible; all she could do was feel. Feel and follow, and sense the reality of that hot hunger, the surprisingly subtle, deeply evocative, seductively physical need. And hold hard against the temptation that streaked through her.

Even while he took arrogance to new heights.

She hadn't thought it possible, but he gathered her more closely, imprinting her soft flesh with the male hardness of his. Ruthlessly confident, he angled his head and tasted her—languorously, unhurriedly—as if he had all the time in the world.

Then he settled to play.

To advance and retreat, to artfully entice her into joining the game. The very idea shocked her to her toes—and sent shards of excitement flying down her nerves. They stretched, tightened. His lips and tongue continued their tantalizing dance.

She responded—tentatively; instead of the aggressive response she expected, his lips softened fractionally, encouragingly. She dared more, returning the pressure of his lips, the sensuous caress of his tongue.

Without even knowing it, she sank into the kiss.

Triumph streaked through Richard; he mentally crowed. He'd laid waste her starchy resistance; she was soft and pliant, pure magic in his arms. She tasted like the sweetest summer wine. The heady sensation went straight to his head.

And straight to his loins.

Staving off the burgeoning ache, he feasted, careful not to startle her, to let her wits surface enough to recognize his liberties. He wasn't fool enough to think she wouldn't break away if he gave her sufficient cause. She was no simple country miss, no naive maid—her three words, her attitude, had reeked of authority. And she wasn't young; no young lady would have had the confidence to command him, of all men, to "*Put me down*." She was not girl, but woman—and she fitted very well, supple and curvaceous in his arms.

How well she was fitting, how tempting her curves were, locked hard against him, registered, and raised his lust to new heights. The soft, silken sway of her heavy hair, a warm, living veil drifting over the backs of his hands, and the perfume—wildflowers, the promise of spring and the fecundity of growing things—that rose from the silky locks, converted lust to pain.

It was he who pulled back and ended the kiss—it was that, or suffer worse agony. For he would have to let her go, untouched, unsampled, his lust unsated; a snowbound churchyard in the depths of a winter's night was a challenge even he balked at.

And, despite the intimate caresses they'd exchanged, he knew she wasn't that sort of lady. He'd breached her walls by sheer brazen recklessness, evoked by her haughty command to put her down. Right now, he'd like to lay her down, but that, he knew, was not to be.

He raised his head.

Her eyes flew wide; she looked at him as if he was a ghost.

"Lady preserve me."

Her words were a fervent whisper; condensed by the cold, they misted the air between them. She searched his face—for what, Richard could not guess; with his customary arrogance, he raised one brow.

Lips, soft and rosy—much rosier now than before—firmed. "By the Lady's veil! This is *madness!*"

She shook her head and pushed against his chest; bemused, Richard set her down carefully, then released her. Frowning absentmindedly, she stepped around and past him, then whirled to face him. "Who *are* you?"

"Richard Cynster." He sketched her an elegant bow. Straightening, he trapped her gaze. "Entirely at your service."

Her eyes snapped. "Do you make a habit of accosting innocent women in graveyards?"

"Only when they walk into my arms."

"I *requested* you to put me down."

"You *ordered* me to put you down—and I did. Eventually."

"Yes. But ..." Her tirade—he was sure it would have been a tirade—died on her lips. She blinked at him. "You're *English!*"

An accusation rather than an observation. Richard arched a brow. "Cynsters are."

Eyes narrowing, she studied his face. "Of Norman descent?"

He smiled, proudly arrogant. "We came over with the Conqueror." His smile deepening, he let his gaze sweep her. "We still like to dabble, of course." Looking up, he trapped her gaze. "To keep our hand in with the occasional conquest."

Even in the weak light, he saw her glare, saw the sparks that flared in her eyes.

"I'll have you know this is all a *very big mistake!*"

With that, she whirled away. Snow crunched, louder than before, as, in a flurry of skirts and cloak, she stalked off. Brows rising, Richard watched her storm through the lychgate, saw the quick, frowning glance she threw him from the shadows beneath. Then, with a toss of her head, chin high, she marched up the road.

Toward the inn.

The ends of Richard's lips lifted. His brows rose another, more considering, notch. Mistake?

He watched until she disappeared from sight, then stirred, straightened his shoulders, and, lips curving in a wolfish smile, strolled unhurriedly in her wake.

CHAPTER

Two

୧୭୬

Richard rose early the next morning. He shaved and dressed, conscious of a familiar excitement—the excitement of the hunt. Creasing the last fold of his cravat, he reached for his diamond pin—a rough shout reached his ears. He stilled—and heard, muffled by the windows tight shut against the winter chill, the unmistakable clack of hooves on cobbles.

Three swift strides had him at the window, looking down through the frosted pane. A heavy travelling carriage stood before the inn door, ostlers holding a pair of strong horses, breaths fogging as they stamped. Boys from the inn wrestled a trunk onto the carriage roof, the innkeeper directing them.

Then a lady emerged from the porch, directly below Richard. The innkeeper sprang to open the carriage door. His bow was respectful, which did not surprise Richard—the lady was his acquaintance of the churchyard.

"Damn!" Eyes on her long tresses, flame bright in the morning, clipped together so they rippled like a river down her back, he swore beneath his breath.

With a regal nod, the lady entered the carriage without a backward glance; she was followed by the older woman Richard had seen in the inn. Just before ascending the carriage steps, the old woman looked back—and up—straight at Richard. He resisted the urge to step back; an instant later, the woman turned and followed her companion into the carriage.

The innkeeper closed the door, the coachman clicked the reins and the carriage lumbered out of the yard. Richard swore some more—his prey was escaping. The carriage reached the end of the village street and turned, not left, toward Crieff, but right—up the road to Keltyhead.

Richard frowned. According to Jessup, his groom and coachman, the narrow, winding Keltyhead road led to McEnery House, and nowhere else.

A discreet tap fell on the door; Worboys entered. Shutting the door, he announced: "The lady after whom you were inquiring has just departed the inn, sir."

"I know that." Richard turned from the window; the carriage was out of sight. "Who is she?"

"A Miss Catriona Hennessy, sir. A connection of the late Mr. McEnery." Worboys's expression turned supercilious. "The innkeep, an ignorant heathen, maintains the lady is a witch, sir."

Richard snorted and turned back to his mirror. Witchy, yes. A witch? It hadn't been any exotic spell that had bewitched him in the night, in the crisp cold of the kirk yard. Memories of sleek, warm, feminine curves, of soft, luscious lips, of an intoxicating kiss, returned . . .

Setting his pin into his cravat, he reached for his coat. "We'll leave as soon as I've breakfasted."

His first sight of McEnery House colored Richard's vision of Seamus McEnery and his mother's last years. Clinging to the wind-whipped side of the mountain, the two-story structure seemed hewn from the rock behind it and weathered in similar fashion, totally uninviting as a suitable habitat for humans. Live ones, anyway—the place could have qualified as a mausoleum. The prevailing impression of hard and cold was emphasized by the lack of any vestige of a garden—even the trees, which might have softened the severe lines, stopped well back from the house as if fearing to draw nearer.

Descending from his carriage, Richard could detect no sign of warmth or life, no light burning in defiance of the dull day, no rich curtains draped elegantly about the sashes. Indeed, the windows were narrow and few, presumably from necessity. It had been cold in Keltyburn, at the foot of the mountain—up here, it was freezing.

The front door opened to Worboys's peremptory knock; Richard ascended the steps, leaving Worboys and two footmen to deal with his luggage. An old butler stood waiting just inside the door.

"Richard Cynster," Richard drawled, and handed him his cane. "Here at the behest of the late Mr. McEnery."

The butler bowed. "The family are in the parlor, sir."

He relieved Richard of his heavy coat, then led the way. Richard followed; the impression of a tomb intensified as they travelled down uncarpeted flagged corridors, through stone archways flanked by columns of solid granite, past door after door shut tight against the world. The chill was pervasive; Richard was contemplating asking for his coat back when the butler halted and opened a door.

Announced, Richard entered.

"Oh! I say." A ruddy-complexioned gentleman with a shock of reddish hair struggled to his feet—he'd been engaged in a game of spillikins with a boy and a girl on the rug before the fire.

It was a scene so much like the ones Richard was accustomed to, his cool expression relaxed. "Don't let me interrupt."

"No, no! That is . . ." Abruptly drawing breath, the man thrust out his hand. "Jamie McEnery." Then, as if recalling the matter with some surprise, he added: "Laird of Keltyhead."

Richard gripped the hand offered him. About three years his junior, Jamie was a good head shorter than he, stocky, with a round face and the sort of expression that could only be called open.

"Did you have a good trip up?"

"Tolerably." Richard glanced at the others seated about the room, a surprising number all garbed in dull mourning.

"Here! Let me introduce you."

Jamie proceeded to do so; Richard smoothly acknowledged Mary, Jamie's wife, a sweet-faced young woman too passive for his tastes, but, he suspected, quite right for Jamie, and their children, Martha and Alister, both of whom watched him through big, round eyes as if they'd never seen anyone like him before. And then there were Jamie's siblings, two whey-faced sisters with their mild husbands and very young, rather sickly looking broods, and last, Jamie's younger brother Malcolm, who appeared not only weak but peevish.

Accepting a chair, Richard had never before felt so much like a large, marauding predator unexpectedly welcomed into a roomful of scrawny chickens. But he hid his teeth and duly took tea to warm him after his journey. The weather provided instant conversation.

"Looks like more snow on the way," Jamie remarked. "Good thing you got here before it."

Richard murmured his assent and sipped his tea.

"It's been particularly cold up here this year," Mary nervously informed him. "But the cities—Edinburgh and Glasgow—are somewhat warmer."

Her sisters-in-law murmured inaudible agreement.

Malcolm stirred, a dissatisfied frown on his face. "I don't know why we can't remove there for winter like our neighbors do. There's nothing to do here."

A tense silence ensued, then Jamie rushed into speech. "Do you shoot? There's good game to be had—Da' always insisted the coverts were kept up to scratch."

With an easy smile, Richard picked up the conversational gauntlet and helped Jamie steer the talk away from the families' obviously straitened circumstances. A quick glance confirmed that the gentlemen's coats and boots were well worn, even patched, the ladies' gowns a far cry from the latest fashions. The younger children's clothes were clearly hand-me-downs, while the coat Malcolm hunched in was a size too big—one of Jamie's doing double duty.

The answer to Malcolm's question was transparent—Seamus's children lived under his chilly roof because they had nowhere else to go. At least, Richard mused, they had this place as a refuge, and Seamus must have left them well provided for; there was no hint of poverty about the house itself, or its servants. Or the quality of the tea.

Finishing his, he set his cup down and wondered, not for the first time, where his witch was hiding. He'd detected no trace of her, or her older shadow, even in the others' faces. He'd seen her witchy face clearly enough in the bright moonlight; the only resemblance she shared with Jamie and his siblings lay in their red hair. And, perhaps, he conceded, the freckles.

Jamie's and Malcolm's faces were a collage of freckles, their sisters' only marginally less affected. His memory of the witch's complexion was of ivory cream, unblemished except for a dusting of freckles over her pert nose. He'd have to check when next he saw her; despite his wish to hasten that event, he made no mention of her. With no idea who she was—where she stood in relation to the family—he was too wise to mention their meeting, or express any interest in others who might be present.

Languidly, he rose, causing a nervous flutter among the ladies.

Jamie immediately rose, too. "Is there anything we can get you? I mean— anything you might need?"

While struggling to strike the right note as head of the family, Jamie had an openness of which Richard approved; he smiled lazily down at him. "No, thank you. I have all I need." Bar an elusive witch.

With an easy smile and his usual faultless grace, he excused himself and withdrew to his room to refresh himself before luncheon.

Richard did not set eyes on his witch until that evening, when she glided into the drawing room, immediately preceding the butler. As that venerable individual intoned the words "Dinner is served," she swept the gathering with a calm and distant smile—until she came to him, standing beside Mary's chair.

Her smile died—stunned astonishment took its place.

Slowly, with deliberate intent, Richard smiled back.

For one quivering instant, her stunned silence held sway, then Jamie stepped forward. "Ah ... Catriona, this is Mr. Cynster. He's been summoned for the reading of the will."

Deserting his face, she fixed her gaze on Jamie's. "He has?" Her tone conveyed much more than a simple question.

Jamie shuffled and shot an apologetic glance at Richard. "Da's first wife made him a bequest. Da' held it until now."

Frowning, she opened her lips to quiz Jamie. Having silently prowled closer, Richard took her hand—she jumped and tried to snatch it back, but he didn't let go.

"Good evening, Miss ..." Richard slanted a questioning glance at Jamie.

Instead, his witch answered, in tones colder than ice. "Miss Hennessy."

Again, she surreptitiously tugged, trying to free her hand; Richard unhurriedly brought his gaze to her face, waited until she looked up, trapped her eyes with his, then smoothly raised her hand. "A pleasure," he purred. Slowly, deliberately, he brushed her knuckles with his lips—and felt the shiver of awareness that raced through her—the shiver she couldn't hide. His smile deepened. "Miss Hennessy."

The look she sent him should have laid him out dead on the Aubusson rug; Richard merely lifted a brow, deliberately arrogant, deliberately provocative. And held onto her hand, and her gaze. "What Jamie is understandably hesitant over explaining, Miss Hennessy, is that Mr. McEnery's first wife was my mother."

Still frowning, she glanced at Jamie, who colored. "Your ...?" Understanding dawned; she looked back at him. "Oh." The veriest hint of pink tinged her ivory cheeks. "I see."

There was, to Richard's surprise, no hint of condemnation, or consternation, in her voice—she didn't even yank her hand away, as he'd fully expected; her slim fingers lay quiescent in his grasp. Her eyes searched his, then she inclined her head, coldly gracious, the action clearly signifying her understanding, and a regal agreement to his right to be present. There was no suggestion in any element of her bearing that she was perturbed at learning he was a bastard.

In all his years, Richard had never met with such calm acceptance.

"Catriona is my father's—" Jamie broke off and cleared his throat. "Actually, *my* ward."

"Ah." Richard smiled urbanely at Catriona. "That explains her presence, then."

He fielded another of her lethal glances, but before he could respond, Mary bustled up and claimed Jamie's arm.

"If you could lead Catriona in, Mr. Cynster?"

With Jamie in tow, Mary led the way; entirely content, Richard placed the intriguing Miss Hennessey's hand on his sleeve and elegantly steered her in their wake.

She glided beside him, a galleon fully armed, queenly detachment hanging about her like a cloak. As they left the drawing room, Richard noted that the older woman had also appeared; she had been standing near the door.

"The lady who accompanies you?"

There was a palpable hesitation, then she elected to answer. "Miss O'Rourke is my companion."

The dining room lay across the cavernous hall; Richard led his fair charge to the chair beside Jamie, at the table's head, then, at Jamie's intimation, took the seat opposite, on Jamie's right. The rest of the family and Miss O'Rourke took their places. The room was large, the table long; the distance between the diners was enough to discourage those conversations not already dampened by the atmosphere. Despite the blaze roaring in the hearth, it was chilly; a sense of long-standing austerity hung over the room.

"Could you pass the condiments?"

With that the limit of conversation, as the courses came and went, Richard used the time to indulge his curiosity about Seamus McEnery. With no other avenue available, he studied Seamus's house, his household, his family, for what insights they could offer of the man.

A cursory inspection of those he'd met earlier told him little more; they were, one and all, meek, mild, self-effacing, their very timidity a comment on Seamus and how he'd reared his children. Miss O'Rourke had an interesting face, deeply lined and unusually weathered for a gentlewoman's; Richard didn't need to study it for long to know she distrusted him deeply. The fact did not perturb him; companions of beautiful ladies generally distrusted him on sight. Which left—Catriona Hennessy.

She was, without doubt, the most interesting body in the room. In a gown of deep lavender silk, with her lustrous locks—neither gold nor plain red, but true copper—piled high on her head, tendrils escaping to frame her face in flames, the round neckline of her gown scooped low enough to give a fair indication of the bounty beneath, her shoulders and arms sweetly turned and encased in skin like ivory satin, she was a sight designed for lecherous eyes.

Richard looked his fill. Her face was a delicate oval, with a straight, little nose and a smooth, wide brow. Her brows and lashes were light brown, framing eyes of vibrant green—something he hadn't been able to see in the moonlight, although he did recall how the gold flecks within the green had flared with indignation. He felt sure they would blaze in anger—and smolder with passion. Her only less-than-perfect feature was her chin; that, Richard considered, was a touch too firm, too determined. Too self-willed. She was of below average height, petite and slender, yet her figure, though sleek and supple, was not boyish. Indeed not. Her figure made his palms itch.

Unrestrained by the usual demands of polite dinner conversation, he surreptitiously let his gaze feast. Only when the desserts were set before them did he sit back and let his social senses take stock. Only then did he notice that while the others occasionally exchanged idle glances and the odd desultory comment, none looked at him, or at Catriona. Indeed, with the sole exception of the silent but watchful, and disapproving, Miss O'Rourke, they all kept their gazes carefully averted, as if fearful of drawing his attention. Only Jamie interacted with either Catriona or himself, and then only stiltedly, when need arose.

Curious, Richard tried to catch Malcolm's eye, and failed; the youth seemed, if anything, to sink further into his chair. Glancing at Catriona, Richard saw her look up and scan the table; everyone took care not to meet her gaze. Unperturbed, she patted her lips with her napkin. Richard focused on the soft pink curves, and remembered, with startling clarity, precisely how they tasted.

Shaking aside the memory, he inwardly shook his head. Apparently Seamus's family were so trenchantly timid, they were moved to treat both Catriona and himself like potentially dangerous animals who might bite if provoked.

Which definitely said something about his witch.

Maybe she really was a witch?

That thought provoked others—like what a witch would be like in bed; he was deep in salacious imaginings when Jamie nervously cleared his throat and turned to Catriona.

"Actually, Catriona, I've been thinking that, now Da's gone and you'll be my ward, that it really would be better—more fitting, I mean—if you were to come and live here."

Caught in the act of swallowing a spoonful of trifle, Catriona stilled, then swallowed, laid down her spoon, and looked directly at Jamie.

"With us, the family," he hurried on. "It must be very lonely at the vale all by yourself."

Catriona's expression grew stern; her green eyes held Jamie's. "Your father thought the same, if you recall?"

It was immediately clear everyone at the table, bar Richard, did; a communal shudder passed around the room, even including the footmen, silent by the walls.

"Luckily," Catriona went on, her gaze still locked with Jamie's, "Seamus thought better of it, and allowed me to live as The Lady wishes, at the manor." She paused, eyes steady, giving everyone time to feel the weight behind her words. Then she raised her brows. "Do you truly wish to set your will against that of The Lady?"

Jamie blanched. "No, no! We just thought you might like to ..." He gestured vaguely.

Catriona looked down and picked up her spoon. "I'm perfectly content at the manor."

The matter was closed. Jamie exchanged a glance with Mary at the other end of the table; she shrugged lightly and grimaced. Other members of the family shot quick glances at Catriona, then rapidly looked away.

Richard didn't; he continued to study her. Her authority was remarkable; she used it like a shield. She'd put it up and Jamie, poor sod, had run headlong into it. Richard recognized the ploy; she'd tried the same with him with her "*Put me down*," but he'd been too experienced to fall for it—she'd been all woman once he'd got his hands on her, soft, warm, and pliant. The thought of having his hands on her again, of having her warm, pliant, feminine flesh beneath him, made him shift in his seat.

And focused his mind even more. On why, exactly, he found her so ... appealing. She wasn't, in fact, classically beautiful; she was more powerfully attractive than that. It was, he decided, noting the independent set of her too-determined chin, the underlying sense of wildness that caught him—caught and focused his hunter's instincts so forcefully. Her aura of mystery, of magic, of feminine forces too powerful for simple words, was an open challenge to a man like him.

A bored rake like him.

She would never have been acceptable within the ton; that hint of the wild was far too strong for society's palate. She was no meek miss; she was different, and used no guile to conceal it. Her confidence, her presence, her authority had led him to think her in her late twenties; now he could see her more clearly, he realized that wasn't so. Early twenties. Which made her assurance and self-confidence even more intriguing. More challenging.

Richard set down his goblet; he'd had enough of cold silence. "Have you lived at this manor long, Miss Hennessy?"

She looked up, faint surprise in her eyes. "All my life, Mr. Cynster."

Richard raised his brows. "Where, exactly, is it?"

"In the Lowlands." When he waited, patently wanting more, she added: "The manor stands in the Vale of Casphairn, which is a valley in the foothills of Merrick." Licking trifle from her spoon, she considered him. "That's—"

"In the Galloway Hills," he returned.

Her brows rose. "Indeed."

"And who is your landlord?"

"No one." When he again raised his brows, she explained: "I own the manor—I inherited it from my parents."

Richard inclined his head. "And this lady you speak of?"

The smile she gave him was ageless. "The Lady." The cadence of her voice changed, investing her words with reverence. "She Who Knows All."

"Ah." Richard blinked. "I see." And he did. Christianity might rule in London and the towns, and in the Parliament, but the auld ways, the doctrines of days past, still held sway in the countryside. He had grown up in rural Cambridgeshire, in the fields and copses, seeing the old women gathering herbs, hearing of their balms and potions that could cure a large spectrum of mortal ills. He'd seen too much to be skeptical, and knew enough to treat any such practitioner with due respect.

She'd held his gaze steadily; Richard saw the gleam of triumph, of victorious smugness in her eyes. She thought she'd successfully warned him off—scared him away. Inwardly, his grin was the very essence of predatory; outwardly, his expression said nothing at all.

"Catriona?"

They both turned to see Mary rising and beckoning; Catriona rose, too, and joined the female exodus to the drawing room, leaving the gentlemen to their port.

Which was, to Richard's immense relief, excellent. Twirling his glass, he considered the ruby liquid within. "So,"—he flicked a glance at Jamie— "Catriona is now in your care?"

Jamie's sigh was heartfelt. "Yes—for another three years. Until she's twenty-five."

"Are her parents long dead?"

"Six years. They were killed in an accident in Glasgow while arranging to buy a cargo—a terrible shock it was."

Richard raised his brows. "An especially big shock for Catriona. She would have been—what? Seventeen?"

"Sixteen. Naturally, Da' wanted her here—the vale's an isolated spot, no place for a lone girl, you'd think."

"She wouldn't come?"

Jamie's face contorted. "Da' made her. She came." He shuddered, and took a long sip of his port. "It was horrific. The arguments—the shouting. I thought Da' would have a seizure, she goaded him that much. I don't think he'd ever had anyone argue back like she did—*I* wouldna dared."

As he drank more port, Jamie's accent emerged; like many Scots of his age, he'd learned to suppress it.

"She didna want to stay—Da' wanted her here. He had plans afoot to marry her well—she needed someone to take care of her lands, he thought."

"Her lands?"

"The vale." Jamie drained his glass. "She owns the whole damned valley from head to mouth. But she wasn't having any of Da's plans. Said she knew what she was doing, she had The Lady to guide her, and she would, on her mother's grave, obey The Lady, not Da'. She was dead set against marriage. Mind you, when those lairds who'd offered for her on the strength of her lands actually met her, they sang a different tune. All the offers dissolved like mist in a strong breeze."

Richard frowned, wondering if Scottish notions of feminine attractions were so different.

"Of course, everyone o' them was imagining bedding her, until they spoke to her." Jamie's lips quirked; he exchanged a conspiratorial glance with Richard. "She scared 'em silly—the beggars came from Edinburgh and Glasgow, or one of the cities, lairds in need of estates. They didna know about The Lady, and to hear Catriona tell it, if they displeased her at all, she wouldha' turned 'em into toads. Or eels. Or some such slimy creature."

Richard grinned. "They believed her?"

"Aye, well—when she wants to be believed, she can be that persuasive."

Recalling the power he'd heard her wield twice, Richard had no difficulty believing that.

"And that other one, Algaria—Miss O'Rourke—was there to help. So,"— Jamie reached for the decanter—"after that, there were no more offers. Da' was livid—Catriona was unmovable. The fighting raged for weeks."

"And?"

"She won." Jamie set down his glass. "She went back to the vale, an' that was that. Da' never spoke of her again. I didna think she'd agree to live here now, but Mary said we should at least ask. Especially after finding the letters."

"Letters?"

"Offers for her lands, rather than her hand. Heaps of 'em. Some from the lairds who'd given up notions of bedding her, others from all over, some from her neighbors in the Lowlands. All, however, for a pittance." Again Jamie drained his glass. "I found the pile in Da's desk—he'd scrawled comments on many." Jamie's lips twisted. "Like 'Bah! Am I a fool?'"

"The land's good?"

"Good?" Jamie set down his glass. "You won't find better in Scotland." He met Richard's eye. "According to Catriona and her people, The Lady sees to that."

Richard raised his brows.

"Aye, well." With a rueful grimace, Jamie pushed back his chair. "We'd best get back to the drawing room."

Entering the long room beside Jamie, Richard paused just beyond the threshold. To one side, Catriona stood chatting to one of Jamie's colorless sisters. Perhaps chatting was the wrong word—from her gestures, lecturing might be nearer the mark. The ever watchful Miss O'Rourke stood silently, hands clasped, by Catriona's shoulder; her gaze, black and expressionless, was already fixed on him. Richard resisted the urge to grin wickedly at her; instead, with his usual grace, he crossed to pay his compliments to his hostess.

Mary was easily flattered, easily flustered; Richard spent some time calming her, until she could smile at him and answer his questions.

"She doesn't seem to see any need for a husband." Her eyes darted to Catriona, then returned to his face. "It seems odd, I know, but she has been running the manor for six years now, and I gather everything goes smoothly." Another darting glance lingered on Catriona's elegant dark lavender gown. "She certainly seems to want for nothing, and she's never made any claim on the McEnerys."

"I'm surprised,"—Richard affected his most indolent drawl—"that there are no local aspirants to her hand. Or does the valley boast only a few souls?"

"Oh, no. The population's quite considerable, I believe. But none of the young men would look to Catriona, you know." Mary regarded him earnestly. "She's their 'lady,' you see. The lady of the vale."

"Ah." Richard nodded, although he didn't see at all, but there was a limit to how far he could question even sweet Mary without raising suspicions. But he wanted to understand who and what Catriona Hennessy was, and how she'd come to be so. She was an intriguing "lady" on a number of fronts; he'd been so bored, she was a breath of fresh air—a fresh taste to his jaded palate.

He glanced her way and saw her look sharply at Algaria O'Rourke as the older woman struggled to suppress a yawn. The conversation that ensued was easy to follow; Catriona, moved by concern, pulled rank and ordered her watchdog to bed. Richard quickly looked away—and felt, a second later, the older woman's suspicious glance. But she went, passing the tea trolley on her way. The butler stationed the trolley before Mary.

"Let me help." Richard collected the first two cups Mary poured. "I'll take them to Miss Hennessy and ..."

"Meg," Mary supplied with a smile. "If you would be so kind."

Richard smiled and moved away.

"Meg? Miss Hennessy?"

Both turned in response to his drawl. Meg's eyes fixed on the cups in his hands. "Oh! Ah ..." She swallowed, and turned a delicate shade of green. "I ... don't think so." She cast a desperate glance at Catriona. "If you'll excuse me?"

With a helpless look at Richard, she hurried across the room and slipped out of the door.

"Well!" Brows high, Richard looked down at the tea. "Is it that bad?"

"Of course not." Catriona relieved him of one cup. "It's just that Meg's increasing and a bit fragile at present. The most unexpected things turn her stomach."

"Is that what you've been so earnestly discussing?"

"Yes."

Richard met Catriona's gaze over the rim of her cup as she sipped; her head barely topped his shoulder, yet her manner proclaimed her belief that she was as powerful, if not more powerful, than he. There was no hint of feminine weakness, or any acknowledgment of susceptibility.

Lowering her cup, she eyed him evenly. "I'm a healer."

The declaration was cool; Richard affected polite surprise. "Oh?" He'd assumed as much, but better she think him an ignorant southerner, a gullible Sassenach, if she were so disposed. "Eye of newt and toe of frog?"

The look she cast him was measuring. "I use herbs and roots, and other lore."

"Do you spend much time hovering over a bubbling cauldron, or is it more like a well-stocked stillroom?"

She drew a tight breath, her gaze on his steadfastly innocent expression, then exhaled. "A stillroom. An *encyclopedic* one."

"Not a cave, then." Bit by bit, Richard drew her out—and with each factual answer, her fridigity melted a fraction more. He held to his harmless, bantering pose, letting his gaze touch her face only briefly, politely. Her hair drew his eyes more frequently, a magnetic beacon. Even among all the redheads in the room, her crowning glory made her stand out. The soft curls shimmered in the candlelight; those about her face and neck jiggled as she moved, exerting the same mesmeric attraction as dancing flames. They held the promise of heat—Richard felt an overwhelming urge to warm his hands in them.

He blinked and forced himself to look away.

"Naturally, there are some things not available locally, but we send out for them."

"Naturally," he murmured. Shifting so he stood beside her, supposedly scanning the room, he glanced swiftly at her profile. The ice had melted significantly; with her flaming tresses and those gold sparks in her eyes, he felt sure there'd be a volcano beneath. For the first time since joining her, he focused intently on her face. "Your lips taste of roses, did you know?"

She stiffened, but didn't disappoint him; the look she shot him over the rim of her cup held fire, not ice. "I thought you would be gentleman enough to forget that incident entirely. Wipe it from your mind."

There was compulsion in her last words; Richard let it flow past him. He smiled lazily down at her. "You have that twisted. I'm far *too* much a gentleman to forget that incident, not even its most minor detail."

"No gentleman would mention it."

"How many gentlemen do you know?"

She sniffed. "You shouldn't have grabbed me like that."

"My dear Miss Hennessy! You walked into my arms."

"You shouldn't have held me like that."

"If I hadn't held you, you would have slipped and fallen on your luscious—"

"And you certainly shouldn't have kissed me."

"That was unavoidable."

She blinked. "Unavoidable?"

Richard looked down, into her green eyes. "Utterly." He held her gaze, then raised his brows. "Of course, you didn't have to kiss me back."

Color rose in her cheeks; she looked back at her cup. "A moment of temporary insanity, immediately regretted."

"Oh?"

She glanced up, hearing danger in his tone, but wasn't quick enough to stop him from stroking, not the nape of her neck, so temptingly exposed, but the coppery curls that caressed her sensitive skin. Unobserved by the company, Richard caressed them.

And she shivered, quivered.

Then hauled in a breath and thrust her empty cup at him. "I find the company entirely too fatiguing—and the journey here was boring in the extreme." Her words were couched in sheet ice, her tone a chill wind blowing straight from the Arctic. "If you'll excuse me, I believe I shall retire."

"Now, *that*," Richard said, taking the cup, "I didn't expect."

She paused in the act of stepping away and shot him a suspicious glance. "What didn't you expect?"

"I didn't expect you to run away." He looked down at her as she studied him, and wondered how she did it. No hint of volcanic heat remained, not even a tiny glow of feminine warmth; she was encased in polar ice, colder than any iceberg. And the air had literally turned chill—the lady of the vale could give the ice-maidens of London lessons. He let the ends of his lips curve. "I'm only teasing you."

It came to him then—no other man had—no other man had ever dared.

She frowned, measuring him and his words. Eventually, she exhaled. "I won't go if you keep your hands to yourself and don't mention our previous encounter. As I told you, that was a complete and utter mistake."

Catriona imbued the last words with conviction, but, as before, it had little effect. He seemed immune, as if he could deflect her suggestive powers easily—an observation that did little to settle her skittish nerves.

When she'd walked into the drawing room and seen him there, his blue gaze direct, as if he'd been waiting for her, she had, for the first time in her life, literally felt faint. Dumbfounded. And ... something else. Something more akin to searing excitement, something that had made her nervous, aware, set alive in a way she'd never been before.

For the first time in a long while, she wasn't sure she could control her world, her situation. She was not at all sure she could control him.

Which, first and last, was the crux of her problem.

She watched as he set their empty cups on a side table, and wished he'd been forced to keep them in his hands. Hands she'd already spent some time studying; long-fingered, elegantly made, they were the hands of an artist, not a warrior. At least, not a simple warrior. Standing beside him, she was all too aware that her bedevilled senses had reported accurately on the man who had stolen a kiss—several kisses—from her. He was large and strong—not the strength of sheer brawn, but a more supple, skillful strength, infinitely more dangerous. There was intelligence in his eyes, and something else besides— the embers of that hot, prowling hunger glowed behind the blue.

He straightened. And nodded to the rest of the company. "Is this all Seamus's family?"

"Yes." She scanned the room's occupants. "They all live here."

"All the time, I understand."

"They have little choice. Seamus was a miser in many ways." She glanced about the room. "You must have noticed the ambience—hopefully, once Jamie and Mary and the others finally realize it's theirs now, and they no longer need Seamus's approval for every penny spent, they'll make it more livable."

"More like a home? Amen to that."

Surprised by his acuity, Catriona glanced up; his polite mask told her nothing.

He trapped her gaze. "You clearly didn't like Seamus. If you won't consider moving here to live, why have you come?"

"I'm here to pay my final respects." She considered, then added, more truthfully: "He was a hard man, but he did as he deemed right. He might have been an adversary, but I did respect him."

"Magnanimous in victory?"

"There was no battle."

"That's not how the locals tell it."

She humphed. "He was misguided—I set him right."

"Misguided because he wanted you to wed?"

"Precisely."

"What have you got against the male of the species?"

How had they got onto this topic? She slanted her tormentor a sharp glance. "Just that—they're male."

"A sorry fact, but most women find there are compensations."

She humphed again, the sound eloquently disbelieving. "Such as?"

"Such as . . ."

His tone registered; she turned and met his eyes—and the glow that danced therein. Her breathing seized; her heartbeat suddenly sounded loud. With an effort, she found breath enough to warn: *"No teasing."*

His lips, untrustworthy things—she tried hard not to focus on them—lifted; his eyes glowed all the more. "A little teasing would do you good." His voice had dropped to a deep purr, sliding over her senses; Catriona detected the power in the words, although she hadn't met its like before. It was... beguiling; instinctively, she resisted. She felt like she was swaying, but knew she hadn't moved.

"You might even find you . . ."—his brows quirked—"enjoy it."

Behind her back, screened from the company, his hand rose; Catriona sensed it with every pore of her skin, every nerve in her body. An inch from her silk-encased form, it rose, slowly skimming without touching, until it reached her neckline and rose . . .

"Don't!" The word was a breathless command; his hand halted, hovering, close, very close, to her quivering curls. If he touched them again . . .

"Very well."

A seductive purr, with no hint of contrition; *he* was being triumphantly magnanimous now. But his hand didn't disappear—it reversed direction. Slowly, so slowly her skin had ample time to prickle and heat, his hand traced her back, down over her shoulderblades, over the slight indentation at her waist, then, even more slowly, over the curve of her hips.

Not once did he touch her, yet when his hand dropped away, she was shaking inside—so badly, as she stepped away and, half-turning, inclined her head in his direction, she could barely form the words: "If you'll excuse me, I should retire."

She left him without meeting his eyes, quite sure of the male triumph she would see there, unsure of her hold on her temper if she did.

Meg had returned; she was sitting, wan-faced, in an armchair. Catriona stopped before her. "Come to my room when you go up—I'll have that potion ready."

"Are you going up now?"

"Yes." Catriona bit off the word, then forced a smile. "I fear the journey here was more fatiguing than I'd thought."

With a regal nod, she swept from the room, conscious, to the very last, of a blue, blue gaze fixed unwaveringly on her back.

CHAPTER
Three

୫ଡ଼ଡ଼ଡ଼

A few minutes before eleven o'clock the next morning, Catriona made her way to the library, whence they'd been summoned to hear Seamus's last testament. She'd breakfasted in her room—because it was warmer there.

The attempt at self-deception worried her, as did its cause. She'd breakfasted privately so she wouldn't have to face Richard Cynster and the power he wielded. Whatever it was. She knew, of course, but she wasn't game to let herself contemplate it. At all. That way lay confusion.

A footman stood before the library door; he opened it and she glided through. And gave thanks that some sensible soul had given orders for the fire to be built up above its usual meager pile. The cavernous fireplace filled one end of the monstrous room, the largest in the house, stretching the length of one entire wing. As the walls were stone and the narrow windows uncurtained, the room was perpetually chill. She'd dressed appropriately in a dress of blue merino wool with long fitted sleeves, but was still grateful for the fire.

Jamie and Mary sat on the *chaise;* the others sat in armchairs on either side, all the seats arrayed in a semicircle facing the fire and, to one side, the huge old desk behind which Seamus had habitually sat. Now, a Perth solicitor sat in Seamus's chair and shuffled papers.

Subsiding into the one vacant armchair, between Meg and Malcolm, Catriona returned the solicitor's polite nod, then acknowledged the others present, only at the very last letting her eyes meet Richard Cynster's.

He sat on the other side of the *chaise,* beyond Mary, filling a chair with an indolent grace in stark contrast to the tentative postures of the other males present. He inclined his head, his expression impassive; Catriona inclined her head in return and forced her eyes elsewhere.

One glance had been enough to fill her mind with a vision far more powerful than the one that had brought her here. He was wearing a blue coat of a deeper hue than her dress, superbly tailored to hug his broad shoulders. A blue-and-black striped silk waistcoat covered a snowy white shirt topped by a beautifully tied cravat. His breeches, of the finest buckskin, clung to long, powerful thighs far too tightly for her comfort; his boots she already knew.

She wished him anywhere else but here; she had to fight to keep her eyes from him. Malcolm, beside her, was not so restrained; slumped in his chair, he gnawed on one knuckle and stared openly at the lounging elegance opposite. Catriona suppressed a waspish urge to tell him he'd never measure up, not while he slouched like that.

Instead, she breathed deeply, and determinedly settled, drawing calmness to her with every breath. Hands clasped in her lap, she reminded herself that she was here by The Lady's orders; perhaps she'd been sent here to meet Richard Cynster to learn what it was she should avoid.

Masterful men.

Denying the urge to glance at one, she fixed her gaze on the solicitor and willed him to get on with his business. He looked up and blinked, then owlishly peered at the mantel clock. "Hurrumph! Yes." He glanced around, clearly counting heads, matching faces against a list before laying it aside. "Well then, if we're all assembled . . .?"

When no one contradicted him, he picked up a long parchment, cleared his throat, and commenced. "I read the words of our client, Seamus McEnery, Laird of Keltyhead, as dictated to our clerk on the fifth of September this year."

He cleared his throat again, and changed his voice; all understood that they were now hearing Seamus's words verbatim.

"'This, my last will and testament, will not be what any of you, gathered here at my request, will be expecting. This is my last chance at influencing things on this earth—to put right what I did wrong, to rectify the omissions I made. With the hindsight of age, I've been moved to use this, my will, to that end.'"

Not surprisingly, a nervous flutter did the rounds of the listeners. Catriona was immune, but even she frowned—what was the wily old badger up to now? Even Richard Cynster, she noticed, shifted slightly.

Settling in his chair, Richard inwardly frowned and struggled to shake off the premonition Seamus's opening paragraph had evoked. He was only a minor player in this scene; there was no reason to imagine those words were aimed at him.

Yet, as the solicitor went on, it seemed he was wrong.

"'My first bequest will close a chapter of my life otherwise long completed. I wish to give into her son's hands the necklace my first wife bequeathed to him. As I have stipulated that he, Richard Melville Cynster, must be here to receive it, it has now served its purpose.'" The solicitor fumbled on the desk, then rose and crossed to Richard.

"Thank you," Richard murmured, lifting the delicate strands from the solicitor's gnarled hands. Gently, he untangled the finely wrought gold links, interspersed with opaque rose pink stones. From the center of the necklace hung a long crystal of amethyst, etched with signs too small for him to make out.

"It was quite out of order for Mr. McEnery to keep it from you," the solicitor whispered. "Please do believe it was entirely against our advice."

Studying the pendant, noting the curious warmth of the stones, Richard nodded absentmindedly. As the solicitor returned to the desk, Richard glanced up—from across the circle of seats, Catriona's gaze was fixed on the pendant. Her absorption was complete; deliberately, he let the crystal hang, then moved it—her gaze remained riveted. The solicitor reseated himself; Richard closed his fist about the pendant. Catriona sighed and looked up; she met his gaze, then calmly looked away. Resisting an urge to raise his brows, Richard pocketed the necklace.

"Now, where were we? Ah ... yes." The solicitor cleared his throat, then warbled: "'As to all the wealth of which I die possessed, property, furniture, and funds, all is to be held in trust for a period of one week from today, the day on which my will is read.'" The man paused, drew breath, then went on in a rush: "'If during that one week, Richard Melville Cynster agrees to marry Catriona Mary Hennessy, the estate will be divided amongst my surviving children, as described below. If, however, by the end of that week, Richard Cynster refuses to marry Catriona Hennessy, my entire estate is to be sold and the funds divided equally between the dioceses of Edinburgh and Glasgow.'"

Shock—absolute and overpowering—held them all silent. For one minute, only the rustle of parchment and the odd crackle from the fire broke the stillness. Richard recovered, if that was the right word, first; he dragged in a huge breath, conscious of a sense of unreality, as if in a crazy dream. He glanced at Catriona, but she wasn't looking at him. Her gaze was fixed in the distance, her expression one of stunned incredulity.

"How could he?" Her vehement question broke the spell; she focused abruptly on the solicitor.

A cacophany of questions and exclamations poured forth. Seamus's family could not take in what their sire had done to them; most of them were helpless, barely coherent.

Seated beside Richard, Mary turned a stricken face to him. "My God—*how* will we manage?" Her eyes filled; she grasped Richard's hand, not in supplication, but for support.

Instinctively, he gave it, curling his fingers about hers and pressing reassuringly. He saw her face as she turned to Jamie, saw the hopelessness that swamped her.

"What will we do?" she all but sobbed as Jamie gathered her into his arms.

As stunned as she, Jamie looked at the solicitor over her head. *"Why?"*

It was, Richard felt, the most pertinent question; the solicitor took it as his cue and waved his hands at the others to hush them. "If I might continue ...?"

They fell silent, and he picked up the will. He drew breath, then looked up, peering over his pince-nez. "This is a most irregular will, so I feel no compunction in breaking with tradition and stating that I and all others in my firm argued most strongly against these provisions, but Mr. McEnery would not be moved. As it stands, the will is legal and, in our opinion, uncontestable by law."

With that, he looked down at the parchment. "'These next words are addressed to my ward, Catriona Mary Hennessy. Regardless of what she might think, it was my duty to see to her future. As in life I was not strong enough to influence her, so in death I am putting her in the way of one who, if half the tales told of him and his clan are true, possesses the requisite talents to deal with her.'"

There followed a detailed description of how the estate was to be divided between Seamus's children in the event Richard agreed to marry Catriona, to which no one listened. The family and Catriona were too busy decrying Seamus's perfidy; Richard was too absorbed in noting that not one of them imagined any other outcome than that the estate would pass to the Church.

By the time the solicitor had reached the end of the will, despair, utter and complete, had taken possssession of the McEnerys. Jamie, swallowing his bitter disappointment, rose to shake the solicitor's hand and thank him. Then he turned away to comfort Mary, distraught and weeping.

"It's iniquitous," she sobbed. "Not even the barest living! And what about the children?"

"Hush, shussh." Jamie tried to soothe her, his expression one of abject defeat.

"He was mad." Malcolm spat the words out. "He's cheated us of everything we'd a right to expect."

Meg and Cordelia were sobbing, their meek spouses incoherent.

Sitting quietly in his chair, untouched by the emotion sweeping his hosts, Richard watched, and listened, and considered. Considered the fact that not one of the company expected him to save them.

Considered Catriona, sleek and slender in deep blue, her hair burning even more brightly in the dull and somber room. She was comforting Meg, counselling her away from hysteria, exuding calm in an almost visible stream. Straining his ears, he listened to her words.

"There's nothing to be done, so there's no sense in working yourself into a state and having a miscarriage. You know as well as anyone I didn't get along with Seamus, but I would never have believed him capable of this. I'm as deeply shocked as you." She continued talking quickly, filling Meg's ears, forcing the woman to listen to her and not descend into excessive tears. "The solicitor says it's a *fait accompli*, so other than calling down curses on Seamus's dead head, there's no use in having the vapors now. We must all get together and see what can be done, what can be salvaged."

She continued, moving the direction of her thoughts, and Meg's and Cordelia's and their husbands', into a more positive vein. But that vein followed the line of what to do to cope with this unexpected shock; at no point did she, or anyone, not even Jamie or Mary when they joined the group, allude to any alternative.

Not once did Catriona glance his way; it was almost as if she'd dismissed him from her mind, forgotten his existence. As if they'd all forgotten him—the dark predator, the interloper, the Cynster in their midst. No one thought to appeal to him.

To them all, not only Catriona, the outcome was a *fait accompli*. They didn't even bother to ask for his decision, his answer to Seamus's challenge.

But then, they were the weak and helpless; he was something else again.

"Ah-hem."

Richard glanced up to see the solicitor, his papers packed, peering at him. His exclamation startled the others to silence.

"If I could have your formal decision, Mr. Cynster, so that we can start finalizing the estate?"

Richard raised his brows. "I have one week to decide, I believe?"

The solicitor blinked, then straightened. "Indeed." He shot a glance at Catriona. "Seven full days is the time the will stipulates."

"Very well." Uncrossing his legs, Richard rose. "You may call on me here, one week from today"—he smiled slightly at the man—"and I will give you my answer then."

Responding to his manner, the solicitor bowed. "As you wish, sir. In accordance with the will, the estate will remain in trust until that time."

Quickly gathering his papers, the solicitor shook hands with Richard, then with Jamie, stunned anew, then, with a general nod to the rest of them, quit the library.

The door shut behind him; the click of the latch echoed through the huge room, through the unnatural stillness. As one, the family turned to stare, dumbfounded, at Richard, all except Catriona; she was already staring at him, through ominously narrowed eyes.

Richard smiled, smoothly, easily. "If you'll excuse me, I believe I'll stretch my legs."

With that, he did so, strolling nonchalantly to the door.

"Don't get your hopes up." Brutally candid, Catriona all but pushed Jamie into a chair in the parlor, then plopped down on the *chaise* facing him. "Now, concentrate," she admonished him, "and tell me everything you know of Richard Cynster."

Still dazed, Jamie shrugged. "He's the son of Da's first wife—hers, and the man the English government sent up here one time. A duke, he was—I've forgotten the title, if I ever heard it." He screwed up his face. "I can't remember much—it was all before I was born. I only know what Da' let slip now and then."

Catriona restrained her temper with an effort. "Just tell me everything you *can* remember." She needed to know the enemy. When Jamie looked blank, she blew out a breath. "All right—questions. Does he live in London?"

"Aye—he came up from there. His valet said so."

"He has a valet?"

"Aye—a very starchy sort."

"What's his reputation?" Catriona blinked. "No—never mind." She muttered beneath her breath: "I know more about that than you." About a man with lips like cool marble, arms that had held her trapped, and a body ... she blinked again. "His family—what do you know of them? Do they acknowledge him openly?"

"Seemingly." Jamie shrugged. "I recall Da' saying the Cynsters were a damned powerful lot—military, mostly, a verra old family. They sent seven to Waterloo—I remember Da' saying as the ton had labelled them invincible because all seven returned with nary a scratch."

Catriona humphed. "Are they wealthy?"

"Aye—I'd say so."

"Prominent in society?"

"Aye—they're well connected and all tha'. There's this group of them—" Jamie broke off, coloring.

Catriona narrowed her eyes. "This group of them?"

Jamie shifted. "It's nothing as . . ." His words trailed away.

"As should concern me?" Catriona held his gaze mercilessly. "Let me be the judge of that. This group?"

She waited; eventually, Jamie capitulated. "Six of them—all cousins. The ton calls them the Bar Cynster."

"And what does this group do?"

Jamie squirmed. "They have reputations. And nicknames. Like Devil, and Demon, and Lucifer."

"I see. And what nickname is Richard Cynster known by?"

Jamie's lips compressed mulishly; Catriona levelled her gaze at him.

"Scandal."

Catriona's lips thinned. "I might have guessed. And no, you need not explain how he came by the title."

Jamie looked relieved. "I dinna recall Da' saying much more—other than they were all right powerful bastards wi' the women, but he would say that, in the circumstances."

Catriona humphed. Right powerful bastards with women—so, thanks to her late guardian's misbegotten notions, here she was, faced with a right powerful bastard who, on top of it all, was in truth a bastard. Did that make him more or less powerful? Somehow, she didn't think the answer was less. She looked at Jamie. "Seamus said nothing else?"

Jamie shook his head. "Other than that it's only fools think they can stand against a Cynster."

Right powerful bastards with women—that, Catriona thought, summed it up. Arms crossed, she paced before the windows of the back parlor, keeping watch over the snow-covered lawn across which Richard Cynster would return to the house.

She could see it all now—what Seamus had intended with his iniquitous will. His final attempt to interfere with her life, from beyond the grave, no less. She wasn't having it, a Cynster or not, powerful bastard or otherwise.

If anything, Richard Cynster's antecedents sounded even worse than she'd imagined. She knew little of the ways of the ton, but the fact that his father's wife, indeed, the whole family, had apparently so readily accepted a bastard into their midst, smacked of male dominance. At the very least, it suggested Cynster wives were weak, mere cyphers to their powerful husbands. Cynster males sounded like tyrants run amok, very likely domestic dictators, accustomed to ruling ruthlessly.

But no man would ever rule her, ruthlessly or otherwise. She would never allow that to happen; the fate of the vale and her people rested on her shoulders. And to fulfill that fate, to achieve her aim on this earth, she needed to remain free, independent, capable of exercising her will as required, capable of acting as her people needed, without the constraint of a conventional marriage. A conventional husband.

A conventional *powerful bastard* of a husband was simply not possible for the lady of the vale.

The distant scrunch of a boot on snow had her peering out the window. It was mid-afternoon; the light was rapidly fading. She saw the dark figure she'd been waiting for emerge from the trees and stroll up the slope, his powerful physique in no way disguised by a heavy, many-caped greatcoat.

Panic clutched her—it had to be panic. It cut off her breathing and left her quivering. Suddenly, the room seemed far too dark. She grabbed a tinderbox and raced around, lighting every candle she could reach. By the time he'd gained the terrace, and she opened the long windows and waved him in, the room was ablaze.

He entered, brushing snowflakes from his black hair, with nothing more than a quirking brow to show he'd noticed her burst of activity. Catriona ignored it. Pressing her hands together, she waited only until he'd shrugged off his coat and turned to lay it aside before stating: "I don't know *what* is going on in your mind, but I *will not* agree to marry you."

The statement was as categorical and definite as she could make it. He straightened and turned toward her.

The room shrank.

The walls pressed in on her; she couldn't breathe, she could barely think. The compulsion to flee—to escape—was strong; stronger still was the mesmeric attraction, the impulse to learn what power it was that set her pulse pounding, her skin tingling, her nerves flickering.

Defiantly she held firm and tilted her chin.

His eyes met hers; there was clear consideration in the blue, but beyond that, his expression told her nothing. Then he moved—toward her, toward the fire—abruptly, Catriona scuttled aside to allow him to warm his hands. While he did so, she struggled to breathe, to think—to suppress the skittering sensations that frazzled her nerves, to prise open the vise that had laid seige to her breathing. Why a large male should evoke such a reaction she did not know—or rather, she didn't like to think. The blacksmith at the vale certainly didn't have the same effect.

He straightened, and she decided it was his movements, so smoothly controlled, so reminiscent of leashed power, like a panther not yet ready to pounce, that most unnerved her. Leaning one arm along the mantelpiece, he looked down at her.

"Why?"

She frowned. "Why what?"

The very ends of his lips twitched. "Why won't you agree to marry me?"

"Because I have no need of a husband." *Especially not a husband like you.* She folded her arms beneath her breasts and focused, solely, on his face. "My role within the vale does not permit the usual relationships a woman of my station might expect to enjoy." She tilted her chin. "I am unmarried by choice, not for lack of offers. It's a sacrifice I have made for my people."

She was rather pleased with that tack; men like the Cynsters understood sacrifice and honor.

His black brows rose; silently he considered her. Then, "Who will inherit your manor, your position, if you do not marry and beget heirs?"

Inwardly, Catriona cursed; outwardly, she merely raised her brows back. "In time, I will, of course, marry for heirs, but I need not do so for many years yet."

"Ah—so you don't have a complete and absolute aversion to marriage?"

Head high, her eyes locked on his, Catriona drew a deep breath and held it. "No," she eventually admitted, and started to pace. "But there are various caveats, conditions, and considerations involved."

"Such as?"

"Such as my devotions to The Lady. And my duties as a healer. You may not realize it, but . . ."

Propped against the mantelpiece, Richard listened to her excuses—all revolved about the duties she saw as devolving to her through her ownership of the manor. She paced incessantly back and forth; he almost ordered her to sit, so he could sit, too, and not tower over her, forcing her to glance up every time she wanted to check his deliberately uninformative countenance, then he realized who her pacing reminded him of. Honoria, Devil's duchess, also paced, in just the same way, skirts swishing in time with her temper. Catriona's skirts were presently swinging with agitated tension; Richard inwardly sighed and leaned more heavily on the mantelpiece.

"So you see," she concluded, swinging to face him, "at present, a husband is simply out of the question."

"No, I don't see." He trapped her gaze. "All you've given me is a litany of your duties, which in no way that I can see preclude a husband."

She had never in her adult life had to explain herself to anyone; that was clearly written in the astonished, slightly hoity expression that infused her green eyes. Then they flared. "I don't have *time* for a husband!" Quick as a flash, she added: "For the arguments, like this one."

"Why should you argue?"

"Why, indeed—but all men argue, and a husband certainly would. He would want me to do things his way, not my way—not The Lady's way."

"Ah—so your real concern is that a husband would interfere with your duties."

"That he'd seek to interfere in *how I perform* my duties." She paused in her pacing and eyed him narrowly. "Gentlemen such as you have a habit of expecting to have your own way in all things. I could not possibly marry such a man."

"Because you want to have your *own* way in *all things?*"

Her eyes flashed. "Because I need to be free to perform my duties—free of any husbandly interference."

Calmly, he considered her. "What if a husband didn't interfere?"

She snorted derisively and resumed her pacing.

Richard's lips twitched. "It is possible, you know."

"That you would let your wife go her own way?" At the far end of her route, she turned and raked him with a dismissively contemptuous glance. "Not even in the vale do pigs fly."

It was no effort not to smile; Richard felt her raking gaze pass over every inch of his body—he had to clamp an immediate hold over his instinctive reaction. Ravishing her wouldn't serve his purpose—he had yet to decide just what his purpose was. Learning more of her would, however, greatly assist in clarifying that point.

"If we married, a man such as I," his tone parodied her distinction, "might, given your position, agree to"—he gestured easily—"accommodate you and your duties." She shot him a skeptical glance; he trapped her gaze. "There's no reason some sort of agreement couldn't be reached."

She considered him, a frown slowly forming in her eyes, then she humphed and turned away.

Richard studied her back, the sweeping line of her spine from her nape to the ripe hemispheres of her bottom. The view was one designed to distract him, attract him—the stiffness of her stance, the sheer challenge of her reluctance, only deepened the magnetic tug.

"You're *not* seriously considering marrying me."

She made the statement, clear and absolute, to the darkness beyond the window.

Richard lowered his arm and leaned back against the mantlepiece. "Aren't I?"

She continued to gaze into the gloaming. "You only claimed the week's grace because we all took it for granted that you would refuse." She paused, then added: "You don't like being taken for granted."

Richard felt his brows rise. "Actually, it was because *you* took me for granted. The others don't count."

The swift glance she shot him was scathing. "I might have known you'd say it was my fault."

"You might have noticed I haven't. You *were* the reason I so promptly claimed the time, but ... on reflection"—his gesture encompassed the woods through which he'd tramped—"I would have claimed it anyway."

She frowned. "Why?"

He studied her and wondered if he could ever explain to anyone how he felt about family. "Let's just say that I've a constitutional dislike of making rushed decisions, and Seamus laid his plans very carefully. He knew I wouldn't appreciate being used as a pawn to disenfranchise his family."

Her frown deepened. "Because of being a bastard?"

"No. Because of being a Cynster."

Her frown grew more puzzled. "I don't understand."

Richard grimaced. "Nor do I. I'm not at all clear, for instance, on why Seamus went to such lengths—such machinations—to get me here, into this bizarre situation."

She humphed and turned back to the window. "That's because you didn't know Seamus. He was forever plotting and scheming—like many men of wealth and position. Indeed, he often spent so much time making plans he never got around to the execution."

Richard raised his brows. "No wonder my father was sent here." Catriona looked her question; he met her gaze. "Cynsters are renowned for action. We might plan, just enough, but our talents lie in the execution. Never ones to drag our heels."

She humphed softly and turned back to the night. After a moment, she raised a hand and started drawing spirals on the cold pane. "I was thinking . . ." She paused; he could hear the grimace in her voice. "Seamus may have envisioned marriage to me as a penance—a sort of deferred punishment—with you paying the price in place of your father."

Richard frowned. "If he thought that, then the joke's on him. It would be no hardship to be married to you."

She turned her head; their gazes locked—everything else did as well. Time, their breathing, even their heartbeats. Desire shimmered, filling the air, heightening senses, tightening nerves.

She drew breath and looked away. "Be that as it may, you *aren't* considering it."

Richard sighed. When would she learn she couldn't sway him with her tone? "Think what you will. But the solicitor's left and won't be back for a week. I won't make my decision until then." He wouldn't be rushed, he wasn't impulsive—and he needed to know more. Of her, and *why* Seamus had made such an iniquitous will.

She humphed and muttered something; he thought it might have been "stubborn as a mule."

Pushing away from the mantelpiece, he strolled toward her, his footfalls muffled by the carpet. As he neared, she whirled, only just suppressing a gasp. She went to step back—and stopped herself. And tilted her chin instead.

Inwardly, he smiled—she looked deliciously ruffled, and it was he who'd done the ruffling. "Don't worry, I'm not about to pounce."

The gold flecks in her eyes flared. "I didn't imagine—"

"Yes, you did." He looked down at her, at her too-wide eyes, at the way her breasts rose and fell. Bringing his eyes back to hers, he grimaced. "If it eases your mind, as my host's ward and a virtuous, unmarried lady, you are effectively removed from my list of potential seductees."

He could follow her thoughts easily in her vibrant eyes.

"Ah, no," he murmured, "that doesn't mean you're safe with me." He smiled. "Just that I won't seduce you without marrying you."

She glared—at this distance, he could feel the heat. It stopped abruptly; an arrested expression filled her eyes. Then she focused on him.

"I just realized ... Seamus only required *you* to agree to marry *me*, not that *I* agree to marry *you*. He knew I wouldn't agree; I'm under no compulsion to obey him." She frowned. "What *did* he imagine he'd achieve?"

Looking down into her upturned face, at her eyes, wide and puzzled, at her lips, warm and slightly parted, Richard fought down an urge to kiss her. "I told you—Seamus made a very thorough study of the Cynsters."

"So?" She searched his face, then his eyes.

"So he knew that, if I publically declare I'll wed you, I will."

Her eyes flew wide, then narrowed to green shards. "That's *ridiculous!* You can't simply declare we'll wed—*I* have to agree. And I won't!"

"*If* I decide to have you ..."—he kept his words deliberate, pausing to let the qualification sink in—"I'll have to change your mind."

"And just how do you imagine doing that?"

The words were flung at him, a challenge, a taunt. Brows slowly rising, his gaze intent, locked on hers, Richard held her trapped—and raised one hand. And deliberately caressed the curl quivering by one ear.

Her ice shattered—she gasped, shivered, and stepped back. The blood drained from her face, then rushed back as she stiffened.

And threw him a sizzling glare. "Forget it!"

She whirled, skirts hissing; spine rigid, she stalked out.

And slammed the door behind her.

CHAPTER
Four

৪৩⁄৩৪

That night, Catriona slept poorly, bedevilled by a vision of a warrior's face. Forced to view that same vision, in the flesh, over the breakfast table, she inwardly sniffed and decided to go for a long ride.

Heading upstairs to change, she met Algaria at the top of the stairs. Algaria's black gaze swept her, then fastened on her face.

"Where are you off to so early?"

"I need some fresh air—how can a place so cold be so stuffy?"

"Hmm." Looking down into the hall, Algaria sniffed disparagingly. "The atmosphere is certainly less than convivial"—she shot a shrewd glance at Catriona—"what with this unnecessary charade."

"Charade?"

"Aye. It's plain as a pikestaff that bastard from below has no real intention to wed—not you, nor, I'll warrant, any woman." Algaria's face was set, the lines deeply etched. "It's clear he's a wastrel and just enjoying himself at our expense. Even Mary holds no hope other than that he'll eventually decline to be a part of Seamus's wild scheme and go back to London. She thinks he's making a show of considering the issue out of politeness."

Catriona stiffened. "Indeed?"

Algaria's lips twitched; she patted Catriona's hand. "No need to take offense—it's what we want, after all." She started down the stairs. "Him to go away and leave you alone."

Catriona stared at the back of Algaria's head; her answering "Hmm" was supposed to be approving—somehow, a hint of disappointment crept in. She shut her ears to it; swinging about, she marched purposefully to her room.

It was the work of a few minutes to don her riding habit, a snugly fitting jacket and full skirt in jewel green twill. Serviceable, it was not especially warm; she hunted through the wardrobe for her old-fashioned fur-lined cloak. Her hair was a problem—in the end, she braided it and looped the braids about her head.

"There!" Satisfied her hair would not come loose no matter how hard she rode, she swung the cloak about her shoulders and headed for the door.

The stables huddled between the main house and the mountain, sheltered from the incessant winds and, at present, the lightly flurrying snow. The day was overcast, but the clouds were too light to deter her; she was accustomed to riding in all weather, whenever her duties called. The views might be grey, but they were visible; the hovering clouds kept the temperature above freezing. While the snow on the bare fields was hoof-deep, on the paths and tracks, the cover was less, and none of it was dangerously icy.

All in all, a perfectly acceptable winter's day to go riding in The Trossachs. That was Catriona's determined thought as, atop a strong chestnut, she clattered out of the stable yard and headed into the trees. She'd ridden often in the few weeks she'd previously spent here as an escape from the battleground of the house; she remembered the tracks well. The one she took wound its way through stands of birch girding the rocky mountainside, eventually meeting another bridle path leading to the summit. Looking forward to a brisk gallop across the clear top of Keltyhead, she urged her mount upward.

The Highlands spread out before her as she emerged from the trees onto the normally wind-swept mountaintop. The earlier breeze had died to nothing more than a whisper, threading sibilantly through the bare boughs. Even the fall of fine snow had ceased. Catriona's spirits soared; scanning the wide views, she drew in a deep breath. Directly before her, an open area thinly covered with rough mountain grass beckoned—she waited for no more. A smile on her face, a "Whoop!" on her lips, she set the chestnut to a canter, then shifted fluidly into a gallop.

Cold, bitterly fresh, the air rushed to greet her. It whipped her cheeks and tugged at her braids. She welcomed it joyously—one of The Lady's simple pleasures. Exhilarated, at one with her mount, she journeyed across the empty space, immersed in the wide silence about her.

She was halfway across the treeless expanse when a heavy clop and a whinny broke the stillness. Glancing back, she saw a familiar tall figure, mounted, watching her from the skirts of the forest. As still and dark as the trees behind him, he studied her. Then he moved; the deep-chested black beneath him stepped out powerfully, on a course to intercept her.

Her breath tangled in her throat; abruptly, Catriona looked forward and urged her mount on. Damn the man! Why couldn't he leave her alone? The thought was shrewish, the smile tugging at her lips much less so—*that* was instinctively feminine, a reflection of the *frisson* of excitement that had shot down her nerves.

Had he followed her?

She plunged on, determined to lose him—he rode much heavier than she. And she knew she rode well; as the end of the open area neared, she considered which of the three tracks ahead, each leading in a different direction over different terrain, would best serve her purpose. That depended on how close he was. She glanced over her shoulder, expecting to see him in the distance—and nearly lost her seat. Eyes widening, she gasped and swung forward. He was only two lengths away!

Lunging onto the nearest path, she raced along it, through twists, around turns, over rocky ground screened by tall trees. She burst into the next clearing at a flat gallop, the chestnut eagerly answering the challenge. They flew across the snowy white ground—but she heard, insistent, persistent, inexorably drawing nearer, the heavy thud of the black's hooves gradually gaining ground, moving alongside.

A quick glance revealed her nemesis riding effortlessly, managing one of Seamus's big stallions with ease. He sat the horse like a god—the warrior of her dreams. The sight stole her breath; abruptly, she looked ahead. Why on earth was she running?

And how, once he caught up with her, would she explain her reckless flight? What excuse could she give for fleeing so precipitously?

Catriona blinked, then, dragging in a breath, slowed the chestnut and wheeled away from the approaching trees. In a smooth arc, she curved back into the clearing; the black followed on the chestnut's heels. She slowed to a walk as they neared a section where the trees fell away. Halting, she crossed her hands on the saddlebow; eyes fixed on the white mountains spread before her, she breathed deeply, then exhaled, forcing her shoulders to relax. "So exhilarating, a quick gallop in these climes." Her expression one of infinite calmness, she looked over her shoulder. "Don't you find it so?"

Blue, blue eyes met hers. One of his black brows slowly arched. "You ride like a hoyden."

His expression remained impassive; she felt sure he intended the remark as a reprimand. Her giddy senses, however, heard it as a compliment—one from a man who rode well; it was an effort to keep a silly grin from her lips. She met his blue gaze with regal assurance. "I ride as I wish."

Her emphasis was subtle, but he heard it; his brow quirked irritatingly higher. "Hell for leather, without fear for life or limb?"

She shrugged as haughtily as she could and returned to surveying the scenery.

"Hmm," he murmured. She could feel his gaze on her face. "I'm beginning to understand Seamus's reasoning."

"Indeed?" She tried to hold them back, but the words tumbled out. "And what do you mean by that?"

"That you've run wild for too long, without anyone to ride rein on you. You need someone to watch over you for your own protection."

"I've been managing my life for the past six years without anyone's help or interference. I haven't needed anyone's protection—why should I need it now?"

"Because ..." And, quite suddenly, Richard saw it all—why, on his death, Seamus had trampled on custom to do all he could to put Catriona into the hands of a strong man, one he knew would protect her. His gaze distant, fixed unseeing on the white peaks before them, he continued: "As time goes on, you'll face different threats, ones you've not yet encountered."

Not yet, because while he'd been alive, Seamus had acted as her protector, albeit from a distance. They'd found the letters, but how many more advances had been made directly? And Jamie was no Seamus—he wouldn't be able to withstand the renewed offers, the guileful entreaties. He'd refer them to Catriona, and then *she* would have to deal with ... all the threats from which Seamus had shielded her.

That was why he, Richard, was here—why Seamus had couched his will as he had.

Frowning, Richard refocused to discover Catriona studying his face. She humphed, then haughtily turned away, pert nose in the air. "Don't let me keep you." With an airy wave, she gestured a dismissal. "I know this area well— I'm quite capable of finding my own way back."

Richard swallowed a laugh. "How reassuring." She slanted him a frowning glance; he responded with a charming smile. "I'm lost."

Her eyes narrowed as she clearly debated whether she dared call him a liar. Deciding against it, she shifted from defense to attack. "It's truly unconscionable of you to raise the family's hopes."

"By considering whether it's possible to help them?" He raised his brows haughtily. "It would be *unconscionable* of me to do otherwise."

She frowned at him. "They're not your family."

"No—but they are *a* family, and as such, command my respect. And my consideration."

They do? She didn't speak them, but the words were clear in her eyes. Richard held her gaze. "I'd vaguely imagined that families lay at the heart of your doctrine, too."

She blinked. "They do."

"Then shouldn't you be considering what you can do to help them? They're weaker, less able, than you or I. And none of this is their doing."

It was a scramble to get back behind her defenses; she accomplished it with a frown and a fictitious shiver. "It's cold to be standing." She looked up. "And there's more snow coming. We'd better return to the house."

Richard made no demur as she turned her horse. He brought the black up alongside the chestnut, then gallantly drew back to amble behind her as she set the chestnut down a steep track. His gaze locked on her hips, swaying deliberately, first this way, then that, he spent the descent, not considering Seamus's family, but the mechanics of releasing them from his iniquitous will.

The behavior of Seamus's family in the drawing room, and over the dinner table, tried Catriona's temper sorely. While clearly of the opinion their cause was hopeless, they nevertheless endeavored to cast her in the most flattering light, to convince a reluctant suitor of her manifold charms. As they were self-effacing, bumbling, and close to helpless, she was forced to rein in her temper—forced to smile tightly rather than annihilate them with a crushing retort, or cut them to ribbons with her saber tongue. Richard noted her simmering—reminiscent of a barely capped volcano—and bided his time.

When they returned to the drawing room, and the tea trolley arrived, no one challenged his suggestion that he take Catriona her cup. As she was, by then, standing stiff and straight, looking out of one of the uncurtained windows, it was doubtful anyone else would have dared. As he strolled up, two cups in his hands, he fixed his gaze, deliberately unreadable, on Algaria O'Rourke's face. Holding fast to her customary position beside Catriona, she returned his stare with a black, unfathomable one of her own.

"Oh, Algaria?"

From behind him, Richard heard Mary call, and saw consternation and indecision infuse Algaria's face.

Halting before her, a pace behind Catriona's back, Richard smiled, all teeth. "I don't bite—at least, not in drawing rooms."

The comment, or perhaps its tone, reached Catriona; she stirred and turned and took the situation in in one glance. Reaching for one of the cups, she grimaced at Algaria. "Oh, go! And you might check on Meg for me."

With one last, warning glance at Richard, Algaria inclined her head and went. Richard watched her retreat, her spine poker-stiff. "Does *she* bite?"

Catriona nearly choked on her tea. "She's a fully fledged disciple—she was my mentor after my mother died. So beware—she might turn you into a toad if you step too far over the line."

Richard sipped, then turned and studied her. She was still simmering. "You can rip up at me, if you like."

The glance she shot him suggested she was seriously considering it. "This is all your fault. While they think there's an outside chance—the most distant possibility—they'll feel compelled to make a push to"—she gestured—"interest you in me."

"You could always explain they don't need to make the effort."

Catriona stiffened; she glanced up—and saw the lurking heat in his eyes. She frowned. "Stop it."

"Stop what?"

"Stop thinking of that kiss in the graveyard."

"Why? It was a very enjoyable kiss, even in a graveyard."

She fought not to wriggle her shoulders, fought not to think of it herself. "It was a mistake."

"So you keep insisting."

"You could end this entire charade, this senseless agony of expectation, by simply stating your mind."

"How can I do that if I don't know it myself?"

She narrowed her eyes at him. "You know perfectly well you'll return to London in a week's time, unencumbered by a wife." He merely raised his brows, with that irritatingly arrogant confidence that never failed to get her goat. She looked away. "You don't want to marry me, any more than I wish to marry you."

Turning his head, he looked down at her; she felt the sudden intensity of his gaze.

"Ah—but I do wish, very much, to bed you, as much, if not more, than you wish me to do so, which might well predispose us to wed."

Stunned, Catriona looked up; politely, he raised his brows, his eyes like blue flame. "Don't you think?"

She snapped her mouth shut. "I do *not!*" Her cheeks burned; she dragged in a breath and looked away, adding through clenched teeth: "I most certainly do *not* wish you to bed me."

He studied her profile; even without looking, she knew his brows rose higher. "*Now* who's lying?"

She straightened, but couldn't meet his eyes. "You're only teasing me."

"Am I?"

The soft words set her nerves skittering. And his fingers settled on the sensitive skin of her nape. She lost her wits, lost her breath. His fingers shifted, in the lightest caress—

She hauled in a breath and whirled to face him. "Stop that!"

"Why?" His expression unreadable, he studied her frown. "You like it."

Biting her tongue against another lie, she forced herself to meet his gaze—to ignore the wild sensations crashing through her. "Given that you *will not* be bedding me, there will be *no reason* for us to wed, and you will go back to London, and Seamus's fortune will go to the Church. Why won't you admit it?"

He raised his brows. "I will admit that if I'm involved at all, a wedding will certainly necessitate a bedding. In your case, to my mind, the two are inseparable—the one will beget the other."

"Very likely." Catriona spoke through gritted teeth. "*However,* as there will be *no wedding*—"

"What's this?"

Before she could focus, let alone gather her wits, he reached for the fine chain that hung about her throat, visible above the neckline of her gown. Before she could catch his hand, he drew the chain free, lifting the pendant from its sanctuary in the valley between her breasts.

And clasped it in his hand, turned it between his long fingers. Catriona froze.

Squinting at the long crystal, he frowned. "It's carved, like the one on my mother's necklace, only of the other stone."

Drawing a shaky breath, Catriona lifted the pendant from his grasp. "Rose quartz." She wondered whether her voice sounded as strained as it felt. She dropped the pendant back into its haven—and nearly gasped in shock at its heat. It had been warm from her flesh, but the heat of his hand had raised its temperature much higher. With a herculean effort, she reassembled her scattered defenses, and retreated behind a haughty wall. "And now, if you've quite finished teasing me—"

The chuckle he gave was the definition of devilish. "Sweet witch, I haven't even started."

His blue eyes held hers; trapped for one instant too long, Catriona felt the hot flames sear her. And felt . . .

"You're a *devil*." She picked up her skirts. "And very definitely no gentleman!"

His lips twitched, just a little at the ends. "Naturally not. I'm a bastard."

He was that—and much more.

And he will father your children.

Catriona awoke with a start, with a gasp that hung, quivering, in the empty dark. About her, the room lay still and silent; the bedcovers lay over her, in tangled disarray. She lay on her back, her heart racing to a beat she did not know, but recognized too well. Her arms lay tensed at her sides, her fingers gripping the sheets.

It took effort to straighten her fingers, to ease her locked muscles. Gradually, the tension holding her decreased; her breathing slowed.

Leaving behind confusion, consternation—and a compulsion that grew stronger by the day, by the hour. And even more by the night.

Night—when she need not—could not—hide from herself, when, in her dreams, her deepest yearnings and unvoiced needs held sway. Overridden, as always, by The Lady's will.

But that was not happening now. Instead, The Lady's will and her own deep yearnings were acting in concert, pushing her forward, into the arms of—

"A man I *can't* marry."

Rolling onto her elbow, Catriona reached for the glass of water on the table by the bed. She sipped; the cool water doused the lingering heat—heat that had flared at the dream of his lips on hers, of the touch of cool marble that incited flame. Heat that had spread through her like forest fire in response to the hot hunger in his eyes, in his soul.

In response to his desire.

Alone in the night, there was no point in denying that, from the first, she had wanted him. Wanted him with a finality, a certainty, an absolute conviction that stunned her. She wanted him in her bed, wanted him to be the one to fill the empty space beside her, to dispel the private loneliness that was a part of her public persona. But from childhood she'd been taught to put her wants below the needs of her people; in this instance, the choice had been clear.

Or so she had thought.

She was no longer so sure. Of anything.

Slumping back in the bed, she focused on the canopy. She had occasionally in the past, in her wild and willful youth, fought The Lady's will; she knew what it felt like. *This* was what it felt like. A draining combination of uncertainty, dissatisfaction, and an overwhelming confusion, from which, no matter how hard she tried, she could not break free.

She was at odds with herself, because she was at odds with fate, with The Lady's will.

Muting a scream of keen frustration, she thumped her pillow, then turned on her side and snuggled down.

It had to be impossible. Had the Lady *seen* him? Did she know what—in this case—she was suggesting? Ordering?

Did she know what she was getting her senior disciple into?

Marriage to a masterful bastard.

The thought froze her mind; she stared, unseeing, into the dark, then shook herself, closed her eyes, and willed herself to sleep—without any more dreams.

She woke late the next morning—too late for breakfast. After taking tea and toast on a tray, she dressed warmly, dragged on her pelisse, and, avoiding Algaria's watchful eye, set out for a long walk. She needed to clear her head.

The day was brighter than the one before; only a sprinkling of snow remained on the paths. Pausing on the side steps, Catriona looked around; seeing no one, she walked briskly to the opening of one of the three paths leading downward, and slipped into the shadows beneath the trees.

Under the spreading branches, cool peace held sway. She swung along, the scrunch of her boots on the crisp, dead leaves the only sound she could hear. The air was fresh and clean; she drew it deep into her lungs. And felt better.

The path swung sharply, descending into a hollow; she rounded the bend—and saw him waiting, leaning negligently against the bole of a tall tree, his greatcoat protecting him against the light breeze that ruffled his black hair.

His eyes were on her, his attitude that of a man waiting for his lover at an assignation previously planned.

As she drew level with him, Catriona was tempted to reach out and lay her hand over his heart, to see if it was beating too quickly. He must have left the house behind her; he must have run down the other path to get here—be here—now. But touching him was out of the question. She raised her brows instead. "Lost again?"

His eyes held hers steadily. "No." He paused, then added: "I was waiting for you."

She returned his gaze consideringly, then humphed, and waved an acceptance of his escort. He fell in beside her as she strolled on, his stride a long prowl. He was so much larger, stronger, than she, his presence weighed heavily on her senses. Catriona drew a tight breath; she looked up at the patches of sky framed by the bare branches. "Do the Cynsters live in London?"

"Yes. Some all of the time, others some of the time."

"And you?"

"All of the time, these days." He scanned their surroundings. "But I grew up in Cambridgeshire, at Somersham Place, the ducal seat."

She threw him a quick glance. "Jamie said your father was a duke."

"Sebastian Sylvester Cynster, 5th Duke of St. Ives."

The affection in his tone was easily heard; she glanced at him again. "You were brought up within the family?"

"Oh, yes."

"And you have an older brother?"

"Devil." When she raised her brows, he grinned and added: "Sylvester Sebastian to *Maman*—Devil to all others."

"I see."

"Devil has the title now. He lives at Somersham with his duchess, Honoria, and his heir."

"Is it a big family?"

"No, if you mean do I have other brothers and sisters, but yes, if you mean is the clan, as you might call it, large."

"There are lots of Cynsters?"

"*More* than enough, as any fond mama in the ton will tell you."

"I see." She was too interested to sound suitably reproving. "So you have—what? Lots of cousins?"

With an ease she hadn't expected, he described them—his uncles and aunts, and their children, led by his four male cousins. After a quick listing of the family's major connections, he enumerated his younger cousins. "Of course," he concluded, "about town, I tend to meet only Amanda and Amelia."

Catriona located them on the mental tree she'd been constructing. "The twins?"

"Hmm."

He frowned and looked down. When he said nothing more, she prompted: "Why are they a worry?"

He glanced at her. "I was just thinking ... both Devil and Vane, who are recently married gentlemen, are unlikely to spend much time in town. And with me up here ..." His frown deepened. "There's Demon, of course, but he might have to visit his stud farm, which leaves it all up to Gabriel and Lucifer." He grimaced. "I just hope Demon remembers to jog their elbows before he leaves town."

"But why do they need to be 'jogged?' Surely, with all your relatives and connections, the twins will be closely watched over."

His expression hardened; he threw her another glance. "There are some dangers extant within the *ton* which are best dealt with by experts."

She opened her eyes wide. "I would have thought you rated more as one of the dangers."

His mask slipped; the warrior showed through. "That's precisely why I—and the others—are the sort of watchers the twins most need."

She could tell—from his eyes, his expression—that he was deadly serious. Nevertheless ... looking ahead, she fought to keep her lips straight—and failed. A gurgle of laughter escaped her.

He shot her a narrow-eyed glance.

She waved placatingly. "It's just the thought of it—the vision of you and your cousins creeping around ballrooms keeping surreptitious watch over two young ladies."

"*Cynster* young ladies."

"Indeed." Tilting her head, she met his gaze. "But what if the twins don't want to be watched—what if, indeed, they possess the same inclinations as you? You come from the same stock—such inclinations aren't restricted to males."

He stopped stock-still and stared at her, then humphed, shook his shoulders, and started to pace once more. Frowning again. "They're too young," he finally stated.

Lips still not straight, Catriona looked away, across the snowy tops of the foothills. After a moment, she mused: "So the family's large, and you were brought up within it—and that's why you see family as important."

She did not look at him, but felt the swift touch of his gaze on her face. Although delivered as a statement, that was, in fact, her principal question: why did a man like him have such strong feelings about family?

They strolled on for a full minute before he replied. "Actually, I think it's the other way around."

Puzzled, she looked up; he trapped her gaze. "The Cynsters are as they are *because* family is important to us." He looked down and they walked on. She didn't try to disguise her interest; she kept her gaze on his face, her mind on his words.

He grimaced lightly. "Cynsters are acquisitive by nature—we *need* possessions—the family motto, after all, is *'To Have and To Hold.'* But even long ago, the motto was not—or not only—a material one." He paused; when he spoke again, he spoke slowly, clearly, his frowning gaze fixed on the snow. "We were always a warrior breed, but we don't fight solely for lands and material wealth. There's an understanding, drummed into us all from our earliest years, that success—true success—means capturing and holding something more. That something more is the future—to excel is very well, but one needs to excel *and survive*. To seize lands is well and good, but we want to hold them for all time. Which means creating and building a family—defending the family that is, and creating the next generation. Because it's the next generation that's our future. Without securing that future, material success is no real success at all."

It seemed as if he'd forgotten her; Catriona walked silently, careful not to disturb his mood. Then he looked up, squinting a little in the glare, his face exactly as she had seen it in her dreams—the far-sighted warrior.

"You could say," he murmured, "that a Cynster without a family is a Cynster who's failed."

They'd reached the end of the ridge; the path turned at the rocky point, which formed a small lookout, then wound back up the slope through the trees. They halted on the point; the wind blew fresh and chill from the white mountaintops before them.

As one, they viewed the majestic sight; unprompted, Catriona pointed out various peaks and landmarks, naming them, citing their significance. Richard listened attentively, blue eyes narrowed against the wind and glare. As he studied the landscape, Catriona surreptitiously studied him.

His expression, she had realized, was very rarely spontaneous, even though he sometimes appeared open and easy. He was, in reality, reserved, his feelings kept close behind his mask—that facade he showed to the world. Whatever reactions he displayed were those he wanted to show; even his glib and ready charm was a carefully cultivated skill.

But when he'd spoken of his family—and of family—his mask had slipped, and she'd seen the man behind, and a little of his vulnerability. The insight had touched her, stirred her—and made her clamp a firm hold over her own reactions before they could carry her away. Richard Cynster, she'd already realized, was temptation incarnate—this morning had added another dimension to his attractiveness.

Quite the last thing she needed.

With a half-suppressed sigh, she turned. "We'd better get back."

Richard turned, and, scanning the path upward, suppressed a sigh of his own. Tightening his grip on his rakish impulses, he gave Catriona his arm up the first section of path, made hazardous by melting snow. Pacing slowly beside her, aware through every pore of her soft warmth, gliding along beside him, and not making any advance whatsoever, had taken considerable effort; speaking of his family, explaining why he felt as he did, while maintaining the distance between them, had required superhuman resolution. But he wasn't yet sure how far he could push her—and he wasn't yet sure if he should.

As he'd foreseen, she slipped on the path; resigned, he caught her against him, unable to deaden the impact of her soft curves against him, let alone his instant reaction. Luckily, she was engrossed in regaining her footing, but when she tumbled against him again, one ripe breast pressing hard against his chest, one hip and sleek thigh riding against his hip, he had to bite his lip against a groan.

When they finally reached the place where the path leveled out, he'd given up hiding his scowl. She stopped to catch her breath; he stopped to let his body ease. Innocently, she regarded the scenery; annoyed, irritated, and mightily frustrated, he regarded her. And resumed his impassive mask. "You do understand why Seamus did as he did, don't you?"

She turned to face him. "Because he was mad?"

Richard let his lips thin. "No." He hesitated, studying her clear eyes. "You're an attractive proposition, both personally and for your lands. You can't be unaware of it. The offers for your hand have apparently been legion, most from men who would sell your vale from under you and treat you with far less respect than is your due. Seamus, more than anyone, was aware of that, so he tried a last throw, a last attempt to see you safe."

She half smiled, her expression, her eyes, full of a feminine superiority expressly designed to goad him—or any male. "Seamus was a tyrant in his own family—it would never have occurred to him that I'm well able to take care of myself."

If she had patted him on the hand and told him not to worry, it would have had the same effect; he didn't bother to suppress his aggravated sigh. "Catriona, you are *incapable* of defending yourself against one determined callow youth, let alone a determined man."

Up went her pert nose. "Rubbish." Green eyes clashed with his. "Besides, The Lady protects me."

"Oh?"

"Indeed—men always think they have the winning hand, simply because they're bigger and stronger."

"And they're wrong?"

"Completely. The Lady has ways of dealing with importunate suitors—and so do I."

Richard sighed and looked away—then abruptly swung back and stepped toward her. She half-shrieked and jumped back—plastering herself helpfully against the bole of a tall tree. He splayed one hand on the bole by her side; with his other hand, he trapped and framed her face. The base of the tree was higher than the path, making her relatively taller. Richard tilted her face to his; with her skirts brushing his boots, and a mere inch between them, he looked down into her wide eyes. "Show me."

Her eyes grew wider as they searched his. Her breasts rose and fell rapidly, straining the fabric of her coat—and still she was breathless. "Show you … what?"

"These ways you and Your Lady have of dealing with importunate suitors." His gaze dropped to her lips; with his thumb, he brushed the lower.

And felt her quiver. Her heart was racing, and he hadn't even kissed her.

The thought prompted the deed; bending his head, he brushed his lips tantalizingly over hers, not sure who he was teasing the most.

"How had you planned to protect yourself against a man who accosts you and kisses you?" He whispered the taunt against her lips, then raised his head—her lips parted fractionally. He sucked in a breath, and went back for more—for a slow, leisurely exploration of her luscious lips, of the soft, warm cavern of her mouth.

And she melted for him—with no hint of a struggle, she welcomed him in, her tongue tangling tentatively with his.

He drew back only to drag in a breath, and, his voice deep and grating, ask: "Just how had you planned to stop a man ravishing you?"

He didn't wait for an answer, but ravished her mouth, taking all she offered, and demanding more. Commanding more. Which she gave.

Unstintingly.

The damned woman had no defenses to speak of.

Some small part of Catriona's mind knew what he was thinking—the rest of her mind didn't care. She'd never expected to have any defense against *him*; she could normally freeze any man with a mere glance, yet from the first, he'd been immune, both to such overt intimidation and to more subtle manipulations. But she certainly wasn't going to explain that—that with him, her defenses, those The Lady had gifted her with, would not, for some misbegotten reason, work.

Even with her head spinning, her wits reeling, she wasn't that daft. She could normally tie men in mental or verbal knots, make them trip over their toes, stutter, wheeze—a whole host of simple difficulties that would send the most confident fleeing.

But not him.

With him, all she could do was run.

But at present, she couldn't run. All she could do was …

Enjoy her ravishment.

Not a difficult task. One her senses recommended.

Wholeheartedly.

At some point, she lifted her arms and wrapped them about his neck, and he moved closer, the pressure of his chest easing her aching breasts. She kissed him back with giddy abandon and felt him shift. Then his hand slid behind her, between the tree and her back, and slid down. Her willful senses leapt as he cradled her bottom, tilting her hips away from the tree. Then he pressed one hard thigh between hers.

She would have pulled back from their kiss and gasped, but he wouldn't let her go—their kiss continued with escalating urgency, an urgency she felt to her bones. Their lips fused, eased, then melded again—his were cool marble, hers burned. He leaned into her—she drew him closer. Her thick pelisse muted the sensation of body meeting body, yet heat still swept through her, wave after wave, increasing in intensity—they had to be melting the snow for yards.

But she didn't pull back—didn't struggle to escape—she returned his kisses with increasing fervor, undismayed by the intimacy he pressed on her, eagerly savoring every nuance, every facet—what else could she do? This was experience, one she might never again enjoy.

So she enjoyed—and encouraged, invited, incited.

And he responded. Ardently.

His desire, his fire, set her aflame. When his hand dropped from her face to close firmly about her breast, she gasped and swayed—her knees literally wobbled. His hand firmed beneath her bottom, supporting her as his long fingers closed and caressed, firming about her nipple, squeezing gently. She arched against him, driven by instinct, by a hot need that was the counterpart of his. His prowling hunger had never been so clear, so forcefully imprinted on her senses. She tasted it in his kiss, felt it in his locked muscles, in the ridge of rampant flesh riding against her belly.

He tilted her hips, lifting her slightly—his thigh pressed deeper between hers, shifting suggestively.

The heat took her—a storm of fire and flame raced through her. She clutched his head wildly, threading her fingers through his thick locks as she angled her lips beneath his.

Crack!

Mere seconds later, or so it seemed, she was stepping carefully along the path a full five yards past the comfortable tree, one hand on Richard's sleeve, the other holding her skirts as she stepped over a tree root, when firm footsteps approached from behind.

They both turned, with wholly false expressions of polite surprise. Catriona could only be thankful for the dappled shadows that hid her face as Algaria's black gaze found her.

Algaria frowned. "I thought you might have got lost."

Refraining from pointing out that she knew these woods better than her mentor, Catriona inclined her head. Carefully—it was still spinning. "I showed Mr. Cynster the lookout. We were on our way back." Via a tree.

She could only just summon enough breath to get the words out; Algaria merely humphed and waved them on.

"Don't wait for me—I'll just plod along slowly."

Catriona flicked a glance at her companion in time to see his lips twitch; she ignored the dangerous light in his eyes. "Very well."

Gracefully haughty, as befitted The Lady's senior disciple, she turned and allowed her nemesis to lead her on. She felt his gaze on her face, but kept her eyes fixed on the path and the scenery; she was still giddy, and flushed, with her senses clamoring. Insistently.

Steadfastly, she ignored them—and the question of what might have happened had Algaria not arrived. Such speculation was not calming, and right now, she needed calm.

Calm to deal with Richard Cynster—and calm to deal with herself. And she wasn't at all sure which would prove more difficult.

His attitude to family had intrigued her, so she'd tried to draw him out, driven by a compulsive need to know more about him, so she could interpret her visions in a more sensible light. Instead, what she'd learned had made her decision harder still—how could she not respond to a man who desired and actively sought to establish a real family?

Yet the rest—all she had learned since they'd left the lookout—had only hardened her resolve to resist him. His facade had slipped long enough to confirm her inner view of him—to confirm his emotional motivation. He was, indeed, a warrior without a cause—the cause he searched for, yearned for, was a family to defend and protect.

Which was all very well, but warriors, especially the hereditary sort, did not hang up their swords in the hall and become simple family men. Far from it. They remained warriors still, to the heart, to the soul.

And warriors ruled.

Inwardly she sighed, and saw the house looming ahead. All she had learned had confirmed her in her resistance, while increasing the temptation to give herself to him—to have him as her lord. But first and last, she was the lady of the vale—she couldn't, simply could not, let him into her life, couldn't let him think of her as part of his cause, no matter how tempting that might be.

And tempting it was. Just how tempting she hadn't understood, not until she'd stood pressed against him under that tree.

They stepped out of the woods and onto the lawn, spotted white with snow; Algaria followed close behind them. Calmer, more determined, Catriona drew a deep breath; she glanced briefly at Richard's face, then looked at the house.

Temptation incarnate was what he was—his attitudes were strongly attractive, his sensuality so compelling he engaged her senses to the exclusion of all else. But his very strength was what stood between them. He was too powerful a personality, too strong a male, to surrender his natural dominance to a wife. A witch-wife at that.

He was a powerfully attractive, family-oriented gentleman, but he was still a warrior to the core.

The house rose before them, cold and grey; she felt his gaze on her face.

"You look pale."

She glanced up and realized he thought she was still reeling. She let cool haughtiness infuse her eyes. "I haven't been sleeping well lately."

She looked ahead; from the corner of her eye, she saw his lips twitch.

"Indeed? Perhaps you should take up the local custom of a dram of whiskey before climbing into bed. Jamie tells me the locals all swear by it."

Catriona humphed. "They'd swear by any 'custom' that means drinking whiskey."

He chuckled. "Understandable—it's good stuff. I hadn't really appreciated it before. I'm a rabid convert to the local custom."

"Converts are always the most rabid," Catriona observed. "But if you really are interested, you should visit the distillery in the valley."

They'd reached the side steps; describing the distillery, she led the way inside.

CHAPTER
Five

ॐ✦ॐ

"Ah—Richard?" Halfway across the front hall, Richard halted and swiveled—Jamie stood uncertainly in a doorway. "I ... ah, wondered if you could spare me a moment of your time?" As lunch had concluded half an hour ago, and as his witch had haughtily declined his invitation to find another tree and, nose in the air, hips seductively swaying, retired to her room, he'd been on his way to the billiards room to while away the afternoon, Richard saw no reason not to smoothly incline his head and stroll through the doorway through which Jamie waved him.

He knew what was coming.

Jamie didn't disappoint him. Closing the door, Jamie followed him into the room and indicated a large chair angled before a desk. Richard sank into the chair, lounging gracefully, balancing one boot on his knee.

His host, however, didn't settle in the chair behind the desk, but paced nervously before the hearth—before Richard. Glancing about, Richard noted the ledgers filling the shelves lining one wall, and the maps and diagrams of the area scattered about the room. This was clearly the estate office, equally clearly Jamie's domain. The room was small but comfortable, much more comfortable than the library Seamus had inhabited.

"I wondered," Jamie eventually began, "whether you've decided yet how you will answer the solicitor next week."

The look he bent on Richard was a plea—not to be saved, but to have the worst told to him.

"I'm afraid," Richard replied in his London drawl, "that I've not yet decided."

Jamie frowned and paced on. "But ... well, it isn't all that likely, is it?"

"As to that," Richard answered, "I really can't say."

In the hall, hugging the shadows, Algaria pressed her ear to the oak panels of the office door. She'd been traversing the gallery upstairs, on her way to Catriona's room to inquire as to the reason for her unusual withdrawal, when she'd heard Jamie speak to Richard in the hall. His intent had been obvious; what she'd heard thus far confirmed it. She was not averse to a little eavesdropping if it served to ease her mind. And Catriona's.

"But you normally reside in London, I understand. I'm afraid Catriona will never live anywhere else but Casphairn Manor."

"So I apprehend."

"And, well, she really is a sort of a witch, you know. Not the sort to change people into toads or eels or whatever she might say, but she really does— can—do strange things—and make other people do strange things."

"Really?"

The tone of that response had Algaria gritting her teeth.

"And doubtless you're accustomed to balls and parties in London—a constant stream of them, I imagine."

"Indeed—a never-ending stream of balls and parties."

The undertone sliding beneath that reply made Algaria frown, but before she could define the emotion, Jamie spoke again.

"And, ah . . ." He coughed. "I daresay there are many ladies—very beautiful ladies—gracing the balls and parties."

Leaning back in the chair, Richard merely inclined his head and kept his face expressionless.

His lack of response made Jamie more nervous. "I understand life at the manor is very quiet—no balls or parties at all. In fact, according to Catriona, it's even quieter than here."

"But not colder." The words left Richard's lips before he'd thought; luckily, Jamie took them only literally.

"True—but it's still very cold." He threw him a searching look. "The Lowlands are a lot colder than London."

"Indubitably."

As Jamie continued highlighting the stark contrasts between the life he imagined Richard led in London—only a slight exaggeration of the truth—and the life he could expect to lead as the lord of Casphairn Manor, Richard politely held to his noncommittal replies. As Jamie was his host, he felt obliged to humor him thus far, but would not commit himself, one way or the other.

He couldn't. He hadn't yet made up his mind.

Commited by a freakish, witch-induced impulse to seriously consider Seamus's proposal, the more he did—the more he learned of Catriona Hennessey—the more he felt inclined to accept. To take up Seamus's gauntlet, accept his challenge, which, day by day, was looking more like an appeal—an appeal to greater strength—the offer of a commission.

A commission for life, admittedly, but he was developing a serious taste for one of the payments that would accrue. The idea of having a witch in his bed for the rest of his life, his to tease, taunt and enjoy as he—and she—pleased, was shaping as a potent inducement.

But he distrusted the entire situation. Fate and Seamus McEnery had conspired to place him in it—he had no reason to trust either. Not on the question of marriage, not given what marriage meant to him.

So he hedged and said nothing—the gentlemanly course.

"Well!" Jamie exhaled as he ground to a halt and somewhat dampeningly concluded: "The truth is, I suppose, that life in the Lowlands, married to a wild witch, would not measure on the same scale as the life of a London swell."

Lids lowered, Richard gravely inclined his head. "Indeed not."

Life with a wild witch was infinitely more alluring.

Out of breath, Algaria reached the top of the stairs just as the office door opened. Silently, she slipped into the shadows of the gallery and headed for Catriona's room.

Her brief tap on the door went unanswered; frowning, she tapped again. When no sound came from within, she frowned even harder and opened the door.

And saw Catriona slumped on the floor.

Smothering a cry, Algaria quickly shut the door and rushed forward; the briefest glance at the items on the table beside which Catriona lay was sufficient to tell her all. Her erstwhile pupil had been scrying, and scrying deep, if her swoon was any guide.

Even as Algaria straightened her limbs, Catriona stirred.

A second later, as a wet cloth passed over her face, she regained full consciousness. Peeking through her lashes, she saw that her attendant was Algaria, and relaxed. "Oh, *hell!*"

Algaria sat back. "Hell?"

Struggling onto one elbow, Catriona waved. "Not you—this whole situation." She'd gone further than mere scrying—she'd literally challenged the powers that be to reconsider, and demanded an unequivocal answer.

The answer she'd received had been more than unequivocal—it had been emphatic.

"Ah, well—the situation has just taken a turn for the better."

"It has?" Catriona frowned as Algaria helped her to her feet. Her mentor's smug expression rang warning bells. "How?"

"In a minute." Algaria steered her to the bed. "Here—just lie back and rest, and I'll tell you all I heard."

Still weak from her exertions—facing She Who Knew All was exceedingly draining—Catriona was very willing to lie down. Algaria sat beside her and proceeded to tell her tale—how she'd listened to Jamie's discussion with Richard Cynster in the office.

Algaria's memory, perfected by the demands of her calling, was exceptional; Catriona had no doubt she was hearing exactly the words that had been said. Algaria's veracity was beyond question, as was her devotion to her own welfare—Catriona knew that for fact. However, in this instance, Algaria's tale gave her a headache.

A massive one.

"So!" Algaria triumphantly concluded. "It's as I said—he's only amusing himself—teasing you, if you like. But he's absolutely certain to go back to London and leave you unwed—he made no attempt to deny it."

"Hmm." Frowning direfully, Catriona massaged her temples.

Studying her face, Algaria's triumphant expression faded. "What is it?"

Catriona glanced at her, then grimaced. "A complication." She saw the questions gathering on Algaria's lips; she stayed them with a raised hand. "I'm too tired to think, just now." After a moment, she continued: "I need to rest, and consider—to see how what I've been told fits with the facts, and how the whole might come together."

Lifting her head, she smiled, a trifle wanly, at Algaria. "Let me rest for an hour or two—come back and wake me for dinner."

Algaria hesitated. "You'll tell me what you learned then?"

With swift understanding of the older woman's fear of being left out, being redundant, Catriona smiled and squeezed her hand. "Before dinner, I'll tell you all."

Dinner time came around far too fast; it seemed to Catriona that she'd barely had time to marshal her thoughts before Algaria returned.

Struggling up against the pillows, she waved Algaria forward. "Come sit and I'll tell you all."

She did, starting from the first visions she'd had, through all her subsequent communcations with The Lady, culminating in the most recent.

As she restated that last, emphatic dictate, Algaria stared. Then frowned. "Just that—no qualifications?"

"Not a one. She could hardly put it more simply: *He will father your children.*" The words still rang in Catriona's mind.

Algaria's frown mirrored her own. "But . . ."

Together, they revisted the problem—concisely; Catriona had been over the same ground on her own so many times her head still hurt.

"But he's *too strong*," Algaria insisted. "He's not the sort of man you *can* marry—he'll never be content to sit back in besotted bliss and let you make the decisions." Bewildered, she shook her head. "But if The Lady says . . ."

"Precisely." Catriona waited patiently while Algaria examined the problem from every angle—her mentor's view in large part mirrored her own.

In the end, Algaria simply shook her head. "I can't make head or tail of it—we'll just have to wait for some sign of how we should proceed."

Catriona caught her eye. "I've just had the next sign. You brought it."

Algaria stared at her, then blinked. "The news that he'll be leaving?"

"Indeed—and if he leaves, just how is he to father a child on me? I can't go chasing him to London, yet, as you say, he seems certain to leave at the end of the week—in all my discussions with him, I've had no indication otherwise."

Algaria shot her a quick glance. "He does seem taken with you, but many men are."

Catriona inclined her head. "As you say—physically, I'm attractive enough, but on further reflection . . ." She considered, then stated: "All he has said and done is consistent with what you overheard—he's considering the possibility because there are various elements in the proposed situation that attract him, but, ultimately, there's nothing I can offer him that he can't, in reality, find in London, with a wife much more suited to his lifestyle."

She felt proud of that assessment—it had taken some soul-searching, and the exercise of brutal candor, to reach it. Richard Cynster was attracted to her for a number of reasons, but she would not, ultimately, be a suitable wife for him. He was too far-sighted not to see it.

"So, what now?" Algaria asked. "If he leaves ..."

Catriona drew in a deep breath. "If he leaves, he leaves—we can do nothing to stop him. Which means ..." She looked at Algaria, waiting for her to reach the same conclusion she had.

This time, her mentor failed her. Totally bemused, Algaria stared at her. "Means what?"

"It means," Catriona declared, getting off the bed to pace, "that I'm to beget a child by him, but we won't be married." She waved aside Algaria's frown. "That, if you think about it, is possibly the perfect solution for me—to have a child outside wedlock. The Lady, you'll notice, does not mention marriage, only the fact that I'm to have a child by him. And you have to admit, if he'd been a stallion, he'd be a prize."

"*Prize?* You're going to ..." Algaria's voice trailed away; aghast, she stared. Then: "How?"

Catriona paced determinedly. "Presumably by going to his bed."

"Yes—but ..." Clearly dumbfounded, Algaria drew a deep breath. "It's not that simple."

Irritated by her lingering uncertainty, *and* her lack of experience, Catriona frowned. "It can't be that hard. He's a rake—the activity should come naturally. And it's the right time of my cycle—all the signs are propitious."

Algaria shook her head. "But what if, after the deed, he changes his mind and decides to stay. You can't be *sure* he'll leave."

"I've thought of that." Catriona paced before the fireplace, all that Richard had said of family still fresh in her mind. And although they hadn't discussed it, she could guess what his stance over abandoning a bastard child would be. She felt some qualms over that, but ... she had always obeyed The Lady, and always would. Besides, Richard's child would not be alone—it would be a much-loved child. Hers. "He won't know."

Algaria simply stared. "He'll father a child on you and he won't know?" She got off the bed and laid a hand on Catriona's forehead.

Irritated, Catriona brushed it aside. "I've thought it through—it can be done—you know that as well as I. It's tricky, admittedly—he must be asleep enough not to consciously remember, and yet his body and senses must be able to respond and perform. A sleeping potion will dull the brain, an aphrodisiac will prime the body. The doses will have to be perfectly judged, one against the other, but if I gauge the amounts correctly, all should go smoothly."

Algaria looked ill, but didn't contradict her—she couldn't; she'd taught her most of that lore herself. She could, however, protest. "You're mad. This will simply not work—too many things can go wrong."

"Nonsense!"

Algaria grew stern, but her underlying fear and concern showed through. "I'll have no part in it—this scheme is as mad as old Seamus's."

"It's what The Lady requires. She will guide me."

Tight-lipped, Algaria shook her head. "You must have misinterpreted."

Catriona drew herself up—she knew Algaria didn't believe that; there was no possiblity she could have misinterpreted such a strong and repeated directive. Folding her arms, she returned her mentor's black stare. "Give me an alternative and I'll consider it—just as long as it results in Richard Melville Cynster being the father of my child."

Slowly, Algaria shook her head. "I'm against it—this *can't* be right."

Aware of her mentor's deep distrust of most men, and ones like Richard Cynster in particular, Catriona didn't argue. "I have The Lady's orders—I'm determined to obey them." She paused, then asked, more gently: "Will you help me?"

Algaria met her gaze, and held it for a full minute. Then, slowly, she shook her head. "No—I cannot. I'll have no part in this—no good will come of it, mark my words." She spoke slowly; she had no alternative to offer and she knew it.

Catriona sighed. "Very well. Leave me—I need to work up the mixture." She had all she needed in her traveling kit, the kit she'd inherited from her mother. She'd religiously replaced each herb and specific as they aged without questioning why each was included in the selection. The aphrodisiac had always been there—it was there now, when she needed it. Along with a powerful sleeping potion.

Algaria trailed to the door; hand on the knob, she paused and looked back.

Sensing her gaze, Catriona looked up, and raised a brow.

Algaria straightened and lifted her chin. "If you bear any love for me, I pray you, *do not go* to Richard Cynster."

Catriona held her black gaze steadily. "The Lady wills it—so I must."

The mechanics of drugging her nemesis proved much easier than she'd expected. Late that night, Catriona paced her bedchamber and waited for the moment of truth—when she would go to his room and discover how successful she had been.

Mixing the potion had been merely a matter of making a series of estimations, all based on her extensive experience. She routinely held the health of the more than two hundred souls who inhabited the vale in her hands—she treated them from birth to death; she knew her herbs. Her only uncertainty lay in gauging her mark's weight—in the end, she'd simply added an extra dash of both potions and prayed fervently to The Lady.

As for getting him to down the drug, the vehicle had been ready to hand— she'd remembered his talk of the whiskey; it was perfect for her needs. The strong, smoky taste would disguise the tang of the herbs, at least to one who was not a connoisseur. She had gauged the amount to add to the decanter so that a good dram would hold enough drug to accomplish what she needed.

Introducing the potion to his decanter had been simplicity itself. She was always the last down to dinner; she simply waited until her usual time, then stopped by his room on the way. Her one tense moment had occurred when she was almost at his door. It had opened, and his servant had come out. Standing still as a statue in the shadows, she had watched him depart, then, barely breathing, smoothly continued on and entered the room.

It was one of the largest bedchambers in the house; the decanter stood on a sideboard beneath one window. It had been the work of a moment to gauge the volume in the decanter and add the required amount of her mixture. Then, stoppering the vial, she'd turned and glided out of the room and down to dinner.

And had had the devil's own time dampening her awareness, her consciousness of what she was up to, especially while under Richard's blue gaze. He'd sensed that she was edgy, so she'd put on a haughty act and prayed he'd see her skittishness as a lingering effect of their morning's kiss.

Catriona humphed and swung about, the skirts of her dressing robe flaring about her. Beneath it, she wore a fine lawn nightgown—she supposed, for him, it should have been silk, but she didn't possess any such apparel. The thought of his hands on her body shielded only by the thin gown made her shiver. She glanced up at the clock on the mantelpiece just as it chimed.

Twelve solid bongs. It was time for her to go. Dragging in a breath past the vise locked about her lungs, she closed her eyes and uttered a brief prayer, then, clutching her robe about her, determinedly headed for the door. To keep her appointment with he who was to father her child.

CHAPTER
Six

〜⊙〜

Two minutes later, Catriona stood in the shadows before Richard's door and stared at the oak panels. An overwhelming sense of fatality weighed heavily upon her; she stood on the threshold of far more than just a room. In opening the door and stepping inside, she would take an irrevocable step into a future only dimly perceived.

Never before had she faced such a choice—such a crucial, life-changing decision.

Shifting, she drew her dressing robe closer and inwardly chided her hesitant self. Of course stepping over the threshold would change her life—getting with child was definitely irrevocable, but quite clearly part of her future. That future lay beyond the door—why was she hesitating?

Because it wasn't just a child who lay beyond the door.

Exasperated, she straightened and reached for the doorknob, simultaneously opening her senses—to detect any hint of warning, any last-minute premonition that her intent was wrong. All she sensed was peace and silence, a deep, quiet steadiness throughout the house.

Drawing a deep breath, she opened the door. It swung noiselessly wide; beyond, the room lay silent and still, lit only by the glow of the fire still flickering in the hearth.

Stepping quietly inside, Catriona closed the door, easing the lock back so it slid home without a sound. Eyes already adjusted to the dark, she scanned the room. The huge four-poster bed stood shrouded in shadows, its head against the corridor wall. The sight held her eyes, her senses. Slowly, on silent slippered feet, she approached the bed.

She was five paces from it when she realized it was empty, the coverlet flat, undisturbed. Eyes flying wide, her breath caught in her throat, she whirled and scanned the room again.

And, from her new position, saw an arm, clad in a dark coat sleeve, wide white cuff golden in the firelight, hanging over the side of the wing chair facing the fire.

The arm hung limply, long, lax fingers almost reaching the floor. Between their tips hung a crystal tumbler, its base balanced on the polished boards.

It was empty.

Drawing a calming breath, Catriona waited for her heart to slow, then, carefully silent, glided forward and rounded the chair.

At least one part of her potion had worked—he was asleep. Asprawl in the chair, his long legs stretched before him, his waistcoat undone, his cravat untied, he still managed to look elegant. Elegantly dissolute, elegantly dangerous. His chest, covered by his fine linen shirt, rose and fell regularly.

Catriona's gaze roamed, then lifted to his face; she studied the lean planes gilded by the firelight—a bronze mask more relaxed than she'd yet seen it. With his eyes shut, it was easier to concentrate on his face, on what it showed. Strength was still there, glaringly apparent even in repose; the hint of not sadness, but a lack of happiness that hung about his well-shaped mouth was not something she'd noticed before.

Inwardly frowning, she committed the sight to memory, then shook herself, and turned her mind to her task. Step one had been accomplished—he was asleep.

Fully dressed.

In the chair before the fire.

A good ten paces from the bed.

Catriona frowned in earnest. "What now?" she muttered under her breath. Hands rising to her hips, she studied him—and considered—and studied him some more. Her head was shaking even before she reached her conclusion: with him asleep, *she'd* have to provide the lead in the upcoming proceedings, and for that, she definitely needed him on the bed. A chair might be possible, but her imagination boggled at the thought.

She glared at her sleeping victim. "I might have known you'd find some way to be difficult," she informed him in a hissed whisper. Bending, she retrieved the tumbler from his fingers before it fell, and turned to set it on a side table. The glass clicked on the polished table top.

Catriona swung back, her eyes flying to Richard's face. The black crescents of his lashes flickered. Then rose.

He looked directly at her.

She froze. Her mind seized; she stopped breathing.

His lips curved, kicking up at the ends first, then curving fully into a beguiling smile. "I might have known you'd turn up in my dreams."

Daring to breathe—just a little—Catriona slowly straightened and finished turning to stand before him. His eyes followed her; as his lids lifted farther, it was clear he was drugged. Ringed by deep blue, his pupils were huge, his gaze unfocused, not sharp and intent as it usually was.

His beguiling smile, both inviting and evocative, deepened. "Only fair, I suppose—the witch of my dreams haunting my dreams."

He was awake, but thought he was dreaming. Catriona blessed The Lady—this way, she could get him to the bed. Letting her features, which had blanked with shock, ease, she smiled back. "I've come to spend the night with you."

His smile changed to a wicked grin. "That's usually my line, but in the circumstances, I'll let you borrow it."

He seemed in no hurry to rise from the chair; smiling still, Catriona held out one hand.

Retrieving his right arm from over the side of the chair, he reached out and grasped her fingers; before she could urge him up, he drew her closer. His gaze swept her, far hotter than the fire at her back.

"You need to get rid of that robe."

Catriona hesitated for only a second; any argument might bring him to his senses. Drawing her fingers from his, still smiling, she raised her hands and lifted the loose robe from her shoulders, then let it slide down her arms.

His dazed blue gaze followed it to the floor, then slowly, very slowly, as if he had all the time in the world, rose, caressing her legs, her thighs, her hips, her breasts—by the time he reached her face her cheeks were flaming.

A situation not helped by the wicked glint in his eyes or his openly lustful smile.

"Good enough to eat."

He made the pronouncement as if he was contemplating doing just that. His gaze slid from her face to rove hungrily again—and Catriona realized that with the fire behind her, her fine nightgown would be translucent.

"Ahh . . . come to the bed." She held out both hands.

His gaze still on her body, he lifted his hands, every movement slow and heavy, as if his limbs were leaden. His fingers closed about hers—then he lifted his blue gaze to her face, to her eyes, and she saw the wicked laughter flare.

"Not yet."

He pulled her into his lap.

Catriona went to shriek—and had to swallow the sound. She tensed to struggle—and had to suppress the impulse. Sharp sound, or a fight, could wake him. She wriggled in his lap and managed to face him. His thighs felt like solid oak beneath hers, his chest, when she placed both palms against it, felt like warm rock. About her, his arms lay heavy and relaxed—they might as well have been steel bands holding her trapped.

They shifted; she felt his fingers slide up the back of her neck, splaying into her thick hair. He angled her head—his lips closed over hers.

Hungrily.

She was kissing him back, exchanging breath for breath, caress for fiery caress, before she had a chance to think. Heat rose, pooling within her, radiating from him. As her wits whirled and desire danced in the air, she didn't think she'd have much trouble carrying out her plan. Provided she could get him to the bed.

With an effort, she drew back from the kiss. He let her go; her head tipped back—and back—as he trailed fire down her throat. "The bed," she gasped. "We have to get to the bed."

"Later."

Catriona's temper kicked in. She opened her mouth—and lost her breath on a gasp as his hands closed possessively about her breasts, protected only by thin lawn. His thumbs circled, then finger and thumb closed tightly. She bit her lip hard, denying her instinctive shriek.

His hands left her breasts and she breathed again. Only to feel long fingers, hard palms, tracing her body, investigating every curve, subtly caressing yet with a deeper purpose—as if he was learning her.

Licking lips suddenly dry, she managed to gasp: "Richard—the bed."

His hands stopped; she sensed his attention—and held her breath. Would he wake? What had she said to focus him so?

Slow and sure, his hands resumed their meandering, imparting heat through her thin gown.

"That's the first time you've said my name." He breathed the words against her jaw, then feathered a kiss across her already swollen lips. "Say it again."

Catriona dragged in a breath too shallow to steady her head; she lifted a hand and brushed back the heavy lock of hair falling across his forehead. "Richard?"

He kissed his name from her lips, then drank deep while his hands continued to roam, tracing breasts, hips, the long muscles of her back, the backs of her thighs, the globes of her bottom. Slowly arousing her—and him. When next he lifted his head, she was quivering. "Richard—take me to your bed." She had no difficulty investing the plea with believable feeling.

His reply was a wicked chuckle—a sound that played havoc with her overstretched nerves.

"Not yet. What's the hurry?" He tipped her chin up and nibbled his way down her throat. "We've all night—and time stands still in dreams, anyway."

Not this one. Catriona struggled to harness her wits. "Just think how much more confortable we'll be in your bed."

"I'm perfectly comfortable here—and so are you. And we're about to be even more comfortable yet."

Catriona righted her head, registering as she did that one large hand was presently cradling her bottom, fondling far too knowingly, leaving her flesh heated, fevered. She looked down—and saw long fingers, dark against the white of her nightgown, artfully slipping the tiny buttons free.

Her eyes flew wide; she sucked in a desperate breath—and lost it in a shuddering, achingly desperate sigh as his hand flicked back the open bodice and his fingers brushed the peak of her swollen breast.

His artful fingers returned, caressing, tracing, teasing, then possessing.

She let her lids fall, felt her bones melt, felt her will evaporate like mist before the sun. But . . ."*The bed*," she whispered.

"Later," he insisted. Cool air caressed her heated breasts as he pressed back her gown and bared them fully. One hand closed firmly, gently kneading. "This is *my* dream. I intend to enjoy it—and you—to the full."

Catriona bit back a groan. Cracking open her lids, she studied his face, lit by the fire's glow. Saw the sleepy smile of lustful anticipation on his lips, felt the heat of desire in his gaze, fixed on her breast, on the throbbing, aching nipple his wicked fingers teased and taunted.

He sensed her gaze, and glanced at her—then smiled, oddly confiding, and returned his attention to her breast. "There are ladies in London who imagine they're cold." His smile deepened—for an instant distinctly predatory. "Some like to believe their flesh is chilled, that their passion is locked in ice." His knowing fingers played over her aching flesh—never forceful, always teasing. His lips twisted, wryly triumphant. "I've melted quite a few of them. There's a knack to it."

As if to demonstrate, he shifted her in his arms, exposing her other breast, simultaneously letting her feel how intimate was his hold on her bottom.

"You, however, are going to be no trouble—you're like that mountain in whose shadow you were born."

Dazed, Catriona blinked. "Merrick?"

"Hmm." He turned his head and looked into her eyes. "Snow and ice on the peak . . ." Looking down, he lifted his hand from her bare breast and trailed his fingers down, over the curve of her stomach, into the hollow at the apex of her thighs. "But fires burn beneath."

Catriona sucked in a breath as his fingers lightly traced the line between her thighs. She couldn't suppress the impulse to squirm, and felt his fingers firm about her bottom. He held her still and continued to play, tracing the long lines of her legs through her fine gown. His touch was tantalizing; she was breathing rapidly—her heart thudding in her throat—when he reached down and caught the gown's hem.

He lifted it slowly, then slid his hand beneath; the gown rose on the back of his hand as he traced, caressed, assessed her ankle, calf, knee, and thigh. He pushed the gown up over her hip, then, with complete and utter absorption, fell to caressing the expanse of thigh thus exposed. Beneath his fingers, a thousand fires sprang up, heating her, dewing her skin.

Caught in his play, as absorbed as he, Catriona knew he was right. She didn't need him to shift her again, so he could study the copper-bright curls at the junction of her thighs, didn't need to feel his fingers stroke them, then part them, then slide past, into her softness.

Didn't need him to look at her with unfocused eyes lit by blue flame and say: "You're just like that mountain—you're a volcano inside." He looked down again. "A dormant one, perhaps." Very gently, he stroked the soft flesh between her thighs, which had parted of their own accord. "I'm going to stir you to life. Until passion pours like lava through your veins. Until you're hot and aching and wet. Until you're so slick and needy, you spread your lovely thighs wide and let me enter you. Fill you. Until I bathe in your heat."

Catriona closed her eyes and felt her body surrender—felt the slickness he drew forth. Felt his fingers slide and glide, over and between the throbbing folds. Then his lips brushed hers. On a gasp, she kissed him back, sliding her hands from where they'd lain passive against his chest, around and about, holding him to her.

The kiss reached deep, then he drew back and chuckled—a wickedly devilish sound. "You're not like those ladies in London at all. The most intriguing thing about you is that you *know* you've fire in your soul."

Eyes closed, her body so heated she felt liquid, Catriona felt him open her, felt him press gently, then slowly, deliberately, slide one long finger into her.

She felt the invasion keenly, felt it in her soul.

Welcomed it in her heart.

He shifted within her, gently stroking; the sudden tension that gripped her eased. She softened about him, about his probing finger, relaxing against him, sinking into his embrace.

"You're not a woman of ice and snow."

She heard his words, and felt them, a breath across her temple, a deep reverberation in his chest. She tightened her hold on him, spreading her hands across his back, hanging on for dear life as if he was a rock anchoring her against the waves of heat beating through her.

Waves he incited with every smooth slick stroke, every subtle twist of his finger, every probing caress.

"You're heat—pure heat. Elemental heat. The heat of the earth, the purest fire."

He was right—she was burning now with a flame hotter than the blue of his eyes. She'd always known this was how it would be—that passion for her would be hot and heated, steamy and searing. How she'd known, she didn't know, but the knowledge had always been there. And it had been so hard to hold the fire in, to quench it, tame it, hide it through all the years she'd waited.

Waited for this.

She was long past asking him to stop and adjourn to the bed. That would necessitate him taking his hands from her, and she couldn't bear that. His hands were pure magic, wicked fingers made to tease her, to light her fires.

And there was a tidal wave of flame bearing down on her.

She cracked open her lids just enough to find his head—to drag his lips to hers. She kissed him deeply, urgently, wantonly. Let her thighs part farther, urged him to reach deeper.

Instead, he drew back. And chuckled wickedly again. "Oh, no. Not yet, sweet witch." He withdrew his hand from between her thighs.

Breasts heaving, Catriona lay back in his arms and stared at him. "What do you mean?" she finally managed to gasp. "Not yet?"

He grinned. "This is my dream, remember. You have to wait until you're frantic."

Lips parted, she stared at him. "I *am* frantic."

The look he bent on her was patronizingly dismissive. "Not *nearly* frantic enough."

With that, he lifted her and set her on her feet between his thighs. Her legs quaked; his hands steadied her. Her gown slithered down to cover her legs; the bodice gaped.

Catriona yanked the two halves together and ignored the teasing quirk of his brow.

Once she'd steadied, he rose—and immediately tottered; *she* had to steady *him*.

His frown was only fleeting; another chuckle banished it. "I must have had more of that whiskey than I'd thought."

All but collapsing under his weight, Catriona, suddenly suspicious, looked up into his face. His eyes met hers, still dark as the night, his gaze still vague and unfocused; his lips were still set in that boyishly open smile.

He was still ... dreaming.

Shifting her feet so she could better support his weight as he slumped, unrestrainedly heavy, against her, Catriona muttered a curse and struggled to ease him around the chair.

"The bed," she stated.

"Oh, indeed," he averred. "It's definitely time for the bed."

His devilish chuckle ensued; she shut her ears against it. If she hadn't known she'd drugged him, she would have thought him drunk—he could barely set one foot before the other. Certainly not in a straight line.

"Keep looking at the bed," she instructed as they lurched heavily toward the door. "Look—it's over there." Exerting all her strength, she managed to turn him and get them back on course.

"Never had such trouble in my life," he said, not sounding terribly concerned. "Usually know precisely where the bed is." After two more heavy steps, he added: "Must be that whiskey. Hope I'm not too drunk to accommodate you."

Gritting her teeth with the effort of holding him steady, Catriona didn't reassure him. And then wished she had.

"Never mind," he murmured, and threw her a lecherous leer. "If I am too debilitated, I'll just tease you until the effect wears off."

Catriona closed her eyes fleetingly and stifled a groan. What had she done? She'd willingly taken the principal role in the dreams of a rake. She must have been mad.

But it was too late to draw back. Far too late. Aside from anything else, no matter how frantic she had to get, she wanted to reach the end of the hot, steamy, heated road he'd started her upon.

She definitely wanted to be hot and needy, and to feel him enter her.

Three more lurching steps and they reached the side of the bed—the opposite side to the one they'd started out for. Catriona was simply relieved. "There!"

Swinging him around so his back was to the bed, she placed both palms against his chest and shoved. He obligingly toppled back across the bed—but took her with him.

Landing half-across him, Catriona couldn't manage even a squeak. She immediately wriggled, fighting free of his arms but not of his hands—they were everywhere. She tried to ignore them. "We have to get you undressed." At least undressed enough.

Predictably, he chuckled. "Be my guest." Flinging both arms wide, he lay back. And grinned.

Catriona narrowed her eyes at him and tugged his cravat free. She flung it over the end of the bed, then, kneeling beside him, grabbed the lapel of his coat. No matter how she tugged, she couldn't get it even close to his shoulder. Exasperated she sat back, and noticed that his chest was quaking, even though his expression remained guileless.

She glared at him. "If you don't help me undress you, I'll leave."

Laughing softly, he rolled onto one shoulder, then sat up. "It's impossible to get a well-cut coat off me without my help."

Catriona humphed. She watched as he shrugged the coat off and sent it to join his cravat. Impelled by she knew not what, she reached out and ran her hands over his chest, pressing aside his waistcoat to explore the wide expanse.

Beneath her questing hands, muscles shifted, rippled, then set. He caught her wrists and yanked her to him, then bent his head and kissed her.

She sank into his embrace, felt the heat surround her, rise within her, lick tantalizingly up her spine as he gathered her closer. With a mind of their own, her fingers quickly undid the buttons of his shirt, then slid inside, spreading wide over warm tight skin, over ridged muscles, hard bands of hair-dusted flesh.

He broke from the kiss with a soft curse. From beneath her lashes, she saw him fight free of both waistcoat and shirt and fling them aside. She also saw one hand drop to his waistband, undoing the buttons there. Closing her eyes quickly, she reached for him, relieved when he captured her lips with his and kissed her witless.

He shifted, coming up on his knees and guiding her back, down onto the bed. She sank back obediently, eyes closed, silently willing him to be quick.

His weight shifted on the bed; she heard the dull thwacks as his shoes, then his trousers hit the floor. She kept her eyes tight shut—she definitely wasn't going to look. Then she felt him beside her; he leaned over her, and his lips covered hers.

He kissed her deeply, commandingly—more intimately than before. He took her mouth as if she'd offered herself; in a way, she supposed she had. The claiming was complete, unrestrained—as if even asleep he knew she was his. His for the taking.

And he took.

Somewhere along the line, she opened her senses, let them reach and tell her what her eyes could not. She set her hands exploring, over the smooth acres of his chest, tight and hard under her hands and roughened by crinkly hair, then over the rounded curves of his shoulders. Flexing her fingers into the steel of his upper arms, she lifted against him, driven by his kiss—he was leaning far over her, his body, hot and hard, a mere inch from hers.

He was lying beside her, his hip against hers, his body radiating heat and a sensuality that wrapped about her, about them, and shielded them from the world.

And still he kissed her, reaching deep, asking for more and taking it. Emboldened, she met his demands—and let her hands stray lower.

To his hip. Fingers reaching, she traced the wide bone, sensed the slightly different texture of his skin. And sensed the sudden hiatus in their kiss—the abrupt refocusing of his senses.

Deliberately, she let her hand fall, fingers languidly trailing over his lower stomach.

His breath hitched—he pulled back from the kiss.

Just as she found him.

Eyes still closed, she touched tentatively, surprised to find such delicate skin. And felt him quiver, then tense. Intrigued, she slowly reached farther, and wrapped her fingers around the heavy length. Every muscle he possessed locked.

The one in her hands throbbed.

Lips curving in a wicked smile, she stroked, and caressed, closed her hands and weighed, then explored farther still.

He broke and caught her hands. "Sweet witch, you're killing me."

The words sounded as if they'd been said through clenched teeth; she gave a wicked chuckle of her own.

Only to have him kiss her voraciously, ravenously, until her wits whirled and she lost touch with reality. Then he drew back.

"Now it's my turn."

He swung over her, kneeling, his knees on either side of hers. Catching the hem of her nightgown, he raised it.

Eyes closed, expectation hammering in her veins, Catriona lay still and waited.

He pulled her gown up to her waist—then straight up to her shoulders, drawing her arms up, clearly intending to wrestle it from her.

Catriona gasped and came alive. Grabbing folds of the gown, she tried to wrestle it back down. He didn't need her naked to—

He chuckled, the sound even more evocative with her head wrapped in her gown, her body fully exposed. To the night, to him.

"Actually," he drawled, "that's an even better idea."

The gown shifted, twisted; Catriona waited half a second, then tried to move her arms, only to find them stuck. Her head, arms and shoulders were wrapped, trapped, in her gown.

"Hmm. *Excellent.*"

The purring drawl had her biting her lip, had her tensing with expectation. An expectation fully borne out when she felt him lower his naked body upon hers. He shifted, sliding lower, his legs outside hers.

"Positively succulent."

She felt his breath against the soft skin of her breasts and wondered what he meant.

The next instant, she arched wildly and nearly screamed as his mouth closed hotly about one nipple. He pressed open-mouthed kisses over her quivering flesh, then lovingly licked each peak to a tight bud—before torturing it with his tongue.

Catriona fought wildly—just to catch her breath. When she finally thought she'd become used to the new sensations, he suckled one nipple fiercely—she screamed and melted anew.

Luckily, the folds of her gown got into her mouth and muffled her shriek. As sanity returned, she realized his attentions hadn't faltered—she hadn't jarred him fully awake. When he suckled her other breast, she was prepared for the lightning bolt—the shocking strike of pure sensation. Her body arched, but she contained her scream.

Panting, gasping, her body afire, she waited, desperately trying to imagine what he would do next.

His lips drifted lower, leaving trails of fire down her body, over her waist. He pressed hot kisses to her stomach; she tensed, then relaxed as the trails continued down her thighs, first one, then the other.

Then he shifted, moving back and away. Senses searching, Catriona placed him kneeling astride her calves. Then she felt his hands close about her knees and lift them, parting her thighs.

After the slightest hesitation, she let him open her; catching her breath, she waited for him to cover her.

Instead, she felt a feathery touch, then feathery kisses dotting along her inner thigh. First one, then the other.

As what he *might* intend broke on her mind, she gasped and tried to clamp her thighs shut, only to find his broad shoulders between.

He chuckled wickedly.

And pressed a long, hot kiss to her damp curls.

"Not yet, sweet witch."

Then he kissed her.

And licked her. And sucked so gently she thought she would die.

Mindless, she threshed, trying to fight her way free of her nightgown; defeated, she tried to sit up—only to feel the heavy weight of his forearm across her waist press her down. Only to feel his other hand slide beneath her bottom and tilt her up. So he could savor her softness more thoroughly.

And savor her he did. Long and slow, languid and devastating, his lips and tongue wove their magic, until fires burned under every inch of her skin, until her bones had melted and her nerves shrivelled and her wits had reduced to ashes. Until she was panting, almost crying in her need.

She was hot, she was needy—she was ready.

She was frantic.

Then he pulled back.

"*Richard!*"

Her cry was weak—a demand and a plea.

He shifted back onto his knees with a satisfied groan; the next instant, he smoothed aside the folds of her gown, searching for her hands. Their fingers touched, and locked; he drew her up so she was sitting.

Catriona swung her legs under her so she was kneeling, too—but before she could push her gown down, he whisked it off over her head. Aghast, she watched it float over the end of the bed.

She looked at her tormentor.

Which was a big mistake.

Fully dressed, he was intimidating. Naked, he was mesmerizing. Fascinatingly, mind-numbingly male—a potent, powerful presence just waiting to claim her.

In all that had led to this moment, she had steadfastly refused to let her mind form any picture—to imagine how he would look naked, without the civilized cloak he wore when he stalked the world. Dragging in a tight breath, she wondered if imagining might have been better—might have better prepared her to face this.

To her mind, to all her senses, he was magnificent, his long, lean frame covered with taut muscle. The sight of him stirred her powerfully, unfurled some primitive emotion in her.

She gulped, and forced her gaze upward, relieved to see his boyish grin still in place.

"That's better."

While her eyes had been roaming, so had his, with very evident results. He reached for her; she tried to hold back but her knees slid across the sheets. To her surprise, he didn't gather her into his arms, but, sinking back on his ankles, stopped her with her knees against his and eased her back so she was sitting as he was, on her ankles, knees wide.

He grinned, his expression the very essence of male sexual expectation. "Next installment."

Her wits long gone, her senses reeling, she couldn't even summon a frown. "Installment?"

His hands closed over her breasts, confident and firm. His thumbs rubbed her tightly budded nipples; her body came instantly alive. Her lids fell of their own accord as she arched lightly, pressing her breasts into his palms. "What do you mean?"

"I want to see how high you can go—how high I can take you before you shatter."

She struggled to frown, struggled to make sense of his words, and couldn't. Not with his hands on her breasts, then roaming her body, her sides, her thighs, quiveringly tight.

Then he stroked her soft curls, then slid long fingers past to stroke her there, where she was hot and molten. Two fingers pressed in and filled her, then retreated; he circled her entrance, then pressed—and she gasped. His fingers slid away, and played, then returned to the same excruciatingly sensitive spot, and pressed again.

White light flared behind her lids. And suddenly, Catriona understood. She grabbed his wrist—and felt, beneath her fingers, the seductive shift of tendon and muscle as he probed her—slowly, deliberately, evocatively.

She snapped open her eyes and looked at his face. Harsh-edged with passion, the planes were set. Fully aroused, his gaze was locked on where his hand worked between her thighs.

She couldn't believe her senses. "You're teasing me? Like *this?*"

He looked up and met her gaze. His was still clouded, his eyes like black pools; if anything, the hold of the drugs was deepening. Then he smiled—the same boyish smile. "I've been itching to sink into you since first I set eyes on you—I've been aroused virtually every minute I've spent in your sight. Being around you, especially every time you put your pert nose in the air, has been torture. I thought I'd give you a dose of your own magic before I ease my pain." His smile grew soft, distinctly dreamy. "And as for this"—he pressed again; Catriona gasped and swayed—"I plan on teasing you a lot more yet."

"A lot *more?*" Aghast, she stared at him and tried to think of what he hadn't yet done.

His grin widened. "When I'm inside you. It'll be long and slow—the most perfect torture for a sexy witch."

Catriona simply stared—what had she done? What had she set in train? He was dreaming. He really *was* dreaming—reality fluidly merging with fantasy. He didn't know what he was doing. He didn't realize he was frightening her, pushing her too far. Making her feel far too much. He didn't know she was real.

She was going to lose her mind if he didn't fill her soon. Simply lay her on her back and take her. Quickly. She could feel the passion mounting, bubbling through her veins, exactly as he had predicted. Her inner fires were raging, she was molten with liquid heat. And she needed to release it.

She wanted him—now, immediately, ten minutes ago. It was her own need that was scaring her, not his.

But he didn't know that—and she couldn't explain. She didn't want to beg. Unexpected panic flared within her.

It must have shown in her face, for he frowned. His fingers slowed, and he cocked his head slightly, studying her. He blinked once, twice—confusion was writ plain in his face. "What is it?"

Catriona opened her lips—but no words came out. What should she say? What should she admit to? He was clearly dazed, increasingly hazy—he was operating on instinct. What sort of instinct did a rake have?

Her gaze locked with his, she moistened her lips, suddenly aware of the huge risk she'd taken. Algaria had tried to warn her, but she hadn't understood. She wasn't in control of this situation—and neither was he.

Which meant she'd thrown herself on the mercy of a rake's true soul, his real, inner self, his true character—and she didn't know what that was.

She was about to find out.

Acting on instinct, she held out her arms to him. "I want you now."

She didn't try to hide the genuineness of her need—her vulnerability. Her only guarantee that she would be safe in so doing was The Lady's insistence that he was the one. Placing her trust in The Lady's judgment, with her arms, with her eyes, she reached for him. "*Please.*"

She didn't see him move, only felt his arms close about her as he gathered her close.

"Sshhh." He held her against him, hot skin to hot skin, and pressed his face into her hair. "I didn't mean to frighten you." His hands stroked her back, soothingly, comfortingly. Cupping her bottom lightly, he shifted against her, his erection riding against her belly. "Put it down to too much imagining. I've been fantasizing for so long about you—how you'd feel"—he slid his hands over her back and hips—"how you'd taste." With his shoulder, he nudged her head up and kissed her—gently, lingeringly—the hunger in him held back, the tangy taste of her still there on his lips and tongue.

Then he raised his head and looked into her face. "I want you in the worst possible way"—he grinned ruefully, boyishness overlaid by passion—"in every way known to man. I want to see you flower for me—spread your legs for me and hold out your arms for me. I want to be inside you more than I want to breathe—I want to feel you rising beneath me as I ride you. And I want to wake and find you beside me—I want to hold you forever." He pressed a kiss to her lips. "I want to *care* for you forever." Lifting his head, he looked into her eyes. "I want to be your lover in all ways—in every sense of the word, and the deed."

Locked in his dark, cloudy gaze, Catriona could only quiver. He'd seduced her all over again. "Come."

It was she who took his hand, she who lay down upon the bed, spread her thighs wide and held out her arms to him.

And he came to her—the invincible warrior without a cause—devoid, because of her scheming, of his mask, the shield he held up to the world. In that instant, when he'd looked into her eyes and made his declaration, he hadn't been capable of lying. He wanted to love her—and to have her love him. Not just physically but in all ways. He wanted her as part of his life—and wanted to be part of hers. She'd needed no higher powers to read the truth—it had been there, transparent in his unshielded eyes.

It was there, written on his soul—and in that moment she'd been able to read the words. The truth. The reality of what he yearned for.

So she welcomed him to her, wrapping her arms about him as he covered her. Nudging her thighs wider, he settled between and fitted himself to her slick sheath. Turning his head, he took one pebbled nipple into his mouth and suckled fiercely; she arched, and he pressed inside her, stretching her.

She tensed and tried to force her muscles to ease. He reached down, between their bodies, and caressed the nubbin he'd earlier teased.

Sensation streaked—jagged lightning striking deep. It broke the banks and set the floodtide raging, molten passion, lava hot, surging, racing through her. And she was caught in the tide, swept up and whirled away, into the pure heat of the moment. She felt him retreat, then powerfully surge, and fill her.

Felt him ride deep to her core.

She melted about him and welcomed him in—into her body, into her heart. She knew it was dangerous—she saw the gaping hole yawning at her feet, but the desire that drove him, the raw need that now filled him, driving him into her again and again—as surely as it had caught him, it caught her. She jumped into the hole without a second thought.

And gave herself to him, opened her body and her senses, and let him fill both. Exquisitely vulnerable, spread beneath his hard strength, held immobile by it, impaled by it, she kissed him wildly, and urged him on.

But not even she could warp his true character; despite the force of the energy flowing so strongly between them, he harnessed it and set himself to please her. Pleasure her.

In a wild and wonderful way.

His surging rhythm became hers, became her very heartbeat. He used his body to love her—she learned to use hers to love him back. He was no gentle teacher, yet he forced nothing but pleasure on her. She raised her knees and gripped his hips, and gave herself up to his loving.

To the joy, the heat, and the escalating pleasure. To the moment that came upon her unawares, and stole her mind, her senses, her very being from her.

And left her floating in a void of delight, anchored only by his heartbeat.

She only just managed to smother her scream; she wasn't even sure she succeeded. She wasn't even sure that she cared.

Richard felt her melt beneath him, felt the last of her contractions fade, sensed her final surrender. With a gasp and a groan, he thrust deep and shut his eyes, blocking out the sight of her, the blazing mane of her hair a frame for her ecstasy, for the expression of pure peace that filled her face.

Racking shudders swamped him; he felt her grip him tight.

He gasped again and surrendered, and followed her into the void.

Later, much later, he lifted from her and drew her into his arms. She turned and snuggled closer, warming him inside and out. He felt his lips lift—he couldn't understand why he felt so pleased. Why he felt so at ease. So complete.

Then he remembered.

But it was just a dream.

With a soft sigh, he closed his eyes and wished dreams could last forever.

CHAPTER
Seven

ॐ⌒ॐ

Richard woke the next morning, very slowly. An age seemed to pass before he felt certain he was in this world, and not some other. He felt disoriented, lethargic. Drained.

If he hadn't known better, he would have said he felt sated. The thought made him frown. The thoughts that followed made him frown even more.

"Rubbish." He looked at the bed beside him. The covers were straight, the pillow still plump. No hint of a bedmate. To prove the point, he lifted the covers and peered down. Beside him, the sheet was not rumpled in the least; it was, in fact, very neat.

Instead of lightening, his frown grew blacker. He shifted his gaze to that part of his anatomy that featured most prominently in his disturbing dream. He gazed at it as if it could answer the wild question in his mind; it simply lay there, in its customary semi-aroused morning state, and told him nothing. He checked, but there was no discernible evidence that it had engaged in any wild nocturnal coupling.

Dropping the covers, Richard lay back on the pillows; crossing his arms above his head, he gazed at the canopy. But the more he let his mind dwell on his dream, the more vivid it became, refusing to fade in the cold morning light. The more he thought of it, the more definite details became, the more intense the sensual memories.

"Ridiculous." Flinging back the covers, he sat up.

He washed and shaved, attended by Worboys, then dressed, shrugged into his coat and headed downstairs. Throughout his ablutions, his dream had refused to get out of his mind, had only grown more vivid. More detailed.

Lips compressed, he stepped off the stairs. Given his recent abstinence, given the witch presently under the same roof, given the fantasies he'd been consciously and unconsciously concocting about her, it probably *wasn't* surprising she'd started inhabiting his dreams.

He strolled into the breakfast parlor, knowing he was late. Exchanging mild nods with the rest of Seamus's dull household, he filled his plate and carried it to the table. The object of his lustful dreams was not present, but she'd proved to be an early riser.

At McEnery House, bright morning chatter was unheard of, which suited his mood. He ate in silence. He was devilishly hungry. He'd cleared half his plate when rushing footsteps sounded in the corridor. Everyone looked up.

Catriona hurried in.

Her gaze collided with his; she stopped as if she'd run into a wall. For one instant, she stared, her expression unreadable.

"Well! I wondered when you'd rouse."

Algaria's dry, disapproving comment broke the spell; Richard couldn't tell who'd thrown it—Catriona or him. Or some other force entirely.

Catriona glanced at Algaria, then approached the table. "I . . . ah, overslept."

"You were dead to the world when I looked in."

"Hmm." Without meeting anyone's eye, Catriona served herself a large portion of the kedgeree the butler offered. Instead of her customary tea and toast. Richard frowned—first at her plate, then at his. And wondered if it was possible for people to share dreams.

It was a horridly dull day, with sleet and snow lashing the house. Denied any chance of a walk to clear her head, Catriona set herself to review the stillroom. Which appeared not to have been reviewed since last she'd visited. The task proved so consuming, she got no chance to devote any sensible thought to the problem she'd seen looming on her horizon.

She hadn't seen it until that morning, when she'd rushed into the breakfast parlor. Not that she could have foreseen it, given she hadn't foreseen the depth of her involvement with Richard.

He who was to father her child.

But she got no chance to think on that, to dwell on how her view of him had changed, and on whether that meant she could, or should, change her plan, or even whether her plan was now safer, or more dangerous.

He'd been confused this morning—and that she hadn't expected. She'd seen it in his eyes as he'd looked at her—a remembrance of the night. Given what had happened, she wasn't surprised; she hadn't expected him to be even partially awake, much less in that peculiar state of a waking dream.

It wasn't, therefore, surprising that he remembered something; his confusion told her he hadn't remembered enough. Enough to be sure it hadn't been a dream.

She was safe, but he was disturbed. She needed to think about that.

"Tie all these up in bunches and hang them properly. And when you've finished with that, you can throw all this away." "All this" was a pile of ancient herbs that had long ago lost their efficacy. Hands on hips, Catriona surveyed the much-improved stillroom, then nodded briskly. "We'll make a start on the oils in the morning."

"Yes, ma'am," the housekeeper and two maids chorused.

Catriona left them to their labors and headed back to the family parlor. Her route lay through a labyrinth of corridors giving onto a narrow gallery overlooking the side drive.

The gallery led to the main wing of the house. She'd started along it before she looked up and saw the large figure standing before one of the long windows looking out at the wintry day. He heard her and turned his head, then turned fully, not precisely blocking her path, but giving the impression he would like to.

Head high, Catriona's steps did not falter. But she slowed as she neared him, suddenly aware of a changed presence in the air, of some blatantly sexual reaction. On his part—and on hers.

She stopped a full yard away, not daring to venture closer, unsure just what the sudden searing impulse to touch him might lead her to do. Keeping her expression mild and uninformative, she lifted her chin and raised a questioning brow.

He looked down at her, his expression as unreadable as hers.

And the hot attraction between them grew stronger, more intense.

It stole her breath and fanned heat over her body. Her nipples crinkled tight; she held her ground and prayed he wouldn't notice.

"I wondered," he eventually said, "if you'd like to stroll." His tone made it clear he wanted her alone, somewhere private so he could investigate what he was feeling. "The conservatory as we have no other choice."

The fact that—even knowing the truth—she actually considered the possibility truly scared her. "Ahh ... I think not." Prudence reasserted itself in a rush; Catriona softened her refusal with a smile. "I must tend to Meg—she's unwell."

"Can't Algaria tend Meg?"

His irritation nearly made her grin; his mask was slipping—the warrior was showing. "No—Meg prefers me."

His lips thinned. "So do I."

Catriona couldn't stop her grin. "She's ill—you're not."

"Much you know." Thrusting his hands in his trouser pockets, he turned and sauntered beside her as she resumed her progress into the main wing.

Catriona shot him a careful glance. "You're not sick."

He raised an arrogant brow. "You can tell just by looking?"

"Generally, yes." She trapped his gaze. "In your case, your aura is very strong, and there's no hint of any illness."

He searched her eyes, then humphed. "When you've finished with Meg, you can come and examine my strength in greater detail."

Catriona fought to keep her lips straight enough to frown. "You're just feeling a trifle under the weather. Perfectly understandable." They'd reached the bottom of the main stairs; with a nod, she indicated the bleak scene beyond the hall windows. "He looked, but didn't seem to see. He stopped before the stairs; she halted on the bottom step and faced him.

"I'd be perfectly all right," he said, meeting her eyes, "if I could just ..."

His words died; desire swept over them, tangible and hot as a desert wind. He stared at her; Catriona held tight to the banister and struggled not to respond, to keep her own mask in place as his wavered.

Then he blinked, frowned, and shook his head. "Never mind."

More shaken than she could allow him to see, Catriona smiled weakly. "Later, perhaps."

He looked at her again, then nodded. "Later."

There was to be no later—not that day. Despite her best intentions, Catriona found herself in constant demand, with Meg, with the children, even with Mary, who was usually as hale as a horse. The tensions in the house, generated by Seamus's iniquitous will, were taking their toll.

The only time she had to herself was the half-hour while she dressed for dinner. Hardly enough time to consider the implications of the unexpected turn her straightforward plan had taken. As she scrambled into her gown, then shook out her hair, brushed it and rebraided it, she swiftly reevaluated her position.

If things had gone as she'd planned, she would have steadfastly avoided Richard during the days, done nothing to give him the slightest reason to change his mind. She had planned to hold aloof until he'd refused Seamus's edict, seen him on the road to London, then headed for the vale. Carrying his child.

Such had been her plan.

Now, however, one small element had gone awry. She needed to adjust. He'd remembered enough of the night to be seriously disturbed. The idea that he might be affected in some way as a result of her machinations was not one she could accept.

She'd have to do something about it.

The first thing she did, on her way down to dinner, last as ever, was to add to his fateful decanter a few drops of another potion, one that would prevent him from remembering any further "dreams."

The second thing she did was stand, rather than flee, when he reentered the drawing room after dinner and stalked straight to her side.

Algaria, beside her, stiffened. Catriona waved her away—she went, reluctantly. Richard barely nodded at her as he took her place.

"Where the devil have you been?"

Catriona opened her eyes wide. "Calming Meg, dosing the children—all six of them—then mixing Mary a potion, then checking the children, then helping Meg get up, then checking the children, then ..." She waved. "My day flew, I'm afraid."

He eyed her narrowly. "I'd hoped to catch up with you after lunch."

Catriona threw him a helpless, apologetic look.

Richard inwardly snorted, and all but glowered at the rest of the company. He'd filled in what probably ranked as the dullest day of his life in the library and in the billiard room, praying that his sudden susceptibility would fade.

It hadn't.

Even now, just standing beside her, his body was literally remembering what hers had felt like pressed against him. Naked—skin to skin. The thought made him hot—hotter than he already was. If she'd been a problem yesterday, with her ability to arouse him, after last night's dream, she qualified as a full blown crisis. "I wanted to speak with you."

About what, he wasn't sure. But he definitely wanted to know if she felt what he did—if she could sense the sheer lust that scorched the air between them. He'd watched her carefully but had detected no especial awareness; he slanted a glance at her now, as, with less than a foot between them, she calmly considered his words. Not a glimmer of consciousness showed.

While all he could think of was how it had felt to slide inside her.

He bit back a groan; it was no use hardening his muscles against the remembered sensations—they were hard enough as it was. "We need to talk."

The glance she threw him was searching. "You're not sick—you don't need my professional advice."

She sounded positive—Richard wasn't so sure. He might not be physically ill, but ... he knew his "dream" was a dream for the simple reason it could not have really happened. The chances of her turning up in his room like that, smiling and saying she'd come to go to bed with him, were, in his estimation, less than nil.

And if that hadn't happened, then the rest certainly hadn't.

But he'd never had memories like this, not even of real events. Real women—ones with whom he *had* shared a bed. Much as he hated to think it, he wasn't at all sure that all the long nights of his lenthy and lustfully successful rakish career weren't coming back to haunt him.

Because he was sure—to his bones—that he knew her in the biblical sense.

He drew in a deep breath and let it out through clenched teeth. "Do you know much about dreams?" He glanced at her. "Can you read them?"

She looked up and met his eyes; he sensed her hesitation. "Sometimes," she eventually replied. "Dreams often mean something, but that something often isn't clear." She considered, then quickly added: "And it's often not the thing it appears as in the dream."

He threw her an exasperated look. "That's a lot of help."

She blinked and considered him. Rather carefully, he thought.

"If you're troubled by some dream, then the best thing to do is set it aside for the moment, because if it *is* supposed to mean something, then that something will become apparent, usually in a few days. Or the dream will disappear."

"Indeed?" Richard raised a brow, then reluctantly nodded. That was probably sound advice—he might as well put it into practice. But first, he needed to stop her from deserting him. He nodded to the tea trolley being stationed before Mary. "I'll get our cups."

Catriona graciously inclined her head and watched him cross the room. And swore she'd start carrying a fan. She was so hot, she was surprised she hadn't spontaneously combusted—gone up in flames right here in Mary's drawing room. The flushes that washed through her came in two forms—hot and hotter. Hot when he wasn't looking directly at her, hotter when he was. The only reason she was still standing here, using every ounce of her will and experience to appear unaffected, was because she'd convinced herself this was the penance she had to pay for the way her plan had affected him—to bear with the countereffect and bring him what ease she could. But . . .

She was desperately in need of her tea.

He returned and handed her her cup; she accepted it and sipped gratefully.

Richard sipped, too, for much the same reason, then set his cup back on its saucer. "Tell me about this role of yours—being the lady of the vale."

Catriona blinked and looked up at him. "The lady of the vale?" When he simply waited, she asked: "You want to know what I do?"

Richard nodded. And saw wariness seep into her eyes.

"Why?"

"Because . . ." He paused, then continued, "I want to know what I'm turning down." If she thought he was considering falling in with Seamus's plan, she'd tell him nothing. He capped the words with one of his teasing smiles, and was rewarded with one of her humphs.

"You don't need to know."

"Where's the harm?" He slanted her a glance—she'd tossed her pert nose in the air again and he was wretchedly uncomfortable. "You're the local healer, but that can't be the summation of your duties, not if you own the vale."

"Of course not."

"I assume you keep control over the rents and sales of produce, but what about the other areas? The livestock, for instance. Do you supervise the breeding yourself, or does someone else help?"

The glance she shot him was part irritation, part resignation. "There are others, of course. Most of the husbandry is dealt with by one of my staff, but the dairy is separate."

"Do you make your own cheese?" By dint of a succession of careful questions, he dragged a reasonable outline of her holdings, and how she managed them, from her. As he'd expected, there were gaps in her management—important areas in which she relied on people who themselves had no real qualifications. She trusted too easily, despite, or perhaps because of, her beliefs.

He'd already proved that.

Catriona answered his questions because she couldn't see any reason not to. And he surprised her—with his insight, his understanding, his experience. In the end, she asked: "How do you know to ask all this?" She frowned at him, grateful the heat between them had ebbed. Not disappeared, but eased. "Do you manage large estates in your spare time?"

He looked mildly bemused. "Spare time?"

"I gathered your conquests in London take up *most* of your time."

"Ahh." Her tart reply amused him. "You forget—I'm a Cynster."

"So?"

His smile started off as teasing, but somewhere along the way turned intent. "You've forgotten," he murmured, "the family motto."

Catriona felt the air about her stir; she was surprised it didn't crackle. She held his gaze and lifted a haughty brow. "Which is?"

"To have . . . and to hold."

The words hung between them, layered with meaning; holding his gaze, Catriona prayed he couldn't see through her mask as easily as she could see through his. She didn't need to be told those words were not just a motto—they were a *raison d'e?^tre*. For them all, perhaps, but especially for him.

The bastard—the warrior without a cause.

Barely able to breathe, she reached for his empty cup. "If you'll excuse me, I must check on Meg."

He let her go without a word, which was just as well. How much longer she could have withstood the temptation to reach out to him—to let him have her as his cause—she didn't like to think.

Nevertheless, later that night, when the last of the midnight chimes died, she once more stood before his closed door—and stared at it. While telling herself, in very plain terms, precisely why she was there.

First and foremost there were The Lady's orders, orders she could not defy. And it was indisputable fact that three nights was the minimum she should spend with him—that was what she would advise any other woman in her place.

And lastly, but, she had to admit, very far from least, there was the simple fact she wanted him. Wanted to lie in his arms again, wanted to miss none of the short time fate had granted them. She wanted to hold him again, the vulnerable warrior, and give herself to him completely—give herself to fill the void in his soul. She couldn't marry him, but that didn't mean that he—and she—couldn't have that.

Even if only in his dreams.

She drew a deep breath and reached for the door handle.

Lying back in his bed, wide awake, Richard stared moodily at the whiskey decanter. He'd gone without his usual nightcap. It had occurred to him that the whiskey—not his normal drop—might be to blame for his over-vivid dreams.

If it was, he'd avoid it. He couldn't handle another day like this, with his body clamoring—reacting—as if something that hadn't happened had. He'd go mad. Some held that the Scots were all insane—witness Seamus. Maybe whiskey was to blame.

The soft swoosh of air as the door opened had him turning his head. The door swung open—not tentatively—and Catriona walked in. She closed the door quietly, then scanned the room—and saw him. The fire had burned low, but he still saw her soft, peculiarly witchy smile.

Every muscle in his body locked; he couldn't breathe. A condition that worsened as, her smile still playing over her face, she walked toward the bed, slipping off her robe—a robe he remembered—as she came. She let the robe fall as she reached the side of the bed. Head on one side, she studied him—still smiling softly.

Absolutely rigid, he watched her, then realized she was searching his face. The light from the fire didn't reach the head of the bed; she might be able to see his eyes were open, but she couldn't possibly read them. If she did, she'd flee.

Instead, her smile deepened. She reached for the covers, then hesitated. Then she shrugged and straightened—and calmly unbuttoned the bodice of her nightgown, grasped the skirt, and drew it off over her head.

Richard sucked in a tortured breath; if he could have moved he'd have pinched himself. But he *knew* he wasn't asleep.

He wasn't dreaming. This was real.

Totally naked, her long tresses hanging free about her shoulders, over her back, her skin—smooth breasts, sleek flanks—gleaming like ivory in the weak light, she lifted the covers and slid in. The dipping of the mattress as she settled beside him triggered an instinctive, almost violent response. He only just managed to suppress it—the primitive urge to roll over, cover her, take her.

His mind was reeling, his wits in disarray, struggling to grasp the fact that this was *real*—that she was, in solid fact, here, in his bed—blissfully naked.

What in all hell was she up to?

He hadn't moved—he didn't dare; if he did, the reins would slip from his grasp, and God alone knew what would happen then. Every muscle quivering with restraint, he looked at her.

And she touched him.

Spread one small, warm hand over his chest, then swept it down to boldy cup him.

After that, hell, God—even her Lady—didn't matter.

He closed his eyes on a long groan. Her fingers tightened; his reins snapped. He caught her hands, first one, then the other, locking them above her head in one of his. In the same movement, he lifted over her, found her lips, and plundered.

One thought burned in his fevered brain—to confirm, beyond all doubt, that *she* had been the woman in his dream. That she'd been the woman he'd brought to life the night before, the woman who'd begged him to take her, then writhed like a wanton in his arms.

He closed his hand over one firm breast and recognized it. Felt it swell, found the tight pebble of her nipple. And recognized that, too. He swept his hand down, tracing curve after curve, of breast, waist, hip and thigh; the globes of her bottom, smooth and perfect, filled his hand. As they had last night.

And she was with him, as she had been last night—hot and urgent, her mouth, her lips, melding with his, her tongue dueling with his. With her arms still anchored above her head, her body arched beneath him, caressing him as he caressed her.

Caught in her heat, driven by wild compulsion, he wedged her thighs wide. And touched her. She was wet, scorchingly hot—she rose to his touch, mutely begging for more. He slid one finger deep and she gasped.

His name.

He drank it from her lips as he pushed her thighs wide, positioned himself between. And slid home.

Braced above her, he let his head fall back as she closed, scalding velvet, about him. He moved within her and she answered, matching him stroke for stroke, taking him deep into her heat, and holding him.

Freed, her hands rose to caress his chest, then strayed to his flexing flanks. She held him lightly, then repositioned her hips and guided him deeper.

He gasped, and came down on his elbows, framed her face and kissed her. Voraciously. The friction between their bodies was driving them both insane—demented with desire.

But he kept them there, held them there, in the heat of the furnace, in the eye of the storm. He prolonged their joining for as long as he could, addicted to the sheer joy of filling her.

Beneath him, Catriona gloried in the exquisite intimacy, in the clear, shining knowledge that this was how it was meant to be. Their bodies moved in a dance older than time, his hard, driving, hers soft, accepting.

Both loving.

The thought came to her on a fractured sigh and a guttural groan; bodies locked, they climbed higher, and higher, both focused totally on sensation—on sensation that went further than the physical, that breached some other plane.

Some plane where each touch became laden with meaning, with feeling, with emotion, where they asked and answered through each caress, through each deep thrust that linked them.

It was a plane where their heartbeats joined and swelled, where bodies ceased to exist and souls, freed, could touch. And be touched.

It was a plane of unlimited joy, unlimited ecstasy. Freed, together, they explored—and lived for every precious moment.

Their fusion, when it came, was all heat, glorious heat, molten rivers pouring through their bodies, down their veins. Bodies locked, they climaxed together, melted together, fused, then, as one, slowly cooled.

Richard returned from the dead first, but was too deeply sated, too shaken, to move. His mind was still in limbo, reeling between truth, reality, and an even greater truth. Her body beneath him, around him, was his anchor; her arms tight about him, she seemed as disinclined to move as he.

It seemed like hours before they could bear to part, slowly, reluctantly, disengaging their limbs. Even then, she turned to him, slipping into his arms as if she belonged there.

Richard held her—and tried to hold back his thoughts, tried not to recognize that greater truth. Tried instead to focus on the far less unnerving fact that it had indeed been she last night—it hadn't been a dream. He wasn't going insane. At least, not in the way he'd thought.

The clock on the stairs struck one. He glanced down at her face and realized she was awake. He hesitated, then said: "Sometimes, dreams don't turn out as you expect."

He felt her exhale slowly, then she whispered, "No." Lifting her head, she stretched up and kissed him, long and lingeringly, then sank back, settling in his arms. "No."

She fell asleep with her head on his shoulder, leaving him frowning into the dark.

CHAPTER
Eight

ॐৎ৩ॐ

S he had the touch of a goddess. He could feel her hands on him, on his
back, on his flanks. On his—Richard awoke with a start. He glanced at the
bed beside him and realized he'd been dreaming. "Or rather," he murmured,
lips thinning, "remembering."

He noted the bed's state—as neat and tidy as the morning before. Scanning
the room, he saw not one sign of his witch's presence. Lying back on the
pillows, he frowned. He wasn't a particularly heavy sleeper, but clearly she
could slide from his arms, even straighten the sheet beside him, without
awakening him. She moved smoothly—gliding rather than walking; her hands
were used to soothing, her gestures always graceful.

He didn't want to think about her hands.

With an oath, he flung back the covers and stalked across the room to the
bellpull. He was in hunter mode again; all he needed to do now was locate his
prey.

He found her in the breakfast parlor, sunnily eating a boiled egg. She greeted
him with a breezy smile. And such transparent happiness he was momentarily
thrown off-balance.

He hesitated, then nodded back and headed for the buffet. After making a
selection of the various meats on offer, he returned to the table, to the chair
opposite hers. Malcolm, morosely munching toast at the table's other end, and
Algaria O'Rourke were the only others down yet.

Catriona's watchdog sat beside her, regarding him with her usual
disapproval; Richard ignored her and ate—while watching Catriona do the
same. Watched her lick egg-yolk from her lower lip, then lick her spoon. Saw
her lips sheening pink when she sipped her tea.

He shifted in his seat, looked down at his plate, and tried to remember how
to fashion a trap.

"Did you have any disturbing dreams last night?"

He looked up; Catriona smiled at him, her green eyes openly studying him. He waited until her gaze reached his eyes. "No." He held her gaze steadily. "In fact, I don't believe I dreamed *anything* last night."

Her smile was glorious, as warming as the sun. "Good."

Richard blinked and inwardly shook himself. "I was wondering—"

"Catriona?"

All looked up; Mary hovered in the doorway, wringing her hands. "If you've finished, could you see to the children? They're so *fractious*."

"Of course." Laying her napkin by her plate, Catriona stood. "Are they still feverish?"

She bustled out, with not even a last look for him; Richard eyed her departing rear through narrowing eyes.

Turning back to his plate, he returned to his plans—the first item on his agenda was a very long ride.

He rode late into the afternoon, until the light was almost gone. Returning to the house, he ordered a late tea to be eaten in his rooms. Worboys arrived with the tray.

And remained to shake out his greatcoat and put away his gloves. And interrogate him.

"Am I right in assuming we'll be departing on the heels of the solicitor, sir?"

"Hmm," Richard answered around a portion of roast beef.

"I must say," Worboys persisted, "that it's been a most *instructive* stay. Makes one appreciate the little joys of London."

Sunk in the armchair before the fire, Richard didn't reply.

"I take it we'll be returning to the capital directly? Or do you intend visiting in Leicestershire?"

"I haven't the faintest notion."

Worboys sniffed, clearly disapproving of such aimlessness. He opened the wardrobe door. While he shuffled coats and straightened sleeves, Richard munched steadily, his gaze on the flames.

And pondered the fate of one witch.

Some part of his mind—the Cynster part of his mind—had, from the first moment he'd set eyes on her, been considering making her his. Ever since the reading of the will, he'd been toying with the prospect. Trying to decide, one way or the other, whether he should seize the opportunity Seamus had created, bow to fate and take a wife—or drive away and leave her behind.

Such had been his state before she'd come to his bed.

Now ... long fingers tightening about the chased goblet, Richard stared at the leaping flames.

"Are you ready to dress for dinner, sir?"

Richard looked up, his features set. "I am indeed."

* * *

Motive. She had to have some reason for coming to his bed.

Crossing the threshold of the drawing room, Richard instantly located Catriona, and strolled, apparently languid, in reality with fell intent, toward her.

She welcomed him with an open smile; he returned it with a wholly deceptive smile of his own.

His memories of their first night were incomplete, yet he was prepared to swear she'd been a virgin. An enthusiastic, eager, ready-to-be-wanton virgin, but a virgin nonetheless. She'd never lain with any man before him.

Which raised one very large question: Why him?

Or was that: Why now?

"I was wondering," he said, as he claimed his now customary place beside her, "where you intend going after we settle this business of the will."

She turned and met his eyes. "Why, to the vale, of course. I never stay away for long—usually not for more than a day."

"You never travel to Edinburgh or Glasgow?"

"Not even Carlisle, and that's closer."

"But you order things—you mentioned you did."

"I have agents call at the vale." She shrugged. "It seems wiser not to flaunt my existence—or that of the vale. We do very well in our anonymity."

"Hmmm." Richard studied her face. "Are there many other families of standing in the vale?"

"Standing?"

"Independent. Not your tenants."

She shook her head. "No—I own the whole vale." Fleetingly, she raised her brows. "We don't even have a curate, because there's no church, of course."

Richard humphed. "How did you escape that? Or did the initial incumbents simply disappear?"

She tried to straighten her lips, but didn't succeed. "The Lady doesn't approve of violence. But the answer to your question is geography. The vale is isolated—indeed, if you don't know it's there, it's not easy to find."

"You must at least have neighbors—the surrounding landowners."

She nodded. "But in the Hills the population is widely scattered." She looked up at him. "It's a lonely existence."

He had the impression she'd intended that last sentence one way, but it had come out another. She held his gaze for an instant, then seemed to draw back. She blinked and looked away, smiling quickly as she reached for one of the cups Mary carried.

Richard perforce smiled at Mary, too, and relieved her of the second cup.

"My dear, I can't thank you enough." Mary looked at Catriona with gratitude in her eyes. "I don't know *how* we would have coped if you hadn't been here—the children would have driven us all insane. Instead, they listened to your stories for the whole afternoon—I don't know how you do it. You're so good with them, even the little ones."

Catriona smiled one of her "lady of the vale" smiles. "It's just part of the healer's art."

Behind his teacup, Richard raised a skeptical brow. The healers he knew often took delight in scaring children, and treated them as patients only grudgingly. Not all healers, any more than all adults, had the patience to bear with children's capriciousness.

"Whatever," Mary said, "we most sincerely appreciate your efforts." She looked hopefully at Catriona. "Are you sure you won't stay?" A shadow passed over her face, then she grimaced. "I don't know where we'll be, after next week"—she shot an apologetic glance at Richard—"but you'll always be welcome wherever we are."

Catriona squeezed her hand. "I know—and don't worry. Things will sort themselves out. But I must return to the vale—I've already been away far longer than I'd expected."

A slight frown, a shadow of concern, momentarily clouded her eyes. Richard noted it. Draining his cup, he inwardly reflected that, whatever else, Catriona Hennessey took her role as lady of the vale seriously.

Perhaps too seriously.

He wanted to know why she'd done it—put some potion in his whiskey, then climbed into his bed. And given herself to him.

Was it simply for experience—or was there more to it than that?

Lying in his bed with the bed curtains drawn, Richard stared into the blackness and listened to the clock on the stairs announce the quarter hours.

And waited for her to come to him.

He didn't know what he felt—his reactions, even after a whole day on horseback in an empty world, were still too violently tangled for him to be sure of them, much less consider them. On the one hand, he felt honored she'd chosen him for whatever reason; on the other, he was furious that she'd dared. And there were other feelings that surged through him whenever he thought of her—and their nocturnal couplings—that went far beyond any rational response. Any response he could understand.

He wanted to know—needed to know—why.

He could, of course, ask—simply wait for her to appear, then put a simple question. If he did, he doubted he'd get an answer. He doubted she'd stay to spend the rest of the night in his arms, either.

On both the previous nights, she'd thought him asleep—drugged. Capable physically, but not *compos mentis*. On the first night, that had indeed been the case. He still couldn't remember all of it—snippets were crystal clear, while other parts were a phantasmagoria of remembered sensation, drowning out all other recollections. He knew he'd spoken, and she'd replied—which was why she hadn't reacted last night, when he'd spoken again. She'd thought he was speaking in his dreams.

And that, after a whole day of planning, was the only avenue he could see that might get him the answer he wanted. If he put the question to her while she was in his arms, and thought him asleep, she would be far less inhibited in answering. She might even tell him the truth.

Not straight away, perhaps, but ...

One thing he did remember from that first night was the way he'd teased her—parts of that burned, beacon bright, in his brain. She'd crumpled very quickly. Which, now he knew her in the biblical sense, wasn't a surprise. She'd bottled up all her hot heat for too long—new to the game, she didn't have the ability to stave off completion for long, to hold back all that suppressed energy.

He'd only just started to torture her—there was a lot more he could do in that vein. And he'd enjoy the doing. As long as she thought him asleep, she'd talk—eventually; he was sure of that. And the longer she resisted, the more he'd enjoy it. And so would she.

Tonight, he'd have his answer. Which was why the bed curtains were drawn.

And why he didn't hear her enter, why he didn't know she was there until the curtains parted. He'd left a gap at the foot of the bed, admitting a weak beam from the fire, just enough so he, with excellent night vision, could see her clearly.

She checked that he was there, lying relaxed beneath the covers, then she looked wonderingly at the curtains all but enclosing the bed.

Her lips lifted in a soft, distinctly witchy smile that had him stiffening. Lifting her hands to her shoulders, she slid her robe off and let it fall. Beneath it, she was naked, all ivory limbs and flaming red hair.

Richard fought the urge to reach for her; he couldn't stop his gaze from devouring her. She sensed it, and looked at him, and smiled.

And, lifting the covers, slid in beside him.

He turned and drew her into his arms before she could touch him. She sighed softly and sank against him, then lifted her face to his.

He kissed her gently, unhurriedly, content to savor the soft warmth of her body pressed freely against his, content to explore the soft warmth of her mouth, his to claim as he willed.

As was she. He held the thought back, channeled his aggression into anticipation, and kept every touch languid. He was supposed to be asleep, making love to her in his dreams.

So he held himself back and let her urgency build, let her grow hot, her skin fevered, her kisses increasingly demanding. He sank back on the pillows and let her take the lead—or at least, let her think she did. Half atop him, she kissed him wildly, and squirmed—heated, silk-encased flesh pressing caress after intimate caress upon him.

He gritted his teeth—and enjoyed every minute.

But he kept her hands high, lacing his fingers through hers to prevent her precipitating events—events he intended orchestrating to the full.

Wrapped in the warm dark, Catriona surrendered to the night, to her deepest desires, and gave herself to him. This was the last night they would share—she was determined to fill it with pleasure, on both the emotional and physical planes. The physical sensations were pure bliss, but for the emotional joy she found in their union, she would sell her very soul.

All but blind in the dense darkness, she could see him only as a deep shadow—closing her eyes, she could sense him more clearly. Dispensing with sight, she explored—by touch, by tactile impression as she lay on top of him. With her hands locked in his, she was acutely aware of the sensations felt through the soft skin of her breasts, midriff and belly. Drinking in the fascinating contrasts—of textures—hot, taut skin roughened by crisp hair—of the innate, readily discernible strength lying so lax, so amenable beneath her—she wriggled, slowly, sensuously. Filling her mind, her memories.

Between them, heat welled, swelled, and hot became hotter.

He seemed content to wallow in the heatwave; with a mental snort, she tugged her fingers from his, framed his face, and kissed him voraciously. Rapaciously.

She sank into the kiss, caught in a sudden flare like a sunspot; her limbs heated still more until she melted against him. Wanted to melt beneath him—have him fuse with her. Sliding her fingers into his hair, she let her lips, her tongue, taunt him, challenge him. Incite him.

Despite responding ardently, he remained supine beneath her. Inwardly cursing the effects of her potion, she avoided his hands and set hers to trace the ridges and hollows of his chest, the heavy bones of his shoulders, the tensed muscles of his upper arms.

His arms locked around her, heavy and warm across her waist—denying her quest to reach lower.

Not that she needed to touch him there—he was already fully aroused. The steely length of him rode against her hip, hot and urgent. That much of him, at least, was cooperating. The rest of him was not.

Shifting, she lay fully atop him, settling his erection between her thighs. She rolled her hips, experimenting until she found the particular shifting slide that most evocatively stroked him.

And felt the muscles in his arms shift, tensing, relaxing, then tensing again, as if he couldn't make up his mind.

Swallowing a curse, she trapped his lips with hers—and put her heart and soul into a slow, deliberate undulation, breasts, hips and thighs—even the curls at the base of her belly—coming into play. Deliberately evocative, she called to him.

And he answered. She felt the wave of response building in his body, felt the need she baited flare and swell. Felt hard become harder, felt tense muscles turn taut.

With a gasp—of relief, of anticipation—she dragged her lips from his and half wriggled, half slid to the side. Puppetlike, his body followed; as she turned on her back, she grasped his upper arm, tugging him over her.

The reins of his lust locked in a grip of iron, Richard followed her lead—let her shift, let her tug—let her believe he was dazedly following her directions as she urged him over her. He complied, moving heavily, unhurriedly.

While she panted, in heat.

Consumed by heat. At his touch, her thighs parted. He swung heavily over her, then let himself down between, then took his time settling himself—and her. Impatient, she arched, and he felt her heat scald him, touch and cling to that most exquisitely sensitive part of him.

He caught his breath—and felt, in his chest, something shift, something lock. With a soft, desperate gasp, she arched again—and he eased into her.

Slowly. Savoring every inch of her hot softness as she stretched to accommodate him, savoring the subtle easing of her body as she accepted him.

She sighed as he sank home, then her hands, tensed on his arms, relaxed. And skimmed down his sides.

He caught them—first one, then the other—letting his weight down on her as he trapped them. And gently but firmly removed the reins from her grasp. Beneath him, she shifted, sinking deeper into the soft mattress, angling her hips to cradle him more effectively.

Tentatively, she lifted her legs, sliding them over his flanks.

"Yes." He breathed the word against her lips as he settled fully upon her. He found her lips with his and took them, took her mouth, then pressed deeper into her.

He drank her instinctive gasp—a gasp of pure pleasure. Inwardly smiling, he drew back, then sank deep again, and felt her flaring response. He set himself to feed it.

To stoke her fires, to drive her frantic. More frantic than she'd ever been.

With each slow, controlled thrust, the flames within her rose higher; he held to a steady, rolling rhythm until she was burning. Until, hot and heated, awash with desire, she rose beneath him, meeting every thrust, her body caressing him, clinging to him, cleaving to him. Until she was aflame, urgent in her wanting, desperate in her need.

Frantic.

Trapped in the heat, Catriona flexed her fingers, trying to slip them from his grasp, frantic to hold him, desperate to draw him to her—to reach the bright pinnacle of physical bliss that hovered on her horizon. Sunk deep in the mattress, she squirmed and panted, trying to get that last inch closer, trying to get him that last fraction of an inch deeper. His fingers, clamped about hers, didn't give, but, to her surging relief, surging expectation, he raised his chest slightly, just enough so her nipples, excruciatingly tight, brushed his chest.

So they were brushed by his chest.

A scream welled in her throat; struggling to lift her heavy lids, she swallowed it as he lifted higher, breaking their kiss. He was a dense shadow looming over her, shoulders and chest surging in a slow, powerful rhythm, a rhythm she could feel in her marrow. In her womb.

With her hands still anchored, one on either side of her head, she gripped his flanks with her thighs, gasping, arching, as he thrust harder, deeper.

Then he drew back farther; lips parted, senses whirling, she waited, quivering, for the next impaling stroke. Only to feel him rock lightly, penetrating her with just the tip of the hard length she wanted buried inside her.

She opened her lips on a protest—instead, she gasped anew as, bending his head, he took one ruched nipple into his mouth. Hips rocking gently, teasingly, he feasted on her swollen breasts, until she was awash on an endless sea. A sea of pure pleasure.

After laving her hot flesh, his lips burned when they again brushed hers.

"Why are you here?"

She wasn't, at first, sure whether he had spoken, or she'd simply heard the words in her head. But his hips stopped rocking; he lay, hot and hard as a brand, just parting the swollen folds about her entrance.

Leaving her empty.

"Because I want you."

After an instant's pause, he started rocking again, once, twice—then he slid into her anew. She sighed, then lost what breath she had left as he pushed deep, then nudged deeper, and let his weight down on her once more.

Richard rode her, just a little deeper, just a little harder, just a fraction more intimately. He was having a hard time clinging to his reins—only rock-hard determination, and his Cynster strength of will—of endurance—allowed him to do it—to see her panting beneath him, her hair a burning veil spread across the pillows, her thighs gripping him urgently as he loved her. She responded without guile, without reticence, without hesitation—with a complete lack of reserve, the strongest feminine spell he'd ever encountered.

Her welcome, every time he sank into her, was bone deep. The temptation to lose himself in her arms, in her body, grew with every passing second.

But he needed to know her reasons, as well as her.

Gradually, he slowed, letting the rhythm stretch—not die, but slow to the point where her frantic need—a need he knew well how to manage—rose to the fore again.

When she whimpered, and squirmed, trying to urge him on, he brushed a kiss to her temple. "Why do you want me? Why me? Why now?"

A frown passed across her face like a breeze rippling corn, then she shook her head and it was gone. She lifted beneath him, wriggling more urgently; swallowing a curse, he impaled her fully again, then kissed her breathless.

And gave her a little more—rode her a little higher up the mountain of desire. Despite his weight, she undulated beneath him, hips rising, meeting him more fully. Letting go of her hands, he grabbed a pillow; releasing her from their kiss, he eased back, lifted her hips and stuffed the pillow beneath them.

Tilting her up so he could sink deeper—without stimulating her to completion. Her breath fractured when he thrust deep—an urgently evocative sound. He shut his ears to it. "Wrap your legs about me."

She did, immediately; arms braced, he held himself over her and drove her up, up, and on to the next level, the next plane of passion. Eagerly, she clung to him, her hands, now free, trailing over his chest and arms, then gripping tight as he delved deeper and pushed her on.

Fingers sinking into flexing sinews, Catriona let her head fall back, lips parted as she struggled to breathe. Senses aswirl, her wits long gone, she surrendered to the whirlpool of sensations he commanded, surrendered to the power she could feel in every thrust that joined them, in every synchronous beat of their hearts. A sense of beauty, of delight, of joy unimaginable hovered—just out of reach.

"Why are you here, with your legs spread wide, locked about my waist—with me buried to the hilt inside you?"

The question floated down to her, a whisper in the night. It was beyond her—eyes closed, she shook her head. And concentrated on the steely flex of his body as it melded with hers.

Powerfully, yet still slowly. In some dim corner of her mind, a hazy, rather acid thought formed: If this was his performance when asleep, what would he be like awake?

A soft moan surprised her—she bit her lip, determined to be quiet. Then gasped as he surged more powerfully, faster, deeper ...

She caught her breath on a strangled gasp—then cried out, in shocked disbelief, when he pulled back and left her. Fighting to raise her lids, she saw him lift fully away from her. Stunned she reached for him, half-sitting—

Large hands caught her and flipped her over, then locked about her hips and pulled her back onto her knees.

And they were everywhere, those large, hard hands—kneading, stroking, squeezing, probing. Until her breasts ached, until her skin glowed, until her nerves were taut and tingling. Until the heat within her was a raging furnace and pure molten need filled her veins. And her loins.

Kneeling behind her, reaching over and around her, a dark, rampantly aroused presence in the night, he bent his head and nipped her ear lobe, then soothed it with his lips. "Lean farther forward."

His hands clamped about her hips as she did, steadying her. Then he nudged her thighs wider, and caressed her—stroked her slick, swollen flesh until it was throbbing anew, until she sobbed his name.

He slid into her—smoothly, easily—filling her deeply, until she was so full of him she could sense him throughout her body. Eyes closed in rapturous delight, she pressed back and took him all.

Richard felt her clamp tight about him; features set, etched with passion, he couldn't smile, not even smugly. She needed him inside her now—if he was not there, she'd feel empty, hot and aching. This way, he could fill her without risking her willfullness getting the upper hand. She couldn't reach heaven this way, not without his active cooperation. Taking her from behind, with her on her knees, he could keep her locked for just a little longer in the web he'd woven—and try again to get the answer to his question.

But first ...

He was going to love her until she couldn't think, until she had no will left to deny him.

So he caressed her, inside and out, using his body, hands, and lips in concert, consciously bringing the full force of his expertise and experience to bear.

He intended to be ruthless.

He filled his hands with her swollen breasts and kneaded, and she whimpered with desire; he shut his ears to the sound, and dotted kisses along her exposed nape. Locating her nipples, he teased and tweaked, until she moaned and sobbed. Nuzzling aside the heavy fall of her hair, he pressed hot open-mouthed kisses along her shoulder, then down her spine.

And all the while he filled her, to a slow, steady rhythm guaranteed to leave her both satisfied and wanting—glorying in what was, and ready to sell her soul—tell the truth—in order to get more.

He was going to be ruthless.

He had already studied her curves—he knew them well. Now, with her on her knees before him, he took in other aspects of her beauty—her delicate bones, the sleek, supple strength of her, the very feminine curve of her spine. The sweet hollow between shoulder and throat, the long sweep of her neck.

Letting his gaze roam, he straightened, hands drifting back to close about her hips. The smooth planes of her back were exquisite, perfect ivory, unblemished, unmarred. Hands trailing farther, he traced the long muscles of her thighs, braced, lightly quivering, flexing slightly as he rode her. His gaze, however, had fixed—on the firm globes of her bottom, ivory hemispheres meeting his body with satisfying force every time he thrust into her, on his staff, rigid and engorged, gleaming with her slickness, sliding effortlessly into her, deep into the embrace of her waiting, willing sheath.

The sight held him entranced. She moaned softly, then rotated her hips, clinging to him, closing like a burning glove about him as he pressed deep.

Richard gasped; he closed his eyes and tightened his death grip on his impulses.

Opening his eyes again, he drew a ragged breath—and leaned forward. And reminded himself to be ruthless.

But the instant his hands curved about her shoulders, then trailed down to cup her breasts, he knew the best he could hope to be—with her—was ruthlessly gentle.

Not even she could worship her Lady with the same devotion with which he worshipped her—felt compelled to worship her. She was his temple, he her priest, serving her. Lavishing attention on her. Helplessly in thrall, drawn deeper with every heated thrust, every caress he pressed on her—and she pressed on him—he was a victim of emotion that bound him to her through this act and yet more deeply, reaching to his soul. Demanding his obedience, his acceptance, his surrender. It was as if some deeply buried part of him recognized her as his mate—and his salvation.

When next he straightened, his breathing was beyond ragged, his control badly frayed. He knew he had a question—it took a moment to recall what it was. With her on her knees before him, with his staff buried in her sweet heat, it was difficult to imagine anything else mattered.

But one thing did. Chest swelling, he set himself to take her up the last stretch of their road. Fingers tightening about her hips, he looked down—and noticed a birthmark, just by his thumb on her right buttock—a strawberry mark in the shape of a butterfly in flight. The size of his thumbnail, the mark showed clearly against her pale skin.

Richard dragged in a deep breath; fingers sinking into her hips, he anchored her, and thrust deep. Again, and again—pushing her high, then higher, swiftly taking her toward the shattering climax that he'd deliberately designed for her. On and on, higher and higher—she panted, then sobbed in her need.

He took her to the last but one step—

And withdrew from her, drawing her up against him, his hands full of her breasts, his throbbing erection riding between the globes of her bottom. He held her upright on her knees against him, and delicately kissed one ear.

The change was so swift, Catriona could barely take it in, barely heard, over the desperate thudding of her heart, his gravelly whisper.

"Why do you want me inside you?"

She couldn't see his face; she was so heated and urgent and needy she couldn't think—yet she heard the warrior's demand in his voice; she answered truthfully.

"Because I need you." The words came out on a sob—a sob of pure need. Raising one hand, she reached back and traced his lean cheek. *"Please, Richard. Now."*

His face was beside hers; she heard a soft hiss, then a smothered curse.

Then he reached around her, grabbing first one pillow, then another, piling them before her, even as his other hand pressed on her back and guided her down. Swiftly, he drew her knees back, and she was lying on her stomach, the piled pillows beneath her hips.

And he was behind her, between her spread thighs, his hips pressing against her bottom. Against skin flickering with heightened nerves, her inner thighs excruciatingly sensitive to the brush of his hair-dusted limbs.

With one thrust, he surged into her.

She screamed with sheer delight. Horrified, she grabbed handfuls of the twisted sheets and held them to her face. And heard him groan—braced above her, his hands planted on either side of her, he drew back, and surged deep—so deep—again.

In bliss—and knowing there was more to come—Catriona closed her eyes, buried her face in the bedclothes, and surrendered—her wits, her senses, her body—to the glory that beckoned. Surrendered to the desire to take him deep and love him, hold him tight and caress him.

He rode her hard, filling her completely, driving her on—straight over a precipice and into the sun.

She screamed as it shattered about her.

Eyes closed tight, braced above her, Richard drank in the lovely sound. Half muffled by the sheets, it was still pure magic; the sound of her ecstasy was pure ecstasy to him. Sunk to the hilt inside her, he held still, rigid, tense as a coiled spring, and savored her contractions, the rippling caress of her body as release swept through her.

He waited, not patiently, but with steely determination, until she eased beneath him, then, gritting his teeth, he leaned forward, grabbed two more pillows, lifted her, and raised her hips still higher.

So he could ride her on, up the next peak—the one she hadn't even guessed existed. When she realized it was there, she joined him—eagerly, wantonly—as focused as he. Heated once more, flushed, her skin dewed, she writhed beneath him, urging him on not with words but with deeds, with the flagrant encouragement of her lush body.

And when he sent her tumbling through the stars again, the effect was cataclysmic. He heard it in her unrestrained scream. The sound caught him up—tugged at his heart, his loins, his soul. Closing his eyes, he filled her completely and swiftly followed her beyond the end of the world.

Catriona awoke, disoriented, not entirely sure she *was* awake. Sweet peace held her; warmth surrounded her—she didn't want to move, to disturb the spell.

But presentiment nagged her—reluctantly, she lifted her lids. And looked into gloomy darkness. Blinking rapidly improved her vision marginally, enough to realize where she still was—where she shouldn't be.

In Richard's bed.

The warmth around her was him. The fact she could see at all warned her that deepest night had passed—morning was not far away.

Wielding a mental whip, she drew a shallow breath—all she could manage with his arm over her waist—and started the process of carefully untangling her limbs from his. This was the third morning she'd had to ease from his arms, but the task wasn't getting any easier with practice.

Eventually, she managed to slide from the bed. Quickly donning her robe, she fastened it, then swiftly straightened the sheet, settled the covers and silently plumped the pillow.

Pausing, she looked down at her companion of the night. He slept sprawled on his stomach, the arm and leg that had been thrown over her now relaxed on the bed. She studied his face, what she could see of it. The harsh planes had eased, but still retained their hardness, the promise of strength; his lashes lay, black crescents on his cheekbones, his lips still firm, purposeful. Even in repose, his face told her little—beyond the fact that here lay a warrior without a cause.

She had to leave him.

Drawing in a deep breath, she reached out to brush back the errant lock of hair that made a habit of falling over his forehead—and stopped herself. For one instant, her hand hovered over the neatened covers, then she sighed and, with a sad grimace, drew it back.

She couldn't risk waking him.

And she could sense the house stirring, tweenies waking in the attics, doors banging in the far distance.

Hugging her robe about her against the morning chill, she took one last, long look—at the husband she couldn't have—then slipped out through the bed curtains.

The instant the curtains closed, Richard opened his eyes. He listened—and heard the faintest of clicks as the door closed. For an instant, he simply stared at the closed curtains, at the empty space beside him, then he drew a huge breath and turned on his back. Crossing his arms behind his head, he stared at the canopy.

He still didn't have his answer—at least, not all of it. But he had learned something through the night. Whatever it was that drove his lust for her—she felt it, too. When they were together, her feelings for him were the counterpart of his feelings for her.

What his feelings for her were, however, was beyond his ability to describe. There was a sensual connection between them, something that invested their lovemaking with a deeper, stronger, more vibrant energy than the norm. He knew all about the norm—he'd had so many women, the difference was stark. Even in her innocence, she must be aware of it—that power that flared between them every time they touched, every time they kissed.

In his case, it was now with him constantly, ready to rear its head every time he set eyes on her. He was even, heaven help him, getting used to it. It had very quickly become a part of him.

Grimacing, he threw back the covers, sat up, and ran his hands over his face. He knew himself too well not to know, not to accept, that he wouldn't readily give it up—cut himself off from that power, from the addictive surge of possessiveness that swept him every time he saw her.

He still didn't know why she'd given herself to him. In the depths of the night, when they'd stirred and untangled their limbs, and she'd wordlessly slid into his arms, he hadn't had the heart to further interrogate her—he'd kissed her, soothed her into sleep, then tightened his arms about her and fallen into blissfully sated slumber himself.

Standing, he stretched, then grimaced. He'd have it out with her tonight. Once she was in his arms. Today, especially after last night, there were other things he needed to do.

The solicitor would return tomorrow.

He waited at the breakfast table until Jamie appeared. His host passed Algaria in the doorway. After waiting, and waiting, for Catriona to appear, Algaria had thrown him a black look that should have flayed him, then risen and gone to search out her erstwhile pupil.

Richard watched her go—Algaria clearly knew where her erstwhile pupil had been spending her nights—then turned to Jamie.

Who looked worried and drawn, obviously exercised by the difficulties of where the family would remove to, how they would cope after tomorrow. Jamie smiled wanly. "Not a particularly fine day, I fear."

Richard hadn't noticed. "Actually, I was wondering if you might appease my curiosity." Before Jamie could ask how, Richard waved languidly at Jamie's plate and picked up his coffee mug. "Once you've finished breakfast."

Malcolm and one of Jamie's nondescript brothers-in-law was present; Richard did not want his plans broadcast, especially not to the ears of his witch. He intended to inform her of his decision in person. Tonight. He was looking forward to it; he would allow no one to spoil his plans.

Jamie ate quickly; together they left the breakfast parlor and strolled into the hall. Jamie paused and looked inquiringly at him. Richard waved toward Jamie's office, and they strolled on, into the corridor.

"I was curious," Richard murmured, "about those letters you mentioned. The ones Seamus received about Catriona and her lands. I've been trying to fathom just why your father wanted me to marry Catriona—if I could see what he'd been handling in relation to her, it might clarify the matter."

Jamie's brows rose. He blinked at Richard, rather owlishly. "I see." He halted outside his office door; Richard halted, too. Jamie cleared his throat. "Are you ... ah ... *considering* ...?"

Richard grimaced lightly. "Considering, yes. But ..." He met Jamie's eyes. "If even that gets to Catriona's ears, life for all of us will be that much harder."

Jamie blinked and straightened. "Indeed." As Richard watched, Jamie's face lost some of its unnatural pallor, as hope, however faint, replaced despondency.

"Those letters?"

"Oh! Yes." Jamie shook himself. "I left them in the library."

The afternoon was dying beyond the library windows before he'd read them all. When Jamie had spoken of a pile of letters, Richard hadn't imagined a pile literally two feet high. And in no order to speak of. He'd spent hours sorting them, then even more hours deciphering the scripts and the demands.

For demands there'd been. Many of them.

Of Seamus's replies there was no record, but from the continuing correspondence, his attitude was clear. He'd done a stalwart job of defending Catriona and her vale.

Heaving a sigh, Richard set the last of the letters back on the stack, then pushed back his chair, opened the large bottom drawer of the desk and set the stack, in two halves, back where Jamie had stored it. Then he sat back in the chair and stared at the three piles he'd separated from the stack and lined up on the blotter.

Each little pile derived from one of Catriona's nearest neighbors. He had earlier taken a break and wandered down the hall to Jamie's office to check the maps. Her neighbors wanted her land. However, contrary to Jamie's recollections, all three still offered marriage—Sir Olwyn Glean to himself, Sir Thomas Jenner to his son, Matthew, while Dougal Douglas had not specified.

All three sets of correspondence were current—all three were at the stage of veiled threats on both sides. Seamus was less than subtle, Glean was patronizing, Jenner pompous, and Douglas the most disturbing, the most pointed.

Richard lit the desk lamp, and reread the letters, every one, then stacked them together. His expression set, his lips a thin line, he considered the pile, then folded it and slipped it into his coat pocket.

In the distance, the dinner gong boomed. Pushing back his chair, Richard rose and headed upstairs to change.

That night, Catriona tossed and turned. Wide awake, she stared at the canopy of her bed, then turned—and tossed—again.

She couldn't get to sleep.

Some devil inside her informed her why—and prodded her. Pointed out it was only a short distance to Richard's room. Richard's bed. Richard's arms.

And all the rest of him.

With a frustrated groan, Catriona shut her ears to the temptation. She had to—she couldn't give into it.

She'd known how it would be—that she would be tempted to go to him, that she would try to tell herself one more night wouldn't matter. But her only justification for going to him as she had was The Lady's orders—and they didn't include extra nights purely for her own indulgence. At this time of her cycle, three nights were enough. The way he'd loved her, that should be *more* than enough. She couldn't justify more.

But she'd known she'd be tempted, so while, in the full light of day, her resolution had held firm, and he'd been ensconced in the library, she'd gone to his room and replaced the drugged brandy with untainted stock. So she couldn't go to him, even if she weakened.

She'd weakened long before the clock struck twelve.

Now it was striking four, and she still hadn't fallen asleep. She hadn't settled in the least. First, she felt hot, then not hot enough. Her body was restless, her emotions disturbed. As for her thoughts ... she would much rather be asleep.

In the forefront of her mind hung the fact that, after tomorrow, when the solitcitor left, she would never see Richard again.

And he would never see his child.

She didn't know which thought made her feel worse.

CHAPTER

Nine

ॐ

Morning eventually dawned. Weary, wrung-out, Catriona dragged herself from her uncomfortable bed. She washed and dressed, then paused before the door—and plastered on a bright, breezy smile before opening it.

As had been her previous habit, she was early to the breakfast table. As the others appeared, she poured tea and helped herself to toast, all the while maintaining her glamor of morning cheer.

Richard saw her smile, her bright eyes, the instant he stalked in. Sweetly sunny, her expression stated she did not have a care in the world.

Little did she know.

Her gaze flew to his face—he saw her eyes widen. Richard suppressed an impulse to snarl. He met her gaze—pinned her for one brief instant—then turned and stalked to the sideboard.

And piled his plate high. He would rather have followed up the threat in that one glance, but there were others present. There was a need for civility— for the cloak of sophisticated behavior he habitually wore. He reminded himself of that—even while he itched to throw the cloak aside.

He was frustrated to the point of violence.

Never in his life had he had to cope with this degree of sexual frustration. Of frustrated intent. As for the emotional side of the coin—he couldn't even think of that. Not without a swirling haze of anger clouding his mind.

His response was not rational—the realization didn't help in the least. When it came to Catriona Hennessey, witch, his thoughts—his feelings— definitely didn't qualify as rational. They were powerful. Strong. And very close to slipping their leash.

Plunking his plate down at the place opposite hers, Richard sat. He met her wide gaze with a hard stare and saw her cheery smile waver. Belatedly remembering what the morning held, he gritted his teeth and looked down at his plate. And kept his gaze lowered as he ate.

She'd fled from him before—he didn't want to look out of the library window and see her carriage rolling down the drive. His plans were otherwise.

"Miss? They be a-waiting ye in the lib'ry."

Catriona whirled, straightening, her attention flying from the child she'd been tucking in. "Already?"

Head poked around the nursery door, the maid nodded, wide-eyed. "Did hear as the s'licitor came early."

Catriona inwardly cursed. "Very well." Turning to the children's nurse, she gave brisk instructions, patted heads all around, then hurried down the long, cold corridors.

She stopped in the front hall to check her reflection in the mirror—what she saw did not reassure her. Her hair was neat, but not as lustrous as usual; the curls at her nape hung limp. As for her eyes, they were overlarge and faded. Washed-out—just like she felt. Her morning gown of rich brown, normally a good color for her, did nothing to disguise her pallor. She was tired; she still felt drained. Not, in all honesty, up to handling the inevitable grief when the final blow *finally* fell and Seamus's maltreated family learned they would have to quit the house. She'd intended to leave this afternoon, but had already revised her plans—she would be needed here for another day at least, to calm Meg and the children most of all.

With a sigh, she braced herself and headed for the library.

The butler opened the door for her; she glided through—and was instantly aware of a presence in the air. An unexpected presence. The hair on her nape lifted; she paused just inside the long room and took stock.

The family—*all of them!*—she inwardly sighed—were gathered before the fireplace as before. Seated at the desk, the solicitor shuffled papers; he glanced at her fleetingly, then looked away.

To where Richard stood, looking out one long window, his back to the room.

Together with the solicitor, Catriona studied that back, elegantly clad in deep blue. Her earlier uneasiness returned—that edgy, nervous feeling that had overtaken her in the breakfast parlor when he'd looked at her so accusingly. As if he had a very large bone to pick with her.

She didn't know—couldn't guess—what it was.

Neither his back, straight and tall, nor his hands, clasped behind him, offered any clues.

And now, on top of that uneasiness, came this other presentiment. A swirling, building sense of impending ... something. Something momentous. The energy was strong, all-pervasive in the room; she couldn't discern its focus. On guard, she glided forward and took the empty seat beside Mary.

In that instant, Richard turned—and looked at her.

She met his gaze—and instantly understood who was the source of that energy. And who its focus. Suddenly breathless, she glanced at the door, then back at him.

Prowling forward to stand by the mantelpiece, he gazed at her steadily, his message transparent. He was now ten feet away, the door was thirty. No escape.

His intention, however, remained unclear.

Catriona dragged in a breath past the now familiar vise locked about her lungs and let haughtiness infuse her expression. Tilting her chin, she returned his regard, then pointedly switched her gaze to the solicitor. And willed him to get on with his business. To get this over and done with, so Richard Cynster could leave, and she could breathe again.

The solicitor coughed, sent a shaggy browed look around the room, then peered at the papers in his hand. "As you are all aware . . ."

His preamble outlined the situation as they knew it; everyone shifted and shuffled and waited for him to get to the point. Eventually, he cleared his throat and looked directly at Richard. "My purpose here today is to ask you, Richard Melville Cynster, if you accept and agree to fulfill the terms of our client Seamus McEnery's will."

"I do so accept and agree."

The words, so unexpected, were uttered so calmly Catriona did not—could not—take them in. Her mind refused to believe her ears.

Apparently similarly afflicted, the solicitor blinked. He peered at his papers, adjusted his spectacles, drew breath, and looked again at Richard. "You declare that you will marry the late Mr. McEnery's ward?"

Richard met his gaze levelly, then looked at Catriona. Trapping her gaze, he spoke evenly, deliberately. "Yes. I will wed Catriona Mary Hennessey, ward of the late Seamus McEnery."

"Good-*oh!*"

Malcolm's gleeful shout led the cacophany; the room erupted with exclamations, heartfelt thanks, outpourings of profound relief.

Catriona barely heard them—her gaze locked with Richard's, she let the tide wash over her and sensed a none-too-subtle shift in the energy around her. Some trap was closing on her—and she couldn't even see what it was.

Despite Jamie thumping him on the back and pumping his hand, despite the questions of the solicitor, Richard's blue gaze didn't waver. Trapped in that steady beam, Catriona slowly rose, much less steadily, to her feet. Putting out one hand, she gripped the chairback and straightened to her full height, so much less than his; unable to help herself, she tilted her chin defiantly.

Gradually, the clamor about them died, as the family belatedly sensed the clash of wills occurring beneath their noses.

Catriona waited until silence reigned, then, in a cool, clear voice, stated: "*I,* however, will not marry you."

A shadow passed through his eyes; the planes of his face set. He shifted— the others stepped quickly from between them. He strolled toward her, his stride his customary prowl. While subtly intimidating, there was no overt threat in his approach. He stopped directly before her, looking down at her, still holding her gaze, then he glanced over his shoulder at the others. "If you'll excuse us?"

He waited for no yea or nay, not from them or her; he grasped her hand— before she could blink he was striding down the long room, towing her with him.

Catriona stifled a vitriolic curse; she had to pace quickly to keep up. But she reined in her temper—there was a definite advantage in putting distance between themselves and the rest of the company.

He didn't stop until they reached the other end of the room, hard up against the wall of bookshelves and flanked by two heavy armchairs and a small table. The instant he released her, she swung to face him. "I will *not* marry you. I've told you why."

"Indeed."

The word was a lethal purr. She blinked and found herself pinned by a stare so hard she literally felt stunned.

"But that was *before* you came to my bed."

Her world tilted. She could hear her heart thudding in her throat. She blinked again, slowly. And opened her lips on a denial—the look in his eyes, burning blue, changed her mind. She lifted her chin. "You'll never get anyone to believe that."

His brows rose. "Oh?"

To her surprise, he glanced around—Meg's sketchbook and pencil lay on the small table. He picked both up; before her puzzled eyes, he opened the book to a blank page and sketched rapidly, then handed the book to her.

"And just how do you plan explaining how I know about this?"

She stared. He'd sketched her birthmark. Her world had already tipped; now it reeled.

He shifted, leaning closer, simultaneously protective and threatening. "I'm sure you can recall the circumstances in which I saw it. You were in my bed, on your knees, totally naked, before me—and I was buried to the hilt in you."

The words, uttered low, forcefully and succinctly, from less than a foot away, battered at her defenses. Catriona felt them weaken, then crack—and felt the emotion, the sensations, all she'd felt at that moment when she'd been in his bed, seep through. And touch her.

It took all her will to shut them out and seal up the break in her shields. She stared, unseeing, at the drawing until she'd regained some degree of calm, then, very slowly, lifted her gaze to his face. "You were awake."

"I was." His face was a mask of hard angles and planes—determination incarnate.

Catriona mentally girded her loins. "Completely awake?"

"*Wide* awake. I didn't touch the whiskey the second night. Or the third."

She studied his face, his eyes, then grimaced, and looked down.

He waited. When she said nothing more, he straightened, and took the sketch book from her hands. "So"—he nodded toward the others—"shall we go and tell them the news?"

She lifted her head. "I haven't changed my mind."

He looked down at her—then stepped closer, towering over her. "Well, *change it.*"

He took another step; eyes locked on his, Catriona backed. She glanced up the room and saw the others watching. Immediately, she stiffened her spine;

switching her gaze back to her tormentor, she halted, raised her hands and pushed against his chest. "Stop that! You're deliberately trying to frighten me."

"I'm *not* trying to frighten you," he growled through clenched teeth. "I'm trying to *intimidate* you—there's a difference."

Catriona glowered. "You don't need to intimidate me—just stop and *think!* You don't want to marry me—you don't want to marry at all. I'm just a woman—just like all the others." She gestured, as if encompassing hordes. "If you just leave, you'll discover I'm like all of the rest of them—you'll forget me within a week."

"Much you know about it."

His tone was contemptuous; his eyes bored into hers. He slapped one hand on the bookshelf by her shoulder, half caging her. Catriona felt the shelves at her back; she stiffened her spine and tilted her chin higher. And kept her eyes locked on his.

Lips compressed, he looked down at her. "Just so you know ... I generally insist that the ladies I consort with have the good sense not to get under my skin. Some try, I admit, but none succeed. They all stay precisely where I want them—at a safe distance. They don't get into my dreams, interfere with my aspirations, challenge my hopes—or my fears." His eyes narrowed. "*You,* however, are different. *You* succeeded in getting under my skin without even trying—before I even knew how witchy you were going to be. Now you're there, you're there to stay." His gaze hardened. "I suggest you accustom yourself to your new position."

Catriona held his gaze. "It sounds as if you'd rather I *wasn't* there—under your skin, as you put it."

He hesitated; a long moment passed before he said, "I'll admit that I'm not certain I approve of our particular closeness—and I definitely don't approve of your initiative. However, the plain truth is, having had you beneath me, I'm not about to let you go." He held her gaze steadily. "It's as simple as that."

Catriona read the truth in his eyes—she frowned and shook her head. "It *can't* be."

"It can." Blue eyes held hers. "Fate's offered you to me on a silver platter—I'm not about to pass."

A fraught moment ensued. Catriona could feel the sensuality that lay between them, a living, vital thing. It radiated heat, almost seemed to have a will of its own—a dangerously compulsive thing. Her eyes locked with his, she drew in a slow, much-needed breath—and tried another tack. "You agreed because you're in a temper."

That, too, she could sense—suppressed rage locked behind his mask. Her own temper flared; she glared at him. "How typically male—you've agreed to marry me, and created goodness knows what legal muddle, all because you're in a foul mood with me over something I've done." She frowned. "I can't imagine what, but it's hardly sufficient reason for creating this much fuss."

He stiffened. "I'm not angry—I'm frustrated. A result, *not* of something you *have* done, but of something you've *neglected* to do."

The words, bitten off, issuing through clenched teeth, held enough force—enough intimidation—to make her step back. The look in his eyes had her pressed against the bookshelves. But she refused to cower—she stared belligerently back at him. "What?"

"You neglected to come to my bed."

The smile he bent upon her reminded her forcibly of Red Riding Hood's wolf. She studied him in growing bewilderment. "You agreed to marry me just because I didn't succumb to your all but legendary charms? Because I wasn't so mindless that I couldn't resist—"

"*No!*" Richard used the tone he'd most recently used to troops at Waterloo. Thankfully, it worked—it cut her off in mid-tirade; he could see where the tirade was headed. His eyes locked warningly on hers, his lips compressed, jaw set, he gripped the bookshelf tightly—and waited. Until he could say, in more reasonable tones: "I meant *I* was sexually frustrated because *I* wanted *you*. *I'm* the one who can't resist. And no, I don't like it that you can."

She blinked at him, studying his eyes, his face. "Oh."

Richard held her wide, slightly wary gaze—and hung on to his temper, to the illusion of civility that was all that stood between her and an effective demonstration of the strongest argument impelling him to marriage. If he gave into the urge to demonstrate, he'd shock Jamie and company to their toes. "I do hope," he said, and despite the polite form, his tone was savage, "that we're now clear on that point. I want to marry you because I want you as my wife."

Catriona nodded; she didn't need any further explanation of that. His feelings—his need—was reaching her in waves. And helping her cause not at all. Clasping her hands before her, she drew a deep breath—and tried desperately to find a chink, some gap, in the wall he was building around her. "But why have you *decided* to marry me? You wanted me from the first, but you decided on marriage only recently."

"Because—" Richard stopped and considered her—then shrugged aside caution and continued: "Because you're a damned witch who walks alone. Rides alone. A sweet, helpless witch who has a touching but thoroughly misplaced confidence in the protective capacity of mystical powers." His face hardened. "But you live in a world of men—and with Seamus's death, your protection from them has gone. Evaporated—and, most telling, you don't even realize it. You haven't even recognized the danger."

She frowned. "What danger?"

"The danger posed by your neighbors." Briefly, succinctly, he elaborated—drew the folded letters from his pocket and showed her the demands, and the threats, Seamus had received. "Look at the last one from Dougal Douglas." He waited while she found it. "You need to read between the lines, but his message is clear enough."

Catriona read the single sheet, crossed and recrossed, then drew in a tight breath. "He'll bring me to the attention of the authorities—church and state—if I don't marry him?"

She looked up, something close to fear in her eyes.

Richard frowned and reclaimed the letters. "Don't worry. There's a simple way to spike his guns."

"There is?"

"Marry me."

"How will that help?"

"If you marry me, your lands legally become mine, so there's no point pursuing you."

Catriona glanced at the letters in his hand. "What if he does anyway—out of spite?"

"If he does, I can guarantee nothing will come of it."

She looked at his face. "Because you're a Cynster?"

"Precisely." Richard hestitated, then added: "Seamus knew he needed a certain type of man for you—one of the right sort, with the right degree of power." He considered, then grimaced. "A Cynster fitted the bill to perfection, and he had one—me—on a chain. To wit, my mother's necklace. Above all he knew that if you give land to a Cynster, he'll never let it go—*'To Have and to Hold'* still rules us. Which meant you'd be safe—if it were mine, I could never bring myself to sell the vale."

He looked into Catriona's eyes and stated what now seemed obvious. "Through all this farce of his will, Seamus had only one true aim: to ensure your continued safety."

"Hmm." She frowned, then grimaced and looked away.

When she said no more, Richard ruthlessly pressed his point. "By making it widely known he was your guardian, Seamus drew all the approaches to him, leaving you undisturbed. But Jamie is no Seamus—he won't be able to deflect those three from their goal. While Seamus was alive, you were shielded—now he's gone, it'll be open season—on you, and your vale."

She glanced at the letters. "I didn't realize. I didn't know."

"You do know." She looked up; Richard tucked the letters back in his pocket and trapped her gaze. "You said it the night before last. *You need me.* You may choose not to acknowledge it consciously, but you do know it. You may not accept it, but that doesn't alter the reality."

Her eyes flared, spitting gold sparks. "*You* are not my keeper!"

He looked down at her; he couldn't help his growl. "Where you're concerned, if the cap fits, I'll wear it."

She glared at him—he gave not an inch. Slowly, her glare faded—she frowned as she studied his eyes.

He studied hers. "Why did you come to my bed?"

Her eyes locked with his, Catriona drew a deep breath. He'd been totally honest—totally open—with her. "Because The Lady willed it."

For one long instant, he stared into her eyes, then his brow rose. "Your Lady told you to come to my bed?"

"Yes." Briefly, she explained.

Richard heard her out in silence. In genuine surprise. He'd expected the answer to be loneliness—something he understood, something he'd instinctively recognized in her. Divine intervention was a little harder to assimilate. As was the possessive lust that roared through him at the thought of her heavy with his child.

He was not at all sure how he felt about her reason, but the opportunity was too good not to seize.

"In that case"—he straightened away from the bookcase—"there's obviously no impediment to our marriage on your side."

She frowned at him. "Why do you imagine that?"

Brows high, he met her gaze. "Children. The Lady told you I was to father your children." She stared at him blankly; he elaborated: "Children. Plural. More than one."

She blinked, then her features blanked completely.

"It's a little hard to imagine how you could have a brood of children by me, without the benefit of marriage."

"Twins." She refocused abruptly on his face. "There's twins in your family—Amanda and Amelia."

Richard shook his head. "Their father's a twin, and their mother has twin brothers. Not at all the same as us."

"But . . ." Catriona stared at him. "The Lady made no mention of marriage."

"The gods don't have such ceremonies—marriage is an institution created by man."

"But . . ." She'd run out of buts.

He sensed it; he studied her, then said, his voice lower, less forceful—more beguiling: "I meant what I said before—that, if we marry, I won't interfere with your role." He searched her eyes, then his gaze steadied. "I swear always to support you in your position, to defer to you as lady of the vale."

He meant it; it was there in his eyes—a promise of fealty only a warrior could make—and then only to his queen. Catriona felt her will swaying, bending . . . she was losing the battle to remain beyond his reach. And losing it on far too many fronts. More than one part of her mind was urging her to rethink—to accept all he offered.

As perhaps The Lady had intended her to.

Her head, mind and senses were whirling. With an effort, she regrouped—looked down and forced herself to strip aside all the complications of his motives and hers. And get to the heart of the matter.

After a quiet moment, she raised her head and looked him in the eye. "You're not going to let me go, are you?"

He looked straight at her—through blue, blue eyes. "No." She considered him. His face hardened. His gaze locked with hers, he softly added: "And you might like to ponder the fact that if you refuse me and bear my child, I'll have an unassailable legal right to that child."

Catriona heard the depth of his commitment, not to her but to their unborn child. "You'd take our child from me?"

His gaze didn't waver; she'd read his answer in his eyes before he stated: "I'd claim any child of mine from the arms of The Lady herself, if she sought to keep it from me."

Dragging in an unsteady breath, Catriona straightened—and felt the trap close firmly, tenderly, but tight. The warrior had secured his cause.

"It won't be as bad as I feared." Catriona dragged her brush through her hair and glanced at Algaria in the mirror. Her erstwhile mentor was agitated to the point of panic. "He's promised to support my position, my role, not undermine it. He didn't have to do that."

"Humph! That's what he says now—just wait until he gets you back to the vale. Once you're big with his child, he'll take over!" Pacing, Algaria swung about. "Do you realize he'll have the power to sell the vale?"

"He won't." In stating it, she was sure of it. "He's landless—a bastard—*and* a Cynster. He's more likely than any other to *keep* the vale—keep it for his children." Protect it for his children. Inwardly smiling, Catriona wielded her brush vigorously.

Algaria had not been present in the library; expecting to leave within a day, she'd been shocked to learn of the impending wedding. And convinced that Richard must have, using some unspecified and utterly inconceivable power, forced Catriona into accepting.

The only power he'd used was simply who he was—who he really was behind his mask; Catriona had tried to explain that, but Algaria wasn't ready to listen.

"I can't believe you've simply acquiesced!" Halting, Algaria stared at her.

"Believe me, there was nothing simple about it. Our discussions ranged over a gamut of issues."

"Did you discuss his character? The fact he'll want to rule—that he'll *need* to rule just as much as he'll need to breathe?"

Sighing, Catriona laid down her brush. "I didn't say it would be easy."

"*Easy?* It's going to be impossible!"

"Algaria." Turning on the stool, Catriona faced her mentor, her second-in-command. "I didn't make the decision lightly. When it came to the point, there were too many convincing reasons why this marriage should be—and few, if any, reasons against." Algaria opened her mouth; Catriona silenced her with an upraised hand. "No—I know about his strength—and so does he. He's vowed to contain it, to use it to support me, not wield it against me." She met Algaria's black gaze steadily. "I intend giving him a chance to fulfill that vow. That's a right he's claimed—and one I cannot justifiably deny him. Until such time as he fails—until he breaks that vow—I do not wish to hear any more on the subject."

She waited, but Algaria, pinch-lipped, said nothing—she started to pace again. "You could have suggested hand-fasting—at least until he shows his true colors."

"I doubt he'd accept it, and you know that's never been our way."

"Marrying men like him has never been our way, either!"

Catriona sighed and let Algaria's agitation slide past her. She didn't share it, but could understand Algaria's state. In common with all disciples of The Lady, Algaria possessed a deep-seated distrust of dominant men—for good and obvious reasons. It was a distrust she had shared, until she'd met Richard Cynster and felt the attraction a strong man could pose, and seen behind his mask to his vulnerabilty. Algaria possessed the talent to see behind his mask, too, but it was pointless to suggest that now. Her erstwhile mentor was too repelled by the vision of strength and dominance to stop and look beyond it.

Considering Algaria, she sighed again. "Times change, and we must change, too. I'm too wise in life's ways to try to resist its flow—the currents carrying me to his arms are considerable. Many more than one, and powerful—The Lady's will and more." Algaria slowed; Catriona caught her eye. "I won't fight fate—I won't fight life. That's not why The Lady put me here."

She held Algaria's black gaze for a moment, then calmly turned back to the mirror and picked up her brush. "I've agreed to marry Richard Cynster before witnesses—we'll be wed as soon as may be." She stroked the brush through her heavy hair; the rhythmic tug on her scalp was soothing. "And then," she murmured, eyes closing, "then, we'll return to the vale."

Tight-lipped, Algaria left her; in a state of unusual mental weariness, Catriona climbed into her bed. The thought of visiting Richard occurred only to be dismissed—she would be his soon enough, and he knew it. Triumphant, he'd been magnanimous in victory—in the drawing room, he'd frowned at her over the teacups and told her to get to bed and get some sleep.

Halfway there, Catriona felt her lips lift. Luckily, no one had been near enough to hear—all the rest of the family had been distracted, struggling to assimilate their "new" state. It was, in fact, their old state—that, perhaps, was one of the positives of the case—that being given their inheritance back, they now viewed it as truly theirs.

Now, hopefully, Mary would get new curtains.

The thought made her smile; she drifted deeper into sleep. More peacefully, more serenely, more reassured than she'd expected.

Things, somehow, would turn out right—so The Lady whispered.

CHAPTER

Ten

೫෮ඁ෮ඁ

They were married by special license, granted by the Bishop of Perth. Three days later, in the kirk in the village, Catriona stood beside Richard Cynster and listened as he vowed to love, honor and protect her. If he did all three, she would be safe; she made her responding vows—to love, honor and obey him—with an open heart.

And felt The Lady's blessing in the shaft of sunshine that broke through the heavy clouds and beamed through the small rose window set high above the altar to bathe them in Her glow.

Richard gathered her in his arms and kissed her—lingeringly. Only when he lifted his head and they turned to walk up the short nave did the sunbeam fade.

By the time they signed the register, then strolled out to the small porch, winter had reclaimed the ascendancy. Clouds laden with snow, grey and churning, stretched from horizon to horizon. A carpet of snow already covered the ground; light flurries whirled on the bitter breeze.

The family followed them to the door, excited and garrulous. Because of Seamus's death, the small private ceremony in the old kirk—all that either she or Richard had wanted—had been agreed to by all. Both the weather and Seamus's death had mitigated against any further revelry. The snows had started in earnest; the passes were slowly filling. Richard and she had been in perfect accord that they should leave immediately after the ceremony, to ensure they weren't snowed in for weeks.

Pausing in the porch, Catriona saw the steamy breaths of their carriage horses rising beyond the lych-gate. She looked up at Richard; he was looking across the graveyard. She followed his gaze—and guessed his thoughts.

"Go!" Lightly, she pushed him. He looked down at her, his mask in place; she ignored it. "Go and say good-bye." She looked inward and afar, then refocused on him. "I don't think either of us will be here again."

He hesitated for an instant more, then nodded and stepped off the porch.

She watched him head for a simple grave by the wall, then swung around and gave her attention to Jamie, Meg and the rest.

Halting before his mother's grave, Richard wondered what she would have thought of him marrying Catriona Hennessy. His mother had been from the Lowlands, too; perhaps she would approve. He gazed at the headstone, studied it carefully, letting the vision sink into his mind.

And recalled his thought, when he'd stood here in the moonlight just before he'd first met his witchy wife.

His wife. The words, even unuttered, sent a streak of unnerving sensation through him, powerful enough to shift the very bedrock of his foundations. Sensation and recollection mingled; eyes narrowing, he gazed at his mother's grave and silently made another vow.

To live life fully.

Straightening, he drew a deep breath and turned. And discovered Catriona waiting a yard behind him. She met his eyes, then looked at the grave. Richard gestured her forward; she came to his side.

For a moment, side by side, they looked at the headstone; inwardly, Richard said good-bye. Then he took Catriona's gloved hand. "Come. It's freezing."

He drew her away. It was she who, halfway down the path, glanced back, then looked at his face, before shifting her gaze forward to where their party waited in the protection of the lych-gate.

They had two carriages—his and hers. Their leave-taking was foreshortened by the increasing snow; within minutes, Richard handed Catriona into his carriage, then followed her in. Jamie shut the door and stepped back. Through the glass, Richard met Jamie's eyes, and, smiling, raised his hand in brief salute. Jamie grinned and saluted back.

"Good-bye!"

"Good luck!"

The carriage lurched; the wedding party, waving madly, fell behind. Sitting back, wrapped in his greatcoat, Richard stretched his legs out and settled his shoulders against the leather seat. Beside him, Catriona flicked out her skirts, then drew her cloak about her. Boots propped on a hot brick wrapped in flannel, she settled her head against the squabs and closed her eyes.

Silence, tinged with expectation, filled the carriage as it rumbled out of the Highlands.

Richard saw no reason to break it—as each mile of white landscape was replaced with the next, his mind was busy listing the various letters he needed to write. The first—a short note to Devil—had already been dispatched, along with Worboys, sent ahead to ensure the comfort of their first night. Informing Devil of his change of status had been easy; informing Helena, Dowager Duchess of St. Ives, would be much less so. Aside from anything else, he would need to break his news in such a way that his stepmother did not immediately appear on the manor's doorstep, seeking to welcome Catriona into the Cynster family in the time-honored way. Oh, no—he wanted time— wanted them to have time—to find their own equilibrium.

To learn how to get on—for him to learn how to manage a witchy wife.

That definitely came first. Helena would have to wait.

"I hope we get to The Boar before nightfall."

Catriona was peering into the whirling white outside.

Richard studied her profile; his lips quirked. Straightening them, he looked ahead. "We'll be staying at The Angel."

"Oh?" Catriona turned. "But . . ." Her words died away.

Turning his head, Richard met her eyes, clear question in his.

"Well"—she gestured—"it's simply that The Angel is a very *superior* house."

"I know. That's why I sent Worboys to secure rooms for us there."

"You did?" She stared at him, then grimaced.

Richard kept his expression mild. "Don't you like The Angel?"

"It's not that. It's just that *superior* also means expensive."

"A fact you need not concern yourself over."

She humphed. "That's all very well, but—"

Richard knew the instant the penny dropped, saw her eyes widen as she finally noticed the luxurious appointments of his carriage—the fine, supple leather, the gleaming brass—finally remembered the lines and deep chests of the four greys between the shafts. Finally considered what she should have long before.

Her eyes, wide and startled, swung to his, her gaze arrested. She opened her lips on hasty words and nearly choked. Clearing her throat, she sat back against the seat and gestured airily. "Are you . . .?"

"Very." Enjoying himself, Richard leaned his head back and closed his eyes. And felt the increasing intensity of her gaze. "How much is very?"

He considered, then said: "Enough to keep me, and you . . . and your vale if need be."

She searched his face, then humphed and sank back. "I didn't realize."

"I know."

"Are the Cynsters *exceedingly* wealthy?"

"Yes." After a moment, he continued, his eyes still closed: "Within the family, my bastardry counts for nothing—my father made provision for me as his second son, which, to all intents and purposes, I am."

She was silent for so long, he wondered what she was thinking.

"Jamie mentioned that you're accepted socially."

The murmured statement held no element of question; opening his eyes, Richard turned his head and looked at her—she was staring out at the snow.

"I expect that means you could have had your choice of all the young ladies from the very best families."

Compelled by the ensuing silence, he replied: "Yes."

"So . . ." She sighed, and turned to meet his eyes. "What will your family think when they learn you've married a Scottish witch?"

He would have quipped that they'd either think he'd lost his senses, or that it served him right, but the shadows in her eyes held him. Compelled him to reach out, slowly, and slide one arm about her. And lift her, with an ease that sent a very definite shiver through her, onto his lap.

"The only thing they'll care about," he murmured, juggling her, "is that I've chosen you."

He would have kissed her, but she stayed him, small hands braced against his chest. "But you haven't." Gratifyingly breathless, she searched his eyes, then blushed lightly. "Chosen me, I mean."

He'd chosen her in the instant he'd first closed his arms about her, in the moonlight near his mother's grave, but he wasn't bewitched enough to admit it; his witch had enough powers as it was. Ignoring her hands, he bent his head and brushed his lips across hers. "You're mine." Breaths mingling, driven, their gazes locked—then, simultaneously, dropped to each other's lips. Searching, hungry, their lips touched again—achingly gentle—then parted. "That's all that matters."

Her lashes fluttered up; for one instant, green eyes met blue, and the air about them shimmered.

She sucked in a quick, shallow breath; in the same instant, he tightened his arms about her, then lowered his head and kissed her.

And she kissed him. With a devastating sweetness, an innocence—as if this were the first time. Which, in some ways, for her, it was. The first time she'd knowingly welcomed him as her lover—a lover fully conscious, wide awake. Richard realized and inwardly groaned, and harnessed his raging desires, savagely hungry after four days' starvation.

He deepened the kiss by gradual degrees, letting them both sink into the caress, into the warmth and heat, into that pleasurable sea. Letting their embers slowly glow stronger, then flicker into flame; with an expert's touch, he fanned the flames until they burned steadily.

She followed his lead readily, openly, without guile. As was her wont, she freely gave all he asked, accepting each intimacy as he offered it, surrendering her mouth to his conquest. He savored her thoroughly, then teased her into making her own demands, into meeting him and matching him, into returning the slow, languid thrusting of his tongue with clinging caresses equally evocative.

But their nerves remained curiously taut, their play curiously charged, as if their first encounter as a married couple was somehow different. Richard sensed it in her, in the tension that invested her slight frame, in the tightness of her breathing—sensed it in himself—an alertness, an awareness, heightened to exquisite sensitivity.

As if their nerves, their bodies, their very beings, thrummed to some magic in the air.

Gently, he lifted her, rearranging her on his lap so that she sat across his legs facing him, one knee on either side of his hips. Locked in their kiss, she barely seemed to notice; pushing her hands up, over his shoulders, she slid her fingers into his hair and angled her lips beneath his.

She moaned when he closed his hands about her breasts. He kneaded and, through the thick fabric of her pelisse, felt the mounds firm and fill his hands. Even with the benefit of a number of hot bricks, even with the heat rising between them, it was too cold to contemplate baring her. Instead, he glided his hands over her in long, sweeping caresses—caresses designed to stir her to life. To love.

When she wriggled impatiently on his thighs, Richard reached between them, found the hem of her skirt, and slid his hand beneath.

He found her—startlingly hot in the cold air in the carriage. She would have pulled back from their kiss but he refused to let her; he kept her lips trapped, filled her mouth with slow, languid thrusts as he stroked her, parted her, penetrated her.

She melted about his fingers; he probed deeper, then stroked gently. She was hot and very ready.

He had to draw back from their kiss to deal with his own clothing. Her questing fingers had already pushed his greatcoat aside and undone both coat and waistcoat. Fingers splayed across the fine linen of his shirt, breasts rising and falling dramatically, her lips swollen and parted, eyes jewel green under heavy lids, she stared dazedly down as he flicked his trouser buttons undone.

They slipped free—abruptly, she lifted her head and stared at him. "What ...?"

The half-squeaked question was eloquent; Richard raised a suggestive brow.

"Here?"

He raised his brow higher. "Where else?"

"But ..." Aghast, she stared at him. Then she looked up at the carriage roof. "Your coachman ..."

"Is paid enough to feign deafness." Ready, Richard reached for her.

She looked back at him and licked her lips, glanced at the seat beside them, then shook her head in disbelief. "How ...?"

He showed her, drawing her fully to him, then easing into her softness. As she fathomed his intention and felt him enter her, she spread her thighs, slid her knees along the cushions, and, with a soft sigh, sank down, impaling herself fully upon him.

As she closed, scalding hot, around him, Richard, watching her face and seeing the expression of sheer relief that washed over her fine features, got the distinct impression that she was as thankful to have him inside her again as he was to be there.

Wrapping his arms about her, one beneath her hips, he took her lips in a searing kiss, then lifted her. Rocked her.

She caught the rhythm quickly. Rising on her knees, she tried to increase the tempo.

"No." Anchoring her hips, he drew her fully down, held her there for a moment, then picked up the rhythm again. "Keep in time with the horses."

She blinked at him, but did; gradually, the steady, rolling rocking became so instinctive they no longer needed to think of it—but could think, instead, solely of the indescribable pleasure of their bodies merging intimately, again and again, in a journey of infinite delight.

Held firmly, closely, Catriona shuddered—with pure pleasure, with sharp excitement. With an unfurling sense of the illicit—of the wild, the unconventional—in her soul and his. Eyes closed, held close in his embrace, their fully dressed state contradicted, contrasted—focused her senses on—the area of their naked engagement. Along the bare inner face of her thighs, all she could feel was the fabric of his trousers, the smooth leather of the seat. Over her flanks and legs, over the curves of her bottom, all she could feel was the shift and glide of her lawn chemise and petticoats.

Only at the core of her, in the soft, swollen, heated flesh between her widespread thighs—only there could she feel him, only there did they touch with no barriers between.

Only there did they merge, sweetly slick, powerfully smooth.

With heightened senses, she reveled in the power inherent in their joining, in the deeply compulsive repetition, in the burgeoning energy rising within them.

Senses wide open, awareness complete, she was deeply conscious that outside the carriage, the world, ice cold and blanketed in white, went on, committed to its own steady rhythm, the unquenchable rhythm of life. Under the snow, life still glowed, seeds warm, fecundity waiting to flower. Just as, beneath their heavy clothes, they—their bodies and their lives—were melding, seeds sown in darkness to flower later—in summer, when the sun returned.

With their own rhythm, the rhythm of their breathing, of their heartbeats, of the constant flexing of their bodies, locked to the rolling gait of the horses plodding through that wintry scene, they, too, became part of it. A natural part of the landscape, the act of their joining invested with the same, intrinsic force that breathed life into the world.

As the snow swirled and the light slowly faded and the horses plodded on, locked in each others arms, their bodies slowly tensing, straining toward shimmering release, they were a piece of the jigsaw of the world at that moment. An essential, necessary piece.

With that certainty investing her mind, her soul, Catriona dragged her lips from his. Laying her head on his shoulder, her forehead by his jaw, she breathed rapidly, raggedly. Her body moved incessantly without her direction, driven by a need she no longer needed to conceal. Didn't know how to conceal.

Caught in the moment, she clung to him, conscious to her toes of the steely strength of him, the hot hard length of him, sliding so effortlessly deep into her core, nudging her womb, soon to fill it, to provide the seed for her fruit.

Need built, then flooded her; she heard herself moan. He shifted and brushed a hot kiss to her temple, then tightened his arms about her and urged her on. Urged her deeper upon him.

She dragged in a desperate breath, and tightened about him, and drew him in—into her body, into her soul.

Into her heart.

She could feel her protective distance dissolving—feel her shields slide away—leaving her defenseless. At her feet, the hole she'd jumped into that first night yawned and beckoned anew—tempting her to recommit to it, to jump in as she had when she'd first given herself to him, when she'd first welcomed him—the warrior—into her body. The second night she'd gone to him had dug the hole deeper, the third night had sealed her fate.

Now, compelled by that same fate, drawn on by a force more powerful than any she'd known, she stepped forward gladly and slid into the dark.

And she was falling.

Through darkness hot with passion, sparking with desire, heated by their yearning bodies. The rush of need rose up and caught her, swept her up and on, a wave lifting her to blessed oblivion. She rode it, rode him, urgently—he met her, reflected her energy and pushed her on. Ever on.

To culmination, to the peak of joy that swelled and welled, then crashed about her, showering her body, her mind with wonder, with release so fragilely beautiful it shimmered in her veins and glowed beneath her skin.

Eyes shut, fingers clenched in his shirt, she muffled her scream against his warm chest. She clung, blissfully buoyed, to the peak for one long instant, then let go.

And floated, at peace.

He gathered her to him, pressed a kiss to her cheek, and filled her even more deeply, even more forcefully. Fully open, she received him joyfully, softly smiling at his deep groan of completion, at the warmth that flooded her womb.

She'd made her decision and stepped into the unknown, and there was nowhere to land but in his arms.

They closed about her, holding her tight.

Shutting her eyes against a sharp rush of emotion, Catriona surrendered and sank into his embrace.

"I take it," Richard drawled, "that that's Merrick looming ahead?"

"Yes." Nose all but pressed to the window, Catriona spared no more than a swift glance for the majestic peak towering over the head of the vale. The carriage rocked and raced on, swiftly pulled by Richard's powerful horses; they were almost home, and she had so many things to think of. "That's the Melchetts' farm." She nodded to a huddle of low-roofed buildings hugging the protection of a rise. "The woods beyond yield most of our firelogs."

She sensed Richard's nod; she kept her eyes glued to the scene beyond the window, as if cataloging all she saw. In reality, her mind was in an unaccustomed, but oddly pleasant whirl—due, of course, to him. They'd crossed into the vale ten minutes before, having left Ayr, on the coast, at first light, after only two nights on the road.

The first, spent at The Angel in Stirling, had opened her eyes to the benefits of traveling with a gentleman—a rich, powerful, protective one. Through Worboys, Richard had made his wishes—their requirements—known; all had happened as he'd decreed. Even Algaria, traveling behind them in the vale's carriage, had muted her unspoken disapproval. Even she had had to appreciate the ease of a private parlor and the quality of an excellent dinner.

Algaria had fallen silent; as the days passed, she'd become withdrawn. Inwardly sighing, Catriona accepted it and waited for her mentor to see the light.

For herself, revelation had already come.

As husband and wife, she and Richard had shared a room, shared a bed, for the past two nights. Time enough, opportunity enough, for her to see what the future might hold. Falling asleep in his arms had been heaven. Waking up there had proved a new delight.

Feeling heat in her cheeks, Catriona inwardly grinned.

She avoided looking at the cause and kept her gaze on the white fields, her hot cheeks close to the cold window.

While her mind remembered all the details, and her wayward senses reveled in recollected sensation.

She'd woken that morning to find him wrapped around her, woken to the sensation of him sliding into her. She'd gasped and clutched the arm wrapped about her waist, only to have him tip her hips back so he could enter her more deeply.

He'd loved her as he always did—slowly, languorously, powerfully. Indefatigably. That seemed to be his style. It was one she found addictive. There was a depth to their intimacy, both physical and emotional, that she hadn't expected.

She'd closed her eyes and drunk it in, let it seep through her and nourish her soul.

Now, she was all but hanging out of the window in her excitement, her eagerness to be home. To start her new life—to have him there, a part of it.

"There!" Like a child, she pointed through the birches, a forest of trunks and bare branches. She glanced over her shoulder at Richard. "That's Casphairn Manor."

He shifted and drew near to peer over her shoulder. "Grey stone?"

Catriona nodded as a turret flashed into view.

"The park looks extensive."

"It is." She glanced at him. "It's necessary to protect the manor from the winds and snows driving off Merrick."

He nodded and sat back again; Catriona turned back to the window. "Another ten minutes and we'll be there." Worry tinged her voice—directly attributable to the sudden, disconcerting thought of whether there was any potential problem she'd failed to foresee, any action she ought to be prepared to take to smooth his entry into the vale, into her life. Inwardly frowning, she stared out the window.

Richard noted her concern, as he'd noted her earlier absorption with her holdings. Her mind was clearly on her fields, on the vale—on her responsibilities, not on him.

His gaze on her profile, he inwardly grimaced. The last two days had gone his way—all his way. She was his on one level at least. But once they gained Casphairn Manor, he'd face new challenges—ones he'd never faced before.

Like keeping his promise not to interfere with her role, with how she ran the vale. Like learning to accept what he meant to her—whatever that was.

That last grated, on his temper, on his Cynster soul. He was not at all sure he appreciated the hand Her Lady had had in bringing about their marriage.

Admittedly, if it hadn't been for such divine intervention, Catriona might not now be his—not on any level. Witch that she was, she was stubborn, willful, and not easily swayed, particularly when it came to matters affecting her calling.

His gaze locked on her face, he felt his features harden, felt determination swell.

It must, he reflected, be his week for making vows.

In this case—her case—he didn't even have to think of the wording, the statement simply rang in his mind. She would, he swore, come to want him on her own account, not because Her Lady had ordained it. She'd want him, all of him, for herself—for what he gave her.

That wasn't, he felt sure, how she felt about him now, how she saw him in relation to herself, but he was a hunter to his soul—he was perfectly prepared to play a waiting game. Prepared to lay snares, carefully camouflaged traps, to persist until she was his.

His in body, as she already was, and his in her mind as well.

His—freely. That was, he suddenly realized, the only way he'd truly have her—the only way he'd know that she truly was his.

As the carriage slowed, rocked, then rumbled through a pair of gateposts and on down a long avenue through the park, Richard watched his new bride—and idly speculated on just how she would tell him—how she would show him—when the time came, and she truly was his.

"Good morning, m'lady! And a good morning it is that brings you home safe and sound."

"Thank you, Mrs. Broom." Taking Richard's hand, Catriona descended the steps of his carriage, and, to her surprise, couldn't exactly place what her housekeeper was thinking. Mrs. Broom was usually easy to read, but the huge grin on her homely face as she beamed up at Richard, all handsomely elegant as usual, defied interpretation.

The sight of an unknown carriage leading her own up the long drive had brought the manor's people running. Maids and stablelads, grooms and workmen, all piled into the courtyard, gathering in a loose crowd about the main steps before which Richard's coachman had pulled up.

Richard had descended first; from the shadows of the carriage, Catriona had watched her people's eyes widen, seen the surprise, the speculation. She'd waited for the distrust, the defensiveness, ready to combat it—but it hadn't yet appeared.

Leaving one hand in Richard's, she gestured with the other, smiling as, with a wave, she gathered her people's attention, then directed it to Richard. "This is my husband, Mr. Richard Cynster. We were married two days ago."

A wave of excitement, a murmur of clear approval, swept the crowd. Catriona smiled at Richard, then smoothly turned to the old man leaning heavily on a stick beside Mrs. Broom. "Allow me to present McArdle."

The old man bowed, slow and deep; when he straightened, a smile wider than any Catriona could recall wreathed his face.

"'Tis a pleasure to welcome you to Casphairn Manor, sir."

Smiling back, Richard inclined his head urbanely. "It's a pleasure to be here, McArdle."

As if some ritual—one *she* was unaware of—had been successfully completed, everyone—all those who had served her since birth, all those who were in her care—relaxed and welcomed Richard Cynster into their midst. Utterly bemused, Catriona felt their warm welcome enfold him. He responded; placing her hand on his sleeve, he turned her. With her at his side, he slowly circled the gathering, so he could meet all her household.

While making the introductions, Catriona studied her staff—one and all, their response to Richard was genuine. They were, indeed, very pleased to see him, to welcome him as her husband. The more he spoke, the more they smiled and grinned. The more she inwardly frowned.

When they were free to go inside, Richard led her up the steps. They passed Algaria, standing silent and withdrawn at the top. Catriona met her black gaze—and instantly knew what she, at least, was thinking.

But Richard's reaction was not feigned, nor part of any plan; as she'd introduced him to a welcome she hadn't foreseen, she'd sensed—known beyond question—that he hadn't foreseen it, either. He'd been as surprised as she, but quick to respond to her people's invitation.

What had her puzzled was what, precisely, that invitation was—and why it had been issued so readily.

Those questions plagued her all day.

By the time the household gathered for dinner, she was seriously disturbed. There was something happening in her small world that she didn't understand, some force stirring over which she had no control. Which was definitely not how it had been, nor how she liked it.

Made uneasy by something she could not name, she glided into the dining hall. Richard prowled at her heels, as he had for most of the afternoon, as she'd shown him about her home. Now his home.

Glancing over her shoulder, Catriona inwardly frowned. The matter of where they would live was something they hadn't actually discussed—she'd simply assumed they would live here. Together. Lady and consort. But she'd assumed wrong on one point—she could be wrong on that issue, too. The thought did not calm her—right now, she needed calm.

Drawing that emotion to her, she smiled at Mrs. Broom and stepped up to the dais. Going to her place at the center of the long table, she graciously waved Richard to the carved chair beside hers. The chair that had stood against the wall, unneeded since her parents' deaths.

Richard held her chair as she sat, then took the chair beside her. Catriona nodded to Mrs. Broom, who clapped her hands for the first course to be served. Maids hurried in, carting piled platters. Unlike the household of gentry elsewhere, at the manor, all the household ate together, as they had for centuries.

Lounging in the chair beside Catriona, Richard studied her people, studied the open and easy manners that pertained between mistress and staff. There was a warmth, a camaraderie present that he previously had encountered only among soldiers; given the vale's isolation, the trials of long winters and wild weather, it was perhaps a good thing—a necessary cohesiveness.

All in all, he approved.

Not so Worboys.

Seated at the table directly below the main one, poor Worboys looked stunned. Inwardly grimacing, Richard made a mental note to expect his resignation. Used to the strict observances pertaining among the best households in the ton, the situation at Casphairn Manor would not meet Worboys's high standards.

And God only knew what the blacking was like.

"Do you care for some wine?"

Turning his head, Richard saw Catriona lift a decanter. Reaching out, he took it from her and studied the golden liquid within. "What is it?"

"Dandelion wine. We make it ourselves."

"Oh." Richard hesitated, then, inwardly grimacing, poured himself a half glass. He passed the decanter to Mrs. Broom, who had slipped into the seat beside him.

"You must tell me," she said, "what your favorite dishes are." She flashed him a wide smile. "So we can see what we can do to accommodate your tastes."

Richard smiled his slow Cynster smile. "How kind of you. I'll give the matter some thought."

She beamed, then turned aside.

Richard turned back to Catriona, but she was absorbed in her meal. Lifting his wineglass, he sipped. Then blinked. Then sipped again, more slowly, savoring the tart taste, the complexities of the bouquet.

Liquid ambrosia.

Straightening, he set his glass down and picked up his soup spoon. "How much of that wine do you have?"

Catriona shot him a glance. "We make as many casks as we can every summer. But we always have some left year to year."

"What do you do with it? The stuff left over?"

Laying down her spoon, she shrugged. "I expect the old casks are still there, in the cellars. I told you they're extensive—they run all the way beneath the main building."

"You can show me tomorrow." When she looked at him suspiciously, he smiled. "Your cellars sound quite fascinating."

She humphed.

A clanging sounded throughout the large room. All turned to where McArdle stood at the end of the main table. When all had quieted, he raised his goblet high. "I propose a toast—to Casphairn Manor. Long may it thrive. To our lady of the vale—long may she reign. And to our lady's new consort, Mister Richard Cynster—a warm welcome to the vale, Sassenach though he might be."

Laughter greeted that last; McArdle grinned and turned to address Catriona and Richard directly. "To you, my lady—and the consort The Lady has sent you."

Wild cheering and clapping rose throughout the hall, echoing from the stone walls and high rafters. Smiling easily, fingers crooked about the stem of his glass, Richard turned his head and cocked a brow at Catriona.

His question was clear; Catriona hesitated, then nodded. She watched as, with nonchalant grace, Richard rose; cradling his goblet, he lifted it high and said, very simply: "To Casphairn Manor."

All drank, as did he. Lowering his glass, he scanned the room, but did not sit down. After a moment, when all attention was again focused on him, on his commanding figure dominating the main table, he said, his voice low but carrying readily through the room: "I make the same pledge to you, and the vale, that I have already made to your lady." A glance directed their attention to her, then he lifted his head and raised his glass. "As consort to your lady, I will honor the ways of the vale and protect you and the vale from all threats."

He drank off his wine, then lowered his glass as clapping erupted from all sides. Heartfelt, the sound rose and rolled over the room. Richard sat— instinctively, Catriona put out a hand to his sleeve. He looked at her—she met his gaze fleetingly, then smiled and looked away.

And wondered at herself—at what he'd made her feel—all of them feel—in those few brief moments, with those few simple words. Magnetic words— she'd felt the tug herself, seen the effect it had had on her household. Her people were very much his already, and he'd only crossed the threshold mere hours ago.

Through the rest of the meal, Catriona pondered that fact. She steadfastly avoided looking at Algaria, but could feel her black glare. And sense her thoughts.

Nevertheless ... she knew, to her bones, that this was how it was meant to be. Quite how their marriage would work out was what she couldn't, at present, see. She'd known Richard for a potent force even before she had met him, which was why she'd believed he was no suitable consort for her. The Lady had deemed otherwise.

Which was all very well but it was *she* who had to cope with his unsettling presence.

Off-balance, uncertain—in severe need of some quiet and calm—she waited until dessert was being cleared, then set aside her napkin. "I'm afraid the journey must have been more tiring than I thought." She smiled at McArdle. "I'm for bed."

"Of course, of course." He started to rise to draw out her chair, then smiled over her head and subsided.

Catriona felt the chair shift and looked around. Richard stood behind her. She smiled at him, then smiled at Mrs. Broom and the rest of the table. "Goodnight."

The others all nodded and smiled. Richard drew her chair farther back; she slipped past, then glided along behind the other chairs, stepped off the dais, and turned through an archway into the corridor leading to the stairs.

The instant she was out of sight of the dining hall, she frowned and looked down. Pondering her state—the uneasiness, the sense of being off-center that had gripped her the moment she'd stepped over her own threshold, Richard by her side—she absentmindedly trailed through the corridors, through the front hall, and climbed the stairs to the gallery and crossed it to her chamber.

Halting before her chamber door, she focused—to find herself standing in deep shadow. She'd forgotten to pick up a candle from the hall table. Luckily, born in this house, she didn't need to see to find her room. She reached for the door latch—

And very nearly screamed when a dark shadow reached past her, gripped the latch, and lifted it.

Hand to her throat, she whirled—even before she saw him, denser than night at her side, she realized who it must be. *"Richard!"*

He stilled; she could feel his frown. "What's the matter?"

The door swung wide, revealing her familiar room, lit by flames leaping in the grate. Catriona gazed in and tried to calm her racing heart. "I didn't realize you were there."

She stepped over the threshold.

"I'll always be here." He followed her in.

Catriona whirled—her heart raced again as she faced him. And realized what he meant. "Ah ... yes. Well ..." Airily gesturing, she turned and walked further into the room. "I'm just not used to it—having someone there."

Truer words she'd never spoken. That was borne in on her as she walked to the fire, scanning the oh-so-familiar, oh-so-comforting furniture, and behind her, heard the latch click. Stopping by the fire, she half turned and glanced at him from beneath her lashes—he was standing just inside the door, studying her.

This was her own private sanctuary. A place he now had the right to enter whenever he chose. Yet another change marriage had wrought—yet another change she would have to accept.

"I ... was tired."

He tilted his head, still studying her. "So you said." With that, he started to stroll, prowling about the room. Like some wild male animal assessing his new home.

Pushing the vison from her, Catriona straightened and jettisoned all thoughts of spending a quiet hour or two considering her state. Considering her husband.

She could hardly do that with him prowling so close.

She could barely *think* with him prowling so close.

His "I'll always be here" was not reassuring.

"Ah ..." Eyeing him as he neared, she forced herself to meet his eyes. "We didn't discuss our sleeping arrangements here."

One black brow rose. "What's to discuss?" Reaching her side, he looked down at her, then crouched to tend the blaze.

Looking down at his head, Catriona felt her temper stir. "We could discuss where you'll sleep, for instance."

"I'll sleep with you."

She bit her tongue—and warned herself of the unwisdom of biting off her nose. "Yes, but what I wondered was whether you would like a chamber of your own."

He seemed to consider that; he remained silent as he piled on logs, building a massive blaze. Then he stood; Catriona only just stopped herself from taking a step back.

Richard looked down at her, then scanned the large room. Despite containing a bureau, dresser, dressing table and chairs, wardrobe and two chests, as well as the reassuringly massive four poster bed, the room was sparsely furnished. They could share it comfortably and still have room to spare. His traveling case, set against one wall, was barely noticeable.

He looked down, into Catriona's eyes. "Will it bother you if I say no?"

The puzzlement that filled her eyes was impossible to mistake. "No, of course . . ."

He raised a brow.

"Well . . ." Abruptly, she glared. "I don't know!"

Unwisely, he grinned.

She slapped him across the chest. "Don't laugh! I've never felt so at sea in my life!"

His grin turned wry. "Why?" Catching her hand, he headed for the bed, towing her, unresisting, behind him.

"I don't know. Well . . . yes, I do. It's you."

Reaching the bed, he turned and sat, pulling her to stand between his thighs. "What about me?"

She frowned at him; holding her gaze, his expression mild and questioning, he set his fingers to the buttons of her carriage dress.

After a long moment, she grimaced. "No—that's not it either."

Frowning absently, she reached for the pin securing his cravat, slipped it free, then slid it into the lapel of his coat. "I'm not sure what it is—just something unsettling—something not quite in its right place." Frowning still, she flicked the ends of his cravat undone, then fell to untwisting the folds.

Richard held his tongue and let her tug his cravat free, then obediently shrugged out of his coat and waistcoat before helping her from her dress. Sitting again, he drew her to him; trapping her between his knees, he started unpicking the laces of her petticoat.

She was still frowning.

"Did my reception surprise you?"

She looked up. He pushed her petticoats down.

"Yes." She met his gaze squarely. "I don't understand it." One hand in his, she stepped from the pile of her skirts. "It was as if you were"—she gestured—"someone they'd been waiting for."

Closing his hands about her waist, Richard drew her back, locking her between his thighs. "That's how they see me, I think."

"But . . . *why?*"

For one minute, he kept his gaze on the tiny buttons of her chemise as he slipped them from their moorings. Then he lifted his gaze and met her eyes.

"Because I think they fear for you—and thus, indirectly, for themselves. I showed you the letters. I imagine, if you asked, you would discover many of your household have their own suspicions of your neighbors and the threat they pose to the vale."

Looking down, he separated the two halves of her chemise, now open to her waist, and drew the sleeves down. She shivered as the cool air touched her flesh, but lowered her arms and slid them free.

Raising his head, he trapped her gaze. "They see me as a protector—for you, the vale, and them."

Her frown wavered, then she grimaced. "I suppose that's what the consort is supposed to be."

"Indeed." Richard closed his hands over her bare breasts and felt her tremble, heard her indrawn breath. Her lids drifted low; he brushed his thumbs over her nipples, and she shuddered.

"The Lady chose me for you, remember." Drawing her closer, he kissed her, then whispered against her lips: "She chose me to be the one to wed you, bed you and get you with child. Chose me to defend and protect you. That's how your people see me—as the one The Lady sent for you."

"Hmmm." Her hands rising to his shoulders, Catriona leaned into the next kiss.

A minute later, he pulled back and urged her on to the bed, divesting himself of his clothes as she slipped between the sheets. Then he joined her, moving immediately over her, spreading her thighs wide and settling between. He fitted himself to her, then, settling heavily upon her, framed her face with both hands and kissed her deeply—as he pressed into her.

He slid fully home, then stopped and lifted his head, breaking their kiss. "I told you I won't undermine your authority." He pressed deeper still, then lowered his head. "Just trust me—it'll all settle into place." In the instant before his lips reclaimed hers, he whispered: "Just like this has."

She couldn't argue with that; as she instinctively eased beneath him, supple and soft as he rode her slowly, deeply, Catriona relaxed, and did as he asked, and put her trust in him.

It wasn't, of course, how she'd imagined things would be. She'd thought to be the assured one, the one to do the reassuring, secure in her position as she eased him into his new role. Instead, the shoe seemed to be on the other foot, with him sliding effortlessly into a role she hadn't known was waiting for him—and having to reassure her of her own.

But here, in their bed, she didn't need reassurance. He'd taught her well, taught her all she needed to know to love him. So she clung to him and gave to him, uncaring of how the future might unfurl.

The future was the province of The Lady; the night—this night—was for them.

Later, much later, in the depths of the night, Richard lay on his back and studied his sleeping wife. His exhausted, sated wife—who had exhausted and sated him. The minutes ticked by as he studied her face, the flawless ivory skin, the wild mane of fire-gold hair.

She was a witch who had bewitched him; he would walk through fire for her, sell his soul and more for her.

And if she couldn't understand that, it didn't really matter, because he couldn't understand it, either.

Sliding deeper into the bed, he gathered her into his arms and felt her warmth sink to his bones. Felt her turn to him in her sleep and curl into his arms.

As his body relaxed, and he drifted into dreams, it occurred to him that few men such as he—strong enough, powerful enough to act as her protector—would agree to wed a witch and then give her free rein.

He had.

He didn't like to think why.

It was almost as if it *had* been preordained—that The Lady had indeed chosen him for her.

CHAPTER
Eleven

৩৩৩৩

Richard woke the next morning as he had the past two—at dawn, reaching for his wife.

This morning, all he found was cold sheets.

"What ...?" Lifting his lids, and his head, he confirmed that the bed beside him was indeed empty. Stifling a curse, he half sat and scanned the room.

There was no sign of Catriona.

Cursing freely, he flung back the covers and stalked to the window. Opening the pane, he pushed back the shutters. Dawn was a glimmer on the distant horizon. Abruptly shutting the window on the morning's chill, he turned back into the room. Scowling ferociously.

"Where the devil has she gone?"

Determined to get an answer, he hauled on buckskin breeches and boots, a warm shirt and a hacking jacket. Tying a kerchief about his throat, his greatcoat over one arm, he strode out of the room.

The front hall and the dining hall were empty; no one was about. Not even a scullery maid clearing the ashes from the huge fireplace in the kitchen. It took him three tries to find the right corridor leading to the back door; finally there, he needed both hands to haul open the heavy oak door—Catriona certainly hadn't gone that way.

Richard paused on the threshold and looked across the cobbled yard, joined to the front courtyard by a wide drive circling the main house. The sun was just rising, streaking light across the world, striking fire from ice crystals dotted like diamonds over the snow. It was cold and chill, but clear, the air invigorating, his breath condensing in gentle puffs before his face. The stables stood directly opposite, on the other side of the yard, a conglomeration of buildings in stone and wood. The manor house itself was of dark grey stone, with steep gables edging the slate roofs and three turrets growing out of the angles of the walls. Irregularly shaped, the main building was large, but surprisingly unified—not the hodge-podge the outbuildings appeared to be.

Everything, however, was neat and tidy, everything in its place.

Except his wife.

Gritting his teeth, Richard shrugged on his greatcoat, then tugged the back door shut. He couldn't see any reason why Catriona would have gone riding, but if he didn't find her soon, he might do the same.

His short tour yesterday with her as his guide had been confined to the reception rooms and gallery, the library, billiard room—a welcome surprise—and her estate office. Punctuated by introductions to a constant stream of staff who had found occasion to pop up in their path, he hadn't seen all that much.

As he strode across the cobbles, the clack of his boot-heels echoed weakly, thrown back by the stone. In the center of the yard, he halted—arrested by sheer beauty. The yard was large; from this position, he had an unimpeded view of the fields leading up to the head of the vale. Directly ahead of him, rising majestically into the sky, stood Merrick, the vale embraced within its foothills. Slowly, he pivoted, until he faced the house; on either side of its bulk, he could see the fields beyond, white-flecked ground stretching away beyond the brown of the park.

The manor was sited on a rise roughly at the center of the vale. To one side, the river that bisected the vale curved about the base of the rise; even under the snow and ice, Richard could hear it murmuring. Between the house and the river lay carefully tended gardens, stone paths wending between what he assumed would be beds of herbs and healing plants. It wasn't hard, in his mind's eye, to see it without snow, to see green instead of brown, to imagine the richness that in summer would be there. Even now, dormant, hibernating under winter's blanket, the sense of vibrant life was strong.

To a Cynster, it was a breathtaking scene. All the land he could see was—if not, in his mind, his—then under his protection.

Drawing in a deep breath, feeling the cold singing through his veins, Richard slowly swung around and resumed his trek to the stables. In the distance, he saw dots ambling across the snowy fields—cattle drifting in and out of crude shelters. He frowned, then reached for the latch of the stable door.

It opened noiselessly—it hadn't, in fact, been fully latched. His frown deepening, Richard drew the door wide. He was about to step through, when hoofbeats came pounding up the slope beyond the stables.

The next instant, a rough-coated chestnut mare swung around the corner and into the yard, Catriona in the saddle. She saw him instantly. Her cheeks were flushed, her wayward curls dancing—her bright eyes grew wary the instant they met his.

"What's the matter?" Drawing rein a few feet away, she asked the question breathlessly.

Richard fought down an urge to roar. "I was looking for you." The words were clipped and steely. "Where the devil have you been?"

"Praying, of course."

Taking in her heavy cloak and the thick leggings she wore beneath her skirts, rucked up as she was riding astride, he caught her mount's bridle as she kicked free of the stirrups. "You pray outside? In this weather?"

"In *all* weathers." Lifting one leg over the chestnut's neck, she prepared to slide down—stifling a curse, he reached up and lifted her to the ground.

And held her before him, trapped between his hands. "Where?"

Her gaze locked on his, she hesitated, then tilted her chin. "There's a circle at the head of the vale."

"A circle?"

Whisking free of his grasp, she nodded and caught the mare's reins.

Suppressing a curse, he reached out and tugged them from her, then gestured for her to precede him. She did—nose in the air, hips swaying provocatively.

For her sake, Richard prayed there were no convenient piles of hay lying loose about the stable. Teeth gritted, he followed her into the warm dark. "Do you go to pray often? Disappear like this, before dawn?" Before he'd woken?

"At least once every week—sometimes more often. But not every day."

Richard gave thanks for small mercies. Her Lady obviously had some understanding of the needs of mortal men. Securing the mare in the stall Cartriona had led him to, he turned to find her tugging the girths free. Then she reached for the saddle.

"Here—let me." He grasped the saddle and lifted it from her and set it atop the stall wall. Turning back, he found her with a currying brush in her hand— he took that, too. And fell to brushing the mare's thick coat.

By the light of a sharp green glare.

"I'm perfectly capable of caring for my own horse."

"I daresay. You might not, however, care for the alternative to letting *me* care for your horse in this instance."

Wariness muted her glare. "Alternative?"

Richard kept his eyes on the mare's hairy hide. "As there's no loose straw about, it'll have to be the wall." Without looking, he gestured with his head. "The corner by the trough might be wise—you could balance with one foot on the edge."

She actually looked—the expression on her face nearly had him throwing the brush aside.

"Then again"—he gripped the brush tightly and put all his pent-up energy into every stroke—"this mangy beast looks like she bites—which doesn't bear thinking of."

Drawing herself up to her full, less-than-adequate height, she stalked around the mare so she could glare at him directly, with the horse a safe bolster between them.

"Why are you so . . ."—she gestured wildly—"whatever it is you are?"

Lips compressed, Richard flicked her a hard stare and brushed on.

Catriona folded her arms and tilted her chin. "Because I went to pray and didn't ask your permission?"

She waited; gradually, the violence behind his brushing abated. His face like stone, he glanced at her over the mare's back. "Not permission—but I need to know where you are, where you go. I can hardly protect you if I don't know where you are."

"I don't need protection while praying—no one in the vale would dare go into the circle. It's hallowed ground."

"Do people from outside the vale know that?"

"I'm as safe within the circle as an archbishop in his cathedral."

"Thomas à Becket was slain before the altar at Canterbury."

She hesitated, then shrugged. And tipped her nose in the air. "That was different."

With a frustrated growl, Richard tossed the currying brush aside, stepped around the mare—and trapped her against the stall wall. Eyes wide, locked on his, all fiery blue, Catriona heroically denied a crazed impulse to glance at the nearby trough.

"Just *tell* me where you're going in future. *Don't* disappear."

Lips thinning, she gave him back glare for glare. "If I wake you in the morning to tell you where I'm going, I won't get there."

His eyes bored into hers while she inwardly dared him to deny it.

Instead, after a fraught moment, he nodded curtly and drew back. "Tell me your plans the night before."

With that, he grasped her elbow and steered her, much less gently than was his wont, out of the stall. Forced to pace quickly by his side, Catriona stared up at him, struggling to make out his features in the stable's dim light.

"Very well," she agreed, as they reached the stable door. "But I don't need any protection while at the circle."

They stepped into the yard; the morning light found his face—illuminating a grim mask. "I'll think about it."

He continued to march her across the cobbles, heading for the house. The tension gripping him, shimmering about her, was beyond Catriona's comprehension.

"What is the matter with you?" Reaching the back doorstep, she swung to face him. "I've agreed to tell you where I go—so what's *this?*" With one finger, she prodded one bicep—locked and as hard as iron.

His chest swelled. "That," he said, his voice very low, issuing through clenched teeth, "is because I'm hungry."

"Well, breakfast should nearly be ready—"

"*Wrong* appetite."

She blinked—and looked into his eyes. And saw the truth simmering. "Great heavens! But ..." She frowned at him. "You *can't* be. What about last night?"

"That was last night. Because you disappeared, I missed my morning snack."

"Morning ...?" She felt her features blank, heard her incredulity ring in her weak: "*Every* morning?"

He grinned—a distinctly feral expression. "Let's just say that for the foreseeable future, it would help. But for now"—hauling open the door, he waved her inside—"why don't we see if I can be distracted with breakfast? Unless, of course, you're in favor of snacking throughout the day?"

For one instant, Catriona simply stared at him, then she glared and tossed her head—and ignored the shivery tendrils of excitement slithering down her spine. "Breakfast," she declared, and swept into the house.

His features like stone, Richard followed her in.

They breakfasted together; in passing pikelets and jam, sharing toast, pouring coffee, the tension between them eased. They were the first to take their seats of those who sat at the main table. Mrs. Broom was fussing, overseeing the serving of the trays; McArdle hobbled in late. Algaria, arriving relatively early, took a seat at the far end and kept her black thoughts to herself.

Sitting back in the carved chair that was now his, Richard idly sipped coffee and watched to see how his wife started her day. Algaria's continued disapproval surprised him; he hoped she'd eventually get over it and accept their marriage, not for his sake, but Catriona's. He saw the hopeful glance Catriona threw the woman and sensed her sigh when it wasn't returned. If he'd thought it would help, he would have spoken to Algaria, but her defensiveness where he was concerned remained marked.

"Have there been any replies to those letters I sent about the grain?"

Catriona's question drew Richard's attention; it was addressed to McArdle.

"Hmm … yes, actually, I believe there were." McArdle frowned. "One or two, at least."

"Well, I'll see those first, then we really must make some headway on the plans for next season's plantings."

"Ahh … Jem's not brought in his figures yet. Nor's Melchett."

"They haven't?" Catriona stared at McArdle. "But we need them to make any sense of it."

McArdle raised brows and shoulders in a comprehensive shrug. "You know how it is—they don't understand what you want, so they hope you'll forget—and so they forget."

Heaving an exasperated sigh, Catriona stood. "I'll see to that later then. But if you've finished, we may as well get started."

As McArdle heaved himself up, Richard reached out and caught Catriona's hand. She turned and raised a brow.

"Don't forget," he murmured, his eyes on hers, his thumb brushing over the back of her hand.

For one instant, she stared at him—and he could see she couldn't decide what he was reminding her of—her agreement to tell him her whereabouts, or his invitation to midday snacks. Then she blinked. And looked at him again. "I'll be in the office for most of the day."

And it was his turn to be uncertain—unsure—just what she meant. She gently tugged and he eased his grip and let her fingers slide from his. She inclined her head, then turned away.

As he watched her glide to the door, he still wasn't sure which she meant.

* * *

He'd decided on the library as his own domain—according to Catriona, only she, and Algaria occasionally, used it. There was a huge, old desk, lovingly polished, and a well-padded chair that accommodated his large frame surprisingly well.

Through the combined efforts of Mrs. Broom and Henderson, a large morose man who filled the position of general factotum, he was supplied with paper, pen and ink. Worboys, looking in on him, departed and returned bearing his seal and a stub of wax. After dispatching a maid to fetch a candle, Worboys cast a haughty, barely approving glance over the leatherbound tomes, then sniffed.

"If you need me, sir, I'll be in your room. Henderson—a nice enough chap if one can cope with his brogue—is organizing to have a second wardrobe moved in. I'll be tending your coats."

Lovingly, Richard had not a doubt. "Very well—I doubt I'll need you much in the coming days." He looked up at Worboys. "We won't be entertaining."

Worboys only just avoided a snort. "It does seem unlikely, sir." With that comment on his new home, Worboys took himself off.

Raising his brows, secretly surprised not to have been presented with Worboys' resignation, Richard turned back to his letters.

He considered, then settled to write a fuller account of his marriage to Devil—the easiest task facing him. He filled in the details he'd omitted in his earlier brief note, but saw no reason to elaborate on his feelings, on the reasons he'd taken the plunge. He was quite sure Devil, having already succumbed, and having lived with the outcome for a year, could fill in the blanks for himself.

And heaven knew Honoria, Devil's duchess, and Helena, Richard's stepmother, certainly would.

Sealing Devil's letter, Richard grimaced and set another blank sheet before him.

He stared at it for half an hour. In the end, he wrote a very careful, exquisitely guarded account, rather shorter on actual facts than the first note he'd sent Devil, but filled instead with the sort of information he knew his stepmother would want to know. That yes, he'd found his mother's grave. A description of the necklace his mother had left him. The fact Catriona had long red hair and green eyes. That it had snowed on the day they had married.

Those sort of things.

He penned them carefully and hoped, without much hope, that she'd be satisfied with that. At least for a while.

With a sigh, he signed his name. He'd told Devil they wouldn't be attending the Christmas celebrations at Somersham this year. He knew without asking that Catriona would prefer to remain here, and even after only one night under this roof, he agreed. Maybe, in years to come, when their life here was more established, they would journey south for those few, family-filled days—he, she and their children.

The thought held him for long moments, then he stirred, sealed his missive to Helena, and turned to his last letter—to Heathcote Montague, man of business, on permanent retainer to all the Cynsters.

That letter was more to his liking—making decisions, dealing with his varied interests, giving directions to enable him to manage them all from the vale—these were positive actions reinforcing his new position, his new role.

He signed that letter with a flourish. Impressing his seal on the melted wax, he waved the letter to cool it, then gathered up all three packets and rose. And set out to discover who collected the mail.

There was no butler as such. Old McArdle retained the title of steward, but from all he'd heard, Richard strongly suspected that Catriona did the bulk of the work herself. Henderson, as factotum, was the most likely to oversee the delivery of letters and parcels. Richard wandered through the corridors toward the back of the house, looking in on small workrooms, finding the butler's pantry—but no Henderson.

Deciding to place the matter—along with his letters—in Worboys's ever efficient hands and only then remembering Henderson's appointment with his henchman in the main bedchamber, Richard headed back toward the stairs.

Somewhere in the depths of the house, a bell clanged.

He was in the corridor heading for the front hall when he heard footsteps cross the tiles, then a heavy creak as the front doors were opened.

"Good morning, Henderson! And where is your mistress? Pray tell her I wish to see her right away. A matter of some seriousness, I fear."

The hearty, emphatically genial tones carried clearly; slowing, Richard halted in the shadows of the archway giving onto the front hall. From there, he could see the large, heavily built gentleman handing his hat to Henderson—and the reluctance with which Henderson accepted it.

"I'll see if the mistress is free, sir."

Piggy eyes in a round, reddened face narrowed slightly. "Now you just tell her it's me, and she'll be free, I'll warrant. Now get a move on, sirrah—don't keep me standing—"

"Sir Olwyn." Catriona's quiet, dignified tones carried clearly down the hall. Richard watched as, having glided from the office, she took up a stance directly before the main stairs. And faced Sir Olwyn calmly.

"Miss Hennessey!" Sir Olwyn's impending scowl was banished by a beaming smile. With over-hearty eagerness, he strode up the hall. "A *pleasure* to see you returned, my dear." Catriona smiled coolly and inclined her head, but offered no hand in greeting; Sir Olwyn only beamed brighter. "I trust your little sojourn in the Highlands passed without mishap?" As if only then recalling what had occasioned her absence, his smile evaporated, to be replaced with an expression of patently false sympathy. "A great loss, I'm sure, your guardian."

"Indeed." Her voice as cold as the snows outside, Catriona inclined her head again. "But—"

"His son has inherited, I understand?"

Catriona drew a patient breath. "Yes. His son Jamie was, indeed, my late guardian's heir. But—"

"Aye, well—he'll want to pay attention to things down here, and that right quickly, I make no doubt." Bluffy earnest again, Sir Olwyn looked at Catriona and shook his head. "I fear, my dear, that I must again lodge a protest—vale cattle have been found wandering *miles* into my fields."

"Indeed?" Brows rising, Catriona turned and looked at McArdle, who had followed her into the hall. He looked steadily back, then gave one of his exaggerated, disclaiming shrugs—this one expressing subtle contempt for the suggestion. Catriona turned back to Sir Olwyn. "I fear, sir, that you must be mistaken. None of our cattle are missing."

"No, no, my dear—of *course* they aren't." Braving the prevailing chill, Sir Olwyn boldly took Catriona's hand and patted it. "My men have strict orders to return them. Many other landowners would not be so lenient, my dear—I do hope you appreciate my concern for you." Cloyingly paternalistic, he smiled into her eyes. "No, no—you losing beasts is not the *point*, sweet lady. The point is that they should *not* have wandered in the *first* place and should certainly *not* have caused damage to *my* fields.

Not thawed in the least, Catriona, very deliberately, withdrew her hand. "What—"

"No, no! Never fear." With a hearty laugh, Sir Olwyn held up one hand. "We'll say no more of it this time. But you really need to pay attention to your stock management, my dear. Of course, being a female, you shouldn't need to worry your pretty head over such matters. A man is what you need, m'dear—"

"I doubt that." With languid ease, Richard strolled into the hall. "At least, not another one."

Sir Olwyn stared, then he bristled. "Who are you?"

Richard raised one brow and looked at Catriona.

With unimpaired calm, she returned her gaze to Sir Olwyn. "Allow me to present Richard Cynster—my husband."

Sir Olwyn blinked, then he goggled. *"Husband?"*

"As I was *trying* to tell you, Sir Olwyn, while in the Highlands, I married."

"Me." Richard smiled—a distinctly Cynster smile.

Sir Olwyn eyed it dubiously. He mouthed a silent "Oh," then flushed and turned to Catriona. "Felicitations, my dear—well! It's quite a surprise." His piggy eyes sharpened; he looked intently at her. "*Quite* a surprise."

"Indeed," Richard drawled, "a surprise all around, I fancy." Smoothly moving forward, he interposed himself between Catriona and Sir Olwyn, ineffably gathering Sir Olwyn within one outstretched arm, turning him and steering him back down the hall. "Glean—it is Sir Olwyn Glean, is it not?— perhaps ... you understand I haven't yet had time to fully acquaint myself with the situation here—we've only just arrived, you see ... where was I? Ah, yes—perhaps you'd be so good as to explain to me how you identified these wandering cattle as originating from the vale. I gather you didn't see them?"

Discovering himself back at the front door, which Henderson had helpfully set wide, Sir Olwyn blinked, then shook himself. And flushed. "Well, no—but—"

"Ah! Your men verified their identities, then. I'm so glad—they'll be able to tell me the farm from which the cattle escaped."

Sir Olwyn flustered. "Well—as to that—"

Catching his eye, Richard dispensed with his drawl. "I will, of course, be taking steps to ensure no similar situation occurs again." He smiled, very slightly, very intently. "I do hope you take my meaning."

Sir Olwyn flushed to the roots of his hair. He threw a stunned look back at Catriona, then grabbed the hat Henderson held out, crammed it on his crown, swung on his heel and clattered down the steps.

Richard watched him go—watched him scramble atop his showy bay and canter out of the courtyard.

At Richard's shoulder, the taciturn Henderson nodded at Glean's departing back. "Good job, that."

Richard thought so. He smiled and handed Henderson his letters, then turned back into the hall. Behind him, Henderson pulled the heavy doors shut.

Catriona hadn't moved from her position before the stairs; Richard strolled up the hall and stopped directly before her.

She met his gaze directly. "Our cattle don't stray beyond the vale—I'd know if they did."

Richard studied her eyes, then nodded. "I'd assumed after reading Glean's letters to Seasmus that all that was so much hot air." He took her hand and turned her toward the stairs.

"Sir Olwyn's always trying to create situations out of nothing."

"Hmmm." Placing her hand on his sleeve, Richard started up the stairs.

Catriona frowned. "Where are we going?"

"To our room." Richard waved ahead. "Henderson and Worboys have been doing a little reorganizing—I think we should see if you approve." He smiled at her, effortlessly charming. "And there's one or two other things I'd like you to consider."

Like the appetite he'd worked up dispensing with Sir Olwyn.

It was time for a midday snack.

Four days later, when Catriona again tried to slip from her husband's arms before dawn, he grunted, held her close for an instant, then let her go—and rolled out of bed as well.

"This is really not necessary," Catriona stated as, ten minutes later, she stood in the dimness of the stable and watched Richard saddle her mare. "I'm perfectly capable of doing it myself."

"Hmm."

Catriona glared. She knew it was useless, but it eased her temper, confused as it was. "You could have stayed nicely warm in bed."

Cinching the girths, he looked up and met her eyes. "There's no point in staying nicely warm in bed if you're not in it."

It was her turn to humph. Gathering the reins, she put her hands to the saddle, intending to scramble up. He was around beside her in a blink; lifting her, he dropped her onto her perch.

Glaring, she reminded herself, was wasted effort. She settled her feet in the stirrups. "I'll be back in less than two hours."

the vale. Nearer at hand, the gardens rolled down to the river, now visible only as a snow ribbon edged by banks of brown.

It was there that she saw him, riding like the wind along the path that followed the river. The horse under him was dappled grey, a flash of silver in the crisp morning light.

Her heart in her throat, Catriona watched, waiting for the inevitable balk, the scream, the rearing and bucking—the inevitable fall.

It didn't happen. Like kindred souls, man and beast flew over the white ground in perfect harmony, every movement a testimony to their innate strength, every line a testimony to their breeding.

She watched until they disappeared into the glare of the morning sun, rising like a silver disc over the mouth of the vale.

She was waiting for him in the stable when he clattered in. He saw her— his brows quirked, then he dismounted. Hands on hips, she watched as he led Thunderer back to his stall and unsaddled the huge grey. Both he and the horse were breathing fast; they were both smiling the same, thoroughly male smile.

Suppressing a humph, she leaned against the open stall door and folded her arms. "How did you manage it?"

Busy brushing the now peaceable stallion, he glanced at her. "It was easy. Thunderer here had simply never had the option put to him."

"What option?"

"The option of staying cooped up in here, or of going for a long run with me on his back."

"I see. And so you simply put this option to him and he agreed?"

"As you saw." Tossing the brush aside, Richard checked the stallion's provisions, then joined her by the stall door.

Arms still crossed, she eyed him broodingly. He was still breathing more rapidly than usual, his chest rising and falling—and he still wore that same, ridiculously pleased-with-himself smile.

He glanced back at Thunderer. "I'll take him for a run every now and then." He looked down at her. "Just to keep him in shape."

His eyes trapped hers—Catriona sucked in a quick breath. They were blue—burning blue—hot with passion and desire. As she stared into their heat, wariness—and expectation—washed over her. No one else was around; all the stable hands were at breakfast.

"Ah ..." Eyes locked on his, she slid sideways, along the open door. He followed, slowly, as if stalking her. But the threat didn't come from him; the knowing lilt to his lips said he knew it. She should, she knew, draw herself up, find her haughty cloak and put it on without delay. Instead, his burning gaze drew forth the exhilaration she'd felt earlier, and sent it singing through her veins. "Breakfast?" she managed, her voice faint.

His eyes held hers; his lips lifted in a slow, slight, very intent smile. "Later."

She'd slid away from the door; reaching out, he swung it shut without looking and continued to follow her, herd her, into the next stall. Which was empty.

Wide-eyed, still backing up, Catriona glanced wildly about. And came up against the wall. She put up her hands, far too weak to hold him back. Even had that been her intent. "Richard?"

It was clearly a question. He answered with actions. And she discovered how useful a feed trough could be.

CHAPTER
Twelve

ॐ♡ॐ

December rolled on, and winter tightened its grip on the vale. Richard's boxes and trunks arrived, sent north by Devil, delivered by a carter anxious to turn his horses about and get home for Christmas.

Along with the boxes came letters—a whole sack of them. Letters for Richard from Devil, Vane and the Dowager, as well as a host of pithy billets from his aunts and female cousins, not amused by his distant wedding, and notes of commiseration from his uncles and ones of sympathy from his unmarried male cousins.

For Catriona came a long letter from Honoria, Devil's duchess, which Richard would have liked to read, but he was never offered the opportunity. After spending a full hour perusing the letter, Catriona folded it up and put it away. In her desk. In a locked drawer. Richard was tempted to pick the lock, but couldn't quite bring himself to do it. What could Honoria have said anyway?

As well as Honoria's letter, Catriona received scented notes from all the Cynster ladies welcoming her into the family. She did not, however, receive any communication from the Dowager, a fact she seemed not to notice, but which Richard noted with some concern.

The only reason Helena would not to write to Catriona was because she was planning on talking to her instead.

It was, he supposed, fair warning.

But fate and the season were on his side; the snows blew hard—the passes were blocked, the highways impassable.

He was safe until the thaw.

Then Christmas was upon them, and he had too much on his plate with the here and now—with absorbing traditions somewhat different from those he knew, with learning how the vale and all the manor celebrated yuletide—to worry about what the future held.

And over and above, through all the merriment and laughter, all the joys and small sorrows, there remained what he considered his principal duty—his principal focus. Learning everything he could about his witchy wife.

Having her in his arms every morning and every night, and in between learning all her strengths, her weaknesses, her foibles, her needs. Learning how he could best support her, as he had vowed to do. Learning how to fit into her life. And how she fitted into his.

It was, he discovered, an absorbing task.

A temporary easing in the weather between Christmas and the New Year saw three travellers appear at the manor's gate. They proved to be a father and his two adult sons, agents for various produce, come to see the lady of the vale.

Catriona received them as old acquaintances. Introduced, Richard smiled politely, then lounged in a chair set back against the office wall and watched how his witchy wife conducted the vale's business.

She was, he learned, no easy mark.

"My dear Mr. Potts, your offer simply will not do. If, as you say, the market is so well supplied, perhaps we should store all our grain for the next year." Catriona glanced at McArdle, sitting at the end of her desk. "Could we do that, do you think?"

"Oh, aye, m'lady." Like a benighted gnome, McArdle nodded sagely. "There's space in the cellars, and we're high and dry here, so there's no fear of it going damp."

"Perhaps that would be best." Catriona turned back to Mr. Potts. "If that's the best offer you can manage?"

"Ah. Well." Mr. Potts all but squirmed. "It's possible we *might*— considering the quality of the vale's grain, you understand—manage some concession on the price."

"Indeed?"

Fifteen minutes of haggling ensued, during which Potts made more than one concession.

"Done," Catriona finally declared. She smiled benignly on all three Pottses. "Perhaps you'd like a glass of our dandelion wine?"

"I don't mind if I do," Mr. Potts agreed. "Very partial to your dandelion wine."

Richard inwardly humphed and made a mental note to take a piece of chalk down to the cellars and inscribe all the remaining barrels of dandelion wine with an instruction that they were not to be broached without his express permission. Then he recalled that he really should gain his wife's approval for such an edict—which led to thoughts of taking her down to the cellars, which led to thoughts . . .

He frowned, and shifted in his seat. Accepting the wine one of the maids served, he directed his attention once more to the Pottses.

"Now, about those cattle you wanted." Potts the elder leaned forward. "I think I can get some young heifers from up Montrose way."

Catriona raised her brows. "None from any nearer? I don't like to have them transported so far."

"Aye, well. Cattle—good breeding stock—are in rare demand these days. Have to take what you can get."

Richard inwardly frowned. As he listened to the discussion—of sources of breeding stock, of prices, of the best breeds for the changing market—he shifted and inwardly frowned harder.

From all he'd heard, all he'd already noted, he knew more about livestock than his witch. Not that she lacked knowledge in general, or an understanding of the vale's present needs—it was more that she lacked experience of what was available in the wider world—a world she, for good reason, eschewed.

The temptation to speak—to butt in and take over—grew; Richard ruthlessly squelched it. If he so much as said a word, all three Pottses would turn to him. From the first, the younger ones had eyed him expectantly—from the looks on their faces now, they would be much more comfortable continuing their discussion of the performance characteristics of breeding stock with him. Man to man.

Richard cared nothing for their sensitivities—he cared much more about his witch, and hers.

He'd sworn not to take the lead, not to take her role, not to interfere with how she ran the vale. He couldn't speak publically, not without her invitation. He couldn't even bring the matter up privately—even there, she might construe it as indicating somewhat less than complete commitment to adhering to his vow.

A vow that, indeed, required complete commitment, required real and constant effort from him to keep it. It was not, after all, a vow a man like him could easily abide by. But he would abide by it—for her.

So he couldn't say anything—not unless she asked. Not unless she invited his comment or sought his views.

And so he sat there, mum, and listened, and itched to set her—and the Pottses—right. To explain that there were other options they ought to consider. Should consider.

But his witch didn't look his way—not once.

He had never felt the constraint of his vow more than he did that day.

The year turned; the weather continued bitter and bleak. Within the manor's stone walls, the lamps burned throughout the dull days, and the fires leapt in every hearth. It was a quiet time, a peaceful time. The men gathered in the dining hall, whiling away the hours with chess and backgammon. The women still had chores—cooking, cleaning, mending—but there was no sense of urgency.

Early in the new year, Catriona took advantage of the quiet and compiled an inventory of the curtains. Which resulted in a list of those she wanted mended or replaced. In search of a seamstress, she wandered into the maze of smaller rooms at the back of the ground floor, her attention focused on the list in her hand.

"Hee, hee, hee!"

The childish giggle stopped her; it was followed by a high-pitched trill of laughter. Curious, she turned from her path and followed the sound of continuing chortles. As she neared the source, she heard a deeper, intermittent rumble.

They were in the old games room. The manor children, of whom there were many, used it as their playroom, the place they spent most of the hard winter. Today, Catriona saw, as she paused in the shadows just outside the open door, that they had a visitor.

Then again, he might just be a hostage.

Trapped in the huge old armchair before the fire, Richard was surrounded by children. The two youngest had clambered onto his lap and cuddled close, one on either side, two others perched on his knees, while still others balanced on the wide arms of the chair. One was even sprawled across the chairback, almost draped over Richard's shoulders. The rest surrounded him, their faces upturned, alight as they hung on his words. His stories.

Folding her arms, Catriona leaned against the door frame and listened.

Listened to tales of boys running wild—a veritable tribe of them, it seemed. Listened to tales of youthful derringdo, of cheeky larks, of dangerous dragons vanquished, of genuine adventures that fate had sent to shape their lives.

The stories were of him and his cousins, she had not a doubt, although he never identified the heroes. The culprits. The demons in disguise.

Catriona wondered how many of his tales were true. She looked at him, so impressively large, his strength still apparent even relaxed as he was, and was tempted to think they all were. His stories were the adventures that had made him what he was.

For long moments, she stood still in the shadows, unremarked as she watched. Watched him, so large and strong, so deeply masculine, open the jewel box of his childhood memories and take them out, one by one, like delicate necklaces of bright gold and beaten silver, to awe, to entertain, to amuse the children.

They were enthralled—they were his. Just as their parents were. She'd noticed that from his first day here—his intrinsic ability to give of himself, and thus inspire devotion, loyalty—his ability to lead. She wasn't sure he recognized it in himself; it was simply an inherent part of him.

As she watched, one of the littlest two, thumb in mouth and almost asleep, started to tip. Without faltering in his recitation, without, apparently, even noticing what he did, Richard cradled the tot in one hand and resettled him more securely against his side.

Catriona stood in the shadows, her gaze on him, on them, her mind full of his stories, her heart full of him, for as long as she dared, then, misty-eyed, retreated without disturbing them.

"Well! I thought I might find you here."

Catriona looked up as Algaria entered the stillroom, and blinked at the expression of joyful confidence that lit her erstwhile mentor's face. "Are you all right?"

"Me?" Algaria smiled. "I'm very well. But I came to ask you the same question."

Catriona straightened. "I'm well, too."

Algaria eyed her straitly. Pointedly. When Catriona remained stubbornly silent, she elucidated: "I wanted to ask if that"—she gestured back into the house; Catriona narrowed her eyes—"*husband* of yours," Algaria sweetly amended, "has succeeded in getting you with child."

Catriona looked down at the herbs she was pounding. "I can't tell yet, can I?"

"Can't you?"

"Not for certain, no."

She did know, of course, but the sheer power of the feelings that surged through her whenever she thought of Richard's child—a tiny speck of life slowly growing within her—shook her so much she couldn't yet bring herself to speak of it. Not until she was absolutely, beyond any doubt or early mishap, sure. And then the first person she would speak to was Richard. Lips firming, she ground up her herbs. "I'll tell you when I am."

"Humph! Well, whatever, it seems as if The Lady's prophesy will, despite all, come to pass. As it always does. I have to admit I didn't think you could be right in deciding you should go to him as you did—it's so transparently obvious that he must never rule here. But The Lady has her ways." With a graceful, devotional gesture, Algaria moved to peer out of the high window. "It all looks like turning out much as you planned."

Grinding the pestle into the mortar, Catriona frowned. "What do you mean—as I'd planned?"

"Why, that he'll get you with child, then leave." Algaria turned from the window and met Catriona's puzzled gaze. "The only thing you didn't foresee correctly is that he'd marry you as well. Really, it's all worked out for the best. This way, you not only get the child, but the formal protection of being a married lady. And all without the bother of a husband—a resident one, anyway."

"But . . ." It took a full minute before Catriona fathomed Algaria's direction. When she did, the knowledge chilled her. "Why do you imagine he's leaving?"

Algaria smiled and patted her hand reassuringly. "You needn't think I have it wrong this time. His man has been with him for more than eight years and he's speaking very openly of their plans to return to London."

"He is?" Catriona gave thanks for the dim light in the stillroom—because of the fumes, only one small lamp was burning. Carefully resting the heavy pestle in the mortar, she gripped the edge of the table. And forced herself to ask: "What is he saying?"

"Oh, no specific details yet. Just that it's apparently their way to spend winter visiting the homes of friends and acquaintances, but that sometime in February, they always return to the capital. For the Season, I understand. Worboys has been regaling the staff with stories of the balls and parties, and all the other entertainments Mr. Cynster customarily enjoys. Without expressly *stating* it, he's given the clear impression that marriage has not changed his master's style. He's expecting they'll be in London before March."

"I see." Wiping her hands, suddenly cold, on her apron, Catriona picked up the pestle again. She kept her gaze on her preparation, avoiding Algaria's bright eyes. "I'm sure The Lady will ensure all goes as it should."

And arrangements that had not been expressly *stated* might not come to pass at all.

That night, Catriona sat before her dressing table brushing her long hair for far longer than was her wont. Long enough for Richard to come in and, after throwing her a lustful smile, start to undress.

Calmly, Catriona brushed and watched him in her mirror. "Your aunts, in their letters, spoke a lot of London. They seem to expect that we'll join them shortly—once the snows melt." Serenely brushing, she watched his brows rise. "For the balls, the parties—the Season."

He grimaced. And dropped his trousers. And stepped out of them.

Then he turned and, stark naked, prowled toward her.

"You don't need to imagine I'll insist that we go."

"You won't?"

"No."

He stopped behind her—all she could see was his bare chest, crisp black hair adorning the heavy muscles. He lifted her hair, spreading it, fanning it over her shoulders, over her breasts. "I'll never force you to leave the vale."

His features had assumed an intent expression she now knew well; reaching out, he took the brush from her hand and laid it on the table.

Her heart thudding in her throat, and throbbing in her loins, she abruptly stood. His hands closed about her waist and held her still; his eyes locked on hers in the mirror.

"Open your nightgown."

The nightgown she wore reached only to her knees; it was fastened down the front with tiny buttons. Barely able to breathe, incapable of taking her eyes from the vision before her, Catriona slowly obeyed.

One by one, the buttons slid free, all the way to her knees. She straightened, and the gown gaped. Revealing the ripe swells of her breasts, the smooth slope of her belly, the long lines of her thighs, the flaming curls between. She stared at the sight, then looked at his face.

And saw the hard planes shift, saw passion lock tight.

Hands tightening about her waist, he lifted her.

"Kneel on the stool."

She did; he straddled her calves. And drew the nightgown from her.

Catriona's eyes flew wide; she couldn't help her shocked gasp.

Immediately he held her, his chest warm against her shoulders and back, his thighs hard, abrasive, against the sensitive skin of her bottom. "Sssh." Head bent, he nuzzled her ear, one dark hand splayed across her midriff, a powerful contrast against her ivory skin.

Shocked to her toes, Catriona felt her senses reel. They were bathed in light—as well as the two candlesticks burning on the dressing table, two candlestands stood on either side, both holding large candles, both lit. She could see the width of his shoulders, clearly visible above and beyond her own, could see the dark, hair-dusted columns of his legs on either side of hers.

Could feel the thick, ridged rod, so flagrantly male, pressed against the cleft between her buttocks.

And felt—and saw—his other hand slide from her hip, under the shimmering veil of her hair, to close firmly about one breast, long fingers curling about her soft flesh.

She moaned softly and let her head fall back against his shoulder. From beneath heavy lids, she watched his fingers flex. Swallowing, she moistened her lips, saw them already parted, already sheening. "The bed?"

"No." He breathed the word against the soft skin of her throat—he was watching his hand on her. "Here."

She shuddered, one small part of her mind desperate to protest, the rest awash with tingling anticipation. Anticipation that steadily built, then silvered into excitement. Into arousal that escalated with each slow sweep of his hands over her flickering skin, with each knowing caress, each expert touch.

He did nothing else but caress her bare body, worshipped it until her skin was flushed rose in the golden candle-glow, and she was quivering with need.

"Lean forward." His voice was a deep, gravelly whisper in her ear. "Place your hands palms down on the table."

She did; he shifted behind her. From under weighted lids, she saw him steady her before him, then reach around her. Splaying one hand across her stomach, he angled her hips back; looking down, he fitted himself to her.

Then, with one slow thrust that threatened to lift her from her knees, he filled her. Stretched her. Completed her.

Fully embedded within her, he leaned forward; his lips brushing her nape, he filled his hands with her breasts. And fondled her swollen flesh as he rocked her. Rocked her slowly, languorously, to heaven.

Until she panted, and moaned, and tried to wriggle her hips—tried to urge him on. His slow rhythm was driving her insane—she wanted him deep, wanted him filling her more forcefully. More rapidly.

She wanted to rush on to the stars.

He straightened; his hands drifted from her breasts to lock about her hips. He anchored her before him, so she couldn't move—and pressed more deeply into her. But he still kept the rhythm slow—slower than she wanted.

So she could feel every inch of his repeated penetrations, was aware to her fingertips of the reined strength of his invasions. Was intimately conscious of the hard, hot rod with which he claimed her, of the slick softness with which she accepted him.

She shuddered and closed her eyes and clamped tightly about him. And sensed his chest swell, sensed his tension tighten. Felt his grip about her hips lock like iron and felt the brush of his thumb over her birthmark. It would be clearly visible in the light, contrasting against the ivory of her buttock, so taut, so tight.

Compulsion forced her to look, to crack open her lids and look at him behind her, his hard body flexing as he loved her. Forced her to study his face, to see the concentration and passion and sheer devotion etched therein, delineating the hard angles gilded by the candles' glow. Forced her to notice her own body, lushly wanton, her skin flushed, her hair wild fire spread over her shoulders and arms, her breasts swollen and tipped with deep rose, her thighs clamped together, her hips rocking only slightly as he filled her. Forced her, at the last, to look at her face, at the expression of sensual abandon stamped on her features, her heavy-lidded eyes, her panting, parted lips.

With a soft moan, she closed her eyes tightly and felt him lift the tempo, felt him start the long crescendo that would carry her to the stars.

And when she reached them, he held her there for long, immeasurable minutes, caught on the cusp of delight—then he joined her, and her heaven was complete.

A week later, Catriona pulled on her heavy cloak, picked up a basket lined with scraps of flannel, and headed out to the large barn. It was three o'clock; the light would soon fade. As she trudged across the yard whipped by lightly flurrying snow, the sun, hidden behind banks of grey cloud, cast the scene in a smoky, pale gold haze.

Struggling against the flurries, she hauled open the single door set in the barn's main doors, then slipped inside. Setting her basket down, she latched the door, then turned, paused to let her eyes adjust to the dimness, then scooped up her basket and headed for the loft ladder.

To find the kitchen cat, who, entirely out of synchrony with the seasons, had given birth somewhere up in the hay.

Gaining the top of the ladder, Catriona swung her basket up, then surveyed the scene—the expanse of hay bales stacked almost to the roof all the way along the loft which stretched down one side of the long barn.

She knew the cat and kittens were in the hay somewhere. She didn't know how she knew—she just did. She also knew that the kittens would die by morning if she didn't find them and take them into the warm kitchen.

With a sigh, she clambered up onto the hay-strewn loft boards and started to search.

The loft extended over the entire barn, over the three separate sections the large building housed. Mentally tossing a coin, she elected to start searching the section nearest, the one over the carriages, carts and ploughs.

Methodically pushing through hay stacks, pressing apart bales, sliding her hand, oh-so-trustingly, into possible dens, she tried to keep her mind on her search and away from its principal preoccupation.

As usual, she failed.

Her husband exerted an almost hypnotic attraction over her thoughts. Over her senses, he wielded absolute control—that, she accepted. But the degree to which she found herself dwelling on him—on his plans—on what his intentions really were—was disconcerting. She'd never before been that linked to anyone, never before felt her happiness dependent on someone else.

She'd been her own mistress for years—being his was changing her in ways she hadn't expected.

In ways she didn't entirely like—in ways she couldn't control.

In moments of weakness, like the present, as she absentmindedly crooned for the cat, when her mind was caught, trapped, in senseless speculation, raising visions that were unnervingly depressing, she'd fallen back on her old habit of lecturing herself. Telling herself, sternly, that what would be, would be.

It only made her feel more helpless, more in the grip of some force beyond her control, as if her life was now tuned to some unknown piper.

Reaching the end of the first section without any sign of the cat, she straightened, pressed out the kinks in her spine, then trailed back to the ladder to fetch her basket. And doggedly glided into the next section—the one over the quartered dairy herd.

She was halfway through that section when she heard voices. Rocking back on her heels, she listened—and heard them again, low, almost murmuring. Curious, she rose and quietly walked into the last section of the loft.

In the back of her mind ran the thought that she might stumble on some illicit assignation—such was her interpretation of the tone of those murmurs. Ready to retreat silently if that proved the case, she inched closer to the loft's edge.

And heard Richard say: "Gently. Easy, sweetheart. Now—let's take it very slowly."

An assenting murmur in a light female tone answered him.

Catriona froze. She turned cold, then burned as temper seared her. What she felt in that instant was beyond her description—but betrayal was there, certainly, as was a furious force she'd never before felt—every bit as green as her eyes. It was that force that fanned the flames of anger into a righteous blaze. Fists clenched, quivering with rage, she marched to the top of the ladder leading down into the last section of the barn.

They heard her footsteps—and looked up.

For one fractured instant, Catriona stared down at her husband and the maid within his arms.

The eight-year-old maid he held balanced on the back of a shaggy coated pony.

Catriona's eyes widened from their angry slits; even while she mentally scrambled to keep her features unrevealing, her lips formed a telltale "Oh." Relief swept her; she teetered and had to take a quick step back from the loft's edge.

Richard's gaze, locked on her face, intensified. He straightened, fluidly swinging the girl down. Only then did Catriona notice the others surrounding the improvised ring, all waiting, obediently silent, for their turn.

"I, ah ..." Weakly, she gestured to the hay-filled loft behind her. "The cat's had kittens."

"Tabitha?" One of the boys broke from the circle and raced to the ladder. "Where?"

"Well, ..." Flustered, Catriona stepped back as the whole riding school swarmed up the ladder. "That's the problem, you see."

The pupils were followed by their teacher who, as was his wont, made the loft shrink as he stepped onto the boards. Catriona backed against the wall of hay and waved down the loft. "She's somewhere up here. We have to find her and take the kittens into the kitchen to keep warm, or they'll die."

The children didn't wait for more. They enthusiastically clambered over the hay, calling the cat, a favorite of theirs.

Leaving her with their teacher. Catriona flicked him a quick glance. "I've searched the first section."

Head tilted, he studied her. "They'll find her." A ferocious sneeze was echoed by two more. He raised his brows. "That, or die trying." He continued to study her; after a moment, he asked: "Have you been up here long?"

Catriona shrugged as nonchalantly as she could and avoided his gaze. "A few minutes." She waved along the loft. "I was at the other end."

"Ah." Straightening, he strolled toward her. He stopped by her side, then, without warning, gathered her into his arms. And kissed her. Very warmly.

Emerging, breathless, some moments later, Catriona blinked at him. "What was that for?"

"Reassurance." He'd lifted his head only to change his hold; as he lowered his lips to hers again, she tried to hold him back.

"The children," she hissed.

"Are busy," he replied—and kissed her again.

"Tabby! Tabby!"

The shrill call had all the children running to one corner of the middle section. None looked back; none saw their lady, flustered and flushed, win free of her consort's arms. And none saw the knowing smile that lifted his lips.

Catriona tried not to notice it either; blotting the sight from her mind, she hurried after the children.

They found five tiny kittens, pathetically shivering, huddling close to their weakened mother's flank. There were ready hands enough to lift the whole family together into the lined basket, which was then carried in procession along the loft, taken down the ladder by Richard as his contribution to the rescue, then entrusted to the care of the eight-year-old maid. Surrounded by her absorbed fellows, she crossed the yard carefully, all the children huddling to protect the cat and her brood from the swirling snow.

The light had all but gone. Catriona stepped out of the barn into a twilight world. Richard pulled the door shut and fastened it, then tugged her cloak around her and anchored her against him, within one arm.

They followed in the children's wake.

"I hope the kittens will recover—they felt very cold. I suppose a little warm milk wouldn't hurt them. I'll have to ask Cook ..."

She blathered on, not once looking up—not once meeting his eyes. Richard held her fast against the wind's tug and, smiling into the swirling snow, steered her toward the kitchen.

He didn't know what woke him—certainly not her footfalls, for she was as silent as a ghost. Perhaps it was the bone-deep knowledge that she was not there, in their bed beside him, where she was supposed to be.

Warm beneath the covers, his limbs heavy with satiation, he lifted his head and saw her, arms crossed tightly over her robe, pacing before the hearth.

The fire had died, leaving only embers to shed their glow upon the room; about them, the house lay silent, asleep.

She was frowning. He watched her pace and gnaw her lower lip, something he'd never seen her do.

"What's the matter?"

She halted; her eyes, widening, flew to his face.

And in that instant, that infinitesimal pause before she replied, he knew she wouldn't tell him.

"I'm sorry. I didn't mean to wake you." She hesitated. When he remained propped on one elbow, watching her, she drifted back to the bed. "Go back to sleep."

He waited until she halted by the side of the bed. "I can't—not with you pacing." Not with her worrying. He could sense it strongly, now; some deep concern that was ruffling her normally unruffleable serenity. "What is it?"

Catriona sighed and shrugged out of her robe. "It's nothing." It was the breeding stock, or lack thereof. But ...

She shouldn't involve him.

When she'd heard his voice, heard him ask, her instinctive impulse had been to tell him, to lay her growing problem on shoulders broader than hers—to share her burden with him. But ... in the back of her mind lurked an unwelcome notion that appealing to him was not the right thing to do. On a number of counts.

Asking him, inviting him to become more deeply involved with running the vale, might not, in the long run, be fair, either to him, or to her. There was a subtle line between offering advice and sage counsel, and making the decisions, determining the final outcome. She had always been taught that strong men, powerful men, had difficulty with that distinction.

Forcing him to face it might not be wise.

And, even if he hadn't said so yet, if he was considering leaving her and journeying to London for the Season, she would be wise to keep her own counsel. Wise to hold him at a distance, in that arena at least. She couldn't afford to start to rely on him only to find him bidding her adieu.

It hadn't escaped her that while he'd promised repeatedly not to force her to leave the vale, he'd never promised to stay. To remain by her side, to face the problems of the vale by her side.

Much as she might now feel a need for a strong shoulder to lean on, a strong arm to rely on, she couldn't afford to let herself develop that sort of vulnerability. Ultimately the vale was her responsibility.

So she summoned a smile and hoped it was reassuring. "It's just a minor vale problem." Dropping her robe, she slid under the covers. He hesitated, then drew her into his arms, settling her against him.

Snuggling her head on his chest, she forced herself to relax against him—forced herself to let her problems lie.

Until she could deal with them alone.

She was being silly. Overly sensitive.

The next morning, pacing before her office window, Catriona berated herself sternly. She still didn't know what she could, or should, do about the breeding stock—it was time she asked Richard for advice.

When viewed in the sane light of morning, the concerns that had prevented her from asking last night no longer seemed sufficient to stop her, excuse her, from taking the sensible course. Such silly sensitivity was unlike her.

She needed help—and she was reasonably sure he could give it. She recalled quite clearly how, at McEnery House, she'd been impressed with his knowledge of farming practices and estate management. It was senseless, in her time of need, not to avail herself of his expertise.

Frowning at the floor, she swung about and paced on.

He'd said nothing about leaving. It therefore behooved her to have faith, rather than credit him with making plans—plans he hadn't discussed with her. There was no reason at all for her to imagine he was leaving; she should assume that he was staying, that he would remain to support her as her consort, and not hie off to enjoy himself—alone—in London. He'd always behaved with consideration—she should recognize that fact.

And if asking him for advice, inviting him to take a more direct interest in the running of the vale, served to bind him to it—and to her—so be it.

Straightening, she drew in a deep breath, drew herself up that last inch, then glided to the door.

He was in the library; from her office, she took a minor corridor, rather than go around through the front hall. The corridor led to a secondary door set into the wall beside the library fireplace.

She reached it, confidence growing with every step, her heart lifting at the thought of asking him what she'd shied away from asking last night, of inviting him that next step deeper into her life. Grasping the doorknob, she turned it—as the door opened noiselessly, she heard voices.

Halting, the door open only a crack, she hesitated, then recognized Richard's deep "humph."

"I imagine I'll start packing in a few days, sir. I don't like to rush things and it is very close to the end of January."

A pause ensued, then Worboys spoke again. "According to Henderson, and Huggins, the thaw should set in any day now. I daresay it may take a week to clear the roads sufficiently, but, of course, the farther south we travel, the more the highways will improve."

"Hmm."

Frozen outside the door, her heart chilling, sinking, Catriona listened as Worboys continued: "The rooms in Jermyn Street will need freshening, of course. I wondered ... perhaps you're thinking of looking in on the Dowager and the duke and duchess? If that were so, I could continue on to town and open up the rooms, ready for your return."

"Hmm."

"You'll want to be well settled before the Richmonds' ball, naturally. If I might suggest ... a few new coats might be in order. And your boots, of course—we'll need to make sure Hoby remembers not to attach those tassles. As for linen ..."

Deep in a letter from Heathcote Montague, Richard let Worboys's monologue drift past him. After eight years, Worboys knew perfectly well when he wasn't attending to him—and *he* knew perfectly well when his henchman was in a quandary.

In Worboys's case, the quandary was simple. He liked it here—and couldn't believe it. He was presently dusting the books on the shelves—in itself a most revealing act—and putting on a good show, trying to convince them both that they were shortly to up stakes and depart, when, in reality, he knew Richard had no such thoughts, and he, himself, did not want to go.

In what he viewed as a primitive backwater, Worboys had discovered heaven.

Not an inamorata in his case, but a household where he fitted in perfectly, like a missing link in a chain. The manor's household was unusual, without the lines of precedence Worboys had lived with all his professional life. Instead, it was a place that operated on friendship—a sort of kinship in serving their lady. It was a household where people had to rely on each other—have faith and confidence in each other—just to get through the yearly round of harsh weather and the short growing season, made even more difficult by their isolation.

It was a place where people felt valued for themselves; the household, in its rustic innocence, had welcomed Worboys to its bosom—and Worboys had fallen in love.

He was presently in deep denial—Richard recognized the signs. So he let Worboys ramble—he was really only talking to himself and convincing no one. Whenever Worboys paused and insisted on some response, he humphed or hmm'd and let it go at that. He saw no benefit in getting drawn into a discussion of things that were not going to happen.

His letter was far more interesting. Spurred by the Pottses' visit, he'd written to Montague, inquiring as to the current state of breeding stock, both in the southern and northern counties. He'd also asked Montague to locate the most highly regarded breeder in the Ridings, just south of the border, not too far from the vale.

"So, sir." Pausing, Worboys drew in a deep breath. "If you just let me know when you've decided on the date, I'll proceed as we've discussed."

Looking up, Richard met Worboys's gaze. "Indeed. When I decide to leave, you'll be the first to know."

Inclining his head gravely, doubtless feeling much better after having got all his useless plans off his chest, Worboys picked up his duster and a pot of wilting flowers, and headed for the door.

Richard waited until it closed before letting his lips curve. Returning to his letter, he read to its end, then, smiling even more, laid it down, and stretched.

And noticed a draft. He glanced around and saw a door, so well fitted in the paneling he hadn't noticed it before, left ajar. Rising, he rounded the desk and crossed to the panel. Opening it farther, he found a dim secondary corridor. Empty. Inwardly shrugging, Richard closed the door—it could have been ajar for a week for all he knew.

Recrossing to the desk, he sat and pulled out a map of the surrounding counties. A Mister Owen Scroggs, cattle breeder extraordinaire, lived at Hexham. How far, Richard wondered, was Hexham from the vale?

If—*when*—his wife finally trusted him enough to ask for his assistance, his support, he wanted to have all the answers. All the right answers, at his fingertips.

CHAPTER
Thirteen

৪৩৺৪

He wasn't, in fact, a patient man.

Ever since receiving the information from Montague, he'd been watching for—waiting for—an opportunity to discuss the matter with his wife. To banish the shadows that seemed to grow, day by day, in her eyes.

Instead, four days later, he'd yet to discover a suitable moment to speak to her. Lounging in an archway not far from her office door, Richard, brooding darkly, kept his gaze on the oak panel and waited some more.

He had a bone-deep aversion to discussing business in their bed. There she remained her usual self, warmly wanton, sweetly taking him in and holding him tight, still insisting on trying to muffle her pleasured screams—he was conscious of a deep reluctance to do anything that might alter the openness that had grown between them there.

But her days were busy; she seemed constantly involved in meetings, or discussions, or in overseeing the household. And if she wasn't actually engaged in the above, she was surrounded by others—by McArdle, Mrs. Broom, or, worse still, Algaria. Even in the odd moments when he would come upon her alone, she was always rushing to be somewhere else.

Worse yet, he was starting to become seriously worried about her health. He was too well attuned to her not to sense the tension, the fragility, she hid beneath her cloak of serenity. He couldn't help but wonder if her pregnancy, which she'd yet to mention to him, was the cause of it—the sudden breathlessness that came upon her, and an emotional brittleness she tried hard to hide.

Those symptoms weren't there when she slid into his arms every night. He couldn't help wonder if, during the days, she was working herself too hard, rather than letting him ease the load so she could take better care of herself— and their child.

The office door opened; McArdle stumped out.

Richard straightened; he waited until McArdle disappeared down the corridor, then swiftly strolled to the office door. He hesitated for a moment, reminding himself that he couldn't demand, then opened the door—and strolled languidly in.

Seated behind her desk, Catriona looked up—Richard smiled easily, charmingly. And tried not to notice the clouds dimming her green eyes. "Are you busy?"

Catriona drew in a deep breath and looked down at the papers before her. "I am, actually. Henderson and Huggins—"

"I won't keep you above a moment."

The words were drawled, nonchalant—unthreatening. Acutely conscious of him, Catriona forced herself to sit back in her chair and wait while he strolled, all idle elegance, to the window.

"Actually, I wondered if I might help you out, as you seem so rushed these days."

Drawing a slow, steadying breath, Catriona turned her head and met his gaze. Swiftly—with a hope she could only just bear to acknowledge—she studied his face. It was an indolent mask of polite indifference; there was no hint of real commitment, real passion—of really wanting to help. No hint that the vale—and she—were seriously important to him.

He smiled, charming as ever, although she noticed the gesture didn't reach his eyes. A languid wave underscored his words: "There's nothing much for me to do here, so I've plenty of time free."

Catriona fought to keep her expression blank, and succeeded. He was bored and could see she was busy, so he'd done the gentlemanly thing and offered to help. She had no trouble shaking her head brusquely and looking back at her letters. "There's really no need. I'm quite capable of handling the vale's business on my own."

The words, uttered in a hard tone, were as much to convince herself of that fact as to decline his *gentlemanly* offer.

He hesitated, then said, a trace of steel in his tones: "As you wish." With a graceful inclination of his head, he strolled out and left her to it.

The thaw arrived.

Two mornings later, Richard lay late in bed, listening to the steady drip of water from the eaves. Catriona had slipped from his arms early, whispering about a confinement, assuring him that she wasn't going out but that the mother-to-be was safe inside the manor.

Staring up at the dark red canopy, Richard tried to keep his thoughts from her, from the leaden feeling that, two days ago, had settled in his gut.

And failed.

Inwardly grimacing, he irritably reminded himself that failure was not something Cynsters indulged in—much less on the scale he was presently wallowing in.

He was failing on all fronts.

The new life he'd envisaged for himself at Catriona's side, once so full of promise and possibilities, had turned into a disappointment. A deep, deadening disappointment—he'd never felt so disillusioned with life as he felt now.

There was nothing for him here—nothing for him to do, nothing for him to be. Boredom now haunted him; his old restlessness—something he'd hoped he'd lost for all time in the kirk at Keltyburn—was growing.

Along with a dark, compelling sense of worthlessness—at least, in this place. In this vale—her vale.

He couldn't understand her.

From night to cockcrow, they were as close as a man and woman could be, but when morning came and she slipped from his arms, it was as if, along with her clothes, she donned some invisible mantle and became "the lady of the vale"—a woman with a calling, a position and a purpose in life, from all of which he was excluded.

While gentlemen of his station did not customarily share their wives' lives, he, very definitely, had expected to share hers. Still wanted to share hers. The prospect of sharing her responsibilities, of sharing it all as a mutual endeavor, and thus having a strong and abiding connection on a daily basis—that was certainly a large part of the attraction he felt for her. She was, he had thought, a woman he could share goals with, share achievements with.

Their marriage hadn't, so far, turned out that way.

He'd been careful of her, careful of pressuring her—he'd given her every chance to ask him for help, for assistance. He'd tried hard not to force her hand—and got nowhere.

For long moments, his gaze locked on the dark red above him, he considered the obvious alternative—the action his Cynster self strongly urged. He could, very easily, take over the reins and steer their marriage into the paths he wanted it to follow. He was not a naturally passive person; he wouldn't normally endure a situation he didn't like. Normally, he'd simply change it.

But . . .

He could forsee two difficulties. The first was that, in taking the reins, he would risk damaging the very thing he most wanted to preserve. He wanted Catriona as a willing life-partner, not as one resenting his dominance.

That, however, while quite bad enough, ranked as the more minor of his difficulties.

The larger, most insurmountable problem, was his vow. The vow he'd made to her—twice—that he would not impinge on her independence, would never seek to override her authority. She'd taken him on trust—she trusted him to keep that vow no matter what. To wrest control from her would betray that trust, in the most damning and damaging way.

There were few things he was sure of in this marriage of theirs, but he knew to his soul that he could never endure the look in her green eyes if he ever betrayed her on that front.

Which meant . . .

He was on a narrow track, high up a mountainside, with unbroken rock to one side and a sheer precipice on the other. He could go forward, or retreat.

Heaving a deep sigh, Richard threw back the covers and got up.

* * *

Cynsters *never* retreated.

The concept was totally alien to him—the very thought offended him at some deep level. So he waited, and trapped her once more in her office, at a time when he knew he could wrest at least two minutes from her busy schedule.

After ambling idly in and exchanging a mild comment about the weather, he looked down at her and asked: "Tell me, my dear, do you have any need of me here?"

He wanted to ask the question brutally—wanted to show her how much she was hurting him by shutting him out of her life, by denying him the chance to give what he felt he could—but he couldn't do it, couldn't let her see how pathetically vulnerable he'd become. So he kept his social mask intact and asked the question lightly, coolly. As if the answer was of no great moment.

Which was how Catriona heard it—that and rather more. To her, it rang as the prelude to his informing her that he was leaving—the polite patter of the executioner before the axe fell.

So she held her own calm like a shield over her weeping heart and smiled, a little weakly, back up at him. "No. There's really nothing for you to do."

Looking down, she forced herself to go on, forced herself to play the role she'd spent hours rehearsing—the role of acquiescent wife. "I daresay you'll be heading to London soon—Huggins heard this morning that the roads to the south are all open, at least as far as Carlisle."

Her head throbbed, her stomach churned, but she continued in the same, lightly distant, tone: "You'll be anxious to see your family, I expect. Your stepmother must be waiting ..." She nearly choked, but swallowed just in time. "And, of course, there'll be the balls and parties."

She continued to enter the figures she'd been transferring from scraps of paper into a ledger—and didn't look up. She didn't dare—if she did, the tears she was holding back would spill over, and then he would know.

Know what he mustn't. Know that she didn't want him to go—that she wanted him here, forever by her side.

But she'd thought it all through very carefully; she had to—absolutely had to—leave him free to leave her. There was no point in binding him to her—to the vale—with ties that would only be resented.

If she could have, she would have stopped herself from falling in love with him, from being in love with him, but it was far too late for that. Even knowing he was leaving, she still couldn't help but wish that she had been the one to change him—the one to focus all his inherent, unconscious qualities—his innate care, his protectiveness, his absentminded kindness—so he became the man he could be.

Her consort.

The Lady had been right—he was made for the position—the real position—but no one could force him to take it. That was a decision he had to make himself, and she couldn't interfere. She had to let him go.

And hope, and pray, that one day he might want what she could give him.

"It must be quite grand," she said, determined to make it easy for him, and easier, therefore, for her, "being in London with all the swells, going to all the balls and parties."

She felt his gaze leave her; a moment of silence ensued. Then he shifted. "Indeed."

She looked up, but he merely inclined his head, his lips lightly curving, and didn't meet her eyes. "I daresay I'll enjoy the balls and parties."

He turned from her and strolled, languid as ever, from the room. Catriona stared at his back, then stared at the door when he closed it behind him. And wondered at his tone, wondered whether her own sensitivity had made her imagine a deep bleakness behind his words.

He'd tried a last throw of the dice—and lost. More than he'd known he had bet.

She had told him there was nothing for him here—and he had to accept her decision. And if he'd needed any urging to leave the field of his defeat, her lightly distant tone as she'd dismissed him and all but wished him on his way had provided it.

Richard didn't know how they had come to this—to this brittle state where it took effort to remain in each other's company. He didn't know—he couldn't imagine—he couldn't even think straight. He couldn't even breathe freely; there was an iron vise locked about his lower chest—every breath was a battle.

How they would get through the night, he hadn't any idea. For the first time since they had married, she was later to bed than he. He waited in the dimness, lit only by the dying fire, and wondered if she really was tending the recently born child and its mother or ... avoiding him.

It was nearly midnight before the door opened; she glanced at the bed only fleetingly, then went to the fire. Richard nearly spoke—nearly called to her—but couldn't think of what to say.

Then he realized she didn't intend sleeping in the armchair; she was simply undressing before the fire.

He watched her—hungrily. Let his eyes feast on her neatly rounded limbs, her skin pearlescent in the fire's flickering light. Drank in the sight of her back, the sleek planes achingly familiar, the globes of her bottom a remembered delight. He stared at her long fire-gold mane as she shook it out, spreading it over her shoulders, as if he could burn the sight into his mind.

Then lost what little breath he had when she turned and, naked—with that glorious unconsciousness she'd displayed from the first—walked to the bed. To where he lay waiting in the dark.

He tensed—expecting her to be tense, too—expecting her to hold herself distantly as she had all day. Instead, she lifted the covers, slid beneath—and slid farther, straight into his arms.

For one moment, his heart stood still, then his arms closed about her. She lifted her lips—he hesitated for only a second before he took them.

Took her—took her mouth as she offered it, took her body as she freely gave it.

If he could have thought, he might have seized the opportunity to ruthlessly, calculatingly, tie her to him with passion—to make her burn so achingly long, so excruciatingly hot, that she would never be able to bid him adieu. Or if she did, would suffer tortures every night without him.

He didn't think—but yet he did. Loved her with such passion, such distilled, poignant force, that she cried. Cried tears of sheer delight, of bliss too great to contain.

All he wanted was to fill his mind, his senses, his heart and soul with her— so inside, she would always be with him.

As he, wherever he was, would, in his mind, always—ever more—be with her.

Beneath him, Catriona clung to him, opened her body and heart to him, knowing full well this might be the last time. If she could have held him with sheer lust she would have—she burned with her need of him and was too desperate to hide it. Desire, unleashed, gave her strength—strength to challenge him on a field that had hitherto been his. Stroked and caressed and loved to flashpoint, still she urged him on—pushed him back and pressed her own wild caresses on him, placed hot, open-mouthed kisses all over his hard body, then, driven by her wildness, took him into her mouth.

And felt the shudder that racked him, the bone deep groan she drew from him.

She loved him with abandon, with her heart, with her soul. Until he, his hands sunk in her hair, helplessly guiding her, suddenly clutched and drew her away. Suddenly sat up, suddenly swung behind her.

And entered her from behind.

Her gasp hung like spun silver in the dark; she arched, clamping tightly about him—he pushed her down, and thrust deeper.

Ultimately, he was stronger—much stronger—than she.

He held her down and raced her straight up the mountain and into earth-shattering delight. Then waited only until her senses were hers again before pressing her on, up the next slope.

Through the dark hours he loved her as he would, and she was his willing slave. She wanted to be everything to him, so she gave all he asked, and offered more.

And he took. He drank from her until she thought she would die, then filled her relentlessly until she did. Until her senses were consumed in a blaze of glory, and she shattered beneath him.

They came together again and again, until there was nothing between them. No space, no feeling, no sense of separate existence. They became, in the dead of that night, one soul melded from the fusion of two.

The final end, when it came, shattered them both, but not even the force of that implosion could undo what the night had wrought.

Richard's return to life—to reality—was a slow, bitter journey.

He couldn't conceive how she could be as she was—so totally abandoned in his arms, yet quite prepared, come the time, to smile sweetly and wave him good-bye.

Lips twisting in bitter self-deprecation, he accepted that he had to have been wrong—that despite his expertise in this theatre, she was an exception. A woman who could love with her heart and soul, without, in fact, loving at all.

He was, it seemed, just like Thunderer—a stud whose physical attributes she appreciated.

She was wrapped half-about him, lying in his arms; he lifted his head and looked at her face, only barely discernible in the dark. She was still on her way back from heaven—he could tell by the lack of tension in her limbs. Lying back again, he waited for her to return to the living. And him.

When she did, however, she simply murmured sleepily and snuggled down, her head on his shoulder, her arm over his chest, one thigh intimately wedged between his.

Richard frowned. "I'll be leaving in the morning."

Catriona heard the words—words she'd been expecting—and felt them in her heart. She'd already heard from her staff of the packing and carriage arrangements. She hesitated for as long as she dared, while frantically wondering what he expected her to say. "I know," she eventually murmured.

The hard body beneath her stiffened fractionally, then, after a second, eased. His chest swelled.

"Well," he said, his tone light but grating, "I suppose there really isn't anything more you need from me, now—at least, not for some time."

He paused; when, bewildered, she said nothing, he continued: "Now you have the child The Lady told you to get from me."

His bitterness rang clearly; bowing her head, biting her lower lip, Catriona accepted it.

She should have told him.

"I ..." How to tell him it had slipped her mind? "Forgot." She rushed on. "It's just that I've been so ..."

"Busy?"

So caught up with *him*. Her temper flashed—a weak flame, but enough to sour her. She'd been so focused on him, she'd totally forgotten the one thing, the one being, that should have been at the center of her consciousness. If she'd needed any proof of how totally obsessed with him she was, how he completely overshadowed everything else in her life, she had it now.

She couldn't think of any response to his rejoinder, so she let it pass. Slowly, she drew her limbs from his and turned away.

Only to be swept by a desolate bleakness, a bone-deep sense of loss. They'd been cheated. A moment that should have been so special, so joyful and filled with love, had instead been soured by hurt and bitterness.

She closed her eyes and tried to sleep; beside her, Richard did the same.

Disillusionment followed them into troubled dreams.

The next day dawned clear, with a brisk breeze scudding clouds over a pale blue sky—a morning bright with the promise of a new season. Perfect for traveling.

Catriona noted the signs from the top of the manor steps and struggled to reconcile them with the heaviness in her heart.

She would normally have gone to pray this morning, but had changed her mind. It was the first time in her life she'd put something else higher than her devotions to The Lady, but she couldn't deny herself her last sight of Richard. It would have to tide her over, probably for months. Possibly until their child was born. And maybe even longer.

Before her, her people scurried to secure the last of Richard's trunks to the carriage roof—he'd left some things behind, for which she was more pathetically grateful than she would ever let anyone know. They would be her only physical link with him in the coming months.

Blinking back the prickling heat behind her lids, she watched the horses—Richard's handsome greys—led up. Her people, unaware of any undercurrents—not, indeed, the sort of folk who were at all susceptible to such subtleties—threw themselves into the final preparations with innocent energy. They simply imagined this was how it was supposed to be; their trust in The Lady—and in her—was complete. The only member of staff who seemed at all put out was, of all people, Worboys. Catriona studied his long face, and wondered, but could reach no conclusion.

Then Richard appeared from the direction of the stables, where he'd gone to bid Thunderer good-bye. He strode across the cobbles, his greatcoat flapping about his gleaming Hessians. He was immaculately dressed as always; as he paused to give orders to the grooms harnessing his greys, Catriona drank in the sight.

Drank in the faintly bored, distant expression on his face, the easy air of ineffable superiority that was so innate a part of him.

He turned and saw her, hesitated, then strode toward her; Catriona looked her fill. To her, he was, quite simply, gorgeous—the most fascinating man she'd ever met.

He was also the eptiome of a bored and restless rake shaking the dust of a too-quiet backwater and an unwanted wife from his highly polished boots. That fact was declared in the hard planes of his face as his eyes met hers, in the cynical set of his lips. Bravely, desperately, holding her cloak of regal assurance in place, Catriona smiled distantly.

"I'll bid you adieu, then. I hope you reach London without mishap."

She lifted her head and met his hard blue gaze directly; that had been the most difficult speech she'd ever made.

Richard studied her eyes, searched them, for some sign all this was a dream. It felt unreal to him—couldn't she sense it? But even more strong than the sense of unreality was the feeling—the compulsion—of inevitability.

It had seemed inevitable they would marry—he'd accepted that and hoped, in his heart, that from their marriage he would gain the stability he'd sought—he'd needed—for so long. Instead, now, it seemed inevitable he would be disappointed in their union, and would, once again, be footless, unanchored, drifting in life's stream. Unconnected to anyone.

He'd thought—hoped—that their marriage would be his salvation. It appeared he'd been wrong; it was therefore inevitable that he would leave.

Would walk away from his wife and leave her to manage on her own.

Uncharacteristic rancor filled him when her eyes gave him no hope, no sign, no encouragement to change his mind and stay. "I'll leave you then."

The words echoed with the bitterness he couldn't hide.

She smiled and held out her hand. "Farewell."

He looked down, into her eyes, trying to fathom, at the last, what shimmered in the vibrant green depths; he took her hand—and felt her fingers slide into his. Felt the touch of her palm, felt her fingertips quiver. And felt—sensed—

"Here you are, sir!"

They both turned to find Mrs. Broom standing beaming just behind them, virtually between them. She held up a packed basket. "Cook and me thought as how you'd be grateful of some real sustenance on the road. Better'n that terrible inn food."

Richard knew for a fact that neither Mrs. Broom nor Cook had ever been to an inn in their lives. It was a measure of how his mind was functioning that that was the only thought he could muster. He felt shaken—and torn—and turned inside out. Taking the basket from Mrs. Broom and summoning a weak smile for her from somewhere, he passed the basket straight to a groom and looked back at Catriona.

Only to see her smile evenly. "Good-bye."

For one instant, he hovered on the brink—of refusing to accept her dismissal, of hauling her into his arms and refusing to let her go, of telling her straitly how things would henceforth be between them—

Her steady smile, her steady eyes—and the black cloud of inevitability—stopped him.

Faultlessly correct, he inclined his head, then turned and strolled nonchalantly down the steps.

Catriona watched him go and felt her heart go with him. Knew to the depths of her soul that she would never be the same—be as strong—without him. He paused to speak to his coachman, then entered the carriage without a backward glance. He sat back and Worboys shut the door; the carriage lurched into motion and headed, gathering speed as it went, down the drive and into the park.

Raising a hand in farewell, one he couldn't see, Catriona murmured a benediction. She watched, silent and still at the top of the steps, ignoring the people trooping past her, until the carriage disappeared into the trees.

Then she went inside, but didn't join her household at breakfast. Instead, she climbed to her turret room, opened the window wide—and watched the carriage carrying her husband from her, until it had passed from the vale.

CHAPTER

Fourteen

ՃⓈⓈՃ

"Oh, no!" Catriona focused on the curtains shielding her window through which she could see light seeping, and groaned. It was morning—*late* morning.

Falling back on her pillows, she stared at the canopy; she had meant to go to the circle this morning, to atone for yesterday's absence, but it was too late now. Drawing in a tight breath, she glanced at the bed beside her. It was a disaster of tangled sheets and rumpled covers—just as it had been the morning before. The cause, however, was quite different.

She hadn't been able to sleep; only as night was fading had she fallen into a restless doze. Which hadn't refreshed her in the least, hadn't prepared her for the day ahead.

Yesterday had dragged; nothing had gone right. She was still as far from finding good breeding cattle as she had been two weeks ago. Two months ago, and more. She needed to find some reasonable stock soon, or miss the chance of improving the herd through the coming season's breeding—an opportunity the vale could ill afford to miss.

But that wasn't what had kept her awake.

The empty space beside her had done that.

Forced her into a neverending round of thinking if, perhaps, she'd done something different, he might still be here, a warm weight beside her—the comfort of her heart. Senseless, useless repetition of their words, her thoughts, her conclusions.

It changed nothing—he was gone.

She sighed, then grimaced, recalling the transparent joy that had transformed Algaria. Ever since Richard had appeared on their horizon, Algaria had been worried, then withdrawn. His departure had more than pleased her—yesterday, she'd been reborn. Yet Catriona was sure he had done nothing to deserve Algaria's censure, or even to rattle her, or confirm her in her views. Other than to be himself.

That, apparently, was enough. Hardly a rational response. Algaria's attitude to Richard now worried her even more than it had. Perhaps there was some deeper purpose behind his leaving, one only The Lady could know.

The possibility didn't make his absence any easier to bear.

The emptiness around her weighed heavily on her heart, making breathing difficult. Dragging in some air, she sat up—and wished she hadn't. For one long instant the room spun, then slowly settled.

Forcing herself to breathe evenly, to concentrate on that, she waited, absolutely still, for the queasiness to pass. She had, it seemed, more misery in store for her than a simple broken heart. When the room had steadied and the hot flush had died, she slowly, carefully stood.

"Wonderful," she muttered, as she crossed to the washstand. "Morning sickness as well."

But she was still the lady of the vale—she had a role to fill, decisions to make, orders to give. She dressed with as much speed as she could muster, then, detouring via the stillroom for some soothing herbs, headed for the dining hall.

Herbal tea and plain toast was the most she could manage—the aromas rising from the plates of others nearly made her gag. She nibbled and sipped, grateful for the warmth of the tea, and tried to ignore, blot out, the smells and sounds around her.

Algaria, of course, noticed. "You're pale," she said, beaming brightly.

"I'm *wretched*," Catriona replied through clenched teeth.

"It's only to be expected."

Catriona turned and met Algaria's black gaze, then realized Algaria was referring, solely, to the consequences of her pregnancy. Algaria wouldn't accept—or even recognize—that Richard's departure was her principal woe. Looking back at her cup, Catriona gritted her teeth. "Don't tell anyone—not until I make the announcement."

"Good heavens—why?" Algaria gestured about them. "It's important news for the vale and the manor—everyone will be delighted."

"Everyone will be *unbearable*." Catriona pressed her lips together, waited for three heartbeats, then, in a more reasonable but still cold tone stated: "The news is important to me, too. I'll make the announcement when I'm ready. I don't want people fussing over me for any longer than necessary." In her present state, her temper wouldn't stand it. "I just want to be left alone to get on with the vale's business."

Algaria raised a shoulder. "As you wish. Now, about those decoctions . . ."

She hadn't thought it possible to miss him more than she had last night—but she was wrong.

By the end of the day, as the light faded from the world, Catriona huddled at her desk, fretfully tugging two shawls about her shoulders.

She was cold to her bones—a cold that came from inside and spread insidiously through her. It was the cold of loneliness, a bone-deep chill. Throughout the day, she'd been rubbing her arms; at lunchtime she'd fetched the extra shawl. Nothing helped.

Worse, she was finding it hard to concentrate, finding it hard to keep her usual serene mask—the face she habitually wore in public as the lady of the vale—in place. Summoning the brightness to put into her smile when she greeted McArdle and the others was very nearly beyond her. Energy was something she no longer had, not in any quantity.

And she needed energy to make her lips curve, to disguise the deadness inside, but supporting her usual sunny disposition was more than she could do. Unfortunately, being the lady of the vale, she couldn't even invent a fictitious malady to account for her state—she was never ill, not in the general way.

Pushing aside the ledgers she'd been studying—the breeding records for the past three years—she sighed. Leaning back in her chair, she closed her eyes. How was she going to cope?

She lay in the chair in the darkened room and opened her senses. But no help came—no suggestion of how she might manage popped into her tired mind.

When she finally opened her eyes and sat up, the one thing she did feel sure of was that the situation was going to get worse.

Dragging herself to her feet, feeling as if the child she carried was seven months older than it was, she straightened, stacked the ledgers neatly, then, setting her shoulders back, lifting her head high, she headed for the door.

While washing and changing for dinner, she grasped the opportunity to lie down—just for a minute.

One minute turned into thirty; by the time she reached the table, it was late. Out of breath, wanting nothing more than to crawl back into her bed, she smiled serenely about the hall and helped herself to lamb collops.

Then pushed them around and around on her plate.

She felt like slumping; only by maintaining a continuous inner lecture did she manage to preserve her facade. But she couldn't eat—she'd lost her appetite. In an effort to conceal her disinterest in the food, she caught Henderson's eye. "What have the children been up to today?" In spite of his dour demeanor, Henderson had a soft spot for the manor's brats.

"Seems like the master'd been teaching some of them to ride, so I took them out to the barn." He grimaced, a depressing sight. "I'm no great horseman, though. I'm thinking they'll have to wait on his return to polish up their skills."

"Hmm." Not wanting to dwell on how long the children might have to wait, Catriona looked along the table at Mrs. Broom and gestured to the steaming apple pie just placed before her, the fruity, spicy aroma much more to her liking than the cold collops a maid had whisked away. "I congratulate you on your new receipe—the spices add a pleasing tang."

Mrs. Broom beamed. "Twas the master suggested it—seems they cook it that way in London town, but it was easy enough to do. Pity he isn't here to enjoy it—he said it was one of his favorites. But we've apples aplenty in the store—I'll make it again when he gets back."

The smile on her face felt tight; Catriona inclined her head gracefully and turned to McArdle. "Has Melchett—"

"Mistress!"

"Mister Henderson!"

"Come *quickly!*"

With those and other cries, the manor children burst into the hall. They were led, as always, by Tom, Cook's redheaded son. He rushed straight to the main table, his gaze locked on Catriona's face. "It's the blacksmith's house, mistress. It's burning!"

"Burning?" Rising, Catriona stared down at Tom. "But ..." She frowned. "It can't be."

Tom bobbed his head urgently. "It *is,* mistress! Flames leaping into the sky, an' all."

Everyone rushed to see. Wide-eyed, Catriona halted on the back step and saw that Tom hadn't lied. The blacksmith's small house, wedged between the forge and the granary, was alight. Angry red flames licked over the wood and stone building, engulfing it from the rear. Beyond, out of sight behind the house, lay open pigpens, presently empty.

As they watched, the flames caught better hold and roared, throwing red sparks high.

Within seconds, the stable yard was a scene of confusion. Pandemonium reigned. People ran this way, then that, bumping into each other and cursing, some running to fetch pails others had already grabbed.

Dragging in a breath, Catriona lifted her head. "Henderson—you and the stablelads to the pump. Huggins, check the stable. Irons, where are you?"

The big blacksmith, a dripping pail in his hand, raised his arm. "Here, ma'am."

"You and all the men start dousing the fire."

"Aye, ma'am."

"All the women—into the kitchens. Grab whatever will hold most water."

They streamed past her; she heard the clatter as the huge pots and pans were collected. They all helped, even Algaria—a deep jam pot gripped tightly, she flung water onto the burning building.

Down on the cobbles, her face lit by the garish glow, Catriona monitored their frantic efforts. Huggins came puffing up. "The horses and animals are well enough—I've left two lads with them."

Her eyes on the flames rising above the cottage, then fanning over to embrace it from behind, Catriona grabbed his arm; she had to scream for him to hear. "Take half the men and start throwing water onto the back. That's where the source is."

Huggins nodded and went. Catriona coughed as billowing smoke gripped her throat. Turning, she surveyed the yard—there was a large crowd waiting, buckets, pails, pots and pans in hand, around the pump. It wasn't hard to guess the problem. The roads had cleared, but it was a long way from spring—the main snows on Merrick had yet to melt, so the river was still at its winter ebb. Only a gentle gush came up through the pump, enough for daily needs, but not enough to fight a fire.

A hot roar at her back had Catriona whirling; she backed as heat hit her like a surging wave.

Sparks and cinders rained down—a real danger for those running close to throw their precious water on the fire. Then came a loud *crack!*—a beam exploded; flaming debris showered down, driving everyone back.

Gasping, Catriona found herself cowering protectively over Tom. "Blankets!" Tom looked up at her—she shook his shoulder. "We need blankets to beat out the sparks. Get the others and fetch the horse blankets from the tack room."

Tom nodded and fled, shrieking through the din for his cohorts to follow him. They did, an unruly band streaking for the stables. They returned in double time, staggering under the weight of the heavy blankets balanced across their arms. Catriona grabbed one and started beating out the flaming cinders. Other women saw and did the same.

Huggins and his band had reached the back of the house; Catriona heard them bellowing for more help. Brushing the back of her hand over her flushed forehead, she looked around. "Jem, Joshua!—take your pails to the back."

They nodded and changed course around the side of the forge.

In the yard, everyone redoubled their efforts, trying to fill the gaps left by those who'd gone to the other front. But the pump would yield only so much. Glancing back through the swirling smoke, Catriona saw Irons had stripped off his shirt and was now bending his back to the pump handle. Henderson was slumped, wheezing, on the water trough—now empty.

"Lady!"

Catriona turned at the tug on her sleeve. Huggins, doubled over and panting, struggling to catch his breath, grimaced up at her.

"'Twas the woodpile behind the house—that's where it started." He paused to drag in another breath, his eyes going to the fiercely burning cottage. "We can douse the pile, but it's almost ashes now. But that won't stop it. The flames have got a good hold on the back wall, particularly on those big lintel beams across the back."

Following his nod, Catriona stared at the huge wooden beams that crossed the cottage, one above the door and window, separating the ground floor from the first, and the other above the first floor, supporting the roof timbers. Matching beams spanned the back.

"It's going to go." Huggins shook his head and slumped forward again. "We can't reach those big beams, and we haven't got enough water even if we could. It's an inferno, up there."

Catriona stared at the greedy flames, then dragged in a huge breath. She coughed and took a firm grip on her wits. And ignored the fright licking at her nerves. "All right." She squeezed Huggins's arm, sending him a little of her hard-won calm. "Tell your men to concentrate on saving the granary and the forge." She hesitated, then added: "The granary first if a choice has to be made."

They couldn't afford to lose the grain and other foodstuffs stored in the granary, their larder for the rest of the winter.

Huggins nodded his understanding and stumbled away to issue her orders. Catriona took one last look at the fiercely burning cottage and went to find

Irons. She found him slumped by the pump; Henderson was manning it again. Grim-faced, his gaze on his burning home, Irons heard her out, then, with a pain-filled grimace, nodded.

"Aye." With an effort, he hauled himself to his feet. "You be right. Cottage can be replaced—granary, and what's in it, can't."

He started bellowing orders himself; Catriona rushed forward once more to take charge close to the house, instructing the waterbearers where to fling their loads.

Her voice hoarse and fading, she grabbed a pot from a maid hard of hearing and showed her where to throw it—at the junction between the walls of the cottage and the granary. Handing the empty pot back to the woman, she paused, wiping the sweat from her brow, trying not to notice the heat washing over her—

She heard a cry.

Not from the yard, but from the cottage.

She stared at the building, the rough stone between the burning beams glowing pink—and told herself she'd imagined it. Prayed she'd imagined it.

But it came again, a whimpering wail that died beneath the flames' roar.

"Oh, *Lady!*" Hand to her mouth, Catriona whirled and searched the host of scurrying women for the blacksmith's wife. And found her, frantically grabbing the older manor children, having to peer through the soot and grime covering their faces to recognize her own. As Catriona watched, the woman grabbed one girl close, hand gripping the slender shoulder like a claw—she saw the woman scream her question, saw the girl shake her head, her own features changing into a mirror of her mother's horror. Then both mother and daughter looked straight at the burning house.

Catriona didn't hesitate. She grabbed a horse blanket from one of the weary beaters and flung it over her head and shoulders. Then she lunged for the closed door of the cottage.

She forced it open, and stepped through—

The flames roared—a wall of heat beat her back.

She staggered and nearly fell; cries and screams from all around filled her ears. Sure of the whimper she'd heard under the roar, she tightened her grip on the blanket and gathered her courage to step forward once more.

Before she could, she was bodily lifted and unceremoniously dumped on her feet ten feet back from where she'd stood. *"Damn, stupid woman!"* was the mildest of the oaths that rang in her ears.

To her stunned amazement, Richard grabbed the singed blanket from her. Then threw it about his head and shoulders and plunged into the cottage himself.

"Richard!" Catriona heard her own scream, saw her hands reach out, grasping, trying to catch him to hold him back—but he was already gone.

Into the flames.

Others ran to her and gathered about, their eyes, like hers, glued to the open doorway. They waited, tense, on their toes, ready to dash closer at the slightest sign.

The heat held them were they were. Waiting. Hoping. Praying.

Catriona prayed the hardest—she'd seen the inside of the cottage. Raging inferno didn't come close to describing it—the whole back wall and the ceiling were a mass of hot, searing flames.

Everyone in the yard fell silent, all gripped by the drama. Into the sudden, unnatural silence came a loud, prolonged creak.

Then the main beam beneath the front of the roof exploded.

Before their horrified eyes, it cracked, once, then again, flames spitting victoriously through the gaps.

A second later, the lower beam, between the ground and upper floor, groaned mightily.

Then, in a vicious splurge, flames spat around the lintel of the door itself. In split seconds, the wood started to glow.

Richard lunged through the door, staggering—a wrapped bundle in his arms, clinging, crying weakly.

Everyone rushed forward—the blacksmith's wife grabbed her child, Irons grabbed both of them in his huge arms and lifted them away. Catriona, Henderson and two of the grooms grabbed Richard, gasping, coughing, struggling to breathe, and hauled him away from the cottage.

On that instant, with a deep, guttural groan like the dying gasp of a tortured animal, the cottage collapsed. Flames shot high; there was a deafening roar. Then the fire settled to crack and consume its prey.

Bare hands smothering the flames flickering in Richard's hair and along his collar and shoulders, Catriona had no time for the cottage.

Richard was not so distracted.

Staring at the furnace growing beside the forge, he finally managed to catch his breath—finally noticed what she was doing. With an oath, he spun and caught her hands—and saw the telltale burns.

"Damn it, woman—don't you have the sense you were born with!"

Stung, Catriona tried to tug her hands free. "You were alight!" She glared at him. "What happened to the blanket?"

"The child needed the protection more than me." Grabbing a full saucepan from a passing waterbearer, Richard plunged Catriona's hands, gripped in one of his, into the cold water. His face like thunder, he dragged her, her wrists locked in one hand, the other holding the water-filled pan, across to the back doorstep.

He forced her to sit. "Stay here." Dumping the pan in her lap, he trapped her gaze. "Stay the hell out of this—leave it to me."

"But—"

He swore through his teeth. "Dammit—which do you think your people— or I—would rather lose—the granary, or you?" He held her gaze, then straightened. "Just *stay here.*"

Without waiting for an answer, he strode away. Into the directionless melee about the pump.

Within seconds, the women were drifting away, pans and pots in hand, uncertain expressions on their faces, all headed to join Catriona. Among them was Algaria. In answer to Catriona's questioning glance, she coldly lifted a shoulder. "He said we were more distraction than help—that the men would do better fighting the fire without worrying if their women and children were safe."

Catriona grimaced; she'd seen more than one of the men stop and hunt through the crowd, or leave their post for a moment to shout orders at their children. The women, as they neared, collected their children as they came. The men, now all gathered about the pump, about Richard, taller than them all, were staring at the burning building, listening intently while Richard pointed and rapidly issued orders.

With a sigh, Catriona lifted her hands from the icy water and studied them. Then she grimaced and put them back into the pot. She looked up at Algaria. "Can you check the baby for me?"

Algaria raised a brow. "Of course." She paused, looking down at Catriona. "That was a foolish thing to do. A few minor burns could hardly harm his black soul."

With that, she turned away and glided, like a black crow, into the house; stunned, her wits too shaken to respond quickly, Catriona stared, open-mouthed, after her.

Then she snapped her lips shut, glared briefly, and swung her gaze back to more important things.

As she looked, the group of men dispersed, breaking into teams which rapidly deployed as bucket lines, one to each side of the cottage, and another streaming into the barren gardens, ultimately linking the river with the back of the cottage. Peering through the dark, Catriona could see men filling buckets with snow, still piled in drifts through the gardens, and passing the buckets up the line, accepting empty buckets back. Some of the field workers came hurrying with shovels, the better to shift the snow.

In the yard, two pairs of grooms staggered along, each pair carrying one of the huge loft ladders. Others rushed to help steady the ladders against the walls of the forge and the granary; they were long enough to reach the roofs.

By the time the ladders were in place, the first filled bucket arrived and was quickly carried up the ladder to be poured down the wall between the granary and the cottage.

At the center of the yard, his face set, Richard viewed their combined efforts. He hoped his witch was praying to Her Lady—they were going to need all the help they could get. The main thrust of the flames through the cottage had been via the central beam running forward to back through the roof, supporting secondary beams which in turn had supported the roof struts. They'd all burned, but now the flames were spreading outward from the center of the cottage, in both directions, licking along the timbers and beams ultimately abutting the walls of the granary and forge.

Luckily, both granary and forge were significantly taller than the cottage wedged between; if that hadn't been so, both would have caught alight by now. They had a chance, a slim one, of saving both buildings, each, in different ways, essential to life at the manor.

Richard strode into the action before the cottage, now all but pulsing with flames. Time and again, he swore at grooms or laborers who sent their bucket loads too far from the vital walls. "We need it where it counts!" he roared up the ladder.

Grasping one bucket, he used his height to send its contents washing over one of the exposed beams in the granary wall. "That," he yelled, pointing to the area, "is where the danger lies."

One of the dangers.

He kept a sharp eye on the men on the ladders, stepping in to rotate them as they, most exposed to the heat rising from the fire, wilted. And when it seemed they were losing the battle for the forge, he went into the garden, grabbed a spade, strode down to the riverbank, and hacked through the softened ice to the water below, uncaring of the iced slush freezing his boots.

Within seconds, Henderson and one of the older grooms were beside him, helping to widen the hole. Then they were bucketing as fast as human hands could manage, sending pails filled with icy slurry up the gardens. Once the faster rate was established, chest heaving, Richard ran back up the slope, grabbing men as he went, positioning them bodily, too out of breath to speak.

As tired as he, but equally determined, they understood; nodding, they formed another bucketline from the river to the front of the forge.

Running back to the yard, Richard paused before the cottage only to rotate the men on the ladders again, then strode quickly to the pump. "Faster," he ordered, as he fetched up beside it. "We need more."

Two wilting farmhands looked at him in dismay. "The river's low—we can't," one of them stammered.

"Low or not," Richard growled, physically displacing them, "faster will still yield more."

He set a new pump rhythm, half again what it had been. "Here"—he passed the pump handle back to the farmhands—"keep it going like that."

They both looked at his face and didn't dare argue. They pumped. Faster. Richard waited to make sure it was fast enough, then nodded, and glanced at the other four men recovering from their shifts. "If you need to, rotate more often. But if you value your hides, *don't slow down.*"

Quite what he meant by that, he neither knew nor cared, but the threat had the desired effect. The group manning the pump lifted their effort and sustained it—long enough to make the vital difference.

On the back step, leaning against the wall, her hands still in the pot of water, Catriona watched it all—the fight to save the manor's buildings. Watched Richard exhort the men to greater efforts, watched him instill his own determination into them. Watched him form them into a coherent force, then direct it at the enemy in the most effective way. Watched him whip them up when they were flagging, when the flames seemed poised to gain the upper hand. Saw them respond, meeting every demand he made of them.

She'd sent the other women and all the children inside, given orders for food to be prepared, for water to be heated. Done all she could to support the effort he was making for her—for them.

Eventually, they won. The flames, denied any hold on the neighboring buildings, spluttered, faded, then died, leaving the cottage a smoldering ruin of glowing embers and charred wood.

They were exhausted.

Richard started sending the men in, the oldest and weakest first, keeping the strongest with him to finish damping down the scene. At the last, when only wisps of smoke and an acrid stench rose from the building, he and Irons hefted grappling hooks, swung them about the ends of the big beams—and brought the whole structure crashing down.

Henderson, Huggins and the handful of grooms still standing used pitchforks to drag, poke and prod the smoldering remains about the yard, spreading them to minimize any chance of fresh fire.

With heavy axes, Richard and Irons weighed into what was left of the cottage, one from either side. By the time they'd finished, there were no contacts remaining between what had been the cottage and either the forge or the granary.

The buildings were secure.

Heaving a huge sigh, Richard leaned on the axe and cast a long look over the scene. Irons came to stand beside him, his axe on his shoulder. Richard glanced at his face. "We'll build it again, although not, I think, just there."

"Aye." Irons scratched his chin. "'Twasn't wise, seemingly. The woodpile at the back didn't help, neither."

"Indeed not." Richard sighed as he straightened. And made a mental note to check where the manor's main woodpile was located. He couldn't remember seeing it; it might well be against the back of the granary. Or the stables. "Seasoned wood should be stored away from farm buildings—we'll need to build another shelter farther back."

"Aye, 'twould be silly not to learn the lessons The Lady sends us." Irons straightened and looked directly at Richard as he held out his hamlike hand for the axe. "I'm in your debt."

Richard smiled wearily; he clapped Iron's broad shoulder as he handed over the axe. "Thank The Lady." He turned away. Lifting his head, he saw Catriona waiting—and murmured, "This is what I'm here for."

They gathered in the aftermath in the dining hall. All were weary, but too keyed up to rest; the effect of what they'd faced had yet to leave them.

Richard took his seat by Catriona's side at the main table and gratefully helped himself to the thick stew and fresh bread Cook and her helpers had labored to provide. A thirty-six-course meal at Prinny's Brighton monstrosity could not possibly have tasted better. Or been more appreciated. Conversation was minimal as both men and women ate, children—all safe—balanced in their laps.

It was Henderson who, as empty plates were cleared and maids hurried to place round cheeses on the tables, voiced the common thought.

"Odd thing, that fire."

Huggins, at the near end of one of the other tables, nodded. "Can't see how it started, myself."

They all looked at Richard. Lounging in his chair, pushed back from the table, with one hand idly resting, unconsciously possessive, on the back of Catriona's chair, he returned their gazes steadily. Then he looked around the room. "Does anyone know of any possible cause?"

Heads shook on all sides.

"Never seen anything like it in all my years," McArdle huffed.

"It was all well-seasoned wood—once lit, it *would* burn. What I can't understand," Richard said, "is how and why it caught alight."

"Aye, there's the mystery." Henderson nodded dourly.

"Midwinter—admittedly it's been dry. And that wood was all under shelter. But ..."

Richard met his eye. "Precisely. *But* ... something must have touched spark to the tinder."

"Aye, but what?"

It was a question no one could answer. They batted it back and forth, until Richard, glancing at Catriona, caught her straightening, caught her in the act of drawing on her reserves to preserve her outward facade. Noting the dark shadows beneath her eyes, the incipient haggardness in her face, he swore beneath his breath and turned back to the others. "Enough. We're merely speculating. Let's sleep on it and see what tomorrow reveals."

All nodded. Many of the household had already dragged their weary bodies from the hall. Without waiting for the others, Richard placed a hand beneath Catriona's elbow and rose, lifting her to her feet beside him.

She blinked, dazed and weary, up at him; jaw setting, Richard denied the impulse to sweep her up in his arms and instead calmly supported her from the dais and into the front hall. Once out of sight of the others, he slid one arm around her; supporting her against him, he steered her up the stairs.

To their bedchamber. He halted before the door, for the first time in his life, not entirely certain of his footing. His welcome. He glanced down at Catriona; she met his gaze—when he didn't open the door, she frowned.

"What is it?"

The same question he'd asked her—the one she'd refused to answer. Richard held her gaze and fought against the compulsion to make the same mistake. "I ..." He paused, then went on: "Perhaps I'd better find a bed elsewhere."

The frown in her eyes grew. "Why? This is our room." Her tone was entirely uncomprehending. Before he could say more, she set the door wide, then glided through; fingers clutching his sooty sleeve, she towed him, unresisting, behind her.

He shut the door. "Catriona—"

"Our clothes are ruined." She looked down at her filthy gown, then turned and looked at him. "And we both need a bath. And your hair needs cutting— it's badly singed at the back. Come on."

She tugged; inwardly sighing, Richard acquiesced. Her eyes were still wide, their expression dazed—he knew shock when he saw it, heard it.

He followed her into the small bathing chamber that gave off their room. A welcome surprise awaited them—some kind souls had slipped upstairs while they were discussing the fire and half-filled the large tub with hot water, now cooled to warm, and set metal pails of steaming water in the hearth where the blaze, stoked high, kept them hot.

"Oh." Catriona stopped and stared.

Richard glanced at her face, then drew up a bathing stool to one side of the fire and sat her upon it. Then he picked up a towel, wrapped it around the handle of one pail, and added it to the tub. After adding all the pails but two, he tested the water; it was perfect, hot but not scorching, just right for easing chilled and tired muscles.

Returning to Catriona, he took her hands and drew her to her feet. She immediately started to unbutton his waistcoat. He sighed and shrugged out of his ruined coats. Once she was absorbed with the buttons on his shirt, he reached around her and tugged her laces free. She didn't notice until he loosened the neckline and started to draw her gown down over her arms.

"No." She tried to tug it up again. "You first."

"No," Richard said, calmly, soothingly. "Both together."

She paused, then looked at the tub; he quickly drew her gown down and freed her hands. She sighed and stepped out of the puddled cambric and kicked it to join his coats. "I suppose we'll fit."

They did, very comfortably. Just before she joined him in the blissfully hot water, Catriona went to a shelf and selected a jar, then returned to sprinkle its contents into the tub. Richard, surfacing from rinsing his hair, tensed as crystals hissed in the water, then relaxed as a delicious herbal scent filled the room.

After returning the jar to the shelf, Catriona stepped into the tub and sank down opposite him, then picked up the flannel. "Turn around." She gestured with her hand. "I'll scrub your back."

Richard complied; he closed his eyes in bliss as she scrubbed and kneaded the stiff muscles. She worked over his shoulders and upper back, then reached below the water.

He heard her hiss—an indrawn hiss of pain. Swinging around, he saw her shake her hand; he caught it—and saw the burned palm. What he said made her wince more.

"Lie back! Rest your hands on the edge." He took the flannel from her and quickly finished his own ablutions, then found the bar of soap she preferred— a tantalizing mix of summer flowers, the scent she always bore—and lathered the flannel.

And proceeded, ignoring her weak complaints, to wash her.

Catriona tried to struggle, then surrendered. She was in shock and she knew it—the shock of the fire—the shock of his totally unexpected return. The shock of seeing him plunge into the burning building, relief at his safe return. The horror of seeing flames licking his hair, the pain of her burned palms. She didn't know what she thought—she didn't know how she should respond, how she should react to any of it.

All she could do was flow with the tide, close her eyes and accept his ministrations, the steady, unhurried sweep of the flannel over her skin.

He was very thorough. Setting her legs wide apart, he sat between; he started with her face, caressing it gently, then laved her neck, then moved on to her shoulders, then extended each arm to lovingly cleanse it, all the way to her fingertips, carefully avoiding her raw palms. Leaving her hands propped on the tub's edge, he reached around her and stroked her shoulders, then the long planes of her back, the curves of her hips, the globes of her bottom in long lazy sweeps, lifting her easily in the water. Setting her down again, he reached for the soap.

From under heavy lids, she studied his face; his expression was deeply calm, like the surface of a fathomless pool. Calm was usually her province, but in the fright and flurry of the evening, she'd misplaced her inherent serenity. She'd lost her calm—but he'd found his. Or, she silently amended, could show his. He wasn't wearing any mask, any social cloak—this was as he was. The warrior who was most at home on the battlefield, in the heart of the fury—that was where he was most at ease. Where he was calmest.

Opening her weary senses, she closed her eyes and shamelessly drank in his calm, and felt it ease her. Let him press calm on her with every smooth caress of the soapy flannel as he gently, lovingly, washed her breasts, her waist, her gently rounded stomach. He moved steadily down, slowly, soothingly, washing every inch of her; by the time he reached her toes, she was floating on a warm tide.

She felt the water shift as he discarded the flannel, then he gripped her wrists and drew her up. Drew her toward him, lifted her so she sat on his thighs, her legs instinctively wrapping around his waist. Her forearms sliding over his shoulders, she blinked her eyes wide as his arms closed around her and his lips found hers.

He kissed her gently, her wet breasts pressed to his wet chest, a thin layer of water sliding between their warmed bodies. Despite their aroused state, it was a soothing kiss. She kissed him back, in the same vein, simply grateful to feel his achingly familiar lips on hers.

Then he rose, lifting her with him; her legs slid down and she was standing beside him. He reached for one of the pails left waiting and rinsed her, then repeated the performance on himself, using the last pail. She went to clamber out, but he was before her. He closed his hands about her waist and lifted her clear, setting her feet on the thick towel laid before the hearth. She accepted the towel he handed her gratefully, and ignored, as best she could, the flush that turned her skin a delicate rose, and the more pointed evidence of his arousal.

Revived, she quickly dried herself, then helped him mop his broad back. Standing behind him, she considered, then swiftly looped the towel around his hips and anchored it. "Sit," she said, prodding him toward the stool. "I want to neaten your hair."

He turned and looked at her with that unfathomable calm in his eyes, but consented to sit. She found a comb and scissors, and started snipping, removing the burnt and singed locks. Then she reached to brush the clipping from his shoulders, stopped, and peered. "You've got burns across your shoulders!"

He wriggled them. "Only minor ones."

"Humph! Well you can sit there a minute more while I salve them." She fetched the right pot from her supplies on the shelf; luckily, her fingers weren't burned, only her palms. She could grip things, could spread and knead; she carefully worked the salve into his burns. Then she stood back and surveyed his back more carefully.

"If you've finished soothing those burns, I have another burning part of my anatomy awaiting your attention."

The gravelly comment jerked her upright. "Yes, well." Quickly, she replaced the pot on the shelf. Half turning, she gestured to the bedchamber. "Come to bed, then."

His gaze fastened on her hand as he stood. "One moment."

He caught her hand, and inspected the raw redness. He swore, glared at her, then towed her back to the shelf. "Where's that salve?"

"My hands will be all right."

"Ah-ha!"

Catriona frowned as he lifted the pot down. "What happened to your burning anatomy?"

"I can suffer a few minutes more. Hold out your hands."

Trapped between him and the door, she had to comply. "This is quite unnecessary."

He glanced at her briefly. "All healers are supposed to be terrible patients."

She humphed, but held her tongue, surprised to find how cool and soothing the salve felt on her scorched flesh. She studied her palms while he returned the pot to the shelf. His left hand appeared; he grasped her right wrist and tugged forward. She stepped forward and looked up—and stubbed her nose on his back. "What ...?"

For answer, he clamped her right forearm beneath his right arm—tight as a vise. She pushed against his back; it was like pushing a mountain. "What are you doing?"

On the words, she felt the soft touch of gauze; she whipped her head around and scanned the shelf—the roll of gauze bandage she kept there was missing.

"Richard!" She tried to wriggle and accomplished nothing. The gauze wound steadily about her hand. She glared at his back. "Stop it!"

He didn't. He was surprisingly deft; when he released her hand, she found herself staring at a perfectly neat bandage, secured by a tight knot. He reached for her other hand—

"No!" She danced back, hiding it behind her.

"Yes!" He stepped forward.

"*I'm* the healer!"

"You're a stubborn witch."

He was unstoppable; despite her protests, despite her active resistance, her left hand, too, was carefully wrapped in gauze, so her fingers were locked together with only her fingertips protruding. Defeated, she stared, first at one mittened hand, then the other. "What . . .? How . . .?"

"There's nothing you need do until morning—that'll give the salve a chance to sink in."

She narrowed her eyes at him.

"Come here. You have ashes in your hair."

He pulled her to the stool; resigned, she sank down and stared at the flames as, standing behind her, he pulled out her pins, searching through the wild mass her hair had become to find them. He shook the long tresses out, then fetched her brush from her dressing table and proceeded to brush out her hair.

"Thank God—or The Lady—there are no burned or singed locks. No thanks, however, to you."

Catriona wisely kept mum and concentrated on the tug of the brush through her long hair, on the soothing, repetitive rhythm. The flames in the hearth burned strongly; she closed her eyes and felt their warmth on her lids, on her naked breasts. With him behind her and the fire before her, she felt secure and warm. Her senses spread, sure and calm; about her, her world had steadied.

"I didn't expect you back—I thought I was dreaming when you appeared in the yard." She made the statement calmly, leaving it to him to respond if he would.

His eyes on the burnished flame of her hair, rippling and glowing beneath each stroke of the brush, Richard drew in a slow breath, then replied: "I got as far as Carlisle. We spent the night there, and I decided I'd made a mistake. I didn't want to go to London—I never did." There was nothing south of the border for him now. He paused, then brushed on. "And if I'd needed any prompting, discovering this morning that, after my arrival at the inn last night, Dougal Douglas had been inquiring after who I was and where I was headed, clarified the position nicely."

"Douglas?"

"Hmm. He lives near there and was in the town when I drove in. He quizzed the ostlers, then made the mistake of approaching Jessup late that night in the tap. Jessup reported his questioning to me this morning."

"And that brought you back?"

Lips compressing, Richard held back the impulse to agree. After three long strokes, he managed to get the truth out. "I'd already decided to return, but the notion that Douglas knew I'd left the vale, leaving you, in his terms, alone, made me hire a horse and ride. I left Worboys and Jessup to follow with the carriage."

"I didn't hear or see you ride in."

"No one did. You were all engrossed with the fire." He gave the lock he was holding an extra tug. "With running into a burning building."

She didn't respond. He brushed on, steadily removing flecks of ash from her bright mane. Under the brush, her hair came alive in his hands, like living fire. Warm, fragrant, gentle fire.

"Will you be staying?"

There were times, Richard decided, when he definitely did not appreciate being married to a witch. To a woman who could hold her demeanor to the calm and serene regardless of her true feelings. He never could tell what she really felt. Her question—surely one of the most vital facing them—had been couched as the most politely distant, totally innocent, query. Which, he decided, after all they'd shared, was too much to accept.

Frowning, he stared at the back of her glossy head. "*That* depends on you."

She clearly expected him to sleep with her—while in this house, he was still, quite obviously, to her, her husband. But what were the boundaries of his role in her eyes?—*that* was something he didn't know, something he needed to find out. Something they needed to discuss.

Abruptly, he stopped brushing. Grasping her shoulders, he drew her around on the stool, then hunkered down before her, so his eyes were level with hers. "Do you want me to stay?"

Catriona searched his eyes—desperately. They viewed her steadily, but told her nothing. "Yes—if you wish to. I mean ..." Dragging in a breath, her gaze locked with his, she rattled on: "If you wished to stay I would be pleased, but I don't want you to think that you must—that I'd be *expecting* you to remain here always ... or, or ... *resenting* ..." She gestured vaguely.

Impatiently, lips thinning, Richard shook his head. "That's not what I asked." He trapped her gaze and held it ruthlessly. "Do you *want* me to stay?"

Wide-eyed, Catriona tried another gesture. "Well! We're man and wife ... I thought ... that is, I imagined it was customary—"

"No!" He closed his eyes; his jaw set. Through set teeth he said: "Catriona, please tell me—do you wish me to stay?"

He opened his eyes—his irate gaze pinned her.

Catriona glared. "Well, of *course,* I want you to stay!" Wildly, she waved her bandaged hands. "I can't even sleep when you're not here! I feel utterly wretched when you're not by. And how on earth I'm supposed to get on if you're not here I don't know—" She broke off as tears filled her eyes.

Richard saw them; the breath trapped in his chest abruptly released in a huge sigh of relief—he reached out, grabbed her, wrapped his arms about her, and buried his face in her hair. And breathed deeply, inhaling the scent he'd so missed the previous night. "Then I'll stay."

After a long, silent moment, she sniffed, and softened in his arms. "You will?"

"Forever." Lifting his head, he brushed her hair from her face and kissed her. Long and lingeringly. "Come to bed."

Her lids lifted; she met his gaze. "Bed?"

Richard grimaced. "Your hands are hurt, remember." He stood, simultaneously lifting her into his arms. He lost his towel in the process; neither of them cared. He carried her to the bed, laid her down gently, freeing her hair, spreading it over the pillows, then, holding her wrists so she wouldn't forget in her passion and harm them, he covered her.

She'd cooled, but when he pressed into her she arched, then arched again and took him in. He settled within her, then drank her soft gasp when he drew back and thrust deep. Three thrusts later, she wriggled beneath him, tilting her hips to better receive him, lifting her legs and clasping his flanks—welcoming him in, holding him to her. Loving him.

Richard slowed, wallowing in the glory, in the intimate caresses she pressed on him. He bent his head and kissed her—she drew him deep there as well.

And so they loved—now slow, then faster, then slow again when the compulsion to savor the moment came upon them. Their bodies shifted and flexed in a dance older than time, hard pressing soft, rough rasping smooth. They lost track of time, of the world about them, of the night beyond their bed. The only things that mattered were each other's pleasure and the soft murmurs of contentment they shared.

And when the spinning stars finally crashed down upon them and took them from the world, they were together, as one, much more deeply than before.

Much more wedded than before.

Sunk deep in her softness, collapsed upon her, Richard's last thought was: At long last, he'd found his home.

Later, in the untrammeled depths of the night, held securely in Richard's arms yet still drifting in a sated sea, Catriona recalled her first sensing of him, recalled his hot hunger—his lustful desire—and his restless longing. She remembered very well that restlessness in his soul, his deep-seated need to belong. She could, she now knew, satisfy his lustful hunger—she could fulfill his other need, too. And thus anchor him here, by her side, satisfied with what she could give him.

She could be his cause, become his life's purpose.

Her initial reading of him, that, quite aside from his strengths, he bore a wound which needed her healer's touch, had been accurate. He did have a deep need for something she could give him—herself, but not just physically; he needed much more than that. He needed her specifically, and that need, even once satisfied, would never die; it would always be a part of him. And if that was so, then if she gave freely, she had no reason to fear losing him.

The only question that remained was how much he understood—whether he would still fight fate—The Lady's will—or accept what she offered him.

She knew he was still awake, still floating in the warm afterglow. She drew in a slow breath, and took her courage in both hands. "Why did you decide to come back?"

The quiet question hung in the dark, a sweetly tolling bell exhorting the truth.

Richard heard and considered the many answers. He'd returned because of the loneliness that had wracked his soul when, last night, he'd slept without her. Tried to sleep without her—without her warmth beside him, without her silken limbs alongside his, the sound of her breathing, soft and low, echoing in his heart. Tried to sleep without the fragrance of her hair sinking through his senses, anchoring him through the night. He hadn't slept at all.

He'd returned even faster after learning of Dougal Douglas, because of the feeling that had churned in his gut, spurring him back from Carlisle. Because of the dread certainty that he should never have left her.

A certainty transmogrified to fact in that horror-filled moment when, clattering wildly into the yard having seen the flames and smoke through the trees, he'd seen his worst nightmare enacted before him—seen her rush into a burning building.

He wasn't about to deny what he felt for her—the depth of what he felt for her—not ever again. He would have to learn to deal with it, learn how to live with it—and so would she.

Not, however, tonight. They were both far too tired to face such a task.

So he searched for a way to answer, some phrase that encompassed the truth. "I came back because this is my place." Turning his head, he pressed a soft kiss to her forehead. "This is where I belong. With you. By your side."

Catriona closed her eyes tight—against tears of relief, of joy, and something more besides. That last welled through her, poured through her, glowing brighter than spun gold.

This was where he belonged—here—by her side. She knew it—thank The Lady, he knew it, too.

CHAPTER
Fifteen

ॐ

Despite the fire and its aftermath, or, perhaps, because of it, they both slept deeply and awoke early, still in each other's arms. The temptation to celebrate the night and its revelations was strong, but . . .

"I have to go to the circle." Her head resting on Richard's chest, Catriona pushed at the heavy arm lying possessively over her waist. "I should have gone two mornings ago—I really must go today."

"I'll go with you." The words were out before Richard thought; he quickly amended: "I'll escort you there—if that's permitted?"

Still trapped under his arm, Catriona wriggled around so she could look into his face. "You'll ride there with me?"

Somewhat warily—was he committing some witchy solecism?—Richard nodded. "I'll wait, and ride back with you."

She searched his eyes, searched his face, then her face transformed, lit by a glorious smile. "Yes—come. I'd like that."

It was all she said before scrambling from the bed; Richard followed, bemused. The smiles she kept beaming his way, even when—especially when—she thought he wasn't watching, tugged at his heart and made him smile, too. By the time they clattered out of the yard, she on her mare, he on Thunderer, she was radiant with delight.

He shook his head at her. "Anyone would think I'd offered to buy you diamonds, not just ride with you to your prayers."

She laughed—a sound so glorious it shook him—touched her heels to her mare's flanks, and headed across the melting snow.

Richard followed, easing Thunderer up alongside her mare. There was no point racing; the mare's short strides were no match for Thunderer's might. So they raced the wind instead, streaking up the vale in the chill of near-dawn, hoofbeats thudding in time with their hearts, breaths steaming as exhilaration overtook them.

Reaching the head of the vale, they slowed; Catriona led the way to an outcropping of rock that formed a natural shelf beside the circle. Sliding from her saddle, she glanced down the vale. The sun was rising in the purple mists beyond the mouth of the vale; the line marking the boundary between night and day, fuzzed by the clouds, advanced, unstoppable, toward them.

"I have to hurry." Breathless, she glanced up at him as he took her reins, then she threw her arms about him, hugged him wildly, then ran for the entrance to the circle.

It was not a simple circle of trees, but a circular grove, grown dense with the centuries. The shadows within swallowed her up as she ran down the dimly lit path. Richard watched until the flickering light of her hair disappeared, then tethered the horses and found a comfortable rock on which to perch.

He was sitting on a lichen-covered boulder appreciating the sunrise when she came running out of the trees, with such joy suffusing her face that just knowing that he, quite aside from The Lady, had played a part in putting it there, warmed his heart. Smiling, he rose, and caught her as she ran full-tilt into his arms. He hugged her, stole a swift kiss, then tossed her to the mare's saddle.

They rode back through the sun-kissed morning, birdcall ringing about them, the chill lifting as the sun struck through the clouds and brought the landscape alive. Snow still stood in drifts across the fields, but brown now showed as well. Behind them, Merrick was still completely mantled, but below the snows, the earth was stirring. Warming. Returning to life.

As they rode side by side into the morning, Richard couldn't suppress the feeling that he, too, had lived through a dark season and was now emerging into the light.

No longer in any hurry, they ambled about the low hummock that hid the manor from sight. Squinting into the silver disc of the sun, they couldn't see the buildings, but knew they were there.

"Hrroooo."

Richard reined in, blinking to clear his vision. Before them stood two of the vale's steers, in less than perfect condition. The cattle blinked sad brown eyes at them, then turned and ambled away. Frowning, Richard watched them go.

He had to start somewhere.

"Catriona—"

"I was just thinking—"

She broke off and looked at him; Richard quelled a grimace and gestured for her to go on.

Hands crossed on her saddlebow, she stared toward the manor. "I was just wondering . . ." She paused; he saw her lips tighten. "If you stay, will you miss the balls and parties?" Swiftly, she glanced at him. "We don't have any, you know."

"Thank heaven—and The Lady, I suspect—for that. I don't give a damn about balls and parties." Considering the statement, Richard raised his brows. "In fact, I haven't cared for them for years." He met Catriona's wide— definitely wondering—gaze and narrowed his eyes. "And I don't give a damn about the incredibly beautiful ladies who attend such events, either."

Her eyes searched his, then her lips formed a silent "Oh" before curving, just a little, at the ends.

Richard fought down an urge to kiss them. "I'm staying—and you can forget any idea that I'll grow bored. There's plenty to keep me busy here—which brings me to what I wanted to discuss with you. The breeding stock."

She grimaced and set the mare plodding slowly on. "I haven't been able to find any source that I consider suitable. Mr. Potts is waiting for—*urging*—my final authority to purchase from his contact at Montrose, but I know it's not right—not what the vale needs."

Richard drew in a long breath. "I have a suggestion." When she looked quickly around at him, he held up a staying hand. "I know I vowed I wouldn't interfere with how you ran things—with how you managed the vale—so if you want to do something different ..." Frowning, he paused, then caught her eye, and drew in a deep breath. "The truth is, your whole situation with livestock badly needs an overhaul. The cattle herd is the most desperate case—they need an immediate injection of good quality stock. But your rams and ewes need weeding out, too, and the dairy herd is only just meeting your needs. You should think of diversifying, too—goats should do well here, and geese. The vale's a reasonably sized holding and while you've managed the crops well, the livestock could do better." Deciding he may as well be hanged for a wolf as a lamb, he added: "And your buildings, fences and shelters need repair and in some cases resiting."

She stared at him, then looked ahead, drew a huge breath and turned back to him.

"I know," Richard said, before she could speak, "I promised no interference, so I can work on each problem with you, behind the scenes."

Catriona frowned and reined in her mare. "That's not—"

"If you prefer, I can just list my suggestions, and you can take it from there." Richard halted Thunderer beside her. "Or if you'd rather, I can talk each matter through with McArdle and the others, and then write to the various dealers in your name and set up the meetings, then you could—"

"*Richard!*"

He looked at her stonily. "What?"

"Your vow!" Catriona glared at him. "I've already *realized* it's senseless to refuse your help with the business side of the vale. While the *spiritual* side of things"—she flung out a hand, encompassing the vale and the circle behind them—"and all healing matters must be left in my hands, I *need* you to help me with the rest."

He stared at her unblinkingly. "You need me?"

Catriona met his gaze directly. "After last night, you need to ask?"

A long moment passed. "But you *didn't* want me to help—I asked, and you said you didn't need my assistance."

Catriona blushed; the mare sidled. "I thought," she confessed, holding his gaze, "that you didn't mean to stay—that you were preparing to leave." She frowned, recalling. "In fact, I came to the library one morning to ask you for help with the breeding stock and heard you talking to Worboys, making plans to leave. That was *before* you offered to help."

Richard frowned. "You were behind that other door in the library?" Catriona nodded; Richard grimaced. "Worboys and his plans." Briefly, he explained.

Catriona sat back in her saddle. "So you never intended to leave at all?"

"Not until you made it impossible to stay." Remembering how she'd made him feel, Richard narrowed his eyes at her. "Do you think that in future, you could just tell me what is really in your witchy mind *without* trying to guess my thoughts first?"

Catriona narrowed her eyes back. "I wouldn't need to guess if you just told me how you felt." She considered his face. "You're very good at hiding your feelings—even from me."

"Humph. I'll take that as a compliment."

"Don't—it's going to have to change."

"Oh?" Brows rising, he looked down at her, arrogantly challenging.

"Indeed." Catriona met his gaze, sheer determination in hers. The horses sidled and stamped—sending them swaying closer. She raised her brows. "I'll make a deal with you. Another set of vows."

Richard's brows quirked, then he grimaced. "Let's make them a little clearer than the last."

"Assuredly—in fact, these vows are designed to ensure future understanding."

Richard eyed her with increasing unease. "What are they?"

Catriona smiled into his eyes and held up her hand. "I vow before The Lady that I will henceforth always speak my mind directly to you—if you will reciprocate in like vein."

Richard studied her eyes, her face, then drew breath, raised his hand, placed it palm to palm with hers, and linked their fingers. "Before Your Lady, I swear I'll . . ."—he hesitated, then grimaced—"try."

Catriona blinked at him, then her lips twitched, then curved, then she threw back her head and laughed. Peal after peal of her glorious laughter rang out; mock-disgruntled, Richard reached for her. "It's not funny, being naturally reticent."

She stopped laughing on a gasp as she landed in his saddle, facing him. "Reticent? *You?*" As his hands ran over her body, then slid beneath her hems, her eyes widened even more. "You don't know the meaning of the word."

Over the next few minutes, he gave her justification and more for that assessment, until she finally gasped, as categorically as she could: "*Richard!* It is *not* possible on a horse."

It was, of course; he demonstrated with an élan that left her shuddering.

Neither of them noticed, on the sun-glazed horizon, a flashing pinprick of light—a reflection off the manor's spyglass as it was lowered and snapped shut.

From the fence near the stables, Algaria stood, watching the two figures locked together on the back of the grey stallion, for two more minutes, then, her face colder than ice, she turned and reentered the house.

* * *

That afternoon, Richard penned a detailed inquiry to Mr. Scroggs of Hexham, describing the breed, age, gender and number of cattle he wished to purchase on behalf of his client, unnamed. That letter was easy—he knew exactly how his father, or Devil, would have worded such a missive. By leaving the identity of the ultimate purchaser unspecified, he left the breeder no facts on which to speculate, and no reason to inflate his prices.

Enclosing the letter with a note instructing Heathcote Montague to forward the letter on, Richard sealed the packet and set it aside. Drawing forth a fresh sheet, he settled to write a more challenging missive—a letter to Mr. Potts.

That letter took him two hours and five sheets, resulting in a brief, single-page epistle. Rereading it, he smiled. After laboring to find the correct tone, the precise colors in which he wished to paint himself, he'd finally taken it into his head to approach the exercise as if he was Catriona's champion, her protector, her right arm. To wit, her consort. *She* was the lady, but he was the one who dealt with beef.

Proud of his handiwork, he rose and went to show her.

He found her, as always, in her office, poring over a collection of lists and detailed maps. She looked up as he entered, and smiled—warmly, welcomingly. Richard grinned. He waved the letter at her. "For your approval."

"Approval?" Her eyes flicking to his face, she took the letter, then glanced at it. "Who ...? Oh—Potts."

Scanning the letter, her expression softened from unreadable, to amused, to one step away from joyful. Reaching the end, she giggled and looked up at Richard. "That's perfect!" She handed the sheet back. "Here—I received this in today's packet."

Richard took the letter she held out and swiftly read it—it was from Potts.

"He's becoming more and more insistent." Catriona heaved a relieved sigh. "I'd laid it aside to talk to you about later, but the truth is, I need to deal with Potts for our grain. He's always been our most active and reliable buyer, so putting him off over the breeding stock, especially when they're so expensive and will bring him a good commission, had started to give me a headache."

"Stop worrying." His gaze on her face, Richard heard the order in his tone, but made no effort to soften it. Maybe it was because she wasn't trying to conceal her feelings from him anymore, but he could now see—and sense— how deeply concerned she'd become over the breeding stock. He knew he was reserved, but with her witchy cloak of seeming serenity, she was every bit as bad.

She smiled up at him; he was relieved to see the clouds gone from her eyes. "I have—now I can leave all that to you." Tilting her head, she asked: "Do you have any sources or definite buys in mind?"

Richard hesitated, then grinned charmingly. "Not yet," he lied.

He'd surprise her—it had suddenly occurred to him that she'd been carrying the problems of the vale on her slight shoulders for more than six years. She was due a pleasant surprise or two. Like an unusual wedding gift—one she couldn't ask the price of, and so couldn't worry how the vale would pay for it.

Still grinning, he twitched his missive to Mr. Potts from her fingers. "I'll get this in the post."

He ambled from the room, leaving her to rotate her crops, perfectly sure that Her Lady would, if not precisely approve, then at least turn a blind eye to lies born of good intent.

The next day saw him outdoors, marking out positions for large shelters for the cattle, both those presently in the vale and those he intended to add to the herd. Together with Irons, Henderson and McAlvie, the herdsman—excited to the point of garrulousness—he hammered short stakes into the ice-hard ground, outlining the buildings, then moved on to mark out a series of yards, pens and races, all linked to the buildings.

"I see, I see." McAlvie nodded briskly. "We can move them in, then move them out, at will and without mixing the groups."

"And we won't need to get them all 'round to the one side, neither," observed Irons.

"That's the idea." Taking a brief rest on the rising slope leading to the house, Richard looked down on their handiwork. "This will let us get the herd in quickly—they won't lose condition as badly as they do at present if they're properly protected. And we'll also be able to get them back out as soon as the snow melts. We can keep them in the yards until there's enough new growth in the pastures."

"Which means they'll be easier to feed, and it'll protect the pastures from too-early grazing." Henderson nodded in dour approval. "Sensible."

"We'll put gates inside, too," Richard said, leading the way back down the slope to the field of their endeavor, "so that once in, you'll be able to bring them out into whatever yard gives access to the fields you want to run them on."

They tramped eagerly after him, McAlvie's expression one of bliss.

In the ensuing days, the new cattle barn became the focus of vale interest. All the farmhands and laborers at the manor threw themselves into its construction with an enthusiasm that grew with it—as its realization revealed its possibilities. Others from the farms dropped by—and stayed to help.

The children, of course, swarmed everywhere, fetching nails and tools, providing unsolicited opinions. Despite the hard ground and the difficulty of sinking foundations, the barn grew apace.

"Oooh!" McAlvie's eyes gleamed as he surveyed the long loft running the length of the barn. "We'll be able to feed by simply pushing half bales over the edge and into the stalls below."

"Not this year," Richard answered caustically, handing him a hammer and directing him to a brace waiting to be secured. "Let's get this up, and the herd under cover, *before* you start to dream."

The end walls of the main barn went up slowly, rock and stone filling the wooden frames. Meanwhile, the long side walls, wooden slats over a complex wooden frame allowing for doors, gates, shutters and runs, took shape. The sound of hammering rang over the vale; with every day the sense of shared purpose grew. Eventually, every man had contributed something—hammered in at least one nail—even old McArdle, who had hobbled down to view the enterprise and hadn't been able to resist.

As a shared distraction in a season usually marked by doing nothing, the men, used to outdoor work, welcomed the chance of activity wholeheartedly, and happily immersed themselves in it. "Better 'n chess," was the general opinion.

Eventually, the women came to see what was afoot.

"Mercy be!" exclaimed Mrs. Broom. "The cattle won't know themselves."

Cook humphed. "Get ideas above their station, shouldn't be surprised."

Catriona came down late in the afternoon, just before the light started to fade. Algaria, dressed, as usual, in unrelieved black, glided in her wake.

"This way, mistress." With a flourish, McAlvie conducted her around his charges' new quarters. "I'm thinking, if they spend winters like this, they'll regain their summer weight in weeks, rather than months."

Nodding, Catriona slowly pivoted, taking in the size of the structure—rather larger than she had supposed. "How many will it hold?"

"Oh, it'll take our present numbers easily."

"Hmm." Discovering a gate before her, Catriona opened it. "What are these for?"

"They," Richard answered, strolling up, "are for channeling the occupants." Taking Catriona's hand, he led her to a ladder left leaning against the loft's edge. "Go up a few steps and you'll see the pattern more easily."

Catriona climbed up, and he explained the flow of traffic through the barn.

"How very useful." Looking down, she smiled at him.

Richard reached up and lifted her down. "Useful is what I do best."

She smiled and pressed his hand; together they strolled to the main doors. Leaving him there with a lingering smile and a promise in her eyes, Catriona started back to the house.

Algaria trudged behind her.

Catriona stopped at the stable yard fence and looked back—at the useful structure her consort had fashioned from the materials and energy lying dormant in the vale. A soft smile curved her lips as she turned away and started across the cobbles.

Algaria, behind her, humphed disgustedly. "Newfangled nonsense!"

As often happened, winter refused to cede its authority without one last freeze. It came literally overnight, a storm that dumped feet of snow over the vale, followed by a cold snap, which froze it all in place.

The cattle barn, while far from finished, was complete enough to house the present herd. McAlvie, warned the day before by both Catriona and Cook's aching joints, had sent his farmhands to all corners of the vale to bring the herd in.

Everyone, both from the manor and the farms, had been there to see the herd, shaggy and gaunt, come plodding and swaying, lowing and mooing, up to the manor. Then McAlvie and his lads turned them down the slope to their new quarters; they'd gone readily, filing in through the main doors, heads up, eyes wide. Those watching had waited, listening for any hint of problems; instead, all they heard was a murmur of contented moos.

That had been yesterday; now, standing by the stable yard fence, Catriona looked down on the snow-shrouded barn. The contented sound still rose from the building. The herd was safe and warm; she could see footsteps sunk deep in the snow leading to the barn and guessed McAlvie's lads had already been out to feed them.

Turning, she surveyed the scene in the yard behind her. Irons was in charge of the team set to clear the pump of snow and ice. Richard was about somewhere; she could hear him issuing orders about sweeping some of the snow from the roofs of the forge and two of the smaller barns. The fall had been heavy; from what she could gather, certain eaves were in danger of snapping under the weight.

All the children had been sternly confined to the house; Catriona could see noses pressed to the window panes of the games room. But she agreed with the edict—every now and then, as the men worked to clear the eaves, a minor avalanche would ensue.

Even she was only there on sufferance. That much was obvious from the frown on Richard's face as he rounded the barn and saw her. He strode up. "I'm sure you must have better things to do than freeze your witchy arse out here."

Catriona grinned. "I'll go inside in a minute. I was just wondering"—she glanced at the games room—"how to best to reward the children. They've been so very good, helping with the barn, among other things."

Richard frowned at the fogged windows. "Why don't you tell them that if they manage to *remain* good until after luncheon, I'll give them another riding lesson?"

Catriona opened her eyes wide. "You will?"

Richard narrowed his eyes at her. "Any further orders, ma'am?"

Catriona giggled. Gripping his coat, she stretched up, kissed his cheek, then his lips fleetingly; then, smiling serenely, keeping her eyes on his to the very last, she drew her shawls about her, and headed back to the house.

Richard watched her go—watched her hips sway provocatively as she crossed the snow. Then he drew a deep breath, wrenched his mind back from where it had wandered, and returned to his task—that of being her right arm.

He had it all done—the eaves all checked, those in danger swept, all the stock checked and safe, paths to the buildings cleared—by lunchtime. Crossing the front hall on his way upstairs to change, he heard Catriona call his name.

She was in her office, seated at her desk with McArdle and a dour man he identified as the recalcitrant Melchett in attendance. Catriona looked up as he entered, and smiled, but a frown lurked in her eyes.

"We've been discussing the crop schedules." With a wave, she indicated the papers and maps spread over her desk. "We were wondering if you had any suggestions to make?"

We who? Aware of a certain tension in the air, Richard frowned and looked down at the lists and field placements. "I suspect," he said, "you'd know better than I."

"We were thinking as how you'd done so much with the cattle, that you might have a few pointers, like, about the crops." Melchett studied Richard unblinkingly.

Richard returned his stare, then glanced at McArdle, then looked back at the maps. "If you asked me about crops and rotation patterns in Cambridgeshire I could give you chapter and verse. But here? There's too many variables in different parts of the country to make facile comparisons. What we grow in the south won't grow so well here. Livestock are different— the principles of sound stock managment are the same anywhere."

"But you must have some ideas," Melchett pressed. "Some principles, like you said."

Resisting the urge to narrow his eyes and put the man firmly in his place, on Catriona's behalf, Richard switched from his instinctive role as Catriona's protector, to that of her champion. "The only real measure of effectiveness in crop farming is the yield per acre. If you had those figures"—he looked at McArdle and raised his brows—"I could tell you if you were doing well, or needed to do more."

"Yields, yields." McArdle flicked pages in a huge worn ledger sitting on the table before him. "Here they are." He turned the ledger around so Richard could read it. "For the last five years."

Richard looked, and looked again. He'd expected to see good figures— Jamie had told him the vale was fertile and did well. But what danced before his widening eyes were yields consistently more than fifty percent above the accepted best. And he'd been raised in some of the highest yielding country in England. He said as much—in tones edged with awe. "These are without doubt the best figures I've ever seen." He returned the tome to McArdle, now grinning widely. Richard glanced at Melchett. "Whatever you've been doing, I'd strongly advise you to keep doing it."

"Oh! Aye—" The big man straightened. "If that's the way of things ..."

Richard straightened and smiled down at Catriona. "I'll leave you to get on with it." Turning away, he added: "Incidentally, remind me to make sure my brother and my cousin Vane have a chance to quiz you when we meet." From the door, Richard caught Catriona's eye. "They'll be very keen to learn the secrets of your agricultural success."

With that, he left them, Catriona with her eyes wide, McArdle still grinning, and Melchett in a much more humble mood.

"Catriona."

On her way through the kitchen to the barn to oversee the children's riding lesson, currently in progress, Catriona halted and swung back to face Algaria, who had followed her down the corridor.

"Corby's just come in." With a graceful gesture, Algaria indicated the front hall. "He says the snow has snapped branches from at least five trees in the orchard. Do you want me to tell him to lop the branches off and seal the scars as usual?"

Catriona opened her mouth to agree, then hesitated. "Corby will be staying the night, won't he?"

"Yes."

"Good." Catriona smiled. "I'll discuss the matter with Richard—tell Corby we'll speak to him this evening."

With her customary regal nod, she whirled; eager to join the fun in the big barn, she hurried on through the kitchens, her smile radiant, happiness lighting her eyes.

Behind her, Algaria stood, silently contained, her black gaze fixed on Catriona as she hurried away. Her suppressed fury vibrated around her, an anger others could sense; the kitchen staff warily gave her a wide berth. Finally drawing in a slow breath, Algaria drew herself up, drew her anger in, and, lips tightly compressed, turned and quit the kitchens.

Leaving Cook, kneading dough, sighing and shaking her head.

"Thank you." Catriona pressed a warm kiss to Richard's lips the instant he settled beside her in their big bed.

"What was that for?"

"For your kind words on the crop yields."

"Kind?" Richard snorted, and wrestled her atop him, sitting her upright, straddling his hips. "Cynsters do not know any kind words when it comes to land. That was the truth. Your yields are absolutely staggering." He started to unbutton her nightgown. "And I was perfectly serious about Devil and Vane wanting to talk to you. They will. They'll be excessively glad I've married you."

"Will they?"

"Hmm." Frowning, Richard struggled with the tiny button at her throat. "They both manage lots of acres. In Devil's case, being Cambridgeshire, it's mostly crops, but Vane farms in Kent—hops, fruit and nuts, mainly."

"Mmm."

The odd sound, one of surprised discovery, had Richard looking into her face. "Mmm what?"

She refocused on him. "Mmm, I'd envisaged your brother and cousins as 'gentlemen about town,' more interested in assessing ladies' contours than the contours of land."

"Ah, well ..." Richard popped the button located between her breasts. "I wouldn't say Cynsters ever totally lose their interest in ladies' contours." He popped the next button and couldn't imagine that being otherwise. "Land, however, is our other obsession—an equally abiding one."

Her gaze abstracted, Catriona considered that. She opened her lips on a question—Richard distracted her by opening her gown. Lifting the sides wide, baring her to his gaze, but leaving it draped on her shoulders. Her hands resting for balance on his arms, she glanced down—a wild sensation of nakedness swept her, stronger, more titillating than if she'd been completely bare. Her skin flushed and prickled, all over. Even over her back and bottom, the backs of her thighs, all still cloaked in the soft lawn of her gown.

But she was naked to him, totally wantonly naked, bathed in the light of the two candles he'd left burning, one on each bedside table. His gaze feasted; she felt it sweep over her—down from her throat, over the full swells of her breasts, growing heavier by the day. Her nipples crinkled tight; his lips curved, too knowingly, then he continued his leisurely perusal, scanning her stomach, taut and quivering, to the bright curls between her widespread thighs—which quivered even more as the heat of his gaze touched her.

Closing his hands about her waist, Richard held her there, delectably displayed before him, while he pondered his next move. He was in no hurry to make it; he knew, very well, what her present position—sitting astride him, displayed, exposed to him—was doing to his sweet witch. She was melting, heating—just behind her flaming curls, she was open and vulnerable, her knees held wide.

He was hardly immune himself. He could feel the silky pressure of her naked inner thighs pressing on either side of his hips, could feel the warm, heating weight of her across his lower stomach. Half an inch behind the taut globes of her bottom, he was achingly rigid.

Then he remembered. Turning, he looked at the beside table; reaching out, he snagged the knob of the drawer, tugged the drawer open, then dipped his fingers inside. "Worboys found this in the pocket of one of my coats."

He drew out his mother's necklace, the finely wrought gold chain interspersed with round, rose pink stones. The amethyst pendant slid from the drawer last, swinging heavily on the chain. Richard held the necklace in both hands, gently shaking the pendant free—and for one wild minute, considered using it to love her. Considered placing it—the heavy, slightly bulbous crystal with its edges smoothed, the numerous round, tumbled stones, each one carrying a certain weight—inside her, sliding it into her warm sheath, stone by stone, each pushing the wider, heavier crystal deeper, each pressing against her soft inner surfaces, drawing the necklace out, pushing it in, until she cried out, until she convulsed.

It was an attractive vision; with a mental sigh, he set it aside—for later. After he'd thought through all the possibilties, developed the idea to its fullest, made plans to extract every last ounce of sensuality from it. *Then* he'd break the news to her. But there was no need to rush, to miss anything. He had all his life to tease her.

With his Cynster smile curving his lips, he looked up and met Catriona's wide gaze. "For you." Raising his arms, he slipped the necklace over her head, then gently lifted her hair free. "A belated bridal gift."

He'd teased her about giving her diamonds—he was rich enough to give her them and more, but ... in his heart, he knew diamonds would mean nothing to her, not at the moment. But she'd been fascinated by the one sight she'd had of his mother's necklace—she would, he felt, appreciate it far more than other jewelry.

He was perfectly right. Wide-eyed, lips parted, Catriona stared down at the necklace as it settled against the soft skin of her chest, the heavy pendant sliding into the valley between her breasts as if it belonged there.

Perhaps it did.

There were times when even she was stunned to silence by The Lady's ways.

She knew her eyes were shining, knew her face glowed as she carefully took the pendant between her fingers and raised it to scan the tiny engravings.

"Do you know what this is?" Her words were hushed, tinged with awe.

She felt Richard's gaze on her face, sensed he was intrigued by her reaction. Eventually, drawing the last lock of her hair free, he answered: "It's my mother's necklace—now yours."

Catriona sucked in a huge breath—truer words he could not have spoken; it was as if The Lady had used him to voice her decision. "It's a disciple's necklace—the engravings say that. They're the same as those on my crystal, committing the wearer to allegiance to The Lady and her teachings. But *this* necklace is from a very senior disciple—more senior than me, or any of the past ladies of the vale." She had to stop, to fight for calm; her heart felt like it might burst with sheer joy. She moistened her lips. "This necklace is much older than mine."

"I knew it was different but similar." Reaching to the other table, Richard drew her necklace, which she left there every night, to him, then held it up between them. "I thought it was the same but with the stones inverted."

Catriona looked at him, then drew in a deep breath and nodded; he was involved in this, he was her consort. She could tell him the facts. "On the surface, of course, it is. But there's a deeper meaning." She caught the pendant of her own necklace. "This is rose quartz, which signifies love, and these"— she pointed to the round purple stones embedded in the chain—"are amethyst, which signifies intelligence. So in this arrangement, the stones mean intelligence driving love, the rose quartz being the focus. However"—pausing, she licked her lips and looked back at the necklace now lying against her skin—"*this* is the way it was supposed to be—used to be—before the supplies of amethyst crystals large enough and fine enough to make the focus crystals ran out."

"So," frowning slightly, Richard followed her thoughts, "this necklace"—he placed his fingers on the necklace lying on her flesh and was surprised at how warm it felt—"signifies intelligence driven by love?"

Catriona nodded. "That was the original meaning. That's The Lady's message, the one every disciple must understand and learn to live by. Love is the principal force—the driving force—behind all; all intelligent acts should be governed by, directed by, love."

After a moment's pause, Richard shifted, and laid Catriona's own necklace aside, then settled back beneath her, studying her rapt expression. Quite obviously, he could not possibly have given her a more meaningful gift. But ... "How did my mother come to have such a necklace?"

Catriona lifted her head and met his gaze. "She must have been a disciple, too." When Richard raised his brows, she nodded. "That's possible. She came from the Lowlands, where there were once many followers of The Lady. It's possible that she was descended from one of the oldest lines of disciples—

that's what the necklace suggests—but that she wasn't trained, or, even if trained, had been forced to marry Seamus."

Richard lay back on the pillows and stared at his witchy wife, stared deep into her green eyes. And wondered . . .

Her eyes widened slightly. "The ways of The Lady are often complex, far-sighted—too intricate for us to understand." Slowly, her gaze locked mesmerizingly on his, she leaned forward. "Stop thinking about it."

The soft command, enforced by an underlying compulsion, fell from her lips; the next instant they touched his in an achingly sweet kiss. Richard inwardly shuddered and decided, for once, to obey.

Decided to follow her lead as she wove her witchy wiles and drew them both deeper into desire, deeper into the heat spiralling upward between them.

Followed her as she shifted, lifted, and drew him deep into the shocking heat of her body, into the furnace of her need. He rose with her as she rode him, sweetly urgent, without guile, in undisguised abandon. Brushing aside her gown, he clamped his hands about her hips, then leaned forward and drew one turgid nipple into his mouth. He laved it—a muted cry was his reward.

He settled to feast on her bounty, pausing now and then to watch their bodies merge, to wonder, sensually dazed, as he gazed at his mother's necklace, now gracing his wife's flushed skin.

Then her heat reached flashpoint and exploded; she clung to the peak, her face awash with sensation, then, with a long, soft, sob of joy, crumpled against him.

Burying his face in her hair, he held her close, anchored her hips against him, and drove into her molten softness, once, twice, and again, savoring to his marrow the sense of completeness that was always his when he was buried within her.

Between them, locked in the valley between her breasts, crushed to his chest, his mother's pendant lay, pulsing with a force that was warm yet owed nothing to any fire's heat.

Closing his eyes, his cheek hard against his wife's fiery hair, Richard dragged in a huge breath and let sensation take him. Just as his mother's necklace had always been destined to find it's way here, to reside with his sweet witch in the vale, he, too, his mother's only child, was destined to find his home, his haven, his salvation, here.

In his witch's arms.

In her.

With a long, shuddering groan, he surrendered to fate.

"Master!"

Richard whirled to see one of the workers from the farm at the mouth of the vale come hurrying across the stable yard. "What is it, Kimpton?"

The man halted before him and touched his cap. "You asked that we should report anything not right, sir."

"I did. What's amiss?"

"The gate on the south paddock." The man looked Richard in the eye. "'Twas fast last night when I did my rounds, but 'twas wide this morning, when my youngest went down that way."

Richard's gaze sharpened. "Did he close it?"

"Aye, sir." The man nodded. "And I checked it, too. Nothing wrong with the latch."

Richard smiled. "Very good. Let's see what happens."

Sir Olwyn Glean arrived just after lunch.

He brusquely thrust his hat at Henderson and charged straight for Catriona's office.

He started blustering the instant he flung open the door. "Miss Hennessey! I really must protest—"

"To whom are you referring, sir?"

Catriona's chill tones brought Sir Olwyn up short; he struggled for an instant to breathe, then drew in a huge breath. And nodded in a belated attempt at polite form.

"Mrs. Cynster."

After her exertions of that morning, let alone all the mornings before, Catriona was of the firm opinion she fully deserved the title. Regally, she inclined her head and folded her hands on her ledger. "To what do I owe this visit, sir?"

"As always," Sir Olwyn declared with relish, "to your cattle! Having them scattered about foraging two and three to a field through winter means you can never keep a sufficiently good eye on them. Fence latches break, or get loose—and then what happens?"

"I have no idea"—Catriona looked at him serenely—"but whatever it is, if the matter concerns the vale's livestock, you should speak with my husband." She waved toward the door. "He's in charge of the herds."

"Much good that is," Sir Olwyn retorted, "with him away in London."

"Oh, no, Sir Olwyn—I'm much nearer than that."

Sir Olwyn jumped and whirled. From just behind him, Richard smiled urbanely, every inch a wolf about to take a large chunk out of a marauding dog.

Catriona fought valiantly to keep a straight face; she nearly choked swallowing her giggle. As for McArdle, he looked down at his closed ledger and didn't look up again. The tips of his ears, however, grew redder and redder.

Smoothly continuing into the room, Richard drawled: "What's this about the vale's cattle?"

Red-faced, Sir Olwyn belligerently spluttered: "The vale's cattle have strayed into my cabbages and ruined the crop."

"Indeed?" Richard's brows rose high. "And when did this happen?"

"Early this morning."

"Ah." Richard turned to Henderson, who stood in the doorway. "Please fetch McAlvie, Henderson."

"Aye, sir."

McAlvie must have been waiting, for he was back with Henderson before the silence in the office stretched too thin.

"Ah, McAlvie." Richard smiled at the herdsman. "Are we missing any cattle this morning?"

McAlvie shook his shaggy head. "No, sir."

"*How* would you know?" Sir Olwyn scornfully interjected. "The vale's cattle wander all the time, especially in winter."

"Mayhap they used to," McAlvie stated, "all the other times when we've paid for your cabbages. Aye, and your corn. But not any more."

Sir Olwyn glowered. "What do you mean—not any more?"

"Precisely that, Sir Olwyn." Deliberately, Richard captured his gaze. "*Not* any more." Then he smiled. "We've instituted a new procedure for managing our cattle through the winter. We have a new barn—the entire herd's been confined there since before the last snowfall, so if any had won loose, the tracks would be easy to see. But they haven't." Richard smiled again. "No tracks. If you'd like to go with McAlvie, I'm sure he'd be happy to count the herd with you and show you about our new facilities."

Sir Olwyn simply stared.

"However," Richard drawled, "to return to your complaint, I'm afraid if any cattle have damaged your cabbages, they really must be your own."

Sir Olwyn's inner struggle showed on his surface—his face mottled, veins stood out on his forehead. He managed not to glare, but only just. All but visibly fuming, he swung on his heel, grabbed his hat from Henderson, went to jam it on his head, and remembered, just in time, to nod briefly to Catriona. Then he forced himself to nod, exceedingly stiffly, to Richard. "Your pardon," he growled. Then he stumped out.

Henderson hurried after him to open and close the front door. Returning to the office, he gruffly declared: "Good riddance, I say!"

Doubled up with laughter, none of the others could speak.

Catriona came early to the dining hall that evening. Sliding into her seat at the main table, she watched as her household—her people—filed in and found their seats, chatting and laughing, faces bright and smiling.

The manor had always been a peaceful place, secure and stable; she was accustomed to the sense of calm serenity that had always hung a comforting blanket over this room. The serenity was still there, but, lately, another element had been added. A certain vigor, a joy in life, an eager confidence to see what tomorrow held.

It was, very definitely, a male quality, owing something to assured strength, to experience, and to sheer energy. At times, it almost sparked with rude vitality. To her heightened, experienced senses, the new force melded and merged with the serenity—primarily her contribution; the result was a household more joyfully alive, more happy and content in its peace, than had existed before.

She knew from whom that new force derived; she had to wonder if he knew he was responsible. On the thought, he entered, pausing to chat with Irons and two of McAlvie's lads.

His hair black in the candlelight, his face so much harder, more angular than any others in sight, his tall figure so vital an amalgam of strength and grace that he threw every other male into the shade, he was the focus of her attention, her mind, her heart.

The focus of her love.

She raised a hand and touched the twin crystals that during the day rode between her breasts. At night, she wore only the older—she would never be without it. It was now a part of her, as it was meant to be. As he was meant to be.

Smiling serenely, she drew her eyes from him. Glancing around, she beckoned to a maid. "Hilda—slip up to our bedchamber and make sure the fire's built high." So the air would be warm when they retired to their bed.

The maid, one with sufficient years to read between the lines, smiled broadly. "Aye, mum—I'll make sure it's a right blaze." Eyes twinkling, she hurried out.

Catriona smiled. Just another little detail married ladies had to deal with. Inwardly grinning, she turned back to survey her people—and enjoy the sight of her husband among them.

CHAPTER
Sixteen

ะ๏๏ะ

Catriona was late down to breakfast the next morning, but not quite as late as had been her wont in recent times. While Richard's morning demands hadn't abated in the slightest, she felt less drained, less exhausted from fulfilling them. Perhaps she was growing used to waking up that way.

Whatever, her energy was at a high as she descended the stairs, her feet tripping, her heart light. Smiling brightly, she swept into the dining hall, beaming at all in sight. At the main table on the dais, Richard was looking down at his plate. Her heart buoyed on a wave of sheer joy, Catriona rounded the table and went to her place beside him.

He sensed her presence and tried to turn her way—tried to straighten his back, tried to lift his head and look at her. Catriona slowed; horrified, she took in his slack features, the pallor of his skin. Hunched, his heavy lids hooding his blue eyes, he made a heroic effort to lift his arm toward her.

He crashed out of his chair.

With a pained cry, Catriona flung herself to her knees beside him. About them, shouts and exclamations rang; chairs scraped as everyone rose. Frantically searching for a pulse at his throat, Catriona barely heard.

Then Worboys pushed through and went heavily down on his knees on Richard's other side. *"Sir!"* The pain in his cry was echoed in Catriona's heart. "He's still alive." A panic like nothing she'd ever known had locked a vise about her lungs. Dragging in what air she could, she framed Richard's face in her hands; with her thumbs, she pried open his lids.

They rose, just enough to confirm her worst fears. He was drugged— heavily, heavily drugged.

She sensed him gather his strength—he blinked and looked directly at her, his eyes focused by sheer force of will. Then, with an even greater effort, he turned his head to Worboys. "Get Devil." He licked his dry lips. *"Immediately!"*

"Yes, of course, sir. But ..."

Worboys' words faded as Richard, with such intense effort it was painful to watch, turned his head until, once more, he was looking at Catriona. Jaw clenching, he lifted one hand, fingers extended, to her, to her face—

A spasm twisted his features; he gave a choked gasp, and his lids fell.

His hand fell, too; his head lolled.

He was unconscious.

Only the slow beat of his heart beneath her palm stopped Catriona from wailing. Others did, believing the worst—she hushed them with a word. "He still lives. Quickly—some wine! Then I'll need to get him to our bed."

That first night was not going to be the worst—Catriona knew it. Richard's life hung by a thread—a steadily fraying one. Only the fact that she'd been there, on the spot when the poison first took hold, had saved him—if she'd been even five minutes later, it would have been too late.

Even now, she might have been too late.

Dragging in a breath, she wrapped her arms about her, and continued her slow pace beside the bed. Before the fire would be warmer, but she didn't dare go so far away. She needed to be close, to do whatever she could quickly, when the time came. It hadn't come yet, but soon, soon . . .

Outside the wind howled and sobbed; she fought not to do the same. She'd done all she could thus far.

Before letting them move him, she'd tipped two glasses of the light morning wine down his throat before his instinct to swallow had faded. All through the day and into the night, she'd painstakingly coaxed liquids into him. Garlic water, honey water, and goat's milk mulled with mustard seed— all the standard remedies. Her efforts had been enough to hold him to life thus far, but it was only the beginning of his battle.

This time, his fate rested squarely in the lap of The Lady.

So she prayed, and paced, and waited—for the crisis she knew must come.

And tried not to think about the other crises looming—the ones to be faced when he regained consciousness, or even before.

The thought that he believed she'd drugged him again, this time with deadly intent, hurt beyond description, but she couldn't interpret his movements, his words, in those instants before he'd lost consciousness in any other way. He'd looked at her so strangely, so intently, so deliberately, then he'd told Worboys to fetch his brother immediately. Then he'd tried to point to her.

Whether the pain that had crossed his face had been due to the drug, or to hurt at her supposed betrayal, she couldn't decide.

But . . . dragging in a huge breath, she pressed her lips tight; kicking her skirts out of her way, she paced on. She was not going to let his temporary insanity get her down. She was not going to waste her time, diffuse her energies, in feeling hurt or insulted, nor in wringing her hands or indulging in tears.

The stupid man couldn't afford it—he might die if she wasn't at her best. At her strongest.

He might die anyway.

Thrusting that thought aside, she reiterated to herself her decision on how best to deal with her husband's mental breakdown. Once his wits returned, she would simply hold him to his vow—and force him to talk to her, and she would talk to him. And keep talking until she had straightened out his wayward thinking. It was, of course, nonsensical to imagine she had poisoned him—no one else in the household, not even Worboys, believed that.

But only Richard knew that she'd drugged him before—she could appreciate that in that dizzy moment when the drug had fought to rip his wits from him, he might have remembered that fact and extrapolated without thinking things through.

She could forgive him—but she wasn't about to let her past misdemeanor combine with his drug-induced daze to set a wall between them.

She would talk until the wall fell down.

There was, however, a hurdle looming in her path—very likely a large hurdle; at least, she imagined his brother would be large. Large and forceful. Powerful. Used to being obeyed, to having his edicts complied with.

Grimacing, Catriona swung about and marched around the bed, just for a change of scenery. Of perspective.

She wasn't now sure she'd done the right thing in encouraging Worboys to carry out Richard's order and summon his brother the duke. At the time, she'd been of the mind that as she'd nothing to hide, there was no reason she couldn't face the inquisition. Unfortunately, *she* hadn't thought things through in that instance—thought about what might happen if Richard's brother—a man known to everyone as Devil and presumably a potent source of authority—insisted on removing Richard from her care. Decreed that Richard, still unconscious, would be better tended in London.

Could she—would she be able to—refuse?

If he was taken away before she made sure he understood she hadn't poisoned him, would she get the chance to right his mind later—would he return if he believed, for whatever twisted reasons, that she was behind his poisoning?

The thought went around and around as she paced up and down. And got nowhere. She couldn't, in fact, concentrate on that point, too overwhelmed by the far more scarifying prospect raised by the possibility of Richard being taken from her care.

If he was, he might not live.

And she doubted she could explain that to his brother, or anyone not acquainted with the ways of The Lady.

Sighing, she halted and reached a hand to Richard's wrist. His pulse was still steady, if far too weak. Once again, she mentally reviewed her treatment, searched for any options she had not yet tried. But she'd done all she could—without knowing the specific poison for certain, she couldn't risk doing any more.

She knew, of course, *who* had poisoned him, but the culprit was no longer in the manor, in the vale, for her to question. It seemed Algaria had slipped the poison—a poison only she and Catriona had access to—into Richard's mug, then left immediately, ostensibly to travel to her own cottage, which she sometimes did, but never without informing Catriona first.

The fact that Algaria hadn't waited to gauge her potion's effect suggested she'd been in no doubt it would work. Quelling a shudder, Catriona resumed her pacing and considered the three possible poisons—hemlock, henbane, and wolfsbane. All were deadly, but the last was the hardest to treat. She couldn't, however, overlook the possiblity that a mixture had been used, so she'd had to combine remedies for all three.

She knew that wouldn't be enough.

Which was why she was there by the bed, would always be there, every minute until he awakened. Until she knew he was safe. She had to be there to anchor him to this world if need be, if his connection with it grew too weak. She'd never done such a thing before, but she knew about the region she mentally dubbed "neither nor." The region in which life ceased to have meaning, the threshold between the real world and that other.

She'd stood on that threshold once before, on the night after her parents had died. Her mother had come to her in her sleep—from the dream state to "neither nor" was no great step. Having died in the arms of a man who had loved her deeply, and who she had loved in return, her mother had had no real cause to linger—she'd held back only to bid her adieu.

So she knew the way to that region, knew it was cold, swirling with chill grey mists, treacherous in that it had no reality to which human senses could cling. Any who stepped into it had to rely on their other senses, and their link to any other in that void would only hold true if there was a strong connection between the two souls—like a mother and child, or a husband and wife bound by love.

If the connection wasn't there, then in trying to reach Richard and hold him to life, she would risk losing herself.

She didn't care—if he died, life wouldn't be worth living, but she'd have to live it anyway, without him. The thought was guaranteed to stiffen her spine, to fire her determination. She would not lose him. Or herself. She had faith enough for both of them—faith in his need of her, as much as in her love for him.

The first trial came in the early watches of the morning, when his breathing slowed and he slipped into the greyness. On her knees beside the bed, Catriona drew in a deep breath and resolutely closed her eyes. With one fist clenched about the twin pendants between her breasts, with the other she held his hand, and followed him, into the void beyond the world.

He was there, but blind and weak, helpless as a day-old kitten; gently, she turned him around and brought him home.

Over the next days, and the next nights, she fought by his side, time and again stepping into that grey nothingness to lead him back, to give him her strength, her life, so he could continue to live.

The effort drained her. She could have done with Algaria beside her, but that, of course, was not to be. About them, the manor lay quiet, hushed, yet she was conscious of a soothing, steady stream of support, of prayers and wishes for his health and hers. Without him, life still went on, but it was as if, with his retreat from their world, the heightened sense of life he'd brought to them had sunk into hibernation.

Mrs. Broom and McArdle brought her food and drink; Worboys was in constant, surprisingly helpful, attendance. He knew his master's state was serious, yet, after that first moment of weakness, he had remained the staunchest in his certainty that Richard would shortly wake hale and whole.

"Invincible, the lot of them," he'd assured her when she'd commented on his unswerving confidence. He'd gone on to relate the Cynsters' successes at Waterloo.

It had given her comfort, and some hope, for which she was grateful.

But she alone knew what harmful forces had been unleashed against him—what powerful poison had been fed to him—and only she could heal him and hold him fast to this world.

With a sickening jolt, Catriona awoke on the third morning after their ordeal had begun.

She'd fallen asleep on her knees by the side of the bed, her arms stretched across Richard. With a start, she jerked upright.

Her heart in her mouth, she stared at his face.

His color was that of one alive, pale, but still with her; she only breathed again after seeing his chest rise shallowly, then fall.

With an immense sigh of relief, she eased back on her knees. He hadn't slipped away from her while she slept.

Thanking The Lady, she struggled to her feet, wincing as cramped muscles protested. She hobbled to a nearby chair and fell into it, her gaze locked on Richard.

He was still held fast by the poison; he still needed her as his anchor.

Catriona sighed, then painfully rose and hobbled to the bellpull. She was going to have to share the watches with others, others she could trust, and put her faith in them to call her the next time he started slipping away.

She couldn't risk falling asleep and leaving him unwatched again.

Courtesy of Mrs. Broom and Cook, she slept the next night through—which was just as well as the morning brought with it a challenge she hadn't expected to face for at least a few more days.

"How on earth did they get here this soon?" Standing beside McArdle on the front steps, she watched the huge black travelling carriage drawn by six powerful black horses come rolling up through the park. There was no need for her to see the crest worked in gold on the carriage's doors to guess who was calling.

"They must ha' traveled through the night—no way elsewise they'd be here now." McArdle's gruff tones held a hint of approval. "Must be right powerfully attached to his brother."

That was Catriona's unwelcome conclusion—dealing with Richard's brother was shaping to be a battle, one she didn't know if she had the strength to win. Suppressing the urge to clutch her pendants, she drew herself up; summoning every last weary ounce of her power, she lifted her chin and prepared to make the acquaintance of her brother-in-law.

As it happened, she was to meet her sister-in-law first. A tall, powerful figure uncurled long legs and stepped down from the carriage the instant it halted, but beyond throwing a hard, raking glance about the courtyard, he didn't advance, but turned back to hand a lady from the carriage—he had to lift her as she was quite clearly not about to wait for the steps to be let down.

The instant her feet touched the cobbles, she glided forward, her gaze fixed on Catriona. The lady was severely but elegantly attired in a warm woolen cloak over a carriage dress of rich brown, chestnut hair escaping from a simple chignon. She was taller than Catriona; her features were fine and presently set in a noncommittal expression. Her gaze was direct, her whole bearing declared she was a lady used to command. Catriona braced as the woman looked down, lifting her hems as she negotiated the steps.

Reaching the top, she dropped her skirts and looked Catriona directly in the eye. "My poor dear."

The next instant, Catriona was enveloped in a scented embrace.

"How dreadful for you! You must let us help in whatever way we can."

Released, Catriona tried to steady her reeling head.

"Is this your steward?" The lady—presumably Honoria, Duchess of St. Ives—smiled kindly at McArdle.

"Yes," Catriona managed. "McArdle."

"A pleasure, Your Grace."

McArdle tried to bend his arthritic spine into a bow of the required degree—Honoria put a hand on his arm. "Oh, no—don't bother. We're family, after all."

McArdle shot her a grateful look.

"If you wouldn't mind, my dear . . . ?"

The deep, rumbling resigned tones had the duchess whirling. "Yes, of course. My dear"—she looked at Catriona and gestured to the presence that had followed her up the steps—"Sylvester—Devil to us all."

Holding her calm before her like a shield, Catriona turned, a welcoming smile on her lips—and had to quell an impulse to take a large step back. She was used to Richard and his towering propensities—Devil was worse—about two inches worse.

She blinked into a hard face that was so much like Richard's it made her heart stop, then she looked into his eyes—a lucent green quite unlike Richard's burning blue. In color. The cast of his harsh features, until then severe, eased. As he smiled, she saw the likeness rise again—in the set of the lips, that untrustworthy glint in the eyes. They were, quite clearly, alike in many ways. She blinked again. "Ah . . ."

Despite his sobriety, his smile held a hint of the devil he must be. "It's a pleasure to meet you, my dear. I thought Richard must have lied but he hasn't." With effortless grace, he captured her hand, planted a kiss on her fingertips, then, his other arm having stolen about her shoulders, bent his head and brushed a perfectly chaste, oddly reassuring kiss on her cheek. "Welcome to the family."

Catriona stared into his eyes. "Th ... thank you." She blinked, and looked at Honoria—who was waiting to catch her eye.

"Don't let it bother you—they're all like that."

Imperiously waving her husband back, she linked arms with Catriona and turned to the door. "Quite clearly my feckless brother-in-law is still alive, or you wouldn't be greeting us so calmly."

"Indeed." Finding herself back in her own hall, Catriona quickly introduced Henderson and Mrs. Broom. She grasped the moment while her overpowering relatives were divesting themselves of their coats to relocate and strengthen her habitual serenity. "Mrs. Broom has prepared a room for you—I'm afraid you'll find the household not quite what you're accustomed to. It's a good deal smaller, of course, and we're also much less formal."

"Oh, good." Handing her gloves to Mrs. Broom, Honoria looked up and smiled. "I'm afraid Cynsters aren't much for formality within the family. And as for this"—with a graceful wave she indicated the house about them—"not being what we're accustomed to, you must remember I was only a lowly governess until just over a year ago."

Catriona blinked. "You were?"

Honoria studied her surprise. "Didn't Richard tell you?" Shaking her head, she linked arms with Catriona; together they turned for the stairs. "Isn't that just like a man—never tells one the important things. I'll have to fill you in."

From behind them, where Devil prowled in their wake, Catriona heard: "Lowly governess? *Lowly?* You've never been lowly in your life."

Despite her woes, Catriona's lips twitched; she couldn't resist glancing at Honoria.

Who waved dismissively. "Don't mind him—he's the worst of them all."

They halted at the foot of the stairs; sobering, Catriona drew her arm from Honoria's and turned to face them both. "As Worboys informed you, Richard was poisoned—precisely with what I don't know, but I've been treating him generally, and ..." Her voice quavered; she broke off and drew in a breath. Lifting her chin, she fixed her gaze on Devil's green eyes. "I want you to know that I had nothing to do with it—I did *not* poison Richard."

They both looked at her, studied her, their expressions blank, their eyes filled with sharp intelligence. Then, just as Catriona was about to speak again—to say something to break the silence—Devil reached out, took her hand, and patted it. "Don't worry—we're here to help. You're obviously overtired."

"Have you been nursing him all by yourself?"

The tone of Honoria's question demanded an answer.

"Well, I ... until yesterday."

"Humph! Just as well we almost crippled the horses to get here. One member of the family in a sickbed is quite enough." Taking Catriona's arm again, Honoria took to the stairs. "Now show us where he is, then you can tell us what needs to be done."

Swept up the stairs by an irresistible force, it was all Catriona could do to steady her whirling head. She'd expected censure, certainly a reserved stiffness, at least some degree of suspicion; instead, all she could sense from her new relatives was a warm tide of sympathy and support. She led them to the turret room, to where Richard lay, straight and still in the bed.

Standing at the foot of the bed, her eyes fixed on Richard's face, she waited while Honoria and Devil greeted Worboys, who had been watching over his master. Then they joined her, one on either side, and looked down at Richard.

"He's still breathing freely and his pulse is steady, but he hasn't regained consciousness since he collapsed."

Catriona heard the tiredness in her voice, and felt, again, Devil's hand slide around hers. He squeezed her fingers gently, comfortingly. She felt Honoria's sympathetic gaze on her face, then sensed an exchanged glance pass over her head.

"I'll sit with him for the next few hours." Devil released her hand.

"Perhaps," Honoria said, "you could show me to our room?"

She didn't really want to leave Richard, but ... Catriona gripped her fingers tightly and lifted her gaze to Devil's face. "If his breathing starts to slow, or grow weaker, you must promise to call me immediately. It's important." Her eyes locked on his, she reinforced that thought. "I might need to ..." She gestured vaguely.

Devil nodded and looked at the bed. "I'll send Worboys or one of the others for you at the slightest sign." Then he looked back, a slight smile curving his long lips. "But if he hasn't already died, the chances are he won't." His gaze drifted to Honoria; the look in his eyes deepened. "There are any number of people who can tell you that Cynsters lead charmed lives."

His comforting gaze came back to her face as Honoria humphed.

"Indeed! Believe me," she said, gently turning Catriona from the bed, "there's little point worrying about them, although, of course, we do." She steered Catriona to the door. "Now come and show me where I can wash— I've been in that carriage for more hours than I care to count."

Ten minutes later, sunk in an armchair in the room Mrs. Broom had readied for the ducal couple, Catriona knew that, far from taking care of her guests, her guests were taking care of her. She was too tired to resist, and they did it so well, so effortlessly. They made it so easy for her to just stop for a moment, to stop thinking and simply be. She needed the rest—so she took it, let the steady flow of Honoria's description of their trip north flow past her, and waited for her guest to finish her ablutions.

That done, as she'd expected, Honoria sank gracefully into the chair beside hers, leaned forward and took one of her hands. "Now tell me—why did you imagine we'd imagine you'd had any hand in poisoning Richard?"

Meeting Honoria's misty-blue gaze, Catriona hesitated, then sighed and closed her eyes. "I got a trifle in advance of myself." Opening her eyes, she looked at Honoria. "You see, I think Richard believes I poisoned him—that might be what he believes when he awakes. I was trying to prepare you for that, trying to assure you he was wrong."

"Well, quite obviously he's wrong—but why would he think such a thing?"

Catriona grimaced. "Possibly because I drugged him once before."

"You did?" Honoria regarded her with more interest than puzzlement. "Why? And how?"

Catriona colored. She tried to hedge, prevaricate, avoid the questions, but, she discovered, Her Grace of St. Ives could be ruthless. Honoria dragged the answers from her—then slumped back in her chair and regarded her with awe. "You're very brave," she eventually stated. "I don't know of many women who would be game to feed an aphrodisiac to a Cynster—and then climb into bed with him."

Catriona raised her brows in resignation. "Blame it on total innocence."

Honoria's lips had yet to return to straight; she shot her a measuring, not-at-all-discouraging, look. "You know, that's really a very good story, but one I fear we'll have to keep within the family—the female part of it, that is."

Having by now realized that Her Grace of St. Ives, having been married to His Grace for more than a year, was unshockable, Catriona accepted the comment with an equanimity that, half an hour before, would have astounded her.

"However, to return to your fears over what Richard might think once he wakes, I really do think that you're underestimating him." Head on one side, Honoria stared past her, clearly considering. "He's not usually thickheaded. And he's certainly not blind—none of them are, although you'll find they sometimes try to pretend they are." She looked directly at Catriona. "Do you have any reason to think he believes you were involved, or is it—forgive me—merely a worry on your part?"

Catriona sighed. "I don't think so." Briefly, she described Richard's actions before he lost consciousness.

"Hmm." Honoria wrinkled her nose. "You could be wrong—it's perfectly possible he had some other, male-Cynster-type reason for sending so emphatically for Devil. And for staring at you in that way. However," she stated, setting her hands on her knees, "that's neither here nor there. If he wakes with such a stupid idea in his head, you may be sure I'll set him right without delay."

Honoria stood and shook out her skirts; rather more wearily, Catriona rose, too. "He might not listen."

"He'll listen to me." Honoria met her eye and grinned. "They all do, you know. It's one of the benefits of being married to Devil. As he's the head of the family, there's always the possibility that I might have the last word."

Despite herself, for the second time that day, Catriona felt her lips twitch. Honoria saw, and smiled. "And now, if you'll do me the honor of listening to me as well, I really think you should rest. Devil and Worboys and I will watch over Richard—you need to gather your strength in case he needs your healer's skills."

Catriona looked into Honoria's eyes and knew she was right. She drew in a deep breath and felt like she was breathing freely for the first time since Richard had collapsed. Putting out a hand to Honoria's, she squeezed gently, blinked quickly, then nodded. "All right."

Smiling, Honoria kissed her cheek. "We'll call you if he needs you."

Catriona slept deeply into the afternoon; she awoke, still worried, but even more determimed to haul her weakened spouse back to this world—and his rightful place at her side.

"He's been unconscious for too long," she declared, pacing once more by his bedside, her gaze on his sleeping face. "We need to do something to rouse him."

"What?" was Devil's only question.

She was about to admit that she didn't know, when a flicker of an eyelid stopped her. She stared at Richard's face, then rushed to the bed. "Richard?"

Another definite flicker—he was trying to respond, but couldn't lift his lids.

Devil, close beside her, placed a hand on her arm when she would have spoken again. "Richard," he said, his tone a warning, "*Maman*'s coming!"

Richard's reaction was clearly visible. He tried desperately to open his eyes, but couldn't. A frown creased his brow, then slowly eased as he drifted back into unconsciousness.

"We can walk him!" Fired anew, Catriona dragged back the covers. "If he can respond, then forcing him to use his muscles will help work the poison from his system."

Devil helped her haul Richard to his feet, but Richard was still too incapable of support his own weight; while Devil could hold him upright, he couldn't make him walk. When Catriona tried to slide under Richard's other arm and help, Devil pulled a lock of her hair. "No!" He frowned at her. "Get Henderson."

There was enough implacability in his face to make her heave an exasperated sigh and run from the room.

Henderson came quickly. With him under one of Richard's arms and Devil under the other, they started walking Richard up and down the room. At first, it was no more than a dragging stagger, as one foot dragged, then fell in front of the other. They walked him for ten minutes, then rested, then tried again. And won a fraction more response from Richard. Heartened, they kept up the treatment, walking, resting, then walking again.

Noticing a flicker of Richard's lashes when she spoke to Henderson, Catriona spoke directly to Richard, exhorting him to greater efforts. But, after a time, he only shook his head irritatedly and became even less cooperative.

"Enough." Devil steered their burden to the bed. "Let's have dinner, then we'll try again."

They did, with greater response but even less cooperation. Richard wanted to be left in peace. He didn't say so, but his meaning was quite clear; he became increasingly difficult to manage, swearing in inventive mumbles at his tormentors.

But he walked—back and forth with increasing control over his limbs. When, all but exhausted himself, Devil called a halt and let Richard fall back across the bed, he had regained enough muscle control to grope blindly back onto the pillows and snuggle down.

Smiling for the first time in five days, Catriona drew up the covers and tucked him in.

As she straightened, Devil draped a brotherly arm about her shoulders and gave her a hug. "If he can remember all those French curses, he'll be back with us soon."

Catriona's smile wavered; she grasped Devil's hand and squeezed. "Thank you."

He grinned and flicked her cheek. "No need. He's mine, too, you know." With that enigmatic comment, he led her to the door. "Honoria's already asleep—she said she'd watch through the small hours. I'll stay here now and wake her about midnight. You can get some sleep, then you can relieve her in the morning."

Catriona hesitated. "Are you sure—"

"Positive." Devil held the door and elegantly waved her through. "I'll see you in the morning."

He did—early in the morning. When Catriona returned to the turret room to relieve Honoria a good hour before dawn, she found, not Honoria, but Devil yawning over a game of Patience set out on the covers beside Richard, still comatose.

Catriona stared at Devil. "What happened to Honoria?"

Devil looked up at her, then squinted at the clock on the mantelpiece. "Good heavens! Is that the time?" He grinned engagingly, but undeniably wearily, up at her. "It seems I forgot to summon my dear wife. Never mind." He stood and stretched. "I'll go and wake her now."

He looked down at Richard. "Time flies when one's having fun, but he never was much of a conversationalist."

With a last, weary smile, he left her.

Shaking her head resignedly, Catriona tugged the armchair into place so, sunk in its comfort, she could see Richard's face. His beard had grown, concealing the gauntness of his cheeks; he looked more than faintly disreputable, slumped almost face down in the bed with his hair falling over his forehead and his arms flung out.

Catriona smiled and pulled her workbasket to her side. They would walk him again after breakfast; she'd ring for Worboys to relieve her, then go and summon Henderson and Irons. With their help, perhaps she could get Richard to throw off the lingering effects of the wolfsbane today.

Looking up at him, she listened to his breathing, steady and even, as familiar as her own. Reassured, she picked up her needle and settled to darn.

Head bent, Catriona was plying her needle in the chair beside the bed when Richard finally managed to lever up his lids. Quite why they'd been so unconscionably heavy he couldn't understand, but, at long last, they'd done what he wanted of them and opened.

The sight of his witchy wife in a pose of sweet domesticity was undeniably pleasant; he drank it in, let it soothe away the last of the panic that had gripped him when he'd drifted in the grey cold and wondered if he would die. He hadn't wanted to die, but he'd been so cold, so weak, he hadn't felt able to cling to life.

But then she'd come, slipping her warm hand in his and leading him back, out of the grey cold and into the warm darkness of their bed. She hadn't wanted him to die either—she hadn't let him go, she'd helped him cling, helped him stay. Helped him live.

He was still here, with her; looking further, he confirmed that he was in their bed, and that morning light was seeping through the curtains. He drew in a deep breath, and brought his gaze back to her well-beloved face—and noticed the dark smudges beneath her eyes. In that instant, she yawned, lifting a hand to smother it, then she blinked her eyes wide and refocused on her darning.

Richard frowned; his witchy wife was undeniably pale, undeniably drawn. She didn't, now he looked more closely, look all that well.

His frown deepened.

Catriona felt it and looked up; startled, the first thing she saw was the blue of his eyes. Her heart soared, only to plummet a second later. He was frowning direfully. At her. He opened his lips—she stayed him with a raised hand. "No! Let me speak first. No matter what you think, I did *not* poison you."

He blinked, but his frown returned immediately. He opened his lips again—

"I realize you might have jumped to that conclusion, and I can see why you might, but you're wrong. It's absolutely ridiculous to imagine that after all you've done for me and the vale, all that's passed between us, that I would suddenly turn around and poison you. If you really think that—"

"I *don't!*"

Catriona blinked and discovered Richard was no longer frowning at her—he was glowering at her.

"Of course, I don't think you poisoned me!" His gaze raked her, then returned to her face; his glower turned black. "What nonsensical notion have you been worrying yourself with?"

When she didn't answer, he swore. "I'd heard women got silly ideas when pregnant, but that takes the prize." He looked at her more closely—then swore again. "Is that what you've been worrying yourself sick over? That I'd be fool enough to think it was you?"

Dazedly, somewhat warily, Catriona nodded. Which brought forth another round of curses.

"What a stupid, foolish notion—"

"Why did you send for your brother, then?"

"So he'd be here to protect *you* if I wasn't about to do it, of course! *Lord—!*"

Running out of curses, he leaned forward, grabbed her hand and hauled her onto the bed. Pins, needle and mending went flying. Catriona gasped as she landed amid the covers.

Before she could react, he'd framed her face and was studying it closely.

"You haven't been taking care of yourself—"

"*You* were the one poisoned—" She struggled to get free, to sit up; even in his weakened state, he held her easily.

"We'll sort that out later. You obviously haven't been getting enough sleep. Pregnant women are supposed to sleep more—I would have thought you'd know that. You've staff and helpers about you ..." He broke off, then looked into her eyes. "How long have I been unconscious?"

"*Five days,*" Catriona informed him.

"Five *days?*" Richard stared at her, then his gaze softened and dropped to her lips ... "No wonder I'm so hungry."

This time, Catriona knew precisely which appetite he was referring to. She opened her lips—but didn't manage to say a word.

He kissed her, gently, tenderly, then with gathering rapaciousness. Catriona felt the covers about her slide, felt the pillows shift, felt his hand slide up her leg to her garter, then stroke the soft skin above. He leaned into her, pressing her deeper into the soft mattress; she clung to the moment, savored it briefly, then thumped him on the shoulder. Hard.

He shifted slightly—she managed to drag her lips free and gasp: "*Richard!* You're not strong enough!"

He raised his head and looked down at her—as if what she'd just said was utterly impossible—then he hesitated, considered, then groaned, grimaced, closed his eyes, and rolled off her.

"Unfortunately, much as it pains me to admit it, I think you might be right."

"Of course, I'm right!" Struggling up on one elbow, Catriona tugged the covers back over him. "You've been at death's door—literally!—for five days. You're not simply going to open your eyes and"—she gestured wildly—"get right back into things."

He caught her eye and waggled his brows at her; ignoring her blush, she humphed. "You just stay there and rest." She went to slide away, to back off the bed, but his arm, around her, didn't give. She looked at his face.

"I'll stay here," he said, gently, reasonably, "provided you stay with me." Catriona frowned; inexorably, he drew her closer. "You need to rest, too." Drawing her down, back into his arms, he settled her head on his shoulder, then pressed a kiss to her forehead. "Just let me hold you while you sleep."

He did. Swamped by relief so deep it shook her, touched that his last conscious thoughts, and now his first, had been for her, wrapped in his arms, with him safe beside her, Catriona slept.

CHAPTER
Seventeen

ॐ⟨⊙⟩ॐ

"I am *not* an invalid!" Richard eyed the mushy food on the tray balanced across his thighs with disgust.

"You are," Catriona declared. "And Cook made that especially for you—she's an expert at building people up."

"I don't need building up." His expression mutinous, Richard poked at the greyish mass with his fork. "I need letting up."

"I think you'll find you're mistaken."

Richard looked up. "Honoria!" His sister-in-law swept in, clearly intending to lend Catriona her support; Richard glanced back at the doorway, and to his relief saw the shadow he wanted darkening the door. "Thank God—come in commonsense."

Brows rising, Devil strolled in. "I don't know that I've ever been called 'common' before." He grinned. "You need a shave."

"Never mind that—have you seen what they're feeding me?"

Devil looked. "Better you than me, brother mine."

"You have to save me." Richard pointed to the mushy mass. "You can't leave me to this fate."

Straightening, Devil looked across the bed—at Catriona, staring mulishly, arms folded; at his wife, her expression implacable, her fine eyes on him. "Hmm—actually, in this case, I think I must defer to higher authority."

Richard stared at him. "You've never done that before."

"Ah—but you weren't married before." Strolling around the bed, Devil collected Honoria in one arm and turned toward the door. Looking back, he added, "And neither was I. I'll come back after lunch."

Richard glared at the empty doorway, flicked a glance at Catriona, then looked down at the mush on his plate. He scooped up a forkful and ate. Swallowing, he frowned at his wife. "I'm only doing this for you, you know."

"Good." Some moments later, she added: "All of it."

Richard complied. Aside from anything else, the food tasted a lot better than it looked—and he was hungry enough to eat a horse.

Both Devil and Honoria returned after lunch, after he'd cleared the tray and Catriona had taken it away.

"I have to say that seeing your eyes open is a great improvement." Devil perched on the end of the bed. "I've had quite enough of watching over you while you sleep."

Richard grinned. Devil was three years older; they'd shared a nursery—his comment harked back to the untold nights when, scared of the dark, he'd only fallen asleep because he'd known Devil was there to protect him from imagined monsters.

"You gave us a shock." Honoria leaned down and kissed his stubbled cheek. "At least you had the good sense to marry a lady who could save you."

Richard smiled and accepted the compliment graciously. Over the next half hour, they exchanged family news, heavily biased toward the emerging talents of one Sebastian Sylvester Cynster, Marquess of Earith, Devil's heir.

"We would have brought him," Honoria declared, "but we didn't know what the state of things here might be."

That, of course, was the cue for Richard to fill them in, which he did in glowing terms, quite unable to contain his satisfaction on that score—his happiness in his new life. "Now you're here, I'll be able to show you around."

"Once you're released from *durance vile*." Devil nodded at the bed.

"Tomorrow," Richard said.

Devil grimaced. "Don't get your hopes up. You didn't seem too strong while we were walking you yesterday."

"Walking me ...?" Richard frowned, then shook his head. "I didn't even know you were here ..." Still frowning, he glanced at Devil. "Actually, I do remember—was it you who warned me *Maman* was coming?"

Devil grinned. "We were testing to see if you'd respond."

Richard shuddered. "Just as long as it's not true." He caught Devil's eye. "You didn't tell her, did you?"

Devil raised his brows exaggeratedly. "What do you think?"

Rising, Honoria shook out her skirts. "Naturally, we left a note."

Devil's head snapped around. "We did?"

Honoria stared at him. "Well, of course. We couldn't simply leave and not tell Helena, not even leave a message—she is his mother, after all."

Richard groaned and fell back against his pillows.

Honoria turned her gaze on him. "She was away with the Ashfordleighs—she'd think it very strange to return to Somersham and find Sebastian alone with the staff. So I simply explained and told her not to worry."

Devil raised his eyes to the ceiling. "Honoria—"

Sudden shouts from outside cut across his words; a second later, the rattle of carriagewheels and the sharp clack of hooves rose from the courtyard.

Richard groaned again; Devil grimaced.

Honoria stared at them. "It can't be."

"It can," Devil assured her.

"It is," Richard gloomily prophesied.

It was. In the courtyard, a cavalcade of two carriages with outriders drew up.

Hearing the commotion as she crossed the front hall on her way back to Richard's side, Catriona went out onto the front porch to investigate.

The scene in the courtyard was bewildering—as if a houseparty from London had lost its way and turned up at the manor. Coachboys, outriders, grooms and maids rushed hither and yon, opening carriage doors and setting steps in place, tugging at the straps that secured bags and trunks to the backs and tops of the carriages. A tall, exceedingly elegant gentleman stepped down from the second carriage; he cast a swift glance about the teeming courtyard—his gaze halted, and lingered, on her, before returning to the scene of chaos about the first carriage. Despite his fairer coloring—brown hair, not black—Catriona felt certain the gentleman was another Cynster.

Just as she felt certain the small, dark-and-silver-haired lady he helped down from the first carriage was the Dowager Duchess of St. Ives—Helena, Richard's stepmother. With the brisk energy of a whirlwind, the Dowager waved the elegant gentleman back to his own carriage, where a second lady was waiting to descend. Behind the Dowager, two young ladies, their lowered hoods revealing a wealth of golden curls, were gaily piling out of the first carriage. Claiming the arm of one of her grooms, the Dowager made straight for the front porch, her cloak billowing about her.

She came up the front steps with the force of a military charge. "My dear!"

Catriona only just had time to brace herself; flinging her arms wide, the Dowager enveloped her in a warm embrace.

"Now you may tell me he is better—he is better, is he not? But of course, he is! You would not otherwise be standing here so calmly, welcoming a garrulous old woman!" Green eyes twinkling, the Dowager hugged her again, then released her; holding both her hands wide, she stepped back and, with every evidence of shrewd consideration, quickly looked her over.

"Oh, yes!" Looking up, the Dowager caught Catriona's eye. "You will do very well for him, I think." She smiled, brilliantly. "And you will not let him down—you will always be there for him, yes?" For one instant, green and hazel eyes held, and touched, then the Dowager beamed. With Gallic exuberance, she kissed Catriona on both cheeks. "Welcome to the family, my dear."

Touched to the heart by the profound love that shone from the Dowager's eyes, Catriona blinked rapidly. "Thank you, ma'am."

"Helena," the Dowager firmly declared. "I am Helena to both my sons' wives. But tell me—Devil and Honoria have arrived, have they not? And how is Richard—is he eating? Has he risen? Has—"

"Aunt Helena, you're liable to give poor Catriona a very strange notion of the family."

Turning, Catriona beheld the elegant gentleman with a graceful lady on his arm. They both smiled warmly; he bowed. "Vane Cynster, my dear—and I assure you we don't all rattle on so."

"I am *not* 'rattling on,'" Helena declared. "I am merely exercising the right of any mother to learn of her son's health."

"But he isn't about to die, is he?" The question came from one of the blonde beauties, now lined up behind the Dowager.

"Surely not Richard?" The second young lady fixed Catriona with huge blue eyes. "But you're a healer aren't you? You'd save him."

There was an element of absolute confidence in that last, uttered with a nod, that touched Catriona anew.

The graceful lady sighed and touched the Dowager's arm. "Perhaps, Helena, if we move inside—I rather think there's another snow shower coming."

Catriona stepped back and gestured the Dowager in; as the Dowager swept majestically across the threshold, the graceful lady touched Catriona's arm and met her glance with a smile.

"I'm Patience, my dear. Recently married to Vane, another of the family's reprobates. And these are Amanda and Amelia—and"—she paused to draw breath and met Catriona's eye—"I'll explain how it all happened later."

They followed the Dowager in; the scene in the hall quickly achieved the same degree of chaos that had held sway in the courtyard. Boxes and trunks were ferried in and piled in corners under Henderson's dour direction. Mrs. Broom looked as stunned as Catriona felt; wide-eyed, the housekeeper struggled to take in her instructions, then rushed off, calling to maids and footmen to open up and air rooms for the latest guests.

A cacophony unlike anything the serene manor had known rose in the hall as the two young ladies checked which bandbox was whose and where the Dowager's shawl had gone; Vane and both coachmen were in earnest discussion with Irons over where to stable the extra horses. The Dowager had discovered McArdle and was inquiring after his stiff limbs as if she'd known him all his life—and he was responding as if she had. Rushing maids and footmen stopped now here, now there, to put a question, then dashed off about their duties.

Catriona stood just inside the front doors and took it all in, let it wash over her. The noise, the boisterousness, the enormous well of energy that swelled within her hall; it was an immensely powerful force. It was there in the swift, neat movements of the Dowager, in the set of her head as she tilted it the better to consider McArdle's replies. There in the crisp directions Vane Cynster issued, in the innate grace, redolent of harnessed power, with which he moved. There in the glow that lit the young ladies' faces and invested their bodies with a taut grace reminiscent of fawns about to spring into flight.

Coming to stand beside her, Patience looked over the hall. "The Cynsters are here—what more need be said?" But she was smiling. She turned to Catriona. "I do apologize for descending on you like this, but as you were going to have to cope with Helena come what may, it's probably just as well the rest of us are here to help you."

The clear affection in Patience's tone, in her eyes, as they returned to the Dowager, stripped her comments of any implied criticism.

"Perhaps," Catriona murmured, "I'd better take her up to see Richard."

Patience nodded. "Do. It'll set her mind at rest. Don't worry about the rest of us." She smiled at Catriona. "If you don't mind, I'll speak directly to your housekeeper if there's any problem—I rather think you must have enough on your plate."

Catriona returned her smile. "Please do." Looking back at the Dowager, she drew in a deep breath. "It's possible I may be rather busy for a while."

With that, she stepped boldly into the fray and fetched up by the Dowager's side. "Helena, if you wish, I'll take you to see Richard—I'm sure he'll be anxious to see you."

The Dowager shot her a shrewd glance. "No, no, *ma petite*—it is I who am anxious to see him. He"—with a Gallic gesture, she dismissed all males—"is but a man. He does not understand these things."

As she took the arm Helena offered, Catriona saw two blonde heads lift; two pairs of blue eyes fastened on them.

"Amelia! Amanda!"

Both heads turned; Patience beckoned. With a sigh and a last look, they went.

"Vane, you can see Richard later—I want to get our rooms sorted out first."

Her gaze on the stairs, Catriona smiled and bore the Dowager upstairs to see her second son.

Richard felt trapped—deserted by Devil and Honoria—left to face his stepmother alone. When the door opened and swung wide, he contemplated groaning and acting much iller than he was, but then he glimpsed his wife's fiery halo and thought better of any deception.

Only God and Her Lady knew where it might land him.

"Richard!" Helena—she who he'd always known as *Maman*—came sweeping down upon him.

Smiling reassuringly, he returned her hug, and squirmed when he glimpsed tears in her eyes. To his relief, she blinked quickly and they were gone, and she beamed her brilliant smile at him.

"*Bon!* You are already much recovered, I can see."

To his surprise, instead of taking possession of him, his sickbed and his room in short order, she contented herself with taking possession of his hand, and cast a questioning glance at Catriona, standing at the end of the bed.

Catriona inclined her head. "He is much better—he was unconscious for five days, but with Devil's help, we managed to walk him so the poison wore off sooner."

"This poison." Helena tilted her head, still regarding Catriona. "How was it given him?"

Catriona looked at Richard. "In his morning coffee."

"And the person who put it there? Will they try again?"

"No." Steadily, Catriona held Richard's gaze. "The poisoner is no longer in the manor, or the vale."

"Ah!" Helena nodded sagely. "They have run to safety, yes?" She looked at Richard, then squeezed his hand. "You will go after them, I know—but not until you are well again, *hein?*"

"I'll be perfectly well by tomorrow." Richard tried to catch Catriona's eye but failed—she was looking at Helena.

"You will know best, of course," his impossible stepmother was saying, "but how quickly he recovers will depend on the poison, yes?"

"Indeed." Looking back at Richard, far too calmly for his liking, Catriona informed him: "You were given wolfsbane, and probably henbane as well. But it's the wolfsbane that's the most lingering. It weakens muscles, and it takes far longer than one thinks to release its effect. For the amount you must have taken in, it would generally take weeks for full recovery."

"Weeks?" Horrified, Richard stared at her.

She smiled reassuringly. "In your case, you have a very robust and ... er, vigorous constitution. If you remain in bed and eat what Cook sends you until you can stand and walk alone, you may be well enough to leave this room inside of a week."

"*Eh, bien*—your wife has spoken. She is the healer here and you must pay attention." Placing his hand under the sheets, Helena covered it and patted his arm. "You will be good and recover quickly, so that I will not worry, no?"

Richard stared at her, then he looked at Catriona and saw the militant light in her eye.

With a long-suffering groan, he sank back into his pillows. He was rolled up—horse, foot and guns.

"Damn it—why couldn't you stop her!" Grumpily, Richard mock-glared at Vane.

Who merely grinned. "Me and which army?" Settling on one corner of the bed, his back against the post, Vane raised a resigned brow. "You've known what she's like all your life."

Richard humphed.

"And if you'd seen what faced us when we arrived at Somersham, you'd be thanking me for managing to leave Mrs. Hull and Webster behind. As it is"— Vane glanced at Devil, similarly ensconced on the other side of the bed—"I'm sure the only reason they consented to remain at Somersham was because Sebastian was there."

Richard looked at Vane in only partly feigned horror, then shook his head. "What I can't understand is what you're all doing here."

"*We,*" Vane said, clearly referring to himself and Patience, "were returning from visiting the Beuclaires in Norwich and thought we'd stop by to tell Devil and Honoria our news."

Devil raised his brows. "What news?"

"The impending extension of our family."

"Really?" Devil grinned and thumped Vane on the shoulder. "Excellent. Another playmate for Sebastian."

Both Richard, beaming and shaking hands with Vane, and Vane himself, stopped and turned to stare at Devil.

"Another?" Vane asked.

Devil grinned even more as he resettled his shoulders against the bedpost. "Well, you didn't think I'd stop at just one, did you?"

They hadn't, but . . . "When?" Richard asked.

Devil shrugged nonchalantly. "Sometime in summer."

Richard hesitated, then raised a brow and sank back. "Sounds like our respective mothers and aunts will be in alt. Nothing they like better than a baby or two." Or three. But he kept his lips shut on that point and looked at Vane. "So what happened when you got to Somersham?"

"We arrived mid-morning, one hour after Helena and the twins, who she's been chaperoning about, got in from the Ashfordleighs—we didn't even get a chance to get out of our coats. Your mother had read Honoria's note and got the bit well and truly between her teeth even before we arrived. Nothing would do but she must rush north to your side—to your deathbed, as she put it. As usual, it was impossible to gainsay her—and, of course, I couldn't let her go rushing through the snow with just the twins for escort. Well," Vane gestured, "you can imagine what it was like. Mrs. Hull on the stairs with Sebastian in her arms declaring you were at death's door. Webster all but wringing his hands and making unhelpful suggestions as to how best to reach the Lowlands. The twins oohing and aahing and trying not to remember Tolly's death. And your mother, center stage, vowing she would fight through drifts on her hands and knees to get to your side in time. In time for what, I didn't ask."

"To make a long story short, I didn't stop them because I couldn't. The push north had gathered so much momentum before we arrived that it was beyond my poor ability to deflect."

Richard grimaced in exasperated understanding. "Couldn't you at least have left the twins behind?"

Vane eyed him straitly. "Have you tried recently to turn the twins—independently or in concert?"

Richard blinked at him. "But they're only girls."

"That's what I keep trying to tell them—they seem to have different ideas."

"Humph!" Richard settled deeper into his prison. "Well, they won't be able to test their wings here—it's as quiet as a nunnery."

An hour later, Catriona presided over the noisiest dinner she could ever recall. It wasn't that anyone raised their voices, or spoke above the tone of polite conversation. But the sudden injection of Cynster elegance, wit and curiosity had spawned innumerable conversations, both at the main table, where all the guests sat, and at all the tables in the hall, filled by her household.

Everyone was chattering animatedly.

The wash of sound did not give her a headache—not at all. It was comforting, in some ill-defined way. There was warmth in the laughter, in the interest and attention, in the real affection so openly displayed. There was a human element the Cynsters had brought to the vale that, somehow, had been missing before. She wasn't quite sure what it was, but . . .

In her habitual role as head of the household, she kept an eye on the courses, making sure her guests needs were met. Everything ran smoothly—indeed, despite the totally unexpected influx, no serious problem had occurred.

Her gaze, at that instant, resting on the Dowager, Catriona inwardly grinned. Everything had gone right, because nothing dared go wrong, not before the Dowager and Honoria. Patience was less forceful a personality, at least on the surface, but even she could command when she wished. She'd called both the twins and her husband to order very effectively that morning.

Catriona inwardly frowned. Vibrant, effective matriarchs did not fit her earlier vision of what Cynster wives must be like. Recalling what had given rise to that transparently inaccurate view, she waited until Honoria, beside her, was free, then caught her eye. "I know," she murmured, leaning closer and lowering her voice, "what the bare circumstances of Richard's birth were. What I can't quite understand"—her gaze flicked to the Dowager—"is how his acceptance into the family came about."

Honoria grinned. "It is difficult to see—unless one has previously met Helena. Then . . . anything becomes possible." She lowered her voice. "Devil told me that when Richard was dumped, a squalling babe of a few months, on the ducal doorstep, Helena heard the ruckus, and before Devil's father had a chance to hide matters, Helena simply—literally—took Richard out of his hands." She paused and sent an affectionate glance up the table to the Dowager. "You see, Helena loves children, but after Devil, she couldn't have any more of her own. The one thing she most yearned for was another— especially another son. So, when Richard arrived, in her inimitable way she decided it was all Providence's doing and claimed him as her own. The trick was, by then, she was well established as Devil's father's duchess—a veritable power within the ton. Quite simply, none had the gall to gainsay her—where was the point? Helena could have socially destroyed most people with nothing more than a raised brow."

"I'm surprised Devil's father was so . . . acquiescent."

"Acquiescent? From all I've heard of him, I doubt the term would apply. But he sincerely loved Helena—the accident that resulted in Richard's birth was more in the way of him comforting Richard's mother than in any intended infidelity. And so he indulged Helena—he loved her enough to allow her the one thing she asked of him in recompense: he allowed her to claim Richard and bring him up as her own, something which unquestionably gave her great and abiding pleasure."

Again, Honoria glanced affectionately at the Dowager. Catriona did the same.

"So," Honoria concluded, "Richard's birth has been an open secret for thirty years, and, really, no one cares any more. He's simply Richard Cynster, Devil's brother—and as the family approve of that, who's to argue?"

Catriona shared a glance with Honoria, then smiled and touched her arm. "Thank you for telling me."

Honoria returned the smile, then looked around, alerted by the deep rumble of her spouse's voice. She promptly called him to order, taking up verbal cudgels in the twins' defense. The head of their house was dissatisfied with their appearance—in what way he refused to clarify.

Catriona stifled a grin. Cynster wives were definitely not mere cyphers, pretty trophies to be displayed on their husbands' arms. With three others in the room, she couldn't escape the conclusion that, for whatever inscrutable male reasons, Cynster men had a soul-deep affinity for strong women.

And, furthermore, despite their occasional comments to the contrary, they wouldn't have it any other way. They took real delight in indulging their wives; one only needed to catch the look in Devil's eyes as they rested on Honoria, or in Vane's as he watched Patience.

Or in Richard's as he watched her.

The realization stopped her thoughts—something inside her quivered. The reason Cynster men so indulged their wives was there in their eyes. Much indulged their wives might be; much loved they certainly were.

And, as Devil loved Honoria, and Vane loved Patience, so Richard loved her.

It was that simple.

Dragging in a tight breath into lungs suddenly parched, Catriona barely heard the flow of noise and chatter about her. Her sight was turned inward.

Richard had fulfilled his vow to play second fiddle to her—to honor and indulge her position as lady of the vale—which was a large concession from a man like him—a warrior like him. She'd realized that from the start—that without such a concession, their marriage could never work, could never be the success they both needed it to be.

He'd made that concession because he loved her.

The sudden clarity, the absolute certainty that filled her mind was dazzling, breathtaking.

She'd known that he needed her, that he now knew he belonged here, in his appointed place at her side. But she hadn't, until that quivering instant, realized that he loved her as well.

Glancing at Devil, she saw him grin and flick a finger to Honoria's cheek, then he turned to address Vane, but his hand closed over Honoria's where it rested on the table. Vane was lounging in his chair, one hand on Patience's back, his fingers idly toying with her curls.

Only by that light in his eyes, and, perhaps, if she had any experience by which to judge, his intensity in their bed, did Richard show his love for her. He was reserved—she'd known that before she'd met him; he always wore a mask in public. He didn't display his love openly, as the others did so easily, apparently without thought. She needed instead to pay attention to his actions, and the motives behind them, to see what force was driving him.

She should, perhaps, have seen it before, but he yielded his secrets grudgingly. That he knew was beyond question; as Honoria had mentioned, Cynster males weren't blind, although they sometimes pretended they were. He had, she recalled, been very definite that he wanted her as his cause.

Turning to speak to the twins, she hugged her newfound discovery to her heart and, throughout dinner, took it out now and then to ponder. To consider. Again and again, she observed that special something that flowed openly between Devil and Honoria, and Vane and Patience—and wanted it for her own.

Quite how she might bring it about—give Richard the confidence he needed to show his love openly, presumably by convincing him she returned it fullfold—was something she'd yet to determine.

But it was something she vowed she would do.

Smiling sunnily, she chatted with the twins—thanks to The Lady, she now had ample time to work on Richard.

The next morning, Richard lay in bed and tried to disguise his fretfulness. Lying in bed doing nothing was his least favorite pastime, but at the moment, that was all he could do. Nothing.

At least he'd managed to coax his wife into sleeping beside him once more; she'd apparently been sleeping in the room next door ever since his poisoning, so as not to disturb him. He had made it very plain that now he'd regained his senses, not having her beside him would disturb him even more. He'd won that round, but no other.

There was no point in arguing—he couldn't stand on his own, much less walk. He'd tried, surreptitiously, in one of the few moments he'd been left alone. Luckily, he'd crashed back on the bed and not the floor. His muscles were not just weak but, as his witchy wife had warned him, still feeling the effects of the poison. Even holding his eyelids up was an effort.

Inwardly cursing she who had drugged him, he kept his face relaxed and listened to Vane's news of shared friends. With his usual instinctive grasp, Devil had refrained from pressing the question of who had poisoned him, waiting until he'd recovered enough to inquire. While Richard and Catriona had not discussed the matter beyond their exchange before Helena, Richard had, with complete confidence, assured Devil that the poisoner was not a threat now, and that he and Catriona would deal with the matter once he'd fully recovered.

Devil had accepted that; Richard knew he could rely on his brother to quash any further interest in the matter. It was definitely a situation he and his witchy wife needed to deal with on their own.

Not, however, yet.

Stifling a sigh, Richard smiled at Vane's description of a race held at Beuclaire Hall. Then he let his gaze drift past his cousin, to where Catriona sat on the windowseat, industriously darning, her hair turned to a blaze of glory by the sunlight streaming in through the window.

At least there was nothing wrong with his eyes.

Five minutes later, heralded by the most peremptory of knocks, the door opened. A tall, broad-shouldered, ineffably elegant figure sauntered in.

His gaze fell first on Catriona—and went no further.

The ends of his long lips lifting in a smile both Richard and Vane knew well, the gentleman advanced, then swept Catriona a bow.

"Gabriel Cynster, my dear."

Catriona instinctively held out her hand; he took it and drew her effortlessly to her feet, into his arms, and kissed her. Raising his head, he smiled wolfishly down at her. "Richard's cousin."

"Another one," Vane commented drily.

Smoothly releasing Catriona and gracefully reseating her with an irresistible smile, Gabriel turned to the bed and raised a languid brow. "You here, too? If I'd known, I wouldn't have half-killed my horse getting here."

Blinking, Catriona picked up her needle, but kept her gaze on the tableau about the bed.

"How the devil did you hear?" Richard asked. "Don't tell me it's common knowledge among the ton."

Halting by the bed, Gabriel looked down at Richard. "Well, you're obviously still alive—Mama must have got her skeins tangled. She was quite adamant I'd find you at death's door." Gracefully, he sat on the end of the bed. "As for the news being bruited about, I can't say, but it wouldn't surprise me. Mama wrote me a series of orders, couched in a manner to discourage disobedience, and bade me hie north at speed. I was at a very select gathering in a hunting lodge in Leicestershire. How the devil she knew where to find me I really don't like to think."

Vane humphed.

Richard grinned sleepily.

Gabriel shook his head. "It's a sad day when one can't even escape to a select, supposedly secret orgy without having one's mother summon one— without a verbal blink."

Both Richard and Vane chuckled. Gabriel raised his brows resignedly.

Catriona shook out her mending and started to fold it. "I'll certainly write to Lady Celia and thank her for her kind thoughts."

A sudden hiatus gripped the three about the bed.

"And now," Catriona declared, "Richard needs to rest."

The three exchanged a meaningful look; Catriona stood and smiled at Vane and Gabriel. "If you would, gentlemen?"

She waved to the door; they left with smooth smiles and no argument. Bustling to the bed, she tucked Richard in. He wished he could frown, but he really was tired.

"Come and lie down with me." He tried to catch her, but he was far too slow.

She whisked away, raised one finger to waggle at him, then changed her mind and smiled. A smile that softened her face and set his pulse racing, a smile that should have sealed her fate—if he'd been in any way up to it.

"Later," she said. "When you're well again."

There was a softness in her eyes, an echo of something in her tone, that eased and soothed his irritation. She drew the curtains and left him; Richard drifted off, into dreams of a highly select orgy, restricted to just two.

* * *

By the next morning, he had really had enough. He felt strong enough while lying relaxed on his back, but even lifting his arms was an effort. He couldn't make love to his wife. He couldn't get out of bed.

As far as he was concerned, he needed practice on both counts.

To that end, he persuaded Devil, so often his partner in crime in days past, now left to bear him company while their ladies took the air in the park, to help him up.

"If I can just get my legs functioning properly . . ."

Ducking one shoulder beneath Richard's arm, Devil helped him balance his weight as he rose from the side of the bed. "Let's try it to the fireplace and back. We need to avoid the window—they might glance back and see us."

Richard grabbed Devil's shoulder and lifted his foot to take the first step—

The door opened. "It's drizzling—" The Dowager, in advance of her daughters-in-law, halted and viewed her sons—caught in an act of disobedience—through narrowing eyes. "What is this?"

They both blushed. The degree of accent in Helena's speech gave them warning she was not amused.

"I would 'ave thought you were both now old enough to 'ave more sense," she declared.

"Sense?" Her expression mirroring her skeptical tone, Honoria stepped around the Dowager. Devil quickly slid Richard back down on the bed and straightened. Honoria marched up to him, met his gaze directly, then took his hand. "Come—I believe you've been relieved of duty here. Permanently." With that, she towed him to the door.

Devil cast a glance back at Richard and shrugged helplessly.

Richard fell back on his pillows with a groan—as the two most important women in his life descended on him.

They lectured and fussed and lectured again, in between tucking him in tenderly. He bore it stoically—with a final sharp but concerned glance, Catriona had to leave him.

Helena pulled up the chair, picked up Catriona's discarded mending, and settled down to watch over him.

Richard sighed. "I promise I won't try to get up again—not until my wife gives her permission."

"Be quiet. Go to sleep."

Helena's stern tone told him she had not forgiven him his indiscretion yet.

Richard swallowed a grunt. After a moment, he said: "You never fuss over Devil."

"That's because he never needed to be fussed over. You do—now be silent and sleep. And leave me to fuss."

Thus adjured, he shut up and found himself, to his surprise, drifting into a doze. Before he succumbed, he asked: "What do you think of Catriona?"

"She's the perfect wife for you. She will fuss very well in my stead."

Richard felt his lips twitch resignedly; he took her advice, shut up and slept.

* * *

He awoke some hours later to discover the twins, one perched in a straight-backed chair to the left, the other in a matching chair to the right, bright blue eyes wide, watching over him.

Astonished, he stared at them. "What the devil are you doing here?"

They smiled. "Guarding you."

Richard glowered; he looked them over, noting the full curves that filled out their bodices, the trim figures revealed by their muslin skirts—and glowered even more. "Your necklines are too low—you'll catch your deaths."

They bent identical disgusted looks on him.

"You're as bad as Devil."

"And Vane."

"*Almost* as bad as Demon—he's been underfoot everywhere we go!"

"What *is* the matter with all of you?"

He humphed and shut his eyes—and refrained from telling them. "This is the Lowlands," he stated incontrovertibly. "It's colder up here." He wondered if Catriona had some spare shawls they could pin over their shoulders, closed to the neck.

Still, at least they were up here, with him, Devil, Vane and Gabriel about, not gallivanting in the south, flaunting themselves like plump lambs before God knew how many hungry wolves, with only Helena for protection.

Keeping his eyes shut, he sank deeper into his bed. Perhaps there was some sense to this madness after all.

CHAPTER
Eighteen

ॐ

The week passed slowly for Richard, confined to his bed, and in a whirl of unaccustomed gaiety for the other inhabitants of the vale. They'd never encountered people like the Cynsters before. Entering the stable yard four mornings later, Catriona was conscious of the smile on her face—it rarely dimmed these days, despite Richard's posioning and what she would, once their guests left, have to face. For now, all was running smoothly, with a bubbling, effervescent sense of life. Thanks to their guests.

They were everywhere, helping with everything, yet they had, with a characteristic tact that was in itself overwhelming, managed to do so without stepping on anyone's sensitivities.

A feat that commanded her respect.

On her way back to the house after checking the still slumbering gardens, she paused to take in the activity in the yard. Devil was there with McAlvie and his lads; beside them, Vane and Corby were mounted, about to ride out to check the orchards. Vane was looking down, Devil was looking up—all the other men seemed not just smaller, but somehow less alive. Then Devil nodded and stepped back. Vane wheeled his mount; with Corby at his heels, he clattered out of the yard. Turning away, Devil collected McAlvie; with the herdsman's lads following close behind, they strode down the slope to the cattle barn.

Smiling to herself, Catriona resumed her progress to the house. Devil watched over the livestock, Vane the orchards. Without the slightest comment, they'd left the crops to her. They'd divided Richard's responsibilities between them and were acting in his stead. As for Gabriel, he'd appointed himself Richard's amanuensis; he was presently sitting with Richard and dealing with the accumulated correspondence concerning his business affairs. She hadn't realized how extensive Richard's investments were until Gabriel had found the pile of letters in the library and come storming upstairs, waving them and insisting Richard deal with them.

She was learning new things every day.

Like the fact that, while in no way susceptible in the common sense, the other women in the vale were very definitely appreciative of men like the Cynsters. A group of them had gathered in the doorway of the dairy to enjoy the sight of Devil and Vane. All the Cynster men drew the same response—they were always so elegantly dressed and shod, yet thought nothing of picking up an axe and splitting logs, or helping with a fence, or herding cows. The local women had grown used to Richard, but ... their wide smiles and their comments, drifting on the breeze—"And there are more of them yet, Cook says." "Oh, my!" as, with smiling nods to her, they turned back into the dairy—suggested they were far from bored with the sight.

Her smile converting to a grin, Catriona climbed the steps and pushed through the heavy back door. Cynsters, she'd decided, were simply larger than life.

Two of them were baking bread. Up to their elbows in flour, Amelia and Amanda stood at the kitchen table, giggling with Cook's girls as they all kneaded dough. All the girls were flushed, Amelia's and Amanda's ringlets were dancing, their huge cornflower blue eyes brilliant with laughter. Even with flour smudges over their pert noses, they were beauties.

Beautiful young English ladies from one of the very best of the old families.

They could still giggle with the best of them. While certainly not unconscious of their charms, neither twin seemed to have a "conscious" bone in her body—while neither would ever forget who they were, they were openly friendly and ready to be pleased.

Cook's girls were in awe, but equally ready to join in the fun.

"Perhaps we could do the loaves in braids—like this." Amelia created a distinctly skewed braid with her dough.

"Aunt Helena likes bread made like that," Amanda explained, "but perhaps we should try some different shapes—braids might not be to the gentlemen's taste."

Smiling broadly, Catriona passed on, leaving them devising all manner of fancy loaves. Those sitting down to lunch would have a new interest.

Heading into the house, she passed the archway to the second kitchen, which housed the main ovens of the manor. And halted—arrested by the sight of two derrieres, side by side, one cloaked in serviceable drab, the other in fashionable twill.

"Hmm—I think it needs a touch more rosemary." Bent over, peering into the dark cavern of the roasting oven, Honoria passed the basting ladle to Cook.

Who nodded her grey head. "P'raps, p'raps. And maybe a pinch more tarragon and a clove or two. Just to pick it up a bit, like."

Neither heard her, neither turned around; both continued to study the roast with absolute concentration. Smiling still, Catriona glided on.

"I have always found that a *soupçon* of lavender in the polish is the perfect touch. It freshens a room without overpowering."

"I do so agree, madam. And it makes the beeswax just that bit softer, to go just that bit farther. Can I help you to a little bit more sherry, Your Grace?"

From the shadows of the corridor, Catriona watched Mrs. Broom refill the sherry glass clasped between the Dowager's fine fingers. A ring of emeralds and diamonds flashed as the Dowager gestured her thanks.

"I have noticed," she said, as Mrs. Broom returned to her chair, "that your silver has a very nice luster. What polish do you use?"

"Ah, well, now—that's a bit of a vale secret, that is. Howsoever, seeing as you're family now ..."

Shaking her head, Catriona glided silently on, storing the moment in her memory to describe to Richard later. The Dowager could very well have sat in the drawing room and commanded Mrs. Broom's presence; instead, she'd elected to take sherry with the housekeeper in her snug little parlor. The better to learn her secrets.

The Dowager was incorrigible.

Her smile wreathing her face, Catriona stepped into the hall—and remembered those she had not seen in her journey through the nether regions. The manor's tribe of children. They'd been noticeably absent—not one small body had she seen, not one shrill shriek had she heard.

Which was not necessarily a good thing.

Where were they? And what were they up to?

She detoured via the games room—and found her answers. Patience was sitting on the rug before the hearth, her elegant skirts spread wide to accommodate the kittens, playing, rolling, batting at fingers and hands. The children were all gathered about, quietly enthralled.

"Ooh, look!" one said in wonder. "This one likes my hair."

"Their claws are sharp."

"Indeed," Patience warned, "and so are their teeth."

She looked up at that moment and saw Catriona—Patience raised her brows in question. Catriona smiled and shook her head.

"Ow!"

Patience turned back. "Now be careful—they're only very young and don't mean to hurt."

With her manor filled to bursting, and yet, at peace, Catriona headed on to the stillroom.

She was there an hour later when Patience put her head around the door. "Can I interrupt?"

Catriona grinned. "Please do—I'm only refreshing the linen sachets."

"Perhaps I could help." Pulling a stool up to the other side of the table at which Catriona sat, Patience settled and picked up one of the small linen bags. "I'll sew them up, if you like."

"You can interrupt me any time," Catriona informed her, pushing the needle and thread over the table. "That's the part I hate."

Once they'd settled to their tasks, Patience said: "Actually, I was wondering if you could recommend anything to help settle my stomach." She caught Catriona's eye and grimaced. "Just in the mornings."

"Ah." Catriona smiled and dusted off her hands. "I have a tea that should help." She had the canister to hand. "It's mainly chamomile."

The family had celebrated Patience and Vane's good news with a boisterous round of toasts around Richard's bed some nights before. Honoria had tried to take a backseat, claiming a second pregnancy was less news than a first—they hadn't let her succeed. However, other than exchanging warm glances, she and Richard had said nothing; both, independently, had felt the need to keep their news to themselves for a time—to savor it fully before sharing it with others. Setting the canister down, she found a cloth bag and filled it with the leaves. "Have the maid brew this for you every morning and drink it before getting out of bed—it should soothe you."

It worked for her.

Patience took the bag gladly. "Thank you. Honoria doesn't seem to be affected—she says she only feels woozy for about a week."

"All women are different," Catriona assured her as she returned to her task of stuffing dried herbs into the linen sachets.

A companionable silence descended, then the door opened; Honoria looked in. She smiled. "There you are. Perfect. I wanted to ask if you had any remedies made up for teething infants." Pulling up another stool to the table, she picked up an empty sachet and started to stuff it. "Sebastian's cut his first two teeth, but the rest seem to be causing him more bother. He gets so fractious—and, if anything, he can out-bellow his father."

Patience chuckled.

Catriona grinned and slipped from her stool. "Cloves should help. I have an ointment made up here somewhere."

While she poked about and found the jar, then filled a smaller jar for Honoria, the other two industriously stuffed and sewed.

"Actually," Honoria said, handing a stuffed sachet to Patience, "when you come to visit I must get you to go through our stillroom. I know the basics, of course, but I'm sure you could give me a few lessons to good effect."

"Hmm." Patience looked around at the neat rows of bottles and jars, all filled, all labelled. "And when you've finished in Cambridgeshire, you can come and visit in Kent."

Ordinarily, she would instantly have said that she never left the vale; instead, visited by an impulse she couldn't define, Catriona smiled warmly. "We'll see."

They all gathered for lunch that day—when the gong sounded, the three ladies left the stillroom where they'd spent a companionable hour finishing the linen sachets and comparing household notes. As she strolled with her sister-in-law and cousin-in-law to the dining hall, Catriona could not recall any similar experience. She'd never been party to such a discussion before, never been exposed to the warmth of shared confidences and freely offered advice.

She'd never felt as close to any other lady as she now did to Honoria and Patience. Yet another revelation of what she had not known could be.

The dining hall was its now customary hub of noise and energy. As she took her seat, she looked over her guests with an affection she'd never before experienced. A growing affection.

They, of course, simply took it as their due; they smiled, grinned and even winked at her, then settled to entertain themselves and everyone else. They were all so powerfully alive, so sure of themselves, so innately confident, yet not high in the instep at all; the manor folk, the vale folk—all her people—had taken them to their hearts.

The Dowager sat beside McArdle and lectured him on taking more exercise, something Catriona had tried to hint to him for years. The Dowager didn't hint—she told him. With extravagant gestures cloaked in Gallic charm.

And, of course, McArdle listened, and nodded his head in agreement.

Cook and Honoria compared notes on the success of their efforts with the roasted meats, while the twins called everyone's attention to the highly varied loaves scattered about the tables, prettily sharing all compliments thus gained with Cook's three girls, who turned beet-red with confusion.

Henderson, Devil and McAlvie sat at another table, deep in discussion of who knew what; farther along, Vane and Gabriel were chatting with Corby, Huggins and the stablelads—about horses if their gestures were any guide.

Outside the weather was still raw and cold, but inside, the manor was aglow with warmth and laughter. Smiling benignly, Catriona looked out over her extended household and silently blessed them, every one.

Later that afternoon, she left Richard, grumbling, to rest, and went out to watch the riding lessons.

Vane had discovered Richard's attempts in that direction—he'd told Devil and Gabriel.

The children were now in alt. They were getting riding lessons every day, sometimes twice a day, from their very own instructors, all ex-cavalry officers. Catriona had learned that last from a breathless Tom, later confirmed by Devil.

"I'm probably the strongest rider," he'd said, "but Demon's the best." He'd glanced down at her and smiled. "You haven't met him yet—he's Vane's brother."

Catriona was quietly grateful Demon hadn't turned up at the manor, too— multiple Cynsters were a lot to get used to all at once.

But they were very good riders—and very good with children.

Slipping unobtrusively into the yard, she perched on the corner of the water trough in its center and watched the three groups into which they'd divided the children. The youngest were with Devil—totally unafraid of him—giggling and laughing as he patiently held them on and taught them how to sit, how to hold the reins. The next group in age, including young Tom, were with Vane, being coached in the rudiments of active riding. The last group, composed of the stablelads and young farmhands who could ride after a fashion but were definitely not up to the Cynster mark, were drilling under Gabriel's eagle eye.

Catriona watched for some time, trying to comprehend the rapport that seemed so effortless, between Cynster men and horses, and also small humans. In the end, she inwardly shrugged, smiled and accepted it—they were, transparently, naturals in both spheres—that was all there was to it.

And she, and all the vale, were going to miss them when they left.

Later that evening, Richard lay on a daybed in their bedchamber, ten feet away from the bed. That was the present limit of his strength, a fact he found disgusting. At least his witchy wife had let him get out of bed; he could now stand, but beyond a few paces, his strength seemed to fail.

Apparently delighted with his mild progress, and finally convinced the poison had departed his system for good, Catriona had brought him up a special herbal brew, guaranteed, so she'd said, to help him regain his strength. Nothing else, she declared, now stood between him and a full recovery.

And freedom. The wild expanse beyond their windows.

The potion tasted vile, but Richard doggedly sipped—and planned how to celebrate his vigor once it returned.

His musings were interrupted by Devil, who opened the door and strolled in, followed by Vane and Gabriel.

"While our wives and esteemed parent are busy hatching plans, we thought we'd come up and commiserate." Devil grinned. "How are you feeling?"

"Better." Draining the last of the potion and swallowing it with a grimace, Richard realized that was true. He set the beaker aside. "I suspect I'll have to endure a few more days, but ..."

"Just make sure you recover fully," Gabriel cautioned. "Be damned if I'm riding this far north again if you suffer a relapse."

Vane chuckled. "Your wife seems convinced you'll be your old self any day, and I rather suspect she knows best."

"Hmm." Richard eyed them speculatively. "Actually, I was just planning a little adventure, so to speak, to celebrate my return to the living."

"Adventure?"

"How little?"

"What sort?"

Richard grinned. "Nothing too outrageous, but we haven't had any serious excursions, not since Waterloo. I don't know about you, but two weeks in a bed has sharpened my appetite."

"*That's* hardly suprising," Devil returned, "in the circumstances. But what about this adventure?"

Richard threw a cushion at him, which landed on target and made him feel much better. "If you don't keep a civil tongue in your head, I won't tell you. I'll just ride off one morning and you'll have to wait until I get back."

"Ride?"

"Where to?"

"I promise to be excessively civil."

"Well . . ."—Richard pulled at his earlobe—"it so happens I'll need help for this venture—at least a couple more riders. If, of course, you think you can spare the time for a little lark before heading south to more civilized climes?"

Devil raised his brows in mock exasperation. "Forget the jokes—what's the plan?"

"Catriona?"

Caught in the act of pushing away from the desk in her office, Catriona looked up. Devil stood in the doorway, with Vane just behind him. "Is anything wrong?" she asked.

"No, no!" Devil entered; Vane followed. Devil smiled ingenuously. "We just wondered if you could spare a few minutes to explain a few things to us."

He wanted something; Catriona could tell by that smile. Calmly settling back in her chair, she waved them to the two chairs facing her. Melchett had just departed, having looked in to tell her all was on track for the spring plantings to be done as she'd directed. Upstairs, Richard was with Worboys, getting dressed for his first attempt at the stairs. Her world was serene, on course. And the two before her were now part of it. "How can I help you?" she asked. "Whatever it is, if it's in my power, naturally, you have only to ask."

Devil's smile broadened. "It's about the crop yields. Richard told me what you achieve here—"

"And Corby happened to mention the tonnage you clear from your orchards—and how old your trees are." Vane raised his brows. "Frankly, if I didn't know he wasn't lying, I'd have said he'd dreamed the figures up."

Catriona smiled. "We do very well, that's true."

"Not very well," Devil corrected her. "Astonishingly well." He met her gaze. "We'd like to know how you manage it."

Catriona held his gaze and swiftly considered her options. She had said she would give them anything in her power; there was no reason she couldn't answer their question. Her only worry was that they wouldn't believe her—or wouldn't have a sufficiently open mind to understand. Then again, they had come to her and asked. And, as one of The Lady's disciples, it behooved her to spread Her message as widely as she could.

Drawing a slow breath, she nodded. "Very well. But you'll need to bear in mind that what I tell you is a . . . a philosophy rather than a prescription." She glanced at Vane. "So the answer is the same for both crops and orchards, indeed, for anything that grows. And the philosophy holds true for all arable lands, whether in the shadow of Merrick, or in Cambridgeshire, or in Kent."

They both nodded. "So . . ." Devil prompted.

"So," she said, "it's a question of balance."

"Balance?"

"What you take out must be put back, if you wish to take out again." Catriona leaned forward, resting her arms on the desk. "Each patch of soil has certain characteristics, certain nutrients which allow it to bear crops of such and such a nature. Once the crop is grown, however, the nutrients used in the bearing are depleted in the soil. If the soil is continually planted, it will continue to deplete and bear poorer and poorer crops until it fails. Crop rotation helps, but even that does not return the nutrients to the soil. So if you want to continuously crop, and crop well, then you need to renew the soil, replace the nutrients used, after each cropping. That's the fundamental point— the need for balance—in and out."

Vane was frowning. "Just go back a minute. Do you mean that for each particular crop, in each particular field, you need to work out a ... a ..."

"An understanding of the balance of the nutrients involved?" Catriona nodded. "Precisely."

"This balance," Devil leaned forward. "How's it measured?"

They questioned her, and she answered and explained; Devil asked for paper and sketched some of his fields—Vane listed the fruits and nuts he grew. They discussed, and even argued, but not once did they doubt, or give any hint that they dismissed her guidance. Quite the opposite.

"I'll try it," Devil declared, "and you'll have to come and talk to my foremen when you visit." He folded the sheet of paper on which he'd jotted notes. "If we can achieve even half of what you do here, I'll die happy."

Considering his own sheet of notes, Vane grinned. "My men are going to think I've taken leave of my senses, but ... it's my fields—and my gain." Looking up, he smiled at Catriona. "Thank you, my dear, for sharing your secret with us."

"Indeed." Rising as she did, Devil waggled his brows at Catriona. "Doubtless the most useful lady's secret I've ever learned."

Laughing, she waved them out; they went with sweeping bows. Sitting back down, she couldn't stop smiling. After a minute, she tidied her desk, then went upstairs to gauge Richard's strength.

"Ah—*there* you are."

Catriona looked up from the garden bed she'd been contemplating, one she hoped would soon show a few green shoots. Gabriel was making his way between the beds toward her, patently trying to see what she'd been studying in the winter brown earth.

"Is there anything there?"

"No." Catriona grinned. "I was merely checking. Is there something you need?"

He straightened and smiled. "Not exactly—I heard of the advice you gave to Devil and Vane."

"Ah, I see." Catriona waved him to join her as she ambled on down the path. "And what do you grow?"

"I don't—at least, not in the same sense." He grinned down at her. "I grow money—from money."

"Oh." Catriona blinked. "I don't think I can give you any advice there."

"Probably not," he affably agreed. "Not but what that balance idea of yours is quite close to the mark—but in investing it's risk and return that create the balance."

Catriona held his gaze. "I'm afraid," she said, "that I don't really know much about investing."

His grin widened. "Few people do—which brings me to my point. In light of your sterling advice to the others—which in turn benefits me, as Devil's wealth underpins the family ducal purse and both he and Vane invest through me, so the more funds they have to put in, the wealthier we all, myself included, become—I'd like to offer you my help in making investments in the same way I help all the rest." He stopped and smiled at her. "You're family now, so it's only fair."

Catriona stared into his eyes, a light hazelly brown, and let his words and his smile warm her. "I . . ." She hesitated, then nodded. "I think I'd like that. Richard invests with you, doesn't he?"

"All the family do. I oversee the investments, and Heathcote Montague, our joint man of business, acts as our executor." Gabriel grinned. "That means I do all the talking and investigating and he takes care of the boring formalities."

Catriona nodded. "Tell me more about what you do. How do these investments of yours work?"

They ambled through the gardens for close to an hour, by which time she'd learned more than enough to know that he, at least, knew precisely what he was talking about. "Very well." With a nod, she halted at the entrance to the gardens. Here was an opportunity to establish the vale's future income for all time. Gabriel would invest their excess funds for her—the income would be there to tide the vale over any lean years, should such ever come to pass. She nodded again and refocused on Gabriel's face. "I'll talk to McArdle and get the funds transferred—Richard will know the direction."

Gabriel's easy smile lit his face; hand over his heart, he bowed. "You won't regret it, I swear." He straightened, eyes twinkling. "Welcome to yet another aspect of our family."

Richard entered the dining hall that evening to a rousing chorus of cheers. The whole household stood and clapped. His slow stroll disguising his lack of strength, he grinned and nodded gracefully, his expression one of amused affability. But when he met Catriona's gaze as he reclaimed his seat beside her, she could see the warmth, the joy, the affectionate acceptance, burning in the blue of his eyes.

She smiled mistily and quickly sat so that he could sit, too. The cheering subsided, and the first course was brought out.

Beneath the table's edge, Richard clasped her hand briefly, then frowned at the serving dish placed before him. "Good heavens! Is that turbot?"

"Hmm-mm." Drawing the dish closer, Catriona heaped some on his plate. "Cook said it was one of your favorite dishes."

"It is." Bemused, Richard stared at it, then looked at her. "But wherever did she get turbot up here?"

Catriona raised her brows haughtily. "We have our ways."

He hesitated, then grinned, and gave his attention to the turbot.

The entire meal was a succession of Richard's favorite dishes—a fact that did not escape him. He caught Cook's eye and saluted her, which made her blush vividly even while she nodded graciously.

He leaned closer to Catriona. "I'd go down and thank her, but ..." He grimaced.

Catriona smiled, and fleetingly leaned her shoulder against his. "You can speak to her tomorrow, or the day after, when next you go through the kitchens."

He trapped her gaze and slowly arched a black brow. "That soon?"

The words hung between them, layered with meaning. The air about them grew dense, shutting everyone else out. Catriona felt her lungs lock. "Oh, I think so," she managed, conscious of that sudden skittering excitement that she hadn't felt for too long. The rest of the room had vanished; all she could see was the blue of his eyes. "You should be able to ... get up ... er, completely, any day now."

His lips quirked; a wicked glint lit his eyes. "You've no idea," he drawled, "how thankful I am to hear that."

Breaking eye contact, Catriona reached for her wineglass and took a much-needed sip. "Yes, well—there you are."

"Hmmm—and where will you be?"

Flat on her back beneath him. "Busy," Catriona stated repressively.

"Oh, I think I can guarantee that," the reprobate she'd married agreed.

Catriona awoke the next morning, and saw—knew—what it was that the Cynsters had brought to the vale. The knowledge came as a revelation—a flash of insight, a crystal clear certainty. And in the same revealing moment, she saw their marriage—hers and Richard's—in its entirety, its full meaning, its full glory. Saw why The Lady had directed her to his arms.

She was there still; she knew, in that moment, that she would remain there for all time. He slept behind her, wrapped around her, his breath, softly huffing, caressing her nape, one arm possessively protective, over her waist.

He'd needed her—to provide an anchor for his restless soul, to give him the home and position he'd needed, to be his warrior's cause.

But she'd needed him, too—in more ways than one. He'd recognized from the beginning, and forced her to see, too, that she needed him to protect her and to ease the burdens that were hers through her responsiblities to the vale. What she hadn't seen—couldn't have seen—and what he may not have guessed, was that she needed more than that.

She needed to learn about family—large ruling families—something she and the vale knew nothing about. With Cynsters all around, she'd observed firsthand the enormous positive energy that, as a group, they commanded. They were not really moral, or religious in any way, yet they all, day by day, act by act, served one goal—the family, both their own smaller groups, as well as the larger whole. While their decisions were usually direct and straightforward, down-to-earth and obvious, they were also far-sighted, always made in the best interests of the family.

From the first, she'd been impressed by the incredible strength of the group, far greater than the sum of its parts. That strength derived from the simple fact that they were all moving in the same direction, all focused on the same ultimate goal.

The Lady's ways were profound.

There'd been no large family at the manor for generations—the lady of the vale had, by custom, only one child, a girl child to take on her mantle. But times were changing—there would be fresh challenges to face, greater challenges. Challenges requiring more than the isolation of the vale to counter them.

Lifting a hand to her breast, Catriona fingered the pendant that hung there—Richard's mother's legacy. Through their marriage, a line older than hers had come into the vale; their child—their first daughter—would be the first of a new line, a greater line, sprung from the merging of the two.

She would be the first of a new family.

Catriona lay still and pondered that fact, while beyond the windows the sun rose. As dawn washed the land, she slipped from Richard's arms and left him softly snoring.

Her revelations were still much in her mind when, later that morning, she repaired to the stillroom.

She'd been there an hour when the door opened and two bright faces looked in.

"May we ask you something?"

Smiling, Catriona waved the twins to stools before the table at which she was working. "How can I help you?"

"We have this burning question," Amanda informed her, wriggling onto the stool.

"We want to know what we should look for in a husband," Amelia stated.

Catriona opened her eyes wide. "That is a big question."

"As you're a healer, we thought you might be able to advise us."

"We're being paraded around at present—you know, so that all the eligible gentlemen can look us over and see if we might suit them."

"But we've decided that that really isn't sensible."

"No. We need to decide if *they* will suit *us*."

Catriona couldn't stop her smile.

"Which," Amanda declared, unabashed, "means we have to decide what it is we should be looking for."

Catriona nodded. "I can see that—I have to say you're approaching this in a very clearheaded way."

"We decided that was the only way to approach it—that's why we've come to see you."

"We can't ask Aunt Helena—she's too old."

"And Honoria was married over a year ago. These days, she's so caught up with being a duchess and taking care of Sebastian, she probably can't remember what she thought was important then."

"And Patience isn't feeling well. And she's rather ... absorbed—as if she's thinking of her new baby."

"But we thought you'd know—you're a healer and they always know everything, and you've only just married Richard, so you should be able to remember why you did."

Unarguable logic. Catriona had to laugh. But her laugh was kindly and gentle; inside, she felt deeply touched, humble, and a little awed. She'd been thinking about how she should learn about "family," as if it was something she could study at a distance—and now here were the twins, reminding her that "family" wasn't at a distance, it was here. She was, their blue eyes declared, already one hub in the giant Cynster web, accepted as such, available to answer questions on matters vitally important to the younger generation. That was how families operated.

Drawing in a breath, she eyed the twins, read the earnestness in their eyes. "As I understand your question," she said, looking down at the paste she was mixing, "you want to know, not why I married Richard, so much as what's important to look for in a prospective husband."

"Precisely."

"That's our dilemma in a nutshell."

"So," Catriona said, "your question is really philosophical, and as such that's something I can answer." Frowning, she swirled the paste with the pestle; the twins remained encouragingly silent.

"A good husband," she declared, "must be protective. That's often the easiest point to ascertain. If he frowns at you when you do something barely reckless, then he's noticing you in that way."

The twins nodded in unison.

Catriona didn't notice, intent on her paste, intent on her answer. "For some reason, the best men also tend to be possessive—and that's also easy to see. He'll scowl at any other eligible men about you and get irritated if you don't pay sufficient attention to him. The *next* point, however, is a difficult one— one you need to be careful to get right. It's often not obvious." She rolled the pestle about. "He should be pleased with you—even proud of you—as you are. He shouldn't seek to change you, or ..." She gestured.

"Think you need to take lessons from his sister in how to go on?"

Catriona looked at Amanda. "Precisely." Amanda's tone, and the militant light in her eye, suggested she'd already stubbed her toe on that step.

"The last point, one which, in your cases especially, I would strongly urge you to consider, is his attitude to family." It was on the tip of her tongue to explain that she hadn't considered that herself—because she hadn't known to do so. But The Lady had ordained her marriage—and The Lady had looked out for her. Pausing in her labors, she studied the twins. "You were born into and raised within a large and close family—not everyone has that advantage. But you would miss it dreadfully, and find life very difficult, if the man you chose did not value your family, and the concept of family, as you do."

Two pairs of huge blue eyes blinked at her; in that instant she knew their thoughts. Family? They weren't aware they valued the concept—it had simply been there, a constant all their lives; they had, perhaps until now, taken it for granted.

"Hmmm." Amanda frowned.

"And, of course," Catriona pointed out, "any gentleman wishing to marry either of you will have to run the gauntlet of your family."

Both girls rolled their eyes.

"As if we could *ever* forget!"

"That's always a worry," Amelia said. "What if the gentleman *we* want doesn't pass the family's inspection?"

Catriona smiled and looked down at her paste. "If the one you want meets those four criteria, I think you'll find the Cynsters will welcome him with open arms."

CHAPTER
Nineteen

ఆధా

Catriona was not called upon to make any declaration on the question of her husband's complete recovery; the next morning, Richard demonstrated his return to full vigor by ensuring he reached the breakfast table a full hour before she did.

When, distinctly breathless, having lifted heavy lids and found him—and the dawn—long gone, Catriona rushed into the dining hall, she was greeted with wide smiles by the other Cynster ladies and knowing grins by the Cynster men. Straightening her spine, she swept up to the main table; her incorrigible spouse uncurled his long length and rose to pull out her chair.

"I wondered when you'd wake."

The words, murmured in a tone of absolute innocence, brushed her ear as she sat; Catriona stifled a too-vivid recollection of what he'd done to ensure she hadn't.

Lifting her gaze, she met the Dowager's bright eyes.

"*Bon!* He is recovered, is he not? So all is well, and we really must return south—the Season will start soon, and Louise will be wanting to take the twins to the modistes."

"Indeed," Honoria agreed. As Patience turned to speak to the twins, Honoria turned to Catriona. "I know you'll understand—I want to get back to Sebastian. We've never before left him for so long."

Catriona smiled serenely, sincerely. "I'm so grateful that you came and have stayed for so long. Naturally, you need to get back. And"—with her eyes she indicated Richard, on her other side, talking to Devil and Vane—"there's really no reason you need stay."

Honoria smiled widely, squeezed her hand in empathy, then looked across the table at Devil. "So we can all leave tomorrow."

"We may as well," Patience agreed, turning from the twins.

His gaze briefly touching Vane's, then Richard's, Devil sat back in his chair. And regarded his wife. "Actually, it's not that simple. I'll need a day or so to talk things over with Richard—there's some matters I've set in train that I need to work through with him."

"And I want to go over the trees in the orchard," Vane said. "There's some grafting work you should consider."

"Don't forget those funds that we must discuss before I leave," Gabriel put in.

Honoria, Patience and the Dowager stared up the table.

"Does this mean," Honoria eventually asked, "that you're not yet ready to leave?"

Devil grinned. "It'll just take a day or two." He transferred his limpid gaze to Catriona. "We wouldn't want Richard to overdo things and suffer a relapse."

All the ladies turned to look at Richard, who returned their scrutiny with a look of helpless innocence. Honoria barely stifled a snort; she stood. "I suppose," she conceded, "a day or two more won't hurt."

Honoria looked up as Patience slid into her chair at the breakfast table the next morning. "Have you seen Devil?"

Patience shook her head. "I was about to ask if you'd seen Vane."

Honoria frowned, then both she and Patience looked up. Gliding more slowly than usual, Catriona joined them. She sank into her carved chair. And looked at the teapot. Then she reached out, lifted the pot, and, with careful concentration, filled her cup. Setting the teapot down, she studied the full cup, then reached for the sugarbowl, and dropped in two lumps.

Honoria grinned and exchanged a swift glance with Patience before turning to Catriona. "Where's Richard?"

Eyes closed as she savored her tea, Catriona shook her head. "I don't know—and I don't want to know. Not until I've recovered."

Honoria grinned; Patience chuckled.

Catriona frowned. "Actually, I vaguely—very vaguely, you understand—recall him saying something about having to be busy about 'Cynster business' today." She cracked open her lids. "I assumed he meant with Gabriel."

They all looked down the table, to the four empty places usually filled by the cousins at breakfast time. From the detritus, it was clear they'd already broken their fast.

Honoria frowned. "They're not in the library. I looked."

Patience frowned, too. "What I can't understand is why Vane left so early—he came down before dawn."

"Devil, too."

Catriona frowned, then shook her head. "I can't recall."

Just then, McArdle appeared, stumping slowly along. With his stiff joints, he was always a late riser. Heading for the end of the table, he stopped by Catriona's chair. "The master asked me to give you this, mistress."

Eyes opening fully, Catriona took the single folded sheet and nodded her thanks; McArdle stumped on. For one instant, she studied the missive; Richard had never written to her before. Unfolding it, she scanned the five lines within—she blinked; her eyes kindled. Lips firming, she set her teacup down with a definite click.

"What is it?" Honoria asked.

"*Just* listen." Drawing a deep breath, Catriona read: "Dear C—Please tell H and P. We have gone to conclude a business deal. We'll be away for four days. You are not to worry. R." She looked at Patience and Honoria. "The 'not' is underlined three times."

They fumed and swore vengeance, then, all three together, they bustled out to the stable.

Catriona led the way. "Huggins—when did the master leave?"

Huggins straightened, letting down the hoof he was checking. "Rode out just at dawn, the boy said."

"And the others?" Honoria asked.

Huggins touched his cap in a half bow. "With him, Your Grace. 'Twas the master, His Grace, and both the other Mister Cynsters, ma'am. They rode out all together."

"Which way?" Catriona demanded.

Huggins nodded to the east. Catriona turned and looked, even though the house blocked her view. She glanced back at Huggins. "They rode *out* of the vale?"

Huggins raised his brows. "Don't know as to that, but they took the road that ways."

"Did they take any provisions?" Patience asked. "Saddlebags, blankets?"

Huggins grimaced. "They saddled their own horses, I believe, ma'am. There's usually only one sleepy lad in the stables that early. I doubt he'd 'ave noticed."

"Never mind. Thank you, Huggins." Catriona motioned the other two away. Together, they crossed the yard and went into the gardens, to where, once past the side of the house, they could look down the vale, into the now well-risen sun. Catriona gestured to the vale's mouth. "If they left near dawn, they'll be well beyond the vale by now."

"Well beyond our reach," Honoria observed darkly.

Patience frowned. "What on earth are they about?"

"And where on earth," Catriona waspishly added, "have they gone to be about it?"

"*Mistress!* Come quickly!"

Three days later, working at the table in the stillroom, Catriona looked up to see Tom jigging in the doorway.

"Come see! Come see!" A smile splitting his face, he beckoned her wildly, then dashed toward the front hall.

Catriona dusted her hands and set off in pursuit.

"What is it?" Patience came out of the library as Tom's running footsteps echoed through the hall.

Catriona lifted her arms in a shrug.

"There's something going on outside." With Patience, Catriona turned to see Honoria hurrying down the stairs. "All the children have rushed down into the park. There's some sort of commotion going on down there."

They all looked at each other, then turned and glided, as fast as dignity allowed, to the front door. Between them, they hauled the door wide, then went out onto the porch.

The sight that met their eyes did not, at first, convey much—they were just in time to glimpse the last of Tom as he flew down the drive into the park. His cohorts, nowhere in sight, were presumably ahead of him. Around both sides of the house, other members of the household and manor farm streamed, deserting the kitchens, the workrooms, the stables and barns, all rushing for the drive.

McArdle stumped up to the steps, nodding toward the park. "We've some new arrivals, seemingly."

His face was relaxed, his lips curving; Catriona was about to quiz him, when she sensed a presence at her back. She turned and beheld the Dowager.

Patience and Honoria moved aside to give her space; in her most regal voice, Helena demanded: "*What* is going on here?"

"*Mooo-rhooo!*"

The bellow had them all turning, staring at where the drive came up from the park. A huge hulking bull came lolloping up out of the trees, a long rope trailing from a ring in his nose. In his wake, a noisy gaggle of children, grooms and farmhands came tumbling, tripping and laughing, calling and screeching. The bull ignored them; sighting the party on the steps, he rolled happily forward, tossing his head, heavy rolls of muscle rippling. Cloven feet clacking loudly on the cobbles, he cantered to the steps, then, planting his front feet wide, came to a skidding halt. He looked the ladies over, then stared directly at Catriona, raised his huge head, uttered a mammoth bellow, shook his head vigorously, then looked down and exhaled in a huge, shuddering snort.

The party on the steps simply stared.

"Got 'im!" The eldest farmhand pounced on the rope, then reeled it in, shortening it to lead the bull away. Looking the animal over, the lad glanced up at Catriona, his eyes shining. "He's a prime 'un, ain't he, mistress?"

"Indeed." Catriona knew enough to know a prize bull when she saw one. "But where . . .?" Looking up, her eyes widened as more cattle came into view. Two yearling bulls led the way, trotting happily along under Gabriel's watchful eye. They were followed by a long line of cows and heifers, ambling contentedly, mooing and lowing; Catriona had lost count by the time three other riders came into view toward the end of the long procession.

Devil and Vane rode on either side of the stream of cattle, keeping them moving, watching for stragglers but even more watching out for the children now running alongside the beasts, hands out to fleetingly touch the soft hides as, heads swinging, the cows plodded on.

Right at the end rode Richard, McAlvie at his stirrup, McAlvie's lads flanking them, striding along, eyes on the cattle, proud grins on their faces.

McAlvie looked fit to burst with enthusiasm. He was talking animatedly to Richard, who, smiling, replied with an indulgent air.

From the instant he appeared, Catriona could look at nothing else; driven by the worry of the past three days, she scanned his tall figure critically, but could see no signs of exhaustion. He rode easily, long limbs relaxed, holding himself in the saddle with his usual indolent grace.

He was well. She knew that even before, reaching the courtyard, he looked up and saw her. The smile that lifted his lips, the light that lit his eyes as he viewed her—despite the distance between them she could feel it like a touch—assured her as little else could that his three days away had done nothing to harm him.

"McAlvie!" Gabriel hailed the herdsman. "Where do you want these two?" He indicated the yearling bulls, now coralled by the crowd to one side of the steps; with a word, McAlvie left Richard and hurried to take charge.

The courtyard was a sea of excitement, of ordered pandemonium, with cows mooing, shifting and stamping, surrounded by the household and farmhands, smiling and pointing, chattering and commenting, all waiting to assist in moving the new herd down to the new cattle barn.

Which, Catriona recalled, had been built large enough to hold them.

But first, by vale tradition, they had to be named. McArdle, by right of being the oldest man in the vale, named the bull Henry. Irons declared one of the yearlings was Rupert; Henderson named the other Oswald. The women deferred to their offspring, and thus were born Rose and Misty, Wobbles and Goldy. Tom frowned and bit his lip, then named his cow Checkers.

And so it went on; called on to approve each and every name, Catriona nodded and smiled and laughed. But her senses were elsewhere, trying, through the noise and bustle, to keep track of Richard. He'd dismounted, but she could no longer see his dark head.

To her right, she was distantly aware of Devil strolling up the steps and being pounced on by Honoria. In accents only a duchess could command, her sister-in-law inquired where they'd been. Devil merely grinned. His gaze intent, he turned her and, deftly blocking her attempts to do otherwise, herded her into the house—all further discussion to be undertaken in private. If he gave her an answer, Catriona didn't hear it.

Behind her, to one side, the Dowager was in earnest discussion with McArdle, gesturing at the herd and asking questions. With a frustrated humph, Patience picked up her skirts and darted down the steps. Vane, handing his reins to one of the grooms, turned as she hurried up. Reaching out, he helped her forward when she would have stopped, one arm sliding around her as he turned her and smoothly guided her toward the gardens.

From her manner, Patience was scolding; from his, Vane wasn't listening.

Brows lifting resignedly, Catriona straightened and scanned the courtyard again. With the cows all named, McAlvie was preparing to move them around the house and down to the barn. People were milling everywhere, but she could usually see Richard easily—he was taller than any of her people. But no dark head stood out. Hands rising to her hips, a frown forming in her eyes, an emptiness in her heart, Catriona reached out with her senses—a talent she rarely used as it disturbed those, like Cook, who had latent talent of their own.

Richard was not in the courtyard in front of her.

"Do you approve of your wedding present?"

The deep purr in her ear, the touch of his breath on the sensitive skin of her temple, came simultaneously with the possessive slide of his hand splaying across her waist and belly. She started, then stilled. He held her, and their child, against him for an instant; she felt his strength envelop her. For one blissful moment, she closed her eyes and let herself slide into it, then his hand slid to her hip and he turned her.

Her eyes snapped open. "Wedding present?"

He was grinning. "I didn't give you one, remember?" The light in his eyes was victorious, triumphant. "I couldn't think what to get you." His gaze softened. "A witch who considers an escort to her prayers as precious as diamonds." Smiling, he tapped her nose with one finger. "It was a challenge— to find something you'd truly appreciate."

A shadow fell across his face; Catriona realized that, with his arm about her waist, he'd steered her back into the front hall.

"You bought me a bull as a wedding present?" She wasn't at all sure she believed that—the herd he'd driven in was worth a small fortune, was probably worth even more than she estimated. The vale could not have afforded that sort of addition to its ailing herd. A fact her husband knew.

"Not just the bull—I bought the whole herd." He looked at her innocently. "Don't you like Henry?"

Catriona smothered a snort. "I daresay he's a very good bull."

"Oh, an excellent bull—I have guarantees and glowing references as to his performance."

His lips were very definitely not straight. The front hall was empty—from outside, a cheer went up as the new herd started their last amble to their new home. Richard's lips curved more definitely, more devilishly; his arm about her tightened. "Why don't we adjourn to our room? I can explain the finer points of Henry's reputation, and you can give me your opinion."

"My opinion?" Arching one brow, Catriona met his glowing gaze. Her feet, of their own accord, were carrying her toward the stairs.

"Your opinion—and, perhaps, a token or two of your affection—your appreciation." His smile had turned devilish with salacious anticipation. "Just to reassure me that you really do like Henry."

Catriona looked into his eyes—the sounds of the crowd walking the new herd to the barn were fading in the distance. She could imagine how victorious their progress up the vale had been—she'd seen any number of workers from the farms among the crowd. And the manor folk had given them a rousing welcome—a hero's welcome. The look in Richard's eyes—the same look she'd glimpsed briefly in Devil's and Vane's—suggested they were expecting a similar welcome from their wives.

Her gaze locked on his, as they reached the top of the stairs, she smiled. Finding his hand, she twined her fingers with his, then, her own eyes alight, she slid her gaze from his and turned toward their chamber. "Come, then—and I'll consider your reward."

He deserved it.

Later, after having overseen his bath and shared a dinner fit for a conqueror which, to her amazement, had arrived without explanation on a tray, Catriona rewarded her husband thoroughly, an exercise that left her totally naked, totally drained, slumped, facedown and boneless, amid the rumpled sheets of their bed.

Much later, she mumbled: "Where did you go?"

Sprawled, similarly naked, beside her, Richard glanced at her face. She hadn't yet opened her eyes, not since he'd shut them for her. He settled back on the pillows and enjoyed the sight—of her luscious ivory back and bottom delectably displayed alongside him. "Hexham."

"Hexham?" A frown tangled Catriona's brows. "That's in England."

"I know."

"You mean those are *English* cattle?"

"The very *best* of English cattle. There's a breeder who lives outside Hexham—we went to visit him."

"Visit?"

Richard chuckled. "I have to admit it felt rather like olden times—raiders from the Lowlands sweeping south to steal cattle. Except, of course, that I paid for them." He considered, then his brows quirked. "Mind you, I'm not sure Mr. Scroggs won't decide we've stolen them anyway—we got them at a very good price."

Catriona lifted her heavy head, and her heavy lids, and stared at him. "Why was that?"

Richard grinned. "Devil's inimitable ways. His presence here was too good an opportunity to pass up—he's a master at negotiating. He doesn't precisely *lean* on people—not physically—but they do tend to give ground. Rather unexpectedly, to them."

Catriona humphed and lowered her head back onto the tangled covers. "We weren't expecting you for another day—you said four in your note."

"Ah, yes." Noting the increasing strength in her voice, Richard's interest in their adventure waned. "We expected to get back today—one day to ride to Hexham, two days to drive the cattle back, but"—he slid down the bed, then swung up and straddled her knees—"we thought if we said four days rather than three, you'd worry less." Sliding his palms along her thighs, he gripped her hips and gently flipped her onto her back. "Or," he said, sitting back on his ankles, his hot gaze roving her delectable nakedness, "at least, not yet have whipped yourselves into a righteous frenzy when we got back on the third day."

So sated she could not tense a single muscle, Catriona lay on her back and stared up at him. "You purposely told us four days, so we wouldn't be prepared to . . . to deal with you as you deserved—"

A swift grin cut off her words; he swooped down and kissed her. "We wanted to surprise you."

For more reasons than one, Catriona knew, but as he kissed her lingeringly again, and eased his long body down over hers, she couldn't summon enough temper to care. He lay on her as they kissed, then eased to one side, lying half over her, half beside her, one dark, hair-dusted thigh wedged between hers.

Propped on one elbow, he turned his head and splayed his hand over her belly. Gently, he stroked, gauged. "Have you told them yet?"

Her gaze on his face, Catriona shook her head. "I ... wanted to wait a little—we haven't had time—"

"I haven't said anything, either." His hand resting heavy over where their child grew, secure within her womb, he turned his head and met her gaze. "I want to think about it—see how things settle—how it feels, if it ... fits."

He looked back at his hand; Catriona studied his face, dark planes gilded by the firelight. Then she raised a hand and gently smoothed back the lock of hair that always fell over his forehead. He looked back at her; she smiled into his eyes. "It fits." Her heart swelling, she held his gaze. "You, me, our child, the manor, the vale—we all fit."

For one long instant, she was lost in the blue—the blue of summer skies over Merrick's high head. Then she smiled, mistily, and traced his cheek. "This is how it's meant to be."

Her gaze had dropped to his lips; half-lifting her head, she rose—he bent his head and their lips met, in a kiss so achingly tender, so honest, so vulnerable, there were tears in her eyes when it ended.

He looked down at her for a moment, then his lips kicked up at the ends. "Come show me." Drawing back, he sat on his haunches and pulled her up to her knees.

"Show you what?" Turning her head, she looked over her shoulder as he swung her about so her back was to him.

His eyes burned, his grin grew wicked as he drew her back, sliding her knees outside of his, drawing her bottom against his ridged abdomen. "Show me how things fit."

He needed little instruction on that point; hot and hard, he pressed into her. Her body flowered and opened for him; she gave a soft sigh as he slid fully home.

He settled her, her thighs over his, her bottom wedged against his hips. Impaled upon him, with his chest against her back and his steely arms around her, she was open and vulnerable; her breasts, her belly, the springy curls at its base, the soft inner surfaces of her thighs, already taut, were his to stroke and fondle, to caress as he willed.

And he willed.

Held almost upright, she couldn't rise much upon him; instead, buried deep within her, he rocked. Slowly, languorously.

Catriona bit her lip against a groan as his fingers tightened about her budded nipples and she felt him surge slowly within her.

Then he chuckled; fingers gripping her hips, he lifted her a little, then slowly thrust upward and filled her. Catriona shivered.

"I was just thinking ..." he murmured.

Flicking a glance over her shoulder, she saw him looking down as he lifted her slightly again.

"We can't risk telling anyone our news yet."

He filled her; Catriona dragged in a desperate breath. "Why not?"

"Because if *Maman* finds out, she might not leave." He drew her fully down and rolled his hips beneath her. He reached for her breasts. "And much as I love her, having Helena about for any appreciable time would try the patience of a saint."

He filled his palms and kneaded.

"Devil seems to manage."

"She doesn't fuss about him."

He started to rock her again, a tantalizingly slow ride. His hands drifted over her skin and she heated, and grew hotter. Grew wilder.

She hadn't yet got used to his manner of loving, of the slow, relentless giving, the gradual, inexorable rise toward bliss. If she tried to run ahead, he would hold her back, prolong the delicious torture until she was all but beyond herself—until, when he let her fly free, she screamed.

She'd had trouble with those screams from the first. She'd tried to muffle them, tried to suppress them, tried to at least keep them within bounds—keep them from disturbing the household. *He* didn't seem to care—but then, as Helena would say, he was a man.

The thought focused her mind on the evidence of that, on the thick, heavy, rigid reality filling her, stretching her, completing her—she felt excitement fuse, felt the thrill shimmer and grow.

Desperately, she opened her eyes and focused—on her dressing table across the room. In the mirror, lit only by the weak light of the fire, she saw him, a dark presence in the shadows behind her, saw her body lift rhythmically in his embrace, saw his body coil and flex, driving hers. Upward. Onward. Into that realm of pleasure where the physical and emotional and spiritual merged. But he kept their journey to a rigidly slow pace. Dragging in a breath, her senses at full stretch, her wits all but scattered, she sought for some distraction—something to help her survive the slow disintegration of senses. "Your nickname."

"Hmm?"

He wasn't listening.

"Scandal," she gasped. She'd heard Devil, Vane and Gabriel all use it to his face, although naturally, all the ladies called him Richard. Clutching the arm wrapped across her hips, she let her head fall back and licked her dry lips. "How did you come by it?"

She'd wanted to know since first she'd heard it. "Why do you want to know?" There was a touch of amusement in his voice—a teasing lilt.

Why? "Because we might go to London. In the circumstances, I think I have a right to know."

"You never leave the vale."

"But you might have to go south for some reason."

After a moment, he chuckled. His steady rocking penetration had not faltered. "It's not what you think."

"Oh?" She was clinging to sanity by her fingernails.

"Devil coined the tag—it wasn't because I cause scandal, but because I was: 'A Scandal That Never Was.'"

Her wits were reeling, her senses fracturing—beneath her heated skin, her nerves had stretched taut. As if he understood, he nuzzled her ear. "Because of Helena's actions in claiming me as hers, I was a scandal that never eventuated."

"Oh." She breathed the syllable—it shattered in the warm stillness as she gasped. And tightened, every muscle coiling.

He bent her forward, drove deeply into her—and sent her flying, tumbling over the edge of the world.

Richard held her before him, heard her scream—listened to it die to a sob. He held still—briefly—buried within her, savoring the strong ripples of her release, then let go his own reins, let his body have its way, and followed her into ecstasy.

By the time she joined the breakfast table the next morning, Catriona was a walking testament to the fact that three days spent primarily out of doors had completely restored Richard's strength.

There was nothing wrong with his stamina; she could swear to that on The Lady's name.

A fact apparently so obvious, no one needed to ask; all the Cynsters were busy with their preparations to leave.

If anything, their leaving created even more commotion than their arrival.

Two hours later, standing on the steps, ready to wave them off, Catriona turned as the Dowager came bustling out, lecturing McArdle to the last.

"Once down to the cattle barn and back at least once a day—I will check in my letters to see that you are doing it."

McArdle's assurance that he wouldn't forget was lost in the clatter as Vane's elegant carriage, drawn by matched greys, came rattling around the house to join the Dowager's carriage and the ducal equipage, both already waiting on the cobbles.

Devil and Honoria had already taken their leave; Richard stood beside Devil as he handed Honoria into their carriage, then, with a last word to Richard, and a last rakish smile and a wave to Catriona, Devil climbed up and Richard shut the door. He paused for a moment, watching Gabriel hand the twins into the Dowager's carriage. His horse tied to the carriage's back, Gabriel would travel with them to Somersham, then escort the twins back to London.

Vane and Patience were heading for London, too, but they would stop at Somersham first to allow Patience to rest before joining Vane's family in the capital. Richard returned Patience's wave as Vane handed her into the carriage; with a salute, Vane followed her in.

A groom shut the door—others scurried around checking straps and harness. Smiling, Richard strolled back to the front steps. He arrived to see Helena release Catriona from one of her extravagant embraces.

"You must promise me you will visit in summer." Clinging to Catriona's hands, Helena looked into her eyes. "The Season, I can understand, might be difficult and not to your liking, but in summer, you must come." She shook Catriona's hands. "You have not been part of a big family before—there is much you yet need to learn."

Catriona saw the worry in Helena's fine eyes; smiling serenely, she leaned forward and touched cheeks. "Of course, we'll come. Exactly when"—she drew one hand free and gestured—"is in the lap of The Lady, but we will come, you may be sure."

Helena searched her eyes briefly, then beamed. "*Bon!* It is good." With that, she pressed Catriona's hand and turned to her second son. "Come—you may lead me to my carriage."

Surprised by his wife's promise, Richard masked his concern and suavely offered his arm.

Helena took it; he led her down the steps and over the cobbles to where Gabriel and the twins were waiting. With a last hug, and a last cling, Helena let him go; accepting Gabriel's hand, she climbed into the carriage. Gabriel followed and Richard shut the door. Helena leaned out of the window as Catriona, who had strolled in their wake, linked her arm with Richard's.

"You will not forget!" Helena wagged a finger at Catriona.

Who laughed. "I won't. June—July—who knows? But sometime in summer."

"Good." Helena beamed her brilliant smile and sat back. The coachman cracked his whip.

"Farewell!"

"Safe journey!"

The carriages rolled smoothly out, the ducal carriage in the lead, followed by the Dowager's with Vane and Patience's carriage bringing up the rear. The grooms and outriders rode alongside, all in the ducal livery. It was a scene from a pageant, a sight the vale had never seen before; the manor household lined the courtyard and the drive, waving their unexpected but very welcome visitors on their way.

Catriona watched them go, waving until the drive dipped and they were lost to view, conscious of a sadness of a type she'd never felt before. She didn't try to push it from her—this was one of the things she needed to learn. Pensive, smiling rather mistily, she let Richard turn her; arm in arm, they strolled back to the house.

She felt his gaze on her face as they climbed the steps. At the top, he halted; looking up, she met his gaze and found it serious and concerned.

He hesitated, then asked: "Did you mean what you said about going to London?"

"Yes." She smiled reassuringly. "I don't intend to let Helena down."

"But ..." He frowned. "I thought you never left the vale—or at least, only under legal edict."

"Ah, well." Her smile deepening, she tried to find words in which to explain something he'd never stopped to think about, something he'd known all his life. Even more, to explain that through the evil of his poisoning, good had come—that having his family here had opened many doors into the future. Not just for the vale, but for the two of them, too. Instead, after searching his eyes, she smiled, deliberately enigmatic; raising a hand, she traced his cheek, then stretched on her toes to plant a kiss by the side of his mouth. "Times change." Turning, she glanced toward the mouth of the vale, to where a collection of dark specks travelled down the road. And smiled. "It's time for the lady of the vale to learn about the wider world."

When the road curved, finally hiding the manor from view, Devil grinned and sat back. An instant later, he reached out an arm, drew his wife to him and kissed her soundly.

"What was that for?" Honoria asked, prepared to be suspicious. She didn't think she'd yet forgiven him for his three-day disappearance, but she couldn't entirely remember what she'd said the night before.

He grinned in unlikely innocence. "Just because."

The carriage jolted; he glanced out of the window. "Well, that's Scandal well settled."

"Hmmm." Honoria closed her eyes and settled against his shoulder. "She's just what he needs."

Devil gazed at the fields and woods beyond the window, then murmured: "This place is what he needs, too. She's given him a home, in the right place, at the right time."

A moment of silence ensued, then, in precisely the same tone, Honoria, her eyes still closed, murmured: "There are times when I could almost imagine you believed in fate."

Devil shot her a sideways glance, one she didn't see. Noting her closed eyes, he let his lips curve, then he looked out of the window—and let the question in her words pass unanswered.

CHAPTER
Twenty

৬⌇৩

Together, Catriona and Richard reentered the front hall. "Excuse me, sir." Henderson came up. "Corby was wondering if he could have a word before he goes back to Lower Farm."

"Of course." Releasing Catriona, Richard beckoned to Corby, who'd hung back by the wall.

By Richard's side, Catriona hesitated, then quietly glided away. Leaving Richard conferring about the orchard fence, she silently made her way upstairs.

She had unfinished business to attend to.

It had been easy to set aside the question of Richard's poisoner while his family—their family—had been here. In truth, it would have been difficult to deal with the matter appropriately while they'd been about.

But they were gone now.

There wasn't a single person in the vale who did not know who had poisoned Richard. But all her people would, with their usual unwavering confidence, leave the matter in her hands—to be settled as The Lady willed.

Which was as it should be, but she wasn't looking forward to it—to what might have to be.

Reaching the top of the stairs, Catriona looked back, down into the hall to where Richard's dark head was bent as he spoke to Corby. She looked for one long moment, then drew in a deep breath, straightened her spine, straightened her shoulders, and turning, headed for their chamber.

Richard knew the instant she left his side. From the corner of his eye, he saw her climb the stairs, her steps slow and measured, saw her reach the top, hesitate as she looked back at him, then quietly walk away.

The instant he finished with Corby, he followed her.

He opened the door to their room and immediately saw her, standing at the end of the bed, pushing a thick shawl into a saddlebag.

She looked up and saw him, then continued with her packing.

He shut the door and advanced on the bed, on her. "Where is she?"

Catriona looked up as he halted beside her; she met his gaze, then raised a questioning brow.

Richard's lips thinned. "Algaria. It's obvious it was she who poisoned me."

Catriona hesitated, then grimaced. "We can't say that for certain."

"It hasn't escaped my notice that, other than you, only she knows enough of those elixirs and potions you store in the stillroom to mix whatever it was in that coffee."

"Wolfsbane. Plus a little henbane. But that doesn't convict her."

"No, but it makes her the obvious suspect." He hesitated, then asked, rather more quietly, "Besides, if it wasn't she, where are you going?"

Her gaze on her saddlebag, Catriona grimaced again.

She heard Richard sigh, then felt him shift. He reached past her, bracing one arm on the bedpost; sliding the other around her, he turned her, trapped her—lifting her hands to his chest, she looked up.

He trapped her gaze. "Don't you trust me yet?" She looked into his eyes and saw nothing but devotion—selfless, committed, and unshakable; with a sigh, she closed her eyes and leaned her forehead on his chest. "You know I do."

"Then I'll come with you. No—" He held up a hand when she looked up, her mouth opened to argue. "Consider me your protector, your champion—your consort. I'll hold myself at your command." He studied her eyes. "In this matter, I won't act without it."

Determination and commitment were etched in his face, enshrined in his blue, blue eyes. Catriona studied them, then drew a deep breath and nodded. "We'll be gone for two days."

Mounted—she on her mare, he on Thunderer—they reached the mouth of the vale just after midday. Richard followed as Catriona turned the mare's head north; he waited until they were trotting steadily before asking: "Where exactly are we going?"

"Algaria has a small cottage." Catriona gestured with her chin. "It's almost directly north. It's not all that far as the crow flies, but the tracks are not easy."

That was an understatement. They followed the road from the vale, a relatively well-surfaced lane, until it joined the road to Ayr. Crossing this, Catriona led the way up a narrow sheep track, the little mare picking her way daintily. Thunderer hurrumphed—and clomped in the mare's wake.

From there on, it was nothing but sheep tracks, barely a trail worn into the rocky ground. Studying the poor land through which they passed, Richard noticed a field, some way away, planted with a low-lying crop. Crossing the field was a straggling line of gaunt cattle.

After considering the sight for a moment, he transferred his gaze to his witchy wife's hips. "Aren't these Sir Olwyn's fields?"

"Yes." She nodded without looking around. "Both to the north and south."

Richard looked to the south, to where the cattle now stood morosely hanging their heads. "Looks like he's just lost some more cabbages."

Catriona looked around, then followed his gaze to the distant field. She studied the evidence, then humphed. "He never would listen when I tried to help him."

Surveying the bleak scene about them, an amazing contrast to the vale, no more than a few miles behind them, Richard raised his brows. "I can see why he wanted to marry you."

Catriona merely humphed again.

They plodded slowly on through the afternoon; Richard called a halt, an enforced rest, on the crest of a small hill. The track wound about the top then descended into shadow. Sitting in the sunshine, he looked across the rocky, largely barren landscape through which they'd travelled. In the distance, a purple haze hid the vale. Catriona came up, dusting her hands on her skirts after feeding dried apples to Thunderer and her mare. With a soft sigh, she slid down beside him, settling against him when he lifted an arm about her shoulders.

They looked out in silence. Eventually, he said: "It's beautiful here. Not pretty, but majestic. It's all so hard, harsh and rocky, it makes a place like the vale all the more wondrous, all the more precious."

Catriona smiled and leaned more heavily against him. "Yes."

They looked some more, then Richard asked: "Are we still on Sir Olwyn's lands?"

"Theoretically yes, but he's never farmed this area. Algaria's cottage lies just inside his northern boundary."

Resting his chin in her hair, Richard frowned. "So Sir Olwyn is Algaria's landlord?"

Catriona looked up at him. "Well—yes, I suppose that's true." Turning back to the scenery, she clasped her hands over his at her waist. After a moment, she sighed. "If there's one thing I know about Algaria, it's that she must have had a very strong reason to poison you. She would not have done it lightly— not just because she didn't like you—not even because she felt so strongly that you weren't the right husband for me."

"She never made any secret of that."

"No—that's not her way. She never hides what she thinks. But to act as she did, she must have had some compelling reason."

Hearing the fervor in her voice, Richard hugged her tighter. "Why are you so sure?"

It was a simple question, accepting rather than dismissive.

"Because the only excuse for any disciple of The Lady to take a life is in the service of others. That is, she must be acting in defense, usually of others."

"Others—such as you?"

Catriona nodded. "Me. Or the people of the vale." After a moment, she sighed. "But that doesn't make sense—because no matter what Algaria *thought* you might do, you haven't *done* anything to harm me or the vale. Quite the opposite."

Turning in his arms, she looked into Richard's face, into his blue eyes. "Can you think of anything—any act at all—that you've committed since coming to the vale that she could misconstrue as a real threat?"

Richard saw the worry in her eyes and knew it wasn't for him. He would have eased even that burden for her if he could. But ... framing her face, he looked deep into her eyes. "Since the day we wed, I've only had one aim in life—your well-being—and that isn't compatible with harming you or the vale."

She sighed; turning her head, she pressed a kiss into his palm, then wriggled around and settled back into his arms. "I know. That's what bothers me so."

They pressed on as the afternoon slowly waned into evening; as the chill in the air deepened, Catriona turned into the mouth of a narrow cleft and pulled up before a rude hut. To Richard's questioning glance, she replied: "We would have made it in a day if we'd started early enough, but we can't go on in the dark."

Richard didn't argue—the track they were now following was little more than a ribbon worn into the rocky hillside, and aside from the cold, there were gullies and clefts aplenty, traps for the unwary. He dismounted, then lifted Catriona down. "What is this place?"

"It's an old shepherd's hut. I doubt it's been used since last I was here."

Unstrapping their bags, Richard glanced at her. "Since last ...? I thought you never left the vale."

Taking the bags from him, Catriona pulled a face. "I don't count my herb trips."

"Herb trips?"

"At least once every spring and again in late summer, I travel to collect herbs and roots which don't grow in the vale."

Unsaddling Thunderer, Richard narrowed his eyes at her. "I foresee a developing interest in botany."

Catriona grinned. Hefting the bags, she threw him a provocative glance. "There's quite a lot I could teach you."

Richard raised his brows. "Indeed?" Hauling the saddle from Thunderer's back, he met her gaze squarely. "Why don't you go and sweep the spiders out, then I'll get a fire going—and you can teach me all you will."

Catriona's grin widened; her eyes danced as she turned away. "Why not?"

Richard watched her hips sway as she climbed to the cottage, then he grinned and turned back to the horses.

The first lessons his witchy wife taught him had nothing to do with botany. The first thing he learned was that despite her delicate appearance and her usually cossetted state, she ranked with the most experienced camp-follower in the not-at-all-easy task of making a rude shepherd's hut seem comfortable and warm. In conjuring a warm and sustaining meal out of what they'd carried in their saddlebags and the roots and leaves she'd gathered before the light died.

In making him feel relaxed and rather cossetted himself.

It was a distinctly pleasant feeling.

Smiling serenely, Catriona watched the heavy muscles in his shoulders ease, watched the glow of comfort suffuse his expression. And inwardly smiled all the more.

She hadn't been sure whether to bring him with her on this journey, not until he'd asked and sworn his allegiance. Then she'd known it was right—that he should be by her side when she faced Algaria at her cottage, and whatever truths awaited them there.

But she could do nothing about Algaria tonight, and, regardless of what transpired with Algaria, her own life would go on—and she had a goal, a personal aim, one vitally important to her.

She needed to show Richard she loved him. Needed to convince him of that fact—drum it through his Cynster skull so that, someday, he would be confident enough to openly show his love for her. She wasn't holding her breath, of course—she knew it would take time. Men as reserved as he did not change their habits overnight. But she was prepared to be patient; she would persevere.

The first thing to do was to start.

And now was as good a time as any.

Sliding the wooden eating bowls back into her saddlebag, she set it aside, then approached Richard where he sat on a round stool before the fire, staring at the flames. Resting her hands lightly on his shoulders, she brushed her lips along his cheek. "Come to bed."

The soft whisper had him standing immediately; he'd already banked the fire. Taking his hand, a soft smile playing on her lips, Catriona led him to the pallet lying on a crude frame in the corner. She'd had him fetch fresh spruce to slide into the dry straw, then she'd covered the whole with a blanket, keeping two others to wrap about them. The warmth in the cottage released a faint tang from the spruce; their warm bodies crushing it would release even more.

Stopping by the bed, he drew his fingers from hers and immediately reached for her laces. Laying aside the warm shawl she'd draped over her shoulders, she let him do what he did so well. He divested her of her gown and petticoats, then considered her fine lawn chemise.

"You might want to keep that on."

Catriona considered her own plans for the night and shook her head. "Not tonight." Quickly, fingers flying, she slid the tiny buttons undone, noting his blink, his sudden stiffening as she opened the bodice. Then she grasped the hem and whisked the chemise off over her head. She dropped it on a stool with the rest of her clothes, then grabbed one waiting blanket, shook it out, and slid onto the bed beneath it.

Richard watched her, blinked at her, then undressed and joined her in record time. He pinched out the candle just before he did, plunging the room into a mysterious dark lit by flickering firelight. The pallet dipped beside her as he stretched beneath the second blanket; he was all dark, mysterious male when he loomed on his elbow beside her. And reached for her.

"No." Catriona braced one hand against his chest when he would have rolled her beneath him. She wriggled the other way, pressing him back to the pallet. "This time, I want to love you—not the other way about."

Richard blinked again and swallowed the reassurance that had risen to his tongue. She always loved him—took him into her body with a joyous delight, a witchy neediness, that was all the loving he needed. But ... if she wanted to love him even more, he'd grit his teeth and bear it. "Just what form," he murmured, as he rolled obediently onto his back, "is this loving of yours going to take?"

"This, for a start." Scrambling over him, Catriona found his lips with hers, and kissed him—gently at first, then with greater confidence as he parted his lips and welcomed her in, playing the role that was usually hers. She took his, wriggling so she was higher over him to deepen the kiss, to coax, to incite, to sexually stir him.

Not that he needed any stirring. Against her thigh, cocooned in the warmth of the blankets, she could feel the steady, pulsing throb of his erection—hard and heavy and all hers. Inwardly grinning, she shifted, trapping it between her thighs, artfully caressing.

It grew hotter, harder. His hands, splayed across her back, tensed.

She pulled back from their kiss. "I want," she whispered, already slightly breathless, "you to tell me what you like."

"What I like?" His voice was a gravelly murmur in her ear. "What I like, sweet witch, is to feel your body close tightly about me, all hot and wet and urgent."

"Hmmm, yes. But before that," she insisted. "Do you like this?" Discovering a flat nipple hidden beneath the crisp mat of his hair, she burrowed her head down and licked it—lovingly.

And felt him tense, just a little, beneath her. "Very nice." The words sounded a touch strained. In wriggling lower, she'd slithered over his erection; it was now cradled in her curls, pulsing against the rounded softness of her belly.

"Good." Artfully sliding this way, then that, using her whole body as well as her hands to caress him, she pressed hot, open-mouthed kisses across his chest, down the ridged muscles of his abdomen, interspersing her kisses with well-placed licks and the occasional suck.

Beneath her, his body was hardening; muscles here and there flickered restlessly. Recalling in fine detail all the caresses he'd pressed on her—and which ones drove her the most demented—Catriona decided that what was good for the goose probably worked equally well with the gander.

The sudden hiss of his indrawn breath as, sliding swiftly further down, she curled her fingers about his rigid length, then caressed it with the warm swells of her breasts, suggested her reasoning was sound. Smiling to herself, she slid further yet, deliberately guiding his long length up from the valley between her breasts, along the smooth skin of her upper chest, then up, sinuously lifting her head to caress him with her throat.

Before turning her head and caressing him with her lips.

He jerked; every muscle in his body locked tight. His hands shifted from her shoulders; his fingers sank into her curls. "Catriona?"

He sounded shocked. Inwardly grinning, Catriona was too busy to answer him. She didn't, however, have any real clue what she was doing, how much pleasure he was feeling, so, after kissing, licking and sucking to her own content, she decided to inquire about his.

"Do you like this?" She planted a soft, wet kiss on his pulsing tip.

Richard bit back a groan. "No," he lied. But he couldn't force his fingers to grip her tresses and haul her away.

"Oh. Well, perhaps you like this better?"

He did; Richard gave up and groaned as she closed her mouth, all soft, hot heat, around him. He withstood her torture for two more, exquisitely wracked minutes, before realizing that, no matter that he could tease her to *extremis,* his own constitution wasn't up to it.

"Catriona—" In an explosive movement, he half-sat—for one fractured instant driving his shaft deeper into her mouth—then he caught her, lifted her, scattering the blankets they no longer needed. They were both burning with an inner heat.

An inner heat that poured over his teased and sensitive flesh as he set her on her knees, straddling his hips.

She blinked down at him. "I was only trying to please you."

He scowled at her; despite the poor light, he could see the witchy smile on her lips. "You please me every time you take me in, you damn witch."

His knowing fingers found her softness, deftly probed, stroked and readied her. It took only one flick to replace his fingers with his throbbing shaft. Gripping her hips, he eased her down, closing his eyes in ecstasy as she slowly slid down and enveloped him.

"That," he stated his voice deep but weak, "is what pleases me the most."

He heard her witchy chuckle, then she rose on him and slid down, clasping him tight again. Sliding his hands about the globes of her derriere, he gripped and helped her rise—and felt the dew spring up beneath his hands as he stroked and caressed.

They settled into their usual slow rhythm; only then did he lift his heavy lids. Small hands braced on his chest, she rode him happily, a serene, definitely witchy, lustfully knowing smile on her lips. Her gaze was fixed on his face, watching, gauging, assessing his response to that ultimate, most intimate caress.

He only just managed to suppress his wolfish grin. He was blessed, and he knew it. "If you really want to please me, one thing you could do is always come to me stark naked, with your hair down." As it currently was, a rich, vibrant corona about her head, rippling fire over her white shoulders and down her slim arms. When he took her from behind, it was like a living veil, sliding sensuously over her back. He loved her hair.

Her eyes glinted; she inclined her head. "Any other requests?"

"Just one. Stop trying to muffle your moans and screams."

She frowned slightly; he smiled winningly and she humphed. "That's all very well for you to say, but if anyone else heard me—well"—she caught his eye and frowned—"it's rather revealing, you know."

He grinned. "I do, indeed, which is why I like to hear them—those little sounds of your appreciation." He gripped her bottom and lifted her high, then thrust deeply into her as he lowered her again. Eyes closing, she bit her lip to hold back a groan. "Like that. They're little sounds of pleasure—and they're precious to me. They're like trophies that I win for pleasuring you." After a moment, he added: "How else do I know if I'm hitting the mark?"

"You *always* hit the mark," Catriona retorted, her lids still too heavy to lift. "You always pleasure me to oblivion."

"Perhaps—but I like to hear you admit it."

Opening her eyes, Catriona studied his as she continued to move upon him. Then he shifted her, pulling her thighs wider so he could sink more deeply into her; a moan welled in her throat—this time, she let it go. And sensed the real pleasure the sound gave him.

"Very well." Leaning forward, she kissed him, letting their hungry lips feast. As she drew back, eyes closed in concentration as he started moving more powerfully beneath her, she mumured, "I'll try."

It wasn't hard, especially given their location, with no one within miles to hear her screams. But he reveled in her commitment and took advantage to the full.

He garnered a whole swag of trophies that night.

Courtesy of Richard's developing fondness for the amenities of the shepherd's hut, it was mid-afteroon before they reached Algaria's cottage.

She'd seen them coming. She stood in the doorway as they rode up, Catriona just a little in the lead. Algaria met Catriona's gaze, then, deliberately, her hands clasped before her, bowed her head. Turning, she went into the cottage, leaving the door open.

Richard dismounted, then lifted Catriona down. She paused, held between his hands, and met his gaze. "Remember your promise."

He grimaced. "I won't forget. I'm your right arm—your protector. I'll follow your lead." He gestured her toward the house.

Drawing a deep breath, drawing herself up, Catriona led the way inside.

It was a two-room cottage, one up, one down, with the kitchen facilities in a lean-to at the rear, and a small stable against the side. Pausing on the threshold to let her eyes adjust, Catriona scanned the room and saw Algaria standing, hands clasped before her, her head still bowed in the attitude of a penitent, on the other side of the deal table with her back to the cold hearth.

Catriona moved into the room, until she stood at the opposite side of the table, facing Algaria. Richard's shadow blocked the light from the door momentarily, then she sensed his presence at her back.

Lifting one hand, she extended it across the table. "Algaria—"

"As you love me, let me speak." Slowly, Algaria lifted her head. She looked first at Richard, standing silent at Catriona's shoulder, then shifted her black gaze to Catriona's face. "I now know what I did was wrong, but at the time, it seemed right—what The Lady required of me. But rather than you, it was I who made the mistakes in interpreting Her signs. I acted wrongly, and I deeply regret the pain and suffering I caused." She drew breath, her gaze locked on Catriona's, and pressed her hands tightly together. "I ask for your understanding and will abide by your judgment."

Lowering her proud head, she looked down.

Catriona waited a moment, then asked: "What made you realize you were wrong?"

Algaria lifted her head; the glance she bent on Richard was hardly affectionate but contained a respect that had not previously been there. "He lived." She looked at Catriona. "If you knew how much wolfsbane I put in that cup ..." She pressed her lips together, flicked Richard another glance, then stated: "Not even your intervention should have been able to save him. Yet he lived. The Lady's intention is clear—she could not have spoken any louder."

Catriona nodded. "As you say. It took him a long time to recover, yet every day longer made his living more remarkable."

Algaria inclined her head and looked down once more. "It is clear The Lady wishes him as your consort—the error of my actions could not be more plain." She lifted her head and met Catriona's gaze levelly. "I am sincerely contrite"—she drew a tight breath—"and ready to accept whatever judgment you make."

"Why?" Catriona asked. "Why did you think it necessary to remove Richard, especially knowing you were acting against my wishes?"

Algaria grimaced. The look she flicked Richard held an element of apology. "Because I believed he was responsible for the fire."

"What?" Catriona felt Richard shift behind her, but true to his word, he held silent. "He was in Carlisle—or riding back—at the time the fire started."

Algaria held up a hand. "Bear with me—I knew that was what we'd been told. However," she paused and drew a deep breath, "if you recall, three days after the fire, we were running low on tansy, and I offered to go and check the patch south of the woods." Catriona nodded; Algaria glanced at Richard. "The patch in the woods always sprouts ahead of the main bed at the manor itself."

Richard inclined his head; Algaria went on: "On that side of the park lives an old man known to us all as Royce. You and he, now I've thought back on it, haven't yet met—he's something of a hermit in winter."

"He's a marvel with animals, particularly with birthing lambs," Catriona put in. "He lives in a small hut on the south side of the park."

"I saw Royce that day when I went looking for the tansy—it was sunny and he was stretching his stiff limbs. He sat on a rock and talked—despite living so alone, he loves to talk to people, so I waited and listened."

"He talked about the fire only in passing—he'd missed all the excitement. He couldn't see the smoke because of the park—he'd only heard about it later. What he *did* say, however, was that on the day when he came to the manor to fetch bones for broth, while returning home, he saw a stranger—a tall, dark-haired gentleman riding a dark horse. This man rode through the park, but not up to the manor. It was late afternoon, heading into evening—the stranger tethered his horse in the park, took something from his saddle pocket, then skirted the manor itself, and went around behind the forge. He didn't see Royce watching. Royce thought it strange, but ..." Algaria grimaced. "He assumed the gentleman was you. Later the gentleman came back, mounted his horse, and rode down the vale—that time, Royce was close enough to see the man had blue eyes." She paused and met Richard's undeniably blue eyes. "I knew Royce got his bones on the day of the fire—I gave them to him myself. He didn't know about the timing of the fire, so he didn't know you didn't apparently arrive until black night."

"You thought it was me?"

Lifting her chin, Algaria nodded. "I reasoned that in order to tighten your hold on Catriona, you'd been seen to leave, then you rode back, earlier than anyone thought, set the fire, waited until it was blazing, then rode in and rescued the situation." She eyed Richard; her lips tightened. "If that had been your plan, from all I saw afterward, it worked."

Richard considered, then nodded. "I can prove it wasn't me. Two of Melchett's lads saw me riding into the vale, and we spoke briefly—we could already see the smoke rising." He could remember that moment of dread panic very well.

Algaria waved dismissively. "I accept without question that my interpretation was wrong—else you would have died. It wasn't you old Royce saw."

"So who was it?" Catriona asked. Algaria lifted her shoulders; in the same instant, Catriona's face lit. "Dougal Douglas!" Swinging about, she looked at Richard. "It must be him."

Richard grimaced. "He fits the general description, but tall, dark-haired, blue-eyed gentlemen aren't really all that rare, even in the Lowlands." He paused, his gaze on Catriona's. "Algaria jumped to an erroneous conclusion—we shouldn't repeat the mistake." He studied her face—he could almost see her intransigence, her witch's wiles working. Inwardly, he sighed. "*But* ... I do know that Dougal Douglas knew I'd left the vale. He thought I was heading south, that I'd be well on the road to London by lunchtime that day."

Her eyes narrowed, Catriona humphed. "I know it was Dougal Douglas." Transferring her gaze to Algaria, she raised her brows. "So you poisoned Richard because you believed he was responsible for the fire?"

Algaria drew herself up. "Yes."

Catriona considered—considered Algaria and her rigid discipline, her rigid pride. Considered Richard, a vital force beside her, his heartbeat as familiar to her as her own. They were both dear to her, both with so much to give. She and the vale needed both of them. Straightening, she turned to Richard. "You have heard all I've heard—you know as much as I know. It was your life Algaria sought to take—as my consort and protector, I give you the right to pass judgment and sentence upon her."

She looked into Richard's eyes, then, without another glance at Algaria, turned and left the cottage.

Leaving Richard staring over the deal table at Algaria.

Who stiffened and lifted her chin proudly, her black gaze smoldering. She was still a potent force—he could sense it—but expecting the worst. Yet the old witch would never beg his pardon, or ask for mercy.

He wasn't inclined to be all that merciful but ... he had survived—and he and his witchy wife were much closer, more one, than they had been. She'd trusted him enough to leave her mentor's fate in his hands.

And, despite the fact that he wasn't at all comfortable with Algaria, she'd behaved much as he, in the same situation, might have himself—although not with poison. A well-aimed fist would have been more his style.

But what to do with her—what possible sentence could he devise? The answer popped into his mind with such vigor, such force, he grinned.

Which made Algaria nervous; he grinned even more. "After much consideration," he stated, "I've decided that the most appropriate penance, the most suitable punishment, will be for you to return to the vale, to act as overall nursemaid to our children." Being responsible for a household of Cynster brats—oh, yes—that was perfect. And he'd so enjoy contributing to her punishment—and she'd so disapprove of the enjoyment he derived from the process. "And," he added, "should you have any spare hours, you must devote them to easing *our* lady's burden by relieving her of some of her healer's chores."

He smiled, rather pleased with himself.

Algaria raised her brows. "That's it?"

Richard nodded—she didn't know anything about Cynsters—she didn't know what she was destined for. When Algaria's face lit with relief, he quickly added: "Just as long as you're quite sure you won't again decide to make away with me."

"What? Fly in the face of The Lady's expressed wishes?" Algaria waved derisively. "That's not a mistake I'm likely to make twice."

"Good." Richard waved himself, gesturing her to the door. "Then I'll leave you to make your peace with our lady."

He was sitting, relaxing, on a stone at the back of the cottage, out of the wind, when Catriona came searching for him. She came up behind him and slid her arms about his shoulders and hugged him.

"Your sentence was inspired—she's so relieved. In fact, she's almost happy. I even saw her smile."

Richard squeezed her arm. "If that pleases you, then I'm glad." He looked out at the rugged hills before them. "Actually, I was thinking of inviting Helena to come for a visit, maybe in November. She can tell Algaria all the stories of what Devil and I and all the rest used to get up to—to prepare her for what's to come."

Catriona chuckled, then sobered. "Incidentally, I remembered, and Algaria does, too, that Dougal Douglas used to visit the vale as a youth. Algaria says his family was keen on a match between him and me."

"Is that so?" Despite his lazy drawl, Richard was already making plans to call on Dougal Douglas. Once he determined who had set the blacksmith's cottage ablaze, he fully intended to exact retribution.

"Well." With a sigh, Catriona straightened. "We'll spend the night here, then start back early tomorrow. We should reach the vale before dusk."

"Good." Richard stood, suddenly eager to be home again, to get his witchy wife back where she belonged. Turning, he gathered Catriona in one arm and they started to stroll back to the cottage. "No one in London would ever believe this—me sitting down to dinner with not one, but two witches."

"*Not* witches." Mock-chidingly, Catriona poked him in the ribs. "Two disciples of The Lady, one of whom is bearing your child."

Richard grinned. "I stand corrected." Tipping up her face, he kissed her—a kiss she returned very sweetly. Then Algaria called from the cottage, and Catriona broke away.

His brows lightly rising, Richard took care to hide his sudden thoughts; when Catriona took his arm and towed him to the cottage, he didn't resist.

The next morning, they left Algaria's cottage at the crack of dawn, Catriona still sleepy, Algaria grouchy, Richard with a wide smile on his face. The attitudes of all three were connected; Algaria had given up her bed for Catriona's use, casting dark looks Richard's way when he'd bid her good night and joined Catriona upstairs. Algaria had slept on the old settle downstairs— that, however, was not the reason she'd slept poorly.

Richard had provided that—provided reason enough for his witchy wife, despite her disapproval, to moan and sob her pleasure for quite half the night.

He was, this morning, in a very good mood.

Keeping Thunderer to a lazy amble, he followed Catriona's mare and Algaria's old grey. The two women rode side by side, talking of herbs and potions.

Richard grinned—and wondered if witches ever talked of anything else.

Idly speculating, he ambled along in pleasant content, his gaze locked on his wife's swinging hips—

Ph-whizz! Thwack!

Thunderer balked and whinnied; Richard abruptly drew rein. Ahead, Catriona and Algaria milled, their faces blanking in shock as they looked back and saw what he was staring at.

A crossbow bolt.

It had whizzed across, a mere inch before his chest, then struck a rock and glanced off. It now lay in the heather, glinting evilly, in the soft morning light.

Fists clenching about the reins, Richard jerked his head up and looked about. Algaria and Catriona followed his lead, visually scouring the slopes below them to their left.

"There!" Algaria pointed to a fleeing rider.

Catriona stood in her stirrups to look. "It's that *fiend* Dougal Douglas!"

"That pestilential man!"

Calmly, Richard scanned the long valley below them. "Wait here!" With that curt order, he swung Thunderer about and tapped his heels to the horse's sides. The huge grey surged, perfectly happy to thunder hell for leather over the heather, leaping small streams, jumping rocks. They descended to the valley on a direct course to intercept the fleeing Douglas like retribution falling from on high.

They met as Richard had planned, with him on Thunderer higher up the slope from Douglas on his black horse. Leaping from Thunderer's saddle, he collected Douglas and rolled, making no attempt to hang on to his prey, more intent on landing safely himself. He managed to avoid hitting his head on any rocks; with only a bruise or two pending, he swung around. And saw Douglas, still prone some yards away, groggily shaking his head. Richard's lips curled. Snarling, he surged to his feet.

Whether Douglas knew what hit him—either what had brought him from his saddle or who it was that hauled him to his feet by his collar, shook him like a rag, then buried a solid fist in his gut—Richard neither knew nor cared. Having a crossbow bolt fired at him gave him, he considered, a certain license.

They were much of a height, much of a size—it was no wonder the old hermit had thought Douglas was him. Richard had no compunction in treating Douglas to a little home-brewed—the way they brewed it south of the border. That first rush took the edge from his fury; grasping the downed Douglas by his collar yet again, he hauled him once more to his feet.

"Was it you," Richard inquired, recalling several incidents that hadn't, to his mind, been sufficiently explained, "who left the paddock gates opened and broke branches in the orchard?"

Gasping and wheezing, Douglas spat out a tooth. "Damn it, mon—she had to be brought to see she needed a mon about the place."

"Ah, well," Richard said, drawing back his fist. "Now she has me." He steadied Douglas, then knocked him down again.

He gave him a moment, then hauled him to his feet again. And shook him until his teeth—those he still had left—rattled. Closing his fist about Douglas's collar, he lifted him, just a little, and, very gently, inquired, "And the fire?"

Dangling and choking, Dougal Douglas rolled his eyes, flailed his arms weakly, then, forced to it, desperately gasped: "No one was supposed to get hurt."

For one instant, Richard saw red—the red glow of the fire as he'd ridden into the courtyard—the red maw that had roared and gaped as he'd seen his wife, her hair bright as the flames, fling a blanket over her head and dash into the fury. "Catriona nearly got caught in the blaze."

His tone sounded distant, even to him; refocusing on Dougals's face, he saw real fear in the man's eyes.

Douglas paled—he struggled frantically.

Catriona rode up to see Richard bury his fist in Dougal Douglas's stomach. The fiend doubled over; Catriona winced as Richard's fist swung up and, with his full weight behind it, crunched into Douglas's jaw. Dougal Douglas fell backward into the heather. And didn't move.

Richard watched, but saw no sign of returning life. Shaking out his fingers, he turned. To see Catriona. He sighed. "Damn it, woman—didn't I tell you—"

Her eyes flew wide. *"Richard!"*

Richard whirled—just as Dougal Douglas came to his feet in a lunge, a knife in his fist. Swift as a thought, Richard sidestepped and caught Douglas's wrist.

Snap!

"*Aargh!*" Dougal Douglas fell to his knees, cradling his broken wrist.
"You *fiend!*"

Abruptly, Richard found himself thrust aside; hands on her hips, green eyes blazing, Catriona interposed herself between Dougal Douglas and him.

"*How dare you?*" Green fire and fury poured over Dougal Douglas. "You were once welcomed as a friend of the vale and *this* is how you repay The Lady's graciousness? You conspire against me and the vale—*worse!* you attempt to harm my chosen consort—the one The Lady finally sent for me. You're an evil worm—a loathsome toad! I've half a mind to turn you into an eel and leave you here to gasp to death, or better yet, to be picked to death by the birds. *That* would be a suitable end for you—a just repayment for your unconscionable acts."

She paused for breath; Douglas, on his knees before her, simply stared. "Damn it, ye daft woman—the man's a damned Sassenach!"

"*Sassenach?* What does *that* have to do with it? He's a *man*—far more of one than you'll ever be." She stepped forward; eyes locked on hers, Dougal Douglas cowered back.

Catriona pointed a finger directly at his nose. "Hear me well." Her voice had changed to one of mezmerizing power. "If you ever again act against me, the vale or any of my people—and especially my consort—those jewels you hide beneath your sporran will shrivel, and shrink, until they're the size of apricot kernels. Then they'll fall off. And as for the rest of your apparatus, should you entertain so much a black thought against any of The Lady's people, it will grow black, too. And wither away. And if you speak ill of anyone from the vale, or even connected with the vale, then for every ill word a boil will grow—on that part of you that has more will than your brain."

She paused for breath; Richard reached out, closed his hands about her shoulders and lifted her aside. Setting her down just behind him, a little to the side, he leaned down so his face was level with hers and whispered: "I think he's got your message. Any more, and he might faint." He glanced at Dougal Douglas, who, aghast and pasty-faced, was watching them both like a trapped rabbit. Richard grinned and turned back to his wife. "Much as I enjoyed your performance, leave the rest to me." He trapped her wide gaze. "It's my job to protect *you*, remember?"

She humphed, and crossed her arms over her chest, and glowered at Dougal Douglas, but she consented to remain silent and still.

Richard turned back to survey their malefactor. "Might I suggest," he said, "that before my wife further develops her theme, you might care to be on your way?" The relief on Douglas's face was plain; he started to get to his feet. Richard stayed him with one raised finger. "However, do make sure that, henceforth, you stay out of our way, and out of the vale. On pain of The Lady's wrath. Furthermore, just in case you're inclined, once you're well away from here, to forget how potentially violent The Lady can be, you would do well to dwell on this, more mortal threat."

All hint of expression leaching from his face, Richard held Dougals's gaze calmly. "All the details of your recent interference in the vale, all the facts plus witnesses' accounts, will be forwarded to my brother, Devil Cynster, His Grace of St. Ives. Should any inexplicable harm subsequently befall anyone in the Vale of Casphairn, it will be laid at your door. And the Cynsters will come after you." He paused, then added, his voice still even and low: "You should also bear in mind that we've centuries of experience in asking for no permissions, but exacting vengeance swiftly—and looking innocent later."

Exactly which one of them Dougal Douglas found more intimidating would have been hard to say. With a dismissive gesture, Richard waved him away. Cradling his wrist, he stumbled to his feet, then lurched off to catch his horse, which was ambling off down the valley.

Richard heard an odd sound from beside him—something between a snort and a cough, crossed with a disgusted humph. He wondered whether his witchy wife was fixing her curse on Dougal Douglas, but decided he didn't need to know—didn't want to know.

He whistled, and Thunderer came ambling up, heartened by his brisk ride. Turning, Richard saw Algaria trotting up, leading Catriona's mare. Draping an arm about Catriona's shoulders, he steered her to the mare.

"It's a great pity we can't lay charges with the magistrate—but we can't." Catriona stopped and looked up, waiting for Richard to lift her to her saddle.

"Indeed not," Algaria agreed. "The last thing we need is to draw official attention to the vale. But your combined threats should hold him." She regarded Richard with real approval. "That last threat of yours was a masterstroke. No matter what curses Catriona levels, men always understand legal threats best."

Richard smiled and lifted Catriona to the saddle—and forebore to point out that his threat was not precisely legal—rather the opposite, in fact—a distinction he felt sure Dougal Douglas had understood. But even more to the point, he could attest that Catriona's curses would make any man think twice. Equipment shrinking, then dropping off, turning black, boils—what else she might have dreamed up he hadn't wanted to hear.

The thought made him shudder as he swung up to his saddle; his wife noticed and looked her question—he smiled and shook his head.

Then he clicked the reins, and they headed home—back to the Vale of Casphairn.

Later that night, snug and safe in their bed, soothed and sated and quietly happy, Richard looked down at his wife's red head, comfortably settled on his chest. Raising one hand, he lifted one fiery lock from her cheek. "Tell me," he murmured, careful to keep his voice low so he wouldn't break the spell, "when you were ranting at Dougal Douglas, were you angry on The Lady's behalf, or your own?"

Catriona humphed and wriggled deeper into his arms, pressing herself to him, holding him tightly. "That was the *third* time I nearly lost you! If you must know, I didn't even *think* of The Lady. Or her edicts. Although in this case, it's really all the same thing. But just because *she* issues the directives, that doesn't mean *I* don't have my own opinions. She sent me to you—you were destined for me. But I agreed to have you. And now you're here and you're mine." She tightened her arms about him. "I'm not letting you go. I want you beside me—and I have no intention of letting anyone interfere, not Sir Olwyn, Dougal Douglas, Algaria, or anyone else!"

Lying back on the pillows, Richard grinned into the dark. After a moment, he murmured: "Incidentally, I'm only half-Sassenach. The other half derives from the Lowlands."

His witchy wife shifted, lifting away from him. "Hmmm . . . interesting." A moment later, she asked: "Which half?"

A week later, Richard was shaken to life—literally—by his witchy wife.

"*Wake up,* do!"

Obligingly, he reached for her.

"No, *no!* Not that! We have to get up! Out of bed, I mean."

She illustrated by leaping out from under the warm covers, letting in a blast of icy air.

Richard groaned feelingly and cracked open his lids. He blinked into deep gloom. "*By The Lady!* It's pitch dark—what the devil's got into you, you daft witch?"

"I'm not daft. Just get up! *Please?* It's important."

He groaned again, with even more feeling—and got up.

Catriona pushed and prodded him into his clothes and down the stairs. Clutching one sleeve, she dragged him into the dining hall, and up onto the dais, and around to the wall behind the main table. She stopped and pointed to a huge old broadsword hanging on the wall. "Can you lift it down?"

Richard looked at it, then at her, then reached for the sword.

It was heavy. As he lowered it and settled his hand about the pommel, he knew it was not just old but ancient. There was no scabbard. But he got no time to dwell on the weapon, because his wife was urging him on.

They went out to the stables and he saddled their sleepy mounts while she held the sword balanced before her. Then they mounted, and he hefted the sword; in the crisp chill of pre-dawn they set out for the circle.

"Tether the horses," Catriona said as he lifted her to the ground. "Then bring the sword."

Richard threw her a glance, but did as she asked. She was gripping and releasing her fingers, her gaze flicking again and again to the line of light slowly advancing up the vale. As far as he could see, she still had plenty of time, and yet . . . his witchy wife was nervous.

The instant he'd finished with the horses and hefted the sword, she gripped his other hand and towed him urgently toward the circle. She didn't drop his hand as they came to the place where he usually sat and waited for her. She didn't stop until they stood at the very entrance to the circle.

Only then did she release his hand and swing to face him.

Catriona looked down the vale, at the slowly advancing line of light; at her back, she could sense the power within the circle start to awaken, to unfurl in anticipation of the first touch of the sun. It was cold and frosty, but the day would be fine. Drawing a deep breath, feeling the age-old power in her veins, she looked up at Richard.

And smiled, unaware that the light of her love filled her face with a glow he found wondrous. Dazzling. A glow he, the warrior, would have moved heaven and earth just to see.

"There's a great deal I have to give thanks for." Her voice was clear, calm, yet vibrant. "As my chosen and accepted consort, as my husband and my lover, it's your right to enter the sacred circle and watch over me while I pray. My father used to stand guard over my mother." She paused, her eyes locked on the blue of his. "Will you perform that office for me?"

It was an offer she needed to make—it was her final acknowledgment that he belonged beside her—always beside her, even here, at the epicenter of her life. They belonged to each other, and nowhere more so than here, before The Lady.

They were one and always would be, both with each other and with the vale.

This, she knew beyond certainty, was how it was meant to be.

Richard stilled. Unable to think, all he could do was feel—sense—the power that held him. And her. He had no wish to break it—to reject it—to fight against its bonds; instead, he welcomed it with all his heart. He drew in a slow breath and wondered at the headiness in the air. "Aye, my lady." Bending his head, he touched his lips to hers, then drew back. "My witchy wife."

He held her sparkling gaze for an instant, then gestured with the sword. "Lead on."

They entered the circle just as the sun reached them, bathing them in her golden glow. He followed her in, hers to the death, the far-sighted warrior who had found his cause.

Epilogue

ᔖᔕᕗ

March 1, 1820
Albemarle Street, London

"And so there you have it." Leaning back in a chair drawn up to the table, Vane raised his ale mug in a toast. "Richard and Catriona—and all the London belles can bid Scandal good-bye."

"Humph!" Languidly asprawl at the other end of the table, resplendent in a navy silk dressing gown embroidered with peacocks, Demon Harry eyed his elder brother with apparent equanimity—and underlying unease. "How's Patience?"

Vane grinned. "Blooming." The sight of his brother's transparent happiness made Demon shift in his seat. "Mama, of course, is *aux anges* over the impending addition."

"Hmm—she would be." Demon wondered whether that would divert her attention from him—he doubted he could rely on it.

"And there's already plans afoot for a huge celebration sometime this summer—Richard and Catriona have committed to coming down, and, of course, all the aunts and connections will want to see them, and the new arrivals."

Demon frowned. He'd missed something. "Arrivals?"

Vane's grin surfaced. "Devil, again—what else? Honoria's due about the same time as Patience, so it'll be quite a summer celebration."

Babies and wives all over. Demon could just imagine.

Having brought him up to date, Vane heard creaks upstairs and, with a raised brow and an understanding smile, made his excuses and left. But instead of repairing upstairs, to further indulge himself with the feminine charms of the luscious body he'd left sprawled in his bed, Demon remained at the table, considering all Vane had told him—chilled, more and more, by the shadow of impending fate.

Which just went to show.

Demon drummed well-manicured fingernails on the table; he was going to have to do something about his situation. The situation he now found himself in.

First Devil, then Vane, now Richard. Who would be next?

There were only three of them left—him, Gabriel and Lucifer—and he was the eldest. There was no doubt in his mind who the aunts and connections would next expect to front the altar.

The odds were narrowing—to a degree he didn't like.

But he'd already made his vows—to himself. He'd vowed he'd never marry—never put his trust, his faith, his heart in any woman's hands. And the notion of limiting himself to one woman sexually was beyond his ability to comprehend. How the others managed to do so—Devil, Vane and now Richard—he couldn't imagine. They certainly hadn't before.

It was one of life's mysteries he had long ago decided he didn't need to unravel.

The question now before him, on this brisk sunny morning, was how to avoid fate—a fate that was steadily closing in on him.

His position wasn't good. Here he was, in London, with the Season about to start, with his mother and all his aunts in residence, with the scent of blood firing them . . .

Drastic action was called for.

Strategic retreat to safer surrounds.

Abruptly ceasing his tattoo on the table, Demon raised his head. "Gillies?"

A moment later, an unprepossessing face popped around the door. "Yessir?"

"Fig out the bays. We're going to Newmarket."

Gillies blinked. "But . . .?" Deliberately, he raised his eyes to the ceiling. "What about the countess?"

"Hmm." Demon looked up, then he grinned and stood, cinching his robe tight. "Give me an hour to satisfy the countess—then be ready to roll."

Newmarket, and assured safety, were only a few hours away, but once there, he'd be starved for the usual rake's fare—he may as well indulge his appetite before leaving.

As he climbed the stairs two at a time, Demon grinned. The countess was no threat—and Newmarket was safe.

He was well on the road to being the one Cynster in all the generations to finally escape fate—and the trap she laid for all Cynsters.

A Rogue's Proposal

The Bar Cynster Family Tree

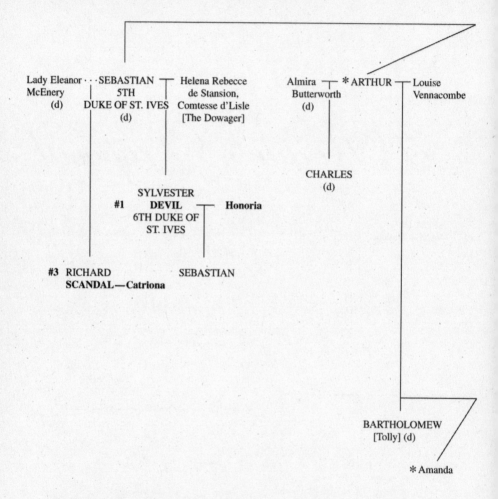

Lady Eleanor · · · SEBASTIAN ⊤ Helena Rebecce
McEnery   5TH   de Stansion,
  (d)   DUKE OF ST. IVES   Comtesse d'Lisle
             (d)   [The Dowager]

Almira ⊤ *ARTHUR ⊤ Louise
Butterworth   Vennacombe
  (d)

             SYLVESTER
     #1   **DEVIL** ⊤ **Honoria**
            6TH DUKE OF
             ST. IVES

CHARLES
  (d)

#3   **RICHARD**   SEBASTIAN
     SCANDAL — Catriona

BARTHOLOMEW
[Tolly] (d)

*Amanda

THE BAR CYNSTER SERIES
#1 *Devil's Bride*
#2 *A Rake's Vow*
#3 *Scandal's Bride*
MALE CYNSTERS named in capitals   * denotes twins

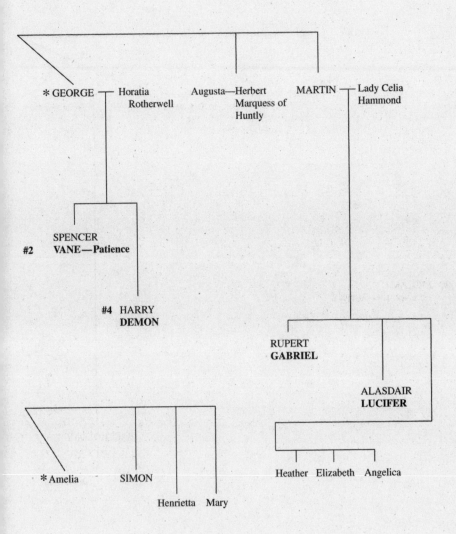

✱ GEORGE —┬— Horatia
          Rotherwell

Augusta—Herbert
        Marquess of
        Huntly

MARTIN —┬— Lady Celia
          Hammond

SPENCER
#2 **VANE—Patience**

#4 **HARRY**
DEMON

RUPERT
GABRIEL

ALASDAIR
LUCIFER

✱ Amelia   SIMON

Henrietta   Mary

Heather   Elizabeth   Angelica

CHAPTER

One

ॐ⋘⊘ॐ

March 1, 1820
Newmarket, Suffolk

U*nfettered freedom!* He'd escaped.

With an arrogant smile, Harold Henry Cynster—Demon to everyone, even to his mother in her weaker moments—drew his curricle to a flourishing halt in the yard behind his Newmarket stable. Tossing the reins to his groom, Gillies, who leaped from the back of the elegant equipage to catch them, Demon stepped down to the cobbles. In a buoyant mood, he ran a loving hand over the glossy bay hide of his leader and scanned the yard with a proprietorial eye.

There was not a scheming mama or disapproving, gimlet-eyed dowager in sight.

Bestowing a last fond pat on his horse's shoulder, Demon headed for the open rear door of the stable. He'd left London at midday, unexpectedly content to have the breeze blow the cloying perfume of a certain lascivious countess from his brain. More than content to leave behind the ballrooms, the parties, and the myriad traps the matchmaking mamas laid for gentlemen such as he. Not that he'd found any difficulty in evading such snares, but, these days, there was a certain scent on the breeze, a presentiment of danger he was too experienced to ignore. ·

First his cousin Devil, then his own brother Vane, and now his closest cousin, Richard—who next of their select band of six, the Bar Cynster as they were called, would fate cause to trip into the arms of a loving wife?

Whoever it was, it wouldn't be him.

Pausing before the open doors of the stable, he swung around, eyes squinting in the slanting sunlight. Some of his horses were ambling in the paddocks with their lads in close attendance. On the Heath beyond, other stables' strings were exercising under the eyes of owners and trainers.

The scene was an exclusively male one. The fact that he felt entirely at home—indeed, could feel himself relaxing—was ironic. He could hardly claim he didn't like women, didn't enjoy their company. Hadn't—didn't—devote considerable time to their conquest.

He couldn't deny he took pleasure in, and derived considerable satisfaction from, those conquests. He was, after all, a Cynster.

He smiled. All that was true. However . . .

Whereas the other members of the Bar Cynster, as wealthy, well-born gentlemen, had accepted the fact that they would marry and establish families in the time-honored tradition, he had vowed to be different. He'd vowed never to marry, never to tempt the fate with which his brother and cousins had fenced and lost. Marriage to fulfill society's obligations was all very well, but to marry a lady one loved had been the baneful fate of all male Cynsters to date.

A baneful fate indeed for a warrior breed—to be forever at the mercy of a woman. A woman who held one's heart, soul and future in her small, delicate hands.

It was enough to make the strongest warrior blanch.

He was having none of it.

Casting a last glance around the neat yard, approving the swept cobbles, the fences in good repair, Demon turned and entered the main stable housing his racing string. Afternoon stables had already commenced—he would view his exercising horses alongside his very capable trainer, Carruthers.

Demon was on his way to his stud farm, located three miles farther south of the racecourse in the gently undulating countryside bordering the Heath. As he had every intention of avoiding marriage for the term of his natural life, and the current atmosphere in London had turned fraught with the Season about to start, and his aunts, as well as his mother, fired with the excitement of weddings, wives and the consequent babies, so he'd elected to lie low and see out the Season from the safe distance of his stud farm and the unthreatening society of Newmarket.

Fate would have no chance to sneak up on him here.

Looking down to avoid the inevitable detritus left by his favored darlings, he strolled unhurriedly up the long central alley. Boxes loomed to his left and right, all presently empty. At the other end of the building, another pair of doors stood open to the Heath. The day was fine, with a light breeze lifting manes and flicking long tails—his horses were out, doing what they did best. Running.

After spending the last hours with the sun warming his shoulders, the stable's shadows felt cool. A chill unexpectedly washed over the back of his shoulders, then coalesced into an icy tingle and slithered all the way down his spine.

Demon frowned and wriggled his shoulders. Reaching the point where the alley widened into the mounting area, he stopped and looked up.

A familiar sight met his eyes—a lad or work rider swinging a leg over the sleek back of one of his champions. The horse was facing away, wide bay rump to him; Demon recognized one of his current favorites, an Irish gelding sure to run well in the coming season. That, however, was not what transfixed him, rooting his boots to the floor.

He could see nothing of the rider bar his back and one leg. The lad wore a cloth cap pulled low on his head, a shabby hacking jacket and baggy corduroy breeches.

Baggy except in one area—where they pulled tight over the rider's rear as he swung his leg over the saddle.

Carruthers stood beside the horse, issuing instructions. The lad dropped into the saddle, then stood in the stirrups to adjust his position. Again, corduroy strained and shifted.

Demon sucked in a breath. Eyes narrowing, jaw firming, he strode forward.

Carruthers slapped the horse's rump. Nodding, the rider trotted the horse, The Mighty Flynn, out into the sunshine.

Carruthers swung around, squinting as Demon came up. "Oh, it's you." Despite the abrupt greeting and the dour tone, there was a wealth of affection in Carruthers's old eyes. "Come to see how they're shaping, have ye?"

Demon nodded, his gaze locked on the rider atop The Mighty Flynn. "Indeed."

With Carruthers, he strolled in the wake of The Flynn, the last of his horses to go out on the Heath.

In silence, Demon watched his horses go through their paces. The Mighty Flynn was given a light workout, walking, trotting, then walking again. Although he noted how his other horses performed, Demon's attention never strayed far from The Flynn.

Beside him, Carruthers was watching his charges avidly. Demon glanced his way, noting his old face, much lined, weathered like well-worn leather, faded brown eyes wide as he weighed every stride, considered every turn. Carruthers never took notes, never needed any reminder of which horse had done what. When his charges came in, he would know precisely how each was faring, and what more was needed to bring them to their best. The most experienced trainer in Newmarket, Carruthers knew his horses better than his children, which was why Demon had pestered and persevered until he'd agreed to train for him, to devote his time exclusively to training Demon's string.

His gaze fastening once more on the big bay, Demon murmured, "The lad on The Flynn—he's new, isn't he?"

"Aye," Carruthers replied, his gaze never leaving the horses. "Lad from down Lidgate way. Ickley did a runner—leastways, I assume he did. He didn't turn up one morning and we haven't seen him since. 'Bout a week later, young Flick turned up, looking for a ride, so I had him up on one of the tetchy ones." Carruthers nodded to where The Flynn was trotting along, pacing neatly with the rest of the string, the small figure on his back managing him with startling ease. "Rode the brute easily. So I put him up on The Flynn. Never seen the horse give his heart so willingly. The lad's got the touch, no doubt about that. Excellent hands, and good bottom."

Demon inwardly admitted he couldn't argue. "Good," however, was not the adjective he'd have used. But he must have been mistaken. Carruthers was a staunch member of the fraternity, quite the last man to let a female on one of his charges, let alone trust her with The Flynn.

And yet ...

There was a niggle, a persistent whisper in his mind, something stronger than suspicion flitting through his brain. And at one level—the one where his senses ruled—he *knew* he wasn't wrong.

No lad had ever had a bottom like that.

The thought reconjured the vision; Demon shifted and inwardly cursed. He'd left the countess only a few hours ago; his lustful demons had no business being awake, much less raising their collective head. "This Flick ..." Saying the name triggered something—a memory? If the lad was local, he might have stumbled across him before. "How long's he been with us?"

Carruthers was still absorbed with the horses, now cooling before walking in. "Be two weeks, now."

"And he pulls his full load?"

"I've only got him on half-pay—didn't really need another hand with the stablework. Only needed him for riding—exercising and the gallops. Turned out that suited him well enough. His mum's not well, so he rides up here, does morning stables, then rides back to Lidgate to keep her company, then comes up again for afternoon stables."

"Hmm." The first horses were returning; Demon drew back into the stable, standing with Carruthers to the side of the mounting area as the stable lads walked their charges in. Most of the lads were known to him. While exchanging greetings and the occasional piece of news, and running knowledgeable eyes over his string, Demon never lost sight of The Flynn.

Flick ambled at the rear of the string. He'd exchanged no more than brief nods and occasional words with the other lads; amid the general camaraderie, Flick appeared a loner. But the other lads seemed to see nothing odd in Flick; they passed him as he walked the huge bay, patting the silky neck and, judging from the horse's twitching ears, murmuring sweet nothings with absolute acceptance. Demon inwardly cursed and wondered, yet again, if he could possibly be wrong.

The Flynn was the last in; Demon stood, hands on hips, to one side of Carruthers in the shadows, shadows rendered even deeper by the sudden brilliance of the westering sun. Flick let the bay have a last prance before settling him and guiding him into the stable. As the first heavy hoof clopped hollowly on the flags, Flick looked up.

Eyes used to the sunshine blinked wide, finding Carruthers, then quickly passing on to fix on Demon. On his face.

Flick reined in, eyes widening even more.

For one, tense instant, rider and owner simply stared.

Jerking the reins, Flick wheeled The Flynn, sending Carruthers a horrified glance. "He's still restless—I'll take him for a quick run." With that, she and The Flynn were gone, leaving only a rush of wind behind them.

"What the—!" Carruthers started forward, then stopped as the futility of any chase registered. Bemused, he turned to Demon. "He's never done anything like that before."

A curse was Demon's only answer; he was already striding along the alley.

He stopped at the first open box, where a lad was easing the girth strap on one of his heavier horses.

"Leave that." Demon shouldered the startled lad aside.

With one tug and a well-placed knee, he recinched the girth. He vaulted into the saddle and backed the horse, fumbling with the stirrup straps.

"Here—I can send one of the lads after him." Carruthers stepped back as Demon trotted the horse past.

"No—leave it to me. I'll straighten the *lad* out."

Demon doubted Carruthers caught the emphasis; he wasn't about to stop and explain. Muttering, he set out in hot pursuit.

The instant his mount cleared the stable door, he dug in his heels; the horse lengthened his stride from trot to canter to gallop. By then, Demon had located his prey. In the far distance, disappearing into the shadows thrown by a stand of trees. Another minute and he'd have lost her.

Jaw setting, he struggled with the stirrups as he pounded along. Curses and oaths colored the wind of his passage. Finally, the stirrups were lengthened enough; he settled properly into the saddle, and the chase began in earnest.

The bobbing figure on the back of The Flynn shot a glance behind, then looked forward. A second later, The Flynn swerved and lengthened his stride.

Demon tacked, trying to close the gap by cutting diagonally across—only to find himself careening toward a stretch of rough. Forced to slow and turn aside, he glanced up—and discovered that Flick had abruptly swung the other way and was making off in a different direction. Instead of shortening, the distance between them had grown.

Jaw clenched, eyes narrowed, Demon forgot about swearing and concentrated on riding. Within two minutes, he'd altered his initial plan—to ride Flick down and demand an explanation—to simply keeping the damned female in sight.

She rode like a demon—even better than he. It didn't seem possible, but . . .

He was a superlative rider, quite possibly the most accomplished of his day. He could ride anything with four legs, mane and tail anywhere, over any terrain. But Flick was leading him a merry dance. And it wasn't simply the fact that his horse was already tired or that he rode much heavier than she. The Flynn was tired, too, and was being ridden harder; Flick was fleeing; he was only following. But she seemed to merge with her mount in that way only other expert riders could understand.

He understood it and couldn't help admiring it grudgingly, even while acknowledging he had not a hope in hell of catching her.

Her. There was no doubt of that now. Lads did not have delicate shoulders and collarbones, swanlike necks, and hands that, even encased in leather gloves, looked small and fine-boned. As for her face, the little he'd glimpsed above the woollen muffler wound about her nose and chin had been more Madonnalike than manlike.

A female called Flick. In the distant recesses of his brain, a memory stirred, too insubstantial to catch and hold. He tried to coax it further into the light, and failed. He was sure he'd never called any female Flick.

She was still a good two furlongs ahead of him, maintaining the distance with ease. They were riding directly west, out onto the less frequented stretches of the Heath. They'd sped past a number of strings out exercising; heads had come up to watch them in surprise. He saw her glance around again; an instant later, she swerved. Grimly determined, Demon squinted into the setting sun and followed in her tracks.

He might not be able to ride her down, but he'd be damned if he'd lose her.

His resolution had, by now, communicated itself quite effectively to Flick. Making a few choice observations about London-bound rakes who came up to their stud farms with not a moment's notice and then proceeded to get in the way, to throw her off her stride, to plunge her into a ridiculous fluster, she irritatedly, and not a little frantically, reviewed her options.

There weren't many. While she could easily ride for another hour, The Flynn couldn't. And the horse Demon was on would fare even worse. And, despite the knot of sheer panic in her stomach, there wasn't any point fleeing, anyway.

She would, one way or another, either now or only marginally later, have to face Demon. She didn't know if he'd recognized her, but in that frozen instant in the stable when his blue gaze had raked her, she'd got the impression he'd seen through her disguise.

In fact, the impression she'd got was that he'd seen right through her clothes—a distinctly unnerving sensation.

Yet even if he hadn't realized she was female, her impulsive reaction had made a confrontation unavoidable. She'd run—and she couldn't possibly explain that, not without giving him, and his memories, far too many hints as to her identity.

Catching her breath on a hiccup, Flick glanced back; he was still there, doggedly following. Turning forward, she noted their location. She'd led him west, then south, skirting the stables and paddocks edging the racecourse, then heading farther onto the open Heath. She glanced at the sun. They had at least an hour before twilight. With all the others back at the stables settling horses for the night, this part of the Heath was now deserted. If she found a spot where they were reasonably screened, it would be as good a place as any for the meeting that, it now seemed, had to be.

Honesty was her only option. In truth, she would prefer it—lies and evasion had never been her style.

A hundred yards ahead, a hedge beckoned. Her memory provided a picture of what lay beyond. The Flynn was tiring; she leaned forward and stroked the glossy neck, whispering words of praise, encouragement and outright flattery into his ear. Then she set him for the hedge.

The Flynn soared over it, landing easily. Flick absorbed the jolt and wheeled left, into the long shadows thrown by a copse. In the space between the hedge and the copse, screened on three sides, she reined in and waited.

And waited.

After five minutes, she started to wonder if Demon had looked away at the crucial moment and not seen where she'd gone. When another minute passed and she sensed no ground-shaking thuds, she frowned and straightened in her saddle. She was about to gather her reins and move out to search for her pursuer when she saw him.

He hadn't jumped the hedge. Despite his wish to catch her, wisdom—care for his horse—had prevailed; he'd gone along the hedge until he'd found a gap. Now he cantered up through the late afternoon, broad shoulders square, long limbs relaxed, head up, the sun striking gold from his burnished curls, his face a grim mask as he scanned the fields ahead, trying to catch sight of her.

Flick froze. It was tempting—so tempting—to sit still. To look her fill, and let him pass by, to worship from afar as she had for years, letting her senses feast while she remained safely hidden. If she made no sound, it was unlikely he would see her. She wouldn't have to face him ... unfortunately, there were too many hurdles along that road. Stiffening her spine, taking a firm grip on her unruly senses, she lifted her chin. "Demon!"

His head snapped around; he wheeled aggressively, then saw her. Even at that distance, his gaze pinned her, then he scanned her surroundings. Apparently satisfied, he set his grey trotting toward her, slowing to a walk as he neared.

He was wearing an elegant morning coat of a blue that matched his eyes; his long thighs, gripping the saddle skirts, were encased in tight buckskin. Ivory shirt, ivory cravat and gleaming Hessians completed the picture. He looked what he was—the very epitome of a London rake.

Flick kept her gaze fixed on his face and wished, very much, that she were taller. The closer he came, the smaller she felt—the more childlike. She was no longer a child, but she'd known him since she had been. It was hard to feel assured. With her cap shading her face, her muffler over her nose and chin, she couldn't imagine how he might see her—as a girl still with pigtails, or as the young lady who'd trenchantly avoided him. She'd been both, but she was neither now. What she was now was on a crusade. A crusade in which she could use his help. If he consented to give it.

Lips firming beneath her muffler, she tilted her chin and met his hard stare.

Demon's memories churned as he walked his horse into the copse's shadow. She'd called him "Demon"—only someone who knew him would do that. Images from the past jumbled and tumbled, glimpses through the years of a child, a girl, who would without a blush call him Demon. Of a girl who could ride—oh, yes, she'd always ridden, but when had she become a maestro?—of a girl he had long ago pegged as having that quality Carruthers described as "good bottom"—that open-hearted courage that bordered on the reckless, but wasn't.

When he stopped his horse, nose to tail with The Flynn, he had her well and truly placed. Not Flick. Felicity.

Eyes like slits, he held her trapped; reaching out, he tugged the concealing muffler from her face.

And found himself looking down at a Botticelli angel.

Found himself drowning in limpid blue eyes paler than his own. Found his gaze irresistibly drawn to lips perfectly formed and tinged the most delicate rose pink he'd ever seen.

He was sinking. Fast. And he wasn't resisting.

Sucking in a breath, he drew back, inwardly shocked at how far under he'd gone. Shaking free of the lingering spell, he scowled at its source. "What the damn hell do you think you're about?"

CHAPTER
Two

❧☙

S he tilted her chin—a delicate, pointy little chin. Set as it was, it looked decidedly stubborn. "I'm masquerading as a stable lad, in your stables, so—"

"What a *damn fool* lark! What the *devil*—"

"It's *not* a lark!" Her blue eyes flashed; her expression turned belligerent. "I'm doing it for the General!"

"The General?" General Sir Gordon Caxton was Demon's neighbor and mentor, and Felicity's—Flick's—guardian. Demon scowled. "You're not going to tell me the General knows about this?"

"Of course not!"

The Flynn shifted; tight-lipped, Demon waited while Flick quieted the big bay.

Her gaze flickered over him, irritated and considering in equal measure, then steadied on his face.

"It's all because of Dillon."

"Dillon?" Dillon was the General's son. Flick and Dillon were of similar age. Demon's most recent memories of Dillon were of a dark-haired youth, swaggering about the General's house, Hillgate End, giving himself airs and undeserved graces.

"Dillon's in trouble."

Demon got the distinct impression she only just avoided adding "again."

"He became involved—inadvertently—with a race-fixing racket."

"*What?*" He bit off the word, then had to settle his mount. The words "race-fixing" sent a chill down his spine.

Flick frowned at him. "That's when jockeys are paid to ease back on a horse, or cause a disruption, or—"

He glared at her. "I *know* what race-fixing entails. That doesn't explain what *you're* doing mixed up in it."

"I'm *not!*" Indignation colored her cheeks.

"*What* are you doing masquerading as a lad, then?"

Her soft blue eyes flashed. "If you'd *stop* interrupting, I'd be able to tell you!"

Demon reined in his temper, set his jaw, and pointedly waited. After a moment's fraught silence, blue eyes locked with blue, Flick nodded and put her pert nose in the air.

"Dillon was approached some weeks ago by a man and asked to take a message to a jockey about the first race of the season. He didn't see any reason he shouldn't, so he agreed. I suspect he thought it would be a lark—or that it made him more involved with the racing—but he agreed to carry the message to the jockey, then didn't. Couldn't. He got a chill and Mrs. Fogarty and I insisted he stay in bed—we took away his clothes, so he had to. Of course, he didn't say *why* he kept trying to struggle up. Not then."

She drew breath. "So the message didn't get passed on. It was an instruction to fix the race, so the race, therefore, wasn't fixed. It now seems that the man who approached Dillon was working for some sort of syndicate—a group of some description—and because the race wasn't fixed and they didn't know it, they lost a lot of money."

"Men came looking for Dillon—rough men. Luckily, Jacobs and Mrs. Fogarty didn't like their style—they said Dillon was away. So now he's in hiding and fears for his life."

Demon exhaled and sat back in his saddle. From what he knew of the unsavory types involved in race-fixing, Dillon had good cause to worry. He studied Flick. "Where's he hiding?"

She straightened, and fixed him with a very direct look. "I can't tell you—not unless you're willing to help us."

Demon returned her gaze with one even more severe, and distinctly more aggravated. "Of *course* I'm going to help you!" What did she think he was? Beneath his breath, he swore. "How's the General going to take it if his only son is charged with race-fixing?"

Flick's expression immediately eased; Demon knew he couldn't have said anything more convincing—not to her. More devoted than a daughter, she was intensely protective of the ageing General. She thought the world of him, as did he. She actually nodded approvingly.

"Precisely. And that, I'm afraid, is one of the things we especially fear, because the man who hired Dillon definitely knew he was the General's son."

Demon inwardly grimaced. The General was the preeminent authority on English and Irish Thoroughbreds and revered throughout the racing industry. The syndicate had planned well. "So where's Dillon hiding?"

Flick considered him, one last measuring glance. "In the tumbledown cottage on the far corner of your land."

"*My* land?"

"It was safer than anywhere on the Caxton estate."

He couldn't argue—the Caxton estate comprised just the house and its surrounding park. The General had a fortune invested in the Funds and needed no farms to distract him. He'd sold off his acres years ago—Demon had bought some of the land himself. He shot a glance at Flick, sitting comfortably astride The Flynn. "My horses, my cottage—what else have you been making free with?"

She blushed slightly but didn't reply. Demon couldn't help but notice how fine her skin was, unblemished ivory silk now tinged a delicate rose. She was a painter's dream; she would have had Botticelli slavering. The idea brought to mind the painter's diaphanously clad angels; in a blink of his mental eye, he had Flick similarly clothed. And the tantalizing question of how that ivory skin, which he'd wager would extend all over her, would look when flushed with passion formed in the forefront of his brain.

Abruptly, he refocused. Good God—what was he thinking? Flick was the General's ward, and not much more than a child. How old was she? He frowned at her. "None of what you've said explains what *you're* doing here, dressed like that, working my latest champion."

"I'm hoping to identify the man who contacted Dillon. Dillon only met him at night—he never saw him well enough to recognize or describe. Now Dillon's not available to act as his messenger, the man will have to contact someone else, someone who can easily speak to the race jockeys."

"So you're hanging around my stables morning and afternoon, hoping this man approaches *you*?" Aghast, he stared at her.

"Not *me*. One of the others—the older lads who know all the race jockeys. I'm there to keep watch and overhear anything I can."

He continued to stare at her while considering all the holes in her story. Clearly, he'd have to fill them in one by one. "How the hell did you persuade Carruthers to hire you? Or doesn't he know?"

"Of *course* he doesn't know. No one does. But it wasn't difficult to get hired. I heard Ickley had disappeared—Dillon was told Ickley had agreed to act as messenger for this season, but changed his mind at the last. That's why they approached Dillon. So I knew Carruthers was shorthanded."

Demon's lips thinned. Flick continued. "So I dressed appropriately"—with a sweeping gesture, she indicated her garb—"and went to see Carruthers. Everyone in Newmarket knows Carruthers can't see well close to, so I didn't think I'd have any difficulty. All I had to do was ride for him and he'd take me on."

Demon swallowed a snort. "What about the others—the other lads, the jockeys? They're not all half-blind."

The look Flick bent on him was the epitome of feminine condescension. "Have you ever stood in a working stable and watched how often the men— lads or trainers—look at each other? The horses, yes, but they never do more than glance at the humans working alongside. The others see me all the time, but they never look. *You're* the only one who looked."

Accusation colored her tone. Demon swallowed his retort that he'd have to have been dead not to look. He also resisted the urge to inform her she should be grateful he had; just the thought of what she'd blithely got herself into, squaring up to expose a race-fixing syndicate, chilled him.

ixing syndicates were dangerous, controlled by men to whom the others meant little. The lives of people like Ickley. Demon made a note to find out what had happened to Ickley. The idea that Flick had self up as Ickley's replacement was enough to turn his hair grey. Gazing at face, on her openly determined expression, it was on the tip of his tongue to terminate her employment immediately.

Recollection of how her chin had set earlier made him hold the words back. Pretty little chin, delicately tapered. And too stubborn by half.

There was a great deal he did not yet know, a great deal he didn't as yet understand.

The horses were cooling, the sun slowly sinking. His mount shifted, coat flickering. Demon drew breath. "Let's get back, then I'll go and see Dillon."

Flick nodded, urging The Flynn into a walk. "I'll come, too. Well, I have to. That's where I change clothes and switch horses."

"Horses?"

She threw him a wary glance. "I couldn't turn up for work riding Jessamy—*that* they'd certainly notice."

Jessamy, Demon recalled, was a dainty mare with exceptional bloodlines; the General had bought her last year. Apparently for Flick. He glanced at her. "So? ..."

She drew breath and looked ahead. "So I borrow the old cob you let run on your back paddock. I don't ride him above a canter, if that. I'm very careful of him."

She looked up. He trapped her gaze. "Anything else you've borrowed?"

Big blue eyes blinked wide. "I don't think so."

"All right. We'll ride these two back, then you climb on the cob and head off. I'll leave in my curricle. I'll drive home, then ride out and join you. I'll meet you by the split oak on the road to Lidgate."

She nodded. "Very well. But we'll need to hurry now. Come on." She leaned forward, effortlessly shifting The Flynn from walk, to trot, to canter.

And left him staring after her. With a curse, he dug in his heels and set out in her wake.

He reached the split oak before her.

By the time she appeared, trotting the old cob, long past his prime, down the middle of the road, Demon had decided that, whatever transpired with Dillon, he would ensure that one point was made clear.

He was in charge from now on. She'd asked for his help; she would get it, but on his terms.

From now on, he'd lead and *she* could follow.

As she neared, her gaze slid from him to his mount, a raking grey hunter who went by the revealing name of Ivan the Terrible. He was a proud and princely beast with a foul, dangerous, potentially lethal temper. As the cob drew closer, Ivan rolled one eye and stamped.

The cob was too old to pay the slightest attention. Flick's brows, however, rose; her gaze passed knowledgeably over Ivan's more positive points as she reined in. "I *know* I haven't seen him before."

Demon made no reply. He waited—and waited—until she finished examining his horse and lifted her gaze to his face. Then he smiled. "I bought him late last year." Flick's eyes, suddenly riveted on his face, widened slightly. She mouthed an "Oh," and looked away.

Side by side, they rode on, the cob doggedly plodding, Ivan placing his hooves with restless disdain. "What did you tell Carruthers?" Flick asked with a sidelong glance. When they'd returned to the stable, Flick had been in the lead. Carruthers had been standing, hands on hips, in the stable door. From behind Flick, Demon had signalled him away; Carruthers had stared, but, as Flick had trotted The Flynn up, he'd stood aside and let her pass without question. By that time, Carruthers and the nightwatchman, a retired jockey, had been the only ones left in the stable.

Handing his mount to the nightwatchman to unsaddle, Demon had set about mollifying Carruthers.

"I told him I knew you as a brat from near Lidgate, and you'd feared that, recognizing you, I'd terminate your employment immediately." The twilight was deepening; they jogged along as fast as the cob could manage. "However, having seen you ride, and being convinced of your fervent wish to work my horses, I said I'd agreed to let you stay on."

Flick frowned. "He came in and all but shooed me off—said he'd settle The Flynn and I should get on home without delay."

"I mentioned that I knew your sick mother and how she'd worry—I instructed Carruthers that you shouldn't pull duties that will keep you late, and that you should leave in plenty of time to reach home before dark."

Although he was examining the scenery and not looking at her, Demon still felt Flick's suspicious glance. It confirmed his opinion that she didn't need to know about the other instructions he'd issued to his trainer. Carruthers, thankfully not an imaginative or garrulous sort, had stared at him, then shrugged and acquiesced.

They left the road and turned into a sunken track between two fields. The cob, sensing home and dinner, broke into a trot; Ivan, forced to remain alongside, accepted the edict with typical bad grace, tossing his head and jerking his reins every few yards.

"He's obviously in need of exercise," Flick remarked.

"I'll give him a run later."

"I'm surprised you let him get into such a bad temper."

Demon stifled an acid retort. "He's been here, I've been in London, and no one can ride him but me."

"Oh."

Lifting her gaze, Flick looked ahead to where the track wended into a small wood; she fell to studying the trees.

From under his lashes, Demon studied her. She'd examined his horse so thoroughly she probably knew his every line, yet she'd barely glanced at him. Ivan was indeed a handsome beast, as were all his cattle, but he wasn't used to taking second place to his mount. Which might seem arrogant, but he knew women—girls and ladies, females of any description—well.

It wasn't simply that she hadn't looked. His senses, well honed through his years on the prowl, could detect not the slightest flicker of consciousness—the minutest suggestion of awareness—in the female riding beside him.

Which, in his experience, was odd. Distinctly odd.

The fact that her lack of awareness was focusing his to a remarkable degree hadn't escaped him. It didn't surprise him; he was a born hunter. When the prey didn't take cover, he—at least that part of him that operated on instinct first, logic second—saw it as a challenge.

Which was, in this case, ridiculous.

There was no reason a girl like Flick, raised quietly in the country, should be aware, in any sexual sense, of a gentleman like him—especially one she'd known all her life.

Demon frowned, tightening the reins as Ivan tried to surge. Disgusted, the big grey snorted; Demon managed not to do the same.

He still had no idea precisely how old she was. He glanced her way, covertly confirming details he'd instinctively noted. She'd always been petite, although he hadn't seen her in recent years. In her present incarnation, he'd only seen her atop a horse, but he doubted her head would clear his shoulder. Her figure remained a mystery, except for her definitely feminine bottom—a classic inverted heart, sleekly rounded. The rest of her was amply disguised by her stable lad's garb. Whether she wore bands about her breasts, as did many devoted female riders, he couldn't tell, but her overall proportions were nice. Slim, slender—she might well be delectable.

On the way back to the stables, she'd tugged her muffler up over her nose and chin so the swath hid most of her face. As for her hair, she'd stuffed it under her cap so thoroughly that, beyond the fact it was as brightly golden as he recalled, he couldn't tell how she wore it. A few short strands had slipped free at her nape, sheening against her collar like spun gold.

Looking forward, he inwardly frowned. It wasn't simply that there were lots of things he didn't yet know about her that bothered him. The very fact he wanted to know bothered him. This was Flick, the General's ward.

General Sir Gordon Caxton had been his mentor in all matters pertaining to horses since he'd been six. That was when, while visiting with his late great-aunt Charlotte, he'd first met the General. Thereafter, whenever he'd been in the locality, he'd spent as much time as possible with the General, learning everything he could about breeding Thoroughbreds. It was due to the General, to his knowledge freely shared and his unstinting encouragement, that he, Demon, was now one of the preeminent breeders of quality horseflesh in the British Isles.

He owed the General a great deal.

A fact he could never forget. He comforted himself with that thought as he trotted beside Flick into the trees beyond which stood the old cottage.

Once a tenant farmer's home, it was now one step away from a ruin. From the rutted lane meandering up to its warped and sagging door, the structure looked uninhabitable. Only on closer inspection could one discern that the roof of the main room was still mostly intact, the four walls enclosing it still standing.

With an imperious gesture, Flick led the way around the cottage. Briefly raising his eyes to the skies, Demon followed, entering a grassy clearing enclosed by trees. A sharp whinny greeted them. Eagerly, Flick urged the cob on. Looking across the clearing, Demon saw Jessamy, a pretty golden-coated mare with pale mane and tail and the most exquisite conformation he'd ever seen. She was tethered on a long rein.

Ivan saw Jessamy, too, and concurred with Demon's assessment. Still held on tight rein, Ivan reared and trumpeted. Only excellent reflexes saved Demon from an embarrassing unseating. Smothering an oath, he wrestled Ivan down, then forced him to the other side of the clearing, ignoring the combined, slightly insulted stares of Flick, Jessamy and the cob.

Dismounting, Demon double-tied Ivan's reins to a large tree. "Behave yourself," he ordered, then turned away, leaving the stallion, head up, staring with complete and absolute absorption across the clearing.

Having turned the cob loose, Flick dumped her saddle on a convenient log and gave Jessamy, who clearly adored her, a fond pat. Then, with another imperious, beckoning wave, she led the way around the far side of the cottage.

Muttering beneath his breath, Demon strode after her.

He rounded the cottage—Flick was nowhere in sight. A lean-to had been tacked onto the cottage on that side. The lean-to hadn't survived as well as the cottage—its outer wall was crumbling and half its roof had disappeared. Flick had ducked through an opening, a door that had never been planned. Hearing her voice in the main room beyond, Demon ducked beneath the canted beams; easing his shoulders through the narrow space, he stepped silently through the debris and entered the cottage proper.

And saw Flick standing beside Dillon Caxton, who was sitting at one end of an old table, blankets wrapped about his shoulders. She was bent over him; as Demon entered, she straightened, frowning, her hand on Dillon's brow. "You don't have any sign of a fever."

Dillon didn't respond, his eyes, large and dark, framed by long black lashes, fixed on Demon. Then he coughed, glanced at Flick, then at Demon. "Ah ... hello. Come in! I'm afraid it's rather cold in here—we daren't light a fire."

Mentally noting that the cottage was *his* property, Demon merely nodded. In such flat countryside, smoke could easily be traced, and smoke rising from an area thought to be uninhabited would certainly attract attention. Holding Dillon's increasingly wary gaze, he strolled the few paces to the other end of the table, to a stool that appeared sufficiently robust to support his weight. "Flick mentioned that there were gentlemen about whose company you were keen to avoid."

Color flooded Dillon's pale cheeks. "Ah, yes. Flick said you'd agreed to help." With one long-fingered hand, he combed back the thick lock of dark hair that fell, in perfect Byronic imitation, across his brow, and he smiled engagingly. "I can't tell you how much I appreciate it."

Demon held Dillon's impossibly innocent gaze for a moment, then hitched up the stool and sat, declining to mention that it was for the General's sake, and Flick's, that he was involving himself in a mess that, as an owner of racing Thoroughbreds, he'd much rather hand straight to the magistrates.

Dillon glanced up at Flick; she was frowning slightly at Demon. "Flick didn't say how much she's told you—"

"Enough for me to understand what's been going on." Resting his arms on the table, Demon looked at Dillon and didn't like what he saw. The fact that Flick was hovering protectively at Dillon's shoulder contributed to his assessment only marginally; much more telling were his memories, observations made over the years, and the facts of the current imbroglio, not as Flick had innocently described them but as he knew they must be.

He didn't doubt she'd faithfully recounted all she'd been told; the truth, he knew, was more damning than that.

His smile held the right degree of male camaraderie to appeal to a youth like Dillon. "I'd like to hear your observations direct. Let's start with your meeting with this character who asked you to carry a message."

"What do you want to know?"

"The how, the when, the where. The words."

"Well, the when was nearly three weeks ago, just before the first race of the year."

"Just before?"

Dillon nodded. "Two days before."

"Two days?" Demon raised his brows. "That seems awfully short notice to arrange a fix, don't you think? The general consensus is that these syndicates lay their plans well in advance. It's something of an imperative, given the number of bookmakers and other supporting characters necessarily involved."

Dillon's eyes blanked. "Oh?" Then his smile flashed. "Actually, the man did say they'd had another messenger—Ickley—he used to work at your stables—lined up to do the job, but he'd changed his mind. So they needed someone else."

"And so they came to you. Why?"

The single word startled Dillon, then he shrugged. "I don't know—I suppose they were looking for someone who knew their way about. Knew the jockeys, and the places to go to rub the right shoulders."

Flick settled onto a stool. She was frowning more definitely, but her frown was now aimed at Dillon.

"Why did you imagine this man didn't just ask you to point out the particular jockey and speak to him himself?"

Dillon's brows drew down sharply; after a moment, he shook his head. "I don't follow."

"Surely you wondered why it was necessary for this man to have a messenger at all?" Demon trapped Dillon's gaze. "If the messages were innocent, why did the man need to hire you—or anyone—to deliver them?"

Dillon's trademark smile flashed. "Ah, but the messages weren't innocent, you see."

"Oh, I do see," Demon assured him. "But you didn't know that before they hired you, did you?"

"Well … no."

"So why didn't you simply tell this man where he could find the jockey? Why be his go-between?"

"Well, because … I suppose I thought he might not want to be seen … well, no."

Demon recaptured Dillon's gaze. "No, indeed. How much did they pay you?"

Every drop of blood drained from Dillon's face; his eyes grew darker, wilder. "I—don't know what you mean."

Demon held his gaze unblinkingly. "This would not, I suggest, be a good time to lie. How much did they pay you?"

Dillon flushed.

Flick sprang to her feet. "You took *money*?" Behind her, the stool clattered on the flags. "You took money to carry a message to fix a race?"

The accusation in her tone would have made the Devil flinch; Dillon did not. "It was only two ponies—just for the one message. I wasn't going to do it any more. That's why they got Ickley."

"Any *more*?" Flick stared at him. "What do you mean 'any more'?"

Dillon's expression turned mulish; Flick leaned both hands on the table and looked him in the eye. "Dillon—*how long*? How long have you been taking money to carry messages for these men?"

He tried to keep silent, tried to withstand the demand in her tone, the scorn in her eyes."Since last summer."

"Last *summer*?" Flick straightened, shoving the table in her agitation. "Good God! *Why*?" She stared at Dillon. "What on earth possessed you?"

Demon held silent; as an avenging angel, Flick had a distinct advantage.

Turning sulky, Dillon pushed back from the table. "It was the money, of course." He attempted a sneer, but it bounced off Flick's righteous fury.

"The General gives you a very generous allowance—why would you want more?"

Dillon laughed brittlely and leaned his arms on the table. He avoided Flick's outraged stare.

Which did nothing to soothe her temper. "And if you needed more, you know you only had to ask. I always have plenty …" Her words trailed away; she blinked, then her eyes blazed. She refocused on Dillon. "You've been gambling at the cockfights again, haven't you?" Scorn—raw disgust—poured through her words. "Your father forbade it, but you couldn't leave it be. And *now*—!" Sheer fury choked her; she gestured wildly.

"Cockfighting's not that bad," Dillon countered, still sulky. "It's not as if it's something other gentlemen don't do." He glanced at Demon.

"Don't look at me," Demon returned. "Not my style at all."

"It's disgusting!" Flick looked directly at Dillon. "You're disgusting, too." She whirled and swooped on a pile of clothes set on an old chest. "I'm going to change."

Demon glimpsed the blue velvet skirts of a stylish riding habit as she stormed past him out into the ruined lean-to.

Silence descended in the main room; Demon let it stretch. He watched Dillon squirm, then stiffen his spine, only to wilt again. When he judged it was time, he quietly said, "I rather think you'd better tell us the whole of it."

Eyes on the table, on the fingertip with which he traced circles on the scratched surface, Dillon drew a shaky breath. "I ran messages the whole autumn season. I owed a cent-per-cent in Bury St. Edmunds—he said I had to pay up before year's end or he'd come and see the General. I had to get the money somewhere. Then the man—the one who brings the messages—found me." He paused, but didn't look up. "I always thought it was the cent-per-cent who nudged him my way, to ensure I'd be in a position to pay."

Demon thought that very likely.

Dillon shrugged. "Anyway, it was easy enough—easy money, I thought."

A choking sound came from the lean-to; Dillon flushed.

"Well, it was easy last year. Then, when the man brought the messages for the last few weeks of races, I told him I wouldn't do it any more. He said, 'We'll see,' and I left it at that. I didn't expect to see him again, but two nights before the first race this year, he found me. At a cockfight."

The sound from the lean-to was eloquent—mingled disbelief, frustration and fury.

Dillon grimaced. "He told me Ickley had balked, and that I'd have to do the job until they could find a 'suitable replacement.' That's how he phrased it." Dillon paused, then offered, "I think that means someone they have some hold over, because he said, bold as brass, that if I didn't agree they'd tell the authorities what I'd done, and make sure everyone knew I was the General's son. Well, I did it. Took the message. And the money. And then I got sick."

Demon could almost have felt sorry for him. Almost. The flies in the ointment were the General, and Flick's sniff of disillusionment that came from behind him.

After a moment, Dillon wearily straightened. "That's all of it." He met Demon's gaze. "I swear. If you'll believe me."

Demon didn't answer. Forearms on the table, he steepled his fingers; it was time to take charge. "As I see it, we have two objectives—one, to keep you out of the syndicate's way until, two, we've identified your contact, traced him back to his masters—the syndicate—and unmasked at least one member of said syndicate, and have enough proof for you to take to the magistrate, so that, in turning yourself in as a witless pawn caught up in a greater game, you can plead for leniency."

He looked up; Dillon blanched, but met his gaze. A moment passed, and Demon raised his brows.

Dillon swallowed, and nodded. "Yes, all right."

"So we need to identify your contact. Flick said you never saw him clearly."

Dillon shook his head. "He was always careful—he'd come up to me as I was leaving the pit in the dark, or come sidling up in the shadows."

Sept. 14 - 16, 2018

**Friday and Saturday
9:30 a.m. to 5 p.m.
Sunday 9:30 a.m. to 4 p.m.**

Event rates apply

Huronia Handweavers Guild

Huronia Spinners Guild

Huronia Branch of the Ontario
Hooking Craft Guild

Orillia Sunshine Rug Hookers

Barrie Modern Quilt Group

Georgian Bay Quilters Guild

Kempenfelt Quilters' Guild

Orillia Quilters' Guild

Quilting Corners Guild, Alliston

Simcoe County Quilters' Guild

Simcoe County Arts & Crafts
Association (SCACA)

Simcoe County Embroidery Guild

Simcoe County Lacemakers

Exhibits and Sales

Demonstrations and
hands-on activities

SCACA Quilt, Rug and Craft Raffle
SCACA Craft Gallery Draw
Embroidery Guild Draw
Huronia Branch of the Ontario Hooking
Craft Guild Draw
Huronia Handweavers Draw

Merchants' Mall
*No ATM on site

Simcoe County Museum
1151 Highway 26, Minesing, Ontario
(5 min. north of Barrie)
(705) 728-3721
museum.simcoe.ca

Connect
and Share

SIMCOE COUNTY
QUILT, RUG
& CRAFT FAIR

To Everything There is a Season
Designed by Marilyn Tardiff and
quilted by Kerry Burke and Rose Bell

Simcoe County Museum
September 14 - 16, 2018

"What's his height, his build?"

"Medium to tall, heavy build." Dillon's frown lifted. "One thing recognizable is his voice—it's oddly rough, like his throat is scratched, and he has a London accent."

Demon nodded, considering. Then he refocused. "Flick's idea is the only reasonable way forward—we'll have to keep watch about the tracks and stables to see who approaches the race jockeys. I'll handle that."

"I'll help."

The statement came from behind him; Demon glanced around, then rose spontaneously to his feet. Luckily, Flick was coldly glaring at Dillon, which allowed him to get his expression back under control before she glanced at him.

When she did, he met her gaze impassively, but he remained standing.

He'd guessed right—her head didn't top his shoulder. Bright, guinea-gold curls formed an aureole about her face; without muffler or cap, he could see the whole clearly, and it took his breath away. Her figure, neat and trim in blue velvet, met with his instant approval. Sleek and svelte, but with firm curves in all the right places. He could now take an oath that she must have worn tight bands to appear as she had before; the swells of her breasts filled the habit's tightly fitting bodice in a distinctly feminine way.

She swept forward with an easy, confident grace, then bent to place her neatly folded stable lad's outfit on the chest, in the process giving him a reminder of why he'd first seen through her disguise.

He blinked and drew in a much needed breath.

She looked like an angel, dressed in blue velvet.

A still very angry angel. She ignored Dillon and faced Demon. "I'll keep your stables under surveillance—you can watch the other stables and other places I can't go."

"There's no need—"

"The more eyes we have watching, the more likely we'll be to see him. And I'll hear things that you, as the owner, won't." She met his gaze steadily. "If they recruited Ickley, there's a good chance they'd like to hobble one of your runners—you'll have quite a few favorites in the races this season."

The Flynn, among others. Demon held her gaze, and saw her chin firm, saw it tilt, saw defiance and sheer stubborn will flash in her eyes.

"That's right," Dillon concurred. "There's a lot of Newmarket to cover, and Flick's already been accepted as one of your lads."

Demon stared, pointedly, at him; Dillon shrugged. "She's in no danger—it's me they're after."

If Demon had been closer, he would have kicked Dillon; eyes narrowing, he was tempted to do it anyway. Only the fact that he hadn't yet determined how Flick saw Dillon—if she reserved the right to kick him to herself, and would fly to Dillon's defense if he administered any of the punishment Dillon so richly deserved—kept him still.

Dillon glanced at Flick. "You could even try riding for some of the other stables."

Flick looked down her nose at him. "I'll stick to Demon's stable—he can look over the others."

Her tone was cold and distant; Dillon shrugged petulantly. "You don't have to help if you don't want to."

He looked down at the table and so missed the fury that poured from Flick's eyes. "Just so we're perfectly clear," she stated, "I am only helping you because of the General—because of what having you taken up, without any evidence of a syndicate to redeem you in any way, will do to him. *That's* why I'm helping you."

Head high, she swung on her heel and stalked out.

Demon paused, looking at Dillon, now staring sulkily at the table. "Stay here. If you value your life, stay out of sight."

Dillon's eyes widened; with a curt nod, Demon followed Flick into the deep twilight.

He found her saddling Jessamy, her movements swift and jerky. He didn't offer to help; he suspected she could saddle up blind—indeed, he wasn't at all sure she wasn't doing that now.

Hurt and anger poured off her; disillusionment shimmered about her. Propping his shoulders against a convenient tree, Demon glanced across the clearing to where Ivan was still standing in exactly the same pose as an hour ago—staring at his new lady love.

Brows quirking, Demon turned back to Flick. Her head was just visible over Jessamy's back. He considered the halo of gold, the delicate features beneath.

She was furious with Dillon, hurt that he hadn't told her the truth, and shocked by the details of that truth. But, once her fury wore thin, what then? She and Dillon were of similar age; they'd grown up together. Precisely what that meant he didn't know, but he had to wonder how accurate her last assertion was. Was she risking her reputation *only* for the General? Or for Dillon as well?

He studied her, but couldn't decide. Whatever the answer, he would shield her as best he could.

He looked up at the stars, just starting to appear, and heard a sniff, instantly suppressed. She was taking a long time with her saddle girths.

"He's young." Why he felt compelled to excuse Dillon he couldn't have said.

"He's two years older than me."

How old did that make her? Demon wished he knew.

"What do you think happened to Ickley?"

Demon silently considered; he didn't imagine her ensuing silence meant she didn't expect an answer. "Either he's gone to ground, in which case the last thing we'd want to do is flush him out, or . . . we'll never know."

She made a small sound, like a hum, in her throat—a muted sound of distress.

Demon straightened away from the tree; in the gathering gloom, he couldn't see her face clearly. At that moment, she stepped back from Jessamy's side, dusting her hands. He strolled around the mare. "You can continue at my stable for the time being—until we catch sight of this contact." If any avenue had offered, he'd have eased her out of his stable, out of Newmarket itself until all danger was past. But ... her stubbornness was a tangible thing.

She turned to face him. "If you try to get rid of me, I'll just get a job in another stable. There's more than one in Newmarket."

None as safe as his. "Carruthers will keep you on until I say otherwise." Which he would the instant they located Dillon's contact. "But you'll be restricted to riding track, morning and afternoon."

"That's the only time that matters, anyway. That's the only time outsiders aren't looked at askance about the Heath."

She was absolutely right.

He'd been going to give her a boost to her saddle; instead, features hardening, he reached for her, closed his hands about her waist and lifted her.

Lust flashed through him like liquid heat—a hot urgency that left him ravenous. He had to force himself to set her neatly in her saddle, to let go, to hold her stirrup while she slipped one small boot into it.

And not drag her back down, into his arms.

He wanted her in his bed.

The realization struck like a kick from one of his Thoroughbreds, leaving him winded and aching. Inwardly shaking. He looked up—and found her looking down at him.

She frowned and shook her reins. "Come on." Wheeling Jessamy, she trotted out of the clearing.

Demon swore. He crossed the clearing in three strides, yanked at Ivan's reins, and then remembered the double knots. He had to stop to undo them, then he vaulted to the saddle.

And followed.

CHAPTER
Three

ॐ

Demon rose before dawn the next morning and rode to his stable to view the morning gallops—and to keep an eye on Flick and her bottom. He felt distinctly aggrieved by the necessity of rising so early, but ... the thought of her, the angel in blue velvet, thundering about disguised as a lad, with all the potential calamities that might ensue, had made dozing off again impossible.

So he stood in the thin mist by Carruthers's side and watched his horses thunder by. The ground shook, the air trembled; the reverberations were as familiar as his heartbeat. The scene was a part of him, and he a part of it—and Flick was in it, too. She flew past, extending The Flynn, exhorting him to greater effort, leaving the other horses behind. Demon's breath caught as she flashed past the post; he felt her thrill—a flaring sense of triumph. It shivered through him, held him effortlessly, then he drew breath and forced himself to look away, to where his other work riders were urging their mounts along.

The fine mist glazed the shoulders of his greatcoat; it darkened his fair hair. Flick made those observations as, slowing The Flynn, she glanced back to where Demon stood. He was looking away, a fact she'd known, or she wouldn't have risked the glance. He'd been watching her almost without pause since he'd arrived, just after she'd taken to the Heath.

Luckily, cursing beneath her breath only reinforced her disguise. But she had to suppress all other signs of agitation so she didn't communicate her sudden nervousness to The Flynn. She'd always felt breathless whenever Demon was about; she'd anticipated some degree of awkwardness, the remnants of her childhood infatuation with him. But not this—this nerve-stretching awareness, the skittery sensation in her stomach. She'd buried deep the suspicion it had something to do—a great deal to do—with the breath-stealing shock she'd felt when he had lifted her to her saddle the previous evening. The last thing she wanted was for The Flynn to make an exhibition of himself under Demon's expert eye. He might see it as a God-given sign to change his mind and relieve her of her duties.

But riding track with him watching proved a far greater trial than performing for Carruthers alone, despite the fact the old curmudgeon was the most exacting trainer on the Heath. There was a certain sharp assessment in Demon's blue gaze that was absent from Carruthers's eyes; as her nervousness grew, she had to wonder if Demon was doing it deliberately—deliberately discomposing her—so she'd make some silly error and give him a reason to send her packing.

Thankfully, all her years of riding had taught her to hide her feelings well; she and The Flynn put on a good show. Wheeling the big bay, she headed back to the stable.

Demon nodded his approval when she walked The Flynn in and halted him in the mounting area. Kicking free of the stirrups, she slid down the horse away from Demon and Carruthers. An apprentice hurried up; he grabbed the reins before she could blink, before she could think, and led The Flynn off to his box, leaving her facing Carruthers, with Demon beside him.

"Good work." Demon's blue eyes held hers; he nodded curtly. "We'll see you this afternoon. Don't be late."

Flick's tongue burned; she had, until now, unsaddled and brushed down The Flynn herself. But her disguise demanded meekness; she ducked her head. "I'll be here." With that gruff declaration, she swung around and, remembering at the last not to walk stiffly, sauntered up the alley to where the cob stood dozing by the door. She scrambled up to her saddle and left without a backward glance—before temptation could get the upper hand.

Behind her, she heard Demon ask Carruthers some question—but she could still feel his gaze on her back.

After seeing Flick safely away, Demon repaired to the coffeehouse in Newmarket High Street favored by the members of the Jockey Club.

He was hailed the instant he crossed the threshold. Returning greetings right and left, he strolled to the counter, ordered a large breakfast, then joined a group comprised mostly of other owners at one of the long tables.

"We're exchanging predictions for the coming season." Patrick McGonnachie, manager of the duke of Beaufort's stable, turned to Demon as he sat. "Currently, of course, we've five times the number of winners as we have races."

"Sounds like a fresh crop," Demon drawled. "That'll keep the General busy."

McGonnachie blinked, then caught his meaning—if horses that hadn't won before made it to the winner's circle, the General would need to investigate their pedigree. McGonnachie shifted. "Ah, yes. Busy indeed."

He looked away up the table; Demon resisted pressing him. McGonnachie, in common with all of Newmarket, knew how close he and the General were. If there was any less-than-felicitous whisper going the rounds concerning the General, McGonnachie wouldn't tell him.

So he ate and listened to the chat about the table, and contributed his share. And bore with easy indifference the good-natured ribbing over his activities in London.

"Need to change your style if you don't want to miss your chance," Old Arthur Trumble, one of the most respected owners, nodded down the table. "Take my advice and spend less time lifting the skirts of London's *mesdames*, and more dealing with the business. The higher the standing of your stud, the more demanding it'll be." He paused to puff on his pipe. "And Lord knows, you look like taking the Breeder's Cup this year."

Two others took immediate exception to that prediction, leaving Demon with no need to reply. He listened, but detected no further suggestion of rumors concerning the General other than McGonnachie's earlier hesitation.

"Mister Figgins is back—did you hear?" Buffy Jeffers leaned forward to look around McGonnachie. "Sawyer ran him in the first—he couldn't wait to see if that leg would hold up, but it did. So your Mighty Flynn will have some decent competition. The handicaps won't be the walk-over they might otherwise have been."

"Oh?" Demon chatted with Buffy about The Flynn's chances, while his mind raced on a different track.

He had wondered how Dillon's syndicate had expected to fix the first race of the year. Run before the start of the spring season, the early races were used to trial horses, generally those new to racing. If that was the case, then fixing meant making sure one specific horse came first, which meant influencing how at least a handful of other horses ran. Bribing multiple jockeys required more money, and was more hazardous, than the alternative way to fix a race. But the other method required one outstanding run—a crowd favorite.

"Tell me," Demon asked, when Buffy paused for breath. "Did Mister Figgins win? You didn't say."

"Romped in," Buffy replied. "Showed the pack a clean pair of heels all the way down the straight."

Demon smiled and let their talk drift into other spheres.

At least he now knew how the syndicate operated; they must have cursed Mister Figgins all the way down the straight. Mister Figgins was the horse the fix should have been applied to; the syndicate would have assumed he'd lose, and their tools—however many bookmakers they'd seduced into their game—would have offered good odds on Mister Figgins, taken huge bets, and, in this case, suffered mammoth losses. That was the one drawback with that method—it could seriously backfire if the bribe wasn't in place, if the race wasn't properly fixed.

Which explained why Dillon was in serious trouble.

After breakfast, in company with the others, Demon strolled across the street and into the Jockey Club. The hallowed precinct was as familiar as his home; he spent the next hour wandering the rooms, chatting to stewards, jockeys and the racing elite—those gentlemen like himself who formed the hub of the English racing world.

Time and again in his idle chats, he sensed a start, or hesitation—a quick skirting around some invisible truth. Long before he ran into Reginald Molesworth, Demon knew beyond doubt that there were rumors afoot.

Reggie, an old friend, didn't wait to be asked. "I say," he said the instant they'd exchanged their usual greetings, "are you free? Let's go get some coffee—The Twig and Bough should be pretty quiet about now." He caught Demon's eye and added, "Something you need to know."

An easy air hiding his interest, Demon acquiesced; together with Reggie, he strolled out of the club and down the street. Ducking his head, he led the way into The Twig and Bough, a coffeehouse that catered more to the genteel elements of the town than to the racing set.

Their appearance left the two serving girls gawking, but the proprietress preened. She quickly bustled out from behind her counter as they claimed seats at a table against the wall. After taking their orders, the woman bobbed and hurried away. By unspoken understanding, Demon and Reggie chatted about inconsequential, tonnish London matters until their coffee and cakes arrived, and the little waitress left them.

Reggie leaned over the table. "Thought you'd want to know." He lowered his voice to a conspiratorial whisper. "Things are being said regarding the household at Hillgate End."

Impassive, Demon asked, "What things?"

"Seems there's some suspicion of races not being run the way they should. Well, there's always talk every time a favorite loses, but recently ..." Reggie stirred his coffee. "There was Trumpeter and The Trojan here last season, and Big Biscuits, Hail Well and The Unicorn at Doncaster. Not to mention The Prime at Ascot. Not so many that it's certain, but it doesn't take a man o' business to work it out. A lot of money changed hands over those losses, and the offered odds in every case ... well, it certainly gives one to think. And that was just the autumn season."

Demon nodded. "Is it official?"

Reggie grimaced. "Yes and no. The Committee think there's a definite question, and they want answers, thank you very much. At present, they're only looking at last autumn, and it's all been kept under wraps, which is why you might not have heard."

Demon shook his head. "I hadn't. Is there any reason to think it went on last spring as well?"

"I gather there is, but the evidence—meaning the offering of odds that could only be considered deliberately encouraging—is not as clear."

"Any guesses as to the Committee's direction?"

Reggie looked up and met Demon's gaze. Reggie's father was on the Committee. "Yes, well, that's why I thought you should know. The jockeys involved, of course, are all as close as clams—they know it's the devil of a case to prove. But it seems young Caxton's been seen about, chatting to the jockeys involved. As he's not previously seemed all that interested in rubbing elbows with the riders, it was noticed. The Committee, not surprisingly, wants to talk to the youngster. Trouble is"—Reggie pulled one earlobe—"the boy's off visiting friends. Given he is the General's son, and no one wants to unnecessarily upset the venerable old gent, the Committee decided to wait until Caxton junior got back, and take him aside on the quiet."

Reggie sighed and continued. "Good plan, of course, but when they made it, they imagined he'd be back inside of a week. That was two weeks ago, and he's still not back. They're uneasy about fronting up at Hillgate End and asking the General where his son is—they'll hold their hand as long as they can. But with the spring season in the offing, they can't wait forever."

Demon met Reggie's deceptively innocent eyes. "I see."

And he did. The message he was getting was not from Reggie, not even from Reggie's father, but from the all-powerful Committee itself.

"You don't have any ... ah, insights to offer, do you?"

After a moment, Demon said, "No. But I can see the Committee's point."

"Hmm." Reggie shot Demon a commiserating look. "Not hard to see, is it?"

"No, indeed." They finished their coffee, paid, then strolled outside. Demon paused on the step.

Reggie stopped beside him. "Where are you headed?"

Demon shot him a glance. "Hillgate End, where else?" He raised his brows. "To see what the situation there is."

"They all think I don't know." General Sir Gordon Caxton sat in the chair behind his desk. "But I follow the race results better than most and although I don't get out to the paddocks much these days, there's nothing wrong with my hearing when I do." He snorted.

Demon, standing before the long windows, watched his longtime friend and mentor fretfully realign his already straight blotter. He'd arrived a quarter of an hour before, and, as was his habit, had come straight to the library. The General had greeted him with open delight. To Demon's well-attuned ear, the General's heartiness had sounded forced. When the first rush of genial exchanges had faded, he'd asked how everything was with his friend. The General's superficial delight evaporated, and he'd made his admission.

"Whispers—and more. About Dillon, of course." The General's chin sank; for a long moment, he stared at the miniature of his late wife, Dillon's mother, that stood on one side of the desk, then he sighed and shifted his gaze to his blotter once more. "Race-fixing." The words were uttered with loathing. "He might, of course, be innocent, but ..." He dragged in an unsteady breath, and shook his head. "I can't say I'm surprised. The boy always lacked backbone— my fault as much as his. I should have taken a firmer stand, applied a firmer hand. But ..." After another long moment, he sighed again. "I hadn't expected this."

There was a wealth of hurt, of confused pain, in the quietly spoken words. Demon's hands fisted; he felt an urgent desire to grab hold of Dillon and iron him out, literally and figuratively, regardless of Flick's sensitivities. The General, despite his lumbering bulk, shaggy brows and martial air, was a benign and gentle man, kindhearted and generous, respected by all who knew him. Demon had visited him regularly for twenty-five years; there had never been any lack of love, of gentle guidance for Dillon. Whatever the General might imagine, Dillon's situation was no fault of his.

The General grimaced. "Felicity, dear girl, and Mrs. Fogarty and Jacobs all try to keep it from me. I haven't let them know there's no need. They'd only fuss more if they knew I knew."

Mrs. Fogarty had been the General's housekeeper for more than thirty years, and Jacobs, the butler, had been with him at least as long. Both, like Felicity, were utterly devoted to the General.

The General looked up at Demon. "Tell me—have you heard anything beyond suspicions?"

Demon held his gaze. "No—nothing more than this." Briefly, he stated all he'd heard in Newmarket that morning.

The General humphed. "As I said, it wouldn't surprise me to learn Dillon was involved. He's away staying with friends—if the Committee's agreeable to wait until he returns, that would be best, I suspect. No need to summon him back. Truth to tell, if I did send a summons, I couldn't be sure he wouldn't bolt."

"It's always been a mystery how Dillon could be so weak a character when he grew up alongside Felicity. She's so ..." The General stopped, then smiled fleetingly at Demon. "Well, the word 'righteous' comes to mind. Turning her from her path, which you may be sure she's fully considered from all angles, is all but impossible. Always was." He sighed fondly. "I used to put it down to her parents being missionaries, but it goes deeper than that. A true character— steadfast and unswerving. That's my Felicity."

His smile faded. "Would that a little of her honesty had rubbed off on Dillon. And some of her steadiness. She's never caused me a moment's worry, but Dillon? Even as a child he was forever in some senseless scrape. The devil of it was, he always looked to Felicity to rescue him—and she always did. Which was all very well when they were children, but Dillon's twenty-two. He should have matured, should have grown beyond these damned larks."

Dillon had graduated from larks to outright crime. Demon stored the insight away, and kept his lips shut.

He'd promised Flick his help; at present, that meant shielding Dillon, leaving him hidden in the ruined cottage. Helping Flick also, he knew, meant shielding the General, even if that hadn't gone unsaid. And while he and Flick were doubtless destined to clash on any number of issues in the coming days—like the details of her involvement in their investigations—he was absolutely as one with her in pledging his soul to spare the General more pain.

If the General knew where Dillon was, regardless of the details, he would be torn, driven by one loyalty—to the industry he'd served for decades—to surrender Dillon to the authorities, while at the same time compelled by the protective instincts of a parent.

Demon knew how it felt to be gripped by conflicting loyalties, but he'd rather leave the weight on his shoulders, where it presently resided, than off-load the problem onto his ageing friend. Facing the windows squarely, he looked over the neat lawns to the shade trees beyond. "I suspect that waiting for Dillon to return is the right tack. Who knows the full story? There might be reasons, mitigating circumstances. It's best to wait and see."

"You're right, of course. And, heaven knows, I've enough to keep me busy." Demon glanced around to see the General tug the heavy record book back onto the blotter. "What with you and your fellows breeding so much Irish into the stock, I've all but had to learn Gaelic."

Demon grinned. A gong sounded.

Both he and the General glanced at the door. "Time for lunch. Why not stay? You can meet Felicity and see if you agree with my assessment."

Demon hesitated. The General frequently invited him to lunch, but in recent years, he hadn't accepted, which was presumably why he'd missed seeing Felicity grow up.

He'd spent the previous evening dredging his memory for every recollection, no matter how minute, trying to find some balance in his unexpectedly tilting world. Trying to ascertain just what his role, his standing, with this new version of Felicity should be. Her age had been a pertinent consideration; physically, she could be anything from eighteen to twenty-four, but her self-confidence and maturity were telling. He'd pegged her at twenty-three.

The General had now told him Dillon was twenty-two, which meant if Flick was two years younger, then she was only twenty. He'd been three years out, but, given the General's assessment, with which he concurred, she might as well be twenty-three.

Twenty-three made her easier to deal with, given he was thirty-one. Thinking of her as twenty made him feel too much like a cradle-snatcher.

But he still couldn't understand why he hadn't sighted her in the last five years. The last time he'd seen her was when, after importing his first Irish stallion, he'd come to give the General the relevant information for the stud records. She'd opened the door to him—a short, thin, gawky schoolgirl with long braids. He'd barely glanced at her, but he had remembered her. He'd been here countless times since, but hadn't seen her. He hadn't, however, stayed for a meal in all those years.

Demon turned from the window. "Yes, why not?" The General would attribute Demon's break with long-standing habit to concern for him, and he would be half-right at that.

So he stayed.

And had the pleasure of seeing Felicity sweep imperiously into the dining parlor, then nearly trip over her toes, and her tongue, deciding how to react to him.

Which was only fair, because he had not a clue how to react to her. Or, more accurately, didn't dare react to her as his instincts suggested. She was, after all—despite all—still the General's ward.

Who had miraculously grown up.

In full light, dressed in ivory muslin sprigged with tiny green leaves, she looked like a nymph of spring come to steal mortals' hearts. Her hair, brushed and neat, glowed like polished gold, a rich frame for the distinctive, eerily angelic beauty of her face.

It was her face that held him, compelled him. The soft blue of her eyes, like a misty sky, drew him, urging him to lose himself in their gentle depths. Her nose was straight, her brow wide, her complexion flawless. Her lips begged to be kissed—delicately bowed, soft pink, the lower lip full and sensual, they were made to be covered by a man's.

By his.

The thought, so unequivocal, shocked him; he drew breath and shook free of the spell. A swift glance, a rake's appraisal of her figure, nearly had him in thrall again.

He resisted. The realization that he'd been bowled over for the first time in his life was enough to shake him to his senses. With his usual grace and an easy smile, he strolled forward and took Flick's hand.

She blinked and very nearly snatched it back.

Demon quashed the urge to raise her quivering fingers to his lips. He let his smile deepen instead. "Good afternoon, my dear. I do hope you don't mind me joining you for lunch?"

She blinked again, and shot a quick glance at the General. "No, of course not."

She blushed, very slightly; Demon forced himself to ignore the intriguing sight. Gracefully, he led her to the table. She claimed the chair by the General's left; he held it for her, then strolled around the table to the place on the General's right, directly opposite her.

The placement couldn't have been more perfect; while chatting with the General, it was perfectly natural that his gaze should frequently pass over her.

She of the swanlike neck and sweetly rounded shoulders, of the pert breasts encased in skin like ivory silk, their upper swells revealed by the scooped neckline of her gown. She was perfectly prim, perfectly proper, and perfectly delectable.

Demon's mouth watered every time he glanced her way.

Flick was very aware of his scrutiny; for some mystical reason, the touch of his gaze actually felt warm. Like a sun-kissed breeze touching her—lightly, enticingly. She tried not to let her awareness show; it was, after all, unsurprising that he found her appearance somewhat changed. The last time he'd seen her, she'd been fifteen, skinny, scrawny, with two long braids hanging down her back. He'd barely registered her existence—she'd stared at him and hadn't been able to stop.

That was the last time she'd allowed herself the liberty; thereafter she made sure that whenever he called, she kept out of his sight. Even if she glimpsed him, she'd force herself to walk the other way—precisely because her impulse lay in the opposite direction. She had far too much pride to stare at him like some silly, lovestruck schoolgirl. Despite the fact that was how he made her feel—hardly surprising, as he'd been her ideal gentleman for so many years—she had a strong aversion to the notion of mooning over him. She was quite sure he got enough of that from other lovestruck girls and all the lovestruck ladies.

She had absolutely no ambition to join their ranks.

So she forced herself to contribute to the conversation about horses and the coming season. Having grown up at Hillgate End, she knew more than enough about both subjects to hold her own. Demon twice tripped over her name, catching himself just in time; she manfully—womanfully—resisted glaring at him the second time it happened. His eyes met hers; one brow quirked and his lips curved teasingly. She pressed her lips tight shut and looked down at her plate.

"Could you pass the vinegar, m'dear."

She looked for the cruet set only to see Demon lift the bottle from the tray further down the table. He offered it to her; she took it—her fingers brushed his. A sharp shock lanced through her. Startled, she nearly dropped the bottle but managed to catch it in time. Carefully, she handed it to the General, then picked up her knife and fork and looked down at her plate. And breathed slowly in and out.

She felt Demon's gaze on her face, on her shoulders, then he turned to the General. "The Mighty Flynn's shaping well. I'm expecting to have another two wins at least from him this season."

"Indeed?"

The General was instantly distracted; Flick breathed a touch easier.

Demon kept the conversation rolling, not a difficult task. Much more difficult was keeping his gaze from Flick; his attention, of course, remained riveted. Ridiculous, of course—she was twenty, for heaven's sake.

But she was there, and utterly fascinating.

He told himself it was the contrast between Flick the righteous, who dressed as a stable lad and single-handedly set out to expose a race-fixing syndicate, and Felicity, the delicate and determinedly proper Botticelli angel.

It was a contrast designed to intrigue him.

"Perhaps," he said as they all stood, the light luncheon disposed of, "Felicity would care to take a turn about the lawns?"

He deliberately phrased the question to give the General an opening to support him. He needn't have bothered. Flick's head came up; she met his gaze.

"That would be pleasant." She glanced at the General. "If you don't need me, sir?"

"No, no!" The General beamed. "I must get back to my books. You go along."

He shooed them toward the open French doors; Demon caught his eye. "I'll drop by if I have any news."

The General's eyes dimmed. "Yes, do." Then he glanced at Flick and his smile returned. Nodding benignly, he headed for the door.

Leaving Flick by her chair, staring at Demon. He raised a brow, and gestured to the French doors. "Shall we?"

She came around the table but didn't pause by his side, didn't wait for him to offer his arm. Instead, she walked straight past, out of the open doors. Demon stared at her back, then shook his head and followed.

She'd paused on the terrace; as soon as he appeared, she led the way down the steps. With his longer stride, he easily caught up with her as she strolled the well-tended lawn. He fell in beside her, sauntering slowly, trying to decide what gambit would work best with an angel. Before he could decide, she spoke.

"*How* am I supposed to hear any comments or see anyone approaching the riders in your stables when I barely spend a moment *in* them?" She cast a darkling glance his way. "I arrived this morning to discover The Flynn already saddled. Carruthers sent me straight out to take The Flynn around for an extended warm-up"—her eyes narrowed—"so he wouldn't still be restless at the end. And then *you* bundled me out of the stable as soon as I rode back in."

"I assumed you would need to get back here." He hadn't, but it was a good excuse. He slanted her a mildly questioning glance. "How are you covering your absences early morning and afternoon?"

"I often go riding first thing in the morning, so that's nothing unusual. If Jessamy's missing from the stable, everyone assumes I'm somewhere about, enjoying the morning. Just as long as I'm back by lunchtime, no one would think to worry."

Slowing as they passed into the shade of the old trees edging the lawn, Flick grimaced. "The afternoons are more difficult, but no one's asked where I ride off to. I suspect Foggy and Jacobs know Dillon's not off with friends, but somewhere close—but if they don't ask, then they can't say if questioned."

"I see." He hesitated, inwardly debating whether to take her hand and place it on his sleeve, forcing her to stroll with him rather than lead the way. But she'd tensed when he'd taken her hand before, and she'd nearly dropped the vinegar. Suppressing a grin, he opted for caution. "There's no reason you can't loiter around the stables after the morning gallops. Not having any chores should give you a freer rein." He had no intention of rescinding the orders he'd given Carruthers. "However, there's no sense in dallying after afternoon stables. At that time, most of the jockeys and hangers-on retire to the taverns."

"There's no reason I can't slouch about the stables until they leave."

Demon inwardly frowned. There was a mulishness in her tone, a sense of rigid purpose in her stance; both had been absent earlier. Earlier in the dining room, when she'd been Felicity, not Flick. Flick was the righteous crusader, Felicity the Botticelli angel.

Slowing, he considered a swath of daffodils nodding their trumpets in the breeze. The odd bluebell and harebell were interspersed, creating a spring carpet stretching under the trees and into the sunshine beyond. He nodded toward the show. "Beautiful, aren't they?"

An angel should respond to natural beauty.

Flick barely glanced at nature's bounty. "Hmm. Have you learned, or heard, anything yet?" She looked into his face. "You did go into town this morning, didn't you?"

He suppressed a frown. "Yes, yes and yes."

She stopped and looked at him expectantly. "Well?"

Frustrated, Demon halted and faced her. "The Committee is waiting for Dillon to return to have a quiet word with him over a number of races last season where the suspiciously priced crowd-favorite didn't win."

Her face blanked. "Oh."

"Indeed. The slumgudgeon didn't even realize that, as he hadn't made a habit of hobnobbing with the riders before, people would notice when he suddenly did."

"But . . ." Flick frowned. "The stewards haven't come asking after him."

"Not the stewards, no. In this instance, they weren't required—any number of the Committee have probably called on the General in the last weeks. Easy enough to learn whether Dillon is here or not."

"That's true." Then her eyes flew wide. "They haven't said anything to the General, have they?"

Demon glanced away. "No, the Committee sees no reason to unnecessarily upset the General, and as yet, they have no proof—just suspicions."

He looked back as Flick sighed with relief. "If they hold off until Dillon can return—"

"They'll hold off as long as they can," he cut in. "But they won't—can't—wait forever. Dillon will have to return as soon as possible—the instant we get enough information to prove the existence of the syndicate."

"So we need to make headway in identifying Dillon's contact. Are the rumors of race-fixing widespread?"

"No. Among the owners and trainers, yes, but amongst others, less so. Some jockeys and stable lads must have suspicions, but they're unlikely to voice them, even to each other."

Flick started to stroll again. "If there's no open talk, no rumors abounding, it's less likely someone will let something slip."

Demon didn't reply; Flick didn't seem to notice. Which, to him, seemed all of a piece. Right now she didn't seem aware of him at all—she seemed to regard him as a benevolent uncle, or some creature equally benign. Which was so far from the truth it was laughable.

It was also irritating.

The Botticelli angel of the dining room, the one who had delicately shivered at his touch, and trembled when his fingers brushed hers, had vanished.

She glanced at him. "Perhaps you could start with the jockeys whose mounts failed last season. I assume, if they've taken a bribe once, they'll be more likely to be approached again?"

"Ordinarily, yes. However, if they've been questioned, however elliptically, by the stewards, one can guarantee their lips will be sealed. With a license in the balance, no jockey's going to incriminate himself."

"There must be some action you can take while I keep watch in your stables."

Demon's eyes widened; he only just stopped himself from replying caustically with rather more information than she needed. "Never mind about me. I'm sure I'll find some useful avenue to explore." He'd already thought of several, but he had no intention of sharing his views. "I'll make a start before I look in on the afternoon's work."

"You could investigate any touts or hangers-on lurking about the other stables' strings."

"Indeed." Demon couldn't help himself—eyes hardening, his gaze openly intent, he lengthened his stride, swung to face her, and halted.

Sucking in a breath, she stopped precipitously, all but teetering in her effort not to run into him. She looked up, blue eyes widening in surprise.

He smiled down at her. "I'll be watching you, too." He held her gaze. "Don't doubt it."

She blinked; to his chagrin, not a flicker of awareness—the consciousness he was deliberately trying to evoke—showed in her soft blue eyes. Instead puzzlement filled them. She searched his face briefly, then shrugged, stepped aside and walked around him. "As you wish, although I can't see why. You know I can handle The Flynn, and Carruthers never misses a stride."

Swallowing a curse, Demon swung on his heel and stalked after her. It wasn't The Flynn that concerned him. Flick clearly considered him unthreatening. While he had no wish to threaten her, he definitely wanted her in his bed, which ought, in his book, to make her nervous, at least a bit wary. But no—not Flick.

Felicity was sensitive—Felicity was sensible. She had the good sense to be aware of him. Felicity had some degree of self-preservation. Flick, as far as he could tell, had none. She hadn't even recognized that he was not a benign uncle, and definitely not the sort of man to be managed by a mere chit.

"It won't," he enunciated, regaining her side, "be The Flynn's performance I'll be watching."

She glanced up and met his eyes, her frown more definite. "There's no need to watch me—I haven't parted company with my saddle for years."

"Be that as it may," he purred, "I assure you that watching you—keeping my gaze firmly glued to your svelte form as you trot about perched on one of my champions—is precisely the sort of behavior that's expected of a gentleman such as I."

"Be that as it may, watching me when you could be observing the hangers-on is silly. A wasted opportunity."

"Not for me."

Flick humphed and looked ahead. He was being deliberately difficult—she could sense his aggravation, cloaked though it was, but she had no idea what had caused it, or why he was making less sense than Dillon. She strolled on. And continued to ignore the fluttery sensations assailing her stomach, and the insistent flickering of her nerves. Along with the other unwanted, unwelcome remnants of her girlish obsession with him.

He'd been her ideal gentleman since she'd been ten and had found a book of Michelangelo's works in the library. She'd found one sculpture that had embodied her vision of a handsome male. Except that Demon was handsomer. His shoulders were wider, his chest broader and more finely muscled, his hips narrower, his legs longer, harder—altogether better defined. As for the rest, she'd surmised from his reputation that he was better endowed there, too. His easygoing attitudes, his love of horses and his involvement with the world of horse racing had all served to deepen her interest.

She hadn't, however, ever made the mistake of imagining he returned it, or ever would. He was eleven years her senior, and could have his pick of the most beautiful and sophisticated ladies in the ton; it would be foolish beyond permission to imagine he would ever look at her. But she would marry one day—one day soon; she was very ready to love and be loved. She was already twenty, waiting, hoping. And if she had her way, she would marry a gentleman exactly like Demon. He, however, was an unattainable idol, entirely beyond her reach.

"This"—she gestured—"shady contact of Dillon's. Presumably he's not a local. Perhaps a search of the hotels and inns—"

"I've already got that in hand."

"Oh." She glanced up and met Demon's gaze; for a moment, his blue eyes remained sharp, keen, then he looked ahead.

"I'll check, but it's unlikely we'll find much by that route. This is, after all, Newmarket, a place that abounds in inns and taverns, and that attracts its fair share of shady characters, most of whom aren't local."

Flick grimaced and looked forward—they'd ambled through the gardens. The stables lay ahead, framed by a series of wooden arches over which wisteria grew. Stepping onto the path leading beneath the arches, she mused, "This contact—who would he be? One of the syndicate, or another pawn?"

"Not one of the syndicate." Demon strolled beside her, his strides long and lazy, his hands, somewhat surprisingly, in his trouser pockets. His gaze was on the gravel. "Whoever they are, the syndicate won't want for money, and the last thing they'd risk is exposure. No—the man will be a hireling. Perhaps a permanent employee. That, for us, would be best."

"So once we identify him, we'll have the best chance of following him back to his masters?"

Demon nodded. Then he looked up and stopped. They'd reached the end of the arches.

Flick glanced up, squinting into the sunlight that shone from over his shoulder. He was looking at her; she couldn't see his features, but she could feel his gaze, could sense his sheer physical presence through every pore. She was used to working with large horses; standing near him reminded her of them—he exuded the same aura of potent physical power, which could, if provoked, be dangerous. Luckily, neither horses nor he posed any danger to her. Inwardly lamenting her continuing sensitivity, she raised a hand and shaded her eyes.

And looked into his.

Her breath caught; for an instant, she felt disoriented—unclear who she was, who he was, and how things really were. Then something shifted in the blue; she blinked, and regained her mental footing. Yet he continued to look at her—not precisely seriously, but intently, the expression in his eyes one she neither recognized nor understood.

She was about to raise a brow when, his gaze still steady on her face, he asked, "Now you know the full story of Dillon's involvement, do you regret agreeing to help him?"

"Regret?" Considering the question, she raised both brows. "I don't think the concept applies. I've always helped him—he's made something of a career of getting into unexpectedly complicated scrapes." She shrugged. "I always imagined he'd grow out of them eventually. He hasn't yet."

Demon considered her face, her open expression, the honesty in her soft blue eyes. They didn't tell him how she felt about Dillon; given her apparent resistance to him, he had to wonder if Dillon was the cause. When she and Dillon were together, she was the dominant party—the one in charge. She'd grown accustomed to Dillon being dependent on her—it was possible she liked it that way. There was no doubt she liked to lead.

Which was all very well, but . . .

"So," she blinked up at him, "what do you imagine will happen next?"

He raised his brows. "Probably not a lot." At least, not in his stables. "However, if you do stumble on any clue, I will, of course, expect to be notified immediately."

"Of course." She lowered her hand and turned toward the stables. "Where will you be?"

Investigating far and wide. "Send a message to the farm—the Shephards always know where to find me."

"I'll send word if I hear anything." She stopped at the edge of the garden and held out her hand. "I'll see you at the stable in a few hours."

Demon took her hand. He lifted his gaze to her eyes—and fell into the blue. Her fingers lay, trusting, quiescent in his grasp. He considered raising them, considered brushing a lingering kiss upon them, considered . . .

Madness and uncertainty clashed.

The moment passed.

He released her hand. With an elegant nod, he turned and, jaw setting, strode for the stables, more conscious with every stride of a demonic desire to capture a Botticelli angel—and take her to his bed.

CHAPTER

Four

౦ళ౧

The next days passed uneventfully; Flick swallowed her impatience and doggedly watched, doggedly listened. She rode morning and afternoon track work every day, then slouched about the stable for as long as she could in the mornings, and until all the stable lads left in the evenings. After three days, the only suspicious character she'd spotted had proved to be one of the lads' cousins, visiting from the north. The only surprising information she'd heard concerned the activities of some redheaded barmaid.

As he'd intimated, Demon had attended all the track work religiously—he'd watched her religiously, too; her sensitivity to his gaze grew more acute by the day. She'd sighed with relief when, within her hearing that morning, he'd told Carruthers that he'd be spending the afternoon about the other stables looking over the competition.

So at three o'clock, she left the General nodding over his records and set off on Jessamy for the cottage—Felicity garbed in her blue velvet riding habit—feeling less trepidatious, certainly more sure of herself. No longer wary of what she might face at the stable.

Dillon was in the clearing when she rode up, the cob placidly munching nearby. She reined in and slid out of her saddle, turned on her heel and marched into the cottage to change—without a single glance at Dillon. He'd have the cob saddled and bridled, and Jessamy unsaddled and tethered, by the time she came out.

She hadn't spoken to him since she'd learned the truth. Every time she'd come by, he'd tried to catch her eye, to smile and make amends.

Struggling out of her velvet skirts, Flick humphed. Dillon was being excessively careful around her—he could be careful for a while more. She hadn't forgiven him for deceiving her—she hadn't forgiven herself for being so gullible. She should have guessed; she knew he wasn't that innocent any more, but the idea that he could have been so comprehensively stupid hadn't entered her head.

Smoothing her curls, she crammed her cap over them. She was exceedingly tired of putting right Dillon's wrongs, of easing his way, but . . .

She sighed. She would continue to shield Dillon if the alternative was upsetting the General. Distress wasn't good for him, as Dr. Thurgood had made very clear. Assuring his tranquility was also one way she could repay him for all he had given her.

A home—a secure, stable place in which to grow up. A steady hand, a steadier heart, and an unwavering confidence in her.

She'd come to Hillgate End a confused seven-year-old, suddenly very much alone. Her Aunt Scroggs, with whom her parents had left her in London, had not been willing to keep her when her temporary need had turned permanent. No one had wanted her until, out of nowhere, the General, a distant connection of her father's, had stepped in, smiled kindly upon her, and taken her into his home.

In the country, where she loved to be, close to horses—her favorite animal.

Coming to Hillgate End had changed her life forever, and all for the better. Even though she hadn't been a pauper, as a child, who knows where she might have ended without the General's kindness, without his care? Thanks to the General, she'd ended here, with a happy life and every opportunity. She owed him a great deal.

Drawing a deep breath, she stepped out of the lean-to. Dillon was waiting, holding the cob, saddled and bridled, close by the log she used for mounting. Flick eyed him steadily as she crossed the yard, but she refused to let him catch her eye. Despite her affection for the General, Dillon, at the moment, she simply endured.

She mounted, gathered the reins, and jogged off without a word.

At least Demon had got the truth out of Dillon. Even though she'd felt foolish for not having seen the inconsistencies in Dillon's story, she could only be glad of Demon's intervention. Since he'd agreed to help, despite his ridiculous insistence on watching her, she'd sensed a lightening of the weight that until his arrival had rested solely on her shoulders. He was there, sharing the load, doing, like her, whatever he could to spare the General. Regardless of anything else, it was a distinct relief.

Reaching the road, she set the cob trotting. At the stable, a lad had The Flynn saddled and waiting; she checked the girths, then with the lad's help, jumped up to perch high on the bay's back. He was used to her now, to the croon of her voice; with the merest urging, he trotted to the door.

Carruthers was waiting. "Take a long walk, then a gentle trot, at least six, then walk him again and bring him in."

Flick nodded and clicked the reins. Afternoon work was always easy; not every trainer even bothered.

She paraded with the rest of the string, listening to the natter of the lads and riders about her, simultaneously scanning the nearby verges of the Heath where the watchers—the hangers-on and the touts, spying out the form for bookmakers or private clients—congregated.

As usual, she was the last to walk her mount in, so she could watch to see if any outsider tried to speak to a rider. None did; no one approached any rider in Demon's string, nor the strings from nearby stables.

Disappointed, starting to question whether she would ever see or hear anything useful, she slid from the saddle and let the stable lad lead The Flynn away. After a moment, she followed.

She helped the lad unsaddle, then left him cleaning the manger while she fetched the feed, then the water. The lad moved on to the next horse he looked after. Flick sighed, and The Flynn turned his huge head and nudged her.

Smiling crookedly, she patted his nose. On impulse, she climbed the box wall and perched atop it, leaning her shoulder against the stable's outer wall. She scanned the boxes, listening to the murmurs and conversations—mostly between lads and their equine charges.

The Flynn nudged her legs; she crooned at him, grinning when he hurrumphed and nodded.

"Oh, fer Gawd's sake—take a hike! I doan wanna hear what you've got ter say, so just piss off, why doan yer?"

Flick straightened so abruptly that she nearly fell off the wall. The words sounded so clear—then she realized she was hearing them through the stable wall. The speaker—she recognized the dulcet tones of one of the top race jockeys—was outside.

"Now, now. If'n you'll just hear me out—"

"I tol' you—I doan wanna hear nuthin' from you! Now push off, afore I set ol' Carruthers on yer!"

"Your loss."

The second speaker had a scratchy voice; it faded away.

Flick scrambled off the wall and tore through the stable, dodging lads with buckets and feed all the way up the alley. They swore at her. She didn't stop. She reached the doors; hugging their edge, she peeped out.

A heavy figure in an old frieze coat was lumbering away along the edge of the Heath, a cloth cap pulled low over his face, his hands sunk in his pockets. She could see little more than Dillon had.

The man was heading for the town.

For one moment, Flick stood in the yard, juggling possibilities. Then she swung around and hurried back into the stable.

Demon ambled into his stable at the end of the working day. Soft snorts and gentle whinnies punctuated breathy sighs as stable lads closed their charges in their boxes. The reek of horse was absolute; Demon barely noticed. He did notice the old cob quietly dozing in one corner, a few handfuls of hay and a bucket close by. Glancing left and right, Demon strolled down the alley.

He stopped by The Flynn's box; the big bay was settled and contentedly munching. Strolling on, he came upon Carruthers, inspecting a filly's hoof.

"Where's Flick?"

Carruthers glanced at him, then snorted. "Gone orf, already. In a pelter, he was. Left his cob—said he'd fetch it later." He looked down at the hoof he was tending.

Demon held back a frown. "Did he say anything else?"

"Nah!" With a deft flick, Carruthers pried a stone free. "Just like the other lads—couldn't wait to get to the Swan and lift a pint."

"The Swan?"

"Or the Bells." Carruthers let the horse's leg down and straightened. "Who knows with lads these days?"

Demon paused; Carruthers watched the filly test the hoof. "So Flick headed into town?"

"Aye—that's what I'm saying. He usually heads off home to Lidgate, quiet as you please, but today he beetled off into town."

"How long ago?"

Carruthers shrugged. "Twenty minutes."

Demon bit back an oath, swung on his heel and strode out of his stable.

He didn't find Flick in the Swan or the Bells, both respectable inns. He found her in the smoke-filled snug of the Fox and Hen, a seedy tavern down a narrow side street. Nursing a full pint pot, she sat sunk in a corner, surrounded by ale-swilling brutes three times her size.

She was trying to look inconspicuous. Thankfully, a dart game was in full swing, and many patrons were still rolling in; the rabble were presently distracted and hadn't started looking around for likely victims.

Jaw set, Demon grabbed a pint from the harassed barman and crossed the room, his size, accentuated by his heavy greatcoat, allowing him to cleave a passage through the crowd. There were others of his ilk present, gentlemen hobnobbing with cits, rubbing shoulders with half-pay officers and racecourse riffraff; his appearance attracted no undue attention.

Reaching the corner table, he ignored Flick's huge eyes. Setting his pot down with a definite click, he sat opposite her. Then he met her gaze. "What the hell are you doing here?"

She glared at him, then flicked her gaze to the next table, then back.

Nonchalantly picking up his pint, Demon sipped, scanning the tables beside them. The nearest held two men, hunched over the table, each with a pint before him. They'd both looked up at the dart game; as Demon turned away, they looked down and resumed their conference.

Meeting Flick's eyes, Demon saw them widen meaningfully. Leaning forward, she hissed, "Listen."

It took a moment to focus his hearing through the din, but once he had, he could hear well enough.

"So which horse and race are we talking about then?" The speaker was a jockey, one Demon had never hired and only knew by distant sight. He doubted the jockey knew him other than by name, but he kept his face averted.

"Hear tell you're down to ride Rowena in the Nell Gwyn Stakes in a couple o'weeks."

The second man's voice, deep and grating, was easy to distinguish beneath the raucous din. Demon lifted his eyes and met Flick's; she nodded, then shifted her attention back to their neighbors.

The jockey took a long pull, then lowered his pot. "Aye—that's right. Where'd you hear? It's not about the course yet."

"Never you mind where I heard—what you should be concentrating on is that because I did hear, you've an opportunity before you."

"Opportunity, is it?" The jockey took another long, slow drink. "How much?"

"Four ponies on delivery."

An eruption of cheers from the dart game had both men looking around. Demon glanced at Flick; eyes wide, she was watching their man—the contact. Under the table, he nudged her boot. She looked at him; he leaned forward. "If you don't stop staring, he'll notice and stare back."

She narrowed her eyes at him, then lowered her gaze to her ale—still untouched. There was another roar from the dart game; everyone looked— even Flick. Swiftly, Demon switched their glasses, leaving his half-full pot for her to nurse. Lifting hers, he drained half; the brew at the Fox and Hen left a lot to be desired, but sitting in a snug amid this sort of crowd nursing a full pot for more than five minutes was enough to invite unwanted attention.

The dart game had concluded. The cheers died and everyone returned to their drinks and conversations.

The jockey looked into his pot as if seeking guidance. "Five ponies."

"Five?" The contact jeered. "You're a mite full of yourself, me lad."

The jockey's expression hardened. "Five. I'm the one on Rowena's back that race, and she'll start it prime favorite. The bets'll be heavy—real heavy. If you want her out of the winner's circle, it'll cost you five."

"Hmm." It was the contact's turn to seek inspiration from his ale. "Five? If you want five, you'll need to keep her out of the places altogether."

"Nah." The jockey shook his head. "Can't do it. If she finishes outside the places, the stewards'll be on my tail, and a whole monkey wouldn't be worth that. I ain't about to blow my license for you. Even bringing her in second ... well, I can do it, but only because Cynster's got a prime filly in the race. Rowena's better, but I can slot her behind the Cynster filly and it'll look all right. But unless there's another runner we ain't seen yet, they're the only possible winners. No way I can drop Rowena out of the places."

The contact frowned, then drained his pot. "All right." He looked the jockey in the eye. "Five ponies for a no win—is it a deal?"

The jockey hesitated, then nodded. "Deal."

"*Aaargh!!*" A bellowed war cry erupted through the noise. Everyone turned to see a furious brute break a jug over his neighbor's head. The jug shattered, the victim slumped. A fist swung out of nowhere, and lifted the assailant from his feet.

And it was on.

Everyone leapt to their feet; chairs crashed, pots went flying. Bodies ricochetted off each other; some thudded on the floor. The melee expanded by the second as more and more patrons launched themselves into the fray.

Demon swung back. Flick, eyes huge, was on her feet in the corner. With an oath, he swept the pots from their table and set it on its side. Reaching across, he grabbed her shoulder. "Get down!"

He forced her down behind the makeshift barricade. One hand on her cap, he pushed her fully down. "Stay there!"

The instant he removed his hand, her head popped up. He swore and reached for her; her already-wide eyes dilated.

He swung around just in time to weave back from a hefty fist. It grazed his jaw—and ignited his temper. Regaining his balance, he plowed a fist into his assailant's gut, then followed with a solid right to the jaw.

The huge walloper teetered sideways, then back, then crashed onto his back amid the ongoing brawl.

"Demon!"

Ducking, he threw his next attacker, managing to shift his feet enough so the bruiser landed against the wall beyond Flick, rather than on top of her.

A jarvey staggered free of the central melee and swung his way. The man met his eyes and stopped, swaying on his feet, then turned and charged back into the heaving mass of bodies and flailing fists.

"Stop it, yer mongrels!" The barman jumped up on the counter, laying about him with a besom. To no avail. The brawlers were well away, enjoying themselves hugely.

Demon looked around. The only door from the snug was diagonally across from their corner, beyond the heaving mass of the fight. The wall to their left hosted two grimy sash windows; thrusting aside tables and chairs, he reached the nearest, forced the catch free, then heaved. After an initial resistance, the sash flew up.

Turning back, he grabbed Flick by the collar, unceremoniously dragged her from her hiding place, then manhandled her out of the window. She tried to climb daintily out; he grabbed her and pushed. She hissed and batted at his hands—he kept grabbing and pushing. She hesitated halfway out, deciding which foot to place where; he slapped a hand beneath her bottom and shoved.

She landed in an inelegant sprawl on the grass.

Flick dragged in a breath; curses burned her tongue, but she didn't have breath enough to utter them. Her bottom burned, too; her cheeks were aflame. Both sets. She glanced back. Demon was halfway through the window. Swearing weakly, she scrambled to her feet, dusting her hands on her thighs— she didn't dare touch her posterior.

The other sash window flew up, and more patrons piled out. Demon appeared beside her; grabbing her elbow, he shoved her away from the inn as others started using their escape route. An orchard rolled down an incline away from the inn—with Demon at her heels, Flick slipped between the trees. The twilight was deepening. Behind them, through the now open windows, they heard shouts, then the piercing whistles of the Watch. Glancing back,

Flick saw more of the inn's customers scrambling through the windows, hurrying to disappear down the orchard's slope.

"Come on!" Demon grabbed her hand, taking the lead, lengthening his stride so she had to scurry to keep up. She tried to wriggle her hand free; he flung her a scowl, tightened his grip, and strode on even faster. She cursed; he must have heard but gave no sign. He dragged her, skipping, half-running, to the end of the orchard, to where a seven-foot wall blocked their way.

He released her as others joined them and immediately started climbing the wall. Flick eyed the wall, then edged closer to Demon. "Is there a gate anywhere?"

He glanced at her, then nodded to the others scrambling up and over. "Doesn't look like it." He hesitated, then stepped to the wall. "Come on—I'll give you a leg up."

Bracing one shoulder against the wall, he formed a cup with his hands. Balancing one hand on the stones, the other on his shoulder, Flick placed her boot in his hands.

He pushed her up. It should have been easy; The Flynn's back was nearly as high as the wall. But the top of the wall was hard and narrow, not smooth and slippery like a saddle. She managed to get half over, with the wall digging into her middle, but her legs still dangled down.

Blowing out a breath, she braced her arms, straightened her spine, and searched with her boots for purchase. But with her hips on the wrong side of the wall, if she straightened too much, she risked falling back down. And if she didn't straighten enough, she couldn't reach any toehold. She teetered, like a seesaw, on the top of the wall.

From beneath her came a long-suffering sigh.

Demon's hand connected with her bottom again. He hefted her up; in the most flustered flurry of her life, cheeks all flaming again, she quickly swung one leg over the wall and sat.

And tried to catch her breath.

He grabbed the wall beside her and hauled himself up. Easily. Astride the wall, he raked her with a glance, then swung his leg over and dropped into the lane.

Flick dragged in a breath and swung her other leg over, then wriggled around and dropped down—before he felt compelled to help her again. She picked herself up and dusted her hands, aware to her toes of the assessing gaze that passed over her. Lifting her head, she met his eyes, ready to be belligerent.

He merely humphed and gestured down the lane.

She fell in beside him, and they strolled to the road. There were too many others about to risk any discussion. When they reached the road, Demon nudged her elbow and nodded up a lane leading to the High Street. "I left my curricle at the Jockey Club."

They changed direction, leaving the others behind.

"You were supposed to send word to me the instant you learned anything."

The words, deathly soft, lethally restrained, floated down to her.

"I would have," she hissed back, "once I had a chance. But who could I send from your stable? Carruthers?"

"Next time, if there's no one to send, bring the message yourself."

"And miss the chance of learning more—like today?"

"Ah, yes. Today. And just how do you imagine you would have survived if I hadn't arrived?"

She studied the small houses lining the road.

"Hmm, let's see."

His purr sank deeper, sliding beneath her skin. Flick resisted an urge to wriggle.

"First we have the question of whether, quite aside from the brawl, you would have escaped notice, given you'd bought a pint and couldn't drink it. Your disguise would have disintegrated rather quickly, revealing to all the fact that the General's ward, Miss Felicity Parteger, was slumming in the Newmarket stews dressed as a lad."

"It was an inn, not a stew."

"For a lady found in it, the difference is academic."

Flick humphed.

"And what might have happened if you'd survived the brawl, with or without being knocked senseless, and landed in the arms of the Watch? One can only wonder what they would have made of you."

"We'll never know," Flick hissed. "The important thing is that we've identified Dillon's contact. Did you see which way he went?"

"No."

She halted. "Perhaps we should go back—"

Demon didn't stop; he reached back, grabbed her arm, and hauled her forward so she marched beside him. "You are not following anyone anywhere." The look he shot her, even muted by the gloom, still stung. "In case it's escaped your notice, following a man like that to his customary haunts is liable to be dangerous for a gentlewoman."

His clipped accents gave the words a definite edge. As they swung into the High Street, Flick put her nose in the air. "You got a good look at him and so did I. We should be able to find him easily, then find out who he works for, and clear up this whole mess. It's our first real discovery."

After a moment, he sighed. "Yes, you're right. But leave the next step to me—or rather Gillies. I'll have him go through the inns and taverns—our man must be putting up at one of them."

Demon looked up as they crossed the High Street; the Jockey Club stood before them. His horses were tied to a tree under the porter's watchful eye. "Get in. I'll drive you back to the stable."

Flick strolled to the curricle and climbed up. Demon went to speak to the porter, then returned, untied the reins, and stepped up to the box seat. He backed the horses, then set them trotting with an expert flick of his wrist.

As they headed down the High Street, Flick tilted her chin. "You'll tell me the instant Gillies discovers anything?"

Demon reached for his whip. The black thong flew out and tickled his leader's ears. The bays stepped out, power in every stride. The curricle shot forward.

Flick grabbed the rail and stifled a curse.

The whip hissed back up the handle, and the carriage rocketed along.

Demon drove back to the stable without uttering a word.

CHAPTER
Five

৪৩ ৩৪

After dinner that evening, Demon retired to the front parlor of his farmhouse to consider the ramifications of all they'd learned. Frowning, he paced before the fireplace, where a small blaze cheerily danced.

His thoughts were not cheery.

He was deeply mired in them when a tap sounded on the curtained window. Dismissing it as an insect or misguided sparrow, he didn't pause, didn't rouse from his reverie.

The tapping came again, this time more insistent.

Demon halted. Raising his head, he stared at the window, then swore and strode across the room. Jerking the curtains aside, he looked down on the face that haunted his dreams. "Dammit—what the *devil* are you doing *here*?"

Flick glared, then mouthed, "Let me in!" and gestured with her hands for him to lift the sash.

He hesitated, then, muttering a string of epithets, opened the catch and flung up the sash.

He was presented with a gloved hand. "Help me in."

Against his better judgment, he did. She was dressed in breeches—not her stable lad attire but a pair of what looked to be Dillon's cast-off inexpressibles, which fitted her far too well for his equanimity. Flick clambered over the sill and into the room. Releasing her hand, he lowered the sash and redrew the curtains. "For God's sake, keep your voice down. Heaven only knows what Mrs. Shephard will think if she hears you—"

"She won't." With a dismissive wave, Flick stepped to the settee and sank down on one arm. "She and Shephard are in the kitchen—I checked."

Demon stared at her—she stared ingenuously back. Deliberately, he thrust both hands into his trouser pockets—against the temptation to lay them on her. "Do you often flit through the twilight dressed like that?"

"Of course not. But I didn't know whether I'd be able to reach you without knocking on the door. Luckily, I saw your shadow on the curtains."

Demon clamped his lips shut. There was no point expostulating that her calmly knocking on his front door and asking his housekeeper, a matronly woman with sharp eyes, to show her into his parlor would have been unwise; she would only argue. Swinging on his heel, he strode back across the room; in the circumstances, the least he should do was put some real distance between them.

Regaining the fireplace, he turned to face her, propping his shoulders against the mantel. "And to what do I owe the pleasure of this visit?"

Her eyes narrowed slightly. "I came to discuss the situation, of course."

He raised one brow. "The situation?"

Flick held his gaze for a moment, then looked down and, with patent determination, removed her gloves. "It seems to me that what we learned today raises a number of issues." Laying the gloves on one thigh, she raised her hands and ticked each point off on her fingers. "First and foremost, if another race is to be fixed, should we warn the authorities? However"—she proceeded to her next finger—"there's the consideration that if we tell the stewards, they may alert the contact and he'll simply disappear, along with all connection to the syndicate. If that happens, we'll lose any chance of redeeming Dillon. Even worse"—she moved to her next finger—"if we inform the stewards and they question that man, it sounds, from what Dillon said, that he'll simply implicate him, and very likely cast him as the instigator of the scheme, thus protecting the syndicate from exposure."

Lifting her head, she looked across the room at the long, lean figure lounging, all brooding elegance, against the mantel. If she'd harbored any doubts that he intended to curtail her involvement in their investigations, his present attitude dispelled them; resistance poured from him in waves. His eyes, his attention, were fixed on her, but he showed no inclination to respond. She tilted her chin. "So, are we going to inform the authorities?"

He continued to study her intently, unwaveringly, but he said nothing. Lips thinning, she raised a brow. "Well?"

"I haven't yet decided."

"Hmm." She ignored his clipped, definitely pointed tone. "That man offered the jockey one hundred and twenty-five pounds—a small fortune for a race jockey. It seems unlikely the jockey will change his mind."

He humphed; she took it as agreement.

"Which means your horse is almost certain to win." Eyes wide, she met his gaze. "That places you in a rather awkward position, doesn't it?"

He straightened; before he could speak she went on. "It's a horrible fix—with Dillon to rescue on the one hand, and your responsibilities to the Jockey Club on the other. I suppose it's a clash between loyalty and honor." In the same even tone, she asked, "Which will you choose?"

Hands sunk in his pockets, he stared at her, then looked down and paced before the fire. "I don't know." He shot her a glance, one dark with irritation. "I was considering the matter when you came through the window."

His look was lightened by a hint of curiosity; she grinned. "I came to help." She ignored his derisive snort. "We need to weigh things up—consider our options."

"I can't see any options." He continued to pace, his gaze on the floor. "That one of my horses is involved is irrelevant—it simply makes things worse. Having learned of an attempt to fix a race, my duty as a member of the Jockey Club is clear. I should inform the Committee."

"How absolute is that duty?"

The glance he sent her was hard. "As absolute as such things can be. I could not, in all honor, let a fixed race run."

"Hmm. I agree it's impossible to let a fixed race *run*—that's quite out of the question. But ..." She let her words trail away, her gaze, questioning, fixed on Demon.

He halted, and looked her way. Then he raised a brow. "But can I—" He broke off, his gaze on her, then briefly inclined his head. "Can *we* legitimately withhold the information until closer to the race, to give ourselves time to follow this contact back to the syndicate?"

"Exactly. That race is next month—more than a couple of weeks away. And the stewards could stop it even if we told them just before the start."

"Not quite, but if we hold back the information until the week before the race, it would leave us five weeks in which to trace the syndicate."

"Five weeks? That's plenty of time."

Demon suppressed a cynical humph. Flick's face was triumphantly aglow; although it was partly at his expense, he had no wish to dim it. When she'd come through the window, he'd been thinking solely in the singular; he was now talking in the plural. Which was what she'd intended; *that* was why she'd come.

Now she sat, perched victorious on the arm of his settee, one boot swinging, a satisfied smile in her eyes. Her understanding of the honor and responsibilities involved in his position intrigued him. She understood racing, the fraternity and its traditions—not something he'd encountered in a woman before.

But discussing such matters with a sweet innocent felt odd. Especially late in the evening, in his front parlor.

Entirely unchaperoned.

He resumed his pacing—this time, in her direction.

"*So*"—she almost bobbed in her eagerness—"how do we find the man we saw this evening? Shouldn't we be trying to locate him?"

He halted beside her, his gaze on her face. "*We* are. At this instant, three of my men are rolling around the town, searching the inns and taverns."

She beamed at him. "Excellent! And then?"

"And then ..." He reached for her hand; she surrendered it readily. Smoothly, he drew her to her feet. "Then we follow him"—holding her gaze, he lowered his voice to a deep purr—"until we learn all we need to know."

Trapped in his gaze, her hand in his, eyes widening, she mouthed an "Oh."

He smiled intently. Wrapping his fingers about her hand, he waited, just a heartbeat, until she trembled.

"We'll find the contact and follow him." His lids veiling his eyes, he lowered his gaze to her lips, soft, sheening, succulent pink. "Until he leads us to the syndicate—and then we'll tell the stewards all *they* need to know."

When he spoke of "we" he didn't mean her—but he'd tell her that tomorrow; no need to mar the night.

Raising his lids, he recaptured her gaze, marvelling at the softness of her clear blue eyes. The two of them stood, handfast, gazes locked, mere inches distant, with her trapped between the settee and him. Without conscious thought, he shifted his fingers, brushing the backs of hers.

Her eyes widened even more; her lips parted slightly. Her breath hitched—

Then she blinked, and narrowed her eyes. Frowning, she tugged her hand free. "I'll leave you now."

Blinking himself, he released her.

She stepped sideways, heading for the window.

He followed. Close.

She glanced back and up at his face, eyes very wide, her breathing too rapid. "I dare say I'll see you tomorrow at the stables."

"You will."

With fluttering hands, she pushed at the curtains. He reached over her head and drew them wide.

She tugged at the sash. To no avail.

He stepped behind her and reached for the handles, one on either of the pane's lower frame.

Trapping her between his arms, between the window and him. His fingers brushed hers, clasped about the handles. She sucked in a breath and snatched her hands away. Then froze as she realized he surrounded her.

Slowly, he raised the sash—all the way up.

As he straightened, she straightened, too. Her spine stiff, she turned her head and looked him in the eye. "I'll bid you a good night."

There was ice and frost in her words. Turning to the window, she sat on the sill; behind her, Demon smiled, slowly, intently.

She swung her legs over and slipped into the darkness. "Good-bye."

Her voice floated back to him; in seconds, she'd become a shadow among many, and then she was gone.

Demon's smile deepened, his lips curving as triumphantly as hers had. She wasn't averse to him—the signs had been there, clear for him to read. He didn't know why she'd pulled back, why she'd shaken free of his hold, but it would be easy to draw her back to him.

And then . . .

He stood at the window for a full five minutes, a smile of anticipation on his lips, staring into the night and dreaming—before reality struck.

Like a bolt.

It transfixed him. Chilled him.

It effectively doused his fire.

Face hardening, he stood in the middle of his parlor and wondered what the hell had got into him.

He rose before dawn and headed for the racecourse, for his stables and Carruthers, who was not at all pleased to learn that he'd lost the services of the best work rider he'd ever employed. For once declining to remain and watch his string exercise, Demon left Carruthers grumbling and set his horses ambling back down the road to his farm. The same road led to the cottage.

Fine mist wreathed the hedgerows and blanketed the meadows; it turned golden as dawn tinged the sky. Flick appeared through the gilded haze, a sleepy stable lad atop the plodding cob, heading in for the start of a new day. Demon reined in his bays and waited for her to reach him.

By the time she halted the cob beside his curricle, she was frowning; deep suspicion glowed in her eyes. He nodded, ineffably polite. "I've tendered your resignation to Carruthers—he doesn't expect to see you again."

Her frown deepened; to her credit, she didn't ask why. "But—"

"The matter's simple. If you hadn't resigned, I would have had to dismiss you." He trapped her gaze and raised a brow. "I thought you'd prefer to resign."

Flick studied his eyes, his face. "Put like that, I don't have much choice."

The ends of his lips lifted fractionally. "None."

"What story did you tell Carruthers?"

"That your ailing mother slipped away, and you'll be joining your aunt's household in London."

"So I'm not even supposed to be in the vicinity?"

"Precisely."

She humphed, but without much heat; they'd found Dillon's contact—she was already thinking ahead. "What about identifying the contact? Have your men turned up anything?"

Because she was watching closely, she saw his hesitation—the swift weighing of his options.

"We've located him, yes." His gaze swept her consideringly. "Gillies is currently doing the honors, with strict instructions to miss nothing. If you'd consent to get properly dressed, perhaps we might confer in more conventional style?"

She raised her brows in question.

His smile—a teasing, alluring temptation to dalliance—flashed. "Go home and change. I'll call at eleven and take you for a tool about the lanes."

"Perfect—we can discuss how best to go on without any risk of being overheard." Flick turned the cob and urged him back toward the cottage. "I'll be ready at eleven."

Her voice floated back to Demon. The reins lax in his hands, he sat in the strengthening sunshine, watching her bob away from him. His smile deepening, he flicked the reins and set his curricle slowly rolling in her wake.

As promised, she was ready and waiting, a vision in mull muslin, a parasol shading her complexion, when he drew his horses to a scrunching halt before the front steps of Hillgate End.

Tying off his reins, he stepped down from the curricle. Face alight, a soft smile on her lips, she eagerly approached. She was too slender to bustle—her movement was more a sweeping glide. Demon watched her advance, his every faculty riveted, effortlessly held in thrall.

Luckily, she didn't know it—she had no idea. Secure in that knowledge, he returned her smile. Taking her hand, he bowed elegantly and handed her up to the box seat. She shuffled across; as he turned to follow, Demon caught sight of a maid hovering by the steps. "I'll return Miss Parteger later in the afternoon—you might mention that to Jacobs."

"Yes, sir." The maid bobbed a curtsy.

Climbing up, he took his seat and met Flick's questioning glance. "Mrs. Shephard packed a hamper so we won't need to return for lunch."

Her eyes widened, then she nodded. "It's turning into a lovely day—a picnic is a very good idea."

Clicking the reins, Demon set the bays pacing, omitting to mention just whose idea it had been.

As he turned out of the drive and the horses stepped out, Flick angled her parasol and glanced at him. "I take it your men located our quarry?"

Demon nodded, taking the turn to Dullingham in style. "He's staying at the Ox and Plough."

"The Ox and Plough?" Flick frowned. "I don't think I know it."

"There's no reason you would. It's a seedy little inn off the main road north of Newmarket."

"Did your man learn the contact's name?"

"He goes by the unenviable name of Bletchley."

"And he's a Londoner?"

"From his accent, that much seems certain." Demon slowed his horses as the hamlet of Dullingham came into view. "Gillies is prepared to swear an oath that Bletchley was born within hearing of Bow bells."

"Which suggests," Flick said, turning impulsively to him, "that the syndicate is London-based."

"That was always on the cards. The most likely base for a group of rich and greedy gentlemen is London, after all."

"Hmm."

When Flick ventured nothing more, Demon glanced at her. She was frowning absentmindedly, her gaze unseeing. It wasn't hard to follow her thoughts. She was considering the syndicate, and the possible need to journey to London to unmask them.

He left her undisturbed, content with her abstraction. As the cottages of Dullingham fell behind, he kept the bays to a steady trot, searching the hedges lining the roadway for the small lane he remembered from years gone by. It appeared on his left; he slowed and turned the bays.

The lane was deeply rutted; despite the strong springs of the carriage, the rocking jerked Flick to attention. Grabbing the front rail, she blinked and looked around. "Good heavens. Where—*oh*! How lovely!"

Demon smiled. "It is a pretty spot."

The lane dwindled to a track; turning the bays onto a stretch of grass, he reined in. "We'll leave the carriage here." He nodded to where willows, lit by the sun, hung catkin-draped limbs over a rippling stream. The babble of the brook filled the rustic stillness; sunlight flashed off the water, shooting rainbows through the air. Between the willows, an expanse of lush grass beckoned. "We can spread the rug by the stream and enjoy the sunshine."

"Oh, yes! I didn't even know this place existed."

Alighting, he handed Flick down, then retrieved the well-stocked luncheon basket and a large plaid rug from the boot. Flick relieved him of the rug; holding it in her arms, she strolled beside him to the grassy bank.

Laying aside her parasol, Flick shook out the rug. Demon helped her spread the heavy folds, then handed her onto it. He waited while she settled, then subsided to lounge, large, lean—all elegantly indolent—beside her.

She had overheard maids exclaiming how their beaux made their hearts go pitter-patter. She'd always thought the description a silly nonsense.

Now she knew better. Her heart was tripping in double time. Definitely pitter-patter.

Reaching for the basket Demon had set by their legs, she hauled it closer. More definitely between them. It was a ridiculous reaction—she knew she was safe with him—but the solidity of the basket made her feel much better. Pulling out the linen napkins Mrs. Shephard had tucked about the food, she uncovered roast chicken, slices of beef, and crisp, fresh rolls. She went to speak, and had to clear her throat. "Would you prefer a leg, or a breast?"

She looked up; her eyes clashed with Demon's, burning blue.

Burning?

She blinked and looked again, but he'd looked away, calmly reaching for the bottle poking out from the basket.

"A leg will do for the moment."

His voice sounded slightly ... strained. Hiding a frown, she watched as he eased the cork from the bottle. It popped free and he looked up, but there was nothing to be read in his eyes or his expression beyond an easy pleasure in the moment. He held out a hand for glasses; pushing aside her uncertainties, she delved into the basket.

Discovering two long flutes, she handed them over; the wine hissed as he filled them. She took the one he offered her, studying the tiny bubbles rising through the straw-colored liquid. "Champagne?"

"Hmm." Raising his glass to her, Demon took a sip. "A suitable toast to Spring."

Flick sipped; the bubbles fizzed on her palate, but the wine slid down her throat very pleasantly. She licked her lips. "Nice."

"Hmm." Demon forced himself to look away from her lips—sheening pink curves that he ached to taste. Inwardly frowning at how definite that ache was, he accepted the chicken leg she handed him, a napkin neatly folded about the bone.

Their fingers brushed; he felt hers quiver—was conscious to his bones of the shivery tremble that raced through her. Focusing on the chicken, he sank his teeth into it, then fixed his gaze on the meadows beyond the stream while she busied herself—calmed herself—laying out their repast. Only when she drew in a breath, took a sip of champagne, then fell to eating, did he glance at her again. "How's Dillon faring?"

She shrugged. "Well enough." After a moment, she volunteered, "I haven't really spoken to him since that evening we learned the truth."

Demon looked back at the stream to hide his satisfaction; he was delighted to hear that her break with Dillon had not yet healed. "Who else knows he's there?" He looked at Flick and frowned. "How does he get food?"

She'd finished her chicken; he watched as she licked her fingers, her wet pink tongue sliding up and around—then she licked her lips. And looked at him.

He managed not to tremble—not to react at all.

"The only one other than us who knows Dillon's at the cottage is Jiggs. He's a footman—he's been at Hillgate End for ... oh, ten years at least. Jiggs takes Dillon food every second day. He told me there's always leftover roast or a pie left wrapped in the larder." She wrinkled her nose.

"I'm quite sure Foggy also knows Dillon's somewhere close."

"Very likely."

They ate and sipped in silence, the tinkling of the brook and the chirp of insects a spring symphony about them. Replete, Demon dusted his hands, then stretched full length on the rug. Folding his arms behind his head, he closed his eyes. "Have you told Dillon anything of our discoveries?"

"I haven't told him anything at all."

From under his lashes, he watched Flick gather up crumbs, then start to repack the basket.

"I decided it wouldn't be wise to tell him we'd found his contact, in case he took it into his head to do something rash—like go into town to see the man himself. It wouldn't do for him to be recognized and taken up for questioning, just when we're making progress."

Demon suppressed a cynical snort. Dillon was no hothead; he was lazy and indolent. Flick was the one who, with eyes wide open, would rush in where wiser souls feared to tread, supremely confident in her ability to pull things off—to make things happen. To unmask the syndicate.

Loyalty, devotion—and good bottom. Her hallmarks.

The thought slid through his brain and captured his attention. Focused it fully on his angel in disguise.

Lifting his lids a fraction more, he studied her; at the moment, she was all angel—a creation from one of his recent dreams. The sunshine turned her hair to blazing glory, framing her face in golden flames. Her cheeks were delicately flushed—from the warmth of the day and the champagne. As she scanned the meadows, her eyes, soft blue, large and wide, were alive with innocent intelligence.

His gaze dropped—to the slender column of her throat, to the firm swells that filled the bodice of her demure gown, rendering it anything but demure. The fall of her dress hid her waist, the folds swathed her hips and thighs, but having seen her so often in breeches, he didn't need the evidence to conjure the vision.

His smile deepening, he let his lids fall, and he relaxed on the rug. He waited until the basket was neatly repacked and, with her arms wrapped around her knees, her half-filled glass in one hand, she settled to enjoy the view.

"It occurs to me," he murmured, "that now we've identified Bletchley and will be following him in earnest, and you no longer need to change clothes and horses morning and afternoon, it would be wise not to go to the cottage at all—just in case Bletchley, or one of his friends, turns the tables on us and follows us back to Dillon. As it's central to our plan to keep Dillon safely hidden, the last thing we want is to lead the syndicate to him."

"Indeed not." Flick considered. "I'll send a message with Jiggs." Staring at the stream, she narrowed her eyes. "I'll say that there's no longer any point in me working at the stables—that we think someone from the syndicate is about and don't want to compromise his safety." She nodded. "That should keep him at the cottage."

Sipping her champagne, Flick abandoned all thoughts of Dillon. Dillon was safe at the cottage, and there he could remain until she and Demon had resolved the imbroglio he had mired them all in. On such a lovely afternoon, she refused to dwell on Dillon. A sense of pleasurable ease held her. A curious warmth, like the glow from a distant fire, enveloped her. It wasn't the breeze, for her curls didn't dance, and it wasn't the sun, for it didn't affect all of her at once. Instead, it washed like a warm wave over her, leaving her relaxed, oddly expectant.

In expectation of what she had no idea.

The fact didn't worry her—with Demon, so large, so physically powerful beside her, nothing on earth could threaten her.

The moment was perfect, serene—and strangely intriguing.

There was something in the air—she sensed it with every pore. Which was odd, for she was hardly a fanciful chit. She was, however, abidingly curious— in this case, abidingly interested. Whatever it was that hung in the air, shimmering like a fairy's spell in the bright sunshine, almost of this world but not quite substantial enough for mortal eyes to see—whatever that was, she wanted to know it, understand it.

Whatever it was, she was experiencing it now.

The buzz of the bees, the murmur of the stream, and that undefined, exciting something held her in silent thrall.

Demon slowly sat up and reached for the basket. She turned to see him draw out the almost empty bottle. He refilled his glass, then glanced at hers, almost empty. He looked at her face, briefly searching her eyes, then reached over and tipped the last of the wine into her flute.

It fizzed; she smiled and took a sip.

The bubbles got up her nose.

She sneezed. He looked up; she waved his concern aside. She took another, more careful sip as he returned the bottle to the basket, leaving it by the side of the rug. That done, he lay back again, this time propping on one elbow, his glass in his other hand.

"So," she asked, shuffling to face him, "how are we going to follow Bletchley?"

His gaze on the stream, Demon fortified himself with a long sip of champagne, then turned his head and met her gaze, studiously ignoring the expanse of ivory skin, the warm swells promising all manner of earthly delights, now mere inches from his face. "It's not a hard task. I've got Gillies and two stablemen rotating the watch. It's a small town—now we know what he looks like, and where he's staying, keeping an eye on him shouldn't overtax us."

"But—" Flick frowned at a nearby willow. "If we don't learn something soon, won't he notice? Seeing a particular stableman forever about will surely make him suspicious. Newmarket stablemen don't have nothing to do."

A warm flush swept her shoulders, her breasts. She looked at Demon; he was looking into his glass, his lids veiling his eyes.

Then he looked at the stream. "You needn't worry. He'll presumably be at the Heath during morning and afternoon stables—I'll watch him there and in the High Street." He drained his glass. "Gillies and the stablemen will watch him in the inns and taverns—they won't be so identifiable in a crowd."

"Hmm. Perhaps." Flick stretched her stockinged feet to the sun. "I'll help, too. About the tracks and in the High Street." She met Demon's gaze as he looked up at her. "He won't suspect a young lady of watching him."

He stared at her for a moment, as if he'd lost the thread of the conversation, then he murmured, "Very likely not." His gaze grew intent; he lifted one hand. "Hold still."

She froze so completely that she stopped breathing. A vise clamped about her lungs; her heart stuttered, skipped, then raced. She held quiveringly still as his fingers slid through the curls above one ear, ruffling the locks as he disengaged . . . something. When he withdrew his hand and showed her a long leaf, flicking it onto the grass, she dragged in a breath and smiled weakly. "Thank you."

His eyes met hers. "My pleasure."

The words were deep, rumbling; the tone set something inside her vibrating. Her gaze trapped in his, she felt flustered panic rise. She looked down and gulped a mouthful of champagne.

The bubbles hit her again; this time, she nearly choked. Eyes watering, she waved a hand before her face and hauled in a much-needed breath. "I'm really not used to this." She lifted her glass. "This is all new to me."

Demon's gaze had remained steady, his eyes on hers. His lips lifted lightly. "Yes, I know."

Flick felt curiously warm, distinctly light-headed. There was a light in Demon's eyes, an understanding she couldn't fathom.

Demon saw confusion grow in her eyes—he looked away, uncertain of how much of his interest, his curious, newfound obsession with innocence, showed in his. He gestured to the sylvan scene before them and looked at her, his expression easy, controlled. "If you haven't been here before, you couldn't have strolled the path by the stream. Shall we?"

"Oh, yes! Let's."

He retrieved her almost empty glass, drained it, then set both glasses back in the basket. Then he rose and held out his hands to her. "Come. We'll investigate."

She gave him her hands; he drew her to her feet, then led her to where a beaten path followed the meandering stream. They strolled along; she ambled beside him, sometimes ahead of him, furling her parasol when it limited her view of his face. Demon was grateful—the parasol had prevented him from watching her—any of her. They saw a mother duck with a gaggle of tiny ducklings, all paddling furiously in her wake; Flick pointed and exclaimed, and smiled delightedly. A sleek trout broke the rippling surface, chasing a fat fly; a kingfisher swooped out of the shade, dazzling them with his brilliant plumage. Flick grabbed his arm in her excitement, then sighed as the bird flew on down the stream.

"There's a bronze dragonfly."

"Where?" She searched the banks.

"Over there." He leaned close; she leaned closer still, following his pointing finger to where the dragonfly hovered above a patch of reeds. Engrossed, she drew in a breath and held it; he did the same.

The scent of her washed through him, sweet, fresh—quite unlike the cloying perfumes to which he was accustomed, to which he was immune. Her fragrance was light, airy; it reminded him of lavender and appleblossom, the essence of spring.

"Ah." The dragonfly darted away, and she exhaled.

His head swam.

She turned to him; they were so close that her skirts brushed his boots. If she took another deep breath, her breasts would touch his coat. His nearness surprised her; she looked up, eyes widening, lips parting on a silent gasp as her breath seized. Her eyes met his—for one fleeting instant, pure awareness invested the soft blue. Then puzzlement seeped in.

He saw it, but had too much to do holding his own desires in check to attempt a distraction. For the last hours, he'd delighted in her—in her innocence, in the fragile beauty of a female untouched, unawakened. He'd seen, sensed, her first glimmerings of consciousness—of him, of herself, of their inherent sensuality.

Sensuality was a quality he'd lived with daily for ten years and more; experiencing it anew, through her innocent eyes, had heightened his own far-from-innocent desires.

Her eyes held his; about them, the pulse of burgeoning spring hummed and throbbed. He felt it in his bones, in his blood. In his loins.

She felt it, too, but she didn't know what it meant. When he said nothing, she relaxed, just a little, and smiled, tentatively yet without the slightest fear. "Perhaps we'd better head back."

He held her gaze for an instant, then forced himself to nod. "Perhaps we had."

His voice had deepened; she threw him another, slightly questioning look. Ignoring it, he took her hand and turned her back along the path.

By the time they regained the swath of green, Flick's puzzlement had grown. Absentmindedly, she helped him fold the rug, then, picking up her parasol, followed him to the curricle.

After stowing the basket and rug, he returned to where she waited by the curricle's side, her frowning gaze fixed on the grass where they'd lain. She looked up as he halted beside her. She said nothing, but her frown was etched in her eyes. He saw it, and read her unvoiced questions with ease.

He had a very good idea what she was feeling—the disconcerting uncertainty, the nervous confusion. She was so open, so trusting, that she thought nothing of showing her vulnerability to him. He knew all the questions crowding her mind—the questions she couldn't begin to formulate.

He knew the answers, too.

She waited, her eyes on his, clearly hoping for some hint as to what it was she sensed. Her stance was both a demand and a plea—a clear wish to know.

Her face was tilted up to him; her tapered chin was firm. Her full lips, tinted delicate rose, beckoned. The soft blue of her eyes, clouded by the first flush of desire, promised heaven and more.

If he'd stopped to think, he would never have risked it, but the web of her innocence held him, compelled him—assured him this was simple, straightforward, uncomplicated.

His eyes locked with hers, he slowly lifted one hand and gently framed her jaw. Her breath caught; deliberately, still moving with mesmerizing slowness, he brushed the pad of his thumb along her lower lip. The contact shook her— and him; he instinctively tightened his hold on his demons. Their gazes held, hers unwaveringly curious.

He drew in a shallow breath and slowly lowered his head, giving her plenty of time to balk. Other than tightening her grip on her parasol, she moved not at all. Her gaze dropped to his lips; she sucked in a breath, only to have it tangle in her throat. Her lashes fluttered, then lowered; her eyes shut on a sigh as his lips touched hers.

It was the most delicate kiss he could remember sharing—a communion of lips, nothing more. Hers were soft, as delicate as they looked, intensely feminine. He brushed them once, twice, then covered them, increasing the pressure only slightly, aware to his bones of her youth.

He was about to draw back, to bring the light caress to an end, when her lips moved beneath his—in clear response, artless, untutored. Enthralling.

She kissed him back—gently, tentatively—her question as clear as it had been in her eyes.

Without thought, he responded, the hand framing her jaw tightening, holding her face steady as he shifted closer, angling his head as he deepened the kiss.

Her lips parted under his.

Just a little—just enough for him to taste her. He ran the tip of his tongue over her lower lip, caressing the soft flesh within, then briefly stroked her tongue, teasing her senses, already taut, quiveringly tight.

They quaked; she shuddered delicately, then stepped closer, so her breasts met his chest, her hips his thighs. Completely trusting, she leaned into him, into his strength.

Demon's head reeled; his blood pounded urgently. The need to close his arms about her—to lock her against him and mold her to him—was almost overwhelming.

But she was too young, too innocent, too new to this game for that.

His demons wailed and demanded—with what wit he had left he fought to deny them.

Even while he fell deeper into their kiss.

Unaware of his problem, Flick reveled in the sudden heat that suffused her, in the heady sense of male strength that surrounded her, in the firm touch of his lips on hers, on the sensual slide of his tongue between her lips.

This was a kiss—the sort of kiss she'd heard maids giggling over, a kiss that slowly curled her toes. It was enthralling, demanding yet unfrightening, an experience of the senses.

The vicar's son had once kissed her—or tried to. That had been nothing like this. There had been no magic shimmering in the air, no skittering sensations assailing her nerves. And none of the excitement slowly growing within her, as if this was a beginning, not an end.

The idea intrigued her, but Demon's lips, firm, almost hard, cool yet imparting heat, effortlessly held her attention, denying all her efforts to think. Leaning against him, her only certainty was a feeling of gratitude—that he'd consented to show her what could be, not just in a kiss but in one glorious afternoon of simple pleasure.

The sort of pleasure a man and a woman could share, if the man knew what he was about. She was immensely grateful to him for explaining, for demonstrating, for enlightening her ignorance. Now, in the future, she'd know what to look for—know where to set her standards.

As for today, she'd enjoyed his tutelage, enjoyed the afternoon—and this kiss. Immensely.

Her unrestrained, open appreciation very nearly overwhelmed Demon. Inwardly shaking with the effort of resisting the powerful instincts that had for so long been a part of him, he finally realized his hand had fallen from her face to her shoulder. Raising his other hand, he gripped her upper arm as well and gently eased her back from him. Then, with gentle care and a reluctance he felt to his soul, he drew back and ended the kiss.

He was breathing too fast. He watched as her lids fluttered, then rose to reveal eyes a much brighter blue than before. She met his gaze; he prayed she couldn't read his state. He attempted a suave smile. "So now you know."

She blinked. Before she could speak, he turned her to the curricle. "Come—we should return to Hillgate End."

He drove her back directly. To his surprise, she was patently unflustered, sitting beside him, her parasol open, sweetly smiling at the sunwashed countryside.

If anyone was flustered, it seemed it was he. He still felt disoriented, nerves and muscles twitching. By the time he turned the bays through the gates of Hillgate End, he was inwardly frowning, and feeling a touch grim.

He wasn't at all sure what had happened that afternoon, especially not who or what had instigated the proceedings. He'd certainly organized to spend a comfortable, enjoyable afternoon with an angel, but he couldn't remember deciding to seduce her.

Things had not gone according to any plan of his.

Which was possibly not surprising—in this sphere, he was a rank amateur. He'd never dallied with anyone so young, so untouched—so damned *innocent*—before. Which was at least half his problem—half the reason he was increasingly attracted to her. She was a very fresh taste to his definitely jaded palate; awakening her was a rare pleasure, a sweet delight.

But seducing an innocent carried responsibility—a heavy, unavoidable responsibility he'd happily steered clear of for all his years. He didn't want to change—had no intention of changing. He was happy with his life as it was.

The taste of her—apple and delicate spice—returned to him, and had him stiffening. Swallowing a curse, he drew the bays up before the front steps. He tied off the reins and stepped down; rounding the carriage, he helped her down.

She smoothed her skirts, then straightened and smiled—gloriously, openly, entirely without guile. "Thank you for a delightful afternoon."

He stared at her, conscious to his bones of a demonic urge to taste her again. It took all his concentration to maintain a suitably impassive mien, to take the hand she held out to him, squeeze it gently—and let go.

With a nod, he turned back to the curricle. "I'll keep you informed of anything we learn. Do convey my respects to the General."

"Yes, of course."

She watched him drive away, a smile on her lips; as the shadows of the drive enclosed him, a frown settled on Demon's face.

He was still frowning when he reached home.

CHAPTER
Six

ꙮ

Demon ran Gillies to earth later that evening in the crowded tap of the Swan; he was nursing a pint and keeping a watchful eye on Bletchley. Their quarry was part of a genial group crowding one corner. Demon slid onto the bench beside Gillies. "Any action?"

"Nah. He went back to the Ox and Plough this afternoon, seemingly to check the post. He got a letter. Looked like he was expecting it."

"Did he leave it there?"

Glancing at Bletchley, Gillies shook his head. "He's got it on him, in an inside waistcoat pocket. He's taking no chances of losing it."

Demon sipped his beer. "What did he do after he got it?"

"Perked up, he did, and bustled right out again, back to the Heath for afternoon stables."

Demon nodded. "I saw him there—it looked like he had Robinson's string in his sights."

"Aye—that's my thought, too." Gillies took another long pull from his pint. "Robinson's got at least two favored runners in the Spring Carnival."

"I didn't see Bletchley approach any of the riders."

"Nor did I."

"Did he make contact with any gentlemen?"

"Not that I saw. And I've had him in sight since he came down the stairs this morning."

Demon nodded, Flick's warning in mind. "Stay at the stud tomorrow. Cross can follow Bletchley to morning stables—I'll take over after that."

"Aye." Gillies drained his pint. "It wouldn't do for him to get too familiar with my face."

Over the next three days, together with Cross and Hills, two of his stablemen, Demon and Gillies kept an unwavering watch on Bletchley. With activity on the Heath increasing in preparation for the Craven meeting—the official Spring Carnival of the English racing calendar—there was reason aplenty for Demon to be about the tracks and stables, evaluating his string and those of his major rivals. From atop Ivan the Terrible, keeping Bletchley in view in the relatively flat, open areas surrounding the Heath was easy; increasingly, it was Demon who kept their quarry in sight for most of the day. Gillies, Cross and Hills took turns keeping an unrelenting but unobtrusive watch at all other times, from the instant Bletchley came down for breakfast, to the time he took his candle and climbed the stairs to bed.

Bletchley remained unaware of their surveillance, his obliviousness at least partly due to his concentration on the job in hand. He was careful not to be too overt in approaching the race jockeys, often spending hours simply watching and noting. Looking, Demon suspected, for any hint of a hold, any susceptibility with which to coerce the selected jockeys into doing his masters' bidding.

On the fourth afternoon, Flick caught up with Demon.

Disguising her irritation at the fact that since leaving her before the manor steps, he'd made not the slightest attempt to see her—to tell her what was going on, what he and his men had discovered—she twirled her open parasol and advanced determinedly across the grass between the walking pens, her gaze fixed unwaveringly on him.

She was twenty yards away when he turned his head and looked directly at her. Leaning against the last pen's fence, he'd been scanning the onlookers watching his and two other stables' strings exercise. His back against the top rung, his hands sunk in his breeches pockets, one leg bent, booted foot braced on the fence's lower rung, he looked subtly dangerous.

Flick inwardly humphed and dismissed the thought of danger. She was impatient—she wanted to be doing something, not sitting on her hands waiting to learn what had happened long after it had. But she'd dealt with Dillon and the General long enough to know how to approach a male. It wouldn't do to show impatience or anger. Instead, smiling sunnily, she strolled to Demon's side, ignoring the frown forming in his eyes. "Isn't it a lovely afternoon?"

"Indeed."

The single word was trenchantly noncommittal; his frown darkened, deepening the blue of his eyes. Still smiling sweetly, she turned and scanned the throng. "Where's Bletchley?"

Straightening, Demon watched her check through the onlookers, then inwardly sighed. "Under the oak to the left. He's wearing a scarlet neckerchief."

She located Bletchley and studied him; against his will, Demon studied her. She was gowned once more in sprig muslin, tiny blue fern fronds scattered over white. The gown, however, barely registered; what was in the gown transfixed his attention, captured his awareness.

All soft curves and creamy complexion, she looked good enough to eat— which was the cause of his frown. The instant she appeared, he'd been struck by an urgent, all but ungovernable, ravenous urge. Which had startled him— his urges were not usually so independent, so totally dismissive, of his will.

As he watched, studied, drank in the sight of her, a light breeze playfully ruffled her curls, setting them dancing; it also ruffled her light skirts, briefly, tantalizingly, molding them to her hips, her thighs, her slender legs. Her heart-shaped bottom.

He looked away and shifted, easing the fullness in his groin.

"Has he approached any gentlemen yet? Or they, him?"

Relocating Bletchley, he shook his head. "It appears his task here—presumably the job Dillon was supposed to do—is to make contact with the jockeys and persuade them to his masters' cause." After a moment, he added, "He received a letter some days ago, which spurred him to renewed activity."

"Orders?"

"Presumably. But I seriously doubt he'll report back to his masters in writing."

"He probably can't write." Flick glanced over her shoulder and met his eye. "So there's still a chance the syndicate—at least one of them—will appear here."

"Yes. To learn of Bletchley's success, if nothing else."

"Hmm." She looked at Bletchley. "I'll take over watching him for the rest of the afternoon." She glanced up at him. "I'm sure you've got other matters to attend to."

He captured her gaze. "Be that as it may—"

"As I've already pointed out, he won't expect a young lady to be watching him—it's the perfect disguise."

"He might not guess that you're watching him, but I can guarantee he'll notice if you follow him."

She swung to face him; he saw her chin firm. "Be *that* as it may—"

"No." The single word, uttered quietly and decisively, brought her up short. Eyes narrowing, she glared up at him; he towered, without apology, over her. "There is no reason whatever for you to be involved."

Her eyes, normally so peacefully lucent, spat sparks. "This was *my* undertaking—*I* invited you to *help*. 'Help' does not mean relegating me to the position of mere cipher."

He held her irate gaze. "You are not a mere cipher—"

"Good!" With a terse nod, she swung back to the Heath. "I'll help you watch Bletchley then."

Weaving back to avoid decapitation by her parasol, Demon swore beneath his breath. Falling back half a step, he glared at her back, her hips, the round swells of her bottom, as she stood, stubbornly intransigent, her back to him.

"Flick—"

"Look! He's heading off."

Glancing up, Demon saw Bletchley quit his position by the oak and amble, with a less-than-convincing show of idleness, toward one of the neighboring stables. Glancing at Flick, already on her toes, about to step out in Bletchley's wake, Demon hesitated, then his eyes narrowed and his lips curved. "As you're so determined to help . . ."

Stepping to her right, he caught her hand and set it on his sleeve, anchoring her close—very close—to his side.

Blinking wildly, she looked up. "What do you mean?" Her voice was gratifyingly breathless.

"If you want to help me watch Bletchley, then you'll have to help provide our disguise." He raised his brows at her. "Just keep that parasol to the side, and as far as possible, keep your face turned to me."

"But how am I to watch Bletchley?"

He strolled; she was forced to stroll beside him. A smile of definite intent on his face, he looked down at her. "You don't need to watch him for us to follow him, but we need to see who he's meeting."

One swift glance ahead verified that Bletchley was heading behind the stable, which, from the horses Demon could see on the Heath, would almost certainly be empty. With Flick's not-exactly-willing assistance, he put his mind to creating a tableau of a couple entirely engrossed with each other, of no possible consequence to Bletchley.

Trapped by his gaze, by the hard palm that held her fingers immobile on his sleeve, by the strength, the power, he so effortlessly wielded, Flick struggled to preserve a facade of normalcy, to slow her breathing and steady her heart. To relax her stiff spine and stroll with passable grace—grace enough to match the reprobate beside her.

The glances he shot ahead, tracking Bletchley, were reassuring, confirming that his intent was indeed to follow the villain and witness any meeting behind the stable. His intent *wasn't* to unnerve her, to send her senses into quivering stasis. That was merely an accident, an unexpected, unintended repercussion. Thankfully, he hadn't noticed; she fought to get her wits back in order and her senses realigned.

"Who do you think he's meeting?" she whispered. Her lungs were still not functioning properly.

"I've no idea." He looked down at her, his heavy lids half obscuring his eyes. His voice had sunk to a deep purr. "Just pray it's a member of the syndicate."

His tone and his sleepy expression were disconcerting, of no help at all in reestablishing her equanimity.

Demon looked up. Bletchley had halted at the corner of the stable. As he watched, Bletchley's gaze swept the throng, then fixed on them. Smoothly, unhurriedly, a wolfish smile curving his lips, he looked down, into Flick's wide eyes. "Smile," he instructed. She did, weakly. His own smile deepening, he raised his free hand; with the back of his knuckles he brushed her cheek.

Her breath caught—she skittered back and blushed; effortlessly, his smile very evident, he drew her back.

"I'm only teasing," he murmured. "It's just play."

"I know," Flick assured him, her heart beating frantically. Unfortunately, he was playing a game with which she was unfamiliar. She tried her best to relax, to smile easily, teasingly, back.

From beneath his lashes, Demon glanced ahead; Bletchley was no longer looking their way. After one last scan of the Heath, he turned and lumbered around the building, out of sight.

Flick's eyes widened; she immediately stepped out. He hauled her up short, pulling her to his side. "No." She looked up, ready to glare; he leaned closer—nearer—so the ebb and flow of their interaction looked like a seductive game. "We don't know," he murmured, his lips close by her temple, "who he's meeting and where they are. They might be behind us."

"Oh." Obedient to his pressure on her arm, Flick, a smile on her lips, steeled herself and leaned against him, her shoulder and upper arm nestling into the warmth of his chest. Then, with the same sweet, inane smile, she eased away as they continued to stroll.

After a moment—after she'd caught her breath—she looked up, into his smiling eyes. "What are you planning to do?"

His lips quirked, very definitely teasing. "Join Bletchley and his friend, of course."

They'd reached the corner of the stable; without pause, Demon continued on, not hugging the shadow of the wall as Bletchley had but strolling on and past, into the clear area behind the stable bounded by a railing fence.

As soon as they had cleared the corner, Flick looked ahead. Demon released her elbow, slid his arm about her waist, drew her against him and kissed her.

She nearly dropped her parasol.

"*Don't* look at him—he'll notice." Demon breathed the injunction against her lips, then kissed her, briefly, again.

Wits reeling, she hauled in a breath. "But—"

"No buts. Just follow my lead and we'll be able to hear everything—and see it all, too." Setting her on her feet, shielded by her open parasol, presently pointed, rather waveringly, at Bletchley, his eyes searched hers, then he added, his voice deep and low, "If you won't behave, I'll have to distract you some more."

She stared at him. Then she cleared her throat. "What do you want me to do?"

"Concentrate on me as if you aren't even aware Bletchley and friend exist."

She kept her gaze glued to his face. "Has his friend arrived?" She hadn't been able to see before he'd kissed her.

"Not yet, but I think someone's drifting this way." Righting her parasol, Demon smiled down at her; his hand resting lightly at her waist, he turned her. Gazes locked, they strolled on, apparently aimlessly.

Bletchley had halted midway along the back of the stable, clearly waiting for someone to join him. From the corner of her eye, Flick saw him frown at them. Demon bent his head and blew in her ear; she squirmed and giggled, entirely spontaneously.

Naturally, he did it again.

With no option but to throw herself into their deception, she giggled and wriggled and squirmed. Laughing, Demon caught her more closely to him, then with a flourish, he whirled her, twirled her—they stopped with him leaning against the railing fence, her before him. His eyes glowed wickedly; his smile was distinctly devilish.

Flick caught her breath on a gasp, a perfectly natural, silly smile on her lips. "What next?" she whispered.

Screened from Bletchley by her parasol, Demon looked down into her eyes. "Put your hand on my shoulder, stretch up and kiss me."

She blinked at him; he raised his brows innocently, the expression in his eyes anything but. "You've done it before."

She had, but that had been different. He'd started it. Still ... it hadn't been difficult.

Fleetingly frowning at him, she placed her free hand on his broad shoulder and stretched up on her toes. Even so, he had to lower his head—balanced precariously on the very tips of her toes, she *had* to lean against him, her breasts to his hard chest, to reach his lips with hers.

She kissed him—just a simple, gentle kiss. When she went to draw back, his hands firmed, one spanning her waist, the other closing about her fingers gripping her parasol. He held her steady as his lips closed over hers.

Tilting her and her parasol to just the right angle, Demon held her before him, and, from beneath his lashes, looked out under the parasol's frilled rim. Bletchley, ten yards away, had been slouching, watching them idly—he doubtless considered Demon a reckless blade set on seducing a sweet country miss. But although he watched, Bletchley wasn't interested. Then he straightened, alert, as another man joined him.

Breaking off the kiss, Demon breathed a curse.

Flick blinked, but he didn't shift, didn't let her down.

"No—don't turn," he hissed as she went to twist her head.

"Who is it?"

His lips, presently at eye level, twisted into a grim grimace. "Another jockey." Disappointment laced his tone.

"Perhaps he has a message from the syndicate."

"Shssh. Listen."

Balanced against him, she strained her ears.

"Let's see if I got this straight."

That had to be the jockey; the voice was clear, not scratchy.

"You'll give me three ponies the day before the Stakes, an' two ponies the day after, if I bring Cyclone in out o' the places. That right?"

"Aye—that's the deal," Bletchley grated. "Take it or leave it."

The jockey was silent, presumably ruminating; Demon looked down at her, then his arm slid further around her, better supporting her against him.

"Relax," he breathed. His lips brushed hers in the lightest of caresses, then the jockey spoke again.

"I'll take it."

"Done."

"That's our cue," Demon said *sotto voce*.

The next instant, he laughed aloud; his arm tightening about her, he swung her around and stood her on her feet. He grinned. "Come along, sweetheart. Wouldn't do for the local gabblemongers to start wondering where we've got to. Let alone what we've been doing."

He spoke loudly enough for Bletchley and the jockey to hear. Flick blushed and ignored their audience completely; locking both hands about her parasol handle, she turned back to the Heath with a swish of her skirts.

With another demonic laugh—one of triumph—Demon, his hand lying proprietorially on her back just a little lower than her waist, ushered her around the stable, back into the safety of the racing throng.

The instant they rounded the corner of the stable, Flick wriggled to dislodge his hand. It only pressed closer.

"We can't drop our roles yet." Demon's murmur stirred the curls above her ear. "Bletchley's following. While he can see us, we'll need to preserve our act."

She shot him a suspicious, distracted look; her bottom was heating.

He smiled, all wolf. "Who knows? An established disguise might come in handy in the following days."

Following *days*? Flick hoped she didn't look as scandalized as she felt; the laughing, teasing look in Demon's eyes suggested otherwise.

To her consternation, Bletchley returned to stand under the oak beside the Heath—and proceeded to watch the exercising strings for the next hour.

So they watched him, while Demon lived up to his nickname and exercised his rakish talents, using ploy after ploy to ruffle her composure. To make her blush and skitter, and act the besotted miss.

Whether it was due to his expertise or otherwise, it grew increasingly easy to act besotted. To relax and laugh and smile. And blush.

He knew just how to tease her, just how to catch her eye and invite her to laugh—at him, at them, at herself. Knew just how to touch her—lightly, fleetingly—so that her senses leapt and her heart galloped faster than any horse on the Heath. When Bletchley, after approaching one other jockey and getting short shrift, finally headed back into the town, she'd blushed more than she ever had before.

Clinging to her parasol as if it were a weapon, and her last defense, she met Demon's eye. "I'll leave you now—I'm sure you can keep him in sight for the rest of the afternoon."

His eyes held hers, their expression difficult to read; for one instant, she thought it was reluctance she glimpsed in the blue—reluctance to set aside their roles.

"I don't need to follow him." Demon looked to the edge of the Heath and raised his hand. Gillies, lounging against a post, nodded and slipped off in Bletchley's wake.

Demon looked back at his companion of the afternoon. "Come—I'll drive you home."

Her gaze trapped in his, she waved to the nearby road. "I have the groom with the gig."

"We can send him on ahead." He raised one brow and reached for her hand. "Surely you'd rather be driven home behind my bays than the nag harnessed to the gig?"

As one who appreciated good horseflesh, her choice was a foregone conclusion. With an inclination of her head that was almost regal, she consented to his scheme, consented to let him hold her by him—to enjoy her freshness—for just a little while more.

He was seated in the armchair before the fire in his front parlor, staring at the flames and seeing her angelic face, her soft blue eyes, and the curious, considering light that flashed in them from time to time, when, once again, she came tapping on his windowpane. Lips setting, he didn't even bother swearing—just rose, set aside the brandy balloon he'd been cradling, and crossed to the window.

This time, when he pulled the curtains aside, he was relieved to see she was wearing skirts—to whit, her riding habit. He raised the sash. "Don't you ever use the door?"

The glance she levelled at him was reproving. "I came to invite you to accompany me to see Dillon."

"I thought we'd agreed not to see him at all."

"That was before. Now we know Bletchley's the contact, and that he's wandering about the Heath, we should warn Dillon and bring him up to date, so he doesn't do anything rash."

Dillon would never put himself to so much bother. The observation burned Demon's tongue, but he swallowed the words. He wasn't at all happy at the notion of Flick riding about the county alone at night, but he knew there was no point trying to talk her out if it. Mentally locating his riding gloves, he reached for the sash. "I'll meet you by the stable."

Pointy chin resolute, she nodded, then slid into the shadows.

Demon closed the window and went to warn the Shephards he was going out for a few hours.

Atop Jessamy, Flick was waiting by the main stable. Demon hauled open the door. In the dimness inside, lit by the shaft of moonlight streaming in through the door, he located his tack and carried it to Ivan's box. The big stallion was surprised to see him, and even more surprised to be saddled and led out. Luckily, before Ivan could consider and decide to protest, he set eyes on Jessamy.

Noting the stallion's fixed stare, Demon grunted and swung up to his saddle. At least he wouldn't have to exercise his talents on Ivan during their ride through the moonlight—Ivan would follow, intent, in Flick's wake.

She, of course, led the way.

They crossed his fields, the night black velvet about them. The cottage appeared deserted, a denser bulk in the deep shadows between the trees. Flick rode into the clearing behind it and dismounted. Demon followed, tethering Ivan well clear of the mare.

A twig cracked.

Flick whirled, squinting at the cottage. "It's us. Me and Demon."

"Oh," came a rather shaky voice from the dark. After a moment, Dillon asked, "Are you coming in?"

"Of course." Flick started for the cottage just as Demon reached her; he followed close on her heels.

"We thought," she said, ducking through the lean-to and stepping into the main room, "that you'd want to know what we've learned."

Dillon looked up, his face lit by the glow of the lantern he'd set alight. "You've identified one of the syndicate?"

Wild hope colored his tone; settling onto a stool by the table, Flick grimaced. "No—not yet."

"Oh." Dillon's face fell. He slumped down in the chair at the table's end.

Drawing off his gloves at the table's other end, Demon studied Dillon, noting his pallor and the lines the last week had etched in his cheeks. It was as if the reality of his situation, now fully realized, and the consequent worry of apprehension and exposure, were eating away at his childish self-absorption. If that was so, then it was all to the good. Drawing out the last rickety stool, Demon sat. "We've discovered your elusive contact."

Dillon looked up, hope gleaming in his eyes. Demon raised his brows at Flick, wondering if she wanted to tell Dillon herself. Instead, she nodded for him to continue. He looked back at Dillon. "Your man's name is Bletchley— he's a Londoner." Briefly, he described their quarry.

Dillon nodded. "Yes—that's him—the man who recruited me. He used to bring me the lists of horses and jockeys."

Flick leaned forward. "And the money?"

Dillon glanced at her, then colored, but continued to meet her eyes. "Yes. He always had my fee."

"No, I mean the money for the jockeys. How did they get paid? Did Bletchley give you their money?"

Dillon frowned. "I don't know how they got paid—I wasn't involved. That's not how it worked when I did it."

"Then how did you do the organizing?" Demon asked.

Dillon shrugged. "It was simple—the list of jockeys told me how much to offer each one. I did, and then reported if they'd accepted. I wasn't involved in getting their money to them after the race."

"After the race," Flick repeated. "What about the payments before the race?"

Dillon's puzzled frown grew. "Before?"

"As a down payment," Demon explained.

Dillon shook his head. "There *weren't* any payments before the race—only the one payment after the deed was done. And someone else took care of that, not me."

Flick frowned. "They've changed their ways."

"That's understandable," Demon said. "They're presently targeting races during the Craven meeting, one of the premier meetings in the calendar. The betting on those races is enormous—one or two fixed races, and they'll make a major killing. That's something the jockeys will know. They'll also know that the risk of being questioned by the stewards is greater—more attention is always paid to the major races during the major meets."

Dillon frowned. "Last season, they didn't try to fix any truly major races."

"It's possible they've been building up to this season—or that they've grown more cocky, more assured, and are now willing to take greater risks in the hope of greater rewards. Regardless, the jockeys for the Spring Carnival races would obviously demand more to pull their mounts." Demon glanced at Dillon. "The going rate for the two races we've heard fixed is five ponies."

"*Five*?" Dillon's brows flew up. "I was only once directed to offer three."

"So the price has gone up, and they're locking the jockeys in by offering some now, some later. Once the first payment's accepted, the jockey's more or less committed, which is less risky for the syndicate." Demon looked at Dillon. "They would, I fancy, be happy to make a down payment to avoid a repetition of what happened in the first race this year."

Dillon slowly nodded. "Yes, I see. This way, the fix is more or less certain."

"Hmm." Flick frowned. "Did you ever hear anything from the jockeys you organized about how they got paid?"

Dillon paled. "Only from one, early last season." He glanced at Demon. "The jockey wasn't too happy—his money was left at his mother's cottage. He didn't feel easy about the syndicate knowing where to find his old mum."

Demon met Dillon's gaze. He didn't like what he was learning. The syndicate sounded disturbingly intelligent—an evil, ruthless and *intelligent* opponent was, in his book, the worst. More of a challenge, but infinitely more dangerous.

That, of course, would normally whet his appetite, stir his Cynster blood. In this case, he only had to look at Flick to inwardly curse and wish the whole damned syndicate to hell. Unfortunately, the way the situation was shaping, it was going to fall to him to escort them there, while simultaneously protecting an angel from the consequences of her almost certain involvement in the syndicate's fall.

While the thought of the syndicate didn't stir his blood, Flick did—in quite a different way, a way he hadn't experienced before. This was not mere lust. He was well acquainted with that demon, and while it was certainly in the chorus, its voice wasn't the loudest. That distinction currently belonged to the impulse to protect her; if he complied with his inner promptings, he'd tie her up, cart her off to a high tower with a single door bearing a large and effective lock, and incarcerate her there until he had slain the dragon she was determined to flush out.

Unfortunately . . .

"We'd better go." She gathered her gloves and stood, her stool grating on the floor.

He rose more slowly, watching the interaction between Flick and Dillon.

Dillon was looking earnestly at her; she tugged on her gloves, then met his gaze. "We'll let you know what we discover—when we discover something. Until then, it's best that you stay out of sight."

Dillon nodded. Reaching out, he caught her hand and squeezed. "Thank you."

She humphed and shook free, but without any heat. "I told you I'm only doing this for the General."

The statement lacked the force of her earlier rendering; Demon doubted even she believed it.

Dillon's lips twisted rather ruefully. "Even so." He looked at Demon and stood. "I owe you a debt I'll never be able to repay."

His expression impassive, Demon met his gaze. "I'll think of something, never fear."

Dillon's eyes widened at his tone; with a curt nod, Demon turned to Flick.

Frowning, she glanced back at Dillon. "We'll look in in a few days." Then she turned and led the way out.

Following on her heels, Demon breathed deeply as they emerged into the night. A quick glance at the sky revealed a black pall—the moon had been engulfed by dark clouds. Within the cottage, the light of the lantern dimmed, then died. Eyes adjusting to the dark, Demon looked around as he strode across the clearing; no other human was anywhere about—just the two of them alone in the night.

Flick didn't wait for help but scrambled into her saddle. Untying Ivan's reins, Demon quickly mounted, holding the stallion steady as Flick trotted Jessamy over.

"I'll ride home through the park. I'll see you on the Heath tomorrow afternoon."

"No."

Surprised, she stared at him. Before she could scowl, he clarified, "I'll ride back to Hillgate End with you. It's after midnight—you shouldn't be out riding alone."

She didn't scowl, but he sensed her resistance. She studied him, then opened her mouth, doubtless to argue, when a breeze wafted through the clearing and set the trees shivering. It moaned, softly, eerily, through the branches, then died away on a sigh, an expiring banshee leaving only the rustling leaves slowly stilling in the deep darkness.

Flick shut her mouth and nodded. "Yes, all right."

Shaking her reins she set out; muttering his by now customary oath, Demon wheeled Ivan and set out to catch up. He did in short order; side by side, they rode across the next field—the last bastion of his domain. Beyond its hedge, directly ahead of them, lay the furthest reaches of the former park of Hillgate End.

There was a spot they both knew where the hedge thinned; they pushed through onto an old bridle path. Flick led the way into the dark shadows beneath the trees.

Although some of the park's paths were kept in good condition for riders, notably Flick, to enjoy, this was not one of them. Bushes pressed close on either side, branches flapped before their faces. They had to walk their mounts—it was too dangerous to even trot. The path was deep in leaf mold; it occasionally dipped, creating the added danger of their horses slipping. They both instinctively guarded their precious mounts, alert to every shift in weight, in muscle, in balance, of the beasts beneath them.

The General had no love of shooting, so the park had become a refuge for wildlife. A badger snuffled and growled as they passed him; later, they heard rustling, then the yips of a fox.

"I didn't realize it would be this bad." Flick ducked beneath a low-hanging branch.

Demon grunted. "I thought this was the route you used to go back and forth to the cottage. Obviously not."

"I normally take the path to the east, but that crosses the stream twice, and after last night's rain, I didn't want to risk Jessamy's knees going up and down slippery banks."

Demon didn't point out that she was risking Jessamy's knees right now— they were deep in the park, with the centuries-old trees forming an impenetrable canopy overhead; he could barely see Flick, let alone any irregularities in the path. Luckily, both Jessamy and Ivan could see better than him. They stepped out confidently; both he and Flick fell back on trust and let their horses find their own way.

After some time had elapsed, he asked, "Doesn't this path cross the stream, too?"

"Yes, but there's a bridge." After a moment, Flick amended, "Well, there *was* a bridge last time I came this way."

Lips thinning, Demon didn't bother asking how long ago that had been; they'd deal with the rotted and possibly ex-bridge when they came to it.

Before they did, it started to rain.

At first, the light pattering on the leaves high above was of little consequence. But the tattoo steadily grew more forceful, then the forest about them started to drip.

Flick shuddered as a series of heavy drops splattered her. Instinctively, she urged Jessamy on.

"No!" Demon scowled through the night. "Hold her steady. It's too dangerous to go faster—you know that."

Her silent acquiescence told him she did. They plodded on, increasingly damp, increasingly cold.

Above them, above the trees, the wind started to rise, to whistle and moan and shake the leaves. Jaw set, Demon searched his memories, trying to gauge how much farther they had to go, but he'd never been on this path before. He didn't know how it meandered, and he couldn't place where it came out. But given the fact that this path crossed the stream only once, and they'd been making very slow progress ...

He didn't like the answers his estimations suggested. They were still a long way from the manor.

Just how far was revealed when they came to a break in the trees, and he saw before them the stream with a narrow log and plank bridge spanning it. And the charcoal maker's hut in the clearing beyond. *That*, he recognized.

Beneath his breath, he swore.

As if in answer, the heavens cracked; the rain positively teemed. Faced with the sudden torrent—a curtain falling between them and the bridge—Jessamy and Flick balked.

Muttering all manner of dire imprecations, Demon swung down. He tied

Ivan's reins to a tree; the stallion, made of stern stuff, seemed unfazed by the downpour. Head up, he sniffed the air and looked toward the bridge.

The bridge that, if not in good condition, would assuredly collapse under his weight.

"Stay back!" Demon yelled at Flick. Pushing past Jessamy, he strode the three paces to the bridge. Ignoring the rain, he checked the structure thoroughly, in the end standing atop its middle and jumping up and down. The timbers didn't creak; the bridge seemed sound enough.

Ducking back through the rain, he nodded at Flick, then freed his reins and was back in the saddle. Despite the downpour, he wasn't soaked; the bridge itself was protected by a huge oak on the stream's opposite bank.

Flick was looking back at him, her brows high. He nodded again. "You cross first."

She nodded and sent Jessamy forward; they clattered across in ordered style. Demon shook Ivan's reins—he bounded forward, keen not to be separated from the mare. His heavy hooves clattered on the planking; in a few swift strides, he was safely across.

Flick was waiting under the spreading branches of the oak; Demon reined in beside her and fixed her with a look calculated to impress on her the unwisdom of arguing with him in his present mood. "There is no possibility that we can ride on to the manor in this."

Eyes wide, she looked at him consideringly, then cast a swift glance at the clearing before them, the surface of which was already playing host to myriad tiny rivulets. "It'll stop soon—these squalls always do."

"Precisely. Which is why we're going to wait in the hut until it does."

Flick eyed the hut and immediately thought of dust, and cobwebs, and spiders. Maybe even mice. Or rats. Then she looked at the steady rain coming down and grimaced. "I suppose it'll only be for an hour or so."

Demon tightened his reins. "There's a small stable tacked on the other side—ride straight there."

Flick shrugged, shook her reins, and did.

A second later, Demon followed.

The small stable was only just big enough to house both horses; with the two of them in there as well, laboring in the darkness to unsaddle, space was in short supply. It was impossible not to bump into each other. Arms brushed breasts, elbows stuck into chests. Searching for a loose strap, Flick inadvertently ran her hand up Demon's thigh—she snatched it back with a mortified "Sorry."

Which was received in fraught silence.

A minute later, reaching out to locate her so he wouldn't hit her when he lifted his saddle from Ivan's back, Demon found his fingers curving about her breast. An incoherent word of apology was all he could manage, too exercised by the battle to drag his hand away.

Flick's only reply was a muted squawk.

Finally, they were done, and the horses, contented enough, were settled side by side, Ivan with a minimum of rein. Flick joined Demon in the doorway, ducking behind him, into the protection afforded by his broad shoulders.

He glanced around at her, then looked back out, peering along the front of the stone cottage. "God only knows what state the inside is in."

"The charcoal makers come every year."

"In autumn," he replied incontrovertibly.

She grimaced.

He sighed. "I'll go and take a look." He glanced over his shoulder. "Do you want to wait here? It's perfectly possible I won't be able to get past the door."

She nodded. "I'll stay here while you check—call if it's all right."

He looked back out, then strode swiftly for the cottage door. An instant later, Flick heard wood grating on stone. She waited, looking out at the steady rain, listening to the dripping silence. Beside her, the horses shifted, heaved horsy sighs, and settled. All she could hear was their steady breathing and the soft patter of the rain.

And a hesistant, furtive rustling in what sounded like straw, coming from the rear of the stable.

Flick stiffened. Wild-eyed, she swung around. Visions of munching rats with evil red eyes filled her brain.

She whirled and fled for the cottage.

The door was ajar; without a thought, she slipped through.

"Stop." It was Demon's voice. "I've found the lantern."

Flick stood just inside the door and calmed her leaping heart. He was large—he had large feet. He'd been clomping around in the cottage for at least three minutes—surely, by now, any resident rodents would have departed.

A scrape of a match on tinder broke the stillness; light flared, then softened, throwing a warm glow about the hut as Demon reset the glass.

Letting out the breath she'd held, Flick looked about. "Well!"

"Indeed." Demon likewise was taking inventory. "Remind me to compliment the charcoal makers when next they're by."

The cottage was neat as a pin, and, bar the inevitable cobwebs, clean. The door had been tight in its frame, and the windows securely shuttered; no unwanted visitors had disturbed the charcoal makers' temporary home.

By extension, however, there was no food left in the cottage to attract vermin. The pots and pans and, most importantly, the kettle, travelled with their owners. There was, however, wood stacked and dry in the woodbox.

Demon glanced at Flick, then moved to the fireplace. "I may as well get a fire going." They were both damp, just this side of wet through.

"Hmm." Flick shut the door, then, rubbing her upper arms, came farther into the cottage. While Demon crouched before the stone hearth, selecting logs and sticks with which to start his blaze, she studied the furniture. There was only one chair—an old armchair from the manor. Beyond it stood three narrow pallets, each sporting a lumpy, tick mattress. Bending down, Flick grasped the wooden strut at the end of the nearest pallet and tugged until the end of the pallet was positioned before the hearth to one side. Satisfied, she sank down upon it. And sighed as she let her shoulders ease.

Demon glanced back, saw what she'd done, and nodded. The next instant, he had a flame laid in the kindling; busily, he coaxed it into a blaze.

Flick sat and watched the flames grow, watched the bright tendrils writhe, then lick along the dark wood. Patiently, Demon fed the flames, laying branch upon twig until the blaze roared.

Heat billowed out, enveloping her, washing through her, driving away the chill locked in her damp clothes. Contentment rolled through her; she sighed and rotated her shoulders, one, then the other, then settled again to watch Demon's hands, steady and sure, pile logs on the fire.

His hands were like the rest of him—large and lean. His long fingers never fumbled. His grip was strong and sure. His movements, she noted, were economical; he rarely used extraneous flourishes, a fact that enhanced the sense of control, of harnessed power, that invested his every act.

He was, now she considered it, a very controlled man.

Only when the flames were voraciously devouring two huge logs did he stand. He stretched, then turned; large and intensely male, he stood looking down at her.

Her gaze fixed on the flames, Flick knew he was studying her; she felt his gaze on her face, hotter than the heat from the flames. She looked away from the fire, to the nook beside the hearth, gathering strength to look up and meet his eyes.

In the dark corner she saw a flicker of movement, a twitch of a whisker.

A pointy nose and two pink-red eyes.

"*Eeeeeehhh!*"

Her shrill scream split the stillness.

With another shriek, she leapt up, straight into Demon's arms.

They locked about her. "What is it?"

"*A rat!*" Eyes glued to the dark cranny, she clung, her fingers sinking into his muscles. She gestured with her chin. "There—by the fireplace." Then she buried her face in his chest. "Make it go away!"

Her plea was a panicked mumble. Demon stared at the small field mouse cowering back against the stones. He stifled a sigh. "Flick—"

"Is it gone?"

This time, he did sigh. "It's only a field mouse attracted to the warmth. It'll leave in a moment."

"Tell me when it does."

He squinted down at her. All he could see was the crown of her curls. Putting his head to the side, he tried to see her face; she had it buried in his chest. She'd somehow insinuated her hands under his coat, and was gripping him, one hand on either side of his back, clinging for dear life.

She was plastered against him, from her forehead to her knees.

And she was trembling.

A faint vibration, the tremor travelled her spine. Instinctively, he tightened his arms about her, then eased his hold to run his hands slowly down and up her back, soothingly stroking.

Bending his head, he murmured into her curls. "It's all right. It'll go in a minute."

He could feel her panicked breathing, her breath hitching in her throat; she didn't answer, but bobbed her head to show she'd heard.

So they stood, locked together before the fire, waiting for the still-petrified mouse to make a move.

Demon had imagined waiting patiently, stoically, but within a minute, stoic was beyond him. The fire, a roaring blaze, had dried him; while Flick had been still chilled when she'd rushed into his arms, his body heat was warming her. Warming her breasts, pressed tight against his chest, warming her hips, plastered to his thighs. She, in turn, was heating him—it wouldn't be long before the largest blaze in the room was not the one in the hearth.

Gritting his teeth, he told himself he could endure it. He doubted she was even aware of his susceptibility; he could manage her easily enough.

The heat between them reached a new high, and her perfume rose to waft about him, to wreathe, then snare, his senses. Making him even more aware of the supple softness in his arms, of the warm breasts crushed to his chest, of the subtle pliancy in her frame that beckoned his hardened senses, of the feminine strength in the arms reaching around him. He snatched a breath—and drew her deep, into his soul. Closing his eyes, locking his jaw, he tried to keep his body from responding.

Entirely unsuccessfully. Hard became harder, tighter, tauter. Inexorably, yet in all innocence, she wound his sensual spring notch after notch.

In desperation, he tried to ease her away—she shook her head frantically and burrowed even deeper into his embrace. Teeth gritted, he used just a little of his strength to shift her, so she was more to his side and no longer in danger of learning, graphically, just how much she was affecting him.

He was in pain and helpless to do anything about it. He was paying for his sins in having dallied with her, teased her, enjoyed her.

But he didn't regret a single moment—then, or now.

The realization puzzled him, momentarily distracted him from the physical plane. Grateful for even such minor relief, he followed the thought, trying to unravel the mystery of why, exactly, Flick so attracted him.

He definitely didn't think of her as just another lady with whom he'd like to dally, no different from those who'd gone before. No other lady had made him feel this protective; none other had tapped the surge of feeling she so effortlessly evoked. That, of all things, was what set her apart—that something she made him feel. She could arouse him effortlessly—in itself a shock—but it was that other emotion that came roaring through him simultaneously with the lust that was so new, so addictive.

It was certainly different—something he'd never felt before. It was as if, in her innocence, she could reach into his soul and touch something innocent there as well—something new, bright, something he'd never known existed within him. Something no other had ever reached, ever touched.

He frowned and tried to shift; she immediately gripped him tighter. Demon inwardly sighed—his protective instincts were well and truly engaged; he couldn't break her hold. Perhaps he should try and think of Flick in the same way he thought of the twins.

That was impossible, yet . . .

Flick the fearless was afraid of mice. He found the thought endearing. Still, as she was truly frightened, the mouse was as good as a dragon. The question was how best to vanquish it—the fear, not the innocent mouse.

Drawing a difficult breath, he grasped Flick's arm and eased her back from him.

"Flick—sweetheart—just look at the mouse. It's a harmless little mouse—it can't eat you."

"It might try."

"Not while I'm here." He brushed his lips to her temple, nudging her face from his chest. "Come—look at it. It's so small."

Warily, she eased her face from his chest; still pressed hard against him, she glanced at the tiny rodent.

"That's right. We'll just watch it until it goes."

A silent minute passed as they watched the field mouse, still frozen, whiskers twitching nervously. Demon couldn't move to scare it away, not with Flick clinging so tightly—she wouldn't appreciate him moving closer to the mouse-dragon.

Finally, reassured by their stillness and silence, the mouse started to edge forward. Flick stiffened. Out of the nook the mouse came, hugging the shadow of the hearth's edge. It reached the corner and paused—

A log cracked—sparks spat and showered in the hearth.

The mouse leapt, and dashed back into the cranny, straight to a small gap between two stones. It squeezed its way between and was gone.

"Quick!" Flick released him. "Block the hole!"

Demon sincerely doubted the field mouse would return, but, snatching a small branch from the woodbox, he swiftly bent and jammed it in the hole. "There. Now you're safe." Rising, he turned.

Flick was mere inches away. She'd followed him to look over his shoulder, to check he'd sealed the hole; now she stood, breathing quickly, all but against him once more.

His gaze had risen no further than her breasts, rising and falling in heightened excitement. Only excellent reflexes saved him from reacting—he locked every muscle, gripped every rein. And, slowly, lifted his gaze to her face.

Flick met his gaze and quivered—she told herself it was the remnants of her fright. But the glow in his darkened eyes—the sight of the embers smoldering in the blue—cut off her breathing, leaving her light-headed, swaying with the impulse to return to his arms, not for their safety but for the comfort her senses insisted she would find there.

Eyes wide, lips parted, her cheeks lightly flushed, she literally teetered on the brink of indiscretion—

His lids lowered, steel shutters cutting off the heat in his eyes; an excruciating awareness raced over her skin, from her breasts all the way to her toes. Her nerves flickered; a prickling sensation swept her. Heat washed in its wake.

She dragged in a breath—

He half turned and gestured to the pallet and the chair. "Which do you prefer?"

She blinked, and struggled to calm her rioting senses, to find her voice. She drew in another breath. "I'll take the pallet—you can have the chair."

He nodded; without meeting her eyes, he waved her to her selected seat. Uncertain—of him, of herself, of what shimmered in the air—she went; sitting on the pallet, she shuffled back and drew up her knees so she could balance her boots on the end strut, out of reach of any further rodents. Hugging her knees, she settled her chin atop them, and stared into the flames.

Demon built up the fire, then subsided into the armchair. He, too, fixed his gaze on the flames, denying the urge to gaze at Flick—to look, to wonder . . .

That moment of unexpected awareness had very nearly defeated him, nearly overcome the defenses he'd erected between her and himself, between her innocence and his demons. Only her abiding innocence—the innocent confusion, laced with equally innocent, equally open, curiosity, in her blue eyes—had saved them. Given him the strength to resist. The effort had left him aching, far more intensely than before. And inwardly shaking, as if his strength had been depleted to dangerously low levels.

Which meant he was in trouble—that matters between them had gone much farther than he'd thought. Than he'd been aware of.

Even now, although he'd recognized the danger, at least half his mind was fully engaged in wondering what having an angel beneath him would be like. In fantasizing, as he had so often that afternoon, about how far her delicate blush extended. But his thoughts of her were no longer merely sensual—they were possessively so. Intent, with an underlying, clawing need that he knew no way of easing, bar one. Which, in this case, by extension, meant . . .

The very thought made him shudder. *Marriage* was not a word he willingly used, not even in his mind.

A rustling had him glancing her way; he watched as, drowsy, her lids heavy, she turned on her side. Tucking her legs up in her skirts, she settled on the mattress, her gaze still fixed on the fire. Demon forced his gaze to follow hers to the flames. And tried, very hard, not to think at all.

Outside, the drops still pattered down in a steady, soaking rain.

When his mind started to wander, he tried to guess the time, but he had no idea how long they'd taken on the path through the park. An hour? Less?

A soft sigh had him turning, looking—after that, he didn't look away.

She was sleeping.

A hand curled beneath her cheek, her long lashes lay still, brown crescents brushing rose-tinted skin. Her lips, slightly parted, sheened softly, their curves the gentlest temptation imaginable. The firelight gilded her jaw and set golden lights in her hair.

Demon looked, and watched—watched the steady swell and ebb of her breathing reflected in the movement of her breasts, tightly encased in blue velvet, watched the ruffle at her throat rise and fall.

He still wasn't sure how she felt about Dillon, but he'd detected no sign of any sensual awareness between them. He'd initially wondered if they were simply too young, too innocent, to have developed that susceptibility, but he now knew Flick, at least, was more than capable of feeling it.

Which brought him to wondering how she saw him . . .

He watched, and pondered. There was no need to look away.

CHAPTER
Seven

ॐ⌘ॐ

He'd seen her face so often in his dreams that he didn't notice when he fell asleep. Her face was his last image before his lids fell—it was the first thing he saw, through the dimness, when he woke.

Frowning, Demon eased his stiff neck and glanced at the fire to see it a pile of cooling ash. He froze, staring at the grey pile, then whipped around to look at the windows.

The heavy shutters were in place, but a thin shaft of pale light edged each slat.

Swearing beneath his breath, he glanced at Flick, still softly sleeping, an angel in repose. Jaw setting, he rose and strode silently to the door. Opening it confirmed his worst fear—the day had dawned.

Drawing the door wide, Demon hauled in a deep breath. The scent of the wet forest flowed into him; he held it in, then slowly exhaled.

A sound behind him had him turning; silent and still in the doorway, he watched Flick awake.

She didn't simply open her eyes. Instead, consiousness slowly invested her features, enlivening her brows, curving her full lips. Eyes still closed, she hummed softly in her throat. Her breasts swelled as she drew in a deep breath, then she stretched languorously, straightening her spine, arching slightly, then she relaxed and her lashes fluttered.

Then, and only then, did her lids slowly rise.

She looked straight at him, then blinked her eyes wide, but no hint of consternation disturbed her content expression. Instead, her lips softened into a sleepily warm smile.

"Is it morning?"

The husky tones of her voice, still drunk with sleep, flowed over him, about him, slid under his skin and seized him. He couldn't speak, couldn't think—he could only want. Want with a searing desire that shocked him, with an absolute possessive need that nearly floored him. Containing that force, reining it in, holding it back, left him rigid. And shaking.

She was still smiling, still waiting for his answer; realizing that, with him framed in the doorway with all light coming from outside, she couldn't see his passion-blank expression, or anything else, he summoned every last ounce of his strength and managed to utter, "Almost."

His tone was harsh and uneven; he didn't wait to see her reaction but turned away to ensure she got no chance to study him further, to see the evidence of that rabid desire. Ostensibly surveying the clearing, he cleared his throat. "I'll get the horses saddled."

With that, he escaped.

Of course, within a few minutes, she came to help.

Ivan was grumpy and fractious; Demon made that his excuse for barely glancing Flick's way. He felt her puzzled gaze; jaw clenched, he ignored it. He didn't even dare help her saddle Jessamy—if she put her hand on his thigh this morning, he couldn't guarantee his reaction—or rather, his *in*action. As soon as he had Ivan's girths tight, he grabbed his bridle and led the restless stallion out of the tight space.

The charcoal makers' hut had been constructed in that particular clearing because it was the natural confluence of four paths through the park. One was the path they'd travelled last night, another led onward to the manor. A third struck across to join the eastern bridle path Flick usually used to reach the ruined cottage and his farm. Halting Ivan in the middle of the clearing, Demon glanced toward the opening of the fourth path, leading in from a small country lane to the west.

To see Hugh Dunstable, the General's middle-aged steward, ambling up through the morning.

Demon froze.

Dunstable had already seen him; smiling, he raised his hand to his hat. "Ah! 'Morning, sir."

Demon nodded easily, urbanely, but he couldn't for the life of him summon a smile. His mind raced while Dunstable's cob plodded closer, ever closer.

"'Spect you got caught in last night's squall." Drawing rein beside him, Dunstable beamed down at him. "No doubt but it was heavy. Got caught out myself, it came up so quick. I'd been off to the Carters, playing a hand of whist— I was on my way back when it hit. I was drenched by the time I reached home."

"As you say." Demon glanced surreptitiously at the shadowed stable. "It was too heavy to risk riding on."

Dunstable snorted. "On these paths? You'd have risked that fine beast."

The fine beast chose that moment to snort, paw and prance, heavily shouldering Dunstable's cob. Demon swore and drew in Ivan's reins. Settling his placid cob, Dunstable chuckled. "Aye—riding him must be an adventure. Not hard to see how you came by your name."

It wasn't his expertise in riding high-bred *horses* that had earned him his nickname, but Demon let the comment pass; he was too busy praying.

Much good it did him. His fervent appeal to the highest authority that Flick would have the sense to remain out of sight was refused; she appeared at that instant, smiling sunnily up at Dunstable as she led Jessamy out.

"Good morning, Mr. Dunstable."

She glanced up at the sky, and so failed to notice the expression on Dunstable's face—sheer shock to begin with, rapidly transmuting into horror, momentarily displaced by speculation, only to revert to righteous horror again.

By the time Flick looked down and cheerily remarked, "And a fine morning it seems to be," Dunstable's features were set in stone, his expression impassive. He mumbled an incoherent reply to Flick; the look in his eyes when he shifted his gaze to Demon was coldly censorious.

Demon reacted in the only way he could—with a high hand. Cool arrogance in his eyes, he met Dunstable's gaze levelly; his expression hard, he raised a challenging brow.

Dunstable, only one step up from a servant, albeit an old and trusted one, was at a loss to know how to respond. Demon regretted putting the old man in his place, but every instinct he possessed refused to let anyone even imagine any ill—any indiscretion—of Flick.

To his relief, she, busy adjusting her stirrups, missed their exchange entirely.

"It looks like the clouds have blown away. I dare say it'll be quite warm by lunchtime." She straightened and glanced around for a log to use as a mounting block.

Demon dropped his reins and crossed to her side; closing his hands about her waist, he lifted her, setting her lightly on Jessamy's back.

That got her attention; she sucked in a breath and blinked at him, then quickly rearranged her legs and her skirts. "Thank you."

Lifting her chin, she fixed her blue eyes on Dunstable. "I can't believe how overgrown the park has become—we must get Hendricks to cut back rather more. Why, you can barely see the sky, even here, even on such a wonderful morning. I rather think—"

She chattered blithely on, unaware that, with her cheeks still delicately flushed from sleep, her hair tousled and her velvet skirts badly crushed, she presented a perfect picture of a youthful damsel who had recently engaged in an energetic morning romp.

Predictably, she led the way along the path to the manor.

Dunstable followed close behind. To give him his due, while remaining stony-faced, he managed to make the appropriate noises whenever Flick paused in her paean to the morning.

Hands on his hips, Demon watched them amble off, then exhaled through his teeth. Returning to the hut, he secured the door, then mounted Ivan. And paused.

For one long moment, he stared down the path at Flick's and Dunstable's backs. Then, lips thinning, jaw firming, he shook Ivan's reins. And followed.

By the time their party reached Hillgate End, Demon had a firm grip on the situation. There was no doubt that he'd compromised Flick, albeit entirely innocently.

He'd caught up with her and Dunstable, only to hear her gaily state that they'd taken shelter soon after the rain had started. So Dunstable now knew that they'd been at the hut, together and alone, from the dead of night to dawn.

Of course, focused on protecting Dillon, Flick had said not a word about what had occasioned her presence, in company with a rake, deep in the park in the middle of the night.

It was no great feat to imagine what Dunstable was thinking. Indeed, it was difficult to conceive of a more damning scenario for a young, unmarried gentlewoman than being discovered at dawn leaving an evening rendezvous in company with a rake of the first order.

Demon had had ample time to consider every facet of their night alone, every nuance, every likely repercussion—their journey to the manor had been slow, the ground very wet, soft beneath their horses' hooves. They'd plodded along, Flick in the lead, followed by Dunstable, with him in the rear. In brooding silence, he'd debated their options—not many—and what that therefore meant, while Flick had entertained Dunstable with her sunny patter.

She'd described the small stable, and exclaimed over the fact that Jessamy and Ivan had been quite dry; she'd continually paused to declaim the wonders of the morning. She had not, however, mentioned the mouse—on consideration, remembering the long moments she'd spent in his arms, he'd decided that was just as well.

God only knew what picture she might paint for Dunstable if she started on that topic.

Finally, they'd reached the manor's grounds; minutes later, they trotted into the stable yard.

Stifling a huge sigh of relief, her mind full of the wonders of a hot bath, Flick reined in. She untangled her legs and skirts from her sidesaddle; she was about to slide to the ground when Demon appeared beside her. He reached for her; his hands closed about her waist, then he lifted her down, and set her on her feet before him.

Quickly catching her breath—she was almost used to the effect of his touch, to the sudden seizing of her lungs—she beamed a sunny smile up at him, and held out her hand. "Thank you so much for taking pity on me last night and seeing me home. I'm really very grateful."

He looked at her—she could read nothing in his eyes, in his oddly set expression. He took her hand, but instead of squeezing it and letting go, he wrapped his fingers about hers and turned. "I'll walk you to the house."

Flick stared at him—at his back. She would have tugged and argued, but Dunstable, having dismounted more slowly, was hovering. Demon started walking—stalking; throwing a bright smile over her shoulder at Dunstable, she had to hurry to keep up.

Striding purposefully, Demon headed up the gravel path, ducking under the wisteria to pass beneath the old trees and cut across the lawn to the terrace. He didn't set her hand on his arm and stroll; instead, he kept his hand locked about hers and towed her along.

Flick tried an outraged glare, but he refused to even notice. His expression was set, determined. Determined on what she had no idea.

Glancing back, she saw Dunstable, watching from beneath the stable arch. She flashed him a reassuring smile and wondered what devil had possessed Demon.

He didn't stop until they were on the terrace, before the open morning room windows. Releasing her, he gestured her inside; with a speaking glance, she stepped over the threshold. Swinging her heavy skirts, she faced him as he followed her into the room. "Why aren't you heading off to the Heath? We have to watch Bletchley."

Halting in front of her, he looked down at her and frowned. "Gillies and the others will keep watching until I arrive to take over. At present, I have matters of greater moment to settle."

She blinked. "You do?"

His jaw set ominously. "I need to speak with the General."

Flick felt her eyes, locked on his, widen. "What about?" She had no idea why, but she was starting to feel uneasy.

Demon saw her question—her lack of understanding—etched in her eyes. Inwardly, he cursed. "I need to talk to him about our current situation."

"Situation? What situation?"

Jaw clenching, he went to step around her; quick as a flash, she blocked his way. "What are you talking about?"

He caught her eye and frowned even more. "I'm talking about the past night, which we spent together, alone." He gave the last two words particular weight; comprehension dawned in her eyes.

Then she blinked and frowned at him. "So?" Her gaze raced over his face. "Nothing—nothing *indiscreet*—happened."

"No," he agreed, his voice tight, controlled, "but only you and I know that. All society will see is that the *potential* for indiscretion was present, and that, in society's eyes, is all that counts."

The sound she made was elementally dismissive. His eyes locked on hers, Demon knew that if she questioned the *potential*, denied it had existed, he'd wring her neck.

She hovered on the brink—he saw it in her eyes. But, after studying his expression, she swung onto a different tack. "But no one knows. Well"—she waved—"only Dunstable, and he didn't imagine anything scandalous had happened."

Stunned, he stared at her. "Tell me, is Dunstable always so stony-faced?"

She grimaced. "Well, he is rather taciturn. I always do most of the talking."

"If you'd done a little more looking this morning, you'd have seen he was shocked to his toes." Again, he went to step past her; again, she blocked his way.

"What are you going to do?"

He didn't want to lay hands on her—didn't want to risk it in his present state. He pinned her with a glare. "I am going to speak to the General, and explain to him exactly what occurred."

"You're not going to tell him about Dillon?"

"No. I'll simply say I came upon you riding alone through my fields late last night, and insisted on escorting you home." He took a step toward her; to keep his face in clear view, she backed away. "I'll leave it to you to explain what you were doing in your saddle at midnight."

She blinked; he pressed his advantage and took another step. She gave ground without noticing. Her eyes, now wide, flicked up to his; before she could interrupt, he stated, "The General will see instantly that, regardless of what truly transpired at the cottage, all society—certainly every matron of standing in Newmarket—will believe you and I spent the best part of the night heating a single pallet in the charcoal makers' hut."

A light blush tinged her cheeks; her gaze flickered, then steadied. Abruptly, she stood her ground. "That's ridiculous." The statement was emphatic. "You didn't lay a finger . . ." Her words trailed away; her gaze blanked.

"On you?" Demon grinned tightly. "Not one—all ten." He trapped her gaze as she refocused. "Can you deny you were in my arms?"

Her lips compressed, her expression turned mutinous, her chin set like rock. Her eyes—those usually soft orbs—positively flared. "That was because of a *mouse!*"

"The cause is irrelevant. As far as society's concerned, having spent the night alone with me, your virtue and reputation are in question. The accepted code of behavior decrees I offer you the protection of my name."

Flick stared at him, then determinedly shook her head. "No."

He looked down at her, and coolly raised his brows. "No?"

"No, that's positively stupid." Flinging her hands in the air, she swung away. "You're blowing this up out of all proportion. Society's not going to say anything because they'll know nothing about it. Dunstable won't talk." Swinging about, she paced back. "I'll see him and explain—" Lifting her head, she saw Demon almost at the door. "No! *Wait!*"

She raced across the room. She would have caught him, but he turned and caught her instead. His hands about her upper arms, he held her away from him. And glared at her.

"There's no point arguing—I'm going to see the General."

His determination was blazoned in his eyes; Flick couldn't mistake it. Her mind raced; she licked her lips. "He'll be at breakfast." Dragging her gaze from his, she sent it skimming down, over his rumpled clothes.

He looked down, too, then frowned; extending one leg, he scowled at the muddy streaks marring his Hessians. And swore. Releasing her, he took stock of his disreputable state. "I can't go in to see him like this."

Flick kept her eyes wide and innocent, and held her tongue. Even when— especially when—his gaze, hard and blue, returned to her face.

After a moment, lips compressed, he nodded. "I'll go home and change— then I'll be back." Eyes narrowing, he held her gaze. "And then we can discuss this fully—with the General."

She merely raised her brows and maintained a strategic silence.

He hesitated, looking into her eyes, then, with a curt nod, turned and stalked out.

Flick watched him go, drifting back to the French doors to watch him stride across the lawn. Only when he'd disappeared into the shadows of the trees did she turn back into the room—grit her teeth, clench her fists, and give vent to a frustrated scream.

"He's *impossible*! *This* is impossible." After a moment, her eyes darkened. "He's out of his mind."

With that, she stalked off to clear the matter up.

Two hours later, Demon drove his bays up the drive of Hillgate End. Under his expert guidance, the curricle came to a flourishing halt immediately before the steps. Handing the reins to the groom who came running, he stepped down. Drawing off his gloves, he strode to the house.

He was perfectly attired in a blue morning coat and ivory breeches, ivory cravat and shirt, with an elegantly restrained blue-and-black-striped waistcoat. His Hessians, another pair, gleamed. His appearance was precisely as he considered it should be, given his errand.

Jacobs opened the door to his knock. Demon returned his greeting with a nod and headed straight for the library. He was somewhat surprised to gain the door without encountering Flick; he'd expected some last-ditch effort on her part to interfere with his plans—his immolation on the altar of the right and proper.

Turning the handle, he opened the door and entered, swiftly scanning the long room for any sign of an angel.

She wasn't there.

The General was, seated as usual at his desk, and sunk behind a huge tome. He looked up as Demon closed the door—and smiled warmly, delightedly.

Demon strolled nearer and saw his mentor's eyes twinkling. Inwardly, he cursed.

The General held up a hand before he could speak. "I know," he declared, "all about it."

Demon came to a dead halt facing the desk. "Flick." His tone was flat. His left hand slowly clenched.

"Eh? Oh, yes—Felicity." The General grinned and leaned back in his chair, waving him to the chair beside the desk. Although Demon moved in that direction, he couldn't sit—he prowled to the window beyond.

The General chuckled. "You needn't worry. A potential imbroglio it might have been, but Felicity took the bit between her teeth and sorted it all out."

"I see." His features under rigid control, his expression utterly bland, Demon turned his head and raised a brow. "How very helpful of her." Even to him, his tones sounded steely. "How did she manage it?"

"Well—" If the General was aware of his tension, he didn't show it; he pushed his chair back the better to beam up at him. "She came straightaway to me, of course, and explained what happened—how she'd felt the need of some air and so gone riding late last night, and forgot the time, and wound up past your farm." The General's smug expression clouded. "Have to say, m'boy, I'm not at all sanguine about her riding off like that alone, but she's promised me she won't do it again." His wide smile returning, he looked up. "One good thing about this little fright she's had, what?"

Demon said nothing; the General grinned and continued, "Luckily, this time, you saw her—very good of you to insist on escorting her home."

"It seemed the least I could do." Especially as it had been him she'd ridden out to see.

"Silly of her to take that old path—Hendricks gave up on it years ago. As for the rain—I can't tell you how relieved I am that you were with her. Goodness knows, she's a reliable miss, but still, she's young, and inclined to press on regardless. Your decision to stop at the hut until the rain passed was unquestionably correct. After that, of course, all the rest followed—no one's fault it happened as it did. Hardly surprising you both fell asleep."

The General looked up and frowned—as severely as he ever did—at him. "And don't think you have to reassure me that nothing happened. I know you—known you from a boy. I *know* nothing untoward occurred. I know my Felicity would be safe with you."

The unexpected fierceness in the General's eyes held him silent; with a satisfied nod, the General sat back.

"Yes, and she told me about the mouse, too. She's petrified of the silly things—always has been. Just what I'd have expected—you had the sensitivity not to laugh at her, but to soothe her. Nothing scandalous there."

Glancing at his desk, the General frowned. "Where were we? Ah, yes. Dunstable. Him coming across you this morning was neither here nor there— he's an old friend and luckily no gabblemonger. Flick insisted on speaking with him after she'd seen me, and he dropped by to see me half an hour ago. Just to reassure me that he would never say a word to harm our Felicity." Grinning, the General glanced up. "Dunstable also asked me to convey his apologies to you for jumping to unwarranted conclusions."

Demon met the General's eye. Flick had plugged every hole, countered every argument.

"So," the General said, his tone one of conclusion, "I hope you can see that I'm perfectly convinced there's no reason for any sacrifice on your part. As you haven't in any way harmed Felicity's reputation, there's absolutely no reason you need offer for her, is there?"

Demon held his gaze, but didn't answer; the General smiled.

"It was all perfectly innocent—and now we'll say nothing more about it, what?" He hauled his tome back into position before him. "Now tell me. I've just been checking these offshoots of the Barbary Arab. What have you heard about this colt, Enderby?"

As if in compensation, the General invited him to lunch. Demon accepted— then, offering to carry word of his joining the table to Jacobs, left the General to his records.

Shutting the library door, Demon paused in the quiet of the corridor, trying, yet again, to regain a sense of equilibrium. He understood what had happened; rationally, logically, he knew all was well. Unfortunately, he didn't feel it. He felt ... deprived.

As if a long-desired object of paramount importance had slipped—been whisked—from his grasp, just as he was about to close his hand.

Frowning, he went to find Jacobs.

He discovered him in the butler's pantry; his message delivered, Demon returned to the front hall and, without a heartbeat's pause, set out to hunt down Flick. Feeling very much like a hungry leopard, he prowled through the downstairs rooms. She would be somewhere close, he was sure, just in case he had raised some quibble she hadn't foreseen and the General had sent for her.

He found her in the garden hall.

She was snipping the stems of flowers and slipping them into a vase. Humming, she tilted her head this way and that, studying her creation. Demon watched her for a full minute, taking in her crisp, cambric morning gown, noting her hair, newly brushed, a gilded frame about her face.

After drinking his fill, he quit the doorway; on silent feet, he approached her.

Flick snipped the stem of a cornflower and considered how best to place it. She held it up, her hand hovering—

Long fingers plucked the bloom from her grasp.

She gasped, but even before her gaze collided with his, she knew who stood beside her. She knew his touch—knew the sense of strength he projected. "Have you seen the General?" she gabbled, frantically trying to slow her racing heart.

"Hmm." Eyes half-closed, he lazily angled the stem this way, then that, then slid it home into the vase. He surveyed his handiwork, then, apparently satisfied, turned to her. "I did see him, yes."

His lazy, indolent—sleepy—expression deceived her not at all; beneath his heavy lids, his eyes were sharp, his gaze incisive. She lifted her chin and picked up the garden shears. "I told you there was no need for any drama."

His lips lifted in a slight smile. "So you did."

Flick stifled a sniff at his tone; she had, indeed, expected his thanks, once he'd had time to consider, to realize what his offer would have meant. She supposed he would marry sometime, but he was only thirty-one, and he definitely didn't want to marry her.

But he made no further comment. Instead, he lounged, shoulders propped against the wall, and, with the same lazy, unnerving air, watched her place her flowers. As the silence stretched, it occurred to her that perhaps he thought she didn't fully appreciate the sacrifice he'd been prepared to make. "It's not that I'm not grateful." She kept her gaze firmly fixed on her blooms.

Her comment succeeded in dissipating a little of his indolence. She felt the sudden focusing of his attention.

"Grateful?"

She continued to snip and set. "For your kind offer to save my reputation. I appreciate it would have entailed a considerable sacrifice on your part—thankfully, there was no need."

His gaze locked on her profile, Demon fought to remain where he was—and not haul her into his arms and kiss her, just to shut her up. "Sacrifice? Actually, I hadn't viewed taking you to wife in quite that light."

"Hadn't you?" She blinked at him in patent surprise, then smiled and turned back to her flowers. "I dare say you would have, once you'd stopped to think the idea through."

Demon simply stared at her. He'd never felt so ... *dismissed* in his life.

"Luckily, there was no reason for worry. I did tell you so."

Luckily for her, what next he might have said, and done, neither of them were destined to learn; Jacobs appeared in the doorway with the information that lunch was awaiting them in the dining parlor.

Flick led the way. Demon no longer expected anything else; he prowled just behind her, making no effort to fully catch up—in his present mood, it was probably wisest if she remained just out of reach.

Lunch was not a success.

Flick grew increasingly impatient with their guest as the meal progressed. He contributed nothing to the conversation beyond answering questions the General threw his way. Instead, broodingly intent, he watched her, as if studying some incomprehensible being of whom he nevertheless disapproved, leaving her to chatter with increasingly feigned brightness until her head ached.

By the time the meal ended and they pushed back their chairs, she was ready to snap at him—if he deigned to give her the chance.

"Well, m'boy—let me know if you detect any weakness in those horses." The General shook hands with Demon, then smiled at Flick. "Why don't you see Demon to the stable, m'dear? It's a lovely day out there." With his usual benign smile, the General waved at the French doors, open to the terrace. "Enjoy the fine weather while you may."

Across the table, Flick met Demon's level gaze. The last thing she wanted to do was, all sweet comfort, accompany him to the stable—she was annoyed with him, at the way he was behaving. It was as if he'd been denied something he wanted, for heaven's sake. He was *sulking*! All because things hadn't gone as he'd planned—because she'd rescripted his grand gesture for him, and he hadn't got to play the role he'd expected. That of heroic sacrifice.

Drawing a deep breath, she held it; lips compressed, she held his gaze challengingly. Very nearly belligerently.

He merely raised one brow—even more challengingly, more defiantly; stepping back, he gestured to the terrace.

Flick could almost hear the gauntlet thud down on the table between them.

Lifting her head, she stepped around the table, preceding him out the doors, down the steps and across the lawn. Pacing briskly, irritatedly, she was halfway across the lawn before she realized he wasn't with her.

Abruptly stopping, she glanced back. He was strolling slowly, leisurely, exceedingly unhurriedly, in her distant wake. Gritting her teeth, she waited, and waited, for him to catch up. The instant he did, she turned and, elevating her nose to an angle worthy of her ire, she matched her pace to his, strolling at crawling pace just ahead of him.

Two paces later, a warm flush washed over her nape, exposed above her neckline. The odd sensation drifted lower, spreading across her shoulders, then sliding down her spine. It lingered in the hollow of her waist, then, at a telling pace, washed lower, and yet lower—

She caught her breath and stopped to brush an imaginary wrinkle from her skirts. The instant Demon drew level with her, she straightened and stepped out—at his side—praying her fading blush was no longer visible.

Biting her tongue against all manner of heated phrases, she preserved a tense silence. He strolled calmly beside her and gave her not one opening to snipe at him.

The grooms saw them as they emerged from beneath the wisteria, and they ran to get his bays.

Halting at the entrance to the stable yard, Flick's patience came to an end. "I can't see why you're not grateful," she hissed. She kept her gaze on the grooms as they fussed with his horses.

"Can't you? Perhaps that's the problem."

"There *isn't* any problem."

"Permit me to disagree." He paused, then added, "Aside from anything else, you're glaring."

She whirled and faced him. "I'm glaring at *you*."

"So I noticed."

"You are *impossible*!"

"*Me*?"

For an instant, his blue eyes blinked wide—she could actually imagine he was sincere in his surprise. Swiftly, his eyes searched hers; his gaze sharpened. "Tell me," he murmured, glancing at the lads harnessing the bays, "do you think to marry Dillon eventually?"

"*Dillon*?" She stared at him, unmindful of the fact that her mouth had fallen open. "Marry *Dillon*? You *are* out of your mind. As if I'd marry such a ... a ... nobody—an inconsequential boy. A man of no real substance. A *nincompoop*! A—"

"All right—forget I asked."

"For your information, I have no intention of marrying *any* gentleman unless I want to. I will certainly not marry simply because of some nonsensical social stricture." Her voice cracked with the effort of screaming in whispers. She drew breath and forged on, "And as for *your* offer—well, you might as well say I must marry because of a *mouse*!"

The bays came trotting up, led by an eager groom. Tersely, Demon nodded his thanks and took the reins. Climbing to the box seat, he sat and looked at her.

Eyes kindling, she tartly remarked, "I can't see *why* you aren't grateful— you know perfectly well you don't *want* to marry me."

He looked down at her, his expression like stone, his eyes hard as blue diamonds. He held her defiant gaze, then his chest swelled.

"You have no idea," he murmured, his diction frighteningly precise, "what I want at all."

He clicked the reins; the bays surged. He swept out of the stable yard and bowled away down the drive.

CHAPTER
Eight

ॐᲐᲗᏜ

"I wondered if you'd care for a drive?" Gasping, Flick whirled; the large vase she was carrying shook, slipped—Demon reached out and steadied it; his fingers brushed hers. Flick trembled. She drew her hands away, leaving him holding the vase. Standing in the sunshine streaming through the gallery windows, she stared at him, disjointed phrases tangling on her tongue. She wanted to rail at him for creeping up on her—again. She wanted to scowl or at least frown—she hadn't forgiven him for his behavior of yesterday.

She wanted to ask what he'd meant by his parting comment. "A drive?" Her head was still whirling.

He shrugged, his lids veiling his eyes. "Just a tool about the lanes for half an hour or so."

She drew in a steadying breath. Twenty-four hours had passed since he'd driven away—twenty-four hours in which she'd thought of little else but him. Swinging to the windows, she looked out on another glorious spring day. Simultaneously, she felt the warm flush she was growing accustomed to slide down her back.

"The breeze is warm. You won't need a spencer."

Just as well; she didn't have one that wouldn't look hideous with this gown—white mull muslin sprinkled with tiny gold and purple daisies. Flick nodded, determination filling her. "A drive would be very nice."

She turned to face him—he was still holding the vase.

"Where do you want this?"

She gestured down the gallery. "If you'll put it on the table at the end, I'll get my parasol and meet you in the hall."

She didn't wait for his nod but headed for her room—her steps eager, her heart lighter, even if she'd yet to meet his eyes directly. They had to get past this silly hitch in their friendship, over the hurdle of yesterday—a drive would be a good start.

A good start to what she was no longer sure by the time Demon turned his bays back up the manor drive. She'd imagined they'd simply slide back to their earlier, easy friendship—she'd expected, after the initial, inevitable stiffness evaporated, to once again encounter the teasing light she'd so often seen in his blue eyes.

Instead ...

Angling her parasol, she studied his face as he tooled the curricle up the drive. Shadows from the enclosing trees wreathed his features, but they did nothing to soften the patriarchal lines of his nose and chin. His was an angular face, high cheekbones shadowing the long planes of his cheeks, a broad forehead above large eyes. A hard face, its austerity seductively flavored by the frankly sensual line of his thin lips, the brooding languor of his heavy lids.

She had never really looked, not so deeply. His had been the face of a man she'd thought she'd known. She was no longer so sure of that.

Realigning her parasol, she looked ahead as they swept out of the trees and bowled along beside the lawns. The end of the drive was in sight, and she'd yet to understand why his teasing looks had been replaced by glances much more direct, much more unnerving. Much more intent. She'd yet to determine where he thought they were heading. Only then could she decide whether she agreed with him or not.

Demon sent the bays into a tight curve so that the curricle fetched up neatly before the steps. He tied off the reins and stepped down, hiding his satisfied smile, along with his awareness of the puzzled looks Flick continued to direct his way.

Strolling around the carriage, he helped her down; releasing her hand, he strolled beside her up the steps. Glancing at her, he met her blue gaze, his expression mild and urbane. "If you would, tell the General that I'm checking into those horses he mentioned yesterday. I'll call on him tomorrow."

She searched his eyes, then nodded. "Yes, of course."

He smiled easily. "I hope you enjoyed our drive."

"Oh—yes. It was very pleasant. Thank you."

His smile deepened. "Your enjoyment is all the thanks I need." Reaching beyond her, he jangled the doorbell. Releasing it, he held her gaze for an instant, then bowed, exquisitely correct. "I'll leave you then. Good-bye."

He turned and strolled down the steps, her hesitant farewell drifting after him. The front door opened as he climbed into the curricle and took up the reins; as he wheeled his team, he glimpsed her, parasol still open, standing on the steps watching him drive away.

His lips curved. It wasn't difficult to envision the look on her face—the puzzled frown in her big blue eyes. Smiling more definitely, he whipped up his horses and headed for the Heath.

He returned to the manor at eleven o'clock the next morning, ostensibly to see the General.

Jacobs opened the door to him; Demon crossed the threshold to discover a sermon in progress. Fittingly, it was being delivered by the vicar's wife, Mrs. Pemberton, a trenchantly good-hearted lady. Her venue was the front hall, her audience Mrs. Fogarty and Jacobs, who, Demon noted, had left the front door wide open. He deduced Mrs. Pemberton was on the point of departure.

His appearance proved a distraction, making Mrs. Pemberton lose her thread. Then she recognized him and regrouped. "Mr. Cynster! *Perfect!*"

Demon suppressed a wince.

Mrs. Pemberton bustled up. "I've just been asking after the General—I understand he's presently 'not to be disturbed.'" Casting a severe glance at Fogarty, Mrs. Pemberton laid a hand on Demon's sleeve. "I have a very important message for him—I would take it most kindly if you would convey it to him when next you have the pleasure of seeing him."

Mrs. Pemberton was no fool. Taking the hand she offered, Demon shook it. "Only too pleased, ma'am." He could hardly refuse.

"Excellent. Now my point is this—" She fixed her eye on Fogarty. "Thank you—I won't need to disturb you further, Mrs. Fogarty."

Fogarty sent a meaningful look Demon's way, then curtsied and withdrew.

Turning, Mrs. Pemberton fixed her sights on Jacobs. "Mr. Cynster will see me to the door. Please convey my compliments to Miss Parteger when she comes in."

Jacobs stiffened but had to bow, close the door, and withdraw, too.

Mrs. Pemberton sighed and met Demon's eye. "I know they're only trying to protect the General, but *really*! He can't simply go to ground in his library all the time—not when he's the guardian of a young lady."

Elegantly, Demon gestured to the padded seat lining the alcove at the rear of the hall. Mrs. Pemberton consented to sit. Folding her hands over her reticule, she fixed her gaze on his face as he sat alongside her.

"My purpose in calling is to bring the General to an understanding of his duties in relation to Miss Parteger. It's all gone reasonably well until now, but she's reached an age where he really needs to take a more *active* role."

Demon raised his brows innocently, encouragingly.

Mrs. Pemberton pursed her lips. "That girl must be nineteen if she's a day, and she barely sets foot outside this house, at least not in a social sense. We— the ladies of the district—have done all we can in sending invitations to Hillgate End, but, thus far, the General has refused to bestir himself." Mrs. Pemberton's double chins firmed. "I'm afraid that's not good enough. It would be a crying shame if that lovely girl is left to molder into an old maid purely because the General won't shake himself out of his library and properly perform his duties as a guardian."

"Hmm," Demon replied, entirely noncommittal.

"I particularly wished to speak with him because I'm hosting a small dance at the vicarage—just for the local young people—three evenings from now. We—the other ladies and I—think it absolutely vital that the General puts more effort into taking Miss Parteger about. How else will the poor girl ever find a husband?"

Spreading her hands, she appealed to Demon; luckily, she didn't expect a reply.

"The dance at the vicarage will be just the way to start—not too many people to overwhelm the child. Will you carry my message to the General? And, perhaps, if you could put the argument that he really needs to pay more attention to Miss Parteger's future?"

Demon met her gaze, then nodded decisively. "I'll see what I can do."

"Good!" Mrs. Pemberton beamed as Demon walked her to the door. "I'll be off, then. If you see her, do mention to Miss Parteger that I called."

Demon inclined his head as Mrs. Pemberton took her leave, considering her parting words.

He would, he decided, tell Miss Parteger she'd called, but not immediately.

Turning, he sauntered toward the library.

Half an hour later, he found Flick in the back parlor. She was ensconced amid the cushions on the settee, her legs curled under her skirts, a dish of shelled nuts on a side table beside her. She was reading a book, utterly absorbed. He watched as, without taking her eyes from the page, she reached out and picked up a nut; without missing a word, she brought the nut to her lips and popped it into her mouth, continuing to read as she crunched.

With Mrs. Pemberton's sermon ringing in his head, he scanned the round blue gown presently concealing Miss Parteger's charms. While her wardrobe would not qualify as "all the crack," there was, to his mind, nothing whatever amiss with her simple gowns. Their very simplicity enhanced, underscored and emphasized the beauty of the body within.

Which, he'd decided, was all definitely to his taste.

The body, the beauty, and her simple gowns.

Pushing away from the doorframe, he strolled into the room.

Flick looked up with a start. "Oh! Hello." She started to smile one of her innocently welcoming smiles, but as he halted before her, full awareness struck, and the tenor of her greeting changed. She still smiled in welcome, but her eyes were watchful, her smile more controlled.

He returned the gesture easily, inwardly pleased that she was, at long last, starting to see him differently. "I've finished talking horses with the General. He invited me to lunch and I've accepted. It's lovely outside—I wondered if you'd care to stroll until the gong?"

With him there, large as life, asking, she really had very little choice. While one part of Flick's mind acidly noted that fact, another part was rejoicing, eager to further explore their new, oddly thrilling, not-quite-safe interaction. She didn't understand it—she'd yet to determine where he thought he was headed. But she wanted to know. "Yes—by all means, let's stroll."

She gave him her hand and let him pull her to her feet. Minutes later, they were on the lawn, ambling side by side.

"Has anything happened with Bletchley?"

Demon shook his head. "All he's done is make tentative overtures toward a number of jockeys."

"Nothing else?"

Again he shook his head. "They seem to be concentrating on the Craven meeting, and that's still weeks away. I suspect the syndicate will have given Bletchley time to make the arrangements—it's possible his masters won't put in an appearance down here just yet."

"You think they'll leave it until closer to the meeting to check on Bletchley's success?"

"Closer, but not too close. It takes time to put all the players in place to milk the maximum return from a fix."

"Hmm." Pondering that fact, and the likelihood that Dillon would have to remain in the ruined cottage for some weeks yet, Flick frowned into the distance.

"Have you ever been to London?"

"London?" She blinked. "Only when I stayed with my aunt just after my parents died. I was only there for a few weeks, I think."

"I confess myself amazed that you've never succumbed to the urge to cut a dash in the capital."

She turned her head and studied him; to her surprise, he wasn't teasing—his gaze was steady, his expression open—well, as open as it ever was. "I ..." She considered, then shrugged. "I've never really thought of it. It's all so far away and unknown. Indeed"—she raised her brows—"I'm not even sure what 'cutting a dash' entails."

Demon grinned. "Being noticed by society due to one's dress, or exploits."

"Or conquests?"

His smile deepened. "That, too."

"Ah, well. That explains my disinterest, then. I'm not particularly interested in any of those things."

Demon couldn't restrain his smile. "A young lady uninterested in dresses and conquests—my dear, you'll break the matchmakers' hearts."

Her expression as she shrugged said she cared not a whit.

"But," he continued, "I'm surprised you don't like dancing—most ladies who enjoy riding also enjoy a turn about the dance floor."

She grimaced. "I haven't spent much time dancing. There aren't a lot of balls around here, you know."

"But there are the usual dances. I vaguely remember my great-aunt prodding me to attend a few many years ago."

"Well, yes—there *are* dances and the odd ball as one might expect. We do get cards periodically. But the General is always so busy."

"Does he even see the cards?"

Flick glanced up, but she could read nothing in his very blue eyes. Still ... she tilted her chin. "I deal with his correspondence. There's no point bothering him with such invitations—he's never attended such affairs."

"Hmm." Demon glanced at her face—what he could see beneath her golden halo. Without warning, he reached for her hand; stepping swiftly, he raised it and twirled her, unsurprised that, startled though she was, she reacted smoothly, graceful and surefooted, innately responsive.

He met her wide eyes as she slowed to a halt, her billowing skirts subsiding. "I really think," he murmured, lowering her hand, "that you'll enjoy dancing."

Flick hid a frown and wondered if that remark was intended to be cryptic. Before she could pursue it, the gong for lunch echoed over the lawn.

Demon offered his arm. "Shall we join the General?"

They did. Sitting at the dining table with the General to her right and Demon opposite was a familiar, comfortable situation. Flick relaxed; her nerves, in recent times slightly tense whenever Demon was near, eased. Chatting with her usual effervescence, she felt subtlely more in control.

Until the General laid down his fork and fixed her with a direct look. "Mrs. Pemberton called this morning."

"Oh?" Flick knew she had—that was why she'd taken refuge in the back parlor. But she was genuinely surprised that the General knew—she, Foggy and Jacobs had a longstanding agreement to ensure the local matrons didn't bother him with their demands.

She scanned the room, but Jacobs had withdrawn. Had Mrs. Pemberton bullied her way past their defenses?

"Hmm," the General went on. "Seems she's giving a dance for the local young people. Us older folk are allowed to come and watch." He caught Flick's startled eye. "I rather think we should attend, don't you?"

Flick didn't—she foresaw all sorts of complications. Including the likelihood of the General learning just how many similar invitations he'd refused in recent times. She glanced at Demon, and was struck by inspiration. "I really don't have anything to wear."

The General chuckled. "I thought you might say that, so I had a word with Mrs. Fogarty—she tells me there's a very good dressmaker in the High Street. She'll go with you tomorrow and see about a dress."

"Oh." Flick blinked. The General was smiling at her, a hopeful question in his eyes. "Er ... thank you."

Delighted, he patted her hand. "I'm quite looking forward to the outing—haven't been about in years, it seems. Used to enjoy it when Margery was alive. Now I'm too old to dance myself, I'm looking forward to sitting and watching you take to the floor."

Flick stared at him; guilt at having deprived him of innocent enjoyment for years tickled at her mind—but she couldn't quite believe it. He *didn't* like socializing—he'd given his opinion on the *mesdames* of the district, and their entertainments, often enough. She couldn't understand what had got into his head. "But ..." She grabbed her last straw. "I don't know any of the local gentlemen well enough to stand up with them."

"Oh, you won't have to worry about that. Demon here has offered to accompany us—he'll stand up with you, teach you a few steps, and all that. Just what you need."

Flick didn't think so. Blank-faced, she looked at Demon. He met her gaze, the quality of the smile in his eyes stating louder than words that it was *he* who had got into the General's head.

Despite the fact that his eyes were blue, Flick saw red. But he had her trussed up tight—no matter how she wriggled, the General stood firm. And as it quickly became clear he was, beneath his placid exterior, gruffly worried about her lack of social experience, she found herself acquiescing with a sweetness entirely out of step with her temper.

Her tormentor, of course, beat a strategic retreat once he'd secured his goal. Flick gritted her teeth—she would now have to learn to dance—*with him*. Excusing himself on the grounds that he wanted to be early to the Heath for afternoon stables, he left them at the table.

All her steel went out of her once he'd gone. She chatted easily with the General, while making a very large, very red mental note to tell his protégé just what she thought of his maneuvering, especially his fostering of the General's worry, the instant she next had a moment alone with him.

That moment did not occur until they were standing by the side of the vicarage drawing room, with every eye in the room upon them. Flick stood, head up, hands lightly clasped, beside the General's chair. Demon, large, lean and hideously elegant, stood immediately by her side.

The stares directed her way, while disconcerting, did not greatly surprise Flick; the vision she presented had stunned her, too. All she'd done was don her new dress and the aquamarine necklace and earrings the General had given her for her last birthday, but the resulting vision that had stared back at her from her mirror had been a revelation.

She'd dutifully gone to the dressmaker with Foggy, a sudden convert to the notion of a dance. The dressmaker, Clotilde, had been surprisingly ready to put aside her other work to create a suitable gown for her. Suitable, Clotilde had insisted, meant pale blue silk, the exact same shade as her eyes. Imagining the cost, she'd demurred, suggesting a fine voile, but Clotilde had waved that aside and named a price that had been impossible to refuse. She'd agreed on the silk, only to be surprised again.

The dress whispered about her, sliding over her in quite a different way from the fine cottons she was used to. It clung, and shifted, and slithered; it was cool and at the same time warm. As for how she appeared in it—she hadn't recognized the slender, golden-haired beauty blinking huge blue eyes at her.

The color of the dress highlighted her eyes, making them appear larger, wider; the texture emphasized curves she normally paid very little attention to.

Demon, on the other hand, had paid a great deal of attention—to her, to those curves, to her eyes. When she'd descended the stairs and found him waiting in the hall, he'd blinked, then slowly smiled. Too intently for her liking. He'd come forward, handing her down the last stairs, then twirling her before him.

As she'd slowed, then halted, he'd trapped her gaze, lifted her hand, and brushed his lips across her fingertips. "Very nice," he'd purred, his blue eyes alight.

She'd felt like a blancmange he was just about to eat. Luckily, the General had appeared, and she'd escaped to fuss over him.

Their journey to Lidgate had been filled with the usual discussion of horses, but once they'd entered the vicarage, that subject was, by tacit agreement, not further pursued. Mrs. Pemberton had greeted them with great good cheer—she'd been particularly delighted to welcome Demon.

Flick slid a glance his way; he was idly scanning the room, slowly filling as more guests arrived. The General had insisted they be on time, so they'd been among the first to arrive. But the rest had followed on their heels; since taking up their positions, they'd had no chance to converse, too busy nodding politely as new arrivals nodded at them.

And stared. Half stared at her—the rest stared at him.

Hardly surprising. He was wearing black, a color that rendered his fair hair a brilliant blond and deepened the blue of his eyes. The severe cut of his coat, pearl satin waistcoat and trousers emphasized his height, the breadth of his shoulders, his long, strong legs. He always looked elegant, but usually in a lazy, negligent way. Tonight, he was every inch the London rake, a predator stepped straight from the ton's ballrooms to prowl the vicarage dance floor.

Flick inwardly grinned at the thought.

As if sensing her gaze, he glanced down at her, then raised a quizzical brow. She hesitated, but with the General so close, she couldn't upbraid him as he deserved for getting her into this—into this room, into this gown, into this situation. With a speaking glance, she elevated her chin and haughtily looked away.

Mrs. Pemberton materialized before them. "Allow me to present Mrs. March and her family from the Grange."

Mrs. March nodded approvingly at Flick's curtsy, smiled appreciatively at Demon's elegant bow, then turned to chat with the General.

"And this is Miss March, who we all know as Kitty."

A young girl in a white dress blushed furiously and curtsied.

"And her friend, Miss Avril Collins."

The second young lady, a brunette in yellow muslin, curtsied rather more assuredly.

"And Henry, who is squiring his sister and Miss Collins tonight."

Henry was obviously a March, as fair as his sister. He blushed furiously while executing the stiffest bow Flick had ever seen. "It's a g-great pleasure, M-Miss Parteger."

Mrs. Pemberton turned away; a second later, together with Mrs. March, she led the General away to where the older guests were gathering to chat and gossip.

"I say—have you lived in these parts long?"

Flick turned to find Henry March earnestly regarding her. His sister, too, lifting her gaze from a perusal of her blue silk gown, looked interested in the question.

Not so Avril Collins, who was brazenly looking interested in Demon.

"Most of my life," Flick answered, her gaze on Avril Collins's face. "I live with the General at Hillgate End, south of the racecourse."

Avril's pouting lips—they *had* to be rouged—lifted in a little smile. "I know," she said on a breathless giggle, one finger reaching out to tap Demon's coat, "that *you* live in London, Mr. Cynster."

Flick glanced at Demon's face. He smiled—not a smile she was used to, but one coolly, distantly polite.

"Actually, I live in London only part of the time. The rest of the time I live near Hillgate End."

"The General keeps a studbook, doesn't he?" Henry March appealed to Flick. "That must be exciting—do you help him keep track of the horses?"

Flick smiled. "It is interesting, but I don't help all that much. Of course, all the talk in the house is about horses."

Henry's eager expression suggested such a household was his idea of heaven.

"Oh, *horses*!" Avril wrinkled her nose and cast an openly inviting glance at Demon. "Don't you find them the most *boring* of creatures?"

"No." Demon met her gaze. "I breed them."

Flick could almost feel sorry for Avril Collins—Demon purposely let the silence stretch for one exceedingly uncomfortable instant, then turned to Henry March. "I own the stud farm to the west of the Lidgate road. Stop by some time if you're interested. If I'm not there, my foreman will show you around. Just mention my name."

"T-thank you," Henry stammered. "I'd l-like that immensely."

Mrs. Pemberton appeared with another group of young people. The fresh round of introductions allowed Kitty March to remove her unfortunate friend. Kitty tugged at her brother's sleeve, but he frowned at her, then returned to his open adoration of Flick.

In that pursuit he was joined by the two male members of the new group, both young gentlemen from nearby estates. Somewhat disconcerted by their soulful looks, Flick did her best to encourage rational conversation, only to be defeated by their patent silliness.

Their silliness, however, was nothing compared to their sisters' witlessness, their vapidity. Flick was not sure which she found more distracting.

"No." She drew a patient breath. "I don't watch every race. The Jockey Club sends all the results to the General."

"Do *you* get to name all the new foals?" One of the young ladies stared wide-eyed up at Demon.

Wearily resigned, he raised his brows. "I suppose I do."

"Oh! That must be so *wonderful*." The young damsel clasped her hands to her breast. "Thinking up sweet names for all those lovely little foals, staggering around on their shaky legs."

Flick immediately looked back at her group of swains. "Do any of you come to Newmarket to see the races?"

She struggled on, racking her brain for topics on which they might have more than two words to contribute. Most of such topics concerned racing, horses and carriages—within minutes, Demon insinuated a comment into their conversation. A minute later, he somehow managed to merge the two groups, which left the young ladies a trifle miffed, but they didn't move away.

Which was a pity, as Mrs. Pemberton arrived with another wave of admirers, both for her and Demon. Flick found herself facing five males, while Demon had his hands full, figuratively speaking, with six young girls. And one not-so-young, not-so-innocent young madam.

"What a delightful surprise, Mr. Cynster, to discover a gentleman of your standing at a gathering such as this. In case you missed my name, I'm Miss Henshaw."

The throaty voice had Flick quickly turning.

"I say—you ride that pretty little mare, don't you? The one with the white hocks."

Distracted, Flick glanced back at one of the new male additions. "Yes. That's Jessamy."

"Do you jump her?"

"Not especially."

"Well, you should. I've seen conformations like that around the traps—she'll do well, mark my words."

Flick shook her head. "Jessamy's not—"

"Dare say you might not know, being a female, but take my word for it—she's got good legs and good stamina." The bluffly genial youth, the local squire's son, grinned at her, the epitome of a patronizing male. "If you like, I could organize a jockey and trainer for you."

"Yes, but—" one of her earnest admirers cut in. "She lives with the General—he keeps the stud records."

"So?" Bluff-and-genial raised a dismissive brow. "What's dusty old records got to do with it? This is horseflesh we're talking about."

A throaty laugh came from beyond Demon. Flick gritted her teeth. "For your information"—her tone stopped all argument and made Bluff-and-genial blink—"Jessamy is an *investment*. As a broodmare, she has arguably the best bloodlines in the country. You may be *very* certain I will not be risking her in any steeplechase."

"Oh," was all Bluff-and-genial dared say.

Flick turned to deal with the throaty-voiced Miss Henshaw—and saw a black-haired beauty, smiling and laughing, leaning close to Demon, her face tipped up to his. She was, Flick saw in that one chilling instant, a lot taller than she herself was—so her face, tilted up, was much closer to Demon's, her lips closer to his—

"Now, my dears!"

Every head in the room lifted; everyone looked to where Mrs. Pemberton stood, clapping her hands for attention. "Now," she reiterated, when everyone was silent, "it's time to find your partners for the first dance."

There was an instant of silence, then a rush as all the young men jockeyed for position. A chorus of invitations and acceptances filled the air.

Flick found herself facing three earnest young men—Bluff-and-genial had been shouldered aside.

"My dear Miss Parteger, if you will—"

"I pray, kind lady, that—"

"If you would honor me with this dance—"

Flick blinked at their youthful faces—they all seemed so *young*. She didn't need to look to know that the seductive Miss Henshaw was batting her long lashes at Demon. She didn't need to look, but she wanted to. She wanted to—

"Actually," a deep drawling voice purred just above her right ear, "Miss Parteger's first dance is mine."

Demon's hand closed firmly about hers; Flick looked up to see him smile with a shatteringly superior air at her youthful admirers. There was no chance in heaven they would argue.

The relief she felt was quite definite, the reasons for it less clear. Luckily, she didn't need to dwell on it. Demon glanced down at her and raised one brow. Gracefully, she inclined her head. He set her hand on his sleeve; the others fell back as he led her onto the rapidly clearing floor.

The dance was to be a cotillion. As Demon led her to a set, Flick whispered, "I know the theory, but I've never actually danced one of these in my life."

He smiled reassuringly. "Just copy what the other lady does. If you wander off in the wrong direction, I'll grab you."

Despite all, despite her dismissive humph, she found that promise comforting.

They took their positions and the music started; despite her worries, she quickly found the rhythm. The dips and sways and hand-clasped twirls were heavily repetitive; it wasn't that hard to keep her place. And Demon's touch was reassuring—every time his fingers closed about hers, he steadied her, even if she wasn't drifting.

As the dance progressed, she felt increasingly assured—assured enough to stop frowning and smile when her eyes touched his. She laughed up at him, over her shoulder, as he twirled her into their final pose, then she sank into an extravagantly deep curtsy as he bowed, equally extravagantly, to her.

Demon raised her; he wondered if she knew how brightly her eyes were shining, how gloriously unabashed, unfettered in her enjoyment she was. She was so different from the other young ladies in the room, all careful to mind their words, their expressions, if not to artfully deploy them. She was unrestrained in her appreciation—something tonnish ladies rarely were. Exuberance, even if honest, was not the ton's way.

It *was* Flick's way—her wide smile and laughing eyes had him smiling, equally honestly, in reply. "And now," he said, and had to draw a deeper breath as he drew her closer and looked into her eyes, "we must return to our duty."

She laughed. "Which duty is that?"

The duty he alluded to was to dance with all the other young people gathered at the vicarage for that purpose. They had barely returned to the side of the room before Flick's hand was solicited for a country dance.

Her other hand still rested on Demon's sleeve. She looked up at him—he smiled reassuringly, squeezed her fingers lightly, then let her go.

As she twirled down the room, Flick noticed Demon twirling, too, with the vicar's daughter. Letting her gaze slide away, she smiled easily at her partner, Henry March.

Dance followed dance, but with time between to allow the dancers to chat. To get to know each other better, to find their feet socially. That was, after all, what the evening was about. The older members of the company sat at the rear of the room, smiling and nodding, watching benignly as their youngsters mingled.

Mrs. Pemberton, her duty as hostess done, sank into a chair beside the General. Luckily, the General was deep in discussion with the vicar; Mrs. Pemberton did not interrupt. Relieved, Flick looked away. Beside her, Demon shifted. Flick looked up, and he caught her eye. And raised a knowing brow. She stared into his eyes, at the comprehension therein, then put her nose in the air and looked away. And struggled to ignore the *frisson* that shot through her when his hand shifted and his fingers brushed hers amid her skirts.

The dances that followed proved a trial. It was increasingly difficult to keep her mind on her steps. As for her eyes, they rarely rested on her partner. Twirling, whirling, she shot glances through the throng, through the constantly moving mass. Looking, searching . . .

She located Demon—he was dancing with Kitty March. Flick relaxed.

The next measure, however, he partnered Miss Henshaw.

Flick collided with another lady in her set, and nearly ended on her bottom. Flustered, she gasped, "I think"—she didn't have to feign her shaking voice—"that I'd better sit out the rest of this dance."

Her partner, a Mr. Drysdale, was only too willing to solicitously help her from the floor.

By the time Demon returned to her side at the end of the dance, as he had at the end of every dance thus far, Flick had herself well in hand. She'd lectured herself more sternly than she ever had in her life.

It was ridiculous! What on earth was she doing—thinking? Watching over him as if she was jealous. How foolish—making a cake of herself like that. Pray God he hadn't noticed, or he'd tease her unmercifully. And she'd deserve it. There was nothing between them—*nothing*!

She greeted him with a cool smile and immediately looked away.

His fingers found hers in her skirts—and tugged. She had to look up and meet his gaze.

It was serious, exceedingly intent. "Are you all right?"

His eyes searched hers; God alone knew what he saw. Flick dragged in a breath—and wished she could drag her gaze from his. "It was just a silly slip. I didn't fall."

A frown darkened his eyes; his lips firmed, but then he nodded and, very slowly, released her hand. "Be more careful—this is, after all, your first time at a dance."

If she'd been feeling at all normal she would have responded to that as it deserved. Instead, the lingering touch of his fingers had blown all her certainties to the wind.

Nothing? If this—the light that turned his eyes dark and smoldering, the sense of protection, of strength, she felt flowing from him, the answering hitch in her breathing, the yearning that grew stronger, day by day, for him—if this was nothing, what would something be like?

More conscious of her heartbeat, of the rise and fall of her breasts than she'd ever been in her life, she looked away.

When she whirled down the next dance, she was conscious of him watching her, aware to her toes of the blue gaze that missed nothing, not a step, not a turn. He was waiting when her partner returned her to the side of the room. As if it was only natural, she slipped into the space beside him.

His gaze swept her face, but he said nothing.

Until the music started up again.

"My dance, I believe."

His tone brooked no argument—from her potential partners, or her. She inclined her head graciously, as if she'd been expecting his claim. Perhaps she had.

For him to dance with her a second time while there were other young ladies he had not yet favored lent the action a particularity it would otherwise not have had—he was clearly singling her out. Despite her lack of social experience, she knew it—and knew beyond doubt that he did, too.

It was a simple country dance that left them partnered throughout, without interaction with other dancers; they had no need to shift their attention from each other. From the instant the music started and their fingers touched, their focus was fixed. For her part, she barely heard the music. She moved instinctively, matching his actions, responding to directing touches so light she felt them more with her senses than with her nerves.

His eyes held her. His gaze, as brilliantly blue as a summer sky, wrapped her in its warmth. And she knew—knew that he was squiring her, deliberately, intentionally. Intent as only he could be. He was wooing her—even if the idea seemed so wild and impossible that her mind could not accept it, her senses did. Her first impulse was to step back—to safety, to a point where she could look about and understand. But while she whirled and twirled, her eyes never leaving his, there was no place of safety, nowhere she could hide from the smoldering glow in his eyes—and the very last thing she wanted to do was run.

His gaze held her effortlessly, yet without compulsion; she was fascinated, and that alone was power enough to keep her whirling. The sliding brush of his fingers as their hands met and parted, the gliding caress, so delicate, as he steered her into a sweeping turn—each was planned deliberately, executed with intent. In that single dance, he wove a net about her—one invisible to the eye but very clear to her senses.

Her nerves tingled, tightened; each heartbeat heightened her awareness. Until his every touch held a temptation and a promise, echoed by their movements in the dance.

She swayed closer, looking up as he drew her nearer, and felt the temptation to surrender. To surrender to the conviction of what he was telling her, to give in and believe that he wanted her to be his wife. And would have her.

The dance moved on, and she drew away, until their fingers barely touched. And heard his promise, unspoken, that if she surrendered she'd enjoy—experience—the full pleasures of the flesh.

He was adept at sending that message, expert at making the temptation grow, and the promise shine and beckon like gold.

The music ended. And they stopped. But the temptation and the promise still shone in his eyes.

She felt like Cinderella when he raised her hand and brushed his lips gently across her fingertips.

CHAPTER
Nine

ॐ

When the next dance commenced, Demon was, courtesy of Mrs. Pemberton, at the opposite end of the room from Flick. Within seconds of their leaving the floor, the vicar's wife had descended on them; with irresistible energy, she'd insisted on taking Demon to introduce him to others of the company.

Her "others" were the collected matrons of the district; Demon was amused to realize their fell purpose in speaking with him was to subtlely encourage his pursuit of Flick.

"She's such a pretty little thing, and quite assured," Mrs. Wallace, of the Hadfield-Wallaces of Dullingham, nodded sagely. "As experienced as you are, you'll have noticed—she's not just in the common way."

Demon smiled, content to let them convince him of the rightness of his cause. He didn't need convincing, but it wouldn't hurt his campaign to have the matrons' support.

Because of his height, he could track Flick's crowning glory. As the ladies' comments continued, he started to chafe at the bit. He understood very well the reasons behind their reactions—those reasons were gathered about Flick like swarming bees about a honeypot.

Their sons looked set to make cakes of themselves over her—their fond mamas could read the script with ease. It was, therefore, in their best interests to have Demon waltz Flick off her feet, out of reach of their moonfaced sons, so said sons could recover quickly and apply themselves to the real business of the upcoming Season—finding themselves suitable wives.

Flick, of course, was highly suitable, but the ladies had accepted that their sons were not in the running, just as they'd accepted that their daughters had no chance of catching Demon's eye. It was therefore best on all counts to get him and Flick quickly paired and out of contention, before they caused any major disruptions to the good ladies' matrimonial plans.

Such was their strategy. As their plans marched so well with his, Demon was perfectly ready to reassure them as to his intentions. "Her knowledge of horses is extensive." He made the comment offhandedly, yet appreciatively. "And, of course, she is the General's ward."

"Indeed," Mrs. Wallace nodded approvingly. "So very appropriate."

"A happy circumstance," Mrs. Pemberton concurred.

With an elegant bow, quite sure they all understood each other well, Demon left them. He ambled down the side of the room, scanning the dancers. He couldn't see Flick.

Halting, he searched more carefully—she wasn't there.

He located the General, chatting with a group of older gentlemen—Flick wasn't with him.

Swallowing a curse directed at milksops who couldn't be trusted to keep a quick-witted girl in line, Demon strolled as swiftly as he could to where he'd last seen her, at the far end of the room. He reached the corner, wondering what had got into her head. Surely her disappearance didn't have anything to do with Bletchley and the syndicate?

The idea that she might have been identified, followed, and lured away chilled him. He shook the thought aside—that was fanciful, unlikely. The main door stood beyond the matrons; he was sure she hadn't gone that way. But the only other doors led deeper into the house.

Where the hell had she gone?

He was searching the throng again when a flicker at the edge of his vision had him turning. The lace curtain over the long window in the corner drifted in a light breeze. The narrow casement was partly open; it extended from head height to a foot above the floor. He couldn't fit through it. Flick, however, was smaller than he.

It took him five minutes to return back up the room, smiling and nodding and avoiding invitations to chat. Regaining the front hall, he slipped out the front door and headed around the side of the vicarage.

The garden beyond the drawing room's corner window was empty. The moon was full; steady silver light illuminated a flagged path and burgeoning flowerbeds edging a neat lawn. Frowning, Demon scanned the shadows, but there were no nooks, no benches set under overhanging boughs—no angel in pale blue communing with the night.

The garden was sunk in silence, the drifting strains of the violins a superficial tune causing barely a ripple in the deep of the night. A lick of fear touched his spine, flicked toward his heart. He was about to turn and retrace his steps, to check she hadn't returned to the drawing room *before* he panicked, when his gaze fell on the hedge lining one side of the lawn.

A path ran beside it, between the lawn and the deep green wall. The hedge was high; he couldn't see over it. Silently, he prowled the wall, searching, wondering if he was wrong in remembering a small courtyard . . .

The opening lay in shadow, just a simple gap in the hedge. He stepped into the gap. And saw her.

The courtyard was a flagged square with a raised central bed in which stood an old magnolia, draping its branches over a small pond. Flick paced slowly back and forth before it, the moonlight washing the blue from her gown, leaving it an unearthly silver.

Demon watched her, transfixed by the sway of her hips, the artless grace with which she turned. Until that instant, he hadn't realized how tightly unnamed fears had seized him; he recognized the tension only as it eased, as relief replaced it.

She felt his gaze and looked up, halting, stiffening—then relaxing as she recognized him. She said nothing, but raised a brow.

"In that gown, in the moonlight, you look like a silver sprite." *Come to steal this mortal's heart.* His voice was gravelly, revealingly deep.

If she noticed, she gave no sign; instead, she looked down at her gown, holding out the skirts to inspect them. "It *is* a very pale blue. I rather like it."

He liked it, too—it was the same pale, pure blue as her eyes. The gown was well worth the price he'd paid. Of course, she'd never know he'd offset the gown's cost. Clotilde was an excellent dressmaker; he made a mental note to send some extra token of appreciation her way.

He hesitated ... but they were here, alone in the moonlight, the violins a distant whisper in the dark. Unhurriedly, he strolled forward, his gaze, intent, on her.

Flick watched him approach, large, elegant—dangerous. The moon silvered his hair, rendering his face harsh in its stark light. The angular planes seemed harder, like pale stone; his eyes were deeply shadowed beneath their heavy lids.

How his presence could be reassuring and unnerving simultaneously she didn't know. Her nerves were tightening, her senses stretching ... The yearning she'd felt as they'd danced returned with a rush.

She'd come here to be quiet, to breathe the cool air, to let it soothe her overheated brain, her flushed skin. She'd come here to ponder. Him. Part of her wondered if she'd read him aright. The rest of her knew she had. But she still couldn't bring herself to believe it.

It was like a fairy tale.

Now he was here .... Her nerves skittered even before she formed the thought. Abruptly, she recalled she was annoyed with him. Folding her arms, she tilted her chin; as he drew near, she narrowed her eyes at him. "*You* conspired with Mrs. Pemberton—Foggy told me she sent her message to the General via you."

He halted before her. "Mrs. Pemberton conjured a vision of you moldering into an old maid—that didn't seem a good idea."

His deep drawl slid over, then under, her skin, effortlessly vanquishing her annoyance. Refusing to shiver, she humphed. "I can't see how an evening like this is going to change things." She gestured toward the house. "I'm certainly not going to find a husband in there."

"No?"

"You saw them. They're so young!"

"Ah—them."

His voice deepened; she sensed that net of fascination flow about her again. His lips curved, lifting just a little at the ends, drawing her mentally closer, nearer. "No," he said, the word a deep rumble. "I agree—you definitely shouldn't marry any of them."

The ensuing pause stretched, then his lids rose and he met her gaze. "There is, however, an alternative."

He said no more, but his meaning was clear, written in the planes of his face, in his eyes. He watched her, his gaze steady; the night held them in soft darkness, alive and yet so silent that she could feel her own pulse filling the air.

Then came the music.

Haunting strains drifted over the lawns, flowed over the hedges. The opening bars of a waltz reached them—he angled his head slightly, then, his gaze never leaving her face, he held out his hands.

"Come—waltz with me."

The net drew tight—she felt its shimmering touch as it settled about her. But he didn't tug; it was her choice to step forward, to accept, if she would.

Flick wondered if she dared. Her senses reached for him—she knew how it felt to be held against his warm chest, how it felt to have his arms close about her, how her hips would settle against his hard thighs. But . . .

"I don't know how."

Her voice was surprisingly even; his lips curved a fraction more.

"I'll teach you"—a hint of wickedness invested his smile—"all you need to know."

She managed not to shiver. She knew very well they weren't talking of a mere waltz—that wasn't the invitation etched in his eyes, the challenge in his stance. Those hands, those arms, that body—she knew what he was offering. And, deep inside, she knew she could never walk away—not without trying, touching. Knowing.

She stepped forward, lifting her arms, tilting her face to his. He drew her to him, one arm sliding possessively about her, the other grasping her right hand. He drew her close, until they touched, until the silk of her bodice brushed his coat. His smile deepened. "Relax, and let your feet follow where they will."

He stepped back, then aside; before she knew it, she was whirling. At first, he took small steps, until she caught the rhythm, then they whirled, swooped, swung, trapped in the music, swept up in the effortless energy of the dance.

Then the mood of the music changed, slowed; they slowed, too. He drew her fractionally closer—she leaned her temple against his chest. "Isn't there some rule that I'm not supposed to waltz before someone or other approves?"

"That only applies in town at a formal ball. Young ladies have to learn to waltz somewhere, or no gentleman would ever stand up with them."

She suppressed a sniff—she hadn't stepped on his toes once. They were revolving slowly, the music soft and low.

It was she who stepped closer, fascinated by the slide of silk between their bodies. And by the heat of him.

He didn't step back. His fingers locked about hers, he laid her hand in the hollow of his shoulder. His arm tightened about her, his hand splaying below her waist, locking her to him so that they moved in truth as one.

His hand burned; so did his thighs as they pressed between hers as he steered her through a shallow turn. Her breasts firm against his coat, she laid her cheek against his chest, and listened to his heart.

Eventually, with a minor flourish they ignored, the music died. Their feet slowed, then halted; for one long instant, they simply stood.

Then she lifted her head and looked into his face. His temptation, his promise, were all around her, a shimmering veil, a glow suffusing her skin. She knew she wasn't imagining it; she didn't know enough to imagine this. She knew what was there, what it was, what might be.

She didn't know why.

So she simply asked, her eyes on his, deeply shadowed by his lids, "Why are you doing this?"

He searched her eyes, then raised one brow. "I would have thought that was obvious." After a moment, he stated, "I'm wooing you—courting you—call it what you will."

"Why?"

"Why else? Because I want you to be my wife."

"Why?"

He hesitated, then his hand left hers. His fingers slid beneath her chin, tipping her face up. His lips closed over hers.

It started as a gentle caress. That satisfied neither of them. Whether it was she or he who deepened the kiss was impossible to say—his lips were suddenly harder, firmer, more demanding; hers were correspondingly softer, more beguiling, more inviting.

Greatly daring, she parted her lips, just a little, then more, thrilled to her toes when he took instant advantage. Angling his head, he tasted her, then, like a conqueror, simply took more.

She shivered, and gave, and welcomed him in; his arms tightened about her, impressing her soft flesh with the hardness of his. She sighed, and felt him drink—her breath was his and his was hers; her head reeled as the kiss went on.

Again, it was she who took the next step, who, in all innocence, stretched her arms up, slid her hands to his nape and sank against him. She felt a rumble in his chest—a groan that never made it to his lips.

Their kiss turned ravenous.

Hot. Hungry.

His lips seared hers; his hunger whipped, and licked, and tempted. She sensed it clearly—there—beneath the smooth control, the elegant facade. Ever bold, she reached for it.

He froze.

The next instant, she was standing, unsteadily, on her feet, the air cool between them. Her breasts ached oddly; all her skin felt hot. She blinked, and focused on him—he was breathing every bit as raggedly as she. He was just recovering faster—her wits were still whirling.

His hands fell from her; it was impossible to read his eyes. "We should get back."

Before she had time to consider, long before she could gather her wits and think, they were back in the drawing room. They mingled with the other guests while she struggled to find her mental feet. Beside her, he was his usual elegant self, cool and disgustingly controlled, while her lips were tingling, her breathing still too shallow. And she ached, bone-deep, with a sense of having been denied.

The next morning, a stack of books under her arm, Flick stepped out of the side door, looking down as she tugged on her gloves—and ran into a brick wall.

"Ooof!" All the breath was knocked out of her. Luckily, the wall was covered in resilient muscle, and had arms that locked around her, preventing her and her books from tumbling to the ground.

She dragged in a breath, her breasts swelling against Demon's soft jacket, then she blew aside the curls that had tumbled into her eyes. The exhalation ruffled the blond locks about his ear.

He stiffened. All over.

Rigid, he awkwardly unlocked his arms, grasped her upper arms, and set her back from him.

She blinked at him. He scowled at her.

"Where are you going?"

His tone, that of one having the right to know, was guaranteed to make her bridle; putting her nose in the air, she stepped around him. "To the lending library."

He smothered a curse, spun on his heel and followed. "I'll take you in my curricle."

Not so much as a by-your-leave! Let alone a "Good morning, my dear, and how are you?" So much for last night! Entirely unimpressed, Flick kept her gaze fixed stubbornly ahead, ruthlessly denying the impulse to glance at him as he ranged alongside. "I'm perfectly capable of returning and selecting my novels myself, thank you."

"I dare say."

His tone was as stubborn as hers.

She opened her mouth to argue—and caught sight of the pair of blacks harnessed to his curricle. Her face softened, her eyes lit. "Oh—what *beauties*!" Her tone was reverent, a fitting tribute to the surely matchless horses impatiently pawing the gravel. "Are they new?"

"Yes." Demon strolled in her wake as she circled the pair, exclaiming over their points. When she paused for breath, he nonchalantly added, "I thought I'd take them for a short outing, just to get them used to town traffic."

Eyes still round, fixed on the blacks' sleek hides, she wasn't paying attention; seizing the moment, he took her hand and helped her into the curricle.

"They hold their heads so well." She settled on the seat. "What's their action like?"

Barely pausing for his answer, she rattled on knowledgeably; by the time she'd run through all her questions and exclamations they were rolling down the drive. Demon kept his gaze on his horses, waiting for her to suddenly realize and berate him for taking advantage. Instead, she set her books on the seat between them and leaned back with a soft sigh.

As the peace unexpectedly lengthened, he shot her a glance; she was sitting easily, one hand braced on the side railing, her gaze fixed, not on the blacks, but on his hands.

She was watching him handle the ribbons, watching his fingers flick and slide along the leather strips. There was an eager light in her eyes, a wistful expression on her face.

He faced forward; a moment later, he clenched his jaw.

Never in his entire career had he let a female drive his cattle.

The blacks, although new, were well broken; thus far, they'd proved well behaved. And he would be sitting beside her.

If he did it once, she'd expect him to do it again.

When riding, she had a more delicate touch on the reins than even he.

Turning out of the manor drive, he set the curricle bowling down the road to Newmarket, but he didn't slacken the reins. Instead, drawing in a breath, he turned to Flick. "Would you like to take the reins for a stretch?"

The look on her face was payment enough for his abused sensibilities—stunned surprise gave way to eager joy, swiftly tempered.

"But ..." She looked at him, hope warring with imminent disappointment. "I've never driven a pair before."

He forced himself to shrug lightly. "It's not that different from a single horse. Here—shift those books and come closer." She did, eagerly sliding along the seat until her thigh brushed his. Ignoring the heat that shot straight to his loins, he transferred the reins to her small hands, keeping his fingers tensioning the leather until he was sure she had them.

"No." Expertly, he relaid the reins across her left palm. "Like that, so you've got simultaneous control over them both with just one hand."

She nodded, looking so excited that he wondered if she could speak at all. Sitting back, one arm along the seat behind her, ready to grab her if anything did go wrong, he watched her, his gaze flicking ahead now and again to check the road. But he knew it well, and so did she.

She had a little difficulty checking the pair for a curve; he gritted his teeth and managed not to reach out and lay his hand over hers. Thereafter, however, she adjusted; gradually, as the fields rolled past, they both relaxed.

There was, he discovered, one benefit in being driven by a lady—one he trusted not to land them in a ditch. He could keep his gaze wholly on her—on her face, on her figure, in this case, neat and trim in cambric. Her hair, those lovely golden curls, was constantly ruffling in the wind of their passage, a living frame for her delicate face.

A face flushed with pleasure, with an excitement he understood. She was thrilled and delighted. He felt decidedly smug.

She cast him a dubious glance as the first stables by the racecourse came into sight. From there on, there would be other horses, people, even dogs about—all things to which the blacks might take exception. Demon nodded; sitting up, he expertly lifted the reins from her hands. He readjusted the reins, letting the blacks know he had them again.

Flick sat back with an ecstatic sigh. She had always—forever—wanted to drive a curricle. And Demon's blacks! They were the most perfect young pair she'd ever seen. Not as powerful as his champion bays, but so very elegant, with their slim legs and long, sleekly arched necks.

And she'd driven them! She could hardly wait to tell the General. And Dillon—he would be green with envy. She sighed again; with a contented smile, she looked around.

Only then did she remember their earlier words—only then did she realize she'd been kidnapped. Lured away. Enticed into a gentleman's curricle with tempting promises and whisked into town.

She slanted a glance at her abductor. He was looking ahead, his expression easy but uninformative. There was nothing to say he'd planned this—that he'd purposely had the blacks put to that morning just so he could distract her.

She wouldn't mind betting he had.

Unfortunately, after enjoying herself so thoroughly, it would be churlish indeed to cavil. So she sat back and enjoyed herself some more, watching as he deftly tacked through the increasing traffic to pull up before the lending library, just off the High Street halfway through the town.

As was usual, the sight of a magnificent pair had drawn a gaggle of boys in their wake. After handing her to the pavement, Demon selected two and, with strict instructions, left the blacks in their care.

That surprised Flick, but she was too wise to show it; carrying her books, she headed for the library door. Demon followed on her heels; he reached over her shoulder and pushed the door wide.

She walked through into familiar surroundings—the wide front bay where two old gentlemen sat, dozing over their history books, the narrow aisles leading away toward the back of what had once been a hall, each aisle lined on both sides with bookshelves crammed to overflowing.

"Hello, Mrs. Higgins," Flick whispered to the large, homely woman who presided over her domain from behind a table near the entrance. "I'm returning these."

"Good, good." Perching her pince-nez on her nose, Mrs. Higgins peered down at the titles. "Ah, yes, and did the General enjoy the Major's biography?"

"He did indeed. He asked me to see if there were any more like it."

"You'll find all we have in the second aisle, dear—about midway down ..." Mrs. Higgins's words trailed away. Looking past Flick, she slowly raised her hand and removed her pince-nez, the better to take in who had strayed into her castle.

"Mr. Cynster's escorting me," Flick explained. Facing Demon, she gestured to the chairs in the front bay. "Would you like to wait there?"

He glanced at the two old gents, then looked back at her, his expression utterly blank. "I'll follow you."

He proceeded to do so, strolling directly behind her as she wandered down the aisles.

Flick tried to ignore him and concentrate on the books, but novels and literary heroes could not compete with the masculine presence prowling in her wake. The more she tried to shut him out, the more he intruded on her mind, on her senses. Which was the very last thing she needed.

She was confused enough about him as it was.

After spending the hours until dawn reliving their second dance, reliving that amazing waltz, and replaying everything they'd said in the moonlight, over her breakfast toast she'd made a firm resolution to put the entire matter from her—and wait and see.

Wait for him to make the next move—and see if it made any more sense than his last.

She had a very strong notion she was misinterpreting, through lack of experience, reading more into his words, his actions, than he intended. He was accustomed to dallying with sophisticated ladies of the ton. Doubtless, that matter of their second dance, and the waltz, and his warm words in the moonlight—and, of course, that kiss—were all simply tonnish dalliance, the way ladies and gentlemen of his ilk entertained themselves of an evening. A form of sophisticated teasing. The more she thought of it, the more that seemed likely.

In which case, the last thing she should do was place any great emphasis on any of it.

Determinedly, she halted before the bookshelf housing her favorite novels—those of Miss Austen and Mrs. Radcliffe. Ignoring the disapproving humph from behind her, she stubbornly scanned the shelves.

Demon propped one shoulder against a bookshelf, slid his hands into his pockets, and watched her with a distinctly jaundiced eye. If she wanted romance, why the hell was she looking at books?

The fact she was didn't auger well for his plans. He watched as she pulled books out and studied them, returning some, retaining others—and wondered if there was any way he could step up his campaign. Unfortunately, she was young and innocent—and strong-willed and stubborn.

Which meant that if he pushed too hard, drove too fast, she might turn skittish and difficult.

Which would slow things down all the more. He'd gentled enough high-couraged horses to know the value of patience. And, of course, this time, there was no question of him not succeeding—he intended to get his ring on her finger no matter how long it took.

This time, he refused to entertain any possibility of defeat. Last time, when he'd turned up at the manor, ready to offer himself up on a sacrificial matrimonial altar, he hadn't known what he was about. He hadn't stopped to think—he'd reacted instinctively to the situation about him. Discovering that Flick had made everything right so there was no need for them to marry had brought him up short. He'd been stunned, but not with joy. He had, in fact, been distinctly unamused, and even less amused by that fact.

That had certainly made him think. He'd spent the next twenty-four hours doing precisely that, doggedly separating his real desires from the disguise of convenience he'd wrapped them in, only to discover that, as usual, his instincts hadn't misled him.

He wanted to marry the chit—never mind why—and having her compromised so innocently had been a convenient, if not perfect, avenue by which to stake his claim. His wish to marry her was not at all innocent—his thoughts, even then, had been colored by desire. His disappointment had been so acute that he'd actually felt hurt, which had annoyed him all the more.

No woman had ever made him feel this uncertain, had made him ache with desire with no surety of relief.

His sudden susceptibility—his need for an angel—was something he wanted dealt with quickly. Once he had her safely wedded and bedded, he was sure he'd feel better—back to his usual, assured, self-reliant, self-confident self.

Which was why he proposed to dog her every step until she agreed to marry him. He could only pray it wouldn't take too long.

With three books in her arms, she finally quit that bookshelf and strolled farther down the aisle. Pushing away from his resting place, Demon ambled after her. She paused to select a cookbook; he glanced at the title as she lifted it down. *Italian Renaissance Recipes.*

"Are you planning to entertain an Italian count?"

She glanced at him. "It's for Foggy—she loves reading recipes." The book was large and heavy; she juggled it, trying to settle it in her arms.

"Here." He reached for the book.

"Oh—thank you." With a grateful smile, she handed him the cookbook and her three novels.

Lips setting, Demon accepted them all, reminding himself that none of his acquaintances, not even Reggie, were likely to come in and discover him wandering the aisles at an angel's beck and call, loaded with cookbooks and romantic novels.

Flick's next stop was the biographies. "The General likes reading about gentlemen connected with horses. The last book I got for him was about a cavalry major." Frowning, she studied the shelves. "Do you know of any work he might find interesting?"

Demon glanced at the leather and gilt spines. "I don't read much."

"Oh?" Brows rising, she looked up. "What do you do of a quiet evening?"

He trapped her wide gaze. "Active endeavors are more to my taste."

A puzzled frown formed in her eyes. "You must relax sometime."

Lips curving, he let his gaze grow intent, let his voice deepen. "The endeavors I favor are guaranteed to relax."

A faint blush tinged her cheeks; she held his gaze for an instant, then raised a haughty brow and looked away.

Inwardly grinning, Demon looked back at the books. At least she no longer viewed him as a benevolent uncle. "What about this one?" Reaching over her head, he tugged a volume free.

"*Colonel J.E. Winsome: Memoirs of a Commander of Horse*," Flick read as he put the book in her hands. She opened it and quickly perused the description at the front. "Oh, yes! This is perfect. It's about the cavalry in the Peninsula War."

"Excellent." Demon straightened. "Can we go now?"

To his relief, Flick nodded. "Yes, that's it."

She led the way to the front of the hall.

Mrs. Higgins pursed her lips in silent disapproval as Demon set the books on her desk. Flick appeared not to notice; she chatted blithely as Mrs. Higgins wrote her selections on a card. Stepping back, Demon cast a last glance around—he wouldn't be paying a second visit if he could help it.

One of the old gentlemen in the overstuffed armchairs had woken; he sent a suspicious look his way, frowning direfully from under shaggy brows.

Turning back to Flick, Demon relieved her of the pile of books she'd just settled in her arms. "Come—I'll drive you home."

Flick smiled, bid Mrs. Higgins good-bye, and preceded him to the door; Demon followed, his gaze on her hips, his mind busy with plans to cure her of all future need for fictional romantic stimulation.

CHAPTER
Ten

৪৩৬৩৩

For Flick, their journey to the library was the start of a most peculiar week. Demon drove her back to the manor by the longest possible route, ostensibly to try the blacks' paces. As he consented to let her handle the ribbons again, she refrained from making any comment on his high-handed arrogance—as it happened, she hadn't had anything better to do.

At least, nothing to compare with the sensation of bowling along, the breeze ruffling her hair, the ribbons taut in her hands. The sheer exhilaration of tooling his curricle, well-sprung and built for speed, with the blacks high-stepping down the lanes, had worked its addictive magic—she was hooked.

When he drew up before the manor, she was smiling so brightly that she couldn't possibly have admonished him.

Which, from the gleam in his eye, was precisely as he'd planned.

He was back the next morning, although this time, it wasn't her he had come to see; he spent an hour with the General, discussing a line of horses the General was investigating. Of course, the General invited him to stay for luncheon, and he accepted.

Later, she strolled with him to the stable. She waited, but, other than an artful comment about enjoying the view—it was a brisk day and her skirts were flapping—he said nothing. His eyes, however, seemed unusually brilliant, his gaze especially attentive; despite the breeze, she didn't feel cold.

Day followed day; his visits highlighted each one. She could never be certain when or where he would appear, which was doubtless why she found herself listening for his footsteps.

And it wasn't just his gaze that was attentive.

Occasionally, he would touch her, just a hand at her back, or a sliding of his fingers from her hand to her wrist. Such touches always made her catch her breath—and flush in a most peculiar way.

Her worst moment came when he called one afternoon and inveigled her into joining him to watch the strings exercising on the Heath—he was still watching Bletchley during morning and afternoon stables.

"Hills and Cross are doing the bulk of it these days. They're less identifiable than Gillies or me."

They were standing by the Heath, she with her hands clasped on the handle of her furled parasol. "Has Bletchley made any further arrangements—fixed any more fixes?"

Demon shook his head. "I'm starting to wonder . . ."

When he said nothing more, she prompted, "What?"

He glanced at her, then grimaced and looked across the close-cropped turf to where his string was going through their paces. Bletchley lounged under his favorite oak; from there, he could see three separate strings working.

"I'm starting to wonder," Demon mused, "whether he's got any more fixes to place. He's been chatting up the jockeys, true enough, but lately it's been more in the nature of ingratiating himself with them. Other than those three fixes we know of, all of which are for major Spring Carnival races, he hasn't made any further arrangements."

"So?"

"So it's possible all the fixes the syndicate want for the Spring Carnival are now in place—just those three. Considering the races involved, they should clear enough for the greediest of men. I'm wondering if Bletchley is simply whiling away time until his masters are due to check with him, and putting in his hours by learning as much as he can about the race jockeys with a view to making his next round of fixes, most likely in a few months—maybe at the July meeting—easier to arrange."

Flick studied Bletchley. "He's looking for weaknesses? Something to give him a hold over the jockeys?"

"Hmm. Possibly."

She knew the instant he switched his gaze from Bletchley to her, knew precisely when his mind shifted from fixes to . . . whatever it was he was thinking about her.

A gentle tug on one curl had her turning her face, only to find him much nearer, closer . . .

"Stop staring at him so deliberately—he'll notice."

"I'm not staring at Bletchley." She was staring at his lips. They curved, then drew fractionally nearer . . .

She stiffened, blinked and dragged her eyes up to his. "Perhaps we'd better stroll." Dalliance was all very well, but she was not about to indulge in any of his mind-whirling kisses—not on the open Heath.

His lips quirked, but he inclined his head. "Perhaps we had."

He turned her; with her hand on his sleeve, they strolled along the Heath's edge—while she hoped he'd exercise his usual initiative and find an empty stable.

To her unreasoning annoyance, he didn't.

The next morning, he took her into town, so they could savor the scones at The Twig and Bough, which he insisted were a cut above excellent. After their repast, they strolled down the High Street, where Mrs. Pemberton beamed at them from her carriage, exchanging gracious greetings.

Flick was quite sure the vicar's wife had never before looked at her with such patent approval.

Which, more than anything else—far more than the insistence of her silly senses or the wonderings of her ill-informed mind—made her question what Demon was about. Really about.

She'd ridden high-bred horses all her life; she'd long ago learned the knack of putting aside all unnerving thoughts and emotions. She had, she thought, been doing an excellent job of ignoring the uncertainties his constant squiring of her had evoked. But after their meeting with Mrs. Pemberton, she could no longer ignore the fact that it really did appear that he was wooing her. Courting her.

Just like he'd said.

Had the moonlight addled his wits—or hers?

The question demanded an answer, not least because his continuing presence was stretching her nerves taut. As it was the same question, albeit in slightly different form, that had been circling in her brain for the past week without answer, there was obviously only one way forward.

And, after all, it *was* Demon—she'd known him nearly all her life. She hadn't shied away from asking for his help with Dillon, and he'd given it. So . . .

She waited until they were rolling down the manor drive the next morning for a tool about the lanes so she could hone her driving skills on his powerful bays. He was still holding the reins. Without giving herself time to think, to balk, she asked, "Why are you behaving like this—spending so much time with me?"

His head whipped around; an incipient frown darkened his eyes. "I told you. I'm wooing you."

She blinked; the storm warning in his eyes wasn't encouraging, but she was determined to have all clear. "Yes," she admitted, evenly, carefully. "But that was just . . ." With one hand, she gestured airily.

His frown crystallized; he slowed the bays. "Just what?"

"Well," she shrugged. "Just that night. In the moonlight."

Demon hauled the bays to a halt. "What about the past days? It's been nearly a week." He was appalled. Swearing, not entirely under his breath, he pulled on the brake, tied off the reins and faced her. "Don't tell me"—narrowing his eyes, he trapped her gaze—"that you haven't noticed. That you haven't been paying attention."

She stared at him, her eyes widening, and widening, as she read the message in his. "You're serious."

Her patent astonishment nearly did him in.

"*Serious?*" He clenched one fist on the railing in front of her, slapped the other on the seat behind her and locked his gaze on her face. "Of *course* I'm serious! What in all creation do you imagine these last days have been about?"

"Well ..." Given the anger vibrating in his tone, Flick decided she'd be wiser not to say. He wasn't yelling—she almost wished he was. His clipped, forcefully enunciated words were somehow more menacing than bellows.

"I am not in the habit of dancing attendance on fresh-faced chits just for the pleasure of their innocent smiles."

She blinked. "I suppose not."

"You may be *certain* not." His jaw hardened to match the rest of his face; his eyes narrowed to slits. "So what the devil have you been imagining?"

If there had been a way of avoiding the question, she'd have taken it, but the look in his eyes declared he wasn't about to drop the subject. And she had been the one to bring it up—and she did still want to know. Holding his gaze, she carefully said, "I thought it was just dalliance."

It was his turn to blink. "Dalliance?"

"A way to fill in the time." Spreading her hands, she shrugged. "For all I know, telling a lady you're wooing her while alone in a courtyard in the moonlight might be standard practice, entirely unremarkable behavior for—"

Caution caught her tongue. She glanced at him; he smiled—all wolf. "For a rake such as I?"

She suppressed a glare. "Yes! How am I supposed to know how you go on?"

Narrow-eyed, he studied her face; his softened not at all. "You may take it from me that when I say I'm courting you, I am." Turning forward, he started to untie the reins.

Flick straightened. "Yes, all right. But you still haven't told me why."

His gaze on his horses, Demon exhaled through set teeth. He released the brake. "Because I want to marry you, of course."

"Yes, but that's what I don't understand. *Why* do you want to marry me?"

He was going to throttle her if she didn't leave off with her whys; jaw setting, he flicked the reins—the bays stepped out. He felt her irate glance.

"You can't expect me to believe you've suddenly taken it into your head that you need to marry me. You didn't even know I existed—well, not other than a pigtailed brat—not until you caught me on The Flynn's back." She swung on the seat to face him. "So *why*?"

Feathering the turn into the road, he set the bays pacing. "I want to marry you because you're the right wife for me." Anticipating her next *why*, he stated, "You're an eligible parti—you're well-born, your connections are commendable. You're the General's ward—you've grown up around here, and you're remarkably knowledgeable about horses." He had his excuses down pat. "All in all, we're an excellent match." He glanced at her sharply. "A fact everyone seems to have realized except you."

She looked ahead, and he turned back to his horses. He wasn't sure he trusted his ears, but he thought she sniffed. She certainly put her nose in the air.

"That sounds horridly cold-blooded to me."

Cold-blooded? He *was* going to throttle her. Just the *thought* of how heated his blood had been, simmering uncomfortably for more than a week, hot need flaring every time she drew close—and as for those times she'd been in his arms, stretched, flush, body to body against him . . .

He set his teeth and heard his jaw crack. His leader jibbed; dragging in a breath, he held it, carefully resettled his horses, then exhaled slowly.

"I also want to marry you"—he forced the words out through gritted teeth—"because I desire you."

He felt her questioning, innocently curious gaze—he wasn't fool enough to meet it—that puzzled look that invited him to demonstrate, to teach her. She'd perfected that look until it could lure even him into deep waters. His gaze locked on his leader's ears, he kept driving.

"What, *exactly*? . . ."

He hauled in a breath. "I want you warming my bed." He wanted her warming *him*. "The fact that I desire you as a man desires a woman is incidental. It merely adds another element to my wooing of you, and our eventual marriage." He quickly changed tacks, focusing on the one aspect he suspected had most contributed to her confusion. She was direct and straightforward—she'd misinterpreted his subtlety. She equated subtleties with playing, with teasing—by definition not serious. "Given your age and lack of experience, as I wish to marry you, a period of courtship is deemed mandatory, during which time my behavior must follow a prescribed pattern."

He was driving dangerously fast. He didn't want to, but he drew back on the reins, slowing to a safer pace. He'd taken a circuitous route; it wasn't necessary to stop and turn in order to return to Hillgate End. Which was just as well. Stopping with him in his present mood and her in her curious one was the definition of unwise.

She'd been listening carefully; he heard the frown in her voice as she repeated, "*Prescribed* pattern."

"Society dictates that I can squire you about, but I can't press my suit too openly, certainly not forcefully. That would be improper. I have to be subtle. I shouldn't tell you how I feel outright—that's not the way things are done. I shouldn't seek to see you in any clandestine manner. I shouldn't kiss you— and I should certainly not mention that I desire you—even let you get any hint of that fact. You're not supposed to know about desire."

He checked the bays for a corner, then set them pacing again. "In fact, this entire *conversation* shouldn't be occurring—Mrs. Pemberton and company would unhesitatingly class it as *exceedingly* improper."

"That's ridiculous! How will I know if I don't ask? And I can't ask anyone else about this—only you."

Demon heard the uncertain note in her voice; much of his tension left him, swamped by a surge of emotion he was growing accustomed to—one Flick and only Flick could evoke. It encompassed an urge to protect, but that wasn't the sum of it.

He sighed, but didn't look at her—he wasn't yet sure how much in control he was, wasn't yet sure he could resist that puzzled, questioning look in her blue eyes. "It's all right to ask me as long as we're alone. You can say whatever you wish to me, but you must be careful not to let anything we discuss privately influence how you behave when we're not private."

Flick nodded. The possibility that he might forbid her to question him, especially about subjects like desire, had shaken her—for an instant she'd feared he would erect a wall between them. Thankfully not.

Yet she still didn't entirely understand.

That he seriously wanted to marry her was hard enough to accept. That he wanted to marry her because he desired her—that was beyond her comprehension. She'd assumed she'd always be a child in his eyes. Apparently not.

As the curricle rolled on, she pondered desire. The whole concept, both in general and specifically, intrigued her. She recalled very well the shimmering net he could throw, the temptation, the promise in the moonlight. Her experience beyond that was nonexistent—all she'd known previously came from overhearing maids comparing notes on their swains. But ... there was one point that, no matter how she construed it, remained unexplained.

Drawing a deep breath, her gaze, like his, fixed on the ribbon of lane stretching before them, she asked, "If you desire me"—she felt her blush heat her cheeks, but she doggedly plowed on—"as a man desires a woman, why do you go rigid when we touch?"

When he didn't immediately answer, she expanded, "Like that night in the courtyard when we kissed—you stopped suddenly. Was that due to society's strictures"—she risked a glance at him—"or something else?"

He went rigid as she looked at him; she could both sense it and see it. Sense the sudden clenching as if it was her own gut, see the muscles beneath his sleeve tense until each band was clearly delineated. As for his face, when she glanced up in surprise, she found it as hard as stone.

Amazed, she lifted a finger and poked his upper arm—it was like stubbing her finger against rock. "Like that." She frowned at him. "Are you sure it's not aversion?"

"It's—*not*—aversion." Demon didn't know how he got the words out; his hands were locked so tightly about the reins that he could only pray the bays didn't choose this particular moment to act up. "Believe me," he reiterated, and had to struggle to draw breath. "It's not aversion."

After a moment, she prompted, "Well?"

He'd told her she could ask. If he didn't get her wed and into bed soon, she might kill him with her questions. He exhaled; his chest felt as tight as a drum. Dredging deep for strength, he took a death grip on his inner demons. His voice almost quavering with the effort of not reacting, he explained, "That night in the moonlight, if I hadn't stopped when I did—hadn't got you back into the drawing room in short order—you would have found yourself ravished under the magnolia in the vicarage courtyard."

"Oh?"

Fascinated consideration rang in her tone.

"I'd even worked out how to accomplish the deed. I would have laid you on the stone edging around the tree and lifted your skirts—you wouldn't have stopped me."

He risked a glance at her; blushing lightly, she shrugged. "We'll never know the truth of that."

He bit back a retort; narrow-eyed, he focused his gaze on her.

She glanced up, met it, and blushed more deeply. She looked ahead. After a moment, she wriggled, shifting on the seat. "All right. I understand about the courtyard, but why does it happen—you freezing like that—now? You even did it yesterday on the Heath when I accidentally bumped into you." Frowning, she looked up. "You can't want to ravish me every time we meet."

Oh, yes, he could. Demon gritted his teeth and let the bays lengthen their stride. "Desire is like a disease—once you've caught it, every further encounter makes it worse."

He was exceedingly thankful when she accepted that comment with a humph. She stared ahead, then he felt another of her considering glances.

"I won't break, you know. I won't have hysterics, or—"

"Very likely." He uttered the words as repressively as he could.

She humphed again. "Well, I still don't understand. If you want to marry me *anyway* . . ."

He couldn't miss her implication—couldn't stop himself from turning his head—and reading, blazoned in the blue of her eyes, her curiosity, and a very definite invitation . . .

Swallowing a virulent curse, he swung his gaze back to the lane. Explaining might just have made things worse. He'd thus far managed to hold his demons in check—but what if she picked up the whip?

Oh no, no, no, no, no. He knew what he was, and what she was, and they were literally eons apart. It would take her years—at least an intensive six months—to even come close to comprehending the level of sexual knowledge he possessed. But he could guess what she was thinking, what route her innocent thoughts had taken. He had to head her off, quash any thoughts she had of jumping into that particular sea feet first. It simply couldn't happen like that. At least, not with him.

Unfortunately, at no point had she become wary of him, much to his disgust. She'd somehow gone from regarding him as an uncle to regarding him as an equal. Which was equally erroneous. His jaw ached, along with most of his body. As for his brain, that simply hurt. "It's not going to happen like that." The effort of explaining things he didn't want to risk thinking about was wearing him down.

"Oh?"

She had those *Oh*s down to a fine art—they always prodded him to explain.

"Desire leads to physical seduction *but*, in your case—in *our* case—that is not going to translate to any quick, rushed, illicit tumble in a courtyard or anywhere else."

He waited for her *Oh*; instead, she asked, "Why?"

Because he was going to train her to be his very own fallen angel. He shook aside the thought. "Because . . ." He struggled, then blinked; if he hadn't been driving, he would have flung up his hands in defeat. Setting his jaw, he reached for the whip. "Because you're an innocent, and you deserve better than that. And *I* know better than that." Oh, yes—this impinged on his ego as well. "I'll seduce you as you deserve to be seduced—*slowly*. Innocence isn't something you should discard like an old shoe. It has a physical value—a passionate value—all its own."

His frown deepening, he kept his gaze fixed on his leader's ears. "Innocence shouldn't be tarnished, it shouldn't be crushed. It should be made to bloom. I know." Those last two words were as much realization as assurance. "Getting innocence to bloom takes time, takes care and attention and expertise." His voice deepened. "It takes passion and desire, commitment and devotion to coax innocence from bud to bloom, to encourage it to unfurl into full flower without a single petal bruised."

Was he still talking of her innocence, or did he mean something more— something of which he was as innocent as she?

To his relief, she said nothing but sat silently and considered. He considered, too—all that he wanted, the totality of his desire.

He was acutely conscious of her sitting beside him. He could feel his own heartbeat, thudding in his chest, pulsing in his fingertips, throbbing in his loins. For long moments, the only sounds about them were the steady clack of the bays' hooves and the repetitive rattle of the wheels.

Then she stirred.

He shot her a glance, saw her frown—saw her open her mouth—

He jerked his gaze forward. "And for God's sake, don't you *dare* ask why."

He felt her glare; from the corner of his eye, he saw her stick her nose in the air, shut her lips, primly fold her hands, and pointedly look over the landscape.

Jaw clenched, he whipped up his horses.

By the time they reached the gates of Hillgate End, he'd regained sufficient use of his brain to remember what he'd intended to tell Flick during the drive.

Setting the bays pacing up the shady avenue, he slanted a glance at her and wondered how much to reveal. Despite his distraction with her, he hadn't forgotten about the syndicate; he knew she hadn't, either.

The truth was, he was growing uneasy. They'd been following Bletchley for weeks and had learned nothing about the syndicate other than that it appeared exceedingly well organized. In the circumstances, he didn't feel happy about fixing all their hopes on Bletchley.

So he'd racked his brain for alternatives. He'd considered requesting help from the rest of the Bar Cynster but had yet to do so. Vane and Patience were in Kent; Gabriel and Lucifer were in London, but needed to keep their eyes on the twins. Richard was, at last report, rather busy with his witch in Scotland. And Devil would be busy with spring planting. Be that as it may, Devil was reasonably close at Somersham. If things got difficult, he'd call on Devil, but, given that all matters to do with racing fell within his particular area of expertise, there seemed little point in summoning aid just yet. He needed to sight the enemy first, before he called in the cavalry.

To which end . . .

He drew the curricle up before the steps with a flourish and stepped down. Taking Flick's hand, he helped her alight, then fell in beside her as she headed for the steps.

"I'm going to London tomorrow—there's some business I need to see to." He stopped at the base of the steps.

Already two steps up, she halted and swung to face him, a whole host of questions in her eyes.

"I'll be back the day after tomorrow, probably late."

"But ... what about Bletchley?"

"Don't worry about him." He trapped her blue gaze. "Gillies, Hills and Cross will keep an eye on him."

Flick blinked at him. "But what if something happens?"

"I doubt it will, but Gillies will know what to do."

Flick had far less confidence in Gillies than she had in his master. However ... she nodded. "Very well." She held out her hand. "I'll wish you a safe journey, then."

Taking her hand, he lifted a brow. "And a speedy return?"

She raised her brows haughtily. "I dare say I'll see you when you get back."

He trapped her gaze. His fingers shifted about her hand—raising it, he turned it and pressed his lips fleetingly to her wrist.

Her pulse leapt; she caught her breath.

He smiled devilishly. "Count on it."

Releasing her hand, he swept her an elegant bow and strode back to his waiting horses.

Flick watched as he leapt up to the seat, then wheeled the bays with matchless authority and set them pacing down the drive. She watched until he disappeared from sight, swallowed up by the shadows beneath the trees.

A frown slowly forming in her eyes, she turned and climbed the steps. The door was unlatched; she went in, closing it behind her. Crossing the hall, she greeted Jacobs with an absentminded smile, then continued on through the house, out on to the terrace and so onto the lawn. The lawn she had so often in recent times strolled with Demon.

If anyone had told her even three weeks before that the thought of not seeing a gentleman for two whole days would dim her mood—would sap her anticipation for those same days—she would have laughed.

She wasn't laughing now.

Not that she was about to succumb to listless lassitude, she had far too much to do. Like deciding how she felt about desire.

She considered the point as she passed beneath the trees and on into the wisteria-shaded walk. Hands clasped behind her, she fell to slowly pacing up and down the gravel.

He wanted to marry her—he intended to marry her. He expected her to say yes—he clearly believed she would.

After this afternoon, and their frank conversation, she at least knew precisely where he stood. He wanted to marry her for all the socially acceptable reasons, and because he desired her.

Which left her facing one very large, formidable question. Would she accept him?

It wasn't a question she'd expected to face. Never in her wildest dreams had she imagined that he, her idol—her ideal gentleman—would want to marry her. Would look at her, a pigtailed brat reborn, and feel desire. The only reason she could state that point, and view the prospect with quite amazing equanimity, was that, deep down, she was still struggling to believe it.

It still seemed like a dream.

But . . .

She knew he was in earnest.

Reaching the end of the walk, she squinted at the clock above the stable arch. There was still an hour before luncheon; all about her was silent, no one else was in sight. Turning, she fell to pacing again, trying to organize her thoughts into a sensible sequence.

The first point she had to consider was obvious. Did she love Demon?

Somewhat to her surprise, the answer was easy.

"I've been secretly in love with him for years," she muttered. The admission left her with a very odd feeling in her stomach.

She was so disconcerted, so startled to find her heart had made up its mind long ago and not told her, that she reached the end of the walk before she could set the point aside, accept that it was decided, and move on.

"Next, does he love me?"

No answer came. She mentally replayed their conversations, but there was nothing he'd said that shed light on that point.

She grimaced. "What if he doesn't love me?"

The answer to that was absolute. If he didn't love her, she couldn't marry him. Her certainty was unshakeable, deeply embedded within her.

To her mind, love and marriage went hand in hand. She knew that wasn't society's view, but it was hers, formed by her own observations. Her parents had loved deeply—it had shown in their faces, in their demeanor, whenever they'd been in the same room. She'd been seven when she'd last seen them, waving good-bye from the rail of their boat as it pulled away from the dock. While their features had blurred with the years, that glow that had always been theirs had not—it still shone strongly in her memory.

They'd left her a fortune, and they'd left her a memory—she was grateful for the fortune, but she valued the memory more. The knowledge of what love and marriage could be was a precious, timeless legacy.

One she would not turn her back on.

She wanted that glow for herself—she always had. She'd grown up with that expectation. From all she'd gleaned about the General and his wife, Margery, theirs, too, had been a union blessed.

Which brought her back to Demon.

Frowning, she paced back and forth, considering his reasons for marrying her. His socially acceptable reasons were all very well, yet superficial and not essential. They could be dismissed, taken for granted.

Which left her with desire.

One minute was enough to summarize all she knew on that subject. Questions like Did desire encompass love? Did love encompass desire? were beyond her ability to answer. Until this past week, she hadn't even known what desire was, and while she now knew what it felt like, her experience of it remained minimal. A fact their recent discussion had emphasized.

There was clearly much she had to learn about desire—love or no love.

For the next half hour, she paced and pondered; by the time the lunch gong sounded, she'd reached one clear conclusion, which raised one simple question. She had, she thought, as she strolled back to the house, made good progress.

Her conclusion was absolute and inviolable—utterly unchangeable. She would marry with love, or not at all. She wanted to love, and be loved in return—it was that or nothing.

As for her question, it was straightforward and pertinent: Was it possible to start with desire—strong desire—and progress to love?

Lifting her face to the sun, she closed her eyes. She felt reassured, certain of what she wanted, how to face what was to come.

If Demon wanted to marry her, wanted her to say yes when he asked for her hand, then he would need to teach her more about desire, and convince her that her question could be answered in the affirmative.

Opening her eyes, she lifted her skirts; climbing the steps, she went in to lunch.

CHAPTER
Eleven

ॐ☙

D emon set out for London just after dawn. He kept the bays up to their bits, eager to reach the capital and the offices of Heathcote Montague, man of business to the Cynsters. After considerable thought, he'd hit upon a possible alternative means of identifying members of the syndicate.

Unbeknown to Flick, he'd visited Dillon and extracted a list of the races he'd fixed. He'd then called in favors from all around Newmarket to get the figures, including various bookmakers' odds, necessary to gauge just how much money had been realized through the fixes. His rough estimations had sent his brows rising high—the amount had been startling enough to suggest Montague might be able to trace it. Even a portion of the total should have left some discernible mark somewhere in the financial capital.

It was worth a try.

The road sped beneath his wheels. Demon's thoughts drifted back—to Flick. Impatience gripped him, a restless urge to hurry.

So he could return to Newmarket.

Lips setting, he shook aside the nagging worry—what possible trouble could she get into in two days? He would remain in London for only one night. Bletchley seemed settled; Gillies had his orders. All would be well.

His gaze fixed on the road ahead, he urged the bays on.

Three hours later, neatly garbed in her velvet riding habit and perched upon Jessamy, Flick went riding on Newmarket Heath.

Naturally, she expected to see Bletchley, idly watching the last of the morning gallops as he had for the past week.

To her consternation, she didn't see him. She couldn't find Gillies, Cross or Hills, either. Sitting straight in her saddle, she scanned the gallops—the rising stretches of turf where the last strings were pounding—then turned to survey the surrounding flats. To no avail.

"Isn't that just typical!" Gathering Jessamy's reins, she wheeled the mare and rode straight into town.

Without any idea what to do, Flick walked Jessamy down the paved street. Most of those about belonged to the racing fraternity—stable lads, grooms, trainers, jockeys. Some knew her and bobbed respectfully; all looked Jessamy over with keen professional eyes. Flick barely noticed.

Where had Bletchley been staying? She couldn't remember the inn's name. Demon had said it wasn't in Newmarket, but somewhere to the north.

But what had happened to Gillies and the others? They'd watched Bletchley for this long without mishap—could he finally have identified them and . . .

And what? She had no idea.

Doggedly, she headed north up the High Street, an ill-formed plan of inquiring at the inns to the north of town in mind. Halfway up the street, she came to the Rutland Arms, the main coaching inn. The mailcoach squatted like a huge black beetle before the inn's main door; she glanced at the passengers waiting to board.

A flash of scarlet caught her eye; abruptly she reined in. A curse from behind had her turning in her saddle. "Oh—I'm so sorry." Blushing, she drew Jessamy aside to let the racing string she'd impeded pass. The long file of horses with lads atop gave her useful cover; screened by them, she peered across the street.

"Yes!" Eyes lighting, Flick saw Bletchley, his red neckerchief a beacon, clamber up to the coach's roof. Then she frowned. "Why is he going to Bury St. Edmunds?"

Raising his yard, the guard blew a warning; the next instant, the coach lurched. Overloaded with men, apparently in rowdy mood, clinging to the roof, it ponderously rolled off up the High Street.

Flick stared after it. While she had no idea *why* Bletchley was heading to Bury St. Edmunds, it seemed unlikely he'd stop anywhere en route. There simply wasn't anywhere en route.

She had to find Gillies, and find out what had happened to him and Hills and Cross. She quickly turned Jessamy south, toward the stud farm.

And spied Gillies mounted on a hack not ten yards away. With a muttered exclamation, she trotted Jessamy over.

"Did you see?" She drew rein beside him. "Bletchley's gone off to Bury St. Edmunds."

"Aye." Gillies's gaze drifted up the street in the wake of the departing coach.

"Well"—Flick settled Jessamy as she danced—"we'd better follow him."

Gillies's gaze snapped to her face. "Follow 'im?"

"Of course." Flick frowned. "Isn't that what you're supposed to be doing?"

Gillies looked uncertain.

"Where are Hills and Cross?" Flick asked impatiently.

"Hills is at the farm—he was last on watch. Cross is over there." Gillies indicated with his chin. "He was watching Bletchley this morning."

Flick located the lugubrious Cross lounging in a doorway across the street.

"Yes, well, now Bletchley has made a move, we'll need to organize to follow him."

"We will?"

Flick stared at Gillies. "What *is* the matter with you? Didn't Demon leave you with orders to follow Bletchley?"

Gillies stared back, then, mute, shook his head.

Flick stared even more; she couldn't imagine what was going on. But Gillies and Cross were out and about. "What *are* your orders?"

Gillies's face fell; his eyes took on the look of a mournful spaniel's. "To follow *you*, miss, and keep you out of trouble."

Only the fact that they were in a crowded public place prevented Flick from giving Gillies her opinion of his master's arrogance. His overweening conceit. His ridiculous male ego.

By the time she, with Gillies and Cross in tow, had retreated to the now empty Heath, she'd calmed down—to simmering. "I don't care *what* orders he gave before he left, he couldn't have foreseen Bletchley leaving. But he has, so we must improvise."

Gillies remained blank-faced. "The master was most particular, miss. He said we was to hold the fort here, and not let—not *make* any rash moves. Anyway, there's no need to follow Bletchley to Bury—chances are, when he wants to hie back to London, he'll come back through here on the coach."

"That's not the *point*!" Flick declared.

"Isn't it?" Standing beside them, Cross squinted up at Flick. "I thought that was it—that we was to watch him in Newmarket and see who he talked to here."

"Not just *here*." Flick drew a calming breath. "We need to see who he talks to *wherever* he goes. He might be going to Bury to meet with his masters."

Cross blinked. "Nah, he'll be—"

Gillies coughed, succumbing to a veritable paroxysm that had both Flick and Cross looking at him in concern. Blinking, he shook his head, waving his hand back and forth in a negative gesture. "It's all right," he said to Flick, but his eyes, bright and sharp, were fixed on Cross.

Cross's expression blanked. "Oh. Ah. Right—well."

Flick frowned at him. "We must organize to pick up the watch on Bletchley when he gets to Bury. The mailcoach takes hours, so we have a little time."

"Ah—it's not that simple, miss." Gillies exchanged a glance with Cross. "Both Cross here and Hills have duties on the farm—they can't simply up and leave for Bury."

"Oh." Flick looked at Cross; he nodded.

"Aye—wouldn't do for us to leave the youngsters unsupervised, like."

Flick grimaced. It was spring, and the stud farm would be a hive of rather serious activity; taking two senior stablemen away at this time was impossible. Especially not from an enterprise as highly regarded as Demon's. Absentmindedly, she settled Jessamy—tail swishing, the mare was growing increasingly restless.

Glancing up, Flick saw Gillies and Cross exchange a look she couldn't interpret; they almost looked pleased. "Well," she stated, "as we can't afford to let Bletchley roam about unwatched, I'll have to go to Bury myself."

Gillies's and Cross's reactions to that were easy to read—their eyes went round and their mouths dropped open.

Gillies recovered first. "But ... but ... you can't go alone." His eyes looked slightly wild.

Flick frowned. "No, but I don't want to take my maid." She looked at Gillies. "You'll have to come, too."

The lugubrious Cross shook his head. "Nah, you don't want to go to Bury just now." He looked hopefully at Flick.

She looked steadily back. "As Bletchley has taken himself off, I expect you should get back to the stud."

Ponderously, Cross nodded. "Aye, I'd better, at that. I'll tell Hills we don' have no pigeon to watch any more."

Tight-lipped, Gillies nodded.

As Cross lumbered off, Flick turned back to Gillies. A militant light in her eye, she transfixed him with a glance. "We had better make some plans over how to watch Bletchley at Bury St. Edmunds."

Gillies stiffened his spine. "Miss, I really don't think—"

"Gillies." Flick didn't raise her voice, but her tone stopped Gillies in his tracks. "I am going to Bury to watch Bletchley. All you need to decide is whether you'll accompany me or not."

Gillies studied her face, then heaved a sigh. "Perhaps, we'd better have a word with Master Dillon. Seeing as it's on his account, an' all."

Flick frowned harder; Gillies sucked in a quick breath. "Who knows? Maybe Master Dillon has some idea of what Bletchley's doing at Bury?"

Flick blinked, then raised her brows. "You're right. Dillon might know—or be able to guess." She looked around. It was lunchtime; the Heath was empty. "I'll need to go home for lunch or they'll miss me. Meet me at the start of the track to the cottage at two."

Resigned, Gillies nodded.

Flick returned the gesture curtly, then loosened her reins, tapped her heels to Jessamy's sides, and raced home.

After polishing off a late lunch at White's, Demon retired to the reading room with a cup of coffee and a large news sheet, behind which he could hide. That last was occasioned by his encounter with the Honorable Edward Ralstrup, an old friend who had joined him for lunch.

"There's a gathering at Hillgarth's tonight. All the usual crowd, of course." Eyes bright, Edward had thrown him an engaging grin. "Nothing like a few highly bred challenges to tune one up for the Season, what?"

"Challenges?" He'd immediately thought of Flick.

Edward's expression was one of blissful anticipation. "The ladies Onslow, Carmichael, Bristow—need I go on? Not, of course, that you'll need to extend yourself—not with the countess champing at the bit."

"The countess?" Reluctantly, he'd dragged his mind back from Newmarket and focused on the woman he'd shown to the door before he'd driven north. "I thought she'd returned to the Continent."

"No, no." Edward winked. "Seems she's conceived an affection for things English, don't you know. Colston had a touch at her—well, word was you'd gone north indefinitely—but it seems she's determined to hold out for ... well, her description was 'something rather *more*.'"

"Oh." He'd been conscious of a definite longing for Newmarket.

His less-than-enthusiastic response hadn't registered with Edward. "After Hillgarth's, if you're still standing, so to speak, there's Mrs. Melton's rout. Quite sure it'll be that, too—plenty of action there. And then tomorrow ..."

He'd let Edward rattle on, while his mind slid back to Newmarket, to the golden-haired angel who was waiting for him, and who didn't know the first thing about matters sensual, let alone "something rather more."

"So—what do you say? Shall I pick you up at eight?"

It had taken all his persuasive talents to convince Edward that he wasn't interested—not in the countess or the many other delights that would be offered him about town. In the end, he'd escaped only by assuring Edward that he had to hie north again at dawn and was not about to risk his horses by staying up all night. As his care for his equine beauties was a byword throughout the ton, Edward had finally accepted that he was serious.

"And," Demon had added, struck by inspiration, "you might oblige me by letting it be known among the brotherhood that I've relinquished all claim on the countess."

"Ooh!" Edward had brightened at that. "I'll do that, yes. Nice bit of sport we should see over that."

Demon certainly hoped so. The countess was a demanding and grasping woman. While her lush body had provided a temporary distraction, one he'd paid handsomely and generously for, he had no doubt that his interest in her had been just that—temporary. Indeed, it had waned on the day he'd headed north.

Sinking into a deep armchair and arranging the news sheet like a wall before him, he settled to sip his coffee and ponder the discovery that life as he had known it—the life of a rakehell in the glittering world of the ton—no longer held any allure. Somewhat to his surprise, he could still imagine attending balls and parties—just as long as he had a certain angel by his side. He would enjoy introducing her to the ton's entertainments, just to see the expression in her wide eyes.

But the ton without Flick?

Anywhere without Flick?

He took a long sip of his coffee. This, he thought darkly, was what happened when fate caught a Cynster in her coils.

He was sitting in London, a town teeming with uncounted beauties, a surprising number of whom would be easily enough persuaded to reveal their charms to him—and he wasn't interested. Not in the beauties—not in their charms, naked or otherwise.

The only woman he was interested in was Flick.

He recalled imagining that it could never happen—that he'd never be satisfied with one woman. But it had. The only woman for him now was Flick.

And she was in Newmarket.

Hopefully behaving herself.

Doing the vases, reading her novels, and twiddling her thumbs.

Possibly thinking about desire.

He shifted in his seat, then frowned. No matter what setting he placed her in, his image of a patient Flick was not convincing.

Ten minutes later, he strode down the steps of White's, his goal the mews close by his lodgings where his bays were presently housed. There was no reason he couldn't leave London immediately. He'd seen Montague that morning, and spent an hour explaining the details of the race-fixing. Montague had done a few quick calculations and concurred with his assessment. The amount of money taken was enormous—it should show up somewhere.

Montague had connections Demon didn't want to know about. He'd left the hard-working agent, who thankfully thrived on financial challenges, with a gleam in his eye. If there was any way to track members of the syndicate through the money they'd taken, Montague would find it.

Which left him free to return to Newmarket, to the watch on Bletchley and his wooing of Flick.

Glancing down, he considered his attire—town rig of trousers, morning coat and shoes. There was no real reason to change. He doubted Flick would even notice, much less make anything of the fact that he hadn't stopped to change before racing back to her side.

Lips twisting wryly, he lengthened his stride and headed straight for the mews.

"Bury St. Edmunds?" Dillon frowned at Flick, then slumped into the chair at the head of the old table. "Why there?"

Flick pulled up a stool, waving Gillies to the other, wishing he was his master instead. "We were hoping you might have some clue. Obviously not."

Dillon shook his head, his expression one of patent bewilderment. "I wouldn't have thought there was any possible attraction in Bury, not for the likes of Bletchley."

"So," Flick stated, her tone businesslike, "we'll need to go to Bury and find out what 'the attraction' is. Like you, I can't see any reason Bletchley would have gone there, *other* than to meet with his masters."

Gillies, who'd been listening carefully, and even more carefully sizing up Dillon, cleared his throat. "There's a prizefight on in Bury St. Edmunds tomorrow morning. That's almost certainly why Bletchley's hied off there. The reigning champion of all England is to take the ring against the latest challenger."

"Really?" Dillon's lassitude fell away—he was suddenly all eager youth. "A *prizefight*," Flick breathed, in the tone of one for whom a light has dawned.

Frowning, Gillies looked from one to the other. "Aye—so there'll be all manner of bucks and bloods and dangerous blades up from London—the town'll be fair crawling with them."

"Damn!" Dillon sat back, a frown in his eyes.

Gillies heaved a sigh of relief.

"Fancy a prizefight so close and I daren't show my face." Dillon grimaced and looked at Flick, clearly inviting her sympathy.

She wasn't looking at him. Grinning, her face alight, she slapped the table. "That's *it*!"

Gillies jumped. "What's it?"

"The prizefight, of course! It's the perfect venue for Bletchley to meet with his masters." Triumph in her eyes, she spread her hands. "It's obvious—members of the syndicate can come up from London and meet with Bletchley without in any way stepping out of their normal roles, their normal pastimes, the places they would normally be found. A prizefight is perfect."

Gillies paled. "No—I don't—"

"You know," Dillon cut in, "you just might be right."

"Of course I'm right." Flick set her riding gloves on the table. "Now we need to work out how to keep an eye on Bletchley at Bury, given there's only me and Gillies to keep watch."

Both Flick and Dillon frowned; Gillies stared at them in patent dismay. "The master won't want you going to any prizefight." He made the statement to Flick, then looked at Dillon.

Dillon wrinkled his nose. "It'll be tricky, but the prizefight must be the venue for Bletchley to meet his masters. Someone's got to watch him."

Gillies dragged in a breath. "I'll go."

Dillon regarded Gillies, then grimaced. "Without belittling your skills, Gillies, it's damned difficult for one person to keep a full-time watch on a target in a crowd."

"Indeed." Flick frowned. "And besides, what if the meeting is held upstairs at the inn, in a private room? I can go upstairs." She turned to Gillies. "You can't."

"Well," Dillon put in, "you won't be able to either, not if you're disguised as a stable lad."

"I'm not going disguised as a lad."

Dillon and Gillies stared at Flick—Dillon with interest, Gillies with trepidation. Flick smiled determinedly. "I'm going as a widow—I have to be able to get a room to stay the night."

"The night?" Dillon queried. Gillies simply stared.

"Most spectators from London will arrive this evening, won't they?" Flick glanced at Gillies.

"Aye." His voice was weak.

"Well, then—if a meeting is to be held, it could be held either tonight or tomorrow—which would probably mean after the fight." Flick frowned. "If I was doing the organizing, I'd hold the meeting tonight. There's bound to be groups gathering to while away the evening—another group meeting in a private parlor would cause no comment. But if they meet tomorrow, after the fight, it'll seem rather odd, won't it?" She glanced at Gillies. "I imagine most of the Londoners will leave from the field?"

Woodenly, Gillies nodded.

"Right, then." Flick nodded curtly. "The Angel's the major inn at Bury—it's likely everyone will gather there. So that's where I'll stay—we'll make that our headquarters. Between us, Gillies and I should be able to keep Bletchley in sight."

"The Angel will be booked out," Gillies protested. "Won't be any way you'll get a room there."

Flick's eyes narrowed. "I'll get a room—don't worry on that score."

"You said you'd go as a widow," Dillon looked at her. "Why a widow?"

Flick's determined smile deepened. "One"—she ticked her points off on her fingers—"men always seem to consider young widows to be in especial need of protection, which will help me get a room. Two, widows can wear concealing veils without raising brows. Three, a widow can travel alone—or at least with only her coachman."

She looked at Gillies. "If you'd rather stay here and await your master, I can get Jonathon to drive me." Jonathon was the Hillgate End coachman.

Very definitely, Gillies shook his head. "I'll stick with you." Under his breath, he grumbled, "Those were my orders. Necks are going to be wrung enough over this without me sticking mine out."

Lifting his head, Gillies looked at Dillon and tried one last time. "The master's not going to like this."

Flick didn't think Demon would approve either, but she wasn't going to point out the obvious.

Dillon, however, did. "Pity Cynster's not here."

"But he's not." Flick swept up her gloves and stood. "So it's up to us to manage." She looked at Gillies. "Come to the manor stable as soon as you can—I want to leave within the hour."

In the well-sprung manor carriage, the trip from Newmarket to Bury St. Edmunds did not take long. They rolled into the town as the last traces of the day were fading from the western sky.

They joined the long queue of curricles, carriages, gigs and carts barely crawling along the main street.

Peering out the carriage window, Flick was amazed at the number of conveyances clogging the usually clear road. The clack of horses' hooves, the snap of whips and innumerable ripe curses filled the air. The pavements were awash with surging masses of men—laborers in drab, country squires in their tweeds, and gentlemen of every hue, from the nattily attired sportsman to the elegant rake, to the brash blades and bucks casting their eyes over any female unwise enough to appear in their sight.

Sitting back, Flick was glad of her thick veil. Not only would it hide her face but it would also hide her blushes. Glancing down, she wished she'd stopped to find a more "widowish" dress—one with a high neckline and voluminous skirts, preferably in dull black. In her haste, she'd donned one of her day gowns, a scooped-necked, highwaisted gown in soft voile in her favorite shade of lavender-blue. In it, she didn't look the least like a widow— she suspected she looked very young.

She would have to remember to keep her cloak fully about her at all times whenever she was out of her room. The cloak, luckily, was perfect— voluminous, heavy and dark with a deep hood. An old trunk in the attic recalled from childhood rummagings had yielded the heavy, black lace veil. Old-fashioned it might be, but it was precisely what she needed—it covered her whole head, her hair as well as her face, obscuring all identifiable features, yet it did not interfere too drastically with her vision.

She was going to need to see, and see well, to play the part she would need to play.

With the veil over her head, and her hood up, the whole secured with two pins, she was certain no one would recognize her. As long as she kept her cloak completely about her, all would be well.

Clutching her black reticule, also liberated from the old trunk, she waited impatiently for the sign of The Angel to appear. The carriage rocked, stopped, then rocked and stopped again. The sound of carriage wheels scraping came to her ears—she promptly shut them to the ensuing curses.

Fixing her gaze on the carriage's wall, she reviewed her plans. She had, she thought, managed well thus far. She'd told the General she'd taken a sudden notion to visit a friend, Melissa Blackthorn, who helpfully lived just beyond Bury St. Edmunds. Over the past ten years, she and Melissa had frequently simply visited, without formal arrangements. The General was always at home, and the Blackthorns were always in residence; there was never any danger of not finding a welcome. So she'd claimed she would visit Melissa and, as usual, stay overnight.

Both the General and Foggy had accepted her decision with a little too much readiness for her liking. The General's understanding smile, his gentle pat on her hand, had left her with the distinct—and she was sure not inaccurate— impression that he thought it was Demon's absence that had prompted her visit to Melissa. That his absence was the cause of her restlessness.

Flick wasn't at all sure how she felt about that—irritated, yes, but in a rather odd way. Frowning, she glanced out of the window and abruptly sat up. They were passing the main courtyard of The Angel, already a sea of men and boys all heading in one direction or another. The majority of visitors were still finding places to lay their heads; Flick prayed, very hard, that she'd be successful in carrying out the next phase of her plan. An instant later, the carriage lurched, then turned, and rumbled under the arch into the stable yard of The Angel.

Where pandemonium reigned.

Gillies hauled the horses to a stop, and two inn boys rushed to the carriage. One pulled open the door and let down the steps; the other ran to the boot. Flick allowed the first to take her hand and help her down; as the second, discovering the boot was empty, returned at a loss, she waved him to the carriage. "My bag is in there."

Her voice was steady; she'd deepened and strengthened her usual tones so that she sounded older, more commanding. It seemed to work; retrieving her one small bag, the inn boys stood respectfully as, having handed the horses over to the ostlers, Gillies came up.

Lifting her arms wide, palms up to encompass the scene, Flick turned dramatically and launched into her charade. "Good gracious, Giles! Just *look* at this crowd! Whatever's afoot?"

Gillies simply stared at her.

One of the inn boys shifted his weight. "It's a prizefight, m'lady. Over on Cobden's field t'morrow mornin'."

"A *prizefight*!" Pressing a hand to her cloaked breast, Flick fell back a step. "Oh, how distressing!" She glanced about, then looked at the inn. "I do hope the innkeeper has a room left—I could not possibly go another mile."

She stared—beneath her veil she glared—at Gillies.

After a moment, he said rather woodenly, "Indeed not, ma'am."

At least he'd remembered to address her as ma'am.

"Come, Giles—we must speak to the innkeeper immediately!" Gesturing dramatically toward the inn's main doors, she picked up her skirts and led the way. Her feminine tones, carrying a hint of imminent distress, had caused more than a few heads to turn, but, as she'd anticipated, the inn boys, responding to her dramatic flair, bustled close, eager to be part of whatever scene was to follow; together with the recently christened Giles, they cleared a path for her to the inn door.

Beyond the door lay a wide reception area fronted by a long counter presently manned by three harassed individuals—the innkeeper, his wife, and his brother. The length of the counter was packed with men—Flick could only catch glimpses of those behind it. Between her and the counter ranged a wall of male shoulders.

It had been years since she'd visited The Angel, but Flick recognized the innkeeper and made a beeline for him, giving wordless thanks when his sharp-eyed wife was called to deal with a customer at the counter's other end. The helpful inn boys, seeing that she'd be swamped, sent up a shout, waving her bag high. "Make way for the lady."

Flick could have kissed them.

Gentlemen's heads turned at the mention of a lady; as they took in her dark cloak and veil, those in her path politely stepped back. Between the inn boys and Gillies, she was conducted to the counter; as she fronted it, however, her escort deferentially stepped back, leaving her surrounded by gentlemen.

All of whom were studying her rather speculatively.

The innkeeper blinked at her; his expression one of concern, he asked, "Aye, ma'am?"

Flick took her courage in both hands.

"Kind sir"—her voice hinted at a quaver—"I have just arrived in your fair town only to discover this crowd before me." Setting her big black reticule on the counter before her, she clasped her hands tight about it so the innkeeper could not miss the huge square-cut topaz she wore on one gloved finger. It was not an expensive stone, but it was impressive in size and style; the innkeeper's eyes duly widened. Casting an agitated glance about her, she declared, "I have already travelled far this day—I cannot go further. My horses, too …" She let the words fade, as if the situation threatened to overwhelm her.

Turning back to the innkeeper, looking into his face, she imploringly put out a hand. "Oh, dear sir, please say you have one more room left for me?"

Her plea caused a hush.

The innkeeper pursed his lips. "Hmm." Brow furrowing, he drew his ledger closer and made a great show of scanning his lists of rooms, all of which Flick knew must already be taken.

Tapping his pencil, he glanced up at her. "Just you, is it, ma'am?"

Flick drew a deep breath. "Yes." She made the word sound very small, very weak. "I …" She drew in another breath and clasped her fingers more tightly on the reticule; the facets of the topaz flashed. "I was recently widowed— well, it's been six months, now, I suppose—I've been travelling … for my health, you understand."

She delivered the words in a slightly breathless rush, with what she hoped was just the right degree of feminine fragility. The innkeeper's lips formed a silent *Oh*, then he nodded and looked down.

Exceedingly glad of her veil, Flick glanced about; the innkeeper's eyes were not the only ones in which calculation gleamed.

"I say, Hodges," one of her neighbors drawled, "you'll have to find a room for the lady—can't possibly send her out into the night."

A deep rumble of assent rose on all sides.

"For the honor of Bury St. Edmunds, if nothing else," some other helpful soul put in.

The innkeeper, who was now scrubbing out and rewriting names on his lists, threw them a distracted frown. That didn't please some of his more arrogant customers. "Aside from the town's honor, what about this house's honor?" Directing a too-smooth smile her way, one rakish buck leaned on the counter. "Surely, Hodges, old chap," he drawled, "you wouldn't want it known that you're the sort of innkeep who turns away helpless widows?"

Flick gritted her teeth and suppressed an impulse to deliver a swift kick to the buck's nearby shin; Hodges was now scowling.

Luckily, he was scowling at the buck. "No need to take that tone, m'lord. I've found the lady a nice room—I hope I know my duty."

He shut his ledger with a snap. Turning, he reached for a key hanging with a full score of others on a board behind the counter. To Flick's consternation, all the gentlemen around her leaned forward, squinting at the board to read the number of her room!

She had, she realized, just saddled herself with a large number of champions, some of whom might be entertaining notions of a reward.

But as the innkeeper turned with a key dangling in his hand, she was too relieved to worry.

"If you'll just come this way, ma'am?" He waved to the end of the counter, to where a wide staircase led upward. Then he turned to the waiting crowd. "You gentlemen won't mind biding your time until I get the lady settled."

It wasn't a question. Grinning behind her veil, Flick glided to the staircase. Hodges, despite being a resident of Bury St. Edmunds, was clearly up to snuff.

Gillies returned to her side to briefly murmur, "I'll go find Bletchley." Then he melted into the ever-increasing crush as the innkeeper joined her.

"This way, ma'am."

Five minutes later, with a great deal of graciousness and enough care to make her feel slightly guilty, she was installed in the very best chamber the inn possessed. Hodges admitted as much when she exclaimed over the size of the room and the superior quality of the furniture.

With a gruff suggestion that she might prefer to have her dinner on a tray to avoid the crowd downstairs—a suggestion with which she readily agreed—he left her.

Flick blew out a breath, then returned to the door and threw the bolt. Crossing to the bed, she sank down upon it; extracting her pins, she pushed back her hood and veil.

And grinned triumphantly.

She'd done it! On the eve of a prizefight, she'd secured a room at the most prominent inn.

Now all she needed to do was find Bletchley—and follow him into his masters' presence.

Leaving Newmarket, Demon headed south, past the racecourse and his stable and on across the empty Heath. As he tickled his leader's ear, then sent the whip hissing back up its handle, the last glow in the west died. Night came slowly, approaching on silent wings, borne on the shadows that reached over the Heath to enfold the country in darkness. Before him lay his stud farm, with its comfortable parlor and one of Mrs. Shephard's excellent country dinners.

Between him and supreme comfort lay Hillgate End.

It was awfully late to pay a social call, but even before he'd formulated an excuse, he checked the bays and turned them up the manor's drive. Flick would be glad he was back early—she could tell him if anything had transpired in his absence. So could Gillies, of course, but he'd rather hear it from Flick. He'd only stay for a minute, just to assure himself all was well.

He brought the curricle to a scrunching halt in the gravel before the steps. A groom or stable lad—he couldn't see in the gloom—came loping across from the stable.

"I'll only be a few minutes," he called as he strode up the steps. Just long enough to see Flick's smile—to see her anticipation of tomorrow come alive.

Jacobs opened the door to his knock.

"Good evening, Jacobs." Crossing the threshold, he drew off his gloves. "Is Miss Parteger about?"

"I'm afraid not, sir." Jacobs closed the door and turned. "She left this afternoon to visit with a friend. I believe she's expected back tomorrow."

Demon managed to keep the frown from his face—he knew it showed in his eyes. "A friend."

"Miss Blackthorn, sir. She and Miss Parteger have been in the way of exchanging visits over the past years."

"I ... see." The proposition that, with Bletchley on the Heath, Flick had abdicated her responsibilities—what she saw as her responsibilities—and had happily gone off to visit a friend, just like any other young lady, was simply too much to swallow. But Jacobs's easy expression declared that he knew no more; with a curt nod, Demon stepped to the door. "Tell her I called when she returns."

Jacobs hauled open the door. "And the General?"

Demon hesitated. "Don't bother him—I'll call and see him tomorrow."

He went swiftly down the steps and strode to his curricle, every instinct he possessed flickering, every nerve jangling. Accepting the reins with a distracted nod, he stepped up to the box seat and sat. Raising his hands to give the bays the office, he glanced at the groom.

And froze.

He frowned. "You're the coachman here, aren't you?"

The man bobbed his head. "Aye, sir." He jerked his head toward the stable. "The lads have gone home, so there's just me and old Henderson."

"But ... if you're here, who's driving Miss Parteger?"

The man blinked. "Why, your man, sir. Gillies."

Light dawned—Demon didn't like what he saw. Jaw setting, he nodded to the coachman. "I see. Thank you."

He sprang the bays; when he reached the road, he set them flying.

Demon found no joy—no news—waiting for him at the farmhouse. Which, he reasoned, meant Gillies imagined they'd be back before the following evening. That didn't tell him where they were now—where they were spending this evening—and, more importantly, what they thought they were doing.

More specifically, what Flick thought she was doing—he doubted Gillies was behind this escapade. He had, however, given his henchman strict instructions not to let Flick out of his sight; it appeared Gillies was following those instructions to the letter.

Which was some small comfort.

After checking with the Shephards, who knew nothing, he paused only to consign the bays into the hands of his head stableman before swinging up to Ivan's back and riding out into the night. Both Hills and Cross lived in cottages north of the Heath—if he had to, he'd track them down, but first he'd check with Dillon.

If something had happened in his absence, it was possible that Flick had sought counsel with Dillon. Whatever had happened might even involve Dillon—*he* might be the reason Flick had needed a carriage. A host of possible scenarios, none of which he liked, fought for prominence in his mind. He pressed Ivan as fast as he dared over the rough trail to the cottage.

He glimpsed a faint light as he entered the clearing; it disappeared by the time he dismounted.

"It's me—Demon."

The glow returned, guiding him through the derelict lean-to and into the cottage proper. Dillon was standing by the table, his hands on the lamp; he looked up, his expression open and eager.

Demon met his eyes. "Where's Flick?"

Dillon grinned. "She's off gallivanting after Bletchley." Dropping into his chair, he waved to a stool. "She's convinced, this time, that Bletchley's going to meet with the syndicate."

Icy fingers clutched Demon's spine. Ignoring the stool, he halted by the table; blank-faced, he looked down at Dillon. "And what do you think?"

Dillon opened his eyes wide. "This time, she might be right." He glanced up as Demon's gloves hit the table; his engaging grin flashed. "A pity you weren't here, but Flick'll be there to see—"

A sound like a growl issued from Demon's throat. He grabbed Dillon by his shirtfront, plucked him out of the chair, shook him like a rat, then took one step and slammed him back against the cottage wall.

The chair crashed, the sound echoing in the stillness. The wall shook.

Wide-eyed, unable to breathe, Dillon stared.

Into Demon's slitted eyes.

Dillon was only a few inches shorter, but he was a great deal slighter. There was nine years between them, and it was measured in muscle. Demon knew he could crush Dillon's windpipe with one forearm—from the look in Dillon's eyes, Dillon knew that, too.

"Where is she?" His words were low, slow and very distinct. "Where is this supposed meeting to take place?"

"Bury," Dillon gasped. His chest heaved. "Bletchley went there—she followed. She was going to try to get a room at The Angel."

"Try to?" The Angel was a very large house.

Dillon licked his lips. "Prizefight."

Demon couldn't believe his ears. "*Prizefight?*"

Dillon tried to nod but couldn't. "Flick thought it was the obvious—the most *likely* place for the syndicate to meet with Bletchley. Heaps of bucks and blades up from London—all the riffraff and the Fancy, too. Well, you know—" He ran out of breath and wheezed, "It seemed like sound reasoning."

"What did Gillies say?"

Dillon glanced at Demon's eyes and paled even more. He dropped his gaze.

When he didn't answer, Demon tensed the muscles in his arms.

Dillon caught his breath in a rush. "He didn't want her to go—he said you wouldn't like it."

"And you? What did you say?"

Dillon tried to shrug. "Well, it seemed like a sensible idea—"

"You call letting a gently reared, twenty-year-old girl go waltzing out to spend the night in an inn filled to the rafters with a prizefight crowd *sensible*?"

A look of petulance passed over Dillon's face. "Well, *someone* had to go. We needed to learn—"

"*You miserable coward!*"

He didn't crush Dillon's windpipe—he hauled him up, shook him once, then slammed him back against the wall. Hard.

Then he released him.

Dillon collapsed in a coughing heap on the floor. Demon looked down at him, sprawled beside his boots. Disgusted and furious in equal measure, he shook his head. "When the devil are you going to grow up and stop hiding behind Flick's skirts?" Turning, he swiped up his gloves. "If I had the time, I'd give you the thrashing you deserve—" He glanced back; when Dillon groggily lifted his head, Demon caught his eye. His lip curled. "Consider it yet another piece of retribution from which Flick has saved you."

He stormed out into the night. Vaulting onto Ivan's back, he set course for The Angel.

CHAPTER
Twelve

❧❧❧

She'd never seen so many men crammed into one space in her life.

Flick stood at her room window and looked down on the sea of male humanity filling the courtyard of The Angel. She'd been right in guessing that the prizefight crowd would congregate at The Angel; the throng seethed as men entered from the street while others drifted into the bars, returning with jugs and glasses. The courtyard of The Angel was the place to be.

Pitch flares had been placed around the courtyard, their flickering light strong enough for her, up in her chamber at the front of the house, to see faces below clearly. She'd snuffed her candles before parting the curtains. Luckily, the windows were hung with lace as well as the heavier drapes; she could stand close to the glass and peer down without risking anyone seeing her.

The noise was amazing. A multilayered rumble, it rose like a cacophany of deep-toned bells struck and rung without order. The occasional gust of laughter erupted, now from one group, then another. From her vantage point, she viewed the scene like some godlike puppeteer.

She'd been watching for close to an hour. The inn's bars were doing a roaring trade; she was grateful the staff had found time to bring up her dinner on a tray. She'd eaten quickly, then the serving girl had returned and taken away the tray. Since then, she'd been watching Bletchley.

He was halfway down the courtyard out in full view, a heavy figure in an old frieze coat, his scarlet neckerchief a useful feature to distinguish him from the many other older men in unfashionable attire. The fashionable and unfashionable mingled freely, their shared interest transcending social bounds. Bletchley stood, feet wide, his bulk balanced, quaffing ale and nodding as those in his circle expounded their theories.

Gillies was watching him, too. Bletchley had gone into the inn twice—Gillies had followed, sliding away from the group he was part of to slip inside. Each time he'd returned to resume his position as Bletchley did the same, a fresh pint in his hand.

Flick shifted her weight, then folded her arms. She was tired of standing, but if she sat, she wouldn't be able to see into the courtyard. The discussions below were gaining in intensity; in a number of groups, she saw money being waved about. There were gentlemen aplenty, well dressed, with the long aristocratic features that screamed wealth and affluence. Flick studied various hard faces, and wondered if they were members of the syndicate. Perhaps it was a group of blades, the most dangerously irresponsible of the younger gentlemen. She'd heard tales of incredible wagers; such men might well need cash, and they didn't appear to possess overmany scruples. But who? Who?

Her gaze passed over the crowd, then returned to Bletchley to see him squinting at an old watch. Tucking it back into his pocket, he drained his pint, collared a harassed serving boy and handed it to him, then, with a nod, excused himself to his cronies and headed away through the crowd.

Flick straightened. Bletchley wasn't heading inside.

Lumbering through the throng, tacking around groups, he made his way toward the far end of the courtyard. Flick lifted her gaze past the masses and looked out beyond the flares at the dark expanse of Angel Hill.

She knew that the long, sloping hill led up to the abbey, although she couldn't see it. The light from the flares ended abruptly just beyond the courtyard; Angel Hill was cloaked in the deep dark of a country night.

"Damn!" Flick relocated Bletchley, still struggling through the crowd. She searched for Gillies and found him; he'd seen Bletchley move, and was on his trail.

Flick sighed with relief—then froze. Someone had grabbed Gillies. He struggled to free himself, only to have more men range about him, smiling and laughing. She caught sight of Gillies's face—he was smiling and laughing, too. He also looked desperate.

One man slung his arm about Gillies's shoulders; another grasped his coat in friendly fashion and started talking nonstop. Flick saw Gillies cast a quick look around—saw him try to turn, but his friends wouldn't let him.

"Oh, *no*!" Aghast, Flick glanced to where Bletchley was nearing the far end of the courtyard, bounded by a few scraggly bushes, then she looked at Gillies, trapped and helpless in the middle of the crowd.

From where Gillies was, he couldn't see Bletchley's direction. He also didn't know where she was—that she could, if he looked her way, direct him. Gillies had lost Bletchley, and there was no way she could set him right—she could hardly fling up the window and shout down.

Lifting her gaze, Flick saw Bletchley reach the courtyard's far boundary. He didn't halt; he didn't look around. Pushing through the low bushes, he stepped out purposefully, into the dark. Heading straight up Angel Hill.

To meet with his masters—she just *knew* it!

Smothering a scream, she whirled and grabbed her cloak. Her veil went flying, disappearing over the edge of the bed; the pins clattered on the floor.

She didn't have time to stop. Dragging the cloak about her, she hauled the deep hood over and down so her face was heavily shadowed. Fingers flicking frantically, she cinched the cloak's laces at her throat, checked to make sure that the cloak was fully about her, then threw the bolt on the door and slipped out, pausing only to lock the door behind her.

Hurrying down the dimly lit corridor, she dredged her memory for all knowledge of the inn. She was on the first floor; the long corridor that crossed hers ended in a side stair leading down to a door just around the corner from the courtyard. Reaching the intersection, she turned and hurried on. Most of the inn's patrons were downstairs; there was no one about. All but running down the narrow carpet, Flick prayed her luck would hold.

She reached the narrow side stair; clinging to the shadows, she descended. The small hall before the side door was empty. She stepped out to cross it—

A door in the wall to her left crashed open. Two maids hurried through, carrying trays of used pots and jugs. They glanced at Flick, plastered back against the wall, but they didn't stop—they rushed on, down the corridor.

Flick dragged in a breath, steadied her pounding heart, and determinedly stepped to the door. It opened easily.

It gave onto a narrow cobbled area around the corner from the courtyard. From her left, noise rolled out and away, into the dark; the flickering flares made little impact on the night beyond.

Closing the door behind her, Flick faced Angel Hill.

Unfortunately, the cobbled area was used to house crates and barrels; it had been extended away from the inn, encroaching on the flank of the hill, where it ended in a high retaining wall. The only way she could gain the hillside and follow Bletchley was to skirt around to her left, cutting through the area dimly lit by the flares.

And risking someone—some man in the courtyard—seeing her.

Flick hesitated. Her back to the wall, safe in her dark cloak in the shadows, she thought of Demon, and Dillon, and the unknown syndicate.

Then she thought of the General.

Drawing a deep breath, she straightened and stepped away from the wall.

She didn't look back—didn't risk the light gleaming on her face or hands. She walked quickly and silently across, skirting the low bushes edging the courtyard and onto the lowest slope of Angel Hill.

Without pause, she walked on, even after the light of the flares had died behind her. Only when the night had swallowed her up and the noise of the courtyard was fading did she stop, draw a deep, reviving breath, and exhale with relief. Then, lifting her skirts, sending fervent thanks to her guardian angel, she hurried on. In Bletchley's wake.

After arranging stabling for Ivan with The Angel's harassed grooms, Demon strolled under the arch separating the courtyard from the stable yard. He stopped and scanned the scene just as Flick appeared briefly in the weak light of the flares on the rising ground on the far side of the courtyard. If he hadn't been looking for her, if she hadn't taken complete possession of his mind, he would have seen nothing more than the outline of a swinging cloak, a shadow against the deeper shadows of the night.

As matters stood, that was enough—he knew it was Flick.

He didn't know where she was going, but that wasn't hard to guess. Swallowing his curses—saving them for later—he stepped into the crowd.

And immediately, inwardly, cursed some more.

He couldn't race after her.

He had more than a few friends there—he'd known of the fight, and would probably have attended if he hadn't been so busy with Flick and her syndicate. His friends, of course, thought he'd come to join them.

"Demon!"

"You took your time. Where're you staying?"

"So—who've you got your money on?"

Adopting an expression of fashionable boredom on his face, Demon answered at random.

If his friends saw him striding into the night, they might follow out of idle curiosity. There was, however, an even greater danger. Many of the young bloods, bucks and blades considered him a man to emulate. If they saw him racing off up Angel Hill, they might send up a hue and cry, and then Flick would find herself enacting the role of fox pursued by a pack of slavering hounds.

Wonderful. This time, Demon vowed, he *would* strangle her.

After he rescued her from whatever danger she was so determinedly marching into.

Mentally gritting his teeth, he smiled and joked; gradually, he made his way to the far side of the courtyard. Only by telling one friend that he was going to join another did he manage to progress at all.

He caught sight of Gillies in the throng; it was instantly apparent his henchman had problems of his own. Demon considered, but detaching Gillies from his mates without attracting attention would prove difficult, and he didn't have the time. Flick had long since disappeared.

Finally reaching the bushes bordering the cobbles, Demon paused to scan the throng. He shifted his weight, first this way, then that, then frowned, turned, surveyed the bushes, then stepped through them. Hopefully, anyone who'd seen him would imagine he was merely caught short and looking to relieve himself.

He walked, definitely but with no panic, out of the circle of the flares.

Then he strode out.

He stopped once the dark had closed around him. He looked back, but could detect no sign of pursuit or interest. Satisfied, he turned back to Angel Hill and the slumbering abbey on the ridge. Somewhere ahead of him Flick was climbing, and, he assumed, ahead of her was Bletchley.

And ahead of Bletchley . . .

Lips thinning, Demon set his jaw and climbed faster.

Higher up the slope, Flick had run out of curses. Which was just as well, because she needed to save her breath. She'd climbed Angel Hill numerous times through her childhood, but she'd never climbed it in the dark. What was in full light an easily conquered slope, at night took on the guise of an obstacle course. The overall slope was even, but the terrain was not—there were dips and ridges, foot-sized holes and sudden ledges, all of which seemed to appear beneath her stumbling feet at the moment she least expected them.

And, to top it all, there was the mist.

Before leaving the inn she'd noticed the night was dark—only when she'd left the comforting flares far behind did she realize that it was, in fact, pitch black. Heavy clouds blanketed the moon; there was not even starlight to light her way. Her only landmark was the abbey and the cathedral tower, denser silhouettes on the crown of the hill, outlined against the ink black sky.

Unfortunately, as she left the town and The Angel behind, she ran into more ribbons of mist wreathing the shoulders of the hill. The higher she went, the thicker the mist became, causing her to lose sight of her landmark. Luckily, the cloud cover was not absolute—the moon occasionally shone through, giving her a chance to get her bearings.

During one such fitful illumination, she saw Bletchley laboring up the slope at least two hundred yards ahead of her. Flick thanked her stars she hadn't lost him. She battled on, slogged on, slowing when the moon again disappeared. Another wide band of mist slowed her even more.

Again the moon sailed free; Flick frantically searched the slope ahead, breathing again only when she sighted Bletchley's lumbering form.

He was much higher now, approaching the abbey. Luckily, the mists thinned toward the crest; she could see him clearly. It rapidly became apparent his goal was not the abbey but a thick stand of bushes surounding three trees a little way below and to the west of the abbey wall.

Flick's urgency eased. Bletchley's meeting with his masters would take more than a few moments. There was no need to scramble and risk alerting them to her presence. Far better to take her time and approach silently.

The clouds cooperated enough for her to see Bletchley round the stand of bushes and disappear from sight. In the time before the clouds caught the moon again, she didn't see him reemerge. In the same interval, she scanned the slope all about the bushes, but saw no one else.

Telling herself that Bletchley would definitely be on the other side of the bushes, she forced herself to climb with care, then slipped silently into the bushes' shadow.

Ears straining, she listened. She heard a gruff word, then nothing more. The moon broke free of the clouds and shone down, lighting up the area. Flick took that as a sign. Metaphorically girding her loins—she'd come too far to retreat—she edged to where she would be able to see around the bushes, exercising supreme care to avoid stepping on twigs, or leaves, or doing anything to warn Bletchley and whoever he was meeting of her presence.

She was successful—Bletchley and his companion remained totally unaware of her.

Then again, they would probably have remained oblivious of anything short of a charge of Hussars.

They were decidedly engrossed.

From the corner of the stand of bushes, Flick looked down on the meeting in progress, first in stunned surprise, then with increasing distaste.

The female Bletchley had come to meet lay flat on her back, her skirts rucked up to her waist, exposing chubby, dimpled white thighs, currently clasped about Bletchley's equally chubby, equally dimpled bare buttocks. Said buttocks were rising and falling in a staccato rhythm, quivering and tensing and shaking like jelly as Bletchley strained up and down, plunging himself into the woman's body.

Despite her carnal innocence, Flick knew what they were about. She knew how animals mated, but she'd never seen humans perform the same act. For one long instant, the sight transfixed her—in horrified fascination.

The sounds that reached her were not words about racing, or horses—certainly not the names she wanted to know. Grunts, gasps, pants and moans were the extent of the conversation.

Disgusted yet inhibited from even muttering an oath, she curled her lip, gritted her teeth on her temper, and swung away. Eyes on the ground, she strode back for the inn, heading downhill, directly away from the bushes.

After all her work—all the risks she'd taken! She had half a mind to scream with vexation and hope the sound gave Bletchley a turn. At precisely the wrong moment.

Men!

She strode into the first swath of mist—and ran right into one.

Her nose stubbed against his chest, burying itself in a soft cravat. She sucked in a breath to scream—and recognized his scent. His arms had locked, iron shackles about her, but as her instinctive rigidity eased, he relaxed his hold. She looked up at him.

He glared down at her. "Where—"

"*Shssh!*" Wriggling free, she tossed her head, indicating the bushes behind her. "Bletchley's back there."

Demon studied her face. "He is?"

Without meeting his eyes, Flick nodded, stepped about him and continued toward the inn. "He's with a woman."

Demon looked toward the bushes, then back at Flick, who was stalking down the slope. "Ah." His lips twitched, but only momentarily. The next instant, he caught up with her. "Actually," he drawled, steel rippling beneath his words, "I didn't come here to discover what Bletchley was about."

She didn't immediately reply, but just strode on. "I followed him here. You were in London. You weren't coming back until tomorrow."

"I changed my mind—a lucky circumstance. If I'd returned tomorrow, God only knows what trouble you might by then have succeeded in bringing down on your head." His clipped accents and the underlying force behind his words held a dire, not-at-all-subtle warning.

Unrepentant, Flick sniffed and gestured back at the bushes. "Obviously, as Bletchley isn't here to meet with the syndicate, I won't be getting into any difficulty."

"It's not Bletchley you need worry about." Demon's voice lowered to a dangerous purr. "*He* was never destined to be the source of your trouble."

A very odd shiver slid down Flick's spine. Demon's fingers closed about her elbow. She considered twisting free, only to feel his fingers tighten into steel shackles. Deciding her wisest course was to ignore him and his hold on her, she haughtily elevated her chin—and allowed him to escort her down the hill.

They covered the distance in silence, a silence that grew increasingly tense as they neared the courtyard. The tone of the gathering had degenerated to raucous, rough and ribald; many of the crowd were weaving on their feet. It was no place for a gently reared lady.

Demon halted beyond the area lit by the flares. "How did you get out?"

"The side door." Flick pointed.

He tugged her hood down to her chin. "Keep your head down." His arm slid around her waist, and he whisked her across the danger zone, into the shadows by the door.

She barely had time to look up before he bundled her through the door and up the stairs. He followed on her heels. On the first-floor landing, he hissed, "Where's your room?"

Flick gestured along the corridor. "Above the main door."

She led the way, but his arm snaked about her waist and yanked her back, anchoring her to his side.

Flick decided not to argue. Or wriggle. The glimpse she'd had of his face as they'd gone through the door had done very strange things to her nerves. His face was always hard, but it presently appeared fashioned from rock. Uncompromising was the term that leapt to mind.

Sounds of revelry gusted up the stairwell. The corridor leading to the front rooms began just before the stairhead.

Then Demon tensed. Flick looked ahead and saw four gentlemen come staggering unsteadily up the stairs. They were well away, rowdy and boisterous; instinctively, she shrank against Demon. He slowed, stopped, then started to turn toward her, shielding her—

Clapping each other on the back and guffawing, the four lurched off down the corridor in the opposite direction. Without, apparently, seeing them.

More voices drifted up the stairs.

With a barely muffled curse, Demon tightened his arm about her and hurried her on, forcing her to half run.

Flick pressed her lips tightly shut and held back her protest. She knew that if she even murmured, he'd throw her over his shoulder and stride on.

Then her door loomed before them. With a silent sigh of relief, she fumbled in her pocket and drew out the key.

Demon filched it from her fingers; he had it in the lock, turned, and the door swinging wide before she could blink.

Brusquely, he shepherded her over the threshold.

Shutting her mouth, Flick narrowed her eyes, elevated her chin, and swept on into the room. She walked straight to the fireplace, then regally swung about. Clasping her hands before her, spine stiff, head erect, she fixed her self-styled protector with a challenging glare.

He'd followed her in and closed the door, but he'd paused with his hand on the latch. His blue gaze raked her—from her head to her toes—then returned, sharp and penetrating, to her face.

She showed no hint of maidenly distress—Demon verified that fact with some relief. Whatever she'd seen of Bletchley's endeavors behind the bushes, she wasn't seriously upset. Indeed, her attention appeared to be fixed on him—which was undoubtedly wise. *He* was presently a far greater threat to her serenity than Bletchley would ever be. He captured her gaze. "Stay here— I'll go and check that Bletchley doesn't go from the arms of his companion to some other meeting." Even to his own ears, his tone sounded lethally flat. "And," he added, "I'll need to speak with Gillies."

A hint of color rose to her cheeks, and her chin rose another notch. Her eyes flashed with what could only be defiance. "The notion to come here was mine—Gillies was good enough to come with me."

"I know it was your idea." Demon heard his words and wondered at their evenness; inside him, ungoverned fury raged. "Gillies would never be such a sapskull as to even suggest bringing you here—into the middle of a *prizefight* crowd." His anger broke through; ruthlessly, he reined it in. "Gillies has only obeyed my orders to stay with you at all times. I'm not about to upbraid him." He held her gaze and quietly stated, "It's not Gillies I'm furious with."

He held her wide eyes for an instant longer, then turned to the door. "I'll be back shortly."

Opening the door, he stepped out, shut it—and locked it.

Flick heard the bolt click home. Lips parting, arms falling to her sides, she stared at the closed door.

Her temper soared.

Just like that! Put into her room and locked in, while he—!

Clenching her fists, she closed her eyes and gave vent to a frustrated scream.

Demon returned to the dim first-floor corridor at the front of the inn two hours later.

To find two young sprigs, decidedly the worse for the inn's ale, serenading outside Flick's door. His footfalls muffled by the corridor runner, he was upon them before they realized, materializing menacingly beside them.

They jumped like scalded cats.

"*Ooh!*"

"*Aaah!*"

Then they blinked and grinned inanely.

"There's a delightful widow behind the door."

"We're attempting to entice her to come out and play, don't y'know."

The first blinked again and stared myopically up at him. "Have you come to join us?"

With satisfying abruptness, Demon disabused them of that notion. He sent them fleeing, stumbling on their way, their egos shredded, their ears burning, their rears bruised courtesy of his rather large shoes. He saw them back to the stairs before returning to Flick's door. In the dimness, it took a few tries to get the key in the lock—eventually, he managed it. Straightening, he turned the key, lifted the latch and stepped inside.

Only lightning-quick reflexes allowed him to catch and hold back the heavy earthenware jug that came swinging down from his left.

Stretched on her toes, her hands clamped about the jug, Flick met his gaze. Darkly.

"Oh. It's you."

Leaving the jug in his hands, she swung away and stalked back across the room. She stopped before the fireplace, before the cheery flames, and swung to face him as she folded her arms.

Demon took in her belligerent stance and mutinous expression, then shut the door. She held her fire while he locked it and set the jug down on a nearby side table.

Then she let loose.

"You locked me in here and left me at the mercy of *those*! . . ." she gestured eloquently. Her eyes flashed. "I've had to endure *two hours* of nonstop caterwauling—no, no—I mustn't forget the *poems*. How *could* I forget the poems?" She flung her arms to the skies. "They were hideous! They didn't even rhyme."

She was unrestrainedly furious. Demon considered the sight.

"Anyway." Abruptly deserting fury, she fixed him with a narrow gaze. "Where did Bletchley go?"

Despite her ordeal with badly phrased poems, she was obviously all right.

"The tap, then to his room." Dropping his gloves on the side table, he pointed upward. "In the attics." Shrugging out of his greatcoat, he dropped it on a chair, noting as he did the large number of lighted candles set about the room. Flick had obviously felt in need of light—and reassurance.

She refolded her arms and frowned at him. "He didn't speak to anyone?"

Glancing around, Demon noted that the chamber was large and commodious, and well-appointed with decent furniture. The bed was long and wide, and made up with pristine linen. "No one of the ilk we're looking for. He didn't speak to anyone beyond the usual taproom chat."

"Hmm." Frowning, Flick watched him as he strolled unhurriedly toward her. "Maybe he did just come here for the prizefight."

"So it appears." His gaze returning to her face, he stopped directly in front of her, trapping her before the hearth. She frowned at him—more with her eyes than her expression. He considered her.

After a moment, she asked, "What are you thinking?"

How much I'd like to undress you, lay you on the bed and . . . "I was wondering," he said, "what it will take to instill into your stubborn head that it is not acceptable for you to go hying off about the countryside chasing villains. *Regardless* of where I, or anyone else, might or might not be."

She humphed and tilted her chin at him. Lifting one hand, Demon closed his fingers firmly about her tapering jaw.

Her eyes widened, then spat sparks. "There's nothing you can say or do that will convince me I don't have as much right as you to go hying after villains."

He raised one brow; his gaze fell to her lips. "Is that so?"

"Yes!"

His lips curved—not with humor but with satisfaction at her challenge—a challenge he was only too willing to meet. Tipping her chin up a fraction more, he lowered his head. "Perhaps we should put that to the test."

He murmured the words against her lips, hesitated for a heartbeat to let his warm breath bring her lips alive—then covered them with his.

She held tight for an instant, then surrendered. Her stiffness eased; her lips softened under his. Although still new to this—to kissing, to giving her lips, her mouth, to him—she was eager; her responses flowed instinctively. She had none of the guile of a more experienced woman—she had a fresh enthusiasm, an innocent ardency that delighted him, enthralled him.

He knew precisely what he was doing—distracting her from villains, from Bletchley and the syndicate, by giving her something else to think about. Something more exciting, more intriguing. He would bring her to life, and pique her curiosity so that she spent her time thinking about him, and this, rather than any villain. Sliding one arm about her waist, he drew her against him.

And deliberately deepened the kiss.

She responded sweetly, tipping her head back, parting her lips, welcoming him in. When his arm tightened in response, locking her to him, she eased against him readily, pert breasts pressing tight to his chest, hips sinking against his thighs. He caught his mental breath, locked an iron fist about his demons' reins, and parted her lips further, so he could artfully, skillfully ravish her soft mouth and take what she offered so freely.

The heady taste of her—so light and fresh, so teasingly alluring—went straight to his head, wreathed his senses, and set his demons straining. Wielding expertise like a whip, he held them back and set himself to enjoy the simple pleasure of her even more.

It wasn't anger that drove him, not even the wish to exercise his will over her and insist she stay out of danger. The compulsion steadily rising in his blood was simple desire—nothing more.

During the hours he'd spent watching Bletchley, speaking with Gillies, his anger had dissipated; his inchoate rage over the risks she'd taken had faded. His knowledge was wide, his imagination consequently well-informed; the visions that, even now, formed too readily were guaranteed to set his teeth on edge. But he'd had time to appreciate her thinking, to realize that, from her point of view, innocent of prizefights, coming here had been not only the obvious step but one she'd felt compelled to take.

He could understand. He still didn't approve, but that was another matter, a different aspect of the day's emotions. His anger had died, but the underlying tension hadn't. The anger had been only a symptom of that deeper emotion—one that felt uncomfortably like fear.

Fear was an emotion no Cynster male handled well. He'd had little experience of it—and he definitely didn't like what he was experiencing now.

That his fear was centered on Flick was obvious; why it should be so was another of those somethings he preferred not to examine.

If he'd known that deciding to bite the bullet and marry would bring all this down on his head, he would have thought twice. Three times. Unfortunately, it was now too late—the notion of giving up Flick, of retreating from marrying her, was unthinkable.

How unthinkable was borne in on him as he briefly released her lips to drag in a breath. Her scent came with it—appleblossom and lavender—a fragrance so innocent it touched his soul, so simple it drove through his defenses, caught and effortlessly focused his desire.

To live without this—without her, without the intense satisfaction experience told him could be his with her—*that* was the definition of unthinkable.

Releasing her jaw, he slid his fingers into her curls and held back a shudder at the sensation of pure silk sliding over the back of his hand. His lips firmed on hers; he angled his head, fingers sliding until he cradled her head, holding her steady so he could do as he wished—and take their kiss still deeper. Into realms she'd never experienced, along paths she'd never trod.

He, however, was *supposed* to be in control.

Shocked, he sensed the reins sliding from his grasp, felt his hunger well. Stunned, he pulled back—forced himself to break the all-too-evocative melding of their lips.

Long enough to drag in a much-needed breath. He couldn't remember when last *his* head had spun. "Umm ..." He blinked. "We'll stay until two o'clock. Then we'll leave. I'll take you home."

He'd worked it all out while watching Bletchley.

Lifting her lids only high enough to locate his lips, Flick nodded, reached up, framed his face, and drew his head back to hers. She knew perfectly well why he was kissing her—he wanted to control her, to render her all weak and limp and acquiescent. She might, indeed, go weak and limp—she might even be a bit distracted—but acquiescent? Just because her body and her wits lost all resolution the instant he had her against him, the second his lips found hers, did not mean her will went the same way.

Which meant that as far as she was concerned, he could kiss her as long as he liked. If he'd decided they had until two o'clock the next morning, she saw no reason to waste any precious minutes.

Being kissed by him was exceedingly nice, exceptionally pleasant. The touch of his lips was enticing, the much bolder caress of his tongue brazenly exciting. It made her feel wild, a touch reckless—oddly restless. That last was due to what lay beyond—all the rest she did not know. His experience was there, in his lips, in the arms that held her so easily, tantalizing, beckoning— simply intriguing.

She offered her lips and he took them again, and her mouth as well. And yet he held back. There was a restraint he placed on his actions, on his hunger, or rather, on letting her see it. She sensed it nevertheless, in his ruthlessly locked muscles, in the tension that held him. But that restraint stood firm, a barrier between her and his greater knowledge. A barrier she could not resist prodding. She was, after all, hardly a chit out of the schoolroom, no matter what he might think.

Brazenly, she leaned into him and wantonly kissed him back—trying this, then that, to see what might best weaken him. Closing her lips about his tongue and sucking was her first success—his attention abruptly focused; his resistance weakened accordingly. Sliding her hands around his neck, locking her fingers at his nape and stretching, sliding, upward against him, worked, too, but—

Abruptly he lifted his head and dragged in a huge breath. He blinked down at her. "Did the innkeeper see your face?" His voice was not entirely steady; he looked a little dazed.

"No." She sank deeper into his arms, sliding her fingertips into his hair. "I was hidden behind my veil the whole time."

"Hmm." He lowered his head and brushed his lips over hers. "I'll go down and pay your shot later. When all's quiet, and there's no one about to hear. There'll be someone at the desk all night tonight. Then we'll leave."

She didn't bother nodding. Her hands fell to his shoulders as he recaptured her lips, and she met his tongue with hers. She could, she decided, happily spend all night kissing him. Pressing herself to him. The thought prompted the deed, but she couldn't get any closer—she was already locked tight, breast to chest, hips to thighs. But . . .

He hesitated, then his lips shifted on hers. The whirlpool of their kiss dragged her deeper, into a vortex of heady sensations—all beckoning, enticing.

The need to get closer welled, swelled—

His resistance irked. If she wanted to marry him—if he wanted to marry her—then she wanted to know more. Deliberately, she stretched upward, flagrantly inciting, kissing him urgently, as evocatively as she knew how—

His arms shifted, then his hands were on her back—large and strong, they slid down, smoothly sweeping down to her waist, to her hips, then down, over the swells of her bottom. He cupped her, held her tight, her curves filling his hands, then he lifted her.

Up and against him—molding her to him so her soft belly cradled the hard ridge of his erection. She would have gasped—not with shock, but delight, a delight wholly new to her—but with lips suddenly ruthless and a demand she felt to her toes, he ravaged her mouth, took all she offered and searched for more.

There was suddenly hunger enough for two, swirling hotly about them.

Flick sank her fingers into his shoulders and hung on—thrilled to her bones as hot became hotter and hard that much harder. Need, want and desire swam through her—passion swept in in their wake. And caught her.

Excitement—even better than the rush of a winning ride—and an anticipation so keen it hurt flooded her, buoyed her—

Tap! Rat-a-tat-tat!

The sharp tattoo startled them both, ending their kiss. Breathing shallowly, they both stared at the door.

Demon straightened, softly cursing. Whoever it was, he would have to find out. It might be about Bletchley. Sliding Flick down until her feet touched the floor, he reluctantly released her luscious bottom and closed his hands about her waist. He seriously doubted she could stand unsupported.

Glancing around, his gaze fell on the solid dressing table against the wall between the mantelpiece and the bed. He glanced at the door, then steered Flick back so she could lean against the dressing table. "Stay there—don't move."

Placed as she was, she couldn't be seen from the door.

She blinked blankly at him, then looked dazedly across the room.

Demon released her; turning, he strode toward the door. Catching a glimpse of himself in the mirror beside the door, he swallowed another curse and slowed, tugging his waistcoat down, resetting his coat and cuffs, then raking his fingers through his hair before reaching for the latch.

He assumed it was Gillies, or one of the inn staff. Whoever it was, he intended getting rid of them fast. Turning the key, he opened the door.

The elegant gentleman who stood on the threshold, an urbane smile rapidly fading, was not a member of the inn's staff. Unfortunately, he was familiar.

Inwardly, Demon cursed, wishing he'd snuffed some of the candles Flick had scattered about the room. At least she was out of sight. Holding the door less than half open, he raised an arrogantly weary brow. "Evening, Selbourne."

"Cynster." Disappointment rang in Lord Selbourne's tone; disgruntlement filled his eyes. His expression, however, remained urbane. "I—" Abruptly, Selbourne's gaze shifted, going past Demon's shoulder. His lordship's eyes widened.

Demon stiffened, his jaw clenching so hard that he thought it would crack. He didn't, however, turn around.

Lord Selbourne's brows rose, coolly, appraisingly, then he glanced consideringly at Demon. And smiled. "—see."

The single word carried a wealth of meaning; Demon comprehended its portent only too well. Face set, he nodded curtly. "Precisely. I fear you'll need to find somewhere else to sleep tonight."

Selbourne sighed. "To the victor, the spoils." With an arch glance directed once again beyond Demon, he turned away. "I'll leave you, dear boy, to get what rest you may."

Biting back an oath—an exceedingly virulent one—Demon managed to shut the door without slamming it. Hands rising to his hips, he stared at the wooden panels; after a moment, the tension in his shoulders eased. Shifted. He blinked, then slowly reached out and turned the key.

The sound of the lock falling home echoed gently—a single knell marking an irrevocable step. Demon turned.

And confirmed that Flick had indeed been unable to resist shifting to the other side of the hearth, to peer about him to see who was at the door.

Selbourne had had a perfect view of her—with her hair ruffled, her gown suggestively crumpled, her lips rosy and swollen from his kisses. Most importantly, she hadn't been wearing hood or veil. Demon stared at her.

She stared back. "Who was that?"

He considered her, then turned back to the door and removed the key. "Fate. Disguised as Lord Selbourne."

CHAPTER
Thirteen

಻ು⁀ಌ

Flick studied him. "Do you know him?"

"Oh, indeed." Slipping the key into his waistcoat pocket, Demon started back toward her. "Everyone in the ton knows Rattletrap Selbourne."

"Rattletrap?"

Stopping directly before her, Demon looked into her eyes. "His tongue runs on wheels."

She searched his eyes, his face; her lips formed a silent *Oh*.

"Which means," he explained, "that at all the balls in London tomorrow evening, the juiciest *bon mot* will be just who the deliciously youthful 'widow' discovered consorting with me at Bury St. Edmunds really was."

Flick stiffened; her eyes flashed. "Don't start that again. Just because he saw me doesn't mean I'm compromised. He doesn't know who I am."

"But he will." Demon tapped her nose with one finger. "That's how Rattletrap secures his invitations—the particular niche he's carved in the bosom of the ton. He ferrets out all the indiscretions committed by the rest of us, and whispers them in the matrons' ears."

He held Flick's gaze steadily. "He'll find out who you are—you're well known in Newmarket, and that will be the first place he'll look. Gillies described the scene you created to get this room—that's precisely how a lady, living near but not in town, desirous of a room in which to meet her lover, would behave."

Flick folded her arms and set her chin stubbornly. "I am *not* compromised."

"You are." Demon didn't blink. "As of the instant Selbourne laid eyes on your face, your situation is the *definition* of compromised."

She narrowed her eyes. After a moment, she stated, "Even if, *theoretically*, I am, that changes nothing."

"On the contrary, it changes a great deal."

"Indeed? Such as?"

He reached out and tugged her hand free; puzzled, she let him raise it.

Catching the other, he lifted both to his shoulders, drawing her nearer. Releasing her hands, he closed his arms about her.

She quickly slid her hands down, bracing them against his chest. "What are you doing?"

He met her gaze, then lowered his head. "Demonstrating how much has changed."

He kissed her—and kept kissing her, not forcefully but persuasively, not ruthlessly but relentlessly, until she surrendered. When she melted against him, he locked his arms about her—and kissed her some more. She responded with her customary eagerness. Steadily, progressively, he retraced their earlier steps until their breathing fragmented, until her hips were pressed tight to his, until heat licked their senses and passion hovered in the wings.

Only then did he lift his head.

Her hands were fisted on his lapels. Her eyes glinted from beneath heavy lids. "You don't *want* to marry me—not really."

Flick made the statement without conviction; tight against him, his rampant arousal riding against her, she could hardly claim ignorance of what he wanted. It was a powerful incentive to give in. *But* ... She wanted him to marry her not just for that, no matter how exciting. She wanted him to marry her for more—for at least one other reason. A more important reason.

Tension invested his face. The same tension held her. His eyes remained on hers, his gaze steadfast, unwaveringly blue. Her lips throbbed. Entirely without her permission, her gaze lowered to his lips—clever lips, lean and strong, just like him. They dipped, and brushed hers.

"I do want to marry you." Again he kissed her—a tantalizing promise as he slid his hands down her back, lifting her against him once more. "I will marry you."

His lips closed on hers, and the kiss turned ravenous. And hot. She could cope with ravishment, but the heat—that welling sense of fire and flame—defeated her. He pressed it on her, and she drank it in. It slid through her veins, through her limbs, through her brain.

And she burned, as did he. There was fire in his touch, in his lips—despite the swelling heat, she couldn't get enough. As her limbs melted and resolution evaporated, she clung to her wits and inwardly cursed. How would she get him to love her if he married her like this?

How to stop him?

As if in answer, he deepened the kiss. Her head spun. Boneless, near to spineless, she sank deeper into his arms, into his strength. Into his shocking heat.

"I've dreamed of marrying you."

The words were a gravelly whisper. He steered her back a few steps; her hips met the dressing table.

"You have?" Breathless, she struggled to lift her lids.

"Mmm-hmm." Propping her against the dressing table, he eased back.

The sudden loss of his hard body against her, all but around her, left her disoriented. She dragged in a breath, watching as he shrugged out of his coat and waistcoat, tossing them on a nearby chair. He returned to her, his hands sliding, then firming about her waist.

"You've dreamed of our wedding?" She found that hard to believe.

His lips kicked up at the ends; his expression remained driven. "My dreams were more concerned with our wedding night."

He drew her to him. Eyes flaring wide, very certain of what she glimpsed in his, she braced her hands against his chest. "No. You know how I feel about marrying for such a reason."

He didn't force her closer, didn't pull her against him and simply melt her resistance. Instead, he ducked his head and dotted gentle kisses along her jaw, over her earlobe. Then his lips slid farther, to caress the sensitive skin beneath her ear.

She shivered.

"Would marrying me be such a hardship?"

He breathed the words against her ear, then drew back just enough so that as she turned, her eyes met his.

Their faces were so close that their breaths mingled. Wide-eyed, Flick looked deep into serious blue eyes, into his perfectly serious, well-beloved face. "No."

He didn't move, didn't grab her in triumph and crow. He simply waited. She studied his eyes, his face, then drew in a shallow breath. About them, the air shimmered, stirring, alive, invested with power. She felt his temptation, his promise, and more. Lifting one hand, she traced the line from one cheekbone to the corner of his lips. Hauling in another breath, she stretched up on her toes and touched her lips to his.

It was madness—a delicious, heady, compulsive madness—a sudden need that seared her, drove her, impelled her. It was impulse—pure, distilled and potent; she had no idea where it would lead.

But she kissed him—invitingly, encouragingly, challengingly. And sank into his arms as they closed about her, sank into his embrace, and into the kiss.

It caught her up, swept her up, and they were back in the fire, back in the flames.

Demon knew very well that she'd simply sprung her horses, that she was riding wild before the wind with no particular goal in mind. It was enough. He was expert enough to ride with her, to set his hand gently on her reins and guide her where he willed.

It took him a moment to work out the details—to plot and plan the where and how. Courtesy of her wildness, her increasingly abandoned kisses, he was already aching, but that was his most minor concern. He'd never made love to an innocent, wild or otherwise—she looked set to test his expertise, his control, to the limit.

Releasing her lips, he firmed his hands about her waist and lifted her, setting her atop the dressing table, giving thanks to whatever rakish god watched over him; the top was the perfect height.

She blinked at him in surprise. Her new position left her face more level with his. Her breasts swelled, then she noticed her skirts straining over her parted knees. She clamped her legs together and quickly shuffled back. Curls in disarray, her lips swollen, her eyes slightly wild, she stared at him. "What—?" She had to stop and haul in another breath. "What are you about?"

He let his lips curve reassuringly; he could do nothing about the fire in his eyes. His gaze locked on hers, he stepped forward, his hips meeting her knees, immobilizing her legs. Lowering his gaze to her chest, he reached for the top button of her bodice. "I'm going to make love to you."

"*What?*" Flick looked down as the first button popped free. His fingers caught the next button—she gasped and closed her hands about his wrists. "Don't be ridiculous."

She hadn't thought this far. And, thanks to him, her wits were frazzled, her brain was overheated. She certainly couldn't think now. She tugged once, then harder, and shifted his hands not at all. He continued to undo her buttons.

"Since by tomorrow evening we can rely on the entire ton believing that I spent tonight in your bed, there's no reason I can see that I shouldn't."

Fleetingly, he met her gaze; his was hot, smoldering blue. Temptation and promise—both glowed clearly; Flick found the sight reassuring.

Reassuring? She was losing her mind—he'd already lost his.

"Besides," he continued, in the same low, sinfully languid tone, "you made it clear you require something more than social stricture to agree to our wedding." The last button slipped free; he looked up and met her gaze. "Consider what follows as my answer to that."

Raising his hands, he framed her face and drew her lips to his. Flick braced herself to deny him—she would not be won over by main force.

But there was no force in his kiss. He nibbled, kissed, tantalizingly teased until, senses whirling, she grabbed him and kissed him back. She sensed his triumph, but she didn't care—in that instant, she needed his lips on hers, needed to feel the fire and flames again, wanted to know, couldn't live without knowing, more.

And she knew he could—would—teach her.

As if in confirmation, he welcomed her in, drew her deep, then toyed with her—incited her. Ignited her.

Until she was consumed by raging heat too hot to be confined within living flesh.

He eased back, his lips still on hers but their kiss no longer so demanding, no longer the focus of his attention. His hands drifted from her face, long fingers trailing down either side of her throat, then spreading over her shoulders. Unhurriedly, those long fingers skimmed down; with the lightest of touches, they flared over her breasts.

Her flesh came alive. Nerves flickered, unfurled—sensitized, they waited, tightening with anticipation.

He drew back from their kiss. Flick kept her eyes shut and struggled to breathe. Slowly, deliberately, he stroked the upper curves of her breasts, then the lower, through the soft fabric of her gown, then his fingers trailed lightly over the peaks, over nipples now excruciatingly tight.

She gasped—his lips returned, drinking the sound. His hands shifted, firming, palms cupping her curves. Gently but intently—inherently possessively—he closed his hands about the soft mounds.

Her breath hitched; his lips shifted on hers, brushed, caressed, reassured.

She felt her breasts swell even more, felt them heat and firm until they ached.

Demon ached, too, but ignored it. Her breasts were small, pert—they fit snugly within his palms. He closed thumb and forefinger about her nipples, and she gasped, and tensed—and tensed. With his lips on hers, soothing her, distracting her, he played, giving her time to grow accustomed to his touch, ruthlessly denying the impulse to brush aside her bodice and bare her to his senses. Eventually, she sighed into his mouth, the tautness in her frame subtly altered to a tension he recognized very well.

She was awakening.

With every controlled sweep of his fingers, every gentle, encouraging squeeze, he drew her further along the road to fulfillment. Hers. And his.

When he released her lips, drew his hands from her breasts and reached for the edges of her bodice, she didn't stop him. She did, however, reach up, too, closing her fingers on the edges below his.

She hesitated.

They were both breathing quickly, heated yet in control of their senses, both very much aware. Supremely conscious of the pounding in his blood, the passion he was holding at bay, he drew in a slow breath, locked his jaw and staved off the urge to rush her. And waited.

Her gaze was fixed on his throat; she dragged in a breath, held it, and looked up, into his eyes.

He had no idea what she saw there—what her swiftly searching gaze discovered; he stared down at her, unable to spare the energy to summon any expression, and prayed she wouldn't balk.

Instead, her chin firmed; her lips curved in a smile of pure feminine assurance tinged with her ever-present innocence. In a gesture almost demure, she dropped her gaze from his; tightening her hold on the open flaps of her bodice, she parted them.

Inwardly reeling, he let go and let her do it. That smile, coupled with her action, had hit him with the force of a fist and left him winded. Captured, transfixed, he watched as she wriggled, sliding first one shoulder free, then the other, then drawing her arms from the tight sleeves.

She glanced shyly, questioningly, up at him; he hauled in a breath and took charge again.

He drew the gown down to her waist, then had to pause to look at her—to take in the smooth expanse of creamy skin showing above her demure chemise, to drink in the beauty of her naked shoulders, her sweetly rounded arms, the delicate structure of her collarbone.

His rakish instincts catalogued points for later examination—where her pulse throbbed at the base of her throat, where her shoulder met her collarbone, the outer swells of her breasts. Her breasts themselves remained screened, albeit incompletely; her nipples peaked tightly beneath the fine chemise, but he couldn't appreciate their color. Soft, pure pink was his guess.

Feeling like a drowning man coming up for air, he hauled in a breath. Lifting his hands, he once more framed her face, and brought her lips to his.

Flick sank into the kiss. The heat welled—she welcomed it, then deliberately let go and slipped into the flow, letting it take her on its tide. If there had been a windmill near, and she'd been wearing a cap, she would have shied it into the sky. She'd made up her mind, made her decision.

She knew he desired her powerfully—it was there in his face, in the hard edge passion set to the angular planes, in the fire that smoldered in his eyes. His desire was palpable, a living thing—hot as the sun, it reached for her as his hands, his arms, his whole body did. She recognized it instinctively—she needed no interpreter to tell her what it was. He wanted her as a man wanted a woman. And she wanted him in the converse way.

As for marrying, he hadn't yet answered her question of whether love could grow from strong desire. Nor had she. But she'd expected no easy declaration of love—not from him. If he said it, he would mean it—she could count on that. But he could only tell her if he knew—and she didn't think he did. However ...

There was a light in his eyes, behind the heated glow, behind the passion and desire—there was a sense in his touch, in his kiss, in all his actions. And while that light shone, and while that sense reached her, she was convinced there was hope.

Hope of love—hope for a marriage invested with love, built on love, with him. She was willing to risk all to claim such a prize. Fate had offered her this chance to secure her deepest, all-but-unrecognized dream—she would take it, grasp it with both hands. And do everything she could to make the dream come true.

She would marry him, but on her terms. He would need to do more than seduce her—teach her about passion, desire and physical intimacy—to get her to say yes. She wasn't, however, about to stop and explain. Tonight was for them—their first night together.

Her first time with him.

When next he drew back, she smiled; lifting her arms, she draped them over his shoulders. His eyes met hers as he slid her closer to the dressing table's edge. He studied her face, his own hard, passion-set; wrapping one arm about her hips, he lifted her and stripped her dress away. Excitement shot through her, searing her veins. Clad in her chemise and petticoats, she dared to meet his eyes. He raised his brows slightly, then slid his hands upward and closed them about her breasts. "Do you like this?"

Her lids fell of their own accord; her head tipped back.

"Yes." She breathed the word, aware only of his clever hands, his clever fingers, as they stroked and gently squeezed. Although muted by fine lawn, his touch burned. His lips returned to hers. Sliding one hand to her back, he urged her nearer, closer to the table's edge.

She complied without thought—thought was beyond her; all she could do was feel. Her senses gloried in unfettered freedom, freed by her decision, freed by the night.

Freed by him. His kiss anchored her to the world, but it was a world of sensation, a world filled with an excitement she'd never known, and a promise of glory she wanted for her own.

Demon captured her lips and kissed her—ravenously—no longer so gentle, so controlled. She was delectable, and so very nearly his—he wanted to devour her. On the thought, his lips slid from hers, tracing the curve of her throat to where her pulse beat hotly. He laved the spot, then sucked lightly; appeased by her gasp, he moved on, sliding his lips along the curve of her collarbone, then shifting lower to the warm swell of her breast.

Through her fine chemise, one pert nipple beckoned; he closed his mouth over it and heard her shocked gasp. But she didn't try to wriggle back—she didn't tell him to stop. So he settled to feast, to wring more shocked gasps from her. Long before he raised his head, he'd succeeded, drawing a chorus of appreciation from her lips.

He kissed them again, parting them fully, ravishing her softness, taking all—demanding more. She met him eagerly, no match for the brutal strength of his passion but with an open eagerness that nearly brought him to his knees.

Abruptly, he stopped kissing her, amazed to find his own breathing as ragged as hers. Nuzzling aside her curls, he slid his lips into the sweet hollow beneath her ear while his fingers swiftly dealt with the laces of her petticoat.

Speed had suddenly become essential. Imperative.

She sighed, a tense exhalation shimmering with reined excitement; the sound literally shook him. The scent of her, rising to torment him, added to his pain. He glanced down at the soft chemise that hid her body from his sight—he longed to strip it away, but experience warned against it. Sitting naked atop a table in full light might be too much for her this time.

All thus far had gone according to his plan. She'd introduced an odd moment or two, but he'd kept them on track. He intended to seduce her but, this time, he needed to do more. He needed to be gentle, and not just because he was excruciatingly aware, to his very fingertips, of her innocence. He wanted her not just once or even twice—he wanted her for all time. So the moment had to be compelling. As powerfully compelling as he could make it—so she would want him again, as eagerly, as enthusiastically as he knew he would want her.

Another challenge—she was full of them. It was one of the things that so attracted him to her.

The laces of her petticoat came free; he loosened the waistband, pushed it down, then swiftly lifted her and swept the garment down her legs. He freed it from her feet, then flung it after her gown. His cravat and shirt followed—as he stepped back to stand against her knees, he flipped off her shoes.

She was waiting, almost shivering with excitement; she raised her arms, lifted her face and welcomed him back with an open-mouthed kiss. He sank into it and let her lead him where she would while he slipped off her garters, then rolled her stockings down, careful not to touch her bare skin. She was so caught up in their kiss, he wasn't sure she noticed when her stockings slipped away, and she was sitting in the candlelight clothed only in her chemise. The fine garment reached to midthigh; he grasped a fold and tugged—she was sitting on it.

Mentally girding his loins, he filled his lungs and wrested back control of their kiss. When he was sure he had all the reins in his grasp, he set his hands on her hips, simply holding her, giving her a moment to grow accustomed to the feel of his hands there. Her chemise was so fine it was no real barrier—to his touch or his senses.

She skittered a little, but calmed almost immediately; as soon as she did, he let his hands wander. Gliding, soothing, tracing, learning, he caressed her thighs, her knees, her calves. Then, gently but firmly, he grasped her knees and eased them apart.

She no longer had them locked together, but she resisted—for a moment. Then, hesitant but willing, she let him move each thigh outward, until he could step between.

Before he could haul in a triumphant breath, one of her hands slid from his shoulder to his chest. Quivering awareness shot through her—and him—when her fingers tangled in his crisp hair, when her hand came to rest tentatively, warm palm on the wide muscle above his heart.

For one long instant, Demon simply existed, focused totally on her—on holding onto the reins of her seduction. Her awakening was becoming an awakening for him—an introduction to delights more intense than any he'd previously known.

The tension that held her so tight, so taut, was, for all that, so intensely fragile; he felt as if, with one wrong move, one wrong breath, he might shatter it. And her.

When her hand shifted, drifted, then gently traced across his chest, he breathed again. Sealing his demon's reins in a death grip, he subtly altered their kiss, encouraging her to explore, relieved, if more tense, when she did.

Gradually, he eased her forward, closer to him, to the edge of the table. Every inch she slid forward pressed her thighs farther apart, until, beneath her chemise, they were wide-spread, held so by his hips.

She was open to him.

It took him a moment or three to shackle his raging lust—a few more to beat back his demons. What came next had to be perfect—it had to be right. Nothing in his life had mattered so much.

Sliding one hand to the small of her back, he settled it there, solid and sure behind her. Then he raised his head fractionally, breaking their kiss, but leaving their lips a mere inch apart. From beneath his lids, he watched her face as, with the same gentle yet deliberate touch he'd used throughout, he dipped his hand beneath her chemise's hem and slid it slowly up the silken length of her thigh.

Her lids flickered; he glimpsed her eyes, wide pupils circled in startling blue. She trembled; her breath caught, then she slowly exhaled. He stroked her thigh, the long quivering muscle, then the delicate inner face—he stroked upward, brushing her lips when she shuddered, letting her cling when, with the backs of his fingers, he caressed her quivering stomach.

Then, very slowly, he let his fingers glide down, tracing the crease at the top of one thigh, then the other, then, easing back from their kiss, he gently pressed two fingers into the silken curls between her thighs.

She sucked in a breath; a sharp quiver lanced through her. Her eyes were shut, but he watched her face, watched the expressions—anticipation, excitement, sharp delight and flaring need—flow across her features as he caressed her, then parted the soft folds and touched her intimately. She was already hot, already plump and swollen; he played, and damp quickly became wet. He found the tight nubbin hidden in its hood; he circled it with a moistened fingertip—her breath hitched, she shuddered; wildly clutching his shoulders, she sought his lips with hers.

He kissed her, but kept the caress light—he wanted her concentrating on his fingers, not his lips. With his hand at her back, he eased her forward another inch, so she was close, very close, to the edge—instinctively, she raised her knees and gripped his hips for balance.

If he could have grinned triumphantly, he would have.

She was fully exposed—to his touch, to him. He touched, caressed, then, very gently, probed her slick, soft flesh. He found her entrance—ignoring the sudden heightening of her tension, he eased one finger in, then, in the instant she caught her breath, slid it slowly, inexorably, into her heat.

She dragged her lips from his on a gasp; he felt the shudder that racked her in his bones. Her body closed hotly about his finger. Recapturing her lips, he kissed her—no longer lightly but deeply, evocatively. He stroked her in the same way.

Flick couldn't think, she couldn't reason—she couldn't imagine how she'd survive. She was hot, so hot; her skin felt afire. The flames that had started deep inside had spread to every extremity; her whole skin felt tight. As for her nerves, they were stretched so taut, so tense in anticipation of his next caress, of the next, deeply intimate invasion, that if it didn't come soon she knew she'd fly apart. If she'd had enough breath left, she would have sobbed.

With pleasure.

She couldn't understand that. She couldn't even think of what he was doing—what she was letting him do to her. Her stunned brain wouldn't hold the mental image. She'd had no idea physical intimacy would prove so shocking. So exciting. So mind-numbing.

So gloriously delicious.

And they hadn't even got to the culmination—the moment when their bodies would join. She knew what that entailed, yet ...

A little knowledge was a dangerous thing.

Luckily, her lover was experienced—exceedingly experienced if her state was any guide. She was panting, squirming, ready to kill for that next bit of sensation, his next caress, the next experience he had in store.

If he didn't hurry up and give it to her, she was quite sure she'd die.

Demon was well aware of her state—not once had he stopped tracking it. He withdrew his finger from her only to slide another in beside it, deliberately stretching her, preparing her. She squirmed and adjusted instantly. He reached deep—her gasp shuddered into a soft sob. She dropped her forehead to his shoulder; he could feel her soft pants hot against his skin.

He no longer needed to hold her to him—there was no chance she would scoot back. Leaving the hand between her thighs still probing in a slow, repetitive rhythm, with the other he slipped the buttons on his trousers and guided them down his hips. He uttered a wordless thanks to fate that he was in his town rig, with shoes, not boots; he toed the shoes off, let his trousers fall, stepped out of them and kicked them away.

She felt him shift—greedy hands grasped his shoulders, hauling him to her. Momentarily off-balance, he went with her pull—then gasped, biting back a groan as his throbbing erection hit the dressing table's edge.

Her thighs were still wide, her knees clamped to his now naked hips. He drew in a breath, nudged her head up, and found her lips again. He caught her up in the kiss, then drew his hand from her slick heat; one hand at her back, he eased her forward a fraction more—until the broad head of his staff nudged into her hot softness.

Abruptly, she drew back from the kiss. Arms locked about his shoulders, she blinked dazedly as their gazes met. She licked her lips, then glanced at the bed. "Aren't we? . . ."

"No." He could hardly speak. The effort of holding still, poised at her entrance, her slickness scalding him like hot honey, was turning his muscles to jelly. "This way will be easier for you this time." She was small; to lie beneath him, trapped by his weight, might not be wise—not for her first time.

Her lips formed an *Oh*—she risked a glance down, but her chemise, stretched across her thighs, blocked her view. She cleared her throat. "How? . . ."

His pained grin never made it to his face. "Easily. Just—like . . ." He pressed nearer, simultaneously drawing her to the very edge of the table—he sank into her. "*This*."

The look on her face was one he would treasure all his life—her eyes widened as he entered her, slowly pushing in, stretching her softness. She was oh, *so* tight, but, to his relief, she didn't freeze, didn't tense. He didn't stop—feeling her untried body ease about him, he penetrated her steadily, inexorably filling her until she'd taken him in to the hilt and he was buried in her sweet heat.

Her fractured "*Oh!*" shivered in the air. Her lids fell—she hauled in a huge breath. *Then* she tensed. Scalding hot, she closed about him, so tight he thought he'd lose his mind. He trapped her lips and only just managed to catch his reins and haul back on the savage urge to ravish her—her mouth, her hot softness, the luscious vessel of her body. Although reeling himself, he caught her senses and steadied her—in so doing, he steadied himself.

Releasing her lips, dragging in a huge breath, clamping a firm hold on his instincts—where she was concerned, too primal, too raw—he anchored her before him, withdrew, and slid home again.

Her maidenhead had been a mere cobweb. That hadn't surprised him; she'd been riding astride all her life and still did. So there'd been no pain, only pleasure as he'd filled her—as he withdrew and filled her again.

His muscles flickered under the strain, but he kept his rhythm very slow so she could grow accustomed to the intimacy, to the slide of his body into hers, to the flexing, regular rhythm, to the elemental repetition.

His breathing sounded ragged in his ears; he was so tense his lungs felt tight. But now he was, at long last, inside her, and she was so tight and hot, and so accepting, he was determined to prolong the sweet torture to the full.

She was very wet, scalding hot; her thighs eased about him as he loved her. Then she wriggled, pressing closer. Clinging to his shoulders, clamping her knees to his hips, she arched, and picked up his rhythm. She matched him, warm and pliant, a female body more delicious, more rewarding, than any he'd known. They could barely breathe, yet their lips fused and held, melding to the same beat as their bodies, the same beat as their hearts.

She was used to riding; he realized what that meant as she continued to meet him, her body supplely flexing in his arms. She could very likely last as long as he could—which was a thought to make a strong man weak.

It only made him more rigid, more engorged. Her murmur as she adjusted was not one of complaint. So he held her lips with his, held her steady before him, and gave her what she deserved—a long, slow ride to delight.

Flick followed his lead eagerly, delighted to find that she could. That the steady rhythm hadn't overwhelmed her, although at first she'd thought it would. That first instant of feeling him deep within her—even now, she gasped at the sensual memory. She still felt their joining keenly, the internal pressure, the fullness that was so strange, especially as she'd never felt empty there before. But now he was riding so smoothly, so deeply, so effortlessly into her, some part of her wits had reengaged.

Certainly not all of them. It was as if the heat between them had reached a new level, another plane, leaving her reeling in pleasured delight but with enough wit to appreciate the sensation. As for her body ...

On a gasp, she pulled back from their kiss to draw in a labored breath, aware of her body arching in his arms—aware to her toes of why. Her skin radiated heat, as did his. But aside from the heat, it was very like riding. She hadn't realized it could be done like this—she was finding it quite easy to cope.

He ducked his head; she felt his lips sear her throat. She clung to his broad shoulders and tipped her head away so he could sear as he would. She lifted her heavy lids to regauge their position—she pressed her hips closer, gripped his hips more tightly and splayed her hands over his back.

And caught sight of the mirror on the wall by the door. Directly opposite.

The reflection in the mirror stole her breath, focused her wits and transfixed her attention. In utter fascination.

She could see his naked back, down to his calves, see the flexing of his spine as he drove into her, see his buttocks clench and ease in time with their riding rhythm.

The view was enthralling.

She couldn't help but remember Bletchley in similar circumstance—which left her feeling like the cat who'd secured the prize cream. There was absolutely no comparison—not at *any* level. Not in the long, taut, steely muscles flexing in back and legs, not in the tight muscles that bunched and thrust, not in the steady, effortless rhythm, and certainly not in the powerful result.

Each deep thrust filled her completely, each movement effective, efficient and seemingly effortless—the outcome of harnessed, concerted power. Controlled power.

Bletchley had flailed and thrashed on top of his woman. In complete and stark contrast was the way Demon filled her. Deeply. Relentlessly. And oh, so repetitively.

Watching him thrust, feeling the result deep within her a split second later, focused her mind on the sensation, and drew her back into the maelstrom. Into the heat, and the swirling build of sensation.

Her lids were falling, her eyes almost shut when he changed his movement into a rolling thrust. She saw it—then felt it. She shut her eyes tight to better savor the moment—then quickly opened them again. To watch, and match her anticipation more acutely to his rhythm, to be ready to make the most of each sliding thrust, to shudder in his arms as he drove more deeply—to eventually let her lids fall as their glorious heat reached a new peak.

It was like riding at flat gallop through a fire.

Excitement, tense and searing, gripped her—along with a driving, compulsively *urgent* need. They were both breathing hard, both reaching deep—for the energy, the strength, to make the final dash.

He turned his head and their lips touched, but only briefly; she felt his hand slide, hot as a brand, up under her chemise. Skin to hot skin, he closed his hand about her breast. His fingers shifted; he found her tightly furled nipple. And pressed.

She cried out—the sound, laden with sharp delight, echoed through the room. His hand shifted on her flesh, and she was burning, burning—incandescent within.

Heat and flames were everywhere, raging through her—molten rivers of pleasure and urgent need flowed, a hot tide, from where they joined. The tide swelled, reaching ever higher, consuming her body, buoying her mind, her senses—lifting them high on a rush of pure passion.

Higher—ever higher.

His hand slid over her fevered flesh, from breast to hip, then around to her rear. He caressed her there—with a smothered gasp, she locked her arms about his shoulders and lifted slightly; instantly, his hand slid lower, caressing her bottom knowingly, evocatively, possessively, then reaching further to trace the line beneath the tight globes.

She shuddered—and felt like she was shattering. Blown apart by the heat and the burgeoning frenzy. He set her down and tipped her back, his hands once again at her hips. He angled them; without thought, she lifted her legs and wrapped them about his waist.

Instantly, he filled her deeply, completely; as he drew back, his fingers slid into the damp curls between her widespread thighs, straight to the nubbin of flesh he'd earlier teased.

He touched her there—and reality shook. She clutched tight—in desperation, she tried to cling to her wits, to her spiralling senses . . .

"Let go." His lips touched hers briefly—hotly. "Throw your heart over."

She heard the raspy order as he touched her again—she obeyed, and soared high.

Her world exploded.

She lost her senses utterly—lost all touch with reality. She was swept up by a force she couldn't describe—hot and powerful, it propelled her into pleasure. Deep, bone-melting pleasure.

It surrounded her like a sea, and left her floating in ecstasy.

To her surprise, her senses returned, heightened but focused solely on him. She felt his hard hands, first gentling, then gripping her, felt the force surge and sweep through his body—and into hers as he drove deep into her molten flesh. She heard his guttural groan as the force caught him, too.

Then he joined her in the void. She felt the warmth of him deep in her womb. Felt the heat of his body beneath her hands as she clung to him, and surrendered.

To the force behind their passion.

Eons later in the depths of the night, she awoke. Slowly, as always. Her mind struggled free of the wisps of sleep, only to slide into mists of confusion.

Her nerves made the dizzying leap from somnolence to excitement— befuddled by sleep, she couldn't understand why. It was full dark. She was lying on her back in the middle of a comfortable bed. A tickling sensation—it had started at the base of her stomach, just above her curls—*that* was what had woken her—was slowly progressing up her body. Over her stomach, past her navel, over her waist, steadily upward.

Some part of her mind was shrieking for her to react—but her limbs were too weighted—pleasurably weighted—for her to make any rash move. The tickling changed to nuzzling beneath her breasts, then warm kisses followed one curve up and over.

Demon's mouth closed over her nipple.

She sucked in a tortured breath and abruptly came to life. Not, however, quite as her mind intended. Held between his hands, she arched, flagrantly offering her breast—he accepted immediately, laving the tip, then taking it deep in his mouth.

Flick heard a soft, strangled cry—then realized it was hers. The searing wetness shocked her anew. Opening her eyes, she looked down. "What—?"

She couldn't see him in the dark, but she could feel him. Her heart hitched, then started to canter as she felt his hair-roughened legs between hers, the solid weight of his hips spreading her thighs wide. The heat of his body as he hovered over her, mere inches distant, sent her heart into a gallop. When she realized that her senses hadn't lied—that there was no longer any garment, no matter how fine, between them, that his wicked lips and wickeder mouth were teasing her bare skin, and that, any second, his hard hot body would lie directly, skin to naked skin, on hers—her heart started to race.

"Relax."

The deep purring murmur came out of the dark as he lifted his head from her breast. After a moment he added, as if to explain, "I want you again."

Those four gravelly words went straight to her heart—then straight to her loins. He'd pushed her chemise up to her arms—when he tugged, she dragged in a massive breath, and obliged, lifting her arms and letting him draw the thin garment off over her head.

Leaving her naked beneath him.

What followed was a second lesson in sheer delight. In the dark of the night, in the depths of the bed, he touched her, caressed her, then, when her body was aching with urgent longing, filled her.

She lay on her back and let sensation wash over her—let her mind supply what she couldn't see. The cotton sheets formed a cocoon about them, cool against her fevered skin. The mattress was thick enough to cushion her against the powerful surges of his possession.

Arms braced, he loomed above her, a shadow lover in the night; he held himself over her as their bodies did what seemed to come naturally. To them both.

She couldn't deny she enjoyed it thoroughly, that she joyfully put her heart and soul into the exercise every bit as much as did he. She enjoyed feeling his body merging with hers, enjoyed the deep sense of completion that came, borne on that final surrender.

Enjoyed the weight of him when he collapsed, spent, upon her.

Enjoyed the feeling of having him so deeply within her.

Demon woke as dawn tinged the sky and crept into the room to lay its pale fingers on the bed. In their light he saw an angel—his angel—sprawled asleep by his side.

She was facing away from him, half on her stomach.

For a long moment, he studied her golden curls while vivid memories rolled through his brain. Then, slowly, careful not to jar her, he came up on one elbow, then reached out and gently lifted the sheet, and drew it down.

She was more perfect than he'd thought—more beautiful than his imagination had been able to conjure. As the light about them strengthened, he looked his fill, drank in the sight of firm curves and slender limbs covered in flawless ivory skin—skin he knew felt like silk to his touch.

And would heat with gratifying swiftness if he touched her.

His gaze had fastened on the smooth hemispheres of her bottom. The thought of her responsiveness coupled with the sight brought him swiftly to attention, and too quickly to the brink of pain.

He gritted his teeth—and tried to think. Tried to reason with his overheated flesh.

All he could recall was her eagerness, her enthusiasm, her honest, open, unrestrained passion.

And the fact that he'd exercised great care in taking her the first time, and she hadn't tensed in the slightest when he'd taken her again.

He shouldn't, of course, have been so demanding as to take her a second time mere hours after the first. But he'd been desperate—visited by an ungovernable urge to reassure himself that it hadn't been a dream. That the most sensual woman he'd met in his life was an innocent Botticelli angel.

If he was wise, he wouldn't think about that—about how she'd responded so ardently, adapted so readily, then joined him in a wild ride. A ride rather wilder and certainly longer than he'd intended.

But she'd enjoyed it—and she'd enjoyed their second ride, too.

Perhaps she'd enjoy a third?

His hand had made contact with her bottom before he'd finished the thought.

Flick woke to discover her bottom flushed and fevered, and Demon's hand sliding beneath her hip. He lifted her, and stuffed a pillow beneath her hips, then eased her down, settling her more definitely on her stomach.

Which seemed rather odd. But then, she was still mostly asleep. "Mmm?" she murmured, making it a question.

He leaned over her, looked into her heavy-lidded eyes, then kissed her shoulder. "Just lie still."

She smiled sleepily, and let her lids fall.

His hand returned to her bottom.

To gently but evocatively caress, leaving a tracery of fire on skin already heated and dewed. Her breath came increasingly fast—when she murmured again, an incoherent question, his hand shifted. Long fingers slid between her thighs, into the soft folds of flesh between. He caressed, then probed—she felt him lean over her, the crisp hair on his chest brushing her back, sending tingling shivers racing through her.

All the way to where his fingers delved.

He smothered a curse, then his fingers left her. He shifted, his weight dipping the bed as he lifted over her. With his legs, he nudged hers wide; grasping her right knee, he drew it up, bending that leg, leaving her knee almost level with her waist—he settled his hips in the space created, hard against her bottom.

She blinked her eyes wide—a large hand came down, palm flat by her shoulder, carrying his weight above her.

Her heart throbbed and leapt to her throat as she felt his weight against her bottom—then stopped as she felt a familiar hardness ease into her.

She gasped as he slid powerfully home. All the way.

Holding still, his hips flush with her bottom, he lowered his head and brushed a kiss on her shoulder. "Are you all right?"

Naked, with him equally naked behind her, joined in a fashion that made her think of stallions and mares, with him throbbing at her center ... she was more than all right. She was on the brink of ecstasy.

"*Yes*." The word came out in a rush, laden with a sweet tension she couldn't disguise. He bent his head and touched his lips to her ear.

"You don't have to do anything. Just lie still."

Then he made love to her until she screamed.

CHAPTER

Fourteen

ဆုၼ်ဳ

"Drive on!" Demon climbed into the manor's carriage; a groom shut the door behind him. The carriage lurched, then rumbled out of The Angel's stable yard.

"Are you *sure* Gillies will be able to cope?" Flick asked. "There's no need for you to escort me all the way to Hillgate End."

Settling beside her, Demon glanced at her, then leaned back against the squabs. "Gillies is perfectly capable of locating Bletchley and following him back to London."

He'd gone down to breakfast and to order a tray to be taken up to Flick, only to find Gillies kicking his heels by the main door. Bletchley, it transpired, had already left for the prizefight field.

"Heard him quizzing the innkeep," Gillies had said, "about the special coaches they've put on, running direct from here to London."

After his lack of activity the previous night, it seemed likely Bletchley had dallied in Newmarket purely to attend the prizefight, but ... they couldn't be certain he didn't have a meeting arranged to take place amid the crowd about the ring. Neither he nor Gillies had believed that—discussing race-fixing surrounded by a crowd containing so many potentially interested ears smacked of rank stupidity, something the syndicate had shown no sign of being. Gillies hadn't followed Bletchley, but waited for orders.

"He went out this morning with the same crew he was chatting with last night, heading straight for the field."

There was an outside chance of a meeting occurring after the prizefight, although given the aftermath of such events, that, too, seemed unlikely. Still ...

Demon had rejigged his plans, sending Gillies after Bletchley to watch and to follow, to London if necessary.

"Gillies knows who to contact in London—we'll set up a watch on Bletchley. He'll have to meet with his masters soon."

Flick humphed impatiently; Demon ignored it. He was relieved that Bletchley was heading south. With him gone, the chances of Flick running headlong into danger were considerably diminished.

With Gillies at the fight, he'd first arranged for a coachman to drive the manor carriage back to Hillgate End, then broken his fast at a leisurely pace, then paid Flick's shot with no explanation whatever, and returned upstairs to escort her, concealingly cloaked and veiled, down to the waiting carriage.

By that time, the fight had started, so there was no one of note left at the inn to witness their joint departure. The only wrinkle in his plan was Ivan the Terrible, presently tied behind the carriage.

Ivan hated being led—especially by a carriage. He was going to be in a foul mood when it came time to ride home.

Demon wasn't, however, disposed to worry about Ivan—before he rode home, he had a number of pressing matters to resolve. The most pressing sat beside him, idly gazing at the scenery, with not the slightest sign of fluster showing in her angelic face.

Which really did surprise him.

He was thirty-one and had bedded scores of women—she was just twenty, and had just spent her first night with a man. Him. Yet her composure was patently genuine. She'd been flustered enough, blushing rosily, when he'd left her in the room and gone to look for breakfast. But by the time he'd returned, she had been perfectly composed, her usual straightforward, openly confident self. Of course, by then, she had dressed.

She'd removed her veil as they'd rolled out of Bury; a quick glance revealed a serene expression, with a slight smile tilting her lips and a soft light in her eyes. As if she was recalling the events of the night and enjoying her memories.

Demon shifted, then looked out of the window—and went over his plans.

Flick was indeed reflecting on the events of the night, and those of the morning, and, further, on how much she'd enjoyed them. She still felt curiously glorious—as if she was glowing all the way to her toes. If this was satiation, she thoroughly approved. Which only made her even more determined on her course.

It seemed clear enough. Demon *could* love her—of that she felt sure. All she needed to do was to make sure he did before she agreed to marry him.

She needed to make him fall in love with her—she would have scoffed at the thought a mere month ago and labelled it an impossible task. Now, however, the prospects looked good. If last night and this morning were any guide, he was already halfway there.

He cared for her—was very careful of her; he clearly enjoyed giving her pleasure. He'd pleasured her to her toes. In a variety of ways. And remained considerate and caring afterward, in his usual overbearing way.

She spent the drive sunk in pleasant memories, but when they rolled through Newmarket, she inwardly shook herself, and sternly told herself to stop thinking of such things. She'd get precious little pleasuring in the days to come—at least until he came to love her.

She slanted a glance at him, then looked away, and rehearsed her plans yet again.

He spoke as they turned through the gates of Hillgate End.

"In case you're wondering, I intend telling the General that, due to an inadvertent circumstance, you and I were seen together in a chamber at The Angel last night by one of the ton's most rabid scandalmongers, and consequently, you've agreed to marry me."

She turned her head and met his eyes. "I haven't."

His face grew hard. "You've done rather a lot since last evening—precisely what is it you don't believe you've done?"

His tone was precise, his words excessively clipped. She ignored the warning. "I haven't agreed to marry you."

The sound he made was frustration incarnate. Abruptly, he sat up. "Flick—you have been well and truly and very thoroughly compromised this time. You have no choice—"

"On the contrary." She held his gaze. "I can still say no."

Demon stared at her, then narrowed his eyes. "Why would you want to say no?"

"I have my reasons."

"Which are?"

She considered him, then said, "I told you I needed something more than mere circumstance to persuade me to marriage. What you did last night wasn't it."

He frowned, then shook his head, his expression turning grim. "Let me rephrase my intention. I'll tell the General what I said before, then, if you still won't agree to our marriage, I'll tell him the rest—how I spent all night in your bed—and half the night in you."

She raised her brows, considered him steadily, then looked away. "You know you'll never tell him that."

Demon stared at her, at her pure profile, at her chin resolutely firm, her nose tip-tilted—and fought down the urge to lay his hands on her.

She was right, of course—he would never do anything to harm her standing with the General, one of the few people she cared about. The General would very likely understand why he'd acted as he had, but he wouldn't understand her refusal. Any more than he did.

Forcing himself to relax, he sank back against the seat and stared out of the window. The horses clopped on.

"What story did you concoct for the household to explain your trip to Bury?" He asked the question without looking at Flick; he felt her glance, then she answered.

"That I was going to see Melissa Blackthorn—her family lives just past Bury. We often visit on the spur of the moment."

Demon considered. "Very well. You intended visiting Miss Blackthorn—Gillies offered to drive you in the hope of seeing the fight, but when you reached Bury, the street was blocked with incoming traffic and you got trapped in the melee. It got dark—you were still trapped. Not being *au fait* with prizefights, you sought refuge at The Angel." He glanced at Flick. "Hopefully, no one will learn of your disguise or your story to gain a room."

She shrugged. "Bury's far enough away—none of the staff have family that far afield."

Demon humphed. "We can but hope. So—you were at The Angel when I arrived, intending to stay for the fight. I saw you . . . and then Lord Selbourne saw us. Thus, this morning, I brought you straight home so we can deal with the current situation." He glanced at Flick. "Can you see any holes?"

She shook her head, then grimaced. "I do hate misleading the General, though."

Demon looked out of the window. "Given we've struggled to avoid all mention of Dillon and the syndicate thus far, I can't see any point mentioning them now." It would only upset the General more to know the current imbroglio was a result of Flick's championing Dillon.

The shadows of the drive fell behind them; ahead, the manor basked in sunshine. The carriage rocked to a stop. Demon opened the door, stepped out, then handed Flick down. Jacobs opened the front door before they knocked; Demon led Flick into the cool hall, then released her.

Mrs. Fogarty came bustling up, fussing about Flick, who slid around her questions easily. Flick cast a watchful, questioning glance at Demon—he met it with his blandest expression. She frowned fleetingly, but had to reorganize her expression to deal with Mrs. Fogarty. With the housekeeper in close attendance, Flick headed to her room.

Demon watched her go, then his lips lifted, just a little at the ends. Challenges—more challenges. Swinging on his heel, he headed for the library.

"So—let me see if I've got this right."

In the chair behind his desk, the General sat back and steepled his fingers. "You and Felicity were *again* caught in an apparently compromising situation, only this time by someone who will take great delight in ruining Felicity's good name. You, however, are perfectly prepared to marry the chit, but she's proving headstrong, and jibbing at the bit. So, instead of pressing marriage on her in such an abrupt manner, you suggest I agree to send her to your mother, Lady Horatia, to enjoy the delights of the Season in London. Under your mother's wing, even without a formal declaration, it will be surmised that she's your intended, but the interlude will give Felicity time to adjust to the position, and accept marriage to you as the sensible course." He looked up at Demon. "Is that right?"

Standing before the windows, Demon nodded. "Naturally, if, in the course of her time in London, she meets any other gentleman and forms a lasting attachment that is returned, I give you my word to release her without complaint. It's her happiness—her reputation—I'm interested in securing."

"Indeed. Hmm." The General's eyes twinkled. "Well then, no reason whatever she should take exception to a sojourn in London. Do her good anyway, to see all she's missed stuck up here with an old man."

The lunch gong boomed; the General chuckled and rose. "Capital notion all around. Let's go tell her, what?"

Demon smiled easily. Beside the General, he strolled toward the dining room.

"London?" Flick stared at Demon, sitting directly opposite across the luncheon table.

"Hmm—the capital. My mother would love to have you stay with her."

It was all so transparent. Flick glanced to her right, to where the General, nodding mildly, was helping himself to more peas. He seemed serenely unconcerned about her reputation, for which she was honestly grateful to Demon; she couldn't have borne it if the old dear had been distressed. Yet she was fairly certain the only reason he was in such fine fettle, knowing her reputation was, if not precisely in shreds, then certainly rather tattered, was because he believed a stay in London under Lady Horatia's wing would make her change her mind and accept his protégé as her husband.

There was a good chance he was right—she certainly hoped so.

And there were a number of good reasons for falling in with Demon's plan. Not least was the fact that Bletchley had gone to London. And while she'd never before felt any interest in tonnish affairs, if she was to marry Demon, then she would need to find her feet in that arena. She was also suddenly insatiably curious as to how, and with whom, he spent his days in London.

Quite aside from all else, if she was going to make him fall in love with her, she needed to be with him.

Her eyes locked on his, she nodded. "Yes—I think I'd like that."

He smiled. "Good. I'll drive you up tomorrow."

"How on earth did that happen?"

Early the next morning, already on the road to London, drawn thence by Demon's powerful bays, Flick swivelled on the curricle's seat and glanced back at Gillies, perched behind. "I thought you were following him?"

Gillies looked pained; Demon answered. "We thought Bletchley was planning to take one of the special coaches back to London from Bury— Gillies heard him asking where to catch them. After watching Bletchley throughout the fight—and learning nothing—at the end, Gillies, quite reasonably, moved to the gate leading back to Bury and waited for Bletchley to pass him. He never did."

"Oh?" Flick glanced back at Gillies.

He grimaced. "He must have caught a ride on some cart back to Newmarket."

"And then hired a horse and, bold as you please, came cantering up the manor drive." Demon set his teeth. That had been too close for his liking— luckily, Bletchley had not seen Flick, nor she, him.

Flick sat back. "I nearly dropped a vase when Jacobs mentioned he'd called, asking after Dillon."

"Thankfully, Jacobs sent him on his way." Demon eased the bays past a farm cart, then let the reins run free. "Bletchley returned to the Rutland Arms and caught the evening mail to London."

"So we've lost him."

He glanced at Flick, relieved to see nothing more than a frown on her face. "For the moment. But we'll come up with him again, never fear."

"London's very big."

"True, but it's possible to keep watch on the likely places Bletchley might meet with a group of gentlemen. The classes don't mix freely at all that many venues. Limmers, Tattersalls, and a few other, less savory haunts."

"Still, isn't it like looking for the proverbial needle?"

Demon hesitated, then grimaced. "There might be another way to identify likely members of the syndicate independent of any meeting, which should make it easier, if a meeting does occur, to track someone to it—and so identify all the syndicate."

"Another way?"

Flick's eyes were firmly fixed on his face. With his gaze on his speeding horses, he outlined his discussions with Heathcote Montague, and what they hoped to discover.

At the end of his explanation, Flick sat back. "Good. So we haven't given up on helping Dillon—it's just that our investigations have changed direction."

"Speaking of Dillon, does he know you've left Newmarket?"

"I sent a message with Jiggs—I told him to tell Dillon that we had to follow up clues in London, that I didn't know when we'd be back, but that he should stay in hiding until we returned. I promised I'd write and tell him what we discover. Jiggs will deliver my letters."

Demon nodded. If nothing else, he'd distanced her from Dillon—while in London, she could concentrate on him, and herself. He was certain his mother would encourage her in that endeavor, while at the same time helpfully denying Flick—a young lady in her charge—the license she would need to pursue Bletchley, the syndicate, or any other villain. Despite the fact both Bletchley and the syndicate were in London, he felt perfectly sanguine about taking Flick there.

As for the danger posed by Lord Selbourne, that was, at least temporarily, in abeyance; his lordship had gone directly into Norfolk to visit with his sister.

The curricle sped south through the bright morning, wheels rolling smoothly along the macadam. Despite losing Bletchley, despite having to revise his plans to accommodate a certain angel's stubbornness, Demon felt in remarkable charity with the world. Their current direction felt right—this was obviously the way to get Flick to say yes. She was, beyond question, already his, but if they had to go through a formal wooing, he was content to remove to London. It was, after all, his home ground. He was looking forward to showing her about—showing her off. Her bright-eyed innocence continued to delight him; through her eyes, he saw aspects of his world he'd long considered boring in an entirely new light.

He slanted a glance at her; the breeze was tugging at her curls, setting her bonnet ribbons twirling. Her eyes were wide, her gaze fixed ahead; her lips, delicate rose, were full, lush, lightly curved. She looked good enough to eat.

Abruptly, he looked ahead, the memory of the taste of her flooding him. Gritting his teeth, he willed the distraction away. He was going to have to keep his demons caged for the foreseeable future—there was no sense in teasing and taunting them. That was the one drawback in placing Flick under his mother's wing—she would be safe from all others, but also safe from him.

Even should she wish otherwise, which was an intriguing, potentially helpful, notion. Mulling over the possibility, he sent his whip out to tickle his leader's ear and urge his horses on.

Beside him, Flick watched the countryside roll past with a keen and eager eye. Anticipation grew with every mile—it was hard to preserve a proper calm. Soon they would reach London; soon, she would see Demon in his other milieu, his other guise. She knew he was considered a rake extraordinaire, yet, until now, her knowledge of him had been restricted to Demon in the country; she had a shrewd notion his tonnish persona would be different from the one she knew. As the miles sped past, she spent the time imagining, envisioning a more graceful, more elegant, more potent presence—the glittering glamor he would assume when in society, a cloak donned over his true character, all the traits so familiar to her.

She couldn't wait to see it.

Despite losing Bletchley, it was impossible to remain sober. Her mood was buoyant, her heart light—she was looking forward to life in a completely new way—facing in a completely unlooked-for direction.

Marriage to Demon—it was a dizzying thought, a dream she had never dared dream. And now she was committed to the enterprise—totally and absolutely. Not that she entertained any doubts about success. In her present mood, that was impossible.

From all she'd heard of London, it would provide the setting—one with the best opportunities—for her to encourage Demon to give her his heart. Then all would be perfect, and her dream would come true.

She sat beside him with barely concealed impatience, waiting for London to appear.

When it did, she blinked. And wrinkled her nose. And winced at the raucous cries. The streets were packed with carriages of every description, the pavements teeming. She had never imagined such close-packed humanity— fresh from the broad plain of Newmarket Heath, she found it disturbing. She felt hemmed in on every side with the sheer weight of humankind. And the noise. And the squalor. And the urchins—everywhere.

She'd lived in London for only a short time before, with her aunt at her London house. She couldn't remember any sights such as those she now saw, but it had, after all, been a long time ago. As Demon concentrated on his horses, deftly tacking through the traffic, she edged closer until she could feel the warmth of his body through her pelisse.

To her relief, the fashionable areas were more as she recalled—quiet streets lined with elegant houses, neat squares with fenced gardens at their centers. Indeed, this part of London was better, neater, more beautiful than her memories. Her aunt had lived in Bloomsbury, which was not nearly as fashionable as Berkeley Square, which was where Demon took her.

He reined in the bays before a large mansion, as imposing as the most imposing she'd seen. As Gillies took the reins and Demon stepped down, Flick stared up at the three-storeyed facade and suddenly knew what "being not quite up to snuff" felt like.

Then Demon took her hand; stilling her fears, she shuffled along the seat and let him hand her to the ground. Clutching her parasol's handle tightly, she took his proffered arm, and climbed the steps beside him.

If the house was imposing, slightly scarifying, the butler, Highthorpe, was worse. He opened the door to Demon's knock and looked down his beaked nose at her.

"Ah, Highthorpe—how's the leg?" With an affectionate smile at the butler, Demon handed Flick over the threshold. "Is her ladyship in?"

"My leg is quite improved, thank you, sir." Holding the door wider, Highthorpe bowed deferentially; he closed it after them, and turned, his starchy demeanor somewhat softer. "Her ladyship, I believe, is in her sanctuary."

Demon's smile deepened. "This is Miss Parteger, Highthorpe. She'll be staying with Mama for the nonce. Gillies will bring her bags around."

It might have been a trick of the light beaming through the fanlight, yet Flick could have sworn a gleam of interest flashed in Highthorpe's eyes. He smiled as he bowed again to her. "Miss. I'll mention to Mrs. Helmsley to prepare a room for you at once—I'll have your bags taken there. No doubt you'll wish to refresh yourself after your journey."

"Thank you." Flick smiled back—Highthorpe suddenly sounded much more comfortable. Demon drew her on.

"I'll leave you in the drawing room while I fetch Mama." He opened a door and ushered her inside.

One glance about the elegant blue-and-white room had her turning back to him. "Are you sure this is a good idea? I could always stay with my aunt—"

"Mama will be delighted to meet you." He made the statement as if she hadn't spoken. "I won't be above a few minutes."

He went out, closing the door behind him. Flick stared at the white painted panels—he didn't come back in. Sighing, she looked around.

She considered the white damask settee, then looked down at her plain, definitely old, outmoded pelisse. Putting one in contact with the other seemed like sacrilege. So she stayed on her feet and shook out her skirts, trying vainly to rearrange them to hide the creases. What would Lady Horatia—the lady who presided over such a well-appointed drawing room—think of her in her far-from-elegant attire?

The point proved academic.

The latch clicked, the door swung wide, and a tall, commandingly elegant lady swept in.

And descended on her, a huge smile on her face, her eyes alight with a welcome Flick could not imagine what she'd done to deserve. But there was no mistaking the warmth with which Lady Horatia embraced her.

"My dear!" Touching a scented cheek to hers, Lady Horatia straightened and held her at arms' length, not to inspect her dowdy pelisse but to look into her face. "I'm so *very* delighted to meet you, and to welcome you to this house. Indeed"—she shot a glance at Demon—"I understand it will be my pleasure to introduce you to the ton." Looking back at Flick, Lady Horatia beamed. "I couldn't be more delighted!"

Flick smiled warmly, gratefully.

Lady Horatia's smile deepened; her blue eyes, very like Demon's, twinkled expressively. "Now we can send Harry away and get acquainted."

Flick blinked, then realized, as Lady Horatia turned to Demon, that she was referring to him.

"You may come back for dinner." Lady Horatia raised a brow—the gesture appeared haughtily teasing. "I presume you are free?"

Demon—Harry—merely smiled. "Of course." He looked at Flick. "I'll see you at seven." With a nod for her and another for his mother, he turned and strolled to the door; it shut softly behind him.

"Well!" Lady Horatia turned to Flick, and smiled exultantly. "At last!"

CHAPTER
Fifteen
〤⊙〤

Despite their languid elegance, when Cynsters acted, things happened in a rush. After luncheon, Horatia whisked Flick into her carriage, off to a family afternoon tea.

"Grosvenor Square's not far," Horatia assured her. "And Helena is going to be as delighted as I to meet you."

"Helena?" Flick sifted through the names Horatia had mentioned over luncheon.

"My sister-in-law. Mother of Sylvester, better known as Devil, now Duke of St. Ives. Helena is the Dowager. She and I only had sons—she, Sylvester and Richard, me, Vane and Harry. Sylvester, Richard and Vane are all married—" Horatia glanced at Flick. "Didn't Harry tell you?"

Flick shook her head; Horatia grimaced. "He always was one to ignore details. So—" Horatia settled back; Flick dutifully paid attention. "Sylvester married Honoria Anstruther-Wetherby over a year ago. Sebastian, their son, is eight months old. Honoria's increasing again, so while they'll doubtless come to town for the Season proper, the ducal couple are presently in Cambridgeshire.

"Which brings us to Vane. He married Patience Debbington last November. Patience is increasing, too, so we don't expect to see them for a few weeks, either. As for Richard, he married *quite* unexpectedly in Scotland before Christmas. There was a spot of bother—Sylvester, Honoria, Vane, Patience and Helena—and a few others—went north, but all seems to have settled comfortably and Helena is in alt at the prospect of more grandchildren.

"However," Horatia declared, reaching her peroration, "as neither Honoria nor Patience, nor Richard's Catriona, were young misses in need of help and guidance, neither Helena nor I have *ever* had a young lady to fuss over." Eyes bright, she patted Flick's hand. "So I'm afraid, my dear, that you'll have to put up with the two of us fussing over you—you're our last chance in that arena, you see."

Flick smiled spontaneously. "On the contrary, I would be glad of your help." Her gaze drifted over the fashionable ladies and gentlemen strolling the pavements. "I've no real idea how one should go on in London." She looked down at her pretty but definitely not chic gown, blushed slightly, and caught Horatia's eye. "Please do hint me in the right direction—I would be very unhappy to be an embarrassment to you and D—Harry."

"Nonsense." Horatia squeezed Flick's hand fondly. "I doubt you could embarrass me if you tried." Her eyes twinkled. "And certainly not my son." Flick blushed; Horatia chuckled. "With a little guidance, a little experience, and a little town bronze, you'll do very well."

Grateful for the reassurance, Flick sat back and wondered how to broach the question uppermost in her mind. Horatia clearly viewed her as a future daughter-in-law, which was what she hoped to be. *But* she hadn't yet accepted Demon, and wouldn't, not until .... Drawing a determined breath, she looked at Horatia. "Did D—Harry explain that I haven't *agreed* ..."

"Oh, indeed. And I can't tell you how grateful I am that you had the wit not to accept him straightaway." Horatia frowned disapprovingly. "These things should take time—time enough to organize a proper wedding, at least. Unfortunately, that's not the way *they* see it." Her tone made it clear she was speaking of the males of the family. "If it's left to them, they'll sweep you past a cleric and into bed with the barest 'by-your-leave!'"

Flick choked; misinterpreting, Horatia patted her hand. "I know you won't mind my plain speaking—you're old enough to understand these things."

Flick went to nod and stopped herself; her blush was because she *did* know, and appreciated Horatia's insight—that was certainly how Demon had imagined it. Only, being him, he'd transposed the cleric and the bed. "I think time—at least a little time—is a necessity in this case."

"Good!" The carriage rocked, then halted; Horatia looked up. "Ah—here we are."

The groom opened the door and let down the steps, then handed Flick, then his mistress, to the pavement. Horatia nodded at the magnificent mansion reached by a sweeping set of steps. "St. Ives House."

The afternoon had turned gloriously fine—tables, chairs and *chaises* were set out on the lawn of the enclosed gardens. At Lady Horatia's side, Flick left the house, stepping past the deferential butler and onto the terrace. She saw a small host of well-dressed ladies, ranging in age from very old to a girl barely out of the schoolroom, congregating on the lawn.

There was not a gentleman in sight.

Parasols dipped and swayed above smart coiffures, protecting delicate complexions. Other ladies simply sat back, glorying in the weak sunshine, smiling, laughing and chatting. While substantial, the noise was not overpowering—indeed, it subtly beckoned. There was a gaiety, a relaxed sense of ease pervading the group, unexpected in conjunction with its blatantly tonnish air. This wasn't fashion and brittle frivolity—this was a fashionable family gathering; the distinction was clear.

The large number of guests was a surprise; Horatia had assured her she would meet only family members and a few close connections. Before she managed to fully grasp the reality, a beautiful older woman came sweeping up to meet them as they descended the steps to the lawn.

"'Oratia!" The Dowager exchanged kisses with her sister-in-law, but her gaze had already moved on to Flick. "And who is this?" A glorious smile and bright eyes softened the abrupt query.

"Allow me to present Miss Felicity Parteger—Helena, Dowager Duchess of St. Ives, my dear."

Flick curtsied deeply. "It's a pleasure to make your acquaintance, Your Grace."

As she straightened, Helena took her hand, directing an arrested, inquiring glance at Horatia.

"Felicity is Gordon Caxton's ward."

With one blink, Helena had the reference pegged. "Ah—the good General." She smiled at Flick. "Is he well?"

"Yes, thank you, ma'am."

With the air of one who could contain herself no longer, Horatia broke in, "Harry brought Felicity up to town. She'll be staying with us in Berkeley Square, and I'll be taking her into society."

Helena's gaze flew to Horatia's face; her smile deepened, and deepened. Looking again at Flick, she positively beamed. "My dear, I am so *very glad* to meet you!"

Before Flick could blink, the Dowager embraced her enthusiastically, then, one arm about her waist, bustled her down the lawn. With a Gallic charm impossible to resist, the Dowager introduced her to her sisters-in-law first, then the older ladies, and eventually the younger ones, two of whom, clearly twins, were adjured to ensure Flick wanted for nothing, including help with names and relationships.

The pair were the most ravishing blonde beauties Flick had ever seen. They had skin like alabaster, eyes like cornflower pools and a wealth of ringlets almost as golden as her own. She expected them to hang back— they might be younger than she, but she was definitely not in their social league. To her surprise, they smiled at her delightedly—every bit as delightedly as their mother and aunts had—and swooped forward to link arms with her.

"Excellent! I thought this party would be just the usual thing—pleasant but hardly exciting. Instead, we get to meet you!"

Flick blinked—she glanced from one to the other, trying to remember which was which. "I've never thought of myself as exciting."

"Hah! You must be, otherwise Demon would never have looked your way."

The second girl laughed. "Don't mind Amanda." She grinned as Flick glanced around. "I'm Amelia. You'll get used to telling us apart—we're not identical."

They weren't, but they were very much alike.

"Tell us," Amelia urged, "how long have you known Demon?"

"We ask," Amanda put in, "because until the last few weeks he's been severely testing our sanity by watching over us at the balls and major parties."

"Indeed. So we know he went up to Newmarket a few weeks ago. Is that where you met him?"

"We did meet at Newmarket," Flick agreed, "but I've lived there since I was seven, and I've known Demon from the first."

Both girls stared at her, then Amanda frowned. "What the devil's he been doing, keeping you hidden away like that?"

"Excuse us for asking, but you are older than us, aren't you? We're eighteen."

"I'm twenty," Flick replied. The twins were taller and certainly more socially assured, but there was a subtle difference; she hadn't imagined herself younger than them.

"So why," Amanda reiterated, "didn't Demon bring you down last year? He's not one for dragging his boots—not him."

"He does tend to drive fast," Flick grinned. "He didn't bring me down last year, because ... well, he didn't really know I existed last year."

That comment, of course, led to further questions, further revelations. Which cleared the way for Flick to ask why Demon had been watching them.

"Sometimes I think it's simply to drive us mad, but truly they can't seem to help themselves, poor dears."

Amanda shook her head. "It's something in the blood."

"Luckily, once they marry, they're not such a bother. They'd still interfere if they could, mind you, but Honoria, Patience and Catriona have so far kept Devil, Vane and Richard out of our way." Amelia looked at Flick. "And now you'll be here to keep Demon occupied."

"With any luck," Amanda added dryly, "the others will find ladies to dote on *before* we become ape-leaders."

Flick grinned. "Surely they can't be *that* inhibiting."

"Oh, can't they?" the twins chorused. They promptly recounted a series of events illustrating their claim, in the process giving Flick vignettes of Demon within the ton—surrounded by beautiful women. Sensing her interest, the twins dismissively waved aside his London conquests.

"Don't worry about them—they never last long, and now he'll be too busy with you."

"Watching over *you*, thank heaven!" Amanda raised her eyes to the skies. "*Only* got two more to go."

Amelia chuckled, and looked at Flick. "Gabriel and Lucifer."

"Who?"

The twins laughed, and explained about their older male cousins, the group known as the Bar Cynster.

"We're not supposed to know about the Bar Cynster, so remember not to mention it to Demon," Amanda warned.

They continued, giving her a potted history of the family—who was whose child, brother, sister. They beckoned the only younger girl over—their cousin, Heather, nearly sixteeen.

"I won't be presented until next year," Heather sighed, "but Mama said I could attend the family events this year. Aunt Louise is giving an informal ball next week."

"You'll be invited," Amanda assured Flick. "We'll make sure your name is on the list."

Amelia stifled a snort. "*Mama* will make sure your name is on the list."

Minutes later, they were summoned to distribute the teacups. Flick did her share, moving easily among the company. Although every lady she paused beside spoke with her, beyond the information Horatia had imparted regarding her visit, not one word was said—not one inference drawn. At least, not within her hearing. Every lady made her feel welcome, and if, by dint of subtle questioning, they extracted her entire life history from her, it was no more than she'd expected. But they were the very opposite of nosy, and certainly not judgmental—their warm approval, their ready acceptance, the protection of the group so openly offered very nearly overwhelmed her.

One very old, very sharp-eyed lady closed a claw about her hand. "If you find yourself in a ballroom, gel, and at a loss what to do, then find one of us—even those flighty flibbertigibbets"—Lady Osbaldestone's black gaze skewered the twins, then she looked up at Flick—"and just ask. The ton can be a confusing place, but that's what family's for—you needn't feel shy."

"Thank you, ma'am." Flick bobbed a curtsy. "I'll remember."

"Good. Now you may give me one of those macaroons. Dare say Clara there would like one, too."

Lady Osbaldestone was not the only one to offer advice and support. Long before the afternoon came to an end and she and Lady Horatia took their leave, amid embraces, waves and plans to meet again, Flick felt she had literally been gathered to the bosom of the Cynster clan.

Settling back in the carriage, Horatia closed her eyes. Flick did the same, and looked back over the afternoon.

They were amazing. She'd known Demon had a large family, but that the Cynsters would prove such a close tribe had been a pleasant surprise. She'd never had a real family—not since her parents had died. She'd never felt part of a continuing whole, a group that had a before and would also have an after, beyond the individual members. She'd been alone since the age of seven. The General, Dillon and the Hillgate End household had become her surrogate family, but this was something very different.

If she married Demon, she would become, once again, part of a real family. One in which there were other women to talk to, to turn to for support; one where, by unspoken accord, the men watched over the young women, even if they weren't their sisters.

In some ways, it was all new to her—in other ways, at some deeper level, it touched a chord that resonated deeply. It felt very right. Opening her eyes, she stared, smiling but unseeing, out of the window, deeply glad at the prospect of becoming a Cynster.

*   *   *

Two mornings later, in a far from glorious mood, Demon gritted his teeth and turned his bays toward the park. For the third time in as many days, he'd arrived at his parents' house only to learn that Miss Parteger was out.

He'd called on the afternoon of the day he'd brought her to town, imagining her sitting alone and forlorn while his mother napped. Instead, they'd been gossiping at his Aunt Helena's—and he knew very well about what. He'd swallowed his disappointment, uneasily surprised that he'd felt it, and reflected that this was precisely why he'd brought Flick to town—so his dear family, especially the female half, could help her make up her mind to marry him. He had no doubt they would do so. They were past masters at engineering weddings. As far as he was concerned, they could exercise their talents on his behalf.

So he'd retired, leaving no message—nothing to alert his too-perceptive mother that he'd been impatient enough to call. He'd arrived promptly for dinner, but discovered that seeing Felicity over a dinner table with his parents present didn't satisfy his appetite.

Yesterday, he'd called at eleven—a perfectly innocuous time. Turning up too close to breakfast would have been too revealing. Highthorpe had looked at him with sympathy and informed him that his mother, his aunt and the young lady had gone shopping.

He knew that meant they'd be away for hours. And they'd be in one of those silly, feminine moods when they returned, wanting to tell him about frills and furbelows, unreceptive to the notion of paying attention to him.

He'd retreated in good order, noting again that this was a part of why he'd brought Flick to town—so she could be seduced by the entertainments available as his wife. Shopping, to the female soul, ranked high as entertainment.

In other arenas, fate was being more helpful; he'd heard on the grapevine that Rattletrap Selbourne had contracted mumps from his sister's offspring and was not expected in town this Season. Selbourne was one complication he could temporarily put from his mind.

Today, he'd arrived at Berkeley Square midmorning, quite sure he'd find Flick waiting to impress him in one of her new gowns.

His mother had taken her off to the park.

He was seriously considering having a very pithy few words with his mother.

Feathering his curricle through the Stanhope Gate, narrowly missing an approaching landau, he tried to rein in his unreasonable temper and still the urgent pounding in his blood. He was surprised at the strength of his reaction, at the sense of deprivation that had seized him. It was, he reassured himself, simply because he'd got used to seeing her daily, nothing else. The effect would wear off, subside.

It would have to. In town, in the lead up to the Season, he would meet her only briefly, in the park under the watchful eyes of the ton's matrons, or in a crowded ballroom, likewise overseen. Private hours such as he'd grown accustomed to in the country were no longer part of their schedule.

Turning into the Avenue, he replaced his grim expression with his usual, politely bored mask.

He found Flick sitting in his mother's barouche, smiling sweetly at a host of gentlemen who, parading with other young ladies on the lawn, were eyeing her speculatively. His mother was deep in conversation with his aunt Helena, whose landau was drawn up alongside.

Smothering a curse, he angled his curricle in behind his mother's carriage and reined in. Gillies came running to hold the bays' heads. Tying off the reins, Demon jumped down and stalked along the verge.

Flick had heard the curricle pull up, and she'd turned; now she smiled, gloriously welcoming. For an instant, he was lost in her eyes, in her glow—his mask slipped; he started to smile, his usual taunting, teasing smile.

He caught himself just in time and substituted an easy, affable expression and a cool smile. Only his eyes, as they met hers, held any heat. If his mother or his sharp-eyed aunt caught a glimpse of that other smile, they'd know a great deal too much.

Flick held out her hand; he took it, bowing easily. "Well met, my dear."

Straightening, he exchanged polite nods with his mother and aunt, then looked back at Flick. He hadn't released her hand. "Can I tempt you to a stroll about the lawns?"

"Oh, yes!" Eagerly, she shifted forward. Demon suddenly understood her interest in the couples on the lawn: simple envy. She was used to riding every day—she would miss the exercise.

His smile deepening, he opened the carriage door. Over Flick's head, his mother glared at him and mouthed "new dress." Inwardly grinning, he helped Flick down, very willing to let his gaze roam. "Is that new?"

She threw him an ingenuous smile. "Yes." Releasing his hand, she twirled, then halted. "Do you like it?"

His gaze had locked on her body, sweetly encased in lavender-blue twill; now he lifted it to her face—and couldn't find words to answer. His chest had seized, his wits scrambled—the pounding in his blood escalated. The sheer glory of her face, her eyes, didn't help—he'd forgotten what it felt like to be smitten by an angel.

His mother and aunt were watching, eagle-eyed; he cleared his throat and managed to smile urbanely. "You look ... extremely fetching." She looked delectable, delicious—and he was suddenly ravenous.

Retaking her hand, he laid it on his sleeve. "We'll take a turn down to the flowerbeds and back."

He heard an amused "humph" from the carriage, but he didn't look back as they strolled onto the lawn, too busy enjoying the sight—and the sensations—of having his angel on his arm again. She smiled up at him—her golden curls caught his eye. "You've had your hair trimmed."

"Yes." She angled her head this way and that so he could appreciate the subtle changes. Her curls had always framed her face, but loosely. Now, by dint of artful clipping, the frame was more complete, more stable—if anything, brighter. "It suits me, I think."

Demon nodded. "It's undeniably elegant." Lowering his gaze, he met her eyes. "I expect it complements your new evening gowns well."

She blinked her eyes wide. "How did you know ...?"

He grinned. "I called yesterday and heard you'd gone shopping. As it appears you've visited a modiste, and I know my mother, the rest is easy."

"Helena came, too. It was ..." She paused, then smiled at him. "Very enjoyable."

Content, Demon returned her smile, then looked ahead.

They strolled in silence, as they had so often on the Heath. Neither felt any pressing need of words, deeply easy in the other's company. Flick felt the breeze ruffle her skirts, felt them flap against Demon's polished Hessians. The steely strength of the muscles beneath her fingers, the sense of strength that reached for her, surrounded her and lapped her about, was blissfully welcome.

She'd missed him. Her singing heart told her that; her exulting senses confirmed it. Tipping her face to the sun, she smiled, aglow with an emotion that could only be love.

She slanted him a glance—only to find him watching her. He blinked, a frown forming in his eyes. Even as she looked, his face hardened.

He looked ahead. "I thought you might like to know what we've discovered about Bletchley."

Guilt struck. In the whirl of the past days, caught up in her own discoveries, she'd forgotten Dillon and his problems. "Yes, of course." Strengthening her voice, she looked ahead. "What have you learned?"

From the corner of her eye, she saw Demon grimace.

"We've confirmed Bletchley arrived on the Newmarket coach. It stops at Aldgate. We checked, but he isn't known in the area." They reached the flowerbeds and turned onto the gravel path beside the display. "Montague—my agent—is organizing a watch on the venues gentlemen use to meet with the riffraff they occasionally hire. If Bletchley appears, we'll pick up his trail again."

Flick frowned. "Is this Mr. Montague the same man you came down to see before?" Demon nodded; she asked, "Has he learned anything by looking for the money?"

"Not yet, but there's a large number of possibilities to check. Stocks, bonds, deposits, foreign transactions—he'll check everywhere. He *has* finalized the approximate sums we're looking for—the amounts taken from each fixed race over the autumn season, and the first race this year."

"Is it a lot?"

Demon met her gaze. "Enormous."

Reaching the walk's end, they turned back across the lawn, passing close by a number of other couples. With easy grace, Demon exchanged cool nods, distant smiles and steered her on. Flick mimicked his politesse with a calmly serene expression.

Once they were free, Demon glanced at her, then lengthened his stride. She kept pace easily, but wondered why he was hurrying.

"The total amount taken is simply so huge," he continued, "it's utterly inconceivable that it won't show up somewhere. That's one encouraging point.

Luckily, we've still got a few weeks before informing the stewards becomes imperative."

"Is there anything I can do?"

"No." He glanced down at her, his expression impassive. "I'll check with Montague in a day or so, if he doesn't contact me." He hesitated, then added, "I'll let you know when we learn anything to the point."

She had to nod—they were almost at the carriage. Glancing at Demon's face, she noted the languidly bored mask that seemed to slide over his features, sensed the steely control that infused his movements, making them appear lazily indifferent. She assumed it was his London persona—his wolf's clothing, as it were.

But she didn't understand why, when he handed her into the carriage and bowed gracefully, he didn't meet her eye.

Horatia tapped his arm. "You'll receive your invitation to an informal ball Louise is giving today. The ball's early next week—I'll expect you to escort myself and Felicity."

Demon blinked. "Won't Papa escort you?" Horatia waved dismissively. "You know your father—he'll want to call at White's on the way." A grim expression flashed in Demon's eyes, then was gone. Resigned, he inclined his head. "As you wish."

As he straightened, his eyes touched Flick's, just for a second, just long enough to reassure her. With a bow to Horatia and Helena, he turned away.

"Don't be late!" Horatia called after him. "We'll be dining there."

A wave showed he'd heard. Taking the reins, he leapt into his curricle, then gravel crunched, and he was gone.

CHAPTER

Sixteen

ॐ

"**J**ust *look at them!*" Amanda hissed disgustedly in Flick's ear, then gracefully twirled away. Amelia took her place. "Even if they're dancing, they still sneak looks." She dipped and swayed, and continued *sotto voce*, "And there's usually one standing on the sidelines, like Demon is now, so if we rip a flounce or tear a ribbon and try to slip away, they still catch us!"

Flick smiled at her partner and linked hands—she gave no sign of having heard the twins' grumblings. They were whirling and twirling their way through a country dance; about them, Louise Cynster's ballroom was filled with all the family presently in London, together with family friends. As the ball was informal, and most guests related to one another, an air of easy gaiety prevailed. There were many younger people present—girls like Heather and younger males, too—which underscored the feeling of a family celebration.

Flick dipped under her partner's hand and smiled at the innocuous young man; the twins did the same, no sign of their disgruntlement showing in their serene faces.

In the days since she'd first met them, they'd spoken at length on the watchful propensities of their male cousins, but Flick hadn't entirely believed them. Now she did. They did watch—she could see how the twins would find it irksome.

While Gabriel and Lucifer had both taken to the floor, they could occasionally be glimpsed through the press, checking on the twins. As for Demon, he stood at the side of the floor, not even bothering with the guise of chatting, his gaze fixed, distinctly intimidating, on their set.

At first glance, it was a wonder any male with an ounce of self-preservatory instinct would dare invite them onto the floor. However, the younger gentlemen—those not much older than the twins themselves—seemed impervious to any threat. As they were truly innocent of entertaining any impure designs on the twins, they seemed to take it for granted they were safe.

Of course, such innocent young men fell far short of the twins' requirements. Which was what was irritating them so. Flick understood; thus far, she'd danced only with the same sort of youthful gentleman—and was utterly bored.

When the dance ended, and they'd thanked and dismissed their too-youthful cavaliers, she linked arms, a twin on each side. "They're only trying to protect you—they've met too many bounders, and so want to warn all such men away from you."

Amelia sighed. "That's all very well, but their definition of 'bounder' is rather wide."

Amanda snorted. "If they think a gentleman has had so much as a single impure thought—a single mental flirt with any less-than-proper idea—then he's a bounder."

"Which tends to thin the ranks rather drastically."

"And is absolutely no help in our campaign."

"Campaign?" Flick stopped beside an alcove hosting three large potted palms.

Amanda glanced about, then took her hand and tugged—they all slipped into the shadowy space behind the palms.

"We've decided ...," Amanda started.

"... after discussions with Catriona," Amelia put in, "the lady of the vale—a sort of wise woman—"

"That we're *not* going to wait patiently, doing nothing but look pretty while suitable gentlemen look us over and debate whether or not to make an offer—"

"No." Amelia lifted her head. "We're going to make our *own* choice."

Amanda's eyes glittered. "We're going to look *them* over, and decide who *we'll* choose, not wait to be chosen."

Flick laughed—an arm about each, she hugged them. "Indeed, from what I've seen thus far, it would definitely be wise to take the matter into your own hands."

"So we think," Amanda declared.

"But tell us." Amelia drew back to study Flick's face. "Did you choose Demon, or did he choose you?"

Flick looked across the ballroom to where Demon stood, to her eyes the most superbly handsome man in the ton. He was wearing black, with ivory shirt and cravat; under the glow of the chandeliers, he looked even more dangerous than in daylight. He was chatting to a gentleman; despite that, Flick knew he knew exactly where she was.

Her lips slowly curved—he looked, and to her senses was, the embodiment of her dream, her desire, a far better reflection than any sculpture, any picture in a book.

She glanced at the twins. "I chose him." She looked across the ballroom. "I was only ten at the time, so I didn't really understand, but ... yes, I definitely chose first."

"Well, there you are." Amanda nodded decisively. "That's all of you— Honoria said she didn't choose first, but she definitely chose. Patience and

Catriona both said they chose first. And so did you. So *choosing* is obviously the best way forward."

Flick glanced at them again, at their beautiful faces, and saw the stubborn wills underneath. She nodded. "Yes, that's probably true." The twins were very much like her.

"We'd better circulate." Amelia nudged them from their nook. "Mama is looking for us."

Adopting easy smiles, they slid into the crowd.

Smiling, Flick separated from the twins; although she forbade herself to scan the room, her senses searched for Demon. Over the last days, she'd seen him only fleetingly at the park, and once, by accident, in Bond Street. They'd exchanged no more than a few whispered phrases about the syndicate. And not once had his ever-so-slightly bored social mask slipped.

They had, however, been in public.

He'd arrived this evening at precisely the right moment to escort them down to the carriage, so they hadn't had a moment in private to catch up—on anything.

Which was becoming frustrating.

As was the fact she couldn't locate him.

She stopped before a bust of Caesar mounted on a pedestal. Dispensing with subtlety, she stretched on her toes and tried to scan the heads—she knew Demon's was somewhere in the room.

From behind, his hand closed on her arm.

She gasped and swung around.

He was standing beside the pedestal—he hadn't been there a moment before. Swiftly, he drew her to him, then swung and drew her past, until she was standing in the shallow alcove behind the pedestal. He faced her, leaning one arm on the pedestal's top, blocking her view.

Flick blinked. The ballroom possessed three semicircular alcoves; before each stood some arrangement, like the palms or the pedestal, leaving a small area behind. Those desirous of a quiet moment could avail themselves of the spot, partially private but in full view of the ballroom.

Looking into Demon's hard-featured face, she smiled gloriously. "Hello—I was looking for you."

His gaze on her face, he hesitated, then said, "I know."

She searched his face, his eyes—she couldn't quite place his tone. "Have you ... ah, learned anything about the money?"

Demon drank in the sight of her, wallowed in the eager, welcoming light in her eyes, basked in the sensual glow that lit her face. She was screened from the ballroom by his shoulders. He drew a deep breath, and shook his head. "No. But we are making progress."

"Oh?" Her gaze lowered, and fixed on his lips; briefly, she moistened hers.

Clenching the fist hidden from the room by the bust, Demon nodded. "Montague has eliminated various securities—financial instruments through which that much money might have been hidden. While so far the results have been negative, we're narrowing our search."

She continued to stare at his lips, then realized they'd stopped moving; catching her breath on a little hitch, she looked up. And blinked. "It seems like we've been chasing the syndicate forever. Catching them seems like a dream." She paused, her eyes softening as they locked with his. Her "Do you think we ever will?" was softer yet.

Demon held her gaze and fought to remain still, to resist the impulse to lean forward, slide one arm about her and bring her against him. To bend his head, set his lips to hers, and answer the question in her eyes. Her gown, a sheath of silver-blue silk caught beneath her breasts with silver cords, then flaring over her hips into skirts that flirted about her ankles, didn't help. Its only claim to modesty lay in a froth of filmy silk gauze artfully looped about the neckline and over the points of her shoulders. It was an effort to remember her question. "Yes." His tone was deep, harsh; she blinked free of his hold, clearly puzzled when she saw his face harden.

The musicians chose that instant to strike up the waltz—he could have cheerfully strangled them with their own strings. Still, that was why they were here, at this moment. He focused on Flick's face, saw the eager light in her eyes, the invitation in her expression. And inwardly cursed. "That's a ..." he drew a tight breath, "very lovely gown."

She looked down. "It's from Cocotte." She spread the silvery skirts and pirouetted in time to the opening bars, then looked at him. "Do you like it?"

"Very much." He could state that honestly, convincingly. When he'd first seen her on the stairs in Berkeley Square, he'd felt winded. The gown flattered her figure so well that he was of the opinion it should be outlawed, but he definitely liked it—and what was in it. So much so that it was impossible for him to take her in his arms and waltz beneath the sharp eyes of his too-interested family.

With one hand, he gestured. "Turn again." It was no hardship to keep his gaze on her hips as she twirled.

"Hmm." He kept his gaze on her skirts, not wanting to see the disappointment gathering in her eyes. She'd told him in the carriage that Emily Cowper, a friend of his mother's, had, in light of her years, given her formal permission to waltz. The waltz was now in full swing. "That's very well cut—slightly different—the way the skirts fall." He was a past master at seduction—couldn't he do better? Next, he'd be talking about the weather.

"Have you heard anything from Newmarket?"

He looked up—he'd heard the soft sigh that had preceded that question; there was no longer any hint of anticipation in her eyes. She looked resigned, yet still gracious. He straightened. "Not specifically. But I have heard from a close acquaintance of a member of the Committee that no one has sighted Dillon yet, nor has anyone spoken to the General."

"Well, that's some relief. I just hope Dillon doesn't do anything stupid while we're in town. I'd better send him a letter tomorrow."

She said nothing more but gazed past the bust to where couples were revolving about the floor. Demon pressed his lips tight shut. However badly he felt about making her miss her first London waltz, he couldn't regret it. Unable to dance with her himself, he couldn't have borne standing by the ballroom's side, watching her in the arms of some other gentleman. He would have turned into an incarnation of his nickname—that was certainly how he felt simply at the thought of her in another man's arms.

It was better for her to miss this waltz. "I heard from Carruthers that The Flynn's shaping well."

That caught her attention. "Oh?"

"He's been pushing him morning and afternoon."

"Carruthers told me he was trying to build his endurance."

"Carruthers wants me to try him in a steeple." He glanced at her. "What do you think?"

Unsurprisingly, she told him. What did surprise him was how detailed her opinion was, how much she understood, how deeply she'd merged with her one-time mount. For the first time in his life, he learned about, and took advice on, one of his horses from a female.

By the time they'd discussed The Flynn's future, and touched on that of the filly Flick had also ridden, the waltz was long over, the next dance about to begin.

A cotillion. Demon turned and beheld a circle of hovering males, all waiting for their chance with Flick. He smiled tightly and turned back to her, still partially hidden by him. His smile softened as he reached for her hand. "Will you grant me the honor of this dance, my dear?"

She looked up and smiled—the gesture lit her face and flooded her eyes. "Of course." She gave him her hand and let him lead her to the floor.

His experience, thankfully, came to the fore—he artfully complimented her, elegantly teased her, all with just the right touch, that of the accomplished rake he was. As only their hands met, and their bodies passed no closer than a handsbreath, she smiled and laughed, but didn't glow. No one watching them, no matter how closely, would have seen anything beyond a young lady responding predictably to an experienced rake's blandishments.

Which was precisely what he wanted them to see.

At the end of the measure, he bowed elegantly and surrendered her to the coterie of admirers, eagerly awaiting their turn. Satisfied he'd weathered the worst of the night and made the best of it, he retreated to the end of the room.

Gabriel and Lucifer joined him there.

"Why do we do this?" Lucifer grumbled. "Amanda all but ripped up at me, little shrew. Just because I insisted on waltzing with her."

"I got the ice treatment," Gabriel returned. "I can't remember when last I waltzed with an iceberg. If ever."

He glanced at Demon. "If this is a taste of what the Season will bring, I think I'll take a holiday."

When Demon, staring over the assembled heads, said nothing, Gabriel followed his gaze to where Flick was holding court. "Hmm," Gabriel murmured. "Didn't see you waltzing, coz."

Demon didn't shift his gaze. "I was otherwise occupied."

"So I noticed—discussing the fate of the Roman legions, no doubt."

Demon grinned and reluctantly deserted the sight of Flick chatting animatedly. She'd taken to social outings like a duck to water. "Actually ..." There was a note in his drawl that brought his cousins' gazes to his face. "I'm investigating a crime." Briefly, he filled them in, told them all he knew of the race-fixing and the syndicate, all he suspected of who they really were.

"Hundreds of thousands," Gabriel repeated. "You're unquestionably right—it's got to show somewhere."

"But," Lucifer countered, "not necessarily where you're looking."

Demon raised a brow invitingly.

"There's collectibles—jewelry's the obvious, but there's paintings, too, and other artifacts."

"You could check on them."

"I'll check—but if those are the sums that should have been appearing over the past months, I'd already have heard." Lucifer grimaced. "Despite the possibility, I doubt collectibles are where the money's gone."

Demon nodded and looked at Gabriel, whose gaze remained distant. "What?"

Gabriel refocused. "I was wondering ..." He shrugged. "I've acquaintances who would know if money's changed hands underground. I'll put the word out. Then, if Montague's covering the legitimate side of business, we should have all avenues through the city covered."

Demon nodded. "Which leaves one large area yet to be canvassed."

"Indeed," Lucifer agreed. "Our own domain, as it were."

"Hmm." Gabriel raised a brow. "So we'll need to flap our ears for any hint of unexpected blunt—old aunts no one heard of before dying, gamblers supposedly under the hatches suddenly resurrected, and so on."

"Anyone sporting any unexpected blunt." Demon nodded decisively. His gaze drifted back to Flick.

Lucifer and Gabriel mumured agreement, then a blond in green silk caught Lucifer's eye—he prowled off in her wake. After a moment, Gabriel tapped Demon's sleeve. "Don't bite—and don't grind your teeth—I'm going to have a word with your guinea-gold delight."

Demon humphed—the Bar Cynster never poached on each other's preserves. He wasn't worried about Gabriel.

He was, however, worrying. Gabriel's description validated his concern. Flick was highly visible, even in a crowd. Her crowning glory drew all eyes—her angelic features held them. In sunlight, her hair was bright gold—in candlelight, it glowed richly, a true yellow gold much more distinctive than the twins' pale gold locks.

She drew eyes wherever she was, wherever she went. Which severely compounded their problem. His problem—he didn't want her to know about it.

It was one of the things he delighted in—her openness—the shining honesty of her joy, her feelings, all displayed in her face for anyone to see.

She was neither ashamed of her feelings nor frightened of them, so she showed them, openly, straightforwardly. Honestly. Accurately.

Therein lay his problem.

When they were close and she focused on him, the sensual connection they shared *glowed* in her face. The heightened awareness, the sensual anticipation, her glorious excitement and eagerness—and her knowledge—showed all too clearly. He'd seen it in the park, a week ago and more recently; he'd seen it tonight, when they'd met in his mother's front hall. The sight warmed him to his toes, sent a medley of emotions wreathing through him; the very last thing he wanted was to dim it. But . . .

She was too mature, too composed, to imagine she was infatuated. No one who viewed her response to him would believe infatuation was the cause. What they would believe was the truth—that they'd already been intimate— he, a rake of extensive experience and she, a very innocent young lady.

To his mind, all blame—if any was to be laid—should rest squarely at his door. Society, unfortunately, wouldn't see it that way.

Her reputation would be shredded—not even the backing of the Cynsters would protect her. For himself, he didn't care—he'd marry her in an instant, but it would be too late; although the furor might fade, it would never be forgotten. Her reputation would be irreparably tarnished—she'd never be welcomed into certain circles.

Their problem, of course, would not have occurred if she'd married him before they came to town, or even agreed to marry him so they could make some announcement. If such was the circumstance, the ton would turn a blind eye. However, now she was here, under his mother's wing, enacting the role of a virtuous young lady. The ton could be vicious—would delight in being vicious—given that scenario.

Watching her confidently chatting and laughing, her heart obviously light, he toyed with the idea of seeing her tomorrow—alone—and explaining the matter fully. She might not believe him at first, but he could call on his mother, and even his aunts, for verification. *They* wouldn't be horrified, but Flick would. She would, he was sure, agree to marry him immediately.

Which was what he wanted, wasn't it?

Lips compressing, he shifted, and wondered when, and why, a woman's wishes—her tender feelings, her inexplicable feminine emotions—had become so important. An unanswerable question, but there was no ducking the fact. He couldn't pressure her to agree in that way.

Straightening, he drew in a breath. If he told her her expression showed too much, she might recognize the danger and agree to marry him purely to avoid any scandal. Which wasn't what he wanted. He wanted her openhearted commitment—a commitment to him, to their future—not an agreement compelled by society's whip.

But if she didn't realize the deeper implications and opt for marriage, then she would try to hide, to dampen, her instinctive reaction. And she might succeed.

He didn't want that to happen, either.

He'd consorted with too many women who manufactured their emotions, who in reality cared little for anyone or anything. Flick's transparent joy was precious to him—had been from the first. He couldn't bring himself to douse the golden glow in her eyes, not even for this.

Which meant . . . he was going to have to find some way to protect her.

He watched her go down a country dance, laughing gaily but without that special delight she reserved just for him. Despite his worry, despite the irony, his lips quirked at the sight. Ambling around the ballroom, his gaze fixed on her—his delight, his desire—he considered how best to protect her good name.

Part of his answer was a drive in the park. Simple, effective—and she wouldn't know enough to realize what he was doing. He drove into Berkeley Square at the earliest possible hour. Ignoring Highthorpe's smugly understanding look, he climbed the stairs to his mother's private parlor, knocked once, then entered.

Seated on the *chaise*, a pair of spectacles perched on her nose, his mother looked up, then smiled. As he'd expected, she was sorting the morning's invitations. Seated on an ottoman before her, Flick was assisting.

"Good morning, Harry—and to what do we owe this pleasure?" Removing her glasses, his mother raised her face for his kiss.

He dutifully obliged, ignoring her teasing look. Straightening, he turned to Flick, who'd quickly risen to her feet.

"I came to ask if Felicity would care for a drive in the park."

Flick's eyes lit up. Her face was transformed by her smile. "That would be delightful." Stepping forward, she held out her hand.

Demon took it—and held it, and her, at a safe distance, ruthlessly denying the urge to draw her—allow her—closer. For one instant, he looked into her face, drank in her eager enthusiasm—then, lids lowering, he smiled urbanely and waved her to the door. "There's a brisk breeze blowing—you'll need your pelisse."

Not for a split second had his polite mask slipped; Flick blinked at him, her smile fading slightly. "Yes, of course." She turned to Horatia. "If it's agreeable to you, ma'am."

"Of course, my dear." Horatia smiled and shooed; Flick bobbed a curtsy and went.

If Demon had had any doubt as to the reality of the threat posed by Flick's revealing countenance, encountering the suddenly sharp gaze of his mother dispelled it. The instant the door shut behind Flick, Horatia shot him a speculative, potentially rigid, disapproving look—but the question to which she wanted an answer was not one she could ask.

And he was, after all, proposing to drive Flick in the park.

As confusion rose in Horatia's eyes, Demon inclined his head with his usual cool grace. "I'll meet Felicity downstairs—I need to walk my horses." Without intercepting Horatia's narrow-eyed look, he turned and made good his escape.

Flick didn't keep him waiting—she came tripping down the stairs as he descended rather more leisurely. Her contempt for feminine preening gave them a rare moment alone. Demon smiled easily, relieved to be able to drop his mask for a moment—he reached for her hand, set it on his sleeve, and drew her close.

She laughed softly, delightedly; smiling gloriously, she turned her face to his. He felt the soft tremor that ran through her, sensed the tensing of her nerves, the tightening of her breathing, the sheer awareness that raced through her as their bodies fleetingly touched. Her eyes widened, pupils distending; her lips parted—her whole face softened. And glowed.

Even in the poor light on the stairs, it was impossible to mistake the sensuality behind the sight. He'd initiated her all too well. She yearned, now, as did he. The temptation to sweep her into his arms, to bend his head and set his lips to hers had never gripped him so hard; need had never driven him so mercilessly.

Drawing an unsteady breath, he glanced down—and spied Highthorpe by the door. He drew back, moving fractionally away, ruthlessly sliding his elegantly bored facade back into place. "Come—the bays will be cooling."

She sensed his withdrawal, but then she saw Highthorpe. She nodded, and strolled down the stairs by his side.

Leaving the house, handing her into the curricle, then driving to the park gave him time to reestablish complete control. Flick remained silent—she'd never been one for aimless chatter—but her pleasure in the outing was in her face, displayed for all to see. Luckily, the curricle was sufficiently wide for there to be a good foot between them, so the display was one of simple joy and happiness, rather than of anything more.

"Have you written to Dillon yet?" With a deft flick, he turned his horses through the park gates.

"Yes, this morning. I told him that while we've temporarily lost Bletchley, we're sure to come up with him again, and that meanwhile, we're searching for the money from the fixed races." Her gaze distant, Flick frowned. "I hope that will keep him at the cottage. We don't want him imagining he's been deserted and so go investigating himself. He's sure to get caught."

Demon glanced at her, then looked forward.

The carriages of the *grandes dames* appeared ahead of them, lining the Avenue. "I've been considering sending The Flynn to Doncaster. How do you think he'd handle the change of track?"

"Doncaster?" Flick pursed her lips, then launched into an animated answer.

It wasn't hard to keep her talking, speculating, arguing, analyzing all the way down the line of fashionable carriages, then all the way back again. He doubted she truly saw the matrons watching them—she certainly didn't notice the interest their appearance provoked, or the meaningful, smugly approving glances exchanged by the senior hostesses. When the ladies whose opinions controlled the reactions of the ton graciously inclined their heads, he responded with a suavity that confirmed their supposition. Flick, without a blink, inclined her head, too, absentmindedly mimicking him, unaware of how her following his lead so smoothly appeared.

"If you're serious about developing The Flynn as a 'chaser," she concluded, "you're going to have to move him to Cheltenham."

"Hmm, possibly."

Turning the bays' heads for the gates, Demon was seized by a sense of triumph. He'd pulled it off—done the deed—made his declaration, albeit unspoken. Every matron they'd passed had heard it loud and clear.

And it hadn't, somewhat to his surprise, abraded his sensitivities—if anything, he felt immeasurably relieved to have so definitively staked his claim. Every matron who mattered now understood he fully intended to marry Miss Felicity Parteger. All would assume there was an understanding between them. Most importantly, the good ladies would see it as entirely proper that he, being so much older than she, with so much more worldly experience, would declare his hand in this fashion, then allow her to enjoy her Season without keeping by her side.

No one would now think it odd if he kept a safe distance between them.

"I'll take you back to Berkeley Square, then I'll call on Montague and see what he's learned."

Flick nodded, the joy in her eyes dimming. "Time is getting on."

CHAPTER
Seventeen

ॐৎ৩৪

Time was indeed passing, but not as Flick had hoped. Four evenings later, she sat in the shadows of Lady Horatia's carriage and tried not to feel let down. Any other young lady would be enjoying herself hugely, caught up in the frantic whirl. She'd been to Almack's, to parties, balls, musicales and soirees. What more could she possibly want?

The answer was sitting on the seat opposite, clothed in his usual black. As the carriage rocked, his shoulders swayed. She could see his fair hair, and the pale oval of his face, but not his features. Her mind, however, supplied them— set in his customary social mask. Ineffably polite with just a touch of cool hauteur, that mask conveyed mild boredom. No hint of interest, sensual or otherwise, was ever permitted to show.

Increasingly, Flick wondered if such interest still existed.

She virtually never saw him in daylight. Since that drive in the park, he hadn't called again, nor had he appeared to stroll the lawns by her side. She appreciated he might be busy with other matters, but she hadn't expected him to bring her here, then leave her so terribly alone.

If it wasn't for the twins' friendship and the warmth of his family, she'd be lost—as alone as she'd been when her parents had died.

Yet she got the distinct impression he still wished to marry her—that everyone expected they'd soon wed. Her words to the twins haunted her; she'd chosen, but she'd yet to declare her choice. If that choice meant leading a life like this, then she wasn't at all sure she could stand it.

The carriage halted, then rocked forward, then halted again, this time under the brilliantly lit portico of Arkdale House. Demon uncoiled his long legs— the door opened and he stepped down, turned and handed her down, then helped his mother from the carriage. Horatia shook out her skirts, smoothed her coiffure, then claimed the butler's arm and swept inside, leaving Demon to lead Flick in.

"Shall we?"

Flick glanced at his face, but it was his mask she saw; his tone held the same boredom. Studiously correct, he offered his arm; inclining her head, she rested her fingertips on his sleeve.

She kept a sweet smile on her lips as they progressed through the door and on up the curving staircase—and tried not to dwell on his stiff stance, his bent arm held away from his body. It was always thus, these days. No longer did he draw her close, as if she was special to him.

They greeted Lady Arkdale, then followed Horatia to a *chaise* by the wall. Demon immediately requested the first cotillion and the first country dance after supper, then melted into the crowd.

Stifling a sigh, Flick held her head high. It was always the same—he assiduously escorted her to every ball, but all that ever came of it was her laying her hand on his sleeve on the way in, one distant cotillion, one even more distant country dance, a stilted supper surrounded by her admirers, a few glimpses through the crowd, then her placing her hand on his sleeve as they departed. How anyone could imagine there was anything between them—anything with the potential to lead to marriage—she couldn't comprehend.

His departure was the signal for her court to gather. Infusing her features with appropriate delight, she set herself to manage the youthful gentlemen who, if she let them, would fawn at her feet.

In no way different from the evenings that had preceded it, this evening, too, rolled on.

"I say—careful!"

"Oh! I'm *so* sorry." Flick blushed, quickly shifted her feet, and smiled apologetically at her partner, an earnest young gentleman, Lord Bristol. They were swinging around the floor in a waltz; unfortunately, she found dancing with anyone but Demon more a trial than a delight.

Because, if she wasn't dancing with him, she was forever trying to catch glimpses of him as he stood conversing by the side of the floor.

It was a dreadful habit, one she deplored, one she lectured herself on constantly. To no avail. If he was there, her eyes were drawn to him—she was helpless to prevent it. Luckily, the ton's ballrooms were large and excessively crowded; a quick glimpse was all she ever caught. Her partners, as far as she knew, had not noticed her fixation.

Even when she stepped on their toes.

Inwardly wincing, she sternly told herself to pay attention. She hated the taste her silly behavior left in her mouth. Once again, she was a besotted girl peering through the banisters for a glimpse of him. Her idol. The one man she'd wanted but who'd been out of her reach. More and more, she was starting to feel he was still out of her reach.

She didn't like watching him, but she did—compulsively. And what she saw brought no joy. There was inevitably a woman by his side, some hideously beautiful lady, head tilted as she looked into his face, her own creasing into smiles as she laughed at some risqué quip. It only needed a glimpse for her to take it all in—the languidly elegant gestures, the saber-witted remarks, the arrogantly seductive lift of a brow.

The women pressed close, and he let them. Some even lifted their white hands to his arms, his shoulders, leaning against him while he charmed and teased, employing the seductive wiles he no longer used on her.

Why she kept looking—fashioning a whip for her own back—she didn't know. But she did.

"Do you think the weather will hold fine tomorrow?"

Flick refocused on Lord Bristol. "I suppose so." The skies had been blue for a week.

"I was hoping I might prevail upon you to honor me and my sisters with your presence on a drive to Richmond."

Flick smiled gently. "Thank you, but I'm afraid Lady Horatia and I are fully committed tomorrow."

"Oh—yes, of course. Just a thought."

Flick let regret tinge her smile—and wished it was Demon who'd asked. She didn't care a fig for the constant round of entertainments; she would have enjoyed a drive to Richmond, but she couldn't encourage Lord Bristol to imagine he had any chance with her.

Supper had come and gone; Demon had coolly claimed her, stiffly escorted her into the supper room, then sat by her side and said not a word as her court endeavored to entertain her. This waltz had followed immediately; she performed without thought, waiting for their revolutions to bring them once more in sight of her obsession. He was standing at the end of the room.

Then Lord Bristol swung her into the turn. She looked—and nearly gasped. Whirling away, she dragged in a breath, struggling to mask her shock. Her lungs constricted; she felt real pain.

Who was she—the woman all but draped over him? She was stunningly beautiful—dark hair piled high over an exquisite face atop a body that flaunted more sumptuous curves than Flick had imagined possible. Much worse, her cloying closeness, the way she looked into his face, positively screamed their relationship.

Blissfully unaware, Lord Bristol swung her up the room. Blankness descended, blessed relief from the clawing, shrieking jealousy that had raked her. The change left her dizzy.

The music faded, the dance came to an end. Lord Bristol released her—she nearly stumbled, only just remembering to curtsy.

Flick knew she was pale. Inside she was trembling. She smiled weakly at Lord Bristol. "Thank you." Turning, she walked into the crowd.

She hadn't known he had a mistress.

That word kept repeating in her mind—incessantly. As she tacked through the crowd all but blind, instinct came to her aid; she headed for a group of potted palms. There was no alcove, but in the shadow cast by the large fronds close by the wall, she found sanctuary.

Not once did she question the correctness of her assumption; she knew she was right. What she didn't know was what to do. She'd never felt so lost in her life.

The man she'd just glimpsed, heavy lids at half-mast as he traded sensuous quips with his mistress, was not the man she'd met on Newmarket Heath—the man to whom she'd willingly given herself in the best bedchamber at The Angel.

Her mind wouldn't work properly—bits of her problem surfaced, but she couldn't see the whole.

"Can't see her at present, but she's a pretty little thing. Quite suitable. Now that Horatia's taken her under her wing, all will, no doubt, go as it should."

The words came from the other side of the palms, in accents of matriarchal approval. Flick blinked.

"Hmm," came a second voice. "Well, one can hardly accuse him of being besotted, can one?"

Flick peeked through the fringed leaves—two old ladies were leaning on their sticks, scanning the ballroom.

"As it should be," the first intoned. "I'm sure it's precisely as Hilary Eckles said—he's had the sense to recognize it's time for him to take a wife, and he's chosen well—a gently reared chit, ward of a friend of the family. It's not a love match, and a good thing, too!"

"Indeed," the second old biddy nodded decisively. "So tiresomely emotional, these love matches. Can't see the sense in them, myself."

"Sense?" The first snorted. "That's because there isn't any to see. Unfortunately, it's the latest fashion."

"Hmm." The second lady paused, then, with a puzzled air, said, "Seems odd for a Cynster to be unfashionable, especially on that point."

"True, but it appears Horatia's boy's the first one in a while to have his head screwed on straight. He may be a hellion but in this, he's displayed uncommon sense. Well"—the lady gestured—"where would *we* have been if we'd allowed love to rule us?"

"Precisely. There's Thelma—let's see what she says."

The two ladies stumped off, leaning heavily on their canes, but Flick no longer felt safe behind the palms. Her head was still spinning; she didn't feel all that well. The withdrawing room seemed her safest option.

She slipped through the crowd, avoiding anyone she knew, especially any Cynsters. Reaching the door to the corridor, she stepped into the shadows. A little maid jumped up from a stool and led her to the room set aside for ladies to refresh themselves.

The room was brightly lit along one side, which was lined with mirrors, leaving the rest of the room heavily shadowed. Accepting a glass of water from the maid, Flick retreated to a chair in the gloom. Sipping the water, she simply sat. Other ladies came and went; no one noticed her in her dim corner. She started to feel better.

Then the door swung wide, and Demon's mistress stepped through. One of the ladies preening before the mirrors saw her; smiling, she turned. "Celeste! And how goes your conquest?"

Celeste had paused dramatically just inside the door; hands rising to her voluptuous hips, she scanned the room. Her gaze stopped, briefly, on Flick, then lifted to her friend. She smiled, a gesture full of feminine sensuality.

"Why it goes, *cherie*—it goes!"

The lady before the mirrors laughed; others smiled, too.

In a sensuous glide that focused attention on her bounteous hips, tiny waist and full breasts, Celeste crossed the room. Stopping before a long mirror, hands on hips, she critically examined her reflection.

Exchanging glances and raised brows, the other ladies departed, all except Celeste and her friend, who was artfully rerouging her lips.

"You have heard, have you not," Celeste's friend murmured, "the rumors that he's to wed?"

"Hmm," Celeste purred. In the mirror, her eyes sought Flick's. "But why should that worry me? I don't want to *marry* him."

Her friend snickered. "We all know what you want, but he might have other ideas—at least once he marries. He is a Cynster after all."

"I do not understand this." Celeste had a definite accent, one Flick couldn't place; it only made her purring voice more sensual, more evocative. "What matter his name?"

"Not his name—his family. Not even that, but ... well, they've all proved remarkably constant as husbands."

Celeste made a moue; she tilted her head—from beneath half-closed lids, her eyes glinted. Deliberately, she leaned toward the mirror, trailing her fingers tantalizingly across the full curves and deep cleavage thus revealed. Then she straightened, gracefully lifting her arms and half turning to examine her bottom, superbly displayed by her satin gown. Then her gaze locked with Flick's. "I suspect," she purred, "that this case will prove an exception."

Feeling more ill than when she'd entered, Flick rose. Summoning strength from she knew not where, she crossed to the table by the door. Shakily, she set the glass down—the click drew the attention of Celeste's friend. As she slipped through the door, Flick glimpsed a horrified face and heard a moaned *"Oh, Lord!"*

The door closed; Flick stood in the dim corridor, the impulse to flee overpowering. But how could she leave? Where could she go? Drawing in a huge breath, she held it and lifted her chin. Defying the sick giddiness that assailed her, refusing to let herself think of what she'd heard, she headed back to the ballroom.

She'd gone no more than three paces when a figure materialized from the shadows.

"There you are, miss! I've been chasing you for hours."

Flick blinked—into the pinched features of her Aunt Scroggs. Clinging to the tattered remnants of her dignity, she bobbed a curtsy. "Good evening, Aunt. I hadn't realized you were here."

"No doubt! You've been far too busy with those young blighters that surround you. Which is precisely what I want to speak to you about."

Wrapping thin fingers about Flick's elbow, Edwina Scroggs looked toward the withdrawing room.

"There are ladies in there." Flick couldn't bear to go back, much less explain why.

"Humph!" Glancing around, Edwina drew her to the side, hard against the tapestry-covered wall. "This will have to do then—there's no one about."

The comment sent an unwelcome chill through Flick; she was already inwardly shivering. Lady Horatia had helped her locate her aunt; she'd visited her early in her stay. There was, however, nothing more than duty between them—her aunt had married socially beneath her and now lived as a penny-pinching widow, despite being relatively affluent.

Edwina Scroggs had been paid by her parents to take her in for the short time they'd expected to be away. The minute news of their deaths had arrived, Mrs. Scroggs had declared she couldn't be expected to house, feed and watch over a girl of seven. She'd literally flung Flick onto the mercy of the wider family—thankfully, the General had been there to catch her.

"It's about all these youngsters you've got sniffing at your skirts." Putting her face close, Edwina hissed, "Forget them, do you hear?" She trapped Flick's startled gaze. "It's my duty to steer you right, and I'd be lacking indeed if I didn't tell you to your face. You're staying with the Cynsters—the word around town is that the son's got his eye on you."

Edwina pressed closer; Flick's lungs seized.

"My advice to you, miss, is to make it his *hands*. You're quick enough—and this is too good a chance to pass up. The family's one of the wealthiest in the land, but they can be high in the instep. So you take my advice and get his ring on your finger the fastest way you know how." Edwina's eyes gleamed. "Seems Cynsters are prime 'uns, always ready to take what they can get. That house is monstrous enough—no difficulty to find a quiet room to—"

"*No!*" Flick pushed past her aunt and fled down the corridor.

She stopped just outside the swath of light spilling from the ballroom. Ignoring the surprise in the little maid's eyes, she pressed a hand to her chest, closed her eyes and struggled to breathe. To hold back the silly tears. To still the pounding in her head.

Cynsters are prime 'uns, always ready to take what they can get.

She managed two breaths, neither deep enough, then heard her aunt's heels tapping, tapping, nearer . . .

Sucking in a breath, she opened her eyes and plunged into the ballroom.

And collided with Demon.

"*Oh!*" She managed to mute her cry, then ducked her head so he couldn't see her face. Reflexively, he caught her, his hands firm about her arms as he steadied her.

In the next heartbeat, his grip tightened. "What's wrong?"

His tone was oddly flat. Flick didn't dare look up—she shook her head. "Nothing."

His grip tightened, his fingers iron shackles about her upper arms. "Dammit, Flick—!"

"It's *nothing*." She squirmed. Because of his size, and because they were standing just inside the door, thus far they'd attracted no attention. "You're hurting me," she hissed.

Immediately, his grip eased. His hands remained on her upper arms, holding her away from him but sliding soothingly up and down, warm palms to her bare skin, slipping beneath the silk folds that formed her sleeves. His touch was so evocative—so tempting; she was wracked by the urge to sob and launch herself into his arms—

She couldn't do that.

Stiffening her spine, she hauled in a breath and lifted her head. "It's nothing," she restated, looking past his shoulder to where couples were milling on the dance floor.

Eyes narrowed, Demon stared over her head, into the shadows of the corridor. "What did your aunt say to upset you?" His voice was even—too even. It sounded deadly, which was precisely how he felt.

Flick shook her head. "*Nothing!*"

He studied her face, but she wouldn't meet his eyes. She was as white as a sheet and ... fragile was the word that leapt to mind. "Was it one of those puppies—the ones yapping at your heels?" If it was, he'd kill them.

"*No!*" She shot him a venomous look; her chin set. "It was *nothing*."

The effort she was making to pull herself together was visible. He didn't move—while he stood before her, she was screened from curious eyes.

"It was nothing," she repeated in a steadier voice.

She was trembling, more inside than outwardly—he could sense it. His impulse was to drag her off to some quiet room where he could wrap her in his arms, wear down her resistance and learn what was wrong—but he didn't trust himself alone with her. Not in his current state. It had been bad enough before. Now ...

He drew in a breath and seized the moments she needed to calm herself to steady his own wracked nerves. And reshackle his demons.

The cross he'd fashioned and willingly taken up was proving much heavier than he'd expected. Not spending any time with her—even by her side in a ballroom—was eating at his control. But he'd set the stage; now he had to play his part and stick by the script he'd written.

For her good, for her protection, he had to keep his distance.

That sentence was hard enough to bear—he didn't need anyone adding to his burden. Bad enough that he'd had to force himself to swallow every instinct he possessed and watch as she waltzed with other men. Until she agreed to marry him and they made a public announcement, he didn't dare waltz with her in public. And, given who he was—a much older, infinitely more experienced rake—and the fact that she was transparently innocent, they could never be private, not until they were formally engaged.

Straightening, he let his arms fall—she shivered at the loss of his touch. Jaw clenching, he drew in a patient breath and waited.

How long he could wait, he didn't know. Every night, the ordeal of the waltz grew worse. Those who'd previously been his partners had tried to tease him onto the floor, but he had no desire to waltz with them. He wanted his angel and only her, but he'd used the others for distraction—not his, but the ton's.

Tonight, it had been Celeste—he'd almost managed to distract himself by giving the salacious countess her *congé* in no uncertain terms, for she'd proved she understood nothing else. Miffed, she'd peeled herself from him and swanned off in a snit, from which he sincerely hoped she never recovered. For one moment, he'd felt good—buoyed by success. Until he'd glanced up and seen Flick in that puppy Bristol's arms.

Half-turning, his gaze raked the dance floor. Couples were forming sets for the next country dance, the second of the dances he permitted himself with Flick. As far as he could tell, all her puppies were somewhere on the floor. So who had upset her?

He looked back at her; she was calmer—a touch of color had returned to her cheeks. "Perhaps we should stroll, rather than dance."

She shot him a startled look. "No! I mean—" Shaking her head wildly, she looked away. "No, let's dance."

She sounded suddenly breathless; Demon narrowed his eyes.

"I owe you a dance—it's on my dance card." Gulping in a breath, she nodded. "That's what you want from me, so let's dance. The music's starting."

He hesitated, then, using his grace to camouflage her state, he bowed and led her to the nearest set.

The instant he took her hand in his, he knew he'd been right to acquiesce—she was so brittlely tense, so fragile, that if he pressed her she'd shatter. She was holding herself together by sheer force of will—all he could do was support her as best he could.

It was just as well he was there. He could perform any dance with his eyes closed, but she'd only learned the steps in the last weeks. She needed to concentrate, but that was presently beyond her. So he guided her as if she was a nervous filly with his hand on her reins. For most of the dance, their hands were locked—by squeezing her fingers, this way or that, he directed her through the figures.

He'd never seen her clumsy before, but she nearly stumbled twice, and bumped into two other ladies.

What the devil was wrong?

Something had changed, not just tonight but gradually. He'd been watching her closely; he wasn't mistaken. There'd been a joy in her eyes, a delight in life, that had, over the past days, slowly faded. Not the sensual glow he fought to avoid eliciting, but something else—something simpler. It had always been there, vibrant, in her eyes. Now, he could barely detect it.

The music ended with a flourish; the dancers bowed and curtsied. Flick turned from the floor and drew in a breath—he knew it was one of relief. He hesitated, then took her hand and placed it on his sleeve. "Come," he said, as she looked up at him. "I'll take you to my mother."

She, too, hesitated, then acquiesced with a small nod.

He didn't let her go until he'd planted her beside the *chaise* where his mother was chatting. Horatia looked up fleetingly, noting Flick's return, but turned back to her conversation immediately. Demon would have said something to her, if he could have thought of what to say. He glanced down at Flick; she still wouldn't meet his eyes. She was still very tense—he didn't dare press her.

Girding his loins for the inner battle he fought each time he left her, he stiffly inclined his head. "I'll leave you to your friends." Then he moved away.

Her court gathered around her almost instantly. Retreating to the wall nearby, Demon studied the group but could detect no reaction on Flick's part; he could discern no threat from any one of her admirers. Indeed, she seemed to treat them as the puppies he'd labelled them, managing them with an absentminded air.

He wanted to stride back and disperse them, but it was hardly acceptable behavior. His mother would never forgive him and Flick might not, either. He couldn't even join her circle; he'd be too utterly out of place within her youthful court, a wolf amidst so many sheep.

The evening, thank God, was nearly over.

Stifling a grunt, he forced himself to stroll farther away, and not stand there staring quite so hungrily at her.

Fate had one last trial in store for him that evening.

He was propping up the wall, minding Flick's business, when a gentleman, every bit as languidly elegant as he, caught sight of him, smiled, then strolled over.

Demon ignored the smile. Grimly, he nodded. "Evening, Chillingworth."

"One would never imagine it a good one from your expression, dear boy." Glancing over the intervening heads to where Flick was passing the time with an enjoyment more apparent than real, Chillingworth's smile deepened. "A tasty little morsel, I grant you, but I never thought you, of them all, would saddle yourself with this."

Demon decided not to understand. "This what?"

"Why—" Chillingworth turned his head and met his eyes. "This torment, of course."

Demon held back a glare, but his eyes narrowed; Chillingworth grinned and looked again at Flick. "Devil, of course, was doomed to run the full race, but the rest of you had far greater latitude. Vane had the sense to avail himself of it and marry Patience away from the ton. Richard—I always considered him the most sane—married his wild witch in Scotland, as far from the mad whirl as it's possible to get. So—" Pondering Flick, Chillingworth mused, "I have to ask myself why—why you've put yourself in line for such punishment." Amused understanding in his eyes, he glanced at Demon. "You must admit it's hardly comfortable."

Demon was not about to admit anything, and certainly not that. That his inner demons were howling with frustration. That he was hardly sleeping, barely eating, and as physically uncomfortable as it was possible to be. He met Chillingworth's gaze steadily. "I'll live."

"Hmm." Chillingworth's lips curved into a full smile. "Your fortitude leaves me quite ..." Turning, he studied Flick. "*Envious.*"

Demon stiffened.

"As you know," Chillingworth murmured, "young innocents have never been my cup of tea." He glanced back and met Demon's stony stare. "However, I've always been in remarkable accord with your family's taste in women." He looked back at Flick. "Perhaps—?"

"*Don't.*"

The single word rang with lethal warning. Chillingworth's head snapped around; he met Demon's eyes. For one instant, despite their elegance, the scene turned primitive, the force resonating between them both primal and violent.

Then Chillingworth's lips curved; triumph gleamed in his eyes. "Perhaps not." Smiling, he inclined his head and turned away.

Inwardly cursing, Demon was damned if he'd let him escape unmarked. "If Devil was doomed, and he was, then so will you be."

Chillingworth chuckled as he strolled away. "Oh, no, dear boy." His words floated back. "I do assure you, *this* will never happen to me."

"Thank you, Highthorpe." After handing over his gloves and cane, Demon strode down the corridor and swung into his parents' dining room.

And came to a dead halt.

His mother's brows rose. "Good morning. And what brings you out this early?"

Surveying the empty chairs about the table, Demon inwardly grimaced. He'd asked for his mother, assuming Flick would be with her. Returning his gaze to Horatia's face, he raised his brows. "Felicity?"

Horatia studied him. "Still abed."

It was past ten. Flick, Demon was certain, would be up at the crack of dawn, regardless of how late she'd been up the night before. She was used to riding early—morning stables started at dawn.

The impulse to ask Horatia to check on her gnawed at him. He resisted only because he couldn't think of any reason for such a peculiar request.

Horatia was watching him, waiting to see if he'd do anything revealing. He actually considered letting her guess. It wouldn't take much to have her leap to the right conclusion; she knew her sons well. But ... there was no guarantee, regardless of how understanding she might be, that she wouldn't, however unintentionally, pressure Flick into accepting him. And he didn't want her to be pressured.

Lips compressing, he nodded curtly. "I'll see you this evening." He was supposed to escort them to a party. He swung on his heel—then paused, and looked back. And met Horatia's eye. "Tell her I called."

Then he left.

He stopped on the pavement, drew in a deep breath, then looked down and pulled on his gloves. In the wee hours, when he'd been lying in bed wracking his brains, he'd remembered Flick's "*that's what you want from me.*"

They'd been talking about a dance—at least, he had. So what had she meant? He didn't want her for a dance partner—at least, not primarily—not for that sort of dance.

He sighed and looked up, tightly gripping his cane. His mind was running hard in predictable grooves. Restraining his impulses, his instincts, never stronger than where she was concerned, was proving harder, more debilitating, day by day. Just how close to the edge of control he was had been demonstrated last night—he'd overheard two of her youthful swains referring to her as "Their Angel." He'd nearly erupted—nearly kicked them and the other yapping puppies away from her skirts, and told them to go find their own angel. She was *his*.

Instead, he'd forced himself to grit his teeth and bear it. How much longer he could manage to do so he really didn't know.

But he couldn't stand on the pavement outside his parents' house for the rest of the day.

Grimacing, he reached into his coat pocket and hauled out the list Montague had drawn up for him in between searching for clues left by the money. Checking the addresses on the list, he set out for the closest.

It was all he could think of to do—to distract himself, to convince himself that it would all work out in the end. The only thing that might give him a smidgen of ease—make him feel he was doing something definite, something meaningful, to further their matrimonial plans.

They would need a house to live in when in London.

A town house, nothing too large, with just the right combination of rooms. He knew what he was looking for. And he knew Flick's tastes ran parallel to his—he felt confident enough to buy her a house for a surprise.

Not a house—a home. Theirs.

CHAPTER
Eighteen

෫෬ඁඔ෯

Yet another ball—Flick wished, very much, that she was back at Hillgate
End, Demon was back at his stud, and life was simple again.

"Miss Parteger, Framley's composed a smashing ode to your eyes. Are you
sure you wouldn't like to hear it?"

"Quite sure." Flick fixed Lord Henderson with a severe glance. "You know
my feelings about poetry."

His lordship looked suitably abashed. "Just thought, perhaps, as it is *your*
eyes . . ."

Flick raised a brow and gave her attention to the next member of her
youthful court seeking to dazzle her. In dealing with the many admirers she'd
gathered without the slightest effort, she tried hard not to be unkind, but they
were so young, so innocuous, so incapable. Of anything, but most especially
of awakening her interest.

Another had done that, very effectively—and then deserted her. She felt her
eyes narrow and quickly forced them wider. "Indeed, sir." She nodded
agreement to Lord Bristol's comment on the rain. Maintaining an expression
of polite interest, she pretended to listen to the chatter while her mind
remained focused on the long, lean figure lounging indolently against the
opposite wall of Lady Henderson's ballroom. She could see him from the
corner of her eye, as usual, along with the beautiful lady fluttering her lashes
at him—also as usual. Admittedly, the lady had a different face every night,
but that didn't, to her mind, change anything; she now viewed such women as
challenges—to be conquered and obliterated.

He wanted to marry her—this morning, lying late abed, she'd decided she
definitely wanted to marry him. Which meant he was going to have to learn to
love her, regardless of what Celeste, Aunt Scroggs or any old biddies might
think. He'd dangled her dream before her eyes. She'd grabbed it, and wasn't
about to let go.

She couldn't relieve her feelings by glaring at him. She toyed with the idea of doing something rash. Like waiting until a waltz started, striding across the room, displacing his lady for the evening, and demanding that he waltz with her.

What would he do? How would he react?

Her fantasies were interrupted by a gentleman who, in a neat maneuever, replaced Lord Bristol at her side.

"My dear Miss Parteger—a pleasure."

Reflexively, Flick gave him her hand; he held it rather longer than necessary. He was older than her other admirers. "I'm afraid, sir"—she retrieved her hand—"that you have the advantage of me."

He smiled. "Philip Remington, my dear, at your service. We met briefly at Lady Hawkridge's last week."

Flick placed him, and inclined her head. At Lady Hawkridge's ball, he'd merely noticed her, though he hadn't shown any particular interest. His gaze had been momentarily arrested by her face, before, with a polite nod, he'd moved on. Now his gaze was much more intent. Not frighteningly so, but she certainly wouldn't confuse him with the callow youths surrounding her.

"I've a question, my dear, if I might be so bold. I fear the ton too easily turns supposition into truth. Confusion is a byword, which makes life unnecessarily complicated."

He delivered the speech with a conspiratorial smile; Flick returned it readily. "Indeed, I often find tonnish ways confusing. What is it you wish to know?"

"A somewhat delicate matter, but ... if I don't ask, how will we ever know?" His gaze caught hers. "I wish to know, my dear, whether rumor is correct, and you and Harry Cynster are engaged."

Flick drew in a breath and lifted her chin. "No. Mr. Cynster and I are not engaged."

Remington smiled and bowed. "Thank you, my dear. I must admit to being very glad to hear that."

His meaning glowed in his eyes. Flick inwardly cursed, even though her pride responded to the warmth; Remington was a distinctly handsome man.

Their words had riveted the attention of other gentlemen idling at the periphery of her circle; like Remington, they were older than her puppies. One pushed through to her side, displacing Lord Henderson. "Framlingham, Miss Parteger. Seeing you amidst the Cynster household, well—we simply assumed, don't you know?"

"I'm a friend of the family," Flick replied repressively. "Lady Horatia has been kind enough to take me around town."

"Ah!"

"Indeed?"

Other gentlemen closed in, relegating her fawning puppies to the outer ranks. Flick stiffened, but, flanked by the courteous and subtly protective Remington and the gruff Framlingham, she quickly realized that her new court was far more entertaining than the last.

Within minutes, she found herself laughing spontaneously. Two other young ladies joined the circle; the conversation shifted to a new level, one of more scintillating repartee.

Stifling a giggle at one of Remington's dry remarks, Flick threw a glance across the room—Demon, she knew, would have appreciated the joke.

He was looking down—into Celeste's face.

Flick caught her breath and swung her gaze back to Remington. After a moment, she exhaled, then drew in another breath, straightened her spine, lifted her chin, and smiled on her new cavaliers.

The next morning, the instant Lady Horatia's carriage halted by the verge of the Avenue, it was swamped.

"Your Grace. Lady Cynster." At the head of a group of six gentlemen and two ladies, Remington bowed to Helena and Horatia, then with a warm smile, bowed to Flick. Straightening, he addressed Horatia. "Could we persuade you, ma'am, to allow Miss Parteger to stroll the lawns in our company?" His gaze switched to Flick. "If, of course, we can tempt her to join us?"

If Demon had been anywhere in sight, Flick would have sat in the carriage and prayed he'd speak with her—but he wasn't. He hadn't appeared in the park in the last week. She'd sent another reassuring letter to Dillon that morning, increasingly worried that he would set out to chase Bletchley himself, and get caught. The General would be devastated. Unfortunately, it wasn't Demon standing before her, ready to reassure her. It was Remington, who knew nothing about her life. Nevertheless, if she walked with Remington, at least she would get to stretch her legs. Returning his smile, she glanced at Horatia. "If you don't mind, ma'am?"

Having shrewdly assessed the group on the lawn, Horatia nodded. "By all means, my dear. A walk will do you good."

"We'll keep within sight of the carriage," Remington assured her.

Horatia nodded, watching as Remington helped Flick to the ground. Flick turned and bobbed a curtsy, then put her hand on Remington's sleeve and joined the others waiting.

"Hmm." Beside Horatia, Helena watched the group as they moved off. "Is that wise, do you think?"

Her eyes on Flick's bright curls, Horatia smiled grimly. "As to that, I can't say, but it should get some action." Turning to Helena, she raised a brow. "Don't you think?"

As had been his habit for the past weeks, Demon spent his day at White's. Montague and the people he'd hired to watch for Bletchley called on him there—he acted as a general, coordinating their searches. For all their efforts, they'd precious little to show. Both the money and Bletchley had to be somewhere—they'd yet to discover where. And time was running out.

Worrying at the problem—not at all enamored of having to admit defeat and inform the Committee about the fixes planned for the Spring Carnival, simultaneously handing Dillon over without any evidence to support his tale—Demon dropped into an armchair in the reading room, picked up a news sheet and opened it in front of his face.

And tried to relax. At least one or two muscles.

He sighed, too aware that every nerve was taut, every muscle half-tensed. He had a serious illness, caused by a Botticelli angel. The cure was obvious, but, given their present state, he was likely to suffer for some weeks yet.

He still had no idea what had upset her; she seemed, however, to have recovered. Unfortunately, there was now a certain coolness in her attitude to him. She seemed to be watching him measuringly. Which made no sense at all. She'd known him for years—she even knew him in the biblical sense—what more did she think to discover?

Suppressing a snort, he flicked out the news sheet. Dealing with that too-revealing glow of hers *had* to be his primary concern. Some might see it as mere encouragement, but only those with poor eyesight. As matters now stood, she was safe from self-incrimination. Reestablishing their previous relationship would simply be a matter of wrapping her in his arms and kissing her witless, once she'd come around to the idea of marrying him. There was no need to worry on that score.

There was no reason to reverse direction and start hovering over her, even had that been an option. The best thing to do was to hold the line—to keep his distance even more rigidly. Just as he had for the last two nights.

Setting his jaw, he forced himself to read the news.

"Hmm—interesting."

Demon looked up; Chillingworth stood beside his chair, regarding him quizzically.

"I have to confess to supreme envy at your coolness under fire."

Demon blinked; every muscle hardened. He searched Chillingworth's face. "What fire?"

Chillingworth's brows rose. "Why, the raging interest in your sweet innocent, of course. Haven't you heard?"

"Heard what?"

"That Remington—you've heard that his acres are mortgaged to the hilt and his pockets entirely to let?"

Demon nodded.

"Apparently he did the unthinkable. In the middle of a ballroom, he asked your dear delight whether she and you were engaged."

Demon swore.

"Precisely. Combined with the fact that supposedly impeccable sources credit her with an income of not less than ten thousand a year, and, well . . ." Demon looked up; Chillingworth met his gaze. "I do wonder, dear boy, that you have time to read the news."

Demon held his gaze for a pregnant instant, then swore viciously. Crumpling the paper, he stood and shoved it at Chillingworth. "My thanks."

Chillingworth smiled and took the paper. "Don't mention it, dear boy. Only too glad to help any of your family into parson's mousetrap."

Demon heard the words, but he didn't waste time thinking of a riposte—there was someone he wanted to see.

"Why the *hell* didn't she—you—*someone* tell me she was a damned heiress? *Ten thousand a year!*" Pacing his mother's parlor, Demon shot her a far from filial look.

Sitting on the *chaise*, engrossed in sorting silks, Horatia didn't see it. "As that's a paltry sum compared to what you have, I can't see why it so concerns you."

"Because she'll have every fortune hunter in town hanging about her!"

Horatia looked up. "But ..." She frowned. "I was under the impression there was an understanding between Felicity and yourself."

Demon gritted his teeth. "There is."

"Well, then." Horatia looked back at her silks.

Fists clenched, Demon hung on to his temper—already sorely tried—and absorbed the fact that his mother was baiting him. "I want to see her," he ground out. Only then did it occur to him that to find Horatia without Flick in attendance at this time of day was odd. A chill touched his spine. "Where is she?"

"The Delacorts invited her to a picnic at Merton. She went down in Lady Hendricks's carriage."

"You let her go *alone*?"

Horatia looked up. "Good heavens, Harry! You know that crew. They're all young, and while both Lady Hendricks and Mrs. Delacort might have sons in need of wealthy wives, as you and Flick already have an understanding, what harm can there possibly be?"

Her blue eyes, fixed on his face, dared him to tell her.

Teeth gritted so hard that his jaw ached, Demon nodded curtly, swung on his heel, and left.

He couldn't do a damned thing about it—the sudden rush of picnics, alfresco luncheons and daytime excursions that swept into the more youthful stratum of the ton.

Standing, arms crossed, against a wall in Lady Monckton's ballroom, Demon eyed the circle gathered about Flick, and only just managed not to glare. It had been bad enough watching a group of helpless puppies fawning about her skirts; the gentlemen now about her were of a different calibre. Many would rank as eligible, some had titles; the majority, however, needed money. And they were all a good few years younger than he. They could, with society's blessing, dance attendance on her, court her assiduously by attending all the picnics and innocent gatherings—all things he could not.

Whoever heard of going on a picnic and taking your own wolf? It simply didn't happen.

For the first time in all his years within the ton, he felt like an outsider looking in. The area of society Flick inhabited was not one he could enter. And she couldn't come to him. Thanks to her unfailing honesty, the distance between them was widening to a chasm.

And he was helpless to prevent it.

He'd been tense before. Now . . .

Securing two dances with her was impossible now; he'd settled for the country dance after supper—it would follow the waltz just starting. Her present partner, he grimly noted, was Remington, one of those he trusted least. Flick didn't share his opinion; she often waltzed with the bounder.

He no longer cared if people noticed he was watching her, but he was nevertheless grateful for the tonnish quirk that held grossly overcrowded ballrooms to be the mark of a successful hostess. This evening, Lady Monckton was an unqualified success, which lent him a little cover.

The idea of using that cover to whisk Flick away, to take her in his arms and kiss her drifted through his mind. Reluctantly, he let the idea go—it was another thing he simply couldn't risk. If anyone saw them, despite his extreme care to date, questions would be asked.

Without conscious direction, his eyes tracked her through the whirl of dancers, fixing on her glorious halo. As he focused on her, she laughed and smiled at Remington. Demon gritted his teeth—unbidden, unwelcome, his promise to the General replayed in his mind. What if . . .

His blood ran cold—he couldn't even finish the thought, couldn't let it form in his brain. The prospect of losing Flick paralysed him.

Abruptly filling his lungs, he shook aside the thought—swiftly replaced it with the image of 12 Clarges Street, the house he'd viewed that morning. It was perfect for him and Flick. It had just the right number of rooms, not too large . . .

His gaze on Flick, his thoughts slowed, stopped, in time with the music. On the other side of the room, Flick and Philip Remington halted; instead of turning toward the *chaise* where Horatia sat, Remington cast a quick glance about, then led Flick through a door. Out of the ballroom.

Demon straightened. "Damn!"

Two matrons beside him turned to glare—he didn't stop to apologize. Moving easily, apparently unhurriedly, he crossed the room. He knew very well the implication of Remington's swift look. Who the hell did the bounder think he was?

"Ah—*darling*."

Celeste stepped into his path. Dark eyes glinting, she lifted a hand—

He stopped her with one look. "Good evening, madam." With a terse nod, he stepped around her and continued on. From behind, he heard a lewd curse in French.

Gaining the corridor that lay beyond the ballroom, he was just in time to see the door at its end close. He paused to dredge up his memories of Monckton House—the room at the end was the library.

He stalked down the corridor, but halted before he reached the end. There was nothing to be gained by rescuing Flick before she realized she needed rescuing.

Opening the door of the room before the library, he entered. Eyes quickly adjusting to the dark, he crossed it, silently opened the French door, and stepped onto the flagged terrace beyond.

Standing in the middle of the library, Flick scanned the pictures on the walls, then looked at her companion. "Where are the etchings?"

The library was made dark by paneling and bookshelves packed with brown books, but a small fire burned cheerily in the grate. Lighted candelabra stood on a table beside the sofa and on a side table by the wall, casting a glow about the room, their flames flickering in the breeze sliding through the French doors open to the terrace. Completing a second survey of the walls, Flick turned to Remington. "These are all paintings."

Remington's smile flashed; she saw his hand shift, heard a click as the door's lock engaged. "My sweet innocent."

There was gentle laughter in his voice as he advanced, smiling, toward her. "You didn't really believe there were any etchings here, did you?"

"Of course, I did. I wouldn't have come otherwise. I'm fond of etchings ..." Her voice faded as she studied his face, then she stiffened and lifted her chin. "I think we should return to the ballroom."

Remington smiled winningly. "Oh, no. Why? Let's just dally here for a short while."

"No." Flick fixed him with a steady, unblinking stare. "I wish you to return me to Lady Horatia."

Remington's expression hardened. "Unfortunately, my dear, I don't wish to do so."

"Don't worry, Remington—I'll escort Miss Parteger back to my mother."

Lounging against the frame of the French doors, Demon drank in their reactions. Flick whirled—relief softened her face, softened her stance. Remington's jaw dropped, then he snapped it shut and glowered belligerently.

"Cynster!"

"Indeed." Straightening, Demon swept Remington a taunting bow. His gaze was steely, as were the undercurrents in his voice. "As you're unable to show Miss Parteger the etchings you promised her, might I suggest you depart? Not just this room, but the house."

Remington snorted, but eyed him uncertainly. Which was wise—Demon would happily take him apart given the slightest provocation. "I'm sure," he drawled, "you can see that's the best way." Strolling forward, he stopped beside Flick and trapped Remington's now wary gaze. "We wouldn't want there to be any whispers—if there were, I'd have to explain how you'd misled Miss Parteger over the existence of etchings in the Monckton House library." Raising his brows, he mused, "Difficult to find a rich wife if you're not invited to the balls any more."

Remington's expression didn't succeed in masking his fury. But he was a good deal shorter and slighter than Demon; swallowing his ire, he nodded, bowed curtly to Flick, then swung on his heel and stalked to the door.

Beside Demon, grateful for his intimidating, reassuring presence, Flick frowningly watched the door close behind Remington. "Is he a fortune hunter?"

"*Yes!*" With an explosive oath, Demon lifted both hands, then appeared not to know what to do with them. With another oath, he swung away, pacing. "*He* is! Half those about you are—some more so than others." His blue gaze stabbed her. "What *did* you imagine would happen once you let it be known how much you're worth?"

Flick blinked. "Worth?"

"You can't be *that* innocent. Now the news is out that you come with ten thousand a year in tow, they're all flocking around. It's a wonder you haven't been mown down in the rush!"

Understanding dawned, along with her temper—she swung to face him. "*How dare you!*" Her voice quavered; she drew in a huge breath. "*I* didn't tell anyone *anything* about my fortune. I haven't spoken about it at all."

Demon halted; hands on hips, he looked at her. Then he scowled. "Well you needn't look at me. I'm hardly likely to fashion a rod for my own back." He started to pace again. "So who spread the news?" He spoke through clenched teeth. "Just tell me, so I can wring their neck."

Flick knew exactly how he felt. "I think it must have been my aunt. She wants me to marry well." She wanted her to marry Demon, so her aunt had let it be known that she was an heiress. She assumed, avaricious as she was, that the news would prompt him to grab her, regardless of how wealthy he was.

"Was that what she said to upset you at that ball?"

She hesitated, then shrugged. "In a way."

Demon glared at her. First his mother, now her aunt. Elderly ladies were lining up to make his life difficult. That, however, wasn't the cause of the black, roiling, clawing rage that filled him, fighting to get loose, spurred by the knowledge of what would have happened if he hadn't been watching her so closely.

"Whatever—*whoever*." He bit off the words. Towering over her, his hands on his hips, he captured her gaze. "Bad enough you're surrounded by a gaggle of fortune hunters—that doesn't excuse your behavior tonight. You know damn well not to go anywhere alone with any man. What the *hell* did you think you were doing?"

Her spine stiffened; her chin rose. Her eyes flashed a warning. "You heard. I happen to like etchings."

"*Etchings!*" Jaw clenched, he only just managed not to roar. "Don't you know what that means?"

"Etchings are prints made from a metal plate on which someone has drawn with a needle."

She capped the comment by putting her pert nose in the air; Demon tightened his fingers about his hips against the urge to tighten them about her. He bent forward, lowering his face so it was closer to hers. "For your information, a gentleman offering to show a lady etchings is the equivalent of him inviting her to admire his family jewels."

Flick blinked. Puzzled, she searched his eyes. "So?"

"*Aargh!*" He swung away. "It's an invitation to intimacy!"

"It is?"

He swung back to see her lip curl.

"How like the fashionable to corrupt a perfectly good word."

"Remington was looking to corrupt *you*."

"Hmm." She looked at him, her expression stony. "But I do like etchings. Do you have any?"

"Yes." The answer was out before he'd thought. When she raised a brow, he grudgingly elaborated, "I have two scenes of Venice." They hung on either side of his bed. When he invited ladies to see his etchings, he meant literally as well as figuratively.

"I don't suppose you'd invite me to see them?"

"No." Not until she agreed to marry him.

"I thought not."

He blinked, and scowled at her. "What's that supposed to mean?" Her cryptic utterances were driving him crazy.

"It means," Flick enunciated, her accents as clipped as his, "that it's become increasingly clear that you want me merely as an ornament, a suitable, acceptable wife to parade on your arm at all the family gatherings. You don't want me *powerfully* at all! That doesn't impress me—and I've been even less impressed by your recent behavior."

"Oh?"

The single, quietly uttered syllable was a portent of danger; she ignored her reactive shiver. "You're never *there*—never about! You don't deign to waltz with me—you've driven me in the park precisely once!" Looking into his face, fists clenched, she let loose her pent-up frustrations. "*You* were the one who insisted on bringing me to London—if you thought this was the way to get me to marry you, you've seriously miscalculated!"

Her eyes narrowed as she looked into his. "Indeed, coming to London has opened my eyes."

"You mean it's shown you how many puppies and fortune hunters you can have at your beck and call."

His growl was a grating rumble she had to concentrate to hear; her reply was a sweet smile. "No," she said, her tone that of one explaining a simple matter to a simpleton. "I don't want puppies or fortune hunters—that wasn't what I meant. I meant I've seen the light about *you*!"

Eyes mere slits, he raised one brow. "Indeed?"

"Oh, indeed!" Buoyed on an outrush of pure release, Flick gestured wildly. "Your women—ladies, I'm sure. Particularly Celeste."

He stiffened. "Celeste?"

There was demand in his tone, along with a clear warning. Flick heeded the first but not the second. "You must remember her—dark hair, dark eyes. *Enormous*—"

"I *know* who Celeste is." The steely words cut her off. "What I want to know is what you know of her."

"Oh, nothing more than anyone with eyes knows." Her own eyes, filled with fury, told him precisely how much that was. "But Celeste is by the way. At least, if we're ever to marry, she will certainly have to be 'by the way.' My principal point, however, is this."

Halting directly in front of him, she looked into his face, and hissed, "*I am not your cousin, to be watched over in this dog-in-the-manger way!*"

He opened his mouth—quick as a flash, she pointed a finger at his nose. "Don't you *dare* interrupt—just listen!"

He shut his mouth; the way his jaw set, she felt reasonably sure he wouldn't open it again soon. She drew in a deep breath. "As you well know, I *am not* some eighteen-year-old innocent." With her eyes, she dared him to contradict her; his lips thinned ominously, but he remained silent.

"I want to talk, walk, waltz and drive—and if you wish to marry *me*, you'd better see it's with *you!*"

She waited, but he remained preternaturally still. A sense of being too close to something dangerous, something barely controlled, tickled her spine. Hauling in a breath, she kept her eyes steady on his, unusually dark in the weak candlelight. "And I will *not* be marrying you unless I'm convinced it's the right thing for me. I will *not* be browbeaten, or pressured in any way."

Demon heard her words through a smothering fog of seething rage. Muscles in his shoulders flickered, twitched—his palms itched. The injustice in her words whipped him. He'd done nothing for any reason other than to protect her. His body was about to explode, held still purely by the force of his will, which was steadily eroding.

She'd paused, searching his face; now she drew herself up and coolly stated, "I will not be managed by you."

Their gazes locked; for one long moment, absolute silence held sway. Neither moved—they barely breathed. The conflagration within him swelled; he locked his jaw, and endured.

"I *refuse*—"

He reached out and pulled her into his arms, cutting the statement off with his lips, drawing whatever repudiation she'd thought to make from her mouth, then he plundered, searched, took all she had and demanded, commanded, more.

He drew her against him, hard against the unforgiving rock his body had become. His mind was a seething cauldron of emotions—rage colliding hotly with passion and other, more elemental needs. He was coming apart—a volcano slowly cracking, outer walls crumbling, blown asunder by a force too long compressed. Only dimly did he recall that he'd wanted to shut her up, wanted to punish her—that wasn't what he wanted now.

Now, he simply wanted.

With a desire so primitive, so primally powerful he literally shook. For one instant, he stood on the cusp, quivering, the last shreds of restraint sliding through his grasp—in that moment of blinding clarity he saw, understood, that he'd asked too much of himself, too much of who he really was. Remington had provided the last straw, piling it on top of more amorphous fears—such as what he would do if she fell in love with someone else. How he would cope if she did.

He'd assumed he could control the thing that was inside him—the emotion she and only she evoked. In that quivering, evanescent instant, he knew he'd assumed wrong.

With the last shreds of his will, he forced his arms to ease just enough to give her leeway to pull away, to escape. Even in extremis, he didn't want to hurt her. If she struggled, or even remained passive, he could fight, hold back, endure, and eventually releash his demons.

She grabbed the chance and pulled her arms from between them; something inside him howled. He braced himself for her shove on his chest—whipped himself to let her go—

Her hands caught his face, framed it. Her lips firmed, then angled under his; her fingers slid into his hair.

She kissed him hungrily. Voraciously. As powerfully demanding as he.

His head spun. Desire exploded. He was lost.

So was she—no angel, now, but a woman wild, demonically demanding, flagrantly inciting—

Madness.

It caught them up—set them free.

Flick gloried in the rush, gloried in the sense of being impossibly alive. Gloried in the hard body against hers, the chest like rock against her aching breasts, the thighs like pillars trapping hers. His lips bruised hers and she exulted; his hard hands held her brutally close, lifting her, rocking her—she only wanted to be closer.

She wanted him more than she wanted to breathe. Flinging her arms about his shoulders, she levered herself up in his punishing embrace, then held tight so their faces were closer, nearly level. His hands wrapped over her bottom, he held her high against him; she could feel the hard ridge of him grinding against her mound.

She wanted him inside her. Here. Now. Immediately. His tongue plundered remorselessly, his lips more ruthlessly demanding than ever before—she had no breath to tell him. Her skirts were just wide enough for her to grip his hips with her thighs; she did, then moved against him.

His breathing hitched; muscles tensed, then quivered. Beneath her hands, he felt like tensile steel, coiled, compressed, ready to let fly.

She moved again. He caught his breath and resumed his heated ravishing of her mouth. But his hands on her bottom shifted; supporting her with one hand, he reached down, caught the hem of her gown, and flicked, sliding first one hand under, then, palm to her bare bottom, changing hands and slipping the other, too, under her silk skirts.

Her fine chemise was short—no impediment. His hands were beneath it from the start. Hauling in a breath, she gripped tighter with her thighs, locked her arms about his neck, and flagrantly wriggled in his hands.

He got the message—his hands drifted, his touch driven, demanding, over the backs of her splayed thighs, over the globes of her bare bottom, then, holding her high with one hand, he slid the other down and around, hard fingers exploring the soft, slick folds between her thighs.

He found her entrance—one finger slid deep. She gasped and arched lightly. The finger left her—a second later, two returned, pressing deep, drawing back, then stabbing once, twice, hard and deep.

She couldn't catch her breath—heat raged beneath her skin. Her body quivered, ready to fly apart. But that wasn't what she wanted.

Locking one arm about his neck, she slid her other hand between them—down to where his engorged flesh throbbed, rampant and hard as iron. She closed her fingers greedily, sliding them down as far as she could—

He groaned. And shuddered. "*God*—!"

Voices reached them. Footsteps steadily approached the library. Panting, senses screaming, Flick turned her head and stared at the door. The unlocked door.

Like the procession of thoughts said to presage death, Demon saw in his mind's eye Remington closing the door behind him. Saw the image he and Flick would present to those nearing the library. They were both beyond dishevelled, barely able to breathe; Flick's arms would never release in time—nor would his.

Three giant strides had them at the French doors; with two more, he got them out of sight.

The library door opened.

Swinging Flick against the wall, he pressed her into the soft creeper—the scent of jasmine wafted about them. Chest heaving, he leaned into her, pinning her there, physically wracked by the effort of exerting his will. His entire body had been focused on doing only one thing—burying himself inside her.

Voices from inside reached them clearly; he couldn't separate the sounds through the drumming in his ears.

He tried to think, but couldn't. Flexing every mental muscle, he tried to pull back from the soft body his rock-hard limbs were holding fast against the creeper-covered stone. And failed. Just thinking about that soft body had hurled him back into the volcano of his need.

Molten desire rose, battered at his senses, broke and consumed his will.

His breathing harsh in the moonlit night, he slowly lifted his head, raised his lids and looked into her face. He expected to see shock, fright—even fear—surely he had to be scaring her? Even fear of discovery—a real possibility—would do; anything to help him hold back from doing what he would do.

Instead, he saw a face sultry with desire, heavy-lidded eyes fixed hungrily on his lips. Saw her swollen lips part, her tongue briefly lick the lower. She felt his gaze and looked up—her eyes searched his briefly, then her chin firmed. "Now."

The demand reached him on a determined whisper. Her lips curved—he could have sworn in ruthless triumph. Then he felt her hand, still trapped between them.

She closed it, slid her fingers down, then up—he closed his eyes and shuddered. Her wicked chuckle was a warm breath against his lips as she trailed her fingers higher—to his waistband. She'd worn male attire herself; in seconds, she'd slipped the buttons and had him free. He leapt in her palm, iron hard, ready to explode.

With a gasping groan he only just suppressed, he reached between them, caught her hand and hauled it up, leaning even harder into her, teeth gritted against the sensation of her silk skirts sliding over his sensitized flesh.

He met her eyes, mere inches from his. If he could have glared, he would have. But his features were set, graven—impossible to shift—hers looked the same way. Driven, muscles locked and quivering, he teetered on the brink—

She met his hard gaze directly, challengingly. "Do it!" she hissed against his lips. Then kissed him ravenously.

The conversation inside the library droned on; mere yards away, in the moonlight on the terrace, hot and frenzied needs held sway. A bare second was all it took for him to lift her skirts, to smooth them up, out of the way. His staff slid seeking between her thighs; she gripped him hard and pulled him to her.

He found her entrance and plunged—drove into her heat—straight into a vortex of shattering need.

His—and hers.

The combination was too powerful for either of them to control; it buffeted them, battered them, drove them. Their bodies bucked and strained, desperate for release, locked in a battle with no foe.

Lips frantically locked to stifle the sounds that clawed their throats, they took all they could, grabbed and held on, clutched for each precious moment—there, against the wall in the moonlight.

The sounds from the library washed over them, gentle, soothing, heightening their awareness.

Of the heated slickness where they joined, of skin too hot to touch, of the raging tide in their blood—of the driven fusing of their bodies.

Crushed blossoms released perfume in a cloud about them—an evocative scent as deeply illicit, deeply intimate as their mating. Gasping, Flick dragged the scent deep. Demon's hips flexed again, ruthlessly driving into her. His lips cut off her glad cry as he plunged. Again and again he filled her—a sword slamming into its sheath. She gripped him lovingly and gloried in the power—the power that drove them both.

The ride was wild—wilder than she'd imagined anything could be. She clung tight, drunk on that power, delirious with speed, drugged with pleasure. Then the peak was before them—they rode faster, gripped by compulsive urgency.

And then they were there—the mountain exploded, erupted, melting them in its massive heat.

No! Don't leave me! Flick silently begged, clinging tightly for one heartbeat, then, accepting that he would have to, she sighed and relaxed her hold.

He withdrew from her; she closed her eyes against the sudden emptiness. Cool air slid between them, chilling her flushed skin. She gripped his shoulder as he shifted, sliding her down, carefully guiding her back to earth.

Her slippers touched cold stone; he flicked her skirts down. They fell easily. She glanced down and was amazed—they were only slightly crushed. He didn't move away; one arm about her, he angled his body, shoulder to hers as he roughly straightened his clothes.

The murmur of voices still flowed from the library; as the pounding in her ears subsided, she could hear two older men swapping tales of long gone battles. The doors to the terrace stood wide, the candlelight a pale swath on the grey flags. If anyone had come to the threshold . . .

Luckily, no one had.

Heat still lapped her; warmth still flowed in her veins. She felt both exhilarated and disappointed—and confused that that was so.

Tightening his arm about her, Demon steered her along the terrace to the next set of doors, also open. Without a word, he helped her over the step and into the dark room.

Her heart leapt—instantly, she stilled it. What was she thinking? Just because she still wanted to hold him, to feel his body naked against hers, to hear his heart beating under her ear, to snuggle close—feel close—to cling— just because she wanted, didn't mean they could. They were at a ball, for heaven's sake!

He drew away from her, quickly tucking in his shirt, doing up his trousers, straightening his cravat and coat. Breathless, giddy, her heart still pounding, she shook out her skirts and smoothed them, wriggled her chemise straight, fluffed out the organza ruffle that traced her neckline and formed her transparent sleeves.

She looked up to discover Demon looking at her; she stared at him hungrily, conscious to her toes of a compulsion to reach out and touch him. Hold him. Although her body hummed with satiation, some other part of her felt . . . deprived. Denied. Still yearning.

Even through the dimness, Demon saw the need in her eyes; he felt it in his gut. He cleared his throat. "We have to go back."

She hesitated, then nodded.

"Do you know where the withdrawing room is?" He spoke in a hushed whisper, conscious of those next door.

"Yes."

"Go there—if anyone comments on you coming from the wrong direction, just say you went out of the other door and got lost." He surveyed her critically. "Put cold water on your lips." Reaching out, he tucked one unruly curl back behind her ear. Ruthlessly squelching the impulse to trail his fingers along her jaw, to fold her in his arms and simply hold her, he lowered his hand. "I'll go directly back."

She nodded, then turned to the door. He opened it, glanced out, then let her through, retreating back into the gloomy room to wait until she'd passed out of sight.

He needed to talk to her, explain things, but he couldn't do it now—not tonight. Thanks to her wantonness, and his, he couldn't think straight—and they had to get back to the ball.

CHAPTER
Nineteen

🙟🙜

Desperate needs called for desperate deeds. Flick knew her needs qualified as desperate, especially after last night. She needed much more from her lover—her prospective husband. She knew what she wanted. The big question was: How to get it?

Surrounded by her court, in the middle of Lady Ashcombe's drawing room, she pretended to listen while inwardly she plotted. She'd come to London with one clear aim: to make Demon fall in love with her. If he'd been going to look at her face and fall down smitten, it would have happened long ago. As it hadn't, she was going to have to do something—take some active steps—to achieve her desired goal.

Insisting he spend more time with her was the logical next step. She'd made a start last night, although they'd got distracted. She'd enjoyed the distraction, as far as it had gone, but that had only made her more determined, more stubbornly set on her course. Such distractions, and the subsequent empty yearning, provided yet more reasons to act soon. She didn't want to find herself in the situation of *having* to agree to his suit. That would leave her with absolutely no leeway to secure her dream. And she definitely wanted to ease the desolate, empty feeling their interlude outside the library had left about her heart.

She was still convinced he could love her if he tried. They had so many things in common. She'd enumerated them at length in her cold bed last night; she felt confident the possibility of love was there.

The first step to making it a reality was to ensure that he spent more time with her. To do that, she needed to speak with him alone. She also wanted to talk to him about Dillon. Recalling how the previous night's interlude had come about, she eyed her would-be suitors measuringly.

Demon saw her proposition Framlingham. His mental imprecations as he strolled to the side door to cut off their escape should have set her ears aflame.

"Oh, ah! Evening, Cynster."

"Framlingham." With a perfunctory nod to Flick, he met his lordship's eyes. "Dissatisfied with her ladyship's entertainments?"

"Ah—" Although bluffly genial, Framlingham was not slow. He shot a glance at Flick. "Miss Parteger needed a breath of fresh air, don't you know."

"Indeed?"

"Indeed," Flick verified. "However, now you're here, I won't need Lord Framlingham's kind escort." She gave Framlingham her hand and smiled sweetly. "Thank you for coming to my aid, my lord."

"Any time—er." Framlingham glanced at Demon. "Pleased to have been of assistance, my dear." With a nod, he beat a hasty retreat.

Demon watched him go, then slowly turned his head and met Flick's limpid gaze. "What are you about?"

She opened her eyes at him. "I would have thought that was obvious. I want to speak with you."

So she'd jerked his leash. Demon clenched his jaw and fought to preserve some semblance of debonair aloofness.

She swung to the door. "Is the garden this way?"

Along with the terrace. "I find it difficult to believe you're in need of fresh air. You're not the wilting sort." She certainly hadn't wilted last night.

"Of course not, but we need to speak privately."

"Indubitably." He bit the word off. "Not, however, out there." He wasn't about to risk a repeat of last night.

Meeting his gaze, she tilted her chin. "Where, then?"

One challenge to which he had an answer. "There's a *chaise* in an alcove over there."

He caught her hand, placed it on his sleeve, and led her through the crowd. Although this was only a party, there were still too many guests crowding the room. It took them some minutes to cross it, time in which his anger faded to resentment—at her action, his reaction, and the ever present, irritating confusion that dogged him.

Never in his life had he had so much trouble with a woman. As on horses, so too in the ballrooms. He was widely acknowledged as clever in the saddle, yet for all his experience, Flick was forever running her own race, perpetually relegating him to following at her heels. He was constantly having to reassess, rethink, readjust, which was not what he'd expected. Unfortunately, there seemed little else he could do.

He had to follow, and *try* to keep *his* hands on their reins. And ignore the nagging feeling that he was out of his depth with her.

Deep inside, he knew it, but he couldn't accept it—he was infinitely more experienced than she. But this was not the young chit he'd made blush under the wisteria, the innocent miss he'd kissed by the banks of the stream, and taught to love at The Angel. This Flick was a conundrum, one he'd yet to work out.

The alcove was deep but open to the room. If they kept their voices down, they could talk freely, but in no real sense were they private.

He handed her to the *chaise*, then sat beside her. "Do you think, next time you wish to speak with me, you could dispense with manipulation and simply send a note?"

She looked him in the eye. "From someone who has so consistently tried to manage me, that's definitely a case of the pot calling the kettle black." Her voice was even but her eyes spat blue sparks.

He waved a hand at the crowd. "Face forward and look bored. Make it appear we're idly chatting while you rest."

Her eyes flared, but she did as he said. "*See?*" she hissed.

"Look bored, not irate." He looked down; her fists were clenched in her lap. "Relax your hands." Despite his irritation, he'd lowered his voice to a cajoling murmur; after an instant's hesitation, her fingers uncurled.

Looking ahead, he drew in a breath, intending to explain, simply, succinctly, that in this sphere he was infinitely more experienced than she, that he knew precisely what he was doing and if she'd only deign to follow his lead, all would be well—

"I want you to spend more time with me."

The demand made him bridle, but he preserved his bored facade. His instinctive response to any outright demand was resistance, but in this case, resistance was tempered by desire. It was a shock to realize he was not at all averse to spending the bulk of his days by her side. He felt his features harden as the implication sank in, while all the reasons he couldn't do so replayed in his mind.

Not least was that sensual glow of hers—if they were frequently together, he'd never preserve a safe distance. And she'd react. On top of that, there was a quality in their interactions now that simply shouldn't be there. For instance, if he leaned closer, she would turn to him, not draw away as an innocent would. Physically, she was completely at ease in his company—womanly, seductively alluring, not nervous and skittish as she should be.

Drawing in a breath, he considered telling her, but … the very last thing he wanted was for her to change.

"No." He spoke decisively. After a moment, he added, "That's not possible."

She didn't, to his surprise, react—didn't turn her head and glare. Instead, she continued to study the room.

It took Flick some time to absorb his words. She'd made her demand expecting an argument, not bald denial. Yet she'd sensed his stiffening the instant the words were out—she'd braced herself to hear something she'd rather not.

Nevertheless … she had trouble taking it in. Trying to understand. What was he telling her?

A sudden premonition swept her—last night she'd accused him of wanting her solely as an ornament. She'd said it to prod him to deny it. He hadn't. Forcing in a breath, she concentrated on not gripping her fingers and wringing them. Had she, from the first, completely misread him—completely misunderstood what this something between them was?

Had she fooled herself into believing he might, one day, love her?

The cold started in her toes and flooded upward; her lungs froze—she felt giddy. But she had to know the truth. She glanced at his face. His features were set, determined. It wasn't his social mask that watched her, but another more stony, more ruthless. She searched his eyes, steady crystalline blue, and found no softness there either. "No?"

The word trembled on her lips. Abruptly, she looked away, struggling to mask the effect of that word—a blow to her unwary heart.

He tensed, shifted, then sat back. After a moment, he said in an even voice, "If you agree to marry me, then I can spend more time with you."

Flick stiffened. "Indeed?" First a blow, then an ultimatum.

In the same controlled tone, he continued, "You know I wish to marry you—that I've been waiting for you to make up your mind. Have you done so?"

She turned her head further away so he couldn't see the fight she waged to keep her hurt from showing.

Demon swallowed a curse. Her agitation reached him clearly, leaving him even more confused than before. But he couldn't reach out and force her to face him—force her to tell him what the devil was wrong. Kept going wrong between them.

He now wished he hadn't pressed for her answer. But he wanted her, and the agony got worse every night. His gaze locked on her curls, he waited, conscious to his bones of that deep wanting, of the contradictions between his mask, his behavior, and his feelings. He wanted to press her, wanted to reassure her. He desperately wanted to tell her the right answer.

One of her curls, the same one he'd often tucked back, had come loose. Raising one hand, he caught it, adjusted it.

And saw his hand shaking.

The sight shook him even more, forcing the vulnerability he'd tried to ignore to the forefront of his mind. His face set; his jaw clenched. A moment later, he demanded, his tone harsh, "Have you decided?"

Flick looked at him, forced herself to meet his hard blue eyes, tried to see behind the ruthless mask. But she could catch no glimpse of what she searched for—this was not the man she loved, the idol of her dreams, the man who'd made long slow love to her all night at The Angel. The man she'd hoped would learn to love her.

Looking away, she drew in a shaky breath and held it. "No—but I think I've made a dreadful mistake."

He stiffened.

She hauled in a tight breath. "If you'll excuse me?" Briefly inclining her head, Flick stood. Demon stood as she did, so winded he wasn't able to speak. He wasn't able to think, let alone do anything to stop her. Stop her leaving him.

Flick walked back to the group she'd earlier left. Within seconds she was surrounded by eligible gentlemen. From the side of the room, Demon watched her.

The word "mistake" burned in his brain. Who had really made it—her, or him? Her rejection—how else was he to take it?—seared him. His eyes narrowed as he saw her nod graciously to some man. Perhaps, this time, he should swallow his pride and take her at her word?

The thought was like acid, eating at his heart.

Then he saw her smile fleetingly—a huge effort all for show; the instant the gentleman looked away, her smile faded, and she glanced surreptitiously his way.

Demon caught that glance—saw the hurt, haunted look in her eyes. He swore and took an impulsive step forward, then recalled where they were. He couldn't cross the room, haul her into his arms and kiss her senseless, much less swear undying devotion.

Suppressing a snarl, rigidly schooling his features to a cast that would allow him to move through the throng, he swung on his heel and left the house.

Every time he tried to manage her, things went wrong.

She refused to run in his harness; she never reacted predictably to the reins. He'd expected to be in control, but that wasn't the way it would be.

Lounging in the doorway of the nursery at 12 Clarges Street, the house he dreamed of bringing Flick to as his wife, Demon looked around the room. Set beneath the eaves, it was of a good size, well lit, well ventilated. As in the light, airy rooms downstairs, he could see Flick here, her curls glowing brighter than the sun as she smiled, shedding her warmth about her.

The house would be cold without her.

He'd be cold without her. As good as dead.

He knew she wanted something from him—something more than a few hours every day. He even knew what that something was. If he wanted to convince her that she'd made no mistake, that her heart was safe with him, he was going to have to give rather more than he had.

He didn't need to hear her say she loved him—he'd known that for some time, at The Angel if not before. But he'd thought of her feelings as a "young" love, youthful, exuberant, relatively immature—easy for him to manage and fulfill without having to expose the depth of his own feelings. He'd even used the mores of the ton to assist him in hiding those—the emotions that at times raged so powerfully he couldn't contain them.

He certainly couldn't manage them. Or her.

His chest swelled as he drew in a deep breath, then slowly exhaled. What lay between them now was an obsession—deep and abiding and impossible to deny—not on her part, or his. She was meant for him and he for her, but if he didn't confront the one thing he most feared, didn't surrender and pay the price, he would lose her.

A prospect the Cynster in him could never, ever accept.

He stood for long moments, gazing unseeing at the empty room. Then he sighed and straightened. He would have to see her alone again, and find out what, precisely, he was going to have to do to get her to agree to be his.

* * *

That evening, together with Horatia, Flick attended Lady Merton's musicale. Musicales were the one social event Demon had flatly refused to attend. Slipping into the room just as the soprano started to wail, Flick winced and tried to block out the thought that her reaction to such music was something else she and Demon shared. They didn't share the most important trait, which was the only one that mattered.

Setting her chin against a deplorable tendency to quiver, she looked along the rows of seats, hunting for an empty one. She'd taken refuge in the withdrawing room to avoid the twins—one look at their bright, cheery expressions and their far-too-sharp eyes and she'd fled. She possessed no mask solid enough to hide her inner misery from them.

She'd expected to sit with Horatia, but she was now surrounded, as were the twins. Looking along the edge of the room, she tried to spot a vacant seat—

"Here, gel!" Clawlike fingers gripped her elbow; surprisingly strong, they drew her back. "Sit and stop flitting—it's distracting!"

Abruptly sitting, Flick found herself on one end of a love seat, the rest of which was occupied by Lady Osbaldestone. "Th-thank you."

Hands crossed over the head of her cane, her ladyship fixed Flick with a piercing black gaze. "You look quite peaked, gel. Not getting enough sleep?"

Flick wished she had a mask to hold in front of her face; the old eyes fixed on hers were even sharper than the twins'. "I'm quite well, thank you."

"Glad to hear it. When's the wedding to be, then, heh?"

Unfortunately, they were sufficiently distant from other guests not to have to remain silent. Shifting her gaze to the singer, Flick fought to quell the tremor in her lips, in her voice. "There isn't going to be a wedding."

"Is that so?" Her ladyship's tone was mildly curious.

Keeping her gaze on the singer, Flick nodded.

"And why is that?"

"Because he doesn't love me."

"Doesn't he?" That was said with considerable surprise.

"No." Flick couldn't think of any more subtle way to put it—even the thought was enough to overset her. Breathing evenly, she tried to ease the knot clutched tight about her heart. It had constricted the previous evening and still hadn't loosened.

Despite all, she still wanted him—wanted desperately to marry him. But how could she? He didn't love her, and wasn't expecting to. The marriage he intended would be a living mockery of all she believed, all she wanted. She couldn't endure being trapped in a loveless, fashionably convenient union. Such a marriage wasn't for her—she simply couldn't do it.

"Humor an old woman, my dear—why do you imagine he doesn't love you?"

After a moment, Flick glanced at Lady Osbaldestone. She was sitting back, calmly waiting, her full attention on her. Despite feeling remarkably close to Horatia, Flick could hardly discuss her son's shortcomings with her kind and generous hostess. But ... recalling her ladyship's first words to her, Flick drew breath and faced forward. "He refuses to give me any of his time—just the polite minimum. He wants to marry me so he'll have a suitable bride—the right ornament on his arm at family gatherings. Because we suit in many ways, he's decided I'm it. He expects to marry me, and—well, from his point of view, that's it."

A sound halfway between a snort and a guffaw came from beside her. "Pardon my plain speaking, my dear, but if that's all you've got against him, I wouldn't, if I was you, be so hasty in your judgments."

Flick shot a puzzled glance at her elderly inquisitor. "You wouldn't?"

"No, indeed." Her ladyship sat back. "You say he won't spend much time by your side—are you sure that shouldn't be '*can't*'?"

Flick blinked. "Why 'can't'?"

"You're young and he's much older—that alone restricts the arenas in which your paths can cross in town. And an even greater restriction stems from his reputation." Her ladyship fixed her with a direct look. "You know about that, do you not?"

Flick colored, but nodded.

"Well, then, if you think about it, you should see there are precious few opportunities for him to spend time with you. He's not here tonight?"

"He doesn't like musicales."

"Yes, well, few gentlemen do—look around." They both did. The soprano screeched, and her ladyship snorted again. "I'm not even sure *I* like musicales. He's generally been squiring you to your evenings' entertainments, hasn't he?"

Flick nodded.

"Then let's think what else he could do. He can't dance attendance on you, because, being who he is, and you who you are, society would raise its brows censoriously. He can't hang about you during the day, in the park or elsewhere—he most certainly can't haunt his parents' house. He can't even join your circle of an evening."

Flick frowned. "Why not?"

"Because society does not approve of gentlemen of his age and experience showing their partiality too openly, any more than it approves of ladies wearing their hearts on their sleeves."

"Oh."

"Indeed. And Harold, just like all the Cynsters, lives and breathes society's rules without even thinking of them—at least when it comes to marriage, specifically anything to do with the lady they wed. They'll happily bend any rule that gets in their high-handed way, but not when it comes to marriage. Don't understand it myself, but I've known three generations, and they've all been the same. You may take my word for it."

Flick grimaced.

"Now, Horatia mentioned you haven't accepted him yet, so that simply lays an extra tax on him. Being a Cynster, he would want to stick by your side, force you to acknowledge him, but he can't. Which, of course, explains why he's been going around tense as an overwound watchspring. I have to say he's toed the line very well—he's doing what society expects of him by keeping a reasonable distance until you accept his offer."

"But how can I learn if he loves me if he's never near?"

"Society is not concerned with love, only its own power. Now, where were we? Ah, yes. Not wanting to make himself, or you, or his family appear outré, and very definitely not wanting society to view your relationship askance, restricts him to half-hour calls in Horatia's presence—and only one or two a week, to meetings in the park, again not too frequently, and escorting you and Horatia to balls. Anything else would be construed as bad ton—something no Cynster has ever been."

"What about riding in the park? He knows I like riding."

Lady Osbaldestone eyed her. "You're from Newmarket, I believe?"

Flick nodded.

"Well, riding in the park means you'll be walking your mount. At the most, you can break into a trot for a short stretch, but that's the limit of what is considered appropriate stimulation for a female on horseback." Flick stared. "So are you surprised he hasn't taken you riding in the park?"

Flick shook her head.

"Ah, well, now you appreciate the intricacies Harold's been juggling for the past weeks. And from his point of view, he doesn't dare put a foot wrong. Most entertaining, it's been." Lady Osbaldestone chuckled and patted Flick's hand. "Now, as to whether he loves you or not, there's one point you've obviously missed."

"Oh?" Flick focused on her face.

"He drove you in the park."

"Yes." Her expression said "So?"

"The Bar Cynster never drive ladies in the park. It's one of those ridiculously high-handed, arrogant, oh-so-male-Cynster decisions, but they simply don't. The only ladies any of them have ever been known to take up behind their vaunted horses in the park are their wives."

Flick frowned. "He never said anything."

"I imagine he didn't, but it was a declaration, nonetheless. By driving you in the park, he made it plain to the ton's hostesses that he intends to offer for you."

Flick considered, then grimaced. "That's hardly a declaration of love."

"No, I grant you. There is, however, the small matter of his current state. Tight as a violin string about to snap. His temper's never been a terribly complacent one—he's not easygoing like Sylvester or Alasdair. His brother Spencer is reserved, but Harold's impatient and stubborn. It's a very revealing thing when such a man willingly and knowingly submits to frustration."

Flick wasn't convinced, but ... "Why did he make this declaration?" She glanced at Lady Osbaldestone. "Presumably he had a reason?"

"Most likely to keep more experienced gentlemen—his peers, if you will—at a distance, even if he wasn't by your side."

"To warn them away, so to speak?"

Lady Osbaldestone nodded. "And then, of course, he kept watch from the other side of every ballroom, just to make sure."

Flick felt her lips twitch.

Lady Osbaldestone saw and nodded. "Just so. There's no reason to have the megrims just because he's not beside you. In terms of his behavior, he's handled this well—I really don't know what more you could want of him. As for love, he's shown possessiveness and protectiveness, both different facets of that emotion, facets gentlemen such as he are more prone to openly demonstrate. But for the facets to shine, the jewel must be there, at the heart. Passion alone won't give the same effect."

"Hmm." Flick wondered.

The singer reached her finale—a single, sustained, piercingly high note. When it ended, everyone clapped, including Flick and Lady Osbaldestone. The audience immediately stood and milled, chatting avidly. Others approached the love seat; Flick rose.

Lady Osbaldestone acknowledged Flick's curtsy. "You think of what I told you, gel—you'll see I'm right, mark my words."

Flick met her old eyes, then nodded and turned away.

Lady Osbaldestone's comments cast matters in a new light, but ... as Horatia's carriage rumbled over the cobbles, Flick grimaced, thankful for the deep shadows that enveloped her. She still didn't know if Demon loved her—could love her—would ever love her. She'd settle for any of those alternatives, but for nothing less.

Looking back over the past weeks, she had to acknowledge his protectiveness and possessiveness, but she wasn't certain that in his case those weren't merely a reflection of his desire. *That* was strong—incredibly, excitingly powerful. But it wasn't love.

His frustration, which she'd recognized as steadily escalating, was to her mind more likely due to frustrated desire, compounded by the fact that she'd yet to accept his offer. She couldn't see love anywhere, no matter how hard she looked.

And while Lady Osbaldestone had explained why he couldn't spend time with her in town as he had in the country, she hadn't explained why, when he was by her side, he still kept distance between them.

As the carriage rumbled through the wide streets, lit by flickering flares, she pondered, and wondered, but always came back to her fundamental question: Did he love her?

Heaving a silent sigh, grateful to Lady Osbaldestone for at least giving her hope again, she fixed her gaze on the passing scenery and considered ways to prod Demon into answering. Despite her usual habit, she balked at asking him directly. What if he said no, but didn't mean it, either because he didn't realize he did, or did realize but wasn't willing to admit it?

Either was possible; she'd never told him how important having his love was to her. It hadn't escaped her notice that he'd got into the habit of using that one small word with her—on this subject, she couldn't risk it. If he said no, her newfound hope would shrivel and die, and her dream would evaporate.

The carriage swung around a corner, tilting her close to the window. Beyond the glass, she saw a group of men standing outside a tavern door. Saw one raise a glass in toast—saw his red neckerchief, saw his face. With a gasp, she righted herself as the carriage straightened.

"Are you alright, dear?" Horatia asked from beside her.

"Yes. Just . . ." Flick blinked. "I must have dozed off."

"Sleep if you will—we've still got a way to go. I'll wake you when we reach Berkeley Square."

Flick nodded, her mind racing, her troubles forgotten. She began to ask Horatia where they were, but she stopped, unable to explain her sudden need of street names. She kept her eyes glued to the streets from then on, but didn't see any signs until they were nearly home.

By then, she'd decided what to do.

Masking her impatience, she waited. The carriage rocked to a halt outside the Cynster house; handed to the pavement, she matched her pace to Horatia's and unhurriedly ascended the steps. As they climbed the stairs, she smothered a yawn. With a sleepy goodnight, she parted from Horatia in the gallery and turned toward her room.

As soon as she'd turned the corner, she picked up her skirts and ran. Hers was the only occupied room in that wing, and she'd forbidden the little maid who helped her to wait up. So there was no one about to see her fly into her room. No one to see her tear to her wardrobe and delve into the cases on its floor. No one to see her shed her beautiful gown and leave it lying on the rug.

No one to see her climb into attire that would have made any lady blush.

Ten minutes later, once more Flick the lad, she crept downstairs. The door was left unlatched until Demon's father came in, usually close to dawn. Until then, Highthorpe polished silver in his pantry, just beyond the baise door. Flick inched down the hall. The front door opened noiselessly—she eased it back just far enough to squeeze through, worried that a draft might alert Highthorpe. Only after she'd closed it again and gently set the latch down did she breathe freely.

Then she darted down the steps and into the street.

She stopped in the shadow of an overhang. Her first impulse was to retrace the carriage's journey, find Bletchley, then follow him through the night. This, however, was London, not Newmarket—it was hardly wise, even dressed as she was, to slink through the streets in the dark.

Accepting reality she headed for Albemarle Street.

CHAPTER
Twenty

ᏬᎧᎧᏬ

Luckily, Albemarle Street wasn't far. She found the narrow house easily enough—Horatia had pointed it out when they'd driven past. Demon lived alone with only Gillies as his general factotum, for which Flick was duly grateful—at least she wouldn't have to cope with strangers.

Slipping through the shadows to the front steps, she noted a lone carriage a few doors down the street. The coachman was shuffling on the box, settling under a blanket; thankfully, his back was to her.

Flick crept up the steps. She reached for the brass knocker, steeling herself to tap gently, but the door gave, just an inch. Catching her breath, she stared at the gap. Splaying her fingers, she gently pushed—the door swung enough for her to slip through.

In the dimness beyond, she looked around, then eased the door closed. She was in a narrow hall, a flight of stairs directly before her. The wall to her right was shared with the next house; to her left lay a closed door, presumably to the parlor. A narrow corridor ran back beside the stairs.

Demon might not be home—there was no light showing beneath the parlor door. Looking up, Flick discerned a faint light low on the landing above. The room upstairs was probably his bedroom.

She bit her lip and considered the narrow stairs.

And heard a sudden scuffle, then the scrape of chair legs on polished boards.

Followed, quite distinctly, by a purring, feminine, highly accented voice: "Harrrrry, my demon . . ."

Flick's feet were on the stairs before she knew it.

From above came a vibrant oath. Then, "What the *devil* are you doing here, Celeste?"

"Why, I've come to keep you company, Harrrry—it's cold tonight. I've come to keep you—*all* of you—warrrrrrm."

Another oath, as heated as the last, answered that. Then came, "This is ridiculous. How did you get in here?"

"Never mind that—*here I am*. You should, at the very least, reward me for my enterprise."

In the shadows on the landing, hard by the door, Flick heard a deep, aggravated, very masculine sigh.

"Celeste, I know English isn't your first language, but no is no in most tongues. I told you at least four times! It's over. *Finis!*"

It sounded as if the words were forced through gritted teeth.

"You don't mean that—how can you?"

Celeste's tone conveyed a purring pout. The soft shushing of silk reached Flick's straining ears—she pressed close, one ear to the panel.

An explosive expletive nearly rocked her on her heels.

"*Dammit!* Don't do that!"

A brief scuffle ensued. A confused medley of muttered oaths mixed with Celeste's increasingly explicit cajoling had Flick frowning—

The door was hauled open.

"*Gillies!*"

Flick jumped—and stared, wide eyed, into Demon's face, watched his snarling expression transform in a blink to utter blankness.

In utter, abject disbelief, Demon stood in his shirtsleeves on the threshold of his bedroom, fury still wreathing his faculties, one hand imprisoning the wrists of his importuning ex-mistress, his gaze locked with the wide blue eyes of his innocent wife-to-be.

For one definable instant, his brain literally reeled.

Flick, thank heaven, was as stunned as he—she stared up at him and uttered not one peep.

Then Gillies shuffled into the hall. "Yessir?"

Demon looked down the stairs. Behind him, Celeste hissed and clawed at his hands. He filled the doorway so she couldn't see Flick, now shrinking back into the corner of the tiny landing, tugging her cap low, pulling her muffler over her face.

Hauling in a breath, he stepped forward and turned, squashing Flick into the corner behind him. "The countess is leaving. *Now.*" He yanked Celeste out of his room and released her; stony-faced, he gestured down the stairs.

Celeste paused for one instant, black eyes spitting fury, then she uttered three virulent words he was quite happy not to understand, stuck her nose in the air, hitched her cloak about her shoulders, and swept down the stairs.

Gillies opened the door. "Your coach awaits, madam."

Without a backward glance, Celeste swept out of the house. Gillies shut the door.

Behind Demon, Flick grinned, having watched the entire proceedings from under his arm.

Then she jumped, plastering herself against the wall as he swung on her and roared, "*And what the damn hell do* you *think you're doing here?*"

"Heh?" Stunned, Gillies looked up. "Good God."

Considering what she could see in Demon's eyes, Flick didn't think God would be much help to her. She could barely remember the answer to his question. "I saw Bletchley."

He blinked and drew marginally back. "Bletchley?"

She nodded. "On one of the corners we passed on the way home from the musicale."

"From Guilford Street?"

She nodded again. "There was a tavern on the corner—he was drinking and chatting to some grooms. *And*"—she paused dramatically—"*he* was in livery, too!"

Which, of course, explained why they hadn't found him, why he hadn't appeared at any of the usual places to meet with the gentlemen of the syndicate. He was, quite possibly, in the household of one of the syndicate.

Demon studied Flick's face while his mind raced. "Gillies?"

"Aye—I'll fetch a hackney." Pulling on his coat, he went out.

Straightening, Demon drew in a huge breath, his gaze steady on Flick's eyes. "Which corner was it?"

"I don't know—I don't know London streets very well." She tilted her chin and looked straight back at him. "I'd know it if I saw it again."

He narrowed his eyes at her; she widened hers and stared back.

Muttering an oath, he spun on his heel. "Wait there."

He fetched his coat, shrugged into it, then escorted her down the stairs and into the hackney. At his order, Gillies came too, scrambling up onto the seat beside the driver.

"Guilford Street. As fast as you can." Demon pulled the door shut and sat back.

The jarvey took him at his word; neither Demon nor Flick spoke as they rattled through the streets and swung around corners. On reaching Guilford Street, Demon told the jarvey to head for Berkeley Square, following the directions he relayed from Flick. Sitting forward, she scanned the streets, unerringly picking out their way.

"It was just a little farther—*there*!" She pointed to the little tavern on the corner. "He was there, standing by that barrel." Bletchley wasn't, unfortunately, there now.

"Sit back." Demon tugged her back from the window, then ordered the jarvey to draw up after the next corner. As the coach rocked to a halt, Gillies swung down and came to the door. With his head, Demon indicated the tavern. "See what you can learn."

Gillies nodded. Hands in his pockets, he sauntered off, whistling tunelessly.

Sinking back against the leather seat, Flick stared into the night. Then she looked down and played with her fingers. Two minutes later, she drew in a deep breath and lifted her head. "The countess is very beautiful, isn't she?"

"No."

Startled, she looked at Demon. "Don't be ridiculous! The woman's gorgeous."

Turning his head, he met her gaze. "Not to me."

Their eyes locked, silence stretched, then he looked down. Lifting one hand, he reached out, tugged one of hers from her lap, and wrapped his long fingers about it. "She—and all the others—they came before you. They no longer matter—they have no meaning." He slid his fingers between hers, then locked their palms together.

"My taste," he continued, his tone even and low as he rested their locked hands on his thigh, "has changed in recent times—since last I visited Newmarket, as a matter of fact."

"Oh?"

"Indeed." There was the ghost of a smile in his voice. "These days, I find gold curls much more attractive than dark locks." Again, he met her eyes, then his gaze drifted over her face. "And features that might have been drawn by Botticelli more beautiful than the merely classical."

Something powerful stirred in the dark between them—Flick felt it. Her heart hitched, then started to canter. Her lips, as his gaze settled on them, started to throb.

"I've discovered that I much prefer the taste of sweet innocence, rather than more exotic offerings."

His voice had deepened to a gravelly rumble that slid, subtly rough, over her flickering nerves.

His chest swelled as he drew breath. His gaze lowered. "And I now find slender limbs and firm, svelte curves much more fascinating—more arousing—than flagrantly abundant charms."

Flick felt his gaze, hot as the sun, sweep her, then it swung up again. He searched her eyes, then lifted his other hand, shoulders shifting as he reached for her face. Fingers closing about her chin, his gaze locked with hers, he held her steady, and slowly, very slowly, leaned closer.

"Unfortunately"—he breathed the word against her yearning lips—"there's only one woman who meets my exacting requirements."

She deserted the sight of his long, lean lips—lifting her lids, she looked into his eyes. "Only one?"

She could barely get the words out.

He held her gaze steadily. "One." His gaze dropped to her lips, then his lids fell as he leaned the last inch nearer. "Only one."

Their lips touched, brushed, molded—

Gillies's tuneless whistle rapidly neared.

Smothering a curse, Demon let her go and sat back.

Flick nearly cursed, too. Flushed, breathless—absolutely ravenous—she struggled to steady her breathing.

Gillies appeared at the door. "It was Bletchley, right enough. He's somebody's groom, but no one there knows who his master is. He's not a regular. The place is the local haunt for the coachmen waiting for their gentlemen to finish at the—" Gillies stopped; his features blanked.

Demon frowned. He leaned forward, looked out at the street, then sank back. "Houses?" he suggested.

Gillies nodded. "Aye—that's it."

Flick glanced along the row of well-tended terrace houses. "Maybe we could learn which houses had guests tonight, then ask who the guests were?"

"I don't think that's a viable option." Demon jerked his head; Gillies leapt at the chance to scramble up top. "On to Berkeley Square."

The carriage lurched forward. Demon sat back and pretended not to notice Flick's scowl.

"I can't see why we couldn't ask at the houses—what harm could there be?" She sat back, folding her arms. "They're perfectly ordinary residences—there must be some way we can inquire."

"I'll put some people onto it tomorrow," Demon lied.

Better a lie than have her decide to investigate herself. That particular row of ordinary residences hosted a number of high-class brothels, none of which would welcome inquiries as to the identity of their evening's guests. "I'll see Montague first thing tomorrow, and swing all our people into the fashionable areas." Inwardly, Demon nodded. Things were starting to make sense.

Flick merely humphed.

Demon had the hackney drop them off just around the corner from Berkeley Square, then take Gillies on to Albemarle Street. He checked the Square, but it was late—there was no one about to see him bring Flick the lad home. He only hoped he could sneak her past Highthorpe.

"Come on." He strolled along the pavement; Flick strolled beside him.

As they climbed the steps to his parents' door, he glanced down at her. "Go straight up the stairs as silently as you can—I'll distract Highthorpe." He gripped the doorknob and turned it—"Damn!" He turned the knob fully and pushed. Nothing happened. He swore. "My father must have come home early. The bolts are set."

Flick stared at the door. "How will I get in?"

Demon sighed. "Through the back parlor." He glanced around, then took her hand. "Come on—I'll show you."

Striding back down the steps, he led her down the narrow gap between his parents' house and the next, into a lane running along the backs of the mansions. A stone wall, more than seven feet tall, lined the lane.

He tried the gate in the wall; it, too, was locked.

Flick eyed the wall and groaned. "Not again."

"'Fraid so. Here." Demon linked his hands. Grumbling, Flick placed her boot in them—he threw her up. As in Newmarket, he had to slap his hand under her bottom and heave her over—she grumbled even more.

Demon caught the top of the wall, hauled himself up, then dropped down to join Flick in the bushes below. Grabbing her hand, he led her through the rhododendrons, across the shadowed lawn, and onto the back terrace. He signalled her to silence, then, using a small knife, he set to work on the French doors of the back parlor. In less than a minute, the lock clicked and the doors swung open.

"There you are." Pocketing the knife, he gestured Flick in. Hesitantly, she crossed the threshold. He stepped in behind her to get off the open terrace—

She clutched his sleeve. "It all looks so different in the dark," she whispered. "I've never been in this room—your mother doesn't sit here." Her fingers tightened; she looked up at him. "How do I get to my room?"

Demon stared at her. He wanted to see her alone—to talk to her privately—but a more formal setting in daylight was imperative, or he'd never get out what he had to say. Not before he forgot himself and kissed her. Screened by the dark, he scowled. "Where's your room?"

"I turn left from the gallery—isn't that the other wing?"

"Yes." Stifling a curse, he locked the French doors, then found her hand. "Come on. I'll take you up."

The house was large, disorientating in the dark, but he'd slipped through its corridors on countless nights past. He'd grown up in this house—he knew his way without looking.

Flick bided her time, trailing him up the stairs and into the long gallery. The curtains at the long windows were open; moonlight streamed in, laying silver swaths across the dark carpet. She waited until they drew abreast of the last window, then she tripped, stumbled—

Demon bent and caught her—

Quick as a flash, she straightened, lifted her arms, framed his face and kissed him, wildly, wantonly—she wasn't going to wait to learn if he was planning to kiss her. What if he wasn't?

Her preemptive action rendered Demon's plans academic. Curses rang in his head—he didn't hear them. Couldn't hear them over the sudden pounding of his blood, the sudden roar of his needs. Her lips were open under his; before he'd even thought, he was deep inside, tasting her, exulting in the sweet mystery of her, drinking her deep.

And she met him—not tentatively or shyly, but with a demand so flagrant it left him giddy.

He pulled back from the kiss to draw in a huge breath, conscious to his toes of the firm swells of her breasts compressed against his expanding chest. He straightened; hands sliding to his nape, she held tight. Eyes glinting under heavy lids, she drew his lips back to hers.

He went readily, urgently hungry for more heady kisses, his pulse pounding in anticipation of the deeper satiation her body, pressed to his in sweet abandon, promised. His arms had locked about her, but it was she who sank against him, a simple surrender so evocative he shook.

Pulling back, he dragged in a breath; dazed, he looked into her face, subtly lit by the moonlight. From under heavy lids, she studied him, then with one finger, traced his lower lip.

"Lady Osbaldestone said you've been keeping your distance because that's what society demands." She arched one fine brow. "Is that right?"

"Yes." He went back for another taste of her, so sweetly intoxicating she was making him drunk. She gave her mouth freely, sliding her tongue around his, then drawing back.

"She said by driving me in the park you made a declaration." She whispered the words against his lips, then kissed him.

This time, it was he who gave, then drew back, rakish senses alert to some subtle shift in the scene. He blinked down at her. Inwardly swearing, he fought to realign his spinning wits. She was, as usual, setting the pace. And he was left scrambling in her wake.

Reaching up, she drew his lips down to hers for another slow, intimate kiss that left them both simmering.

"Did you intend the drive in the park as a declaration?"

"Yes."

His lips were back on hers. She pulled away. "Why?"

"Because I wanted you." Relentless, he drew her back.

For long moments, silence reigned; locked together, they heated, then burned. When next they broke for breath they were panting. Hearts racing, eyes dark and wild under heavy lids, they paused, lips not quite touching.

"Lady Osbaldestone said you would have wanted to pressure me—why didn't you?"

He shuddered; the supple strength of her, so much less than his, struck through to his bones and left him weak. Aching to have her. "God knows."

He went to kiss her, but she stopped him—by running one hand down one locked bicep, then up, across his shoulder and his chest. Stopping with her palm over his heart, she splayed her fingers and tried to press them in—they made no impression on the already tensed muscle.

"She said you were frustrated." She looked up into his eyes. "Is she right?"

He sucked in a breath and tensed even more. "Yes!"

"Is that why you won't let me close—near—even when we're together?"

He hesitated, looking deep into her eyes. "Put that down to the violence of my feelings. I was afraid they'd show." He was never, *ever*, going to tell her she glowed.

As if in vindication, she did. He swooped and took her mouth—she surrendered it eagerly, sinking deeper against him, openly, joyously, feeding his need. Her lips were soft under his, her tongue ready to tangle; he took what she freely gave and returned it full-fold.

"I couldn't bear to see you surrounded by those puppies—and the others were even worse."

"You should have rescued me—carried me off. I didn't want them."

"I didn't know—you hadn't said."

Where the words were coming from, he didn't know, but they were suddenly flowing. "I hate seeing you waltz with other men."

"I won't—not ever again."

"Good." After another searching kiss, he added, "Just because I'm not forever by your side doesn't mean that's not precisely where I want to be."

Her "Mmm" sounded deeply content. She softened in his arms; his breath hitched, his wits reeled—even in her breeches, her body flowed with the promise of warm silk over his erection. He gritted his teeth and heard himself admit, "I nearly went mad thinking you would fall in love with one of them—prefer one of them—over me."

She drew back. In the moonlight he saw surprise and shock in her face, then her expression softened; slowly, she smiled at him—glowed at him. "That won't ever happen."

He looked into her eyes, and thanked God, fate—whoever had arranged it. She loved him—and she knew it. Perhaps he could leave it at that, now he'd admitted so much, and soothed her silly fears that his caution had been disinterest, that his towering restraint had been coolness. He studied her eyes, basked in her glow. Perhaps he could leave things to ease by themselves . . .

A second later, his chest swelled; he bent his head and kissed her—deeply, demandingly, until he knew her head was spinning, her wits in disarray. Then he drew back and whispered against her lips, "I wanted to ask . . ."

Drawing back a fraction further, he drank in the sight of her angelic face— the finely drawn features, smooth ivory skin, swollen, rosy lips, large eyes lustrous under heavy lids, her bright curls gleaming gold even in the moonlight. Her cap had disappeared, as had her muffler. As had his wits. "I hadn't meant it to be like this. You had engagements all day today—I was going to call on you tomorrow to speak to you formally."

Her lips curved; her arms tightened about his neck. "I prefer this." Arching lightly, she pressed against him; he caught his breath. "What were you going to ask?"

Flick waited, and wondered, with what little wit she still possessed. She felt so happy, so reassured. So wanted. Deeply, sincerely, uncontrollably wanted.

His eyes held hers—she both sensed and felt him steeling himself.

"What will it take to make you say yes?" After a moment, he clarified, "What do you want from me? What do you want me to do?"

She wanted his heart—she wanted him to lay it at her feet. Flick heard the words in her head, which was suddenly spinning much too fast. She dragged in a too-shallow breath—

"Just tell me." His voice was so low she felt it more than heard it.

Eyes wide, she held his darkened gaze and dazedly considered it— considered asking the one question she'd told herself she never could. Searching his face, she saw his strength, and a new, more visible devotion, both unswerving, unfailing—there for her to lean on. Neither surprised her. What did—what made her breath catch and her head swim—was the raw hunger in his eyes, in the harsh planes of his face; for the first time, she saw his naked need. She shivered, deeply thrilled by the sight, shaken by its consequence.

He'd asked for the price of her heart. She would have to tell him it was his.

Drawing in a deep breath, she steadied, calmed. This was, without doubt, the highest fence she'd ever faced. She felt his arms about her, felt his heart thudding against her breast. Her eyes locked with his, so dark in the night, she drew in a last breath, and threw her heart over. "I need to know—to believe— that you love me." Her lungs seized; she forced in a quick breath. "If you love me, I'll say yes."

His expression didn't change. He looked at her for a long, long moment. She could feel her heart thudding in her throat. Then he shifted, one arm sliding more completely around her, holding her locked against him; with the other, he lifted her hand from his shoulder. He held her gaze, then carried her hand to his lips.

His kiss seared the back of her hand.

"I could say 'I love you'—and I do." Raising his lids, he met her gaze. "But it's not that simple ... not for me. I never wanted a wife." He drew in a breath. "I never wanted to love—not you, not any woman. I never wanted to risk it—never wanted to be forced to find out if I could handle the strain. In my family, loving's not easy—it's not a simple sunny thing that makes one merely happy. Love for us—for me—was always going to be dramatic—powerful, unsettling—an ungovernable force. A force that controls me, not the other way about. I knew I wouldn't like it—" His eyes met hers. "And I don't. But ... it isn't, it appears, something I have a choice about."

His lips twisted. "I thought I was safe—that I had defenses in place, strong and inviolable, far too steely for any mere woman to break through. And none did, not for years." He paused. "Until you.

"I can't remember inviting you in, or ever opening the gates—I just turned around one day and you were there—a part of me." He hesitated, studying her eyes, then his face hardened, his voice deepened. "I don't know what will convince you, but I won't ever let you go. You're mine—the only woman I could ever imagine marrying. You can share my life. You know a hock from a fetlock—you know as much about riding as I do. You can be a partner in my enterprises, not a distant spectator standing at the periphery. You'll stand at the center of it all, by my side.

"And I'll want you there always, by my side—in the ton as much as at Newmarket. I want to build a life with you—to have a home with you, to have children with you."

He paused; Flick held her breath, very conscious of the steely tension investing his muscles, of the brutal strength holding her gently trapped, of the power in his voice, in his eyes, so totally focused on her.

Releasing her hand, he tucked one stray curl back behind her ear. "That's what you mean to me." The words were gravelly, raw, compelling. "You're the one I want—now and forever. The only future I want lies with you."

Demon drew breath and looked into her eyes, and saw tears welling bright against the blue. He inwardly quaked, unsure if they meant victory or defeat. He swallowed and asked, his voice barely audible, "Have I convinced you?"

She searched his face, then smiled—glowed. "I'll tell you tomorrow."

His hands, one at her waist, the other at her hip, tightened—he forced them to relax. Disappointment welled, but ... she seemed happy. Deeply content. If anything, her glow had reached new heights, new depths.

He studied her eyes, hard to read in the silvery light, then forced himself to nod. "I'll call on you midmorning." He raised her hand and pressed an ardent kiss to her palm. If he had to wait, that was all he dared do.

Steeling himself, he eased his arms from her.

Instantly, she clutched—her eyes flew wide.

"No! Don't go!" Flick locked her eyes on his. "I want you with me tonight."

She didn't want to tell him her decision in words—she could never match his exposition. She intended telling him in a more direct fashion—in a manner she was sure he'd understand. Words could wait until tomorrow. Tonight . . .

He grimaced lightly. "Flick, sweetheart, much as I want you, this is my parents' house, and—"

She cut him off with a kiss—the most potent one she could muster.

Long before she stopped for breath, Demon had forgotten the point of his argument—he'd lost the reins of their carriage long ago. The only point he was capable of contemplating lay at the juncture of her thighs, but . . . deeply ingrained honor forced him to pull back, catch his breath—

She touched him.

Inexpertly, not firmly enough—but she was learning. He shuddered, groaned—and caught her hand. "Flick—!"

She wriggled—he had to move quickly to catch her other hand before she reduced him to quivering helplessness.

"Dammit, woman—you're supposed to be innocent!"

Her warm chuckle was the very opposite. "I gave you my innocence at The Angel—don't you remember?"

"How could I forget? Every damned minute of that night is engraved on my brain."

She grinned. "Like an etching?"

"If an etching can convey sensations as well, then yes." The memories had warmed him, tortured him, for weeks.

Her grin widened. "In that case, you must recall that I'm not a sweet innocent any more." Her expression softened, and glowed. "I gave you my innocence. It was a gift—won't you accept it?"

Demon stared into her lovely face—he couldn't think.

She dropped her gaze to his lips. "If you won't stay with me here, I'll come back to your lodgings."

"No."

"I'll follow you—you can't stop me." Her lips curved; she met his eyes. "I want to see your etchings."

Demon looked down into eyes so blatantly full of love he wondered how he could have doubted her answer. She loved him, and always had, regardless of whether he loved her. But he did love her—desperately. Which meant they'd marry soon. Why was he holding her away?

He blinked. The next instant, he released her hands, wrapped his arms about her, and pulled her hard against him. "God, you are so *stubborn*!"

He kissed her—powerfully, passionately, deliberately letting the reins go— feeling her tug them from his grasp and fling them aside.

At some point in the subsequent heated exchange, they surfaced long enough to turn the corner of the gallery and find the door to her room. Once inside, he leaned back against the door—and let her have her way with him. It was a new experience, and oddly precious—to have a woman so wantonly, ravenously, set on ravishing him.

He reveled in it, in the hot kisses she pressed on him, in the greedy clutch of her fingers on his naked chest. She'd wrecked his cravat, crushed his coat and waistcoat—his shirt had lost buttons. When she hummed in her throat and reached for his waistband, he summoned enough strength to back her to the bed. "Not yet." Catching her hands, he stayed her. "I want to see you first."

Despite having had her more than once, he hadn't, yet, had a chance to sate his senses as he wished, and view her totally naked. He wanted that—and he wanted it now.

She blinked as he sat on the bed and drew her to stand between his thighs. "See me?"

"Hmm." He didn't elaborate—she'd catch on soon enough. At The Angel, he'd seen her naked back, but not her naked front—not in any degree of light. Her male attire made undressing her easy—he had her clad only in a whisper-fine chemise in less than a minute.

By then her eyes were round.

He stood. She stepped back, swiftly scanning the room, noting the lighted candles on her dresser and bedside table, the flickering glow cast by the fire. Dispensing with his coat, cravat, waistcoat and shirt took a minute—his boots and stockings took one more.

Then he sat on the bed again, thighs wide. She turned to look at him, then shyly smiled. All but swaying with the force, the steady pounding, of desire, he went to move—to reach out and draw her to him—

She moved first.

With that same, shy smile on her lips, she grasped the hem of her chemise, and slowly drew it off over her head.

His chest locked—if his life had depended on not looking at her—not visually devouring her—he'd have died.

He wasn't sure he hadn't—he couldn't breathe, couldn't think—he certainly couldn't move. Every muscle had seized, poised, ready …. It took enormous effort to drag in a breath, to drag his gaze upward from the lithe sweeps of her thighs, from the golden nest of curls at their apex, over the smooth curve of her stomach, up over her waist—one he could span with his hands—to the swells of her breasts, high, pert, and tipped with rose.

Her nipples puckered as his gaze touched them; he felt his lips curve, and knew his smile was hungry.

He was ravenous—aching to have her, to haul her into his arms and possess her, sink his throbbing staff deep into her softness, to ride her into sweet oblivion.

She still held her chemise in one hand, but she didn't clutch it close, didn't try to hide from his hot gaze. She shivered, but let him look his fill; when his gaze reached her face, she met his eyes.

There was no mistaking her glow—it was invitation and known delight—it held a siren's allure, and the confidence of a woman well-loved.

If she ever looked at another man like that she would break his heart. The vulnerability washed over him—he acknowledged it, accepted it and let it pass. Reaching out, he took her chemise from her, let it fall to the floor, then curved his hand about her hip.

He urged her to him and she came—shy but not hesitant. Her hands came to rest on his shoulders; he slid his about her waist and held her, sensing the supple strength of her, then he looked up, trapped her gaze, and slid both palms down, over her hips, over the firm spheres of her bottom. He spread his fingers and cupped her, caressed her, kneaded gently—within seconds, her skin dewed and heated. Her pupils dilated, her lids half lowered; she caught her breath and tensed slightly.

Holding her gaze, refusing to let her break the contact, he left one hand evocatively fondling, tracing the smooth curves and hidden valleys, brushing the backs of her thighs. His other hand he placed palm flat on her belly. She sucked in a breath, and tensed even more. Ruthlessly holding her gaze, he slowly slid his hand up, brushing the sensitive underside of one breast with the backs of his fingers, then closing his hand about the firm mound.

She gasped softly; her lids fluttered, then fell. He smiled and kneaded, stroked and tweaked, all the time watching desire flow across her face. Her lips parted. Her tongue slipped out to moisten them; her breath came in little rushes, not yet pants, but with urgency building. Her lashes fluttered as she felt him learn her, explore her.

With a wolfish smile, he bent his head.

Her shocked gasp rang through the room. She clutched his head, fingers gripping tight as he rasped his tongue over the nipple he'd suckled, torturing it even more. She was soon panting in earnest, the sound sweetly evocative.

He drew back. Desire had flooded her, changing her skin from flawless ivory to rose. Sliding his hand down over her waist, he watched her face as he gently kneaded her taut belly, then reached lower, spearing his fingers through her soft curls, pressing into the soft flesh behind.

She was already wet, swollen and ready—he stroked, and she shuddered. And leaned against one thigh, caught his shoulder for balance.

Before he could blink, she hauled in a breath, opened her eyes, and reached for his buttons. Her nimble fingers slid them free; she reached in—

He closed his eyes and groaned.

She closed her hand and he shuddered. His hands fell from her; head bowed, hands fisted, he endured as she eased her hold and went searching, exploring.

He gritted his teeth. He didn't want to open his eyes—his lids still lifted, just enough so he could see her slender arm, wrist-deep in his open breeches, fine muscles flexing as she stroked and squeezed.

Then she reached deep.

The groan she ripped from him was one of real pain—he was achingly hard, throbbing fit to explode.

Her other hand pushed at his chest. "Lie back."

He did, falling flat on his back, chest heaving as he struggled for breath—control was far beyond him. Her hand left him—he cursed the loss of her touch.

"Just a minute."

In disbelief, he felt her tugging at his breeches. This was nothing like what he'd had planned, but ... with a defeated groan, he lifted his hips and let her strip them from him. She got them halfway down, then froze.

Only then did he recall she'd never seen what she'd so successfully accommodated four times thus far.

Oh, God! He levered his lids up—she was standing between his thighs, completely naked, staring, absolutely mesmerized, at his groin. At his rather large member, thick as her wrist, which was presently standing at full attention out of its nest of brown hair.

Stifling a groan, he tensed to sit up, to grab her before she jumped away— to calm her, soothe her, reassure her—

In that instant, the stunned look on her face dissolved into a glorious smile—a wicked, purely sensual, blatantly eager light danced in her eyes. Releasing his breeches, she reached for him—

"*No!*"

Chest heaving, he lay on the bed and gazed at her in absolute horror. Her fingers had stopped mere inches from his staff, which was growing more painfully rigid by the second. He glanced at her face.

She opened her eyes wide and raised her brows back. She didn't get close to looking innocent—it was pure sensual challenge that flashed in her eyes. When he didn't immediately respond—just lay there looking at her, stupefied and at her mercy—her chin firmed.

He hauled in a breath. "All right—but for God's sake get these off me first."

She chuckled wickedly and did, quickly easing the tight breeches down his long legs, then hauling them off his feet.

He used the moment to gather his strength—she was going to kill him.

His breeches hit the floor; the next instant, she clambered eagerly onto the bed—and surprised him again. He'd assumed she'd come to his side—instead, she climbed up between his thighs, settling herself on her knees directly before what was clearly her present obsession.

He sucked in a breath—it got trapped in his lungs; they seized as she seized him. Too gently. On a groan, he reached down and closed his hand about hers, showing her how much pressure to exert. As in all things, she learned quickly. After that, all he could do was lie back and think of England. Of Lady Osbaldestone—of anything that might distract him. Not that anything did—it was utterly impossible to detach himself from her touch, from her increasingly explicit caresses. With the fingers of one hand wrapped about his rigid length, she reached to his chest, running her warm hand over taut muscles that tensed and tightened even more.

Then she leaned over him—she couldn't reach his mouth—she did reach his flat nipples. When he jerked, she chuckled—when he moaned, she only licked harder. With gay abandon, she spread hot, wet, open-mouthed kisses across his chest, then nibbled her way down, over his ridged abdomen.

He went rigid when she nuzzled along the trail of hair leading down from his navel—

And nearly died when she closed her hot mouth about his head.

He caught her, gripping her arms tight, fighting a desperate battle not to buck and push himself deeper. Dizzy, almost faint, he clenched his jaw, and hauled in three deep breaths, even while he gloried in the intimate caress.

Then he slid his hands further, gripped and lifted her.

Her eyes went wide as he held her briefly above him while he brought his legs inside hers.

"Didn't you like it?"

He met her gaze briefly. "Too much." He bit the words off—he wasn't up to talking. He set her down astride his hips. "I need to be inside you."

He was nudging into her as he spoke, muscles bunching, flickering, veins cording as he fought to be gentle. He should have readied her more, eased her more, but . . .

He glanced up—she met his gaze, studied his eyes fleetingly, then she smiled, gloriously wanton, and gave her wicked little chuckle. Setting her hands on his chest for balance, she leaned forward, just a little.

She flowered and opened for him. Before he could catch his breath and thrust upward, she sank down, not in a rush—he was too big for that—but slowly. Her lids fell; her breath caught. Frowning in concentration, her lower lip caught between her teeth, she eased herself down on him, inch by steady inch, even tucking her rear deeper to take him all. She enveloped him in hot, wet silk, slick with her own passion; when she was fully impaled, she released the breath she'd held—and tightened firmly about him.

After that, he couldn't remember anything clearly—just startling moments of achingly sweet sensuality, a delight he'd never experienced before. As she rode him, loved him, used her body to pleasure him, he lay back, conquered—defeated—and surrendered and simply took. He let her set the pace, let her gallop, rush, or amble as she would. While she moved over him, rising and falling, he let his hands roam, refreshing his memory, learning more—feasting on the knowledge, reveling in the intimacy.

And when, flushed and panting, she convulsed about him, collapsing, sated, into his arms, he decided this had to be heaven. Only an angel could have given him so much.

He held her, soothed her, waited until she'd caught her breath before he rolled her beneath him. Pushing her thighs wide, he thrust heavily, deeply; she caught her breath and opened wide, then clung.

She stayed with him as he rode her, reaching up to stroke his chest. Briefly meeting his eyes, she smiled—a cat who'd savored a whole bowlful of cream. "I love you." Her eyes drifted shut on the whisper; her smile remained on her face.

"I know," he murmured, then closed his eyes and concentrated on loving her back.

A soft, smug smile flirted about her lips. Two minutes later, it died.

She blinked, and shot him a surprised look, immediately wiped from her face as she gasped and arched beneath him. He stifled a groan as she tensed, and tightened about him once more. He was fully engorged and so deeply inside her he was going to lose his mind.

She lost hers first, coming apart in a series of small explosions, a shatteringly long, rolling release.

He continued to ride her, hard and deep, waiting until she eased, until all tension leached from her limbs, until, open and possessed, she lay beneath him, her body accepting him with no resistance—in that instant just before she started drifting, just before he joined her in the void, he leaned down, and kissed her gently.

"I love you, too."

CHAPTER

Twenty-one

৩৩৩

The instincts of years hadn't died—Demon woke long before anyone else in the house. And instantly remembered his last words. He tensed, waiting for horror to engulf him—instead, all he felt was a warm peace, a subtle sense that all was right in his world. For long moments, he simply lay there, luxuriating in that feeling.

A ticking inner clock finally prompted him to move. It wasn't yet dawn, but he had to leave soon. Turning on his side, he studied the angel snuggled beside him. He'd fallen asleep still inside her; during the night, he'd woken and disengaged, then gently settled her to sleep by his side.

How she woke was one of the delights already imprinted—etched—on his mind. Smiling, he gently tugged the sheet from her slack grasp and lifted it.

Flick woke to the sensation of him parting her thighs, to the sweet stroking of his finger in the soft flesh between. She never woke quickly—she simply couldn't do it. By the time her breathing had accelerated enough for her to lift her lids, she was hot and wet, aching and empty. In the instant before she would have tensed to move, he shifted over her, one hand pressing beneath her bottom to tilt her up, his hard thighs pressing hers wide.

He entered her—solid and hard and hot. He pushed in, and stretched her, filled her until she gasped, clutched and clung. He rode her and she joined him, their bodies locked together, driven and driving, seeking, climbing, racing until their hearts almost burst and glory rained upon them.

Flat on her back, gasping in the aftermath, she felt him still high and hard inside her. He hung over her, on his elbows, head bowed, chest working like a bellows. They were both hot, skins slick. The hair on his chest abraded her nipples—in her sensitized state, she could feel his hair elsewhere—on his forearms and calves, on his stomach, at his groin. Their limbs touched—everywhere; they were as intimately joined as it was possible to be. She had never been more physically aware of him—or herself.

His heart, thudding against her breast, slowed. Raising his head, he looked at her. "Have I convinced you?"

She lifted her lids and looked into his eyes, then deliberately tensed, tightening all about him, smiled, and let her lids fall. "Yes."

He groaned, moaned, dropped his forehead to hers—and predictably convinced her all over again.

As he left her room in a rush, flitting through the corridors like a thief to slip out of the side door before any maid caught sight of him, Demon swore on his soul that he'd never again underestimate an angel.

His morning was busy, but he was back in Berkeley Square by eleven, confident that now the Season was in full swing, his mother would not yet be down. As he'd requested before he'd left, Flick was waiting—she came gliding down the stairs as Highthorpe opened the door.

The light in her eyes, that glow in her face, took his breath away. As she crossed the hall toward him, the sun shone through the fanlight full upon her—it was all he could do not to pull her into his arms and kiss her senseless. If Highthorpe hadn't been standing in silent majesty beside him, he would have.

Flick seemed to sense his thoughts; the glance she shot him as she glided straight past and out of the door was designed to torment.

"We'll be back late in the afternoon." Demon threw the comment back at Highthorpe as he followed her down the steps. He caught her on the pavement and lifted her into his curricle.

Flick glanced at the empty pillion. "No Gillies?"

"He's off visiting his peers all over town." Retrieving the reins and rewarding the urchin who'd held them, Demon joined her; he set the bays pacing smartly. "I spoke to Montague—we've people everywhere. Now we know where to look, we'll find Bletchley. And his masters." He took a corner in style. "And not before time."

Flick glanced at him. "I had wondered ..."

The Spring Carnival was next week. Demon grimaced. "I should have gone back and seen the Committee this week, but ... I kept hoping we'd find something—at least one link, one fact, to support Dillon's story. As things stand, we should locate Bletchley by tomorrow evening at the latest—if he's anywhere within the ton, he won't be able to hide. As soon as we have any further information, I'll go back to Newmarket—at the very latest, on Sunday." He glanced at Flick. "Will you come with me?"

She blinked and opened her eyes wide. "Of course."

Suppressing a grin, he looked to his horses. "We haven't found any trace of the money—not anywhere—which is odd. We now think it has to be moving through the ton as wagers and overt expenditure. But no one's been throwing large sums around unexpectedly."

He flicked the reins; the bays stretched their legs. As they passed the gates of the park, he added, "I'd assumed the syndicate was too clever to use their own servants, but it's possible that, when both Dillon and Ickley declined to provide the necessary services so close to the Spring Carnival, they had no choice but to send someone already to hand—someone they trusted."

"So Bletchley's gentleman might be a member of the syndicate?"

"Possibly. Bletchley's a pawn, but he may still be being used at a distance. As a gentleman's groom, he'd have plenty of opportunity to meet with other gentlemen—just a word here and there wouldn't register as odd. There'd be no need for formal meetings."

Flick nodded. "I'll write to Dillon and tell him we'll be back by Sunday." Relief rang in her tone. A moment later, she realized her surroundings weren't familiar. "Where are we going?"

Demon glanced at her. "There's a sale at Tattersalls—carriage horses mostly. A pair of high-steppers I wouldn't mind picking up. I thought you might like to watch."

"Oh, *yes*! Tattersalls! I've heard so much about it, but I've never been there. Where is it?"

Her continuing eager queries left Demon in no doubt that he'd discovered the one woman in all England who would rather watch a horse auction than stroll down Bond Street. When, incapable of hiding his appreciation, he said as much, Flick blinked at him in blank bemusement.

"Well, of course—don't be ridiculous. These are *horses*!"

By mutual agreement, he bid on a pair of sweet-tempered, high-stepping greys, rather too finely boned for his taste—he didn't tell Flick they were for her. When they were knocked down to him, she was absolutely thrilled—she spent the time while he arranged to have them delivered to Newmarket making their acquaintance. He all but had to drag her away.

"Come on, or we'll never make it to Richmond."

"Richmond?" Consenting at last to let him lead her from the yard, she stared at him. "Why there?"

He looked down into her eyes. "So I can have you to myself."

He did, throughout a glorious day filled with simple pleasures, simple delights. They went first to the Star and Garter on the hill, to partake of a light luncheon. Settling her skirts at a table for two by a window overlooking the parklands, Flick noted that the other diners were definitely noticing them. She raised a brow at Demon. "Shouldn't we have some sort of chaperon for this type of outing?" Her tone was merely curious, certainly not complaining.

He met her gaze, then reached into his pocket. "I took this to the *Gazette*—it'll be run tomorrow." He handed her a slip of paper. "I didn't think you'd object."

Flick smoothed out the slip, read the words upon it, then smiled. "No—of course not." Refolding it, she handed the paper back—it contained a brief statement of their engagement. "So does that mean we can go about alone without trampling on society's toes?"

"Yes, thank heaven." After a moment, he amended, "Well, within reason."

Reason included a long ramble in the park, under the huge oaks and beeches. They fed the deer, then, hands locked, ambled on through the sunshine. They walked and talked—not of Dillon and the syndicate, or society—but of their plans, their hopes, their aspirations for the shared life before them. They laughed and teased—and shared brief, stolen, tantalizing kisses, screened by the trees. Those kisses left them trembling, suddenly too aware; in unstated accord, they turned back to the carriage and their talk turned to their wedding, and when it was to be.

As soon as possible was their unanimous decision.

As Demon had expected, his mother was waiting when they returned to Berkeley Square.

"Her ladyship is in the upstairs parlor," Highthorpe intoned. "She wished to see you immediately you returned, sir."

"Thank you, Highthorpe." Still smiling, Demon ignored Flick's questioning look; taking her hand, he led her up the stairs.

Reaching Horatia's private parlor, he knocked, then opened the door and sauntered through, towing Flick behind him.

Horatia, head already raised, fixed him with a look so severe—so filled with menacing portent—he should have been struck to stone.

Demon grinned. "How long does it take to arrange a wedding?"

The next afternoon, Flick went for a drive in the park with Horatia and Helena. The notice of her engagement to Demon had appeared that morning; Horatia was in alt. Indeed, she'd been so happy and excited on their behalf last night that they'd cancelled their evening's plans and dined unfashionably *en famille* so they could discuss their impending nuptials. As Demon's only stipulation was that it had to be soon, and she had nothing more to add, Horatia was beside herself with plans.

Naturally, Helena had been immediately informed—she'd appeared in Berkeley Square for breakfast, ready to join in the fun. She was presently seated in the carriage beside Horatia; both were regally dispensing information to the senior matrons of the ton, all of whom made a point of stopping by the carriage to comment, and compliment, and graciously bestow their approval.

Flick sat back, endeavored to look pretty, and smilingly accepted the ladies' good wishes. According to Helena and Horatia, that was all she was required to do.

Thus mildly occupied, Flick scanned the scene and wondered if Demon would appear. She doubted it—he didn't seem enamored of this facet of the ton. Indeed, she'd got the distinct impression that as soon as they were wed, he intended to whisk her back to Newmarket, to his farmhouse, and keep her there for the foreseeable future.

That plan met with her complete approval.

Lips quirking, she glanced at the carriageway, at the high-perch phaeton bowling smoothly toward them along the Avenue. The horses caught her eye; she viewed the high-stepping blacks with educated appreciation, then glanced at the carriage—spanking new, black picked out with gold—not showy but exceedingly elegant.

Idly wondering, she lifted her gaze to the gentleman holding the reins, but she didn't know him. He was older than Demon, brown hair curling tightly above a face that was startling in its cold handsomeness. His features were classical—a wide brow and patrician nose set between thin cheeks; his skin was very white. His eyes were cold under their heavy lids; his thin mouth was unsmiling. Overall, his expression was of overweening arrogance, as if even those blue bloods lining the Avenue were beneath his notice.

Flick mentally raised her brows as the equipage swept past; she was about to look away when her gaze touched the liveried groom up behind. *Bletchley*!

Flick turned to Horatia. "Who is that gentleman—the one who just drove past?"

Horatia looked. "Sir Percival Stratton." She waved dismissively. "Very definitely not one of our circle." She returned to Lady Hastings.

Flick smiled at her ladyship, but behind her demure facade, her mind raced. Sir Percival Stratton—she remembered the name. It took her a moment to recall from where—an invitation sent to Vane Cynster's house, redirected to his parents as Vane and Patience were still in Kent.

Sir Percival was giving a masquerade that evening.

Flick could barely contain her impatience. The instant she and her two soon-to-be relatives regained the Cynster front hall, she excused herself and quickly climbed the stairs—then rushed to reach the parlor ahead of Horatia and Helena. Quickly shutting the door, she raced to the mantelpiece and rifled through the pile of cards set on its end. She'd been helping Horatia answer the invitations; she'd seen Sir Percival's while sorting the cards one morning, and put it with the others for Vane and Patience. Finding it, she tucked it into the folds of her shawl, then sank down on a chair as the door opened and Helena and Horatia swept in. Flick smiled. "I thought, after all, that I might join you for tea."

She did, then excused herself, saying she would rest. Helena would soon leave, then Horatia would rest, too. They all had a full evening of engagements—a dinner and two balls.

That gave her a few hours in which to think what to do.

On the window seat in her bedchamber, she studied the heavy white card, inscribed with bold, black lettering. The invitation was addressed to Mr. Cynster, not Mr. and Mrs. Cynster; Sir Percival must not have realized that Vane had married. Sir Percival's masquerade was to commence at eight o'clock. Unfortunately, it was to be held at Stratton Hall, at Twickenham.

Twickenham was beyond Richmond, which meant it would take hours to get there.

Jaw firming, Flick jumped up, crossed to the bellpull, and sent a footman in search of Demon.

The footman returned, not with Demon but Gillies. He joined Flick in the back parlor.

"Where's Demon?" she asked baldly the instant the door shut behind the footman.

Gillies shrugged. "He was meeting with Montague, and then had some business in the city—he didn't say where."

Flick mentally cursed and fell to pacing. "We're due at a dinner at eight." Which meant there was no reason Demon would hurry home before six. She shot a glance at Gillies. "How long will it take for a carriage to travel from here to Twickenham?"

"Two and a half, perhaps three hours."

"That's what I thought." She paced back, then forth, then halted and faced Gillies. "I've found Bletchley. But ..." Quickly, she filled him in. "So you see, it's absolutely imperative that one of us is there from the start, in case the syndicate decide to meet. Well"—she gestured—"a masquerade—what more perfect venue for a quiet meeting on the side? And even if the syndicate don't meet, it's vital we move quickly—we'll need to search Stratton's house for evidence and this is the perfect way to gain entry, the perfect opportunity to poke around."

When Gillies simply stared at her as if he couldn't believe his ears, she folded her arms and fixed him with a stern look. "As there's no way of knowing when Demon will return, we'll have to leave a message and go on ahead. One of us must be there from the start." She glanced at the mantel clock—it was already after four. "I wish to leave promptly at five. Can you arrange for a carriage?"

Gillies looked pained. "You sure you wouldn't like to reconsider? He's not going to like you hying off on your own."

"Rubbish! It's just a masquerade, and he'll follow soon enough."

"But—"

"If you won't drive me, I'll take a hackney."

Gillies heaved a put-upon sigh. "All right, all right."

"Can you get a carriage?"

"I'll borrow her ladyship's second carriage—that's easy enough."

"Good." Flick considered, then added, "Leave a note saying where we've gone and why in Albemarle Street—I'll leave one here, too. One for Demon, and another for Lady Horatia. That should make all smooth."

Gillies's expression was the epitome of doubtful, but he bowed and left her.

Gillies returned driving Lady Horatia's second carriage, a small, black, restrained affair; he handed Flick into its dimness at just after five o'clock.

Settling back, Flick mentally nodded. Everything was going according to plan. By the time she'd convinced Gillies and returned upstairs, her little maid had returned from the attics with a full black domino and a wonderful, fanciful, feathered black mask. Both were now lying on the seat beside her. The evening was warm, heavy clouds hanging oppressively low. She would don her disguise when they reached Stratton Hall; she was sure no one would see through it.

Indeed, the mask looked quite nice on her, the black heightening the gold of her hair. She grinned. Despite the seriousness of what she was doing, of the syndicate and the danger, she felt a welling thrill of excitement—at last, they were close. At last, she was doing.

With mounting anticipation, she considered what lay ahead. She'd never been to a masquerade before—while such entertainments had once been commonplace, they didn't, it seemed, feature much these days. Idly, she wondered why, and put it down to changing fashions.

Regardless, she was confident that she'd cope. She'd been to heaps of balls and parties; she knew the ropes. And Demon would follow as soon as he got home—there was very little chance of anything going wrong.

Thunder rumbled, low, menacing, yet still distant. Closing her eyes, Flick smiled.

Gillies had stated that Demon wouldn't like her going into danger. Lady Osbaldestone had warned her that he was protective—she already knew that was true. She rather suspected she would be hearing a sound just like that thunder much nearer at hand once he caught up with her.

Not that she was shaking in her slippers. She sincerely hoped he never realized that his reaction was no deterrent. If there was something she felt she needed to do, she would do it—and gladly pay his price later. Ease and soothe his possessiveness. Just as she had at The Angel.

Swaying as the carriage rocked along, she wondered what his price would be tonight.

Demon returned home just after six, with a silly grin on his face and the deed to 12 Clarges Street in his pocket.

Only to find, stoically rigid on his doorstep, one of the footmen from Berkeley Square. The message the footman carried was almost hysterical.

He strode into his mother's parlor five minutes later. "What's the matter?" She hadn't said in her note—mostly a bleat about him never forgiving her, which was so out of character that he'd been seriously alarmed. The sight of her prostrate, sniffing what looked suspiciously like smelling salts, didn't ease his mind. "What the devil's going on?"

"I don't *know!*" Verging on the tearful, Horatia sat up. "Felicity's gone off to Stratton's masquerade. Here—read this." She waved a badly crushed note at him. "Oh—and there's one for you, too."

Demon accepted both. He barely glanced at hers before setting it aside and opening the missive Flick had left for him. As he'd expected, it was much more informative.

"She asked me who Stratton was this afternoon in the park, but I never *dreamed*—" Horatia lifted both hands in the air. "Well—who would have? If I'd known she'd take such a silly notion into her head, I would never have let her out of my sight!"

Demon returned to the note Flick had left her. "What have you done about your evening's entertainments?"

"She suggested I excuse her on the grounds of her having a headache—I've excused us *both* on the grounds of *me* having a headache—which I have!"

Demon glanced at her. "Stop worrying. She'll be all right."

"How do you know?" Suddenly noticing his relative calm, Horatia narrowed her eyes at him. "What's going on?"

"Nothing to get in a flap about." Returning her note, Demon pocketed his. Flick had told Horatia she'd been seized by a desperate longing to attend a masquerade, so had gone to Stratton Hall, expecting him to join her there. "I know what Stratton's masquerades are like." The admission made Horatia narrow her eyes even more; imperturbably, he continued, "I'll go after her immediately—she'll only be there an hour or so before I catch up with her."

Although clearly relieved, Horatia continued to frown. "I thought you'd be ropeable." She snorted. "All very well for *me* not to worry—why aren't *you* worried?"

He was, but ... Demon raised his brows resignedly. "Let's just say I'm growing accustomed to the sensation."

He left his mother with her brows flying, and returned to Albemarle Street. Gillies's note gave him more details. Pausing only to extract his own invitation to Stratton's masquerade from the edge of his mantelpiece mirror, and to unearth his old domino and a simple half-mask, he hailed a hackney, and, once again, set out in Flick's wake.

Within two minutes of haughtily sweeping into Stratton Hall, Flick realized that no amount of tonnish balls and parties could ever have prepared her for Sir Percival's masquerade.

Two giant blackamoors wearing only loincloths, turbans, and a quantity of gold, each carrying a wicked-looking cutlass, stood guard, arms akimbo, in the front hall, flanking the main doors to the ballroom. Inside the enormous room running the length of the house the scene was similarly exotic. Blue silk flecked with gold stars draped the ceiling; the walls were an Arabian Nights' dream of silks, brocades and brass ornaments.

Mindful of her disguise, she didn't pause on the threshold and stare—spine straight, chin tilted at an imperious angle, she stepped straight into the crowd.

In the room's center, an elaborate fountain splashed; Flick saw guests filling glasses with the water—then realized it was champagne. The fountain was ringed with tables displaying delicacies galore; other tables elsewhere were similarly loaded with the most expensive fare—seafood, pheasant, caviar, quails' eggs—she even saw a roast peacock stuffed with truffles.

Wine was flowing freely, as were other spirits—the spirits of the guests were rising in response. Nearing the room's end, she heard a violin, and glimpsed a string quartet playing in the conservatory beyond the ballroom.

There were guests everywhere. Even behind their masks and cloaked in dominos, the women were remarkable—she'd yet to see one who was less than stunning. The men were gentlemen all—she heard it in their accents, invariably refined, and saw it in their clothes—many wore their dominos loose, more like a cloak, in some cases thrown rakishly back over one shoulder.

From the end of the room, Flick circled, searching for Stratton. The long windows giving onto the terrace had been left open to the sultry night. Black clouds raced, roiling across the sky. Thunder rumbled intermittently, but the storm was still some distance away.

"Well, well ... and what do we have here?"

Flick whirled—and found herself pinned by Stratton's cold eyes.

"Hmm ... a woodland sprite, perhaps, come to enliven the evening?" His thin lips curved but there was no warmth in his smile.

His gaze left her face to openly rove over her; Flick quelled a shiver. "I'm searching for a friend."

A calculating gleam entered Stratton's eyes. "I'll be happy to oblige, my dear, once the festivities begin." He lifted a hand. Flick instinctively recoiled but he was too fast. He caught her chin and tilted her face this way, then that, as if he could see through her mask. He was certainly aware of her resistance; it seemed to please him. Then he released her. "Yes—I'll keep an eye out for you later."

Flick didn't even attempt a smile. Luckily, Stratton's attention was claimed by some other lady; Flick seized the moment and slipped away.

The swelling crowd was growing restive. Flick plunged into it, purposefully crossing the room, leaving Stratton before the windows. In addition to the main ballroom door, there were three other doors leading into the house. Guests were arriving via the main door; thus far, she'd seen only footmen using the other doors. The masquerade was getting underway—while the noise exceeded that of the usual ton ball, it had yet to reach raucous.

Flick halted midway down the inner wall, with the fountain and its surrounding melee directly between herself and Stratton. He was reasonably tall—she could see him. She hoped he couldn't see her. From where she stood, she could keep watch on the doors leading into the house—if any meeting was to be held, she doubted it would be convened in the increasingly crowded ballroom.

Until Demon joined her, watching for any sign of a suspicious gathering was the best she could do. Her heart slowing, she relieved the urge to scrub at where Stratton had touched her chin. Settling against the wall, she kept a wary eye on him.

The gathering before her grew increasingly licentious—the guests might be wealthy and well-born, but she was quick to see why masquerades no longer found favor with the *grandes dames*. Even after spending two nights in Demon's arms, some of what she saw still shocked her. Luckily, there were rules of some sort. Despite the way some other ladies were behaving, letting gentlemen freely grope beneath their dominos, all the gentlemen present *were* gentlemen—those who paused to speak with her as she stood quietly by the wall treated her with courtesy, albeit, like Stratton, with a certain predatory intent.

She recognized that intent well enough, but most moved on once she made it clear she was in immediate expectation of being joined by her particular gentleman.

Unfortunately, there were exceptions to every rule.

"I say—your gentleman not here yet?" One predatory rogue lounged close. "Just realized you're still waiting—a pity to waste time, such a pretty little thing like you."

He reached out and flicked a feather on her mask; Flick swayed back, her frown concealed by the mask.

"Indeed." The rogue's friend appeared on her other side, his gaze trailing speculatively down her length. "What say we retire to one of the rooms along the hall, and you can show me and my friend here just how pretty you are, hmm?" He looked up, cool eyes searching hers. "You can always come back and meet your gentleman later."

He moved closer, as did the first rogue, crowding her between them. "I don't think my particular gentleman would like that," Flick stated.

"We weren't suggesting you tell him, sweetheart," the first all but whispered in her ear.

Flick turned her head to him, then had to turn the other way as his friend did the same thing.

"We wouldn't want to cause any ructions—just a friendly bit of slap and tickle to keep my friend and me going until the orgy starts."

Orgy? Flick's jaw dropped.

"That's it—just think of it as a case of mutual tummy-rubbing. Here we are, with our peckers twitching but the action some way off—"

"And here *you* are, a plump little pigeon just waiting to be plucked, but with your chosen plucker not yet in sight."

"Right—a bit of hot fumbling and a few good pokes would ease things all around. What do you say?"

They both leaned closer, voices low, increasingly hoarse as they whispered, in quick fire exchanges, a stream of suggestive suggestions directly into Flick's ears.

Behind her mask, her eyes grew rounder, and rounder. Toes? *Tongues?* Rods ...

Flick had had enough. First Stratton, now these two. They'd pressed close; jerking both elbows outward, she jabbed them in the ribs. They fell back gasping—she whirled on them. "I have never met with such arrogant presumption in my life! You should be ashamed of yourselves—propositioning a lady in such terms! And without the slightest invitation! Just think how horrified your poor mamas would be if they ever heard you speaking like that." They stared at her as if she'd gone mad; Flick glared, then hissed, "And as for your twitching appendages, I suggest you take them for a long walk in the rain—*that* should cure them of their indisposition!"

She glared one last time, then swung on her heel—

And collided with another male.

Hers. His arms closed about her before she bounced off. Clutching his domino, she looked up into his masked face. For a moment, his gaze remained levelled over her head, then he glanced down.

Flick frowned. "How did you recognize me?"

She was the only woman there with hair like spun gold and she drew his senses like a lodestone. Demon narrowed his eyes. "What in *heaven* possessed you—"

"Ssh!" Her eyes darted about. "Here—kiss me." Stretching on her toes, she did the honors. As their lips parted, she whispered, "This appears to be a bacchanal-by-another-name—we have to do our best to fit in." Sliding her arms beneath his domino, she sank against him.

Demon gritted his teeth and backed her into the space she'd recently vacated.

"Those two gentlemen who were talking to me—you'll never guess what—" She broke off. "Where did they go?"

"They suddenly remembered pressing engagements elsewhere."

"Oh?"

She shot him a glance. Demon ignored it, and her distraction. "What I want to know is why you thought fit—" He broke off on a hiss, sucking in a breath as she twined her arms about his neck and shifted her hips against him.

He stared blankly down at her—she smiled, and laid her head on his chest.

"I found Bletchley. He's Sir Percival's groom."

He studied her eyes, lit with anticipation, with expectant excitement, and inwardly sighed. "So your note said." Gathering her more comfortably into his arms, he shifted so he could view the room. "I suppose you've decided the syndicate will meet tonight."

"It's the perfect occasion."

He could hardly disagree—looking over the sea of heads, he noted the spontaneous distractions arising here and there in the crowd. "Those attending wouldn't even risk being recognized." He looked down and met her gaze. "Let's take a look around—Stratton's occasions are always open house." Aside from anything else, he wanted her away from the center of activity, although, as things went, Sir Percival's masquerade had a long way yet to go.

Boldly curving a palm about her bottom, he steered her toward the nearest door. Glancing down, he met her shocked glance, and raised a far from innocent brow. "We have to do our best to fit in."

He flexed his fingers—behind her mask, her eyes flared, then a dangerous glint entered the soft blue. Before he could stop her, she swayed close, slipped one slim hand through the opening of his domino and stroked, tantalizingly, up his length.

Sucking in a breath, he froze; she chuckled wickedly. Catching his hand, she swung to the door. "Come along." The look she threw him as she led him out would have convinced the most suspicious observer that her fell aim was entirely in keeping with Sir Percival's masquerade.

Drawing a steadying breath, Demon went along with her charade while considering a few elaborations to her scheme. Once in the corridor, he drew her closer, settling her within his arm, his hand returning to its former, stridently possessive position. Any others coming upon them in the dimly lit corridors would simply see two revellers searching for a quiet nook.

Many others were doing the same. Pausing before every door, Demon urged Flick to kiss him, then opened the door and half stumbled in, scanning the room without releasing her, mumbling an incoherent apology and swinging straight back out again if it was already occupied. All the downstairs rooms were, some hosting groups; despite his best efforts, it was impossible to completely screen Flick from the frolics in progress. At first, she stiffened with shock—by the time they'd covered all the downstairs rooms, her reaction had changed to one of curiosity.

A fact he tried not to think about. Some of what she was seeing she was definitely not up to. Yet.

"No meetings," Flick murmured as they turned back to the front hall. "Couldn't we just watch Stratton, then follow when he leaves the ballroom?"

"That might not help us. Remember what I said about Bletchley's employer not necessarily being one of the syndicate?"

Flick frowned. "Stratton's phaeton is brand new—his horses would have done you credit."

"Maybe so, but while Stratton's a deuced cold fish, he's also exceedingly wealthy." Demon gestured to their surroundings. "He inherited a massive fortune."

Flick grimaced. "He seemed such a promising candidate."

"Yes, well—" Reaching the hall, Demon turned her up the stairs. "I think we should check all the rooms."

Other couples, flushed and subtly dishevelled, laughing breathlessly, were descending the stairs as they went up. Demon drew Flick suggestively close as they climbed—with her one step ahead of him, their bodies slid against each other as they ascended.

They reached the gallery. Flick paused and whispered breathlessly, "Shouldn't we be checking outside? If it's not Stratton but some of his guests come to meet with Bletchley, wouldn't they use the garden?"

"It's raining—it started as I arrived. I think we can assume no meeting had taken place earlier. Now, it'll have to be held indoors—in some area open to the guests."

They continued their search. Some of the bedrooms and suites were occupied, others were empty. While they stumbled upon meetings aplenty, none were of the type they sought. Flick's shoulders had slumped long before they reached the last door at the end of the last corridor.

Demon tested the handle, then carefully turned it fully and tried the door. "It's locked." He started to turn back; Flick stood in the way, frowning at the locked door.

"Why locked?" She glanced back up the corridor. "His bedroom wasn't locked." She looked at the door behind which two couples were engaged in an energetic romp on Stratton's huge bed. "Nor was his dressing room or study." She nodded at each of those doors, then turned to stare at the last door. "Why would he lock this room and not any other in the house?"

Demon looked at her face, at her stubbornly set chin, and sighed. Placing his ear to the panel, he listened, then glanced down at the bottom of the door; no telltale strip of light showed. "There's no one in there."

"Let's look," Flick urged. "Can you unlock it?"

Demon considered reiterating that Stratton was not a good candidate for race-fixer, but her sudden excitement was infectious. He drew out the small tool he carried everywhere—a multi-pronged pick and knife useful for destoning horses' hooves. In less than a minute, he had the door open. The room within was empty; standing back, he let Flick in. Glancing back up the corridor, he confirmed it was empty, then shut the door behind them.

A warm glow suffused the room. Flick adjusted the wick on a lamp set on a wide desk, then reset the glass. They both looked around.

"An office." Demon glanced at ledgers and books of accounts filling one bookshelf. It wasn't a large room. A padded leather chair stood behind the desk; a wooden chair faced it. One wall was filled with windows looking out over the river—they presently displayed a landscape of driving rain and thick grey clouds backlit by sheet lightning. Thunder rumbled, drawing nearer.

"Half a library, too." Flick considered the wall of bookshelves opposite the windows. "I wonder why he keeps them up here. The library was barely half full."

Demon turned from the elemental rage outside and sauntered to the shelves. Scanning the titles, he found familiar volumes on various games of chance, and a few not so familiar on card-sharping techniques and ways of weighting the odds in some forms of wagering. Frowning, he looked more closely, eventually hunkering down to read the titles of the volumes on the lowest shelf. "Interesting."

His voice had changed—he read the titles again, then rose and turned to the desk, his frame radiating purpose.

Flick looked at him questioningly. He met her gaze as he joined her behind the desk, shrugging off his domino, slipping off his mask.

"Those"—with his head he indicated the bottom shelf of books—"are the full race records for the past two years."

Flick blinked. "The *full* records?"

Demon nodded and pulled open the top desk drawer.

"Not something one finds in your usual library. *I* don't even have a set."

"How? . . ." Without finishing her question, Flick drew out the top drawer on her side of the desk.

"A set went missing last year—never to be found. But he's also added the most recent volumes—those from last season."

"A most useful tool for fixing races."

"Indeed. Look for anything that even mentions horses."

They were the ideal team for the task—they both knew the names of all recent winners, as well as those expected to win in the upcoming season. They sifted through every drawer, examined every single piece of paper.

"Nothing." Blowing an errant curl from her forehead, Flick turned and sat on the desk.

Grimacing, Demon dropped into the padded chair. Without enthusiasm, he lifted the last item from the bottom drawer, a leather-bound ledger. Propping it on the desk, he opened it and scanned the entries. After a moment, he snorted. "That phaeton is new, and he paid a pretty penny for it. As for the horses, he definitely paid too much."

"Anything else?"

"Caviar's gone up two pounds an ounce in the last year—his account-keeping habits are as stultifyingly rigid as he is. He enters every single transaction—even the lost wagers he's paid."

Studying the grim set of his face, Flick grimaced. "No entries under race-fixing, I take it?"

Demon started to shake his head, but he froze as one particular figure danced before his eyes. Slowly straightening, he flicked back a page, then another . . .

"What is it?"

"Remind me we owe Montague an enormous bonus." If it hadn't been for the agent's accuracy, he'd never have seen it. "Those amounts we were looking for—the sums cleared from each fixed race?"

"Yes?"

"They show up here. According to this, they're his main source of income."

"I thought you said he was rich."

Flicking back through the ledger, Demon bit back a curse. "He was—he must have lost it." He tapped an entry. "His income from the Funds was miniscule last year, then it ends. There've been huge debts paid—Hazard, at a guess." He looked up. "He never went to the wall—no one realized he'd been rolled up because he substituted income from race-fixing to cover his lost investment income. He's always been a lavish spender—nothing appeared to have changed. He simply carried on as he always had."

"Except he corrupted and blackmailed Dillon, and jockeys, and goodness knows what happened to Ickley."

"Or any others." Demon studied the ledger. "This is too wieldy to smuggle out." He flicked through the pages, then laid the book on the desk and ripped out five pages.

"Will that do?"

"I think so—they show the amounts from three fixed races going in, and five major purchases that can be traced to Stratton, as well as four very large debts paid to members of the ton who I'm sure will verify from whom they received those sums. On top of that, his writing's distinctive." He scanned the pages, then folded them and stowed them in the inner pocket of his coat. He returned the ledger to the bottom drawer. "We'll take the pages to Newmarket tomorrow—with any luck, he won't notice they're missing."

He shut the drawer and looked at Flick.

A board creaked in the corridor—footsteps paused, some way away—then quickly, purposefully, strode toward the office.

CHAPTER
Twenty-two

ॐ

What occurred next happened so quickly that to Flick it was just a blur. Demon stood, shifted her to the desk's center, her back to the door, yanked the neck ties of her domino free, and flung the garment off so it pooled about her. He tugged—a button on her bodice popped, then he hauled her gown and chemise down, dragging her sleeves down her arms, fully exposing her shoulders and breasts.

"Free your arms—lean back on them."

His words were a sibilant hiss—instinctively, she obeyed. He sat before her, throwing her skirts up, pushing her knees wide.

The door opened. He clamped his mouth over one nipple; Flick gasped— his mouth was hot!

He licked, and suckled, and slid his hand between her thighs, slid his long fingers into her soft flesh, stroking, then probing ...

Flick moaned; her arms locked. She let her head roll back, helplessly arching as he suckled and probed simultaneously.

Then he lifted his head, looking beyond her. She forced her lids up—in the glow from the lamp bathing her bare breasts, sheening the skin showing above her garters, his eyes were glazed, dazed, as he blinked at the door.

"Problem, Stratton?"

Flick didn't look around—Demon's fingers were still playing teasingly between her thighs. It wasn't hard to imagine the tableau their host was seeing as he stood in the doorway. From her quivering back it must be clear she was bare to the waist, and that, with her skirts rucked up so, she must, to Demon, be exposed below as well. The only thing she was still truly wearing was her feathered mask.

She could barely breathe, all too conscious of the slick wetness Demon's long fingers were reveling in. Her heart thudded in her throat; excitement sizzled in her veins.

Sir Percival's hesitation was palpable. In the stillness, she heard the rain pelting the windows, heard her own ragged breathing. Then he shifted, and drawled, "No, no. Do carry on."

The door clicked softly shut; Flick hauled in a relieved breath—and promptly lost it as Demon's mouth closed over her nipple again. He suckled strongly—she barely restrained her shriek. "Demon?" Her voice shook.

He suckled more fiercely.

"*Harry!*"

Two fingers slid deep, probing evocatively.

She arched—on a long, shuddering gasp, she managed, "*Here?*"

"Hmm." He stood, easing her back to lie across the desk.

"But ..." Flat on her back, she licked her dry lips. "Stratton might come back."

"All the more reason," he whispered, leaning over her, cupping her breasts as he kissed her. She parted her lips and he surged within; he kneaded her aching flesh, fingers tightening momentarily about her ruched nipples before his hands drifted away.

Clinging to her senses, her tongue sliding about his, she felt him unbutton his trousers, then his hands closed about her hips, anchoring her as he stepped closer, between her widespread thighs. She felt the pressure as his rigid flesh parted her swollen folds, then found her entrance.

"All the more convincing," he purred against her lips.

Straightening, he looked down at her, the wicked curve to his lips elementally male.

Dazed, she stared up at him. "Stratton might be dangerous!"

Curtailing his perusal of her quivering body held taut between his hands, he met her gaze and lifted a brow. "Adds a certain recklessness to the situation, don't you think?"

Think? She couldn't think.

He grinned. "Don't tell me you're not game?"

"Game?" She could barely gasp the word. With him poised just inside her, she was frantic. One step away from spontaneous combustion. But game? Lips and chin firming, she dragged in a breath, lifted her legs and wrapped them about his hips. "Don't be ridiculous."

She pulled him to her—then gasped, arched—frantically gripped his forearms as he pushed steadily, inexorably, all the way in until he filled her.

That sense of incredible fullness was still new, still startling. She caught her breath and clamped down, feeling him hot and hard, buried deep within her. His lids fell, his jaw locked, then, fingers tightening about her hips, he eased back, then surged anew.

As usual, he was in no hurry—he teased her, tormented her—tortured her. Held before him, virtually naked but for her mask, she squirmed, panted, moaned, then screamed as the world fell away and she was consumed by glory. The storm beyond the windows swallowed her wild cries as he flicked a sensual whip and drove her on, into a landscape of illicit delight, of pleasures honed to excruciating sharpness by the very real presence of danger.

His hands roamed, hard and demanding; she writhed and begged, wanton in her pleading.

And when she came apart for the last time, senses fragmenting beneath his onslaught, he followed swiftly, joining her in that delicious void—only, too quickly, to draw her back. He drew away from her; chest still heaving, he straightened his clothes, then hers.

Struggling to coordinate her wits, let alone her limbs, she helped as best she could. If they didn't reappear in the ballroom soon, Stratton would notice—and start to wonder.

They returned downstairs, Demon holding her close against him. They reentered the ballroom, but didn't go far—propping his shoulders against the wall, Demon cradled her against him, her cheek against his chest, then bent his head and kissed her. Soothingly, calmingly.

Distractingly. Despite that, as her senses returned, Flick heard catcalls, whistles, suggestions called out—clearly to some exhibition at the room's center. From the associated sounds, and some of the suggestions, it wasn't hard to imagine what that exhibition entailed. With Demon's arms around her, she couldn't see—she didn't try to look.

After fifteen or so minutes, when their hearts had slowed to their normal pace, Demon glanced around the room, then looked down at her. "We've been seen and duly noted," he murmured. "Now we can leave."

They did in short order, their bodies still thrumming, their spirits soaring, the evidence they'd sought for weeks at long last in their possession.

Demon called in Berkeley Square at eight the next morning; Flick was waiting in the front hall, her packed bags at her feet, a glorious smile on her face. Within minutes, they were away, the bays pacing swiftly, Gillies up behind.

"You were right about your mother stopping her scolding when I told her we'd rely on her and Helena to make all the wedding arrangements."

Demon snorted. "That was a foregone conclusion—she could hardly scold while in alt. It's her dream come true—to organize a wedding."

"I'm only glad, after all her worrying, that we could leave her so happy."

Demon merely snorted—distinctly unfilially—again.

Two minutes later, in a quiet street, he drew in to the curb, tossed the reins to Gillies, and jumped down. Flick looked around. "What . . .?"

Demon impatiently waved her to him; she shuffled along the seat and he lifted her down. "I want to show you something." Taking her hand, he led her up the steps of the nearest house—a gentleman's residence with a portico held aloft by two columns. In the portico, he pulled a set of keys from his pocket, selected one, opened the front door, and pushed it wide. With an elegant bow, he waved her in, merely lifting his brows at her questioning look.

Wondering, Flick entered a pleasant rectangular hall—from the echoes and absence of furniture it was apparent the house stood empty. Pausing in the middle of the hall, she turned and raised her brows.

Demon waved her on. "Look around."

She did, starting with the reception rooms opening from the front hall, then on up the stairs, going faster and faster as excitement gripped her. The pleasant, welcoming aura that hung in the hall recurred throughout the rooms, all airy and gracious, the morning sun streaming in through large windows. The master bedroom was large, the other bedrooms more than adequate; she eventually reached the nursery, under the eaves.

"Oh! This is wonderful!" She darted down the corridor that led to the small bedrooms, then crossed to peek into the nanny's domain. Then, her heart swelling so much she thought it would burst, she turned and looked at Demon, lounging, all rakish elegance, in the doorway, watching her. She met his gaze, smiling but watchful.

He studied her face, then raised one brow. "Do you like it?"

Flick let her heart fill her eyes; her smile was ecstatic. "It's wonderful— perfect!" Reining in her excitement, she asked, "How much is it? Could we possibly ...?"

His slow smile warmed her. Drawing his hand from his pocket, he held up the keys. "It's ours—we'll live here while in town."

"*Oh!*" Flick flew at him, hugged him wildly, kissed him soundly—then raced off again. She didn't need further explanation—this would be their home—this the nursery they would fill with their children. After the last weeks, she knew family was a vital part of him, the central concept around which he was focused. Even if he didn't know it, she did—this, from him, was the ultimate declaration—she needed no further vows. This—the home, the family—would be *theirs*.

Demon grinned and watched her. He still found her joy deeply refreshing, her open delight infectious. As he trailed her once more through the house, he wryly admitted he could now understand why so many generations of his forebears had found pleasure in indulging their wives.

That had been an abiding mystery before—it no longer was. He—Demon by name, demon by nature—had been vanquished by an angel. He no longer viewed her as innocent and youthful in the sense of being less able than he. After last night, he knew she could match him in any venture, any challenge. She was the wife for him.

And so here he was, trailing in her wake. She led—he followed, with his hand oh-so-lightly on her reins. What he'd found with her he'd found with no other—she was his and he was hers, and that was how it had to be. It was that simple. This was love—he was long past denying it.

Regaining the drawing room, she stopped at its center. "We'll have to shop for furniture."

Demon quelled a shudder. He followed her in, slid one arm around her waist, drew her against him, paused for one instant to watch the sudden flaring of awareness in her eyes, then kissed her.

She sank into his embrace; he tightened it about her. The kiss deepened— and they said all they needed with their lips, their bodies, their hearts. For one long moment, they clung, then he lifted his head.

The evidence he carried in his pocket crackled.

His chest swelled as he drew in a breath; she looked up—he met her eyes. "Let's take these to Newmarket." So they could get on with the rest of their lives.

She nodded briskly. They disengaged, straightened their clothes, then hurried out to the curricle.

By ten o'clock, they were bowling northward, the enclosed spaces of London far behind. Joyfully, Flick breathed deep, then turned her face to the sun. "We'll have to go to Hillgate End first—to tell the General and Dillon."

"I'll drive to the farm. We can leave your things there for the moment, ride to the cottage and collect Dillon, ride on to the manor and tell the General, then go straight on to the Jockey Club. I want to get that information before the Committee as soon as possible." His face hardened; he reached for the whip.

Flick wondered if his grim urgency stemmed from concern for the industry he'd so long been a part of, or from the nebulous feeling that they hadn't, yet, defeated Stratton. That feeling hadn't left her since Stratton had walked in on them last night—like a specter, it hovered at her shoulder, growing blacker, weightier. As they rounded a curve, she looked back, but there was no one there.

They drove through Newmarket in the early afternoon and headed straight for the farm. While Demon organized their horses, Flick hurried upstairs and changed into her riding habit. In less than half an hour, they were riding into the clearing behind the ruined cottage.

"It's us, Dillon," Flick called as she slid from the saddle. "Me and Demon. We're back!"

Her excitement rang in her voice. Dillon appeared through the lean-to, struggling to contain the hope lightening his haggard features.

One glance was enough to tell Demon that Dillon had changed—somewhere, somehow, he'd found some backbone. He said nothing, however, but joined Flick as she headed for the cottage.

Even before she reached him, Dillon stiffened. Demon had never seen him stand so tall, so determined. Fists clenched at his sides, he met Flick's gaze directly. "I've been to see the General."

She blinked and stopped before him. "You have?"

"I told him all about it—the whole story—so you don't need to lie for me—cover up for me—any more. I should have done that at the start."

He looked Demon straight in the eyes. "Papa and I decided to wait until tomorrow in case you found anything, but we'll be going to see the Committee regardless."

Demon met his eyes and nodded, his approval sincere.

"But we *have* found something." Flick gripped Dillon's arm. "We've learned who the syndicate is and we've enough proof to show the Committee!"

One hand at her back, Demon urged her in. "Let's take our revelations indoors."

Neither Dillon nor Flick argued. If they had, Demon couldn't have explained who he thought might overhear. But he was edgy, and had been since he'd looked into Stratton's cold eyes the previous evening.

That Stratton had noticed them the instant they'd regained the ballroom had him worried. Stratton was known as cold and detached—he might well prove a formidable enemy. If there had been any way to safely leave Flick somewhere well out of the action, he'd have snatched the opportunity. But there wasn't. That being so, the safest place for her was with him.

In the cottage, Dillon faced them. "I've written a detailed account of my involvement, first to last—just the bare facts." He looked grim. "It's hardly pleasant reading, but at least it's honest."

Flick smiled. Her inner happiness radiated from her, all but lighting up the cottage. She laid a hand on Dillon's arm. "We've proof of the syndicate."

Dillon looked at her, then at Demon; his expression said he hardly dared hope. "Who are they?"

"Not they—that was our error. It's a syndicate of one." Briefly, Demon explained. "I have to hand it to him—his execution was almost flawless. Only his greed—the fact he fixed too many races—brought the scheme to light. If he'd been content with the money from one or two major races a year ..." He shrugged. "But Stratton's lifestyle calls for rather more blunt than that."

Reaching into his pocket, Demon drew out their evidence. "This was the key." He smoothed out a sheet on the table. Flick hadn't seen it before; together with Dillon, she crowded close.

"I gathered all the details I could about the betting on the fixed races, and my agent, Montague, worked out the amounts cleared from each one. He's a wizard. If he hadn't got it right—very close to exact—I would never have recognized the figures in Stratton's ledger."

Unfolding the sheets he'd torn from Stratton's account book, Demon laid them alongside Montague's sheet. "See?" Tapping various figures in Stratton's income column, he pointed to similar figures on the other sheet. "The dates match, too." Both Dillon and Flick glanced from one sheet to the others, nodding as they took it in.

"Can we prove these are Stratton's accounts?" Dillon looked up.

Demon pointed to certain entries in the expenditure column. "These purchases of a phaeton, and here the pair to go with it—and even more these—lost wagers paid to gentlemen of the ton—can be proved to have been Stratton. With virtually the exact money from the races listed as income on the same pages, it's hard to argue any case other than it was Stratton behind the race-fixing. These"—he gestured to the papers—"are all the evidence we need."

Heeeee—crash!

With a tearing scream, the main door flew in, kicked off its rusting hinges to slam down on the floor. The whole cottage shook. Demon grabbed Flick as they backed up, eyes watering, coughing as dust reared and washed over them.

"How exceedingly foolish of you."

The words, clipped, precise and totally devoid of all feeling, came from the man silhouetted in the doorway.

The bright sunlight outside haloed him; they couldn't see his features. Flick and Demon recognized him instantly.

Eyes on the long barrelled pistol in Stratton's right hand, Demon tried to push Flick behind him. Unfortunately, they'd backed up against the hearth with its low chimney coping.

"Just remain where you are." Stratton stepped over the threshold. He barely glanced at the papers lying scattered on the table, evidence enough to put him in Newgate, a long way from the luxury to which he was accustomed.

Demon tensed, praying Stratton would look at the papers—take his eye off him just for an instant . . .

Stratton hesitated, but didn't. "You've been far too clever. Much too clever for your own good. If I didn't have such a suspicious nature, you might even have succeeded, but I checked my ledger at four o'clock this morning. By six, I was on the road to Newmarket. I knew you wouldn't dally. It was just a matter of time before you appeared."

"And if we'd gone directly to the Jockey Club?"

"That," Stratton admitted, "would have been exceedingly messy. Luckily, you drove straight through. It was easy to follow you on horseback. Equally easy to guess that, if I was patient, you'd lead me to the one player still eluding me." He inclined his head toward Dillon, but the pistol, aimed directly at Flick's chest, didn't waver. He studied her for a moment, then sighed. "Such a pity, but after that little exposition, I fear I'll have to make away with you all."

"And how," Demon asked, "do you imagine explaining that?"

Stratton raised a brow. "Explaining? Why should I explain anything?"

"Others know I've been investigating you in connection with the race-fixing."

"Do they now?" Stratton remained very still, his eyes steady on Demon's face, his aim never faltering from Flick's chest. Then his thin lips eased. "How unfortunate—for Bletchley." Stratton's jaw set. He lifted his arm, straightening it, aiming the pistol at Demon—

Flick screamed.

She flung herself at Demon, clinging to his chest, shoving him back against the chimney.

Stratton's eyes widened—his finger had already tightened about the trigger.

Dillon stepped across Flick—the pistol discharged. The explosion echoed deafeningly between the cottage walls.

Demon and Flick froze, locked together before the chimney. Demon had frenziedly tried to wrestle Flick to the side, knowing he'd be too late—

They both continued to breathe, each searingly conscious the other was still alive. They turned their heads and looked—

Dillon slowly crumpled to the floor.

"Damn!" Stratton dropped the pistol.

Demon released Flick. She dropped to the floor beside Dillon. His face a mask of vengeance, Demon went for Stratton and nearly fell as his boots tangled in Flick's skirts. He grabbed the table to steady himself and saw Stratton pull another, smaller pistol from his greatcoat pocket, saw him aim at him—

"Here! Wait a minute!" Ducking through the lean-to, Bletchley lumbered in. "What's this about things being unfortunate for me?"

Belligerent as a bull, he made straight for Stratton.

Without a blink, Stratton swung his arm farther and shot Bletchley.

Demon vaulted the table.

Stratton swung to face him, raising his riding quirt—

Demon's right cross snapped his head back with a satisfying *scrunch*. He followed up with a left, but Stratton was already on his way down. His head hit the flags with a thud. After one glance at Bletchley's slumped form, Demon leaned over Stratton.

He was unconscious, his aristocratic jaw at an odd, very painful-looking angle. Demon considered, but restrained himself from rearranging any more of his features. Wrecking Stratton's cravat without the slightest compunction, he dumped him on his face, hauled his arms back, secured them, then tied them to his ankles. Satisfied Stratton was no longer a threat, Demon glanced over the table. Flick was staunching a wound on Dillon's shoulder.

Turning to Bletchley, Demon eased him onto his back. Stratton had been rushed, his aim fractionally off. Bletchley would live, hopefully to sing of his master's infamy. Right now, all he could do was moan.

Demon left him to it—he wasn't bleeding badly enough to be in any real danger.

From what little he'd glimpsed, Dillon was.

Rounding the table, Demon joined Flick, on her knees beside Dillon. She'd eased him onto his back. Her face white as a sheet, she struggled to contain her trembling as she pressed her wadded petticoat down hard on his wound. Demon glanced at her face, then looked at Dillon. "Ease back—let me see the wound."

Relaxing her arms, she leaned back. Demon lifted the wad and quickly looked, then replaced it. His face easing, he looked at Flick as she reapplied pressure to the wound.

"It's bad, but he'll live."

Blank-faced, she looked at him. Demon put his arm around her shoulders and hugged. "Stratton was aiming for me. Dillon's shorter than I am—the ball's in his shoulder; it hasn't even touched his lung. He'll be all right once we get the doctor to him."

She searched his eyes; some of the cold blankness left her face. She looked down at Dillon. "He's been such a fool, but I don't want to lose him—not now."

Demon hugged her tighter and pressed a kiss into her curls. He wasn't all that calm himself, but he knew what she meant. If Dillon hadn't come good at the last—hadn't become man enough to, for once, shield Flick rather than expecting the reverse, Flick would have died.

His arm still about her, his cheek against her golden curls, Demon closed his eyes tight and again told himself—the being who dwelled deep inside— that it really was all right, that Flick was still with him, that he hadn't lost his angel so soon after finding her. Flick was a lot shorter than he was—if Dillon hadn't shielded her, Stratton's bullet would have hit her in the back of her beautiful head.

He really couldn't think of it—not without coming apart—so he pushed the image away, locked it deep inside. Lifting his head, he looked down at Dillon, to whom he now owed more than his life. Flick was still staunching the flow of blood, but it seemed to be easing. Demon considered, then looked into her face. She was still pale, but composed.

Part of him wanted to shake her—to swear and rant at her for throwing herself across him; the saner part realized there really was no point. She would simply set her little chin and get that stubborn look on her face and refuse to pay the slightest attention. And she'd do it again in a blink.

The realization only made him want to hug her, hold her tight, keep her forever safe in his arms.

Drawing a deep breath, he reached out and gently tugged her hands from the bloody pad. "Come." She turned to him; he met her gaze. "Leave that to me—you're going to have to ride for help."

Sorting it out took the rest of the day. Flick rode to the farm—Gillies and the Shephards took over from there, summoning the doctor, the magistrate and constable while Flick rode to Hillgate End. She stayed with the General, soothing and reassuring, until the doctor's gig arrived from the cottage with Demon driving and Dillon in the back.

They got Dillon inside—the doctor, a veteran of the Peninsula Wars, had extracted the bullet at the cottage, so Dillon was quickly made comfortable. He was still unconscious—the doctor warned he probably wouldn't wake until the next day. Mrs. Fogarty installed herself at his bedside; the General, after seeing his son still breathing, and hearing from both Flick and Demon of Dillon's bravery, finally consented to retire to the library.

The magistrate and the constable met them there; the members of the Committee, at Newmarket for the Spring Carnival that week, joined them. Tabling Dillon's account, then an explanation of the investigations that had resulted in Montague's estimations, then laying out Stratton's accounts for all to see, Demon led the assembled company through the details of Sir Percival's race-fixing racket.

While Dillon's involvement was frowned upon, in light of the greater crimes involved and his clear repentance, his misdemeanors were set aside, to be dealt with later by the Committee, once he was fully recovered. At present, they had greater fish to fry—the extent of Stratton's manipulation of their industry fired them with fury. They left, faces stiff, vowing to make an example of him. An aim Demon openly supported.

The instant they'd gone, the General slumped. Flick fussed and fretted and worried him into bed; Jacobs assured her he would watch over him. Leaving the General propped on his pillows, Flick paused in the corridor; shutting the General's door behind him, Demon studied her face, then walked to her side and drew her into his arms.

She stood stiffly for an instant, then the iron will and sheer stubbornness that had kept her going until then dissolved. She sank into his arms, sliding hers about him, laying her cheek against his chest.

Then she started to shake.

Demon carried her downstairs and coaxed a small glass of brandy past her lips. Her color improved marginally, but he didn't like the distant look in her eyes. He racked his brain for something with which to distract her.

"Come on." Abruptly standing, he drew her to her feet. "Let's go back to the farmhouse. Your luggage is there, remember? Mrs. Shephard can feed us, then you can look around and decide what changes you'd like to make."

She blinked at him. "Changes?"

He towed her to the door. "Remodelling, redecorating—how should I know?"

They rode back. He watched her every step of the way, but she was steady in her saddle. His staff were very pleased to see them; it instantly became clear Gillies had spread their news. Which was probably just as well, as Demon had every intention of dining alone with his angel.

Mrs. Shephard was on her mettle, laying a nourishing meal quickly before them. Demon was relieved to note Flick's appetite hadn't evaporated. They sat quietly as the evening lengthened, making comments at random, slowly winding down.

Finishing his port, Demon rose, rounded the table, and drew Flick to her feet. "Come—I'll give you the grand tour." He showed her all around the ground floor, then climbed the stairs; his tour ended in his bedroom, above the parlor at whose window she used to come a-tapping.

Much, much later, Flick lolled, utterly naked, in Demon's big bed. She had, she decided, never felt more comfortable, more at peace, more at home, in her life.

"Come on." A sharp smack on her bottom followed. "We'd better get dressed and I'll drive you home."

Flick didn't look around. She didn't lift her head—she sank it deeper into the pillow and shook it. "You can drive me home early in the morning, can't you?"

Lounging beside her, as naked as she, Demon looked down at her—what he could see of her—the tousled guinea gold curls gilding his pillow, one sweetly rounded shoulder and delicately curved arm, one slender leg, and one firm, absolutely perfect buttock, all clothed in the silkiest ivory skin, presently lightly flushed. All the rest of her—all that he'd enjoyed for the past several hours—was provocatively draped in his satin sheets.

She was going to be a never-ending challenge, demanding all his skill to let her run as free as she wished, with only the very lightest hand on her reins.

A slow smile curved his lips as he reached for the sheet. "Yes—I suppose I can."

Epilogue

April 30, 1820
St. Georges Church, Hanover Square

Everyone attended. The Duke and Duchess of St. Ives sat in the first row, with the Dowager beside them. Vane, of course, was best man; he and Patience had returned to London the week before. Of all the family and its myriad connections, only Richard and Catriona hadn't been able to attend, and that only because of the short notice.

The twins were Flick's bridesmaids, with Heather, Henrietta, Elizabeth, Angelica and little Mary as flower girls. Such a crowd had been needed, Demon had discovered, to manage Flick's long train. But from the instant she'd appeared and walked down the nave to join him, to the moment they were pronounced man and wife, he couldn't recall any detail beyond the sheer beauty of her angelic face.

Now, beside him on the pavement before the ton's favored church, an angel in truth in pearl-encrusted silk, she glowed with transparent joy; he couldn't have felt more proud or more favored by fate. Crowds of well-wishers flocked about them as they paused before their carriage. All the family and much of the ton had turned up to see yet another Cynster tie the knot—they were all about to adjourn to Berkeley Square for the wedding breakfast.

His mother was in tears—positive floods of happiness.

Halting before him, she stretched up to place a motherly kiss on his cheek, then she sniffed, and quavered, "I'm so glad I made you promise not to marry in any hole-and-corner fashion." She dabbed at her overflowing eyes. "You've made me so happy," she sobbed.

Helplessly, he looked at her, then looked at his father.

Who grinned and clapped him on the back. "Play your cards right, and you'll be able to live on this for years."

Demon grinned back, shook his hand, then glanced again at Horatia. Today had been the happiest, proudest day of his life—one he wouldn't have missed for the world. Despite his earlier view of marriage, he was now much wiser. But he wasn't fool enough to tell his mother that—instead, he leaned down and kissed her cheek.

Instantly suspicious, she stopped crying and stared at him; his father chuckled and drew her away.

Grinning, Demon turned to have a word with the General and Dillon, standing beside Flick on his other side. Dillon was a far cry from the petulant youth of only a few months ago; now he stood straight and tall, unafraid to meet any man's eye. The Committee had agreed that in reparation for his crime—one against the industry—he would act as a clerk to the Jockey Club, and assist in keeping the breeding register up to date. In his spare time, of his own accord, he'd taken up the task of managing the General's investments, giving his father more time for his research. Seeing them together now, father and son side by side as they chatted with Flick, Demon sensed a closeness, a bond that hadn't been there—or not openly so—before.

Sliding his arm around Flick, he smiled and held out his hand to Dillon.

Above the bustle, lounging against one of the pillars of the church porch, Lucifer looked down on the gathering. In particular, on the twins. "They're going to be much worse after this, you realize."

"Hmm." Beside him, Gabriel resignedly raised his brows. "I've never understood what it is about weddings that so excites the mating instinct of females."

"Whatever it is, you only need to look at them to see its effect. They look ready to grab anything in breeches."

"Luckily, most of us here are related."

"Or, in their view, too old to count."

They continued watching the twins, perfect pictures of delight in cornflower blue gowns the same color as their eyes, their pale ringlets dancing in the breeze. They'd been hovering not far from Flick. Now they pushed forward to hug her frantically as she and Demon prepared to enter the waiting carriage. Flick returned their hugs affectionately—even from the porch, it was easy to discern her reasssuring words: "Your time will come—never doubt it."

To Gabriel and Lucifer, those words held a different ring.

Gabriel quelled an odd shiver. "It's not going to be easy, now it's just you and me."

"Devil and Vane will help out."

"When they're allowed to."

Lucifer's dark blue gaze shifted to Honoria and Patience, standing chatting to one side. "There is that. Still, we should be able to manage it—don't you think?"

Gabriel didn't answer, well aware they hadn't been talking solely about the twins.

At that moment, Demon handed Flick into the carriage. A cheer went up from all the onlookers. Demon turned to acknowledge it—to exchange a round of last comments with Devil and Vane. They laughed, and fell back; Demon reached for the carriage door.

Then he looked up, directly at them—the last unmarried members of the Bar Cynster. A slow, rakish, too-knowing smile lit his face; holding their gazes, he raised a hand and saluted them, paused for one last instant, then turned, ducked and entered the carriage.

Barely hearing the cheers and huzzahs as the carriage rumbled off, Gabriel stood in the porch as if turned to stone. In his mind rang the words *Your time will come—never doubt it.* Not, this time, in Flick's soft voice, but in Demon's much more forceful tones. He blinked and shook aside the horrendous thought, then shivered in earnest as a chill touched his spine.

Exactly as if someone had walked on his grave.

Disguising his shiver as a wriggle of his shoulders, he resettled his cuffs, then glanced at his brother. "Come on—we'd better do the honors *vis-à-vis* the twins, before they find some bounder to accompany them instead."

With a nod, Lucifer followed him down the church steps.

In the carriage rocking over the cobbles toward Berkeley Square, Flick was in her husband's arms. "Demon! Be careful!" She tried vainly to right her headdress. "We'll be greeting our guests soon."

"We're ahead of them," Demon pointed out, and kissed her again.

Flick inwardly sighed and forgot about her headdress, forgot about everything as she sank into his embrace. Possessive, protective, passionately loving—he was all she'd ever wanted. She loved him with all her soul. As she kissed him back, she felt the glow her parents had always had infuse her and Demon, enfolding them in its warmth. With this marriage, this man, this husband and lover, she'd seized her parents' legacy—now, they'd make it their own.

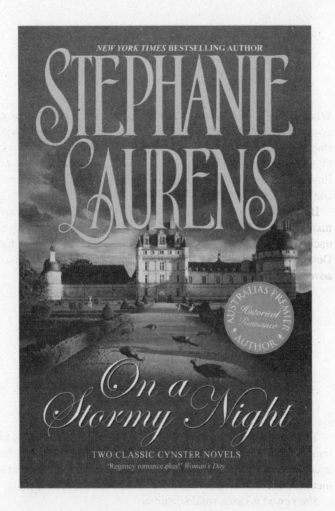

NEW YORK TIMES BESTSELLING AUTHOR

STEPHANIE
LAURENS

On a
Stormy Night

TWO CLASSIC CYNSTER NOVELS

'Regency romance.plus!' *Woman's Day*

On A Stormy Night

Two classic Cynster novels

Devil's Bride

STEPHANIE LAURENS

When Devil, the most infamous member of the Cynster family, is caught in a compromising position with plucky governess Honoria Wetherby, he astonishes the entire town by offering her his hand in marriage. As society's mamas swoon at the loss of England's most eligible bachelor, Devil's infamous Cynster cousins begin to place wagers on the wedding date.

But Honoria isn't about to bend to society's demands and marry a man just because they've been found together unchaperoned. She craves adventure. But could her passion for Devil cause her to embrace the enchanting peril of a lifelong adventure of the heart?

A Rake's Vow

STEPHANIE LAURENS

He vowed he'd never marry …

To Vane Cynster, Bellamy Hall seems like the perfect place to temporarily hide from London's husband hunters. But when he encounters irresistible Patience Debbington, Vane realises he's met his match.

She vowed no man would catch her …

Patience isn't about to succumb to Vane's sensuous propositions. Yes, his kisses leave her dizzy and his caresses make her melt; but Patience has promised herself she'll never become vulnerable to a broken heart.

Is this one vow that was meant to be broken?

NEW YORK TIMES BESTSELLING AUTHOR

STEPHANIE LAURENS

AUSTRALIA'S PREMIER
Historical Romance
AUTHOR

The Truth About Love

The Truth About Love

STEPHANIE LAURENS

Gerrard Debbington is one of the chosen few – a Cynster. One of the most eligible gentlemen in the *ton*, Gerrard is besieged by offers from London's most sought-after beauties, but as the ton's foremost artistic lion, there's only one offer he wants to accept – the chance to paint the fantastical but seldom-seen gardens of reclusive Lord Tregonning's Hellebore Hall.

That chance is dangled before Gerrard, but to grasp it he must fulfill Lord Tregonning's demand that he also create an open and honest portrait of the man's daughter. Gerrard loathes the idea of wasting his time and talents on some simpering miss, but with no alternative, he agrees …

Only to discover that Jacqueline Tregonning inspires him as no other lady has. Gerrard is stunned by the deep emotions she stirs and captivated by her passionate nature and innate goodness.

But something is horribly wrong at Hellebore Hall …

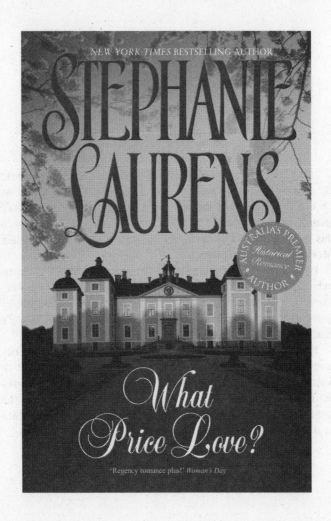

What Price Love?

STEPHANIE LAURENS

Dillon Caxton, protégé of Demon Cynster, is disillusioned with love, jaded by the knowledge that ladies desire his handsome face and figure rather than the man. But as one of the elected guardians of the sport of kings, he has more pressing matters on his mind, namely a criminal scheme set to wreak havoc on the world he's sworn to protect.

Enter Lady Priscilla Dalloway. She has no time for the men who swoon at her feet, seeing her only as a trophy to be won. Arriving in Newmarket to rescue her brother, unwittingly embroiled in some illicit scheme, she is forced to seek Dillon's assistance.

Beginning as antagonists, the pair continue as co-conspirators, eventually progressing to lovers as they seek to identify the villain behind the illicit scheme. Along the way each learns what love can bring them, ultimately facing the question of what sacrifices they will make in order to secure that love.

AVON
ROMANCE CLUB

Become a member today ❤ Enjoy the benefits

❤ **What is the Avon Romance Club?**

The Avon Romance Club is a club designed for anyone who loves to read quality romance. Membership is FREE and it entitles you to a range of exclusive offers, benefits and prizes.

❤ **Why should I join?**

• Avon Loyalty program
• Quarterly newsletter
• Giveaways, competitions, sneak previews & reviews

❤ **How do I become a member?**

It's easy and it's free. Simply complete the details below, detach stub and post to:

The Avon Romance Club
HarperCollins*Publishers*
25 Ryde Road, Pymble
NSW 2073
or register online at www.harpercollins.com.au/avon

Join today and you will receive a free copy of a bestselling Avon title as our gift to you!

Please return completed portion to: Avon Romance Club, HarperCollins*Publishers*
25 Ryde Road, Pymble NSW 2073

Name: _____

Address: _____

State: _____ Postcode: _____

Phone No: _____

Email: _____

Sex: Female ☐   Male ☐   Age: _____ (optional)

How many romance novels do you purchase each month? _____ (optional)